Cousin Jack

a novel

by

Daniel Mason

Alexander Associates

Cornwall PL23 1AR UK.

Alexander Associates

4 South Street, Fowey, Cornwall PL23 1AR. UK.

First Published 1996

Cousin Jack

by

Daniel Mason

ISBN 1 899526 65 X

Printed and bound in Great Britain by
Biddles Ltd, Guildford and King's Lynn

Synopsis

Cousin Jack
a novel by Daniel Mason

Cousin Jack is a novel of the Cornish migration to California, of the American dream, of the land, and of a life-long passion that dominates two people.

The story begins in 1858. Jack Trevenna says good-bye to Susan, his cousin and confidant, and leaves the tin and copper mines of his native Cornwall to try his luck in the Californian gold fields. With Nick, his brother, a profligate but gifted mining engineer, Joseph, his grim, masterful father, and his uncle Jesse, Susan's sensitive, unpredictable father, Jack spends two years prospecting in the Sierra foothills near Grass Valley. In 1860, the Trevennas become shareholders in the North Star, a hard-rock gold mine that becomes enviably profitable under the direction of the Sterling brothers in spite of the bickering between the partners.

After Joseph is killed by a runaway ore car, Jesse sends to Cornwall for his children and his wife, the compassionate and mystical Zennora. Jack and Susan fall in love, but she scorns his resolution to settle in America, so she allows Jesse to arrange for her to marry Hannibal Carne, one of his partners, who plans to return to England. Hannibal betrays her by becoming an American citizen, the couple grow increasingly estranged, and Susan has a brief affair with Jack, who has married another woman.

After the Sterlings arrange a lucrative but controversial sale of the North Star, Hannibal broods over a series of disappointing ventures while Jack devotes himself to a variety of fashionable investment schemes, ranging from the Pony Express to the first automobiles.

One by one, Susan loses the men in her life. Jack takes his family back to Cornwall. Jesse becomes embroiled in the Giant Powder strike of 1868 and then goes mad and dies in an asylum. Nick flees to Australia to avoid his creditors. Hannibal succumbs to typhoid fever.

When Jack returns to Grass Valley, Susan is furious with him for not standing by her, so he settles in San Francisco.

Susan is now head of the family in Grass Valley. Jack visits her frequently, but they quarrel: he sees California as the land of limitless opportunity, while she comes to perceive it as the site of foolhardy and disastrous exploitation. During the hydraulic controversy of the early 1880s, she and Zennora, much to Jack's dismay, enlist as spies against the mining companies. When the Live Yankee, one of Hannibal's lost hopes, finally strikes a vein, Susan becomes a woman of means and influence, and she helps her sons set up small businesses even though two resent her assistance and one turns a local hotel into an extravagant fiasco. She prevents her brother from deserting his family to run off to the Klondike, but he, despondent over his failure to live up to his father's example, hangs himself.

In April of 1906, feeling weary of Grass Valley, she visits Jack in order to consider settling in San Francisco. They survive the earthquake and fire, but while she sees the catastrophe as the doom of the Californian dream, he plans to make a fortune by rebuilding the city. Horrified at his blind opportunism, she returns to Grass Valley, and the lovers never see each other again.

In the course of the story, Jack has brief encounters with Bret Harte, Leland Stanford, Lotta Crabtree, Mark Twain, Ada Menken, David Belasco, James O'Neill, Ulysses Grant, Black Bart, Theodore Roosevelt and Enrico Caruso.

Cousin Jack

Foreword

Although a great deal of contemporary fiction has Cornwall and the Cornish as its theme (from the internationally-renowned works of Daphne du Maurier to the *Poldark* romances), very few authors have responded to the challenge and opportunities offered by the Cornish abroad. This is all the more surprising, given the extensive treatment afforded the Cornish diaspora by historians and others in recent years. In America and in Australia, and increasingly in South Africa and New Zealand too, the extraordinary story of the Cousin Jacks and Jennies - the emigrant Cornish communities - has been rediscovered and recorded in loving detail by university scholars, local and family historians, and the ever-growing multiplicity of overseas Cornish Associations.

Now, however, Daniel Mason has come forward to fill the gap - and he has done so magnificently. In this carefully crafted novel, he deploys his expertise as a a specialist in the Arts (he is Professor of Academic Theatre at the California State University) but he also demonstrates his deep understanding of the Cornish emigrant experience. He combines literary skill with sound historical judgement, so that *Cousin Jack* more than lives up to the expectations inherent in its evocative title - it positively oozes authenticity.

The scope of *Cousin Jack* is on the grand scale, a veritable blockbuster which will delight all those with a taste for the vast panorama of an epic tale well-told. Daniel Mason has trail-blazed a new dimension in Cornish literature, an innovation that can only serve to bring the Cornish diaspora to an even wider reading public. He has shown the way for what must be surely an important new genre in the realms of Cornish fiction, and a significant addition to the burgeoning literature of the American West.

Dr Philip Payton,
Reader in Cornish Studies and
Director,
Institute of Cornish Studies,
University of Exeter,
Redruth, Cornwall, UK.

1
The White Fox
1858

Then the earth fell, and he ran.

Seven weeks had passed since New Year's, and Jack Trevenna had spent every day of it deep down in Wheal Vor, the vast tin mine in Cornwall. The first streamers, forgotten centuries before, had found the ore beneath the shining river water and picked the gravel beds clean before their grandsons' grandsons, tracing the lodes, sank shafts down into the warm darkness, remote from the spiny furze that shivered in the freshening breeze. They delved until they found more water than rock and so abandoned the site for fresh ground. The mine lay neglected until Watt's steam engine appeared, a huffing, oily contraption that could pump dry a shaft as deep as three hundred fathoms. The miners slowly returned to Wheal Vor, and in 1853, a new company of adventurers, tight-lipped gentlemen, bought the workings. They hired a team of captains, who posted notices in Helston and Breage, and in Tregunnow and Rinsey and Hendra, promising good wages for strong, reliable men. The crews mounted an 85-inch engine on Trelawney's Shaft and a 100-inch monster on Crease's Shaft, and the pumps brought out so much water that the men had to scoop out three ponds to hold it. They rebuilt the engine houses, the counting-house, the store room and the engineer's shop, and they built a new sawmill and re-thatched the old timber houses. They cleaned out the old tunnels, running a new series of ladders down the footway shaft, bringing out the rubble from the stopes of the main levels, and clearing out the debris from the winzes, the air shafts that would make it barely possible for the men to breathe. By Christmas of 1857, both Trelawney's and Crease's shafts were dry down to their sumps, and Wheal Vor was once again a subterranean warren, with new drifts reaching out to travel beside the lode as it dipped and turned. Beneath the surface, far from the salty wind, a thousand men and boys chipped away at the unrelenting rock, doggedly taking the black tin from the granite and hoisting it up "to grass," to the surface, where the bal-maidens, their spreading white hats bobbing like moths' wings, broke the fragments with their long-handled hammers and sent carloads to the stamp mills that crushed the ore, separated the metal, and dumped the rubble and sludge in a pit where there had once been a green field.

Yet there were rumors that the new company hadn't found all of the old workings, that a rich lode, with a system of clear tunnels, lay to the south-

Cousin Jack

west of the main operation, towards the sea. Just a week before Christmas, Jack had climbed down to the lowest level and found the dead end, a quiet corner far from the pitches that the underground captains deemed profitable. The air was hot and steaming, and he wiped the sweat off of his neck before sticking his candle on his helmet to gaze at the rock before him. He turned his head from side to side to watch the dim light flickering off of the stone. If nothing lay behind that rock wall, he had little to lose. Yet if the stories were true, then he might earn more than any man he knew and perhaps even get out of the mines and astonish everyone by becoming an adventurer himself. He reached out and laid his palm on the rock, feeling the rough, implacable mass, and closed his eyes. He imagined the tin embedded in the lode, waiting among drifts and shafts that no one had traversed for over a century. Then he opened his eyes, and there was only the dark rock, absolutely solid, sitting dully before him. He wiped the sweat off of his face, turned to look back up the tunnel, and abruptly froze with his rag halfway down his cheek.

Not ten yards away stood a fox. The animal shone in the candle light, pure white from muzzle to tail except for a pink nose and eyes that gleamed red, deep in their sockets, brighter than the feeble flame wavering above Jack's forehead. The miner and the fox stared at each other for several long moments, not moving, scarcely breathing. Then the fox flicked its brush once, twice, and trotted right past Jack, so close that it nearly grazed him, and climbed lightly, delicately up the rock wall and disappeared through a crevice. Jack stood amazed for a moment or two, then caught his breath and reached up to where the fox had vanished. The rock was as solid as when he had first seen it; there was neither chink nor passage.

He laughed aloud. His father had told tales of animals appearing, impossibly, deep in the mines. He had never really believed the stories, and he didn't believe them now: there were no white foxes cavorting in Wheal Vor. He grinned to himself, and spoke to the silent rock. "I be half cracky!" He chuckled at the idea and studied the dead end once again. Pisky foxes or no, the stone seemed promising. During the next few days, be brought several of his friends down, and four of them agreed to join him to form a pare, or crew, to work the site. He said nothing about the white fox.

At the January auction, the grass captain—the senior superintendent, who worked at the surface—smiled when Jack made his bid, and the purser laughed aloud when the older men stared incredulously. The adventurers were glad to take the money, even the ridiculously low price that Jack offered, and gave the pare all rights to the pitch for six months, a commitment of unprecedented length that announced their scorn to everyone. One of the miners, his back bent and his arms knotted with years of drilling, muttered something about Jack being "fair mazed," and from then on, the cockier ones referred to him as "Mazejerry Jack," snickering among themselves whenever his pare started down the footway ladders towards the pitch that no one wanted. The tutmen shrugged their shoulders when Jack asked for counsel about digging the new tunnel; two of them offered to do the job for a price, as they would for the company, but Jack's pare had no money, so they kept digging, drilling and blasting on their own.

The others followed Jack because at seventeen he was the eldest, and because he seemed to understand the rock. On other pitches, even their fathers and uncles had begun to rely on Jack's sense of where the lode would turn, of how much powder to use, of when to shore up a drift and when to trust the rock not to cave in on them. He seemed to know when the rock ahead was tary ground, a stretch that would permit easy drilling but might crumble at an inopportune moment, and when it was elvan, the hard, fine-grained stone that made the safest tunnels if only a man had the patience to hammer through it. In the seven weeks they had spent searching for the lost workings, no one in the pare had been so much as bruised. After each new blast, Jack was the first to go back into the drift, not minding the black powder fumes that choked the others, reaching out to feel the raw rock wall with his left hand, and tapping it here and there with a small hammer he carried in his right. He then beckoned to the others, directing them to wedge in a timber or to clear away the deads, the worthless broken rocks that they'd haul out of their way later. They trusted him, but in spite of the stories they told their families about Jack Trevenna and his sense of the rock, they knew that his luck was just that, and that someday the drift would mock his confidence. A wall would collapse, a ceiling would fall, or a blast would shake down more than they anticipated, and a man would get hurt and maybe killed. They also knew that the lost workings might not be there at all, and that they would extend their drift into blind rock until they finally lost interest and moved on to proven pitches, leaving the dead end there as a token of their willingness to take a chance.

For better than a month, they worked double cores, staying down for fourteen and fifteen hours at a stretch, pausing only for a few bites of cold pasty, the heavy turnover filled with potatoes and onions, and a few gulps of water. Jack divided the pare into teams of two, with the youngest boy, only twelve years old, left over for clearing away the small rubble and bringing tools into position. They drove the borers into the rock, six inches, then twelve, then two feet, one man holding the drill and the other swinging the heavy sledge, metal against metal, metal against rock, so hard that each man's ears rang and the man with the sledge, after half an hour, felt his hands and forearms tingle and go numb. Then they would trade places and continue. When the hole was deep enough, the boy cleaned it out with a swab stick, and Jack made a cartridge out of paper and tallow, letting a candle drip to seal the seams, filling it with black powder and tamping it down into the hole. He inserted a fuse, called to the others to retreat, and lit the trailing end with his candle, then running to join the rest, all huddled against the rock, nestling into crevices or behind outcroppings, waiting for the blast. Then they would clear away the rubble, extend the drift as far as pick and wedges and shovel could manage, and prepare to drill and blast again.

February was waning, and although the pare had lost its initial enthusiasm, the men were still willing to go on. Jack had guided the tunnel into a slow, rising left turn, reaching up to where he believed the old workings might lie. As the tunnel inclined, the results of each blast more and more resembled a cave-in as the fragments fell and rolled rather than simply scattering. The boy clearing rubble liked the grade, for he could roll his barrow down it and back into the main level, but a man driving a drill, straining to balance against the slope, found that each swing of the hammer threatened to tip him over.

They had nearly reached the end of their second core of the day when Jack went in after a blast. He reached up as always, left hand free, right hand balancing the little hammer, and he noticed something different about the rock. It was darker than usual, and it shone. He slipped off his gloves to feel the stone. It was wet, wetter than he expected, and not from any drip or underground rivulet. It was soaked clear through, and the damp was cool, not lukewarm. He wiped his hands across his bare chest, gestured to the others to stay well back, and stood there, finding his footing amidst the deads and the rab so he could stare steadily into the end of the drift. He reached out and tapped with his hammer, and a bit of rock fell away. There was no seepage, but more black wetness. He turned around and stepped slowly back down the slope, kicking away the scattered rocks in his path. He turned up again, considered, and reached down to pick up the shovel lying at his feet. He balanced the tool in his hands for a moment or two, choosing a spot, and drove it with an underhanded motion into the center of the dark wetness. Immediately, a stream of water squirted out from the rock, narrow but powerful, shooting twenty feet over Jack's shoulder and back down the drift. Then the whole ceiling collapsed.

He had no time to turn or even to shout a warning; the surprise of the cave-in and the force of the water behind it threw him into a skidding back somersault that took him down the steepest gradient of the drift and onto a portion that he and the others had cleaned and worn smooth. He scrambled, and as he found his footing and turned to dash back through the tunnel, he saw the rest of the pare ahead of him, already sprinting in hopes of staying ahead of the rushing water. They could not think of their tools, or think at all; they simply ran and ran. The falling rock and the ravening surge set up a roar that filled the tunnel, echoing off of the hard walls and pressing in on the fleeing men like an extended peal of thunder, but thunder that surrounded them and hammered them at close range. If they could get past the point where they had begun extending the drift, the point where they had started their rising incline, they would be running uphill and so might climb above the gathering flood.

Jack raced after the others. The one nearest to him was the boy, lagging behind a bit, unable to pump his shorter legs fast enough to keep up with the rest. Just as Jack reached him, he looked over his shoulder, not at Jack, for the din completely covered the sound of his approach, but at the pursuing water. As he turned, his balance shifted ever so slightly, and his shoulder grazed an outcropping that he might have seen if he had kept his eyes front. The contact slowed him down, and as Jack whisked past, he realized that the boy was losing his footing, and he caught a glimpse of his face, not frightened, but astonished, still frozen in reaction to the initial surprise of the cave-in. Jack did not dare pause or look back; he kept running as fast as he could, looking ahead, unblinking, to find a clear path through the tunnel. One man's candle was, miraculously, still burning, so there was a faint light, just enough to see ahead.

They were running up the slope now, following the established drift, and in another ten seconds, they reached a winze, with its ladder stretching up to safety and air. The first man threw himself up the rungs, with the second so close that they were nearly climbing together. The third grabbed for the base of the ladder, but as Jack approached, he realized, in an instant, that he would have to find another way. If he waited for all three to climb up and out of the way, the water would surely reach him, and if it were a heavy flood—no one knew how much water they had released—when it found the winze it would crush the ladder and spout up the rising shaft like a geyser, battering and drowning anyone inside. His only chance was to reach the main shaft, which plunged beneath their level and down to the sump; there, the water might drain away and so spare him.

He ran and ran, screaming now against the titanic thunder that beat him about the head and ears, screaming like a wild animal, beyond terror, all instinct. There was no light at all now—the man with the candle had been the second one up the winze—so Jack ran through the black void, feeling water under his feet and spray on his back, and he gulped for air, even the hot, stifling air of the mine. He reached the shaft, sensing the change in the space rather than seeing it, and sprang up the ladder, scrambling for a foothold, commanding his hands to keep hold of the rungs and not to slip, and he was pulling himself up when the torrent struck.

He was wrapped around the ladder, still screaming, even though he could not hear himself, for the rising gush had surrounded and enfolded him.

Cousin Jack

He was embedded in water, like a fly in amber, but amber that raged and brought fragments of rock to lacerate his head and hands and chest in the turbulence. Finally, he could scream no more, but he refused to breathe, more out of reflex than will, and he held on, waiting to see whether he could wait long enough. Then, unbelievably, there was air, and he gasped, a long, shuddering struggle to fill his aching lungs. The water fell away, still roiling, and the thunder receded. The sump had taken the flood, leaving Jack clutching the ladder and choking like a half-drowned cat.

An hour later, the furious grass captain made sure that "Mazejerry Jack" knew, for good and all, that he and everyone else in the mine had been unbelievably lucky. Only three men had died: the boy and the third man up the winze from Jack's own pare, and another miner who had happened to stop near the sump for a doze and was caught unawares. The other two men in Jack's pare had been carried home, too shaken and bruised to walk. If the cave-in and flood had occurred at a higher level, or closer to the main workings, many more might have died, either drowned in the torrent or hurled against the rock walls and shattered. Drenched and exhausted, Jack huddled, scrumped up with the cold, at the brace of the footway shaft while the older man paced this way and that, pausing now and then to shake a fist or a finger in the delinquent's face. Only a greedy boy, a rank novice, would drive as far as that without dropping an adit, a drain shaft, towards the sump, and only a bulk-headed fool would have thrust his spade into a soaking wet wall lying above his head. Incensed and nearly babbling, the captain fell back on insults that he'd heard his grandfather use: "You gommock! Ye're a regular cake! A noggy! A pattick!" A nearby group of curious miners grinned at the quaint language. The accident had been a calamity, but they knew that the captain was right: it could have been much worse. None of the dead men had a family to support, and the mine itself hadn't been damaged. Any man who went down a shaft knew he was taking risks, and it was a rare week when at least one man wasn't carried out, broken from a plunge, or crushed by falling rock. "Mazejerry Jack" may have driven too far, but no miner knew exactly what he'd find in a pitch until he was done digging it out.

Spent, the captain folded his arms while the two underground captains told him what they had seen below. Shivering, still wearing his wet flannel trousers and huddled in a scrap of canvas that someone had thrown over him, Jack tried to listen, but all he could hear was the pursuing water, a thundering roar that still pealed in his head. The wind passed right through him, a gale that had driven in from the north Atlantic, measured the open claw of Mount's Bay and scudded easily across the two miles of treeless fields to the mouth of the main shaft. The grass captain walked over and yanked Jack to his feet. "Ye're comin' down with me."

Most of the water had poured down into the sump at the bottom of

Crease's Shaft, and the big engine, its massive bob rocking unperturbed, had already drawn much of it up to the surface. Jack climbed down the ladder first, for none of the captains wanted an exhausted, disgraced man climbing above them where he might lose his footing and take them all to the bottom. Down they went, back into the heat and the stifling closeness of the lower tunnels. Finally, they reached the 200-fathom level, and one of the underground captain's assistants was waiting there to guide them into Jack's drift. He stared at the younger miner for a moment, then gestured to him to go ahead of the rest; the passage was still awash, and if there were any pitfalls, better that Jack be the one to find them. When they reached the bottom of the grade, the water came up to their chests, and every man shivered, trying to control his breathing, but by the time they reached the point of the cave-in, there was only a shallow trickle as the last overflow ran down the slope. Jack stopped there, and the three captains pushed past him to hold their lanterns up into the opening.

The water had blown a hole eight feet wide and twenty feet long, ripping out several feet of what had been the ceiling of Jack's drift, and opening in farther than his pare had blasted. The first underground captain shone his lantern this way and that, and he reached out with a hammer to tap the rock and test it for stability. Satisfied, he handed off his lantern and lifted himself up. The others followed, and finally Jack scrambled up to see what nearly two months of hard work had revealed.

The five men stood in a natural cave that looked to be about eighty feet long and shaped like a flattened egg, the perimeter forming a rough ellipse, thirty feet wide at most, the floor alternately smooth and uneven, and the ceiling arching gently above them, reaching a height of twelve feet in the center and tapering off in all directions. It wasn't an old workings at all, but a geologic bubble, the sort of formation that was found in one out of five of the larger mines in west Cornwall. Over the years, it had filled with ground water that filtered down from the surface, forming a subterranean reservoir with no surface, just water encased in rock, and Jack's drift had emptied it out. Some such caverns did, indeed, lead to rich lodes, and Jack stood in the center, gazing about him, while the three captains and the assistant fanned out around the vault, shining their lanterns up at the walls, tapping here and there on the wet rock, and cursing whenever they lost their footing and slipped on the slick floor. They spent nearly an hour inspecting every bit of the cave, and when they were finished, they gathered near the entrance to confer. Finally, the grass captain walked over to Jack, raised the lantern, and studied his face for a few moments before speaking.

"There be nothin', Trevenna—not even tailings. Tidden worth sendin' good men down t' this 'ere 'ere. An' if I see yer pare down 'ere agin, I'll turn out the whole kit." He spat down near Jack's feet. "As fer you—ye're out o' this pitch. I won't even fine ye. Just split along out o' 'ere, and Wheal Vor'll be done with ye." He spat again, walked over to the entrance, climbed down, and was gone. The other captains followed.

The underground captain's assistant waited until they were gone, and then turned to the sodden young miner. "'Twas a mumchance, Jack—no man can know what lies in th' rock. But ye're in a kicklish way with th' capp'n, so clember up outa 'ere and get on 'ome. Maybe ye can find a pitch at Tin Croft or Dolcoath." He climbed down after the others and disappeared up the drift, leaving Jack alone with a small candle.

He stood silently for a moment, beyond disappointment and beyond grief, and walked over to where he could reach up and touch the rock. It felt as deep and as solid as the earth itself. He slammed his fist against the hard mass and cried out at the pain. Then he bit his lip and left the cave to wade through the pointless drift and climb ladder after ladder, up to grass. He changed out of his soaking, filthy flannels, leaving them in a grimy heap in a corner, and did the best he could to wash himself before putting on his other clothes. His pare had been sharing a one-room stone cottage with dirt floor and thatched roof, a hovel set on a lonely knob of the moor less than a mile from the mine, but he didn't want to go back there to face his two surviving friends. He sat on a bench, counting the few shillings he had left in his pocket and considering whether he should walk to Helston, just two miles to the southeast, when he heard someone calling his name. He looked up to see a man approaching from the other end of the changing house.

"It's Aunt Mary, Jack. Yer fayther is askin' for ye." Jack stared at him for a moment, puzzled, and then realized what the message meant. His grandmother had been ailing when he saw her last, and now she must be dying, so his family had summoned him. The walk to Camborne would take two hours if he hurried, and he looked up at the dull, grey sky, trying to guess the time of day. His pare had been working the afternoon and overnight cores, so the drift must have collapsed two or three hours before the winter dawn. It now would be shortly after noon, and Jack had not slept for twenty-four hours, but he rose to his feet and set off on the road heading north by northeast, across the moor, passing villages, mines, and the walled pastures and woodlands of the manors.

The cobbled streets of Camborne seemed filled with water-carts that clattered past the great old market building and the curving rows of shops. The town was surrounded by some of the deepest tin and copper mines in Cornwall—the Great Condurrow, Cook's Kitchen, Tin Croft, Carn Brea, and the six scattered shafts of the Dolcoath—and their steam engines had pumped out the workings so thoroughly that even if a farmer's well stayed wet, the water in the pail supported a sour scum. Many of the townspeople bought their drinking water from carters who filled their ten-gallon barrels from the headwaters of the River Tratheag, stealing it before it had a chance to drain into Falmouth Harbor. The air was grimy, too, for the day was oddly still and the breeze from the northern shore, not four miles away, hadn't freshened enough to carry out the soot and grit from the mines' great smoke-stacks and mills. Jack kept walking, past the shops to the cottages and houses where the miners and their families lived, neat two-story dwellings with evenly-spaced, white-framed windows and roofs tightly hipped against the seaborne squalls, all behind tidy gardens and little rock walls. He turned up Cross Street and found the familiar house of grey stone sitting behind the rose bushes, all pruned back for the winter. He trudged up the walk and let himself in the front door.

The heavy curtains were drawn across the windows, shutting out the light and muffling the slow, uneven tick-tock of hooves on the stones of the street. One candle burned in the parlor, and beneath it, crouched on the polished oaken floor, a little boy quietly rolled a hard woollen ball to an even younger girl. They looked up at Jack apprehensively, as if expecting a rebuke. The room was as clean as a church altar, and the chairs showed fresh brush marks on the heavy, napped fabric. The door on the far wall swung open, and Jack looked over to see his brother, Frederick, his sullen mouth set resentfully. He beckoned, and Jack followed. The bedroom was so full of people that he could scarcely get through the doorway, but he wedged himself in.

Mary Trevenna lay beneath the arched canopy of her four-poster bed, nearly buried in layers of quilts. Her long grey hair straggled off of one side of her pillow, and her creased eyelids were closed. The skin of her face was as dry as a crumbling leaf, and at the corner of her open mouth there was a drop of spittle that barely quivered as she pulled in each breath and then released it, exhausted. Six decades had passed since she left the fishing village of St. Agnes to marry a copper miner from Crowan. She tolerated him for thirteen years, bore ten children, and then, one fair morning, made the long walk to the head of a shaft to see him lying in an ore car, so lacerated by the explosion that she could not with complete confidence identify his body. Suddenly autonomous, she dispassionately asserted an authority over her children that grew stronger as they grew older, no matter that some left home, married and had families of their own. To obtain Mary's consent was not the point; no one could act without her firm approval and active support. Now they had come to ask leave to go on without her.

At the head of the bed knelt Elizabeth, the elder daughter, praying si-lently, wearing full mourning for her husband, a copper miner who was crushed in a cave-in at Cook's Kitchen only two months since. Next to her stood Jack's own parents, Joseph and Margaret, his mother maintaining a discreet but firm grip on the shoulder of young Nicholas, whose face bulged red with the immense effort of keeping still, while little Charles stared, transfixed by his dying grandmother. On the other side of the bed stood Mary's unmarried children, Richard and Anne, and in the corner opposite the door was Jack's uncle, Jesse, standing with his wife, Zennora, and their three children: Susan, Bessie and Joseph. Although the winter was fading and the still air outside was hardly cold, all in the room wore their heaviest, most formal clothing. The air was more stifling than in the deepest drift in the deepest mine in Penwith.

Elizabeth finished her prayer, reached up for Joseph's hand, and slowly rose to her feet. She took a hymnal from the bedside table, pulled back the narrow ribbon that marked a certain page, and began to sing:

> Shrinking from the cold hand of death,
> I soon shall gather up my feet;
> Shall soon resign this fleeting breath,
> And die—my fathers' God to meet.

The others joined in; first the women, then the men, and, timidly, the children. Margaret tapped Nicholas on the shoulder, and even he sang.

> O that, without a ling'ring groan,
> I may the welcome word receive;
> My body with my charge lay down,
> And cease at once to work and live.

Jack looked at Susan, wishing she would look in his direction, but the girl stood as though in church, head tilted delicately to one side, the steady candlelight setting off the firm, neat chin and the high cheekbones. She kept gazing down at the motionless figure beneath the quilts.

> Walk with me through the dreadful shade,
> And, certified that thou are mine,
> My spirit, calm and undismay'd,
> I shall into thy hands resign.

Elizabeth daubed the corner of Mary's mouth with a handkerchief, and knelt to pray again.

A minute passed by, and two, and three, and five, and ten, and yet they stood without moving. Margaret kept both hands firmly on Nicholas' shoulders, and little Joseph leaned against Zennora, who put her arms around him. Jack's head ached and his legs began to cramp; the room was suffocating him. He looked at his father, but Joseph's face was a bearded mask turned impassively towards the bed. Susan seemed mesmerized; the delicately tilted eyes glistened.

The White Fox, 1858

Finally, the old woman released a breath with a soft, extended squeak. She paused for a long beat, then drew in another, slowly and harshly, and let it go so completely that the little body seemed to collapse and wilt. Elizabeth kept praying while Richard stepped in to close his mother's eyes and pat the quilt into place under her chin.

> Spirit, leave thy house of clay;
> Ling'ring dust, resign thy breath;
> Spirit, cast thy chains away;
> Dust, be thou dissolved in death:—
> Thus the mighty Saviour speaks,
> While the faithful Christian dies;
> Thus the bonds of life he breaks,
> And the ransom'd captive flies.

The children from the parlor peeked in the doorway, and Elizabeth beckoned to them.

> Pris'ner, long detain'd below,
> Pris'ner, now with freedom blest,
> Welcome from a world of woe;
> Welcome to a land of rest:—
> Thus the choir of angels sing,
> As they bear the soul on high,
> While with hallelujahs ring
> All the regions of the sky.

Susan finally glanced over at Jack and she opened her eyes just a little wider to acknowledge him.

> Grave, the guardian of our dust,
> Grave, the treasury of the skies,
> Every atom of thy trust
> Rests in hope again to rise:
> Hark! the judgement-trumpet calls—
> Soul, rebuild thy house of clay;
> Immortality thy walls,
> And eternity thy day.

Joseph and Margaret approached the bed, looked down at the shriveled face, and turned to collect the boys and leave the room. Jack waited next to the door while Jesse and Zennora led their children out, and then he followed them as the others gathered around the deathbed.

No one spoke. After a moment, Joseph strode to the front of the house, drew the curtains away from one window, and turned to find Margaret pursing her lips at him. He raised his eyebrows briefly, said nothing, and gave his back to her, staring through the glass, his big hands, with their heavy, stubby fingers and the two broken knuckles, clasped behind his back.

11

Cousin Jack

Zennora tapped Susan on the shoulder and pointed to the little ones, who had come back into the parlor and were crouched in a corner; they were pale, and the boy's lower lip was trembling. Elizabeth, their mother, would surely stay at the death-bed for another hour, praying and singing hymns. Susan drew a chair into the corner, tucked a lock of wavy brown hair back into place, and invited the children to sit on her lap. The boy climbed up immediately and nestled in the older girl's arms, pressing himself against her flat chest and whimpering. His little sister stood obstinately, unwilling to accept the affection, but equally unwilling to walk away from the prospect. Susan reached out and stroked her hair.

The light in the dooryard began to fade, and the clock struck five. As if reminded, Joseph turned from the window. "John—what of yer pitch?"

Jack flushed, hesitated, considered a lie, and instead confessed. "There was nothin' there. We drove out too far, we 'oled into a 'ouse o' water, and got a good dousing."

Joseph shook his head, but it was Jesse who asked, "'ow many men?"

Jack glanced at the women, not wanting to answer, but then he realized that Joseph's eyes were close on him. "Two. Two men and a boy."

Jesse sighed. "It might've been worse."

Joseph kept gazing at Jack as though assessing him. "So you've nothin' now at Wheal Vor."

"No, fayther, nothin' at all." Jack now felt that everyone in the room was staring at him. Then his father released him, turning to look out the window at the dwindling day.

Joseph had delved for tin and copper for over thirty years, ever since he was a boy, and he had, early on, made a peace with the mines, giving his strength and his patience and expecting in return no more than a decent, reliable living. The Trevenna family had always been careful, training each son thoroughly, and skill had combined with luck so that they had suffered fewer calamities than most. The captains were always gratified to see the Trevennas appear at an auction, and were glad to assign them a good pitch at a fair price. Joseph had worked in most of the mines near Camborne and Crowan, and now, as one of the older and more experienced men in the region, he could look forward to picking his pare and his pitch for the next ten years or so, until he retired. He was rooted. Yet he had begun to realize that he was also indentured, bound to spend his future in the same villages, mines and shafts as in the past. His own father had died without straying outside of Penwith and Kerrier, the westernmost "hundreds," or sections, of the county, and Joseph himself had never been east of the River Fal, nor had he, in his few trips on the fishing boats that worked out of St. Ives, sailed out of sight of the Cornish coast. Like the men of his father's time, he spoke of traveling to London or even to Plymouth as "going to England." He had never permitted himself to consider the possibilities, tacitly using his familial duties as a sort of shield or excuse, and, ever since they had buried his father, deferring to his mother. Now she was dead, and he was the eldest of her children; if there was initiative to claim, it was his. He gazed through the bubbled panes as the light from the cold, featureless sky waned like the strength in a man's legs at the end of a hard core. The houses and gardens on Cross Street were slowly disappearing into the twilight as though they had never been there, the insubstantial lairs of wraiths. He turned and looked at his brother. "Jesse—I think our time be now."

Margaret gasped. Jesse glanced over at Zennora, who seemed perfectly composed, sitting with one arm around Bessie and the other hand on young Joseph's shoulder. Jack looked around the room, wondering what his father meant.

Margaret finally found words. "'ow can you be sayin' such a thing, Joseph Trevenna? To leave 'ere? To leave Dolcoath?"

Jack was intrigued. "Where're ye goin', Fayther? Australia?" His older sister, Louisa, had left Camborne three years earlier to settle in Victoria with her new husband. Her letters had fascinated him with accounts of promising mines, of seasons turned backwards, and of trees taller than anyone in Cornwall had ever seen.

"No," said Joseph. "Not Australia. America." He waited for a beat, pulling them in. "California." There was a hush, a pause. Then they all began talking all at once.

Everyone in Camborne knew someone who had sailed for California since the gold strike in 1848. The first parties were composed mostly of young men, youths with no families, who left impulsively, drawn by fabulous tales and rumors that they read in newspapers and heard in taverns. Then the stories began to change. Prospecting was no longer a matter of wading lazily into a clear mountain stream under the soft shade of pine boughs swaying in a warm breeze, there to pick out pure nuggets with your fingers. The mining had become serious and even organized. There were companies sinking shafts into the Sierra granite, and those companies needed not dilletante gentlemen from New York, London and Lisbon, but men with skill and experience; not wanderers who sought to pick up a fortune in a day and lose it at the San Francisco gaming tables, but men who were willing to work for years at a stretch and knew how to blast into the quartz veins that held the metal. Even the hard-rock miners, men with few illusions, found something newly seductive in the promise of gold. Tin and copper were sensible, utilitarian and familiar, but when gold appeared in a man's dreams, it left an inimitable glitter as an unforgettable, tantalizing residue. The work, they reasoned, might be the same, but the potential rewards were much greater. That the gold lay in California made the idea all the more attractive, for after news of Marshall's discovery reached England, the men of Cornwall had laid aside their hymnals to pass from hand to hand the tempting reports by Dana and Frémont. Even more compelling were the letters that arrived, stained and crumpled, with the San Francisco postmark. The letters circulated among the extended families, and by 1858, everyone in the mining district could cite a cousin, or the cousin of a close friend, who had confirmed the wealth lying in the Sierra foothills, the abundance of water and farmland and crystalline sunshine, and, perhaps most tempting of all, the freedom for a man to stake a claim and work it on his own account. Even serious, stable miners, who had long bent their thoughts to pitch, pare, family and chapel, began to dream and speculate.

Margaret fought Joseph bitterly. She had listened to him ruminate on the possibilities in California, but had dismissed his speculations as inconsequential, the idle musings of a tired man staring into his fire at the end of the day. She knew that many families had separated, the men going to work abroad and send money home, but she had not yet reconciled herself to Louisa's absence, and she could no more conceive of her family scattering than of herself leaving Cornwall behind. Now she felt cornered, trapped in a house of mourning, surrounded by Joseph's brothers and sisters, cut off from her own parents and left to contest this folly by herself. Jack had already proved himself restless, and in two or three years, she predicted, Nicholas would be even worse. She drew young Charles into her body with both hands and faced her husband.

How could he think of leaving now? With his mother gone, he was the head of the family, a role which brought both responsibility and prosperity, for the old lady had left him a third of her money and a half-share in the house where the younger, unmarried brother and sister would continue to live. There was the widowed Elizabeth and her two babies—who would ensure their comfort if he went off? He had two sons still living at home, and another just starting out, not to mention a wife. Besides, the mines in Penwith were doing well, quite well. Copper production was rising and prices were high; the manufacturers in Birmingham couldn't get enough of it. The adventurers were getting £75 a ton for black tin, and nearly £140 a ton for the metal. Joseph might hope to be appointed an underground captain soon, which meant not only a salary but also a share of the profits; perhaps not a large one, but a share just the same. Even if he kept working as a tributer, the price of the ore and the richness of the lode meant that each day's work would be worth more than it had been. Finally she subsided, worn, panting a little.

Joseph had lived with this woman for over twenty years, and he had kept his bargain with her, just as she had kept hers with him. There had been nothing remarkable about their marriage—they had cared for each other, but

The White Fox, 1858

without passion, they had worked for each other, but without sacrifice, and they had raised four children and buried three others, always going on, trudging back and forth between mine and market, kitchen and chapel. Now he saw her as being as much a part of this rocky peninsula as the towns and the moors, the mines and the fisheries, the churches and the markets, the surf and the furze. He still had energy to spend, and he had spent enough here.

"I'm goin' t' California, Margaret. I'm takin' Nicholas with me, and John. I'll ask Frederick, but 'e's told me 'e's bound for Australia. You an' Charles can come if ye wish, or ye can stop 'ere 'til we return." He neither invited nor allowed a response, but turned to Jesse. "And you?"

Jesse looked over at Zennora, who nodded calmly, and back at his elder brother. "I'll join ye, Joseph. I can be ready within th' week."

Betrayed and indignant, Margaret broke into tears, but Joseph had made up his mind and would not be moved. She refused any comfort, and when Richard opened the door, curious about the commotion, she scolded him and sent him back to his prayers. Finally, she took Charles by the hand and dragged him out the front door and down the walk into the moonless night. Joseph scratched his chin through his beard and told Jack to follow her and see her home safely. The boy stopped at the doorway, glanced furtively over his shoulder at his father, and turned his head towards the corner where Susan sat with the little ones. Joseph, watching, could read nothing in the girl's face as she looked back at his son, so he turned to confer with Jesse as the boy walked out and shut the door behind him.

By mid-morning, the breeze had blown away the clouds, and the sun shone out of a clear, cold sky, warming Susan's face as she waited in the Gwennap Pit. The place had first appeared as a sinkhole, formed when the tunnels beneath so weakened the rock that it could no longer support the surface in its original shape. John Wesley had first preached there in 1762, and forty years later, a committee of pious mine captains had graded the dish, surrounding the perimeter with a six-foot stone wall sixty fathoms around and nearly twenty across, and stepping down the grade in grassy concentric rings to the bottom level. On each Whit Monday, the faithful would gather from twenty miles around to sit in the fragrant spring air and sing hymns. During the rest of the year, the Pit lay quiet and peaceful, so Zennora and Margaret had brought their children here for picnics, letting them run up and down the rings and tumble on the grass, safe from the wind that blew across the top of the dish.

Susan lay on her back and gazed up at the sky stretching over her, a perfect canopy. A small flock of birds flew past, tracing the distance from one side of the Pit to the other, reaching their beaks and driving with their wings as they slashed across the blue surface, heading west. Where would they come to rest? They might be heading for the beaches of St. Ives Bay, or they might only stop at a nearby farm, there to raid the henyard for seed and hector the wife for crumbs. Jesse had once taken her to the top of Mulfra Hill, where they could see Mount's Bay to the south and the rocky coast to the north, and she had fancied that if she could soar like a bird, just for a few moments, then she'd be able to see the surf crashing at Land's End, or twenty-five miles farther out at the Isles of Scilly. She closed her eyes and tried to imagine, as if she were a traveling gull, the length of Cornwall, with salt water on both sides and England keeping a firm grip to the east.

She heard a shout, and looked up to see Jack climbing over the wall and leaping down the thirteen steps to where she lay in the center. He came to rest on all fours, rather like a great puppy, panting and sweating. Susan sat up and brushed the bits of grass from her dress. She looked at him. "Will ye really go?" Jack grinned and nodded, and Susan turned away. He tried to see into her face, but her expression told him nothing.

When they were little, they had played like the others, but one afternoon, their mothers looked up from the picnic basket and the somersaulting children to see the two of them sitting against the perimeter wall, their heads bent in towards each other, he picking at the grass between his knees and she slowly twirling a bit of clover. The women glanced over from time to time, and they smiled to see that Jack was talking away, perhaps using a bit of a stick to scrape a hole in the dirt, while Susan listened, now gazing out beyond the rim of the Pit, now counting the blades in a clump of grass, and now serving as shepherd to the ants and beetles that passed among the tufts. The picnics had dwindled as the children grew older, but Jack and Susan kept meeting at the Pit, neither secretly nor openly, but simply without mentioning it to anyone.

Margaret had kept Jack out of the mines until he reached his fourteenth birthday, and while he was proud to fall into the stolid adult routine—the steaming pasty thrust into the can at dawn, the long, matter-of-fact core in a dim tunnel, and the complete exhaustion at the end of the day—he still felt more comfortable with the children, and like a traveler who eagerly but furtively opens a letter from home, he looked forward to these private encounters with Susan, for he had discovered that she would listen, offering neither advice nor judgement, as he puzzled through his new experiences. When something caught her particular attention, she would lift her gaze and he would stop, fighting the catch in his throat as he wondered at the eyes that reminded him of slate a hundred fathoms down, just as grey and just as deceptive.

Susan had found their clandestine meetings irresistible because Jack, still as familiar as a boy, now walked with the men, and he surely must know something that would bring clarity to her apprehensive imaginings. Now fourteen years old, she was moving into a future that her parents presented as safe and predictable, and their casual claims served only to increase her conviction that everything they told her sprang from a quiet conspiracy. Everyone took for granted—although without speaking of it explicitly— that she, like the other women, would slip easily into a role and a pattern that she found bewildering: she would marry a miner, if not from Camborne, then from Crowan or some other nearby parish, and raise sons who would become miners and daughters who would marry other women's mining sons. Her life would be composed of family, of Sunday services, of market days and of occasional festivals. She found the prospect alternately appalling and unconvincing.

Jack seemed to understand the rock so well, feeling safe and secure in the shafts which had become so familiar to him, while she found the land, especially the mines and everything connected with them, to be completely alien. The more she pondered the rocky shores and the granite outcroppings, the more estranged she felt. She found no enchantment in the mines, no soul in the rock. The workings seemed just that, great holes that led to more holes, with armies of men that brought out carts full of stones, some to be crushed and some to be cast aside, some to be sold and some to be scattered. Jack seemed to sense a mystery that remained dark to her, and she longed for magic. Zennora had raised her with legends and fairy tales, and she could not believe that Cornwall, with its ancient farms and fishing villages, its holy wells and stone chapels, its scattered spreading oaks and silent Druidical piles, was nothing more than a collection of excavations. On Sundays, she heard in the hymns something more than the words and the music could plausibly offer, but just as she felt on the verge of reaching the light, the moment dissipated. She perceived in the faces around her a sense of the unseen—the look in her father's eyes when he weighed a lump of ore in his hand, or the calm set of her mother's mouth as she shored up the rock wall that surrounded her garden. For them, she thought, flesh and stone and spirit became one. Yet Susan felt none of this.

She looked back into his face, always so open, always so curious, the blue eyes hiding nothing at all. She took a deep breath and let it out in a long sigh. "So ye're goin' to California." He looked down at her fingers, twisting and twining a bit of wet grass, and took her hand in his. She looked up, intrigued, and they locked fingers. For the first time in years, he had her complete attention, and he looked full into her eyes, waiting, just as she waited. Then he stood, lifted her to her feet, and watched her brush off her skirt, and the two of them climbed the Pit to scale the wall and head home.

2
The Journey
1858

Jack awoke to see his father's beard looming above him, and he quickly pulled on his clothes to help load a neighbor's wagon with their baggage, trudging back and forth in the grey light before dawn. Then he pulled away from his mother's insistent embrace to climb over the sideboard and squeeze in among the bundles in the back. The rocking motion and the squeaking wheels almost put him to sleep before they reached Redruth, but he roused himself to empty the wagon and board the small Cornish local for Plymouth. The next leg was the daily line towards London that crossed moors and downs to leave them at Bristol, where they found an inn and a short night's sleep before another early rising for the trip to Liverpool. All that day, Jack sat pressed against the window, the other men fitted tightly into the bench next to him, and gazed out at the passing countryside, a strange land. They clattered steadily across the Severn, through the green, misty farmlands of Hereford, Shropshire and Cheshire, and past strange villages and troops of smudged laborers walking home from the steel mills near Birmingham. The train skirted outcroppings of the woods that divided the Midlands from Wales, the branches of the trees still black and bare in the damp, and spanned the River Mersey to enter the Liverpool yard, the engine finding its way confidently through the burgeoning maze of tracks. As the dusk gathered around them, Joseph led them to the wharf, where they boarded the *Kangaroo*. The engineer got up steam at first light, and the captain caught the early tide out of the harbor. The Trevennas gathered at the rail, but they lost interest in the strange city and went below for their breakfast. Only Jack remained, fascinated with the receding coastline and the throb of the engines that drove them down St. George's Channel and on into the north Atlantic.

There was little to relieve the tedium of the two-week trip to New York. They were traveling second-class, and so claimed four adjacent bunks in a room that slept twenty men, none of whom displayed any interest in them. Between meals, the great dining cabin was free for passengers to use, so Joseph spent much of his time making drawings in a pocket notebook, a record of the shafts and tunnels of the mines where he had been working, and Jesse sat studying a geography of the world or thumbing through the Bible that his mother had given him as a boy. Nick investigated every inch of the ship, climbing down ladders and walking along passageways to try each door.

The Journey, 1858

Jack spent most of his time on deck, usually as far forward as the crew's work would afford him a space. He had known miners who had been fishermen, and while crouching in the darkness for their croust, the quick meal in the middle of the core, they had talked wistfully of warping out of the harbor to cast their nets into the heaving foam, but Jack had listened only out of courtesy, hearing no wonder to compare with the subterranean architecture around him. Now, compelled to spend six weeks on the surface, and far from land at that, he found himself helplessly beguiled, gazing for hours at the grey-green hillocks and dales that surrounded the *Kangaroo*, emerging and then vanishing, giving transient shape to the water, as though a landscape had come alive and, like the passengers and their vessel, traveled across the face of the earth.

In the afternoons, when the cold wind eased, Jesse climbed up to the deck to walk. He was ten years younger than Joseph, not so heavily built and more inclined to talk and smile, but still as solid as the rock in the floor of a drift, committed to going down into the mines every workday, providing for his family, cherishing his children, and attending Methodist services on Sunday. Yet Susan had told Jack that Jesse, on a day when Dolcoath shut down to repair the pumps, had walked the twenty miles out to Land's End for no apparent reason except to watch water contend with rock in the frothy, turbulent pools. On her tenth birthday, Jesse had given her a piece of lavender quartz that he had found in a drift. He had spent evening after evening chipping away at the lump with a small chisel and a light hammer, shaping it as a jeweler shapes a gem, then re-shaping it again to find all of its fractures and veins, and finally trimming it to the size and form of a small egg, each tiny facet leading evenly into the next to form the gentle arches of the oval. He had given it to her almost casually, choosing a moment when they were alone together, but she treasured it. Her stories had piqued Jack's interest, and now, with neither work nor distraction at hand, he asked Jesse why he was going to California.

His uncle looked at him, grinned, and turned to stare out over the grey waves. "Well, yer fayther persuaded me t' read Dana. That's an eloquent man, and I imagine that Joseph takes 'im very, very seriously."

Jack interrupted. "'e 'as a copy with 'im."

"I don't doubt it. Yer fayther's a sound man, but sometimes 'e lets 'imself see somethin' beyond the wall o' th' shaft. Yet I can't believe that California is th' venturesome garden Dana makes it out t' be. No, John, I'm goin' fer th' mines. If men like us can bring th' gold out o' th' rock, then I can do better there than in Penwith. If not, then I'll be bound 'ome again, 'ome fer th' copper and th' tin."

Jack nodded, studying the railing in front of him, and turned to find his uncle looking sidelong down at him, then shifting his glance furtively away.

Cousin Jack

The look puzzled Jack, but he said nothing about it.

The question had troubled Jesse more than he wanted his inquisitive nephew to know. He did not really know why he was leaving home and family to travel so far away. He was doing well in the copper mines, as well as Joseph, and he was devoted to Zennora, so there was no reason for him to leave Cornwall. Yet there was something in California that drew him. Just after they were married, he and Zennora had gone to Helston for the Furry Dance, and he had thrown himself into the mad procession with increasing abandon, finally so ecstatic that she, in desperation, the dance being done, had slapped his cheek to bring him back. He had announced that he was going to California to take advantage of the rich strike, but he chose that reason because it was what everyone else would expect and the one they would most likely accept. Only Zennora truly knew that he was compelled and driven in a way and by a force that he could not control. Somehow, he had to go to California, whether to find something there or to satisfy some unseemly wanderlust, she could not say, but she knew that he could not rest until he had made the journey and confronted whatever he found there.

The *Kangaroo* arrived in New York City to find docks just as noisy and crowded as the ones they had left, with teams of longshoremen hurrying crates and bundles from hold to cart, or cart to hold, and agents rushing up and down the wharves and in and out of warehouses and offices. The Trevennas disembarked to walk through streets that smelled like horses, the scant breeze leaving the heavy coal-fire smoke drifting sluggishly above them in dirty grey wisps. They passed out of the dockyard district and into a series of narrow alleys lined with shops and residences. None of the Americans simply walked; they marched, they strode, they rushed and they scrambled. Once the visitors stepped off of a curb and hesitated, looking down the street to get their bearings, and started at the crack of a whip and the sudden clopping of a horse bearing down on them. A butcher's wagon had pulled around the corner and nearly run them down, and the teamster called out to them in an unmistakably Irish voice to get out of the road or climb in the back, take their choice. Hardly waiting for them to give him room, he pulled the wagon up, taking the place where they had been standing, and leaped down to unload his cargo, taking no notice of the surprised Cornishmen, shouldering halves of mutton as though they were mere legs of lamb and trotting into the shop with each one, all the while chewing the stub of a cigar. After a few blocks, they crossed an avenue and entered a neighborhood with wider houses and carefully-kept dooryards, but the people, men and women alike, still stepped out crisply, eyes fixed straight ahead on a point thirty yards ahead, and dodging out of their adamantly straight trajectories with slight impatience and no slackening of speed. Even the horses trotted along resolutely, whether pulling a buggy or carrying a boldly mustached rider.

The Journey, 1858

They cast off the next morning and made their way down to the mouth of the Hudson and through the Narrows with a full complement: eight hundred passengers stuffed into every available bunk and cabin. The ship was crowded now; on fine afternoons, the deck was too full of people for a man to walk freely, and on cold or wet days, every seat in the dining-saloon was taken. Joseph seemed not to mind, taking to his bunk as though he were a thousand feet underground, wedged into a shelf in a narrow vein, and he firmly insisted that Nick follow his example. Jesse lay in his bunk for hours, paging through his Bible or writing long letters to Zennora. Jack stayed near them for two days but then, unable to lie still any longer, went above to trace his way through the clusters of people idling on deck.

Just south of Cape Hatteras, the *Kangaroo* steamed into a storm, and the captain sent his officers around to request that all passengers retire to their cabins for their own safety and to leave the decks clear for the crew. The Trevennas wedged their belongings into secure corners as the water slapped against the porthole and the faint sound of unhappy moaning seeped through the bulkheads from the forward steerage compartment. Joseph had just finished repacking part of his trunk when he noticed that Jack was missing. They waited five minutes, then fifteen, and then half an hour before Jesse suggested that they try to find him. Joseph held his brother in his bunk with a look, then swung himself out to drop on the deck and lace up his boots. He checked with the purser, and the man assured him that he'd seen no one wandering about and that due to the ship being so full, there was little chance that the missing man was riding out the storm in someone else's cabin. He gave Joseph permission to search on deck, but tersely ordered him to stay well clear of the railing.

Joseph climbed up the companionway and stood at the top for a moment, surprised by the violence of the wind and the spray. For a moment, he felt as though he had reached the mouth of the main shaft at Cook's Kitchen on a gusty day, with the wind chasing itself across the narrow peninsula from the Mount to St. Ives' Bay and back again, and carrying the slashing rain and the salt smell down all the mines in between. Yet no man had ever come to grass to find the sett, the grounds of the mine, heaving like this. He looked past the rail to find a ridge of water which disappeared in the next moment as the *Kangaroo* climbed out of a trough and seemed to swing up high enough to engulf him as the steamer slid down into another. He wiped the salt water out of his eyes and tried to get his stomach under control so he could look around for his son. He slowly groped his way aft, hanging onto the superstructure every step of the way, and then around the port side and forward. Just when he was about to go below again and try to persuade the purser to send a couple of crewmen around to search, he found him.

Jack was standing as far forward as possible, at the very precipice of the deck. Joseph could not imagine how he could keep from losing his footing and sliding helplessly over the side, but he realized, squinching his eyes to peer through the spume and sparge, that the boy was lashed to a stanchion behind and to the railing before. Secured, he was free to lift his chin to the wind and raise his arms as the water flew around him. He was wearing a sou'wester—doubtless a loan from the same crewman who had lashed him into position—but he'd lost the headgear, and from the collar up, he was completely soaked. Still, as Joseph could see when he turned his head to look at a giant wave that appeared off to port, he was grinning with delight. The spare tip of a wave flicked at the ship and slapped Jack full in the face, and as soon as he caught his breath, he laughed, wiping the salt water from his eyes and tasting it on his fingers. The waters rose and fell as the steamer pitched and rolled in the storm, and Jack lifted his hands as though imposing his will on the sea-surge.

Joseph paused, one arm looped through a safety ring, and stared at his son, forgetting about his anxiety, anger and apprehension. Jack was a daring miner, sometimes too cocky for his own safety, but Joseph had always accepted his boldness as a natural consequence of growing up among the mines. Few men in Kerrier and Penwith stopped to consider the enormity of their everyday labors; even after a cave-in, the crews went down the next day as though nothing had happened. For all that, there was something solid and secure about going underground that made this ocean travel seem fool-hardy. The sea was capricious in a way that stone was not. When a fall of rock caught a pare, it was usually because someone had used too much powder, or failed to prop up a drift, or hadn't bothered to spend enough time finding out if the walls were solid or just tary ground, broken and ready to collapse. Only rarely did a man die because the earth itself betrayed him. Yet the sea, thought Joseph, might do anything, with no more than a strong breath of wind and a twitch of a current that no one could see until it tossed a vessel like a chip in a swollen river. Jack had somehow made himself free of the sea, daring wind and water to take him out. Joseph took a deep breath, then slowly pulled himself to the companionway and down to his cabin. By morning, the storm had passed on.

The *Kangaroo* steamed into the Caribbean, through the Windward Passage and past Jamaica towards Central America. On the tenth day out of New York, Jack lay in his bunk wearing little more than a shirt and dreaming of a summer afternoon at Gwennap Pit. Then he realized that Nick was shaking him gently by the shoulder, calling to him to wake up. The brothers ran on deck and gazed ahead.

At first, Jack saw nothing but a grey blur on the horizon, like a muddled fog bank. Then, off to port, the sun rose, and suddenly green flecks glowed, suspended over the water in the distance, and spread down to meet the sea.

The Journey, 1858

It was the Isthmus, its jungle highlands catching the first light of day and bringing it down to the valleys and villages below. As the *Kangaroo* made its final approach into Aspinwall, the sea breeze subsided and Jack caught his first scent of the land: lush and green, much richer than a harvest of hay in England, but also thick and heavy. His empty stomach began to turn; he closed his eyes, trying to control the nausea, but he could not get a breath of fresh air. They had been at sea for nearly four weeks, and this land smell, this odor of mold and rot, was overpowering. There was a line of warehouses on the far side of the wharf, but beyond them Jack could see a swamp, its still waters wreathed in a mist that rose in response to the morning sun but then floated indecisively in the absolutely still air. On the dock below, piles of iron chain showed rust everywhere, and reddish-brown streaks and stains marred the recently shiny tin on the warehouses. On the roofs, vultures stretched their necks and flapped their wings slowly, as though trying to catch enough wind to soar, but then subsided, perching glumly and staring down at the ship coming into port. The captain called out an order, and seamen fore and aft threw lines down toward the pier, where men slowly stooped to pick up the bights and throw them over the waiting butts. The dockhands' skins were darker than Jack had ever seen, ranging from the color of coffee grounds to a deep mahogany. Some had black, nappy hair, cut close to their heads, while others had dirty, dark brown locks falling heavily to their shoulders. A light rain began to fall, but the men on the dock seemed not to notice.

The captain shut down his engines and a bell warned the passengers to disembark. The Trevennas gathered their luggage and followed the others, walking down the gangway and along the dock to the railroad station. To one side of it was the City Hotel, where men and women alike slept on cots set outside on the long verandahs. A man walking next to him grinned and suggested they spend the day in the bar and wait for the next train to Panamá. "They say whiskey's the best thing to keep off the yellow fever!" But they kept walking through the shower, wavering now, and up the steps to the waiting train. Nick exclaimed incredulously at the fare—$25 apiece—but Joseph paid it without a word, and the Trevennas barely had time to arrange themselves in one end of a car before the train lurched into motion, starting up the canyon of the Chagres to make the three-hour journey to Panamá.

The rain forest was a peaceful riot of iridescent green leaves and spectacularly gaudy flowers, with strange fruits hanging far above the tangled thicket of undergrowth. Jack saw a small troop of marmosets scrambling up and down a gently leaning trunk, chattering to each other and screaming at the puffing engine. Towards mid-morning, the train chugged past a village, a cluster of bamboo huts with roofs of thatched palm leaves, set perfectly against the jewel tones of the jungle. Then he noticed the sagging walls and caved-in roofs, the stagnant pools steeping in oozing blue mud, and the gangs of sullen monkeys picking listlessly at heaps of rotting offal. A lone man crouched in the doorway of a hut, wearing nothing but a bright orange shirt, his dark skin and disheveled hair smeared with mud. He stared straight ahead, his mouth hanging open, noticing neither the nibbling monkeys nor the passing train with its crowd of gaping white men. The sun shone more and more brightly, and Jack realized that they were emerging from the heavy green shade of the forest. The tone of the engine changed slightly and the track turned to the right. Jack looked out of the window and saw, about fifteen miles away, the shining blue water of the Bay of Panamá. The train descended into the city.

The town had spread haphazardly up from the port, piling on top of itself in its haste to make room for more saloons, more faro games, more brothels, and especially more ramshackle hotels for the travelers. The narrow streets twisted unpredictably between dirty, decaying adobe buildings, and the rough, worn stones made casual gutters for the stinking slops that oozed and dribbled down to the sea. Whenever the track interrupted a cart path, the passengers stared at one or two waiting donkey carts, usually laden with vegetables and fruits stuffed into bushel baskets woven of palm fronds, each attended by a tired, apathetic man with a wide straw hat and a black mustache that dominated his brown face. The smell of the city was rank; even stronger than at Aspinwall. Then the engine slowed, and the back alleys of the city gave way to the fringes of the train yard. As the Trevennas climbed down onto the platform, Jack thought he could smell the sea air again, and he let the freshness draw him along, following the others until they reached the quay where their ship lay waiting. Far above the gangway, a man with a fiery red beard and a black-billed blue cap looked them over with glaring eyes and called down to the agent on the dock to ask how many more were coming. Almost as soon as the Trevennas found their second-class cabin, they heard an accumulating volley of cries and answers, and Jack ran out onto the deck to watch the *Golden Age* weigh anchor and get up steam for San Francisco.

The ship followed the lane up the coast, past the beaches of Nicaragua and the Gulf of Fonseca, and farther northwest until it reached the first landfall at Acapulco. The warm sun and cool breezes brought the passengers out of their stuffy, crowded cabins, and the water was so calm that no one complained of feeling seasick. The tables in the vast dining-saloon were filled with the best that the galley could provide: fresh duck and lamb, roast kid, strange new fish, puddings and cakes, fresh eggs, green corn and peas newly hulled, oranges and bananas, raisins and filberts. Men brushed their shoes and hats, and women brought out parasols they had been saving for California. Jack and Nick spent hours at the railing, gazing as though mesmerized at the bow cutting through the blue-green water. Once they saw a school of dolphins that kept pace with them for nearly an hour.

At each port, the captain invited the passengers to disembark, so Jack wandered the seaside streets of Manzanillo, San Blas and Mazatlán, never tiring of the peasants' costumes—the men in their dirty white trousers and smocks, with straw sandals and straw hats, and the women muffled in their black skirts and dark shawls, but with splashes of embroidered colors in unfamiliar patterns—and the adobe houses, built one up against the other, the thick walls pushing in on the narrow, spiralling streets. On the first day, he returned to the ship with a small terra-cotta figurine, but Joseph was so annoyed with him for wasting their money and adding to their baggage that from then on he brought only mangoes, pineapples and small red bananas.

Joseph had little attention to spare for Jack, because Nick's latest escapade had preoccupied him. The boy had asked for permission to go ashore, and his father had given him a few bits of silver in case of emergency. But before disembarking, Nick had stopped to watch a pair of well-dressed Americans, each smoking a cigar and wearing a pair of soft, calf-length boots, who were betting on which sea gull would first fly away from the top of the wheelhouse. Fascinated, he remained, and finally persuaded them to let him wager with his small change. After four hours of good luck and bad, he had doubled his money, and so ran back to Joseph and Jesse, expecting their praise. Instead, Joseph slammed his fist against a bulkhead and marched below to his cabin, leaving Jesse to explain their disapproval. Nick stood with his jaw hanging open and the confused hurt displayed on his face; he barely spoke for the rest of the voyage.

In the refulgent Pacific sunshine, the passengers seemed to glow, and even the *Golden Age*, a new vessel painted in clean colors, glistened and shimmered. They left Mazatlán and rounded Cabo San Lucas to reach up the barren coastline of Baja California, and the sun set directly in front of them, dipping into the ocean like a hot coal. The mandarin light tinted each expectant face, sprinkled even the darker heads with glistening highlights, and turned the officers' blue uniforms to opaque black.

Their first American landfall was San Diego, but the captain paused only long enough to take on fresh coal and water, leaving the passengers tantalized by white, sandy beaches and pale green lagoons. They steamed up the coast, past the offshore islands and into cooler waters, where they stopped at Monterey, just for an hour in the middle of the night, before heading north for their final destination.

Jack was standing near the starboard bow, watching the coastline, barely visible above the waves, when the *Golden Age* began a slow turn and he looked ahead to realize that there was a break in the hills. The quartermaster settled on his new course, and there, its headlands dipped in fog, was the Golden Gate, green grass running up the slope on the northern side, and a rocky bluff marking the southern edge. A flock of seagulls rode the swells, and as the ship drew nearer, the birds stretched their wings and sprang up, out of the kelp and seaweed, to trace patterns in the air and glide on the breeze. One of them came to rest on the anchor windlass, cocking its head to look at the new arrivals before calling out and lifting its wings to the sky again.

The Trevennas stood at the rail as the ship warped into the dock. Beyond the dockside warehouses spread new buildings, wood and stone and brick, with flat roofs set over rows of windows, some crowned with keystones in gentle arches, spaced as evenly as the tap of a hammer. Jack looked back at the bay behind them; through the thickets of masts and spars—delicate skeletons of clippers resting before the rush to China or New York—he could see green islands, and beyond them, the blue hills rising up from the other side of the water. He jumped at a sudden report from the upper deck; an officer had organized a small gun crew to fire a salute to announce, redundantly, their arrival. Joseph led the family down the gangplank, through the crowd of express wagons and hand carts, and past the agents' booths and the lines of cabs and coaches, and on towards the center of the city. As they trudged along the boardwalk, weaving a path through urgent men in suits and sailors striding two and three across, Jack could hear fragments of conversations, phrases of Spanish and Portuguese, French and Italian, and of languages he had never heard before. They passed rooms and courtyards, their doors thrown open to the street, where men sat eating meals, some alone and some in groups, eagerly leaning across the tables and gesticulating at each other with full mouths. Finally, Joseph stopped at a stone building on Dupont Street, laid down a few coins on the counter, and nodded to the others to follow him upstairs, where they found a room bare of furniture except for four mattresses laid on the floor. They set down their luggage, double-locked the door, and clattered down the stairs and out onto the street, where Joseph and Jesse headed back to the wharf, hoping to arrange their passage to Sacramento.

Jack and Nick strolled up the street, trying to fit in by matching the pace of the other pedestrians and not looking around too obviously. Every man walked as though he were late for an appointment on the far side of town, and no one seemed to notice anyone else. Every shop and office seemed full and busy; men walked in and out of doors, back and forth before tall counters, and around display cases and wide tables. In nearly every block, an express wagon stood pulled up to one side, its horse calmly grinding its teeth while a team of men trotted to and fro with crates and bundles, and drays, cabs and smart buggies passed by with surprising speed, each driver assessing a gap with a glance and casually turning to check the clearance as he spun along. On one corner, strangely placid, was a new stone church.

The boys were the only ones who stopped to stare at a man who wore a complete costume from the days before the war with Bonaparte. His coat, waistcoat and knee breeches were all in black velvet, with shining white lace setting off his neck and wrists. Brass buckles shone from his low-cut shoes, and his three-cornered hat displayed not only gold piping around the curving edge but also an embroidered medallion of an eagle, its wings spread in challenge, between the numerals "17" and "76." In one hand, he carried an elegant sword cane that he swung and flourished as he proceeded down the boardwalk, and those he passed, while apparently not noticing him at all, maneuvered so that he could continue his stately parade uninhibited.

After a while, they stopped in front of a shaving saloon to look up through the plate glass window at the barber tending to a customer. Nick grinned and dug an elbow into Jack's ribs. Accepting the challenge, Jack climbed the stairs and walked into the room, where a Negro in striped shirtsleeves approached, his teeth gleaming, and drew him over to sit in a purple velvet chair. As the Negro offered a tufted stool for his feet, the barber, a man with thick red forearms and curled auburn mustachios, asked whether he wanted a shampoo. Jack looked over at Nick, who was leaning against the door jamb with his arms folded, and Nick nodded. The barber took his head in both hands, massaging his scalp with the pads of his fingers, all the way from the hairline to the back of the neck. The Negro took him to a marble washstand, where he draped towels over his shoulders, politely invited him to lean over, and rinsed his head under a gush of lukewarm water from a brass tap, scrubbing with a pair of brushes to move the hair this way and that in the flow. Jack opened his eyes carefully under the torrent and saw the water flowing brown down the drain. The Negro gently raised him to a standing position, took a third towel and dried his head all over, scrubbing and rubbing so that he panted in Jack's face; sour sage and rank onions. He soaked Jack's head all over again, patted it dry, and sprinkled eau de Cologne from crown to nape. Jack reached up to wipe some of it out of his ears, and he could see Nick laughing from the doorway. His guide led him back to the velvet chair, where the barber twirled one wheel to raise him off the floor, and another to lower his head and raise his feet until he was nearly prone. The barber assailed his head with a comb and a pair of scissors, occasionally stepping back to assess the results or twirling the chair to regard his client in the mirror that nearly covered the nearby wall. Whenever he made a decision, he dug in the comb and started the scissors snipping at arm's length, bringing them in, the metal snicking together rapidly, until he reached the locks he had selected. Then he spun the chair again, raised Jack's head just long enough for him to regard the stranger in the mirror and nod approval, and lowered him down again before washing his hands in a basin. The Negro slapped Jack's face with hot water and covered his cheeks and chin with lather from a brush. The barber laid his hands on Jack's jaw, pressing his fingers through the lather and lightly massaging the stubble as though to soften it. Then, with surprisingly few strokes, he scraped Jack's face clean with a long razor, and when he was finished, the Negro wiped away the remaining lather and returned the customer to earth. Nick paid them both and took Jack to a high bench where two Frenchmen, each wielding a pair of stiff brushes, first scrubbed the dirt off of the boys' boots and then rubbed in dollops of black polish that they buffed to a shine wherever the worn leather would stand it. Back on the boardwalk, Jack reached up to feel his chin, strangely small and clearly defined. The breeze felt cool on his skin, and he realized that he smelled sweet.

When they returned to the hotel, Joseph announced that in honor of their arrival, they would dine at a fine establishment. They brushed each other off—Jesse smiled when he noticed the boys' boots—and walked around the corner to a parlor with white linen table cloths and shining silver. An impassive waiter offered each man a menu written in swirling letters. Jack realized that most of the dishes were listed in French, and he looked up, wondering what to do. Joseph was frowning at the card and Nick was simply staring at it, but Jesse winked and beckoned to the waiter, who grudgingly translated. There were bear, elk, deer and antelope; wild birds like quail, brant, snipe, plover, curlew and crane; and fresh salmon and trout. Everything, the waiter assured them, was found locally and provided especially for the management by private arrangement. Joseph shook his head over the profusion and insisted on ordering roast beef. Jesse asked for a venison steak while Jack, suddenly wanting something as unusual as possible, chose a dish made from a turtle. Nick, trying not to appear overwhelmed, announced that he would have "Fricassée de Lapin," but when the plate arrived, the other men stared and then burst out laughing, for the little skinned carcass, still blackened from roasting and dressed in some sort of brown sauce, was clearly the remains of a common tree squirrel.

They left the dining hall to discover that Dupont Street had come alive. There was hardly any wheeled traffic now, and well-dressed men and women had claimed the street as their promenade. Doors that Jack had earlier taken for discreet warehouse entrances were now wide open, revealing gambling houses: the Bella Union, the Empire and the El Dorado. He and Nick managed to lag behind the others and stop in one doorway to look inside. There were Chinese, some wearing red silk and others blue cotton, bent over a dished table, throwing dice and chattering loudly at each other. At another table, men smoking cigars and shouting in English bet on the cards that a shirtsleeved dealer slid out of a shoe. In the center of the room was a tall counter ringed by Mexicans wearing tight suits with many buttons, their dark hair shining in the light of the crystal chandelier hanging above them. Jack stepped in closer and lifted his chin to see one of the Mexicans turn a card, look across at his opponent, and reach out to gather in several small leather pouches that looked worthless. The other man looked down at the disappearing pouches, glanced up at the winner, and without even a shrug, tossed the butt of his thin cigar into the nearest spittoon and began to cut the end off of another.

Nick moved farther and farther into the room until he managed to find an empty chair. No sooner had he sat down than a young woman swept around from behind the monte table and perched on his knee. She smiled down into his startled face, resting one arm across the back of his shoulders and, with her free hand, slowly and lightly running the tips of her fingers from his collar up to his earlobe and then to his cheekbone. "My name is Angèle." Her hair was a confection of brown falls and curls, softly presenting rouged cheeks, precisely painted lips and slanted dark eyes with arched eyebrows. Her arms were bare, and her green silk dress scooped so low in front that Jack could see the swell of her breasts as she slouched down to tickle Nick under the chin. Her shoes were scuffed and scarred, and the hem of her gown was torn and stained.

Jack felt a hand fall on his shoulder, and he turned to see his father, with Jesse behind him. Joseph pulled Jack down onto the boardwalk and stepped up onto the main floor. "Nicky!"

Nick jerked his head like a startled fox, and when he saw his father standing there, he scrambled to his feet, dumping the girl so quickly that she nearly fell. Joseph reached in and pulled his son out of the room and down into the street, where Jesse caught him. The Trevennas continued back to the hotel, but Jack looked back to see the girl standing in the doorway pointing her finger and calling sharply, "Give me an ounce!"

On the following morning, Joseph quietly announced that they would all go to meet a man who knew something about the mines northeast of Sacramento. They walked along Market Street towards the Bay, and whenever Jack and Nick lingered to look at something, one of the older men would reach out and push them along. Although the boys tried to pay attention to the meeting, Jack found himself glancing out the windows at any shadow that passed by. Back on the street, his father hurried them along, but near a corner they found their way almost completely blocked by a small crowd of men and women who were smiling and craning their necks to see something. In the center of the gathering, people were laughing. Even Joseph was curious, so they pushed through until they could see.

There on the steps of a theatre stood a burly man with a massive head and a full beard. He wore a uniform of navy blue broadcloth, trimmed with brass buttons and heavy gilt epaulettes, topped off with a crumpled kepi decorated with red braided piping. He had apparently finished some sort of introduction and now unrolled a dirty piece of paper in order to read in a gravelly voice:

Cousin Jack

"Whereas, certain parties having assumed prerogatives, pertaining only to my Royal self, and whereas, in the furtherance of such assumption, they have printed and circulated treasonable and rebellious documents, circulars, sermons and proclamations, calculated to distract and divide the allegiance of my subjects . . . "

Jesse turned to the man standing next to him and whispered, "Is this a play?"

The man chuckled. "No, it's Norton. Crazy, but harmless. Oh—listen!"

The burly man had not stopped reading.

"Now, Therefore, I, Emperor Norton the First, do hereby command that no notice shall be paid to proclamations issued by Pretenders to my authority, ability, and regal position. And it is further commanded, that any violation of this command shall be reported to me, in order that I may banish the offender from my Kingdom. Given in San Francisco, this day, the twenty-first of April, eighteen-hundred and fifty-eight."

The crowd applauded and waved their hats in the air, and the burly man walked solemnly through the crowd, nodding and occasionally shaking hands. His path took him right to Jack, who was too startled to move out of the way.

Emperor Norton lifted his chin to regard the young man from underneath eyebrows that bristled out from below his forehead. "Ah?"

Jack, not knowing what else to do, said, "Good day, sir."

Emperor Norton's eyebrows rose. "An Englishman? Always a pleasure. Please proffer my warmest regards to Victoria." He moved past and continued his journey through his smiling subjects.

The Trevennas followed Joseph out to the street, where he shook his head. "We're sailin' t' Sacramento tonight." They boarded the *Antelope* that evening and steamed up the Bay until, under the pale moonlight, Jack could see that the bay hills had closed in to become riverbanks. He fell asleep before they arrived.

On the following morning, Joseph once again took them in tow, leading them up and down Front Street so he could meet with assayers, agents, and men in banks. Jack found the place distracting; not as cosmopolitan as San Francisco, but just as busy, with wagons lumbering up and down the rutted roads and messenger boys skipping lightly past. By mid-afternoon, he had slowly realized that everyone they met or observed seemed to be involved in serving the mines in some way—shipping supplies, arranging financing, processing gold, and so forth. Even the farmers seemed to have planted their fields only to feed the miners who brought the metal up out of the ground.

The Trevennas dined at a plain table in their boarding house, but Joseph reluctantly agreed, after a quiet conversation with Jesse, that Nick and Jack might go for a walk on their own, exacting from them solemn promises not to get into trouble and to return no later than 9 p.m. He even insisted that they empty their pockets, and he took care that each of them left with only six shillings.

The boys wandered up and down the waterfront for a while and then decided to have a beer. They were standing at the bar, sipping from their glasses, when a man with bushy sidewhiskers and a full mustache walked up to stand next to them. He raised a finger to the bar man, who nodded casually, reached underneath for a brown bottle of whiskey, poured a drink, waited while the customer drank it down, then poured him another and left the bottle on the bar. The newcomer took a swallow from his glass, let out a breath, set his wide-brimmed hat on the bar and turned to look at the two boys. His curly black hair was carefully parted on one side, and he wore a plum-colored velvet waistcoat over a perfectly white shirt, all underneath a worn, travel-stained coat that fell past to his muddy, calf-length boots. When he pulled the coat back to hook one thumb into his belt, Jack could see the revolver resting in the holster at his thigh. He scanned Jack and Nick up and down, aiming his long nose at each in turn, then shook his head. "You're not miners."

"But we are," protested Jack.

The man smiled slightly. "Ah—just arrived?" The boys nodded. "My God—I can hardly remember. So, you've come to the new Golconda. Where are you bound?"

Jack and Nick looked at each other. "Somewhere near Grass Valley."

The man nodded. "Going for the climate, are you?" The boys did not know what to say, but Jack thought the man was smiling. "Here, let me buy you a drink. Nathaniel!" He summoned the bar man, who poured two more beers. "Just put it down, Nathaniel, put it down. You know I'm good for it." The bar man shook his head and went back to polishing glasses. "My name is Harte." He offered his hand to Jack and then Nick, who introduced themselves. "English?"

"Cornish."

Harte's eyebrows rose slightly. "Cornish. Well." He took another swallow from his whiskey. "You must be careful."

"Careful?" asked Nick.

"Certainly. There are highwaymen. Bandits. Murieta himself considers Grass Valley part of his territory. But then," Harte smiled, "he thinks that Wells, Fargo are his personal transport agents." Another swallow of whiskey. "But what about you?"

"We're goin' up t' mine."

Harte smiled ruefully. "Yes, yes, of course, but still . . . Anything might happen. Hard to say." He lifted the bottle and replenished his glass. "You say you're here to work, here to bring out the gold. Living in the diggings—bark roofs, adobe chimneys. Looking for color. Greenhorns' luck. They tell me that some of the old prospectors still roam the hills, still pack their pans and bedrolls on the backs of their faithful donkeys. Do you know . . . do you know that some of those men stay in the hills for months at a time? Following the streams up to the very heart of the high Sierra, the Sierra Nevada, the snowy mountains. The wall between California and the rest. Into the heart of the crest. Deep inside. Searching for the glint, the shining." He looked into Jack's eyes. "One man stayed up there alone for two years, and came down to a settlement, a camp, really, only to see a child. *To see a child!* He stood there on the street, fingers locked in his long beard, his hat drooping from so many rains, his suspenders cutting a groove in the red shirt over his back, thin from undereating, his eyes hollow but hopeful, waiting for the child to pass by. He had heard a rumor; it might not be true. There might be no one. But there was. The child came out of a hotel, holding its mother's hand, and they walked up the road, finding the only dry path in the ruts. The prospector stood in the mud, watching, and when they passed opposite him . . . they *stopped!* They looked right at him, mother and child. The child gazed at him with innocent eyes, all pink cheeks and golden curls. The child smiled, and the prospector felt as though he might burst. Then they went on, and the prospector stood there, tears streaming from his eyes. The other men on the street brought out their handkerchiefs, nodding their heads and averting their faces. Finally, two of them took that man, that prospector, into a hotel, where the landlord gave him a room, and a bath, and clean sheets, and one of the women of the town held his hand as he curled up underneath those blankets and finally fell asleep. But the next morning, he packed his burro again and set out for the streams, the streams of gold."

Jack found that his cheeks were wet, and he brought out his handkerchief. Nick had turned his head away and seemed to be sniffling. "Is that really true?" asked Jack.

Harte looked at him for a long moment, the compassion for the lonely prospector suffusing his face. Then he turned and poured himself another drink. "It's crap. But they buy it in San Francisco. Pray God they'll buy it in New York some day." With that, he took his hat and strode out into the evening.

Joseph spent most of the following day finishing his business in Sacramento, but by the time the sun set, the Trevennas were sitting in a stage coach, listening to the horses begin the long, slow climb up into the foothills.

3
Red Dog
1858

The light was bright, too bright, and Jack lifted his hand to block out the glare, wondering where his father had found such a lantern to bring down to the fifth level. Then he realized that the beams were filtering through feathery black branches and his left arm had become tangled in the blankets. He rolled over and propped himself up on one elbow.

He was lying in a small, musty tent, and the flap of canvas that served as the front door was hanging askew, leaving a small opening. Through it, he could see that the rising sun was barely reaching over the grassy ridge on the far side of a small, shallow valley. The pine branches above Jack's head seemed gilded, their green needles darkly metallic, and he held his hand up to the light to discover that his fingers glowed orange. He turned his palm into the beam and away, contemplating the ruddy translucence of his skin, but then the saffron flush faded, leaving only white warmth. Jack looked around him; the others were still asleep: Joseph with his head thrown back and his jaw hanging open, Jesse lying serenely on his side, and Nick curled up like a cat. Jack quietly peeled back his blankets, found his boots, and carried them outside to put them on and lace them up. Then he walked down through the trees towards the tents and cabins of Red Dog.

The village had appeared, abruptly, several years earlier when a company of prospectors made a rich strike on Raccoon Creek, a small brook that meandered through a wide, green meadow before rushing across a granite moraine and down a steep gorge towards Grass Valley, a town about five miles away. They staked their claims and pitched their tents above the gravel bars where they worked their sluice boxes. As news of the strike spread, more miners rode in, quickly pacing out the statutory one hundred feet per man and setting up hasty camps to guard their new hopes. One man began serving whiskey from a broken plank resting across two wobbly barrels, and as his business prospered, he set up adjoining tents, then built a wooden shed, and finally raised a two-story building that served as the settlement's first saloon and boarding house. Two other men began bringing in mule trains loaded with provisions, and when there were enough prospective customers camped in the meadow, they, too, opened a store and brought in lumber to build a small warehouse with a long counter running across one doorway. The strike played out after only two years, but Red Dog had become the base camp for all the miners working in that area, those who lived in tents just beyond the shops, and those who unrolled their blankets on the long brown needles beneath the tall pine trees that rose above the nearby hillsides.

Jack found his way to the wagon trail that still served as Red Dog's main street, a chaos of ruts arranged in a lazy curve well above the creek and any likely mining claims. Some of the façades were attached to new, wooden buildings, while others were mere scaffoldings supporting display crates, signs and crude doorways, the frameworks lashed securely to large tents. There were shops selling hardware and miners' equipment—potbellied stoves, tin pans, sand-colored crockery, rope in all lengths and sizes, blasting powder and fuses, knives, shovels, pickaxes, canvas hoses, brass nozzles, small sluice boxes, flannel shirts, broad-brimmed hats and winter gear—and those offering provisions—stacked bags of rice and flour, smaller sacks of tobacco, coffee, tea and sugar, hanging hams and sides of bacon, small crocks of butter and kegs of lard, bottles of "genuine" French brandy and "choice" wines, and feed for mules and horses. Hanging above the porch of one small cabin was a neatly-lettered sign informing passers-by that Edward W. Milford, banker and notary public, would gladly assay the miners' gold, weigh it, purchase it and ship it to San Francisco, and would also serve as the local freight agent for Wells, Fargo & Co. There were similar signs announcing that Red Dog had a barber who would shave the miners, a boot maker who would repair their shoes, and a druggist who would prepare the prescriptions that the physician—a man who had practiced medicine in Maryland, came west in '49 and now lingered, lost—had promised would cure their ailments. When the miners disagreed on the ownership of a claim, or when a partnership needed to be formed or dissolved, one of Red Dog's three lawyers arranged their affairs. A livery stable, set halfway down the row of shops, offered to keep horses or to rent a variety of heavy wagons, or, for special occasions, a smart, two-seater buggy. Scattered among these various enterprises were no less than fourteen saloons ranging from a lean-to where the proprietor served shots of green whiskey in tin cups, to the bar opening onto the lobby of the Red Dog Hotel, by far the most imposing edifice in town, a two-story masterpiece of planking, hasty gingerbread and bright paint, with a small but genteel lounge appointed with a plate-glass mirror set behind rows of sparkling decanters, two polished oak tables with comfortable leather chairs, and a few carefully-placed spittoons intended to encourage the miners to respect the thick, colorful rugs that the proprietor, who called himself Professor Kennedy, had shipped around the Horn. Most of the shopkeepers and professionals lived there, and when an ambitious, earnest man made the rounds of an evening, telling stories, listening to news, seeking advice and making deals, he generally ended his tour with one foot resting on Kennedy's polished brass rail.

Red Dog, 1858

The Trevennas spent the following weeks exploring every hill and ravine in the area. Joseph set the itinerary, and his interest was specific: he wanted to study every mining operation he could find, whether working or abandoned. On some mornings, he split the family, sending Jesse one direction while he went another, each brother taking one of the younger men with him. In the evenings, Jesse read his Bible until dark, but Joseph visited the saloons of Red Dog, drinking as little as possible while gathering as much information as he could find. Late one afternoon, just before dinner, he brought three visitors back to the tent: William Pascoe, an older man who had been mining since he was a small boy, and his sons, James and Will. Joseph introduced them as cousins, connected somehow through his mother's family, and as old friends. At Cook's Kitchen, years earlier, William had given Joseph his first underground job, as his helper.

Jack found that he had time to spare, so while his father investigated the mines, he studied the people of Red Dog. Nearly all of them were young men, younger than his father, and except for those running businesses, every one, apparently, was a miner. They came to town to buy provisions, repair their equipment, bring bags of dust to the assayer, or visit the saloons, but they never stayed long, always eager to get back to their claims, where they worked from dawn to dusk. There were but few families in Red Dog, but many of the men had left wives and children in places like New York, Pennsylvania, Ohio, Tennessee and Missouri. Temporarily single, they lived with their mining partners, each little group sharing food and shelter. The hills were full of meadows that seemed fertile and well-watered, but no one seemed interested in farming. Every man was bent on taking as much gold as he could find and then returning to the East to live in comfort; even the merchants seemed to regard their situation as temporary. Actual cash was scarce, so the men did their business with promises and small sacks of gold dust.

One afternoon, Jack walked farther than usual and crossed over a saddle to find a cluster of tents and cabins that he had never seen before. He slowed as he realized that every man he saw was Chinese. He had noticed Chinese miners in shops and saloons, and he had occasionally wondered where they lived; this must be their own village, set apart from the rest. There were men crouched over cooking fires, sitting under trees with their pipes, and looking out from under tent flaps and out of doorways as the stranger walked past them. Jack blinked at the repeated pattern of black, slitted eyes, high sallow forehead and neat black braid reaching halfway down the back. Each man turned his head to follow the white man with the round blue eyes and pale, wavy hair until Jack reached the last cabin and a man stepped out of the doorway to block his path. The challenger was exactly as tall as he, so they stood nose to nose. Fascinated, Jack was barely able to notice that he, like all the other men in this little camp, wore a loose blue smock and matching trousers. The two stood, motionless, for several moments. Finally, the man slowly lifted a hand and took Jack's lapel between the thumb and forefinger.

"Washee washee?" Jack did not understand. "Me washee you shirt? One dollah hap dozen—me washee you camp. Sabbee?" Jack had heard the Chinese chatter in the main camp, but none had ever addressed him and the pidgin was completely unexpected. The other man seemed to understand the problem and frowned a bit. Then his face relaxed into a hint of a smile. Still holding Jack's lapel, he leaned in and sniffed the shirt. He quickly drew his head back and winced, holding his nose and fanning the air in front of him. Then he broke the pose and pointed firmly at Jack's shirt. "Washee washee!"

As Jack gaped at the sudden performance, the camp behind him erupted into a roar of laughter, and suddenly he understood. The man was offering to do his laundry, even to take on the dirty clothes for his "camp"—his family—at the rate of one dollar for six shirts. Jack smiled, the other man smiled, and while the rest of the Chinese laughed and chattered, the two shook hands on the deal.

Jack took a large load to the laundry man the next evening, another the next, and then smaller bundles every few days. He soon discovered that most of the Americans gave their laundry to the Chinese, but that nearly all of them refused to visit the Chinese camp, so that each day, Chinese men, their pigtails swinging, would carry baskets through the shops and around to the tents and cabins of the white men, picking up mounds of dirty, wadded clothing, and returning with bundles of clean shirts wrapped in paper, folded and tucked securely so they would need no string. Jack chose to carry the wash himself, for the Chinese village fascinated him. The residents soon grew accustomed to him, and rather than stare, as they had done the first time, they went about their business, chattering in a language whose very sounds Jack could not fathom at all. The laundry man's name was Ah Choy, and he apparently found Jack amusing, for he grinned at him whenever he appeared. When Jack indicated an interest in his abacus, he chuckled and showed him how it worked, flicking the beads along the wires to add up the Trevennas' bill. Jack tried to work the contraption himself, but he slid the beads so slowly that Ah Choy and his friends laughed and shook their heads. The business seemed to be doing quite well—there were always stacks of clean laundry piled high on his counter, and at least two assistants ran back and forth to the white men's camp—but nothing about Ah Choy's tent or his clothing suggested prosperity greater than his neighbors. Jack could not shake the feeling that the man knew more than he chose to reveal. Once Jack brought Jesse with him, and while they were waiting for an assistant to add up their bill, Jack took the moment to point out this and that about the Chinese camp, but noticed Ah Choy listening attentively, with knowing eyes, to the English conversation. As soon as Jack shifted his gaze, the man grinned, waved his arms, and chattered in his most outrageous pidgin.

One evening when Jack was walking back from the Chinese camp, he happened to glance through the swinging doors of a saloon to see Nick leaning across the bar and smiling at a woman on the other side. She was tall, with black hair, opaque brown eyes, a nose as straight as a pine tree, and skin the color of manzanita bark. Nick tapped the bar and said something to her, and she smiled, not discreetly, like the fashionable women Jack had seen in San Francisco, but freely, with all of her white teeth showing. She laughed and shifted her position, and Jack could see that she was nursing a tiny baby, nearly invisible under the brightly-colored shawl she wore over her shoulders. Next to her, too short to see over the bar, was a small boy, who disappeared into her skirts as Jack approached. Noticing the boy's retreat, Nick turned and looked over his shoulder.

"Jack! Come over 'ere." He drained his glass, set it down, and slid his foot off the rail. "Jack, this is Antonia García."

Jack offered his hand, and the woman took it, saying something that he could not understand. She laughed when she saw his eyebrows rise, and said, "I am very pleased to meet you, Señor Trevenna. What would you like to drink?" Her pronunciation reminded him of a man he had met in San Blas, a melon farmer.

"Bring 'im a beer," said Nick, and the woman reached under the bar to bring out a bottle and a glass, still cradling the nursing child with one arm. Nick opened the bottle, poured the glass full, and slid it over. "Antonia runs this place."

Jack tasted his drink. "All by yourself?"

She smiled. "There is a man who sleeps in back." She offered no further explanation.

"Not as fancy as the 'otel," said Nick, "but I like it."

She patted him on the arm. "You are a very nice boy."

Nick laughed. "Not a boy. No, not a boy. Not any more. I'm a miner."

"And where is your claim, *señor* miner?" asked the woman. She shifted the baby to her other breast without uncovering herself, and Jack realized that he was trying not to stare at her.

"My claim? My claim." Nick considered. "We'll see. Our fayther 'as been takin' us out fer nearly a month lookin' at every claim in th' district. Surely there's a claim fer me out there."

Three men approached the bar, and one of them growled something in Spanish. The woman lost her smile, her full lips going aloof. They were Mexicans, their smoky faces like those Jack had seen in the streets of Manzanillo, with black mustaches covering their upper lips. Yet instead of white peasant costumes, these men wore heavy, dark clothes, stained at the knees and elbows with red earth, the pants tucked into heavy leather boots. Each had a wide-brimmed black hat pulled low over his eyes and a wool cape thrown over one shoulder against the cold Sierra night. Two of them wore leather chaps rubbed smooth along the insides of their legs, and all three looked as though they had been sleeping in the open for many days. One of them put his hands up on the bar, and in the shadow beneath his cape, Jack could barely see a wide, tooled leather belt, a holster, and the handle of a pistol.

The leader spoke again, and the woman reached under the bar with her free hand to bring out three squat glasses and a bottle. She spoke a couple of words, flat and low, and held the bottle firmly while the leader pulled out the stopper. She poured the whiskey, quickly and accurately, and slid the bottle to her side of the bar while the men drank. One finished in a gulp, slammed the heavy glass down on the bar, and grunted. The woman poured again. The men finished drinking and, wiping their mustaches on the backs of their hands, scanned the room. The leader looked down at Jack, who turned away, staring at the polished decanters on the counter behind the woman. The leader said something to the others, and they looked at Jack and chuckled. Jack realized that Nick had been gazing down into his beer ever since the men had appeared.

As the men turned to go, one tossed a heavy coin on the bar that rang as it landed. The woman picked it up and spoke, her voice tight. They stopped, and the leader asked her a question. She answered, he shrugged and half-smiled at one of the others, and she spoke again, rapidly, on and on, her inflection surging as she raised her free hand to flick her fingers toward the bar, at the baby, at the boy, still fastened to her skirts, at the three Mexicans, at the two brothers, and at the miners sitting at rude tables in the corners and near the doorway, all now carefully, motionlessly watching. One of the men said something, pointing to the coin in the woman's hand, and she answered him, drawing her lips back from her teeth and biting off the words, now stabbing her finger repeatedly at the three men. The motion jarred the infant, so it stopped suckling and began to cry reproachfully. She stopped scolding the men and cuddled the child, her face still angry. One of the men walked back to the bar, took the coin, and in its place left a small leather pouch. Then he reached across and lifted her chin with his thumb, caressing her with the leather of the glove. She glared at him and lifted her head away. He slapped his hand down on the bar, covering the sack, and then lifted it, open palm towards the woman to show that he was taking nothing with him. Then he turned and walked through the swinging doors, his two companions following him.

Jack looked around the room and realized that there were two other Mexicans sitting in the far corner. The rest were white men, and a few of them were glancing at the Mexicans and muttering to each other. The Mexicans finished their drinks quickly and walked out, keeping their eyes stiffly on the doorway as they left. The woman called to them, a sing-song, cheerful farewell. The rest of the miners relaxed and continued their conversations.

"Who were those men?" Jack asked his brother.

Nick shook his head, but the woman answered. "Many times they come in here, but now they pay what they owe." She picked up the leather sack and tucked it in with the baby, who was once again suckling happily.

"One o' them was wearin' a gun," said Jack.

"*Sí*," replied the woman. "But he will not use it." She curled her lip. "He is nothing. They are miners, but not very good, so they think if they ride together and drink like that, then people will respect them." She shifted the baby a little and looked up again. "Your brother tells me he is a very great miner." She grinned at Nick, who was swirling the last of the beer in his glass.

Jack smiled. "'is old nana would 'a' said that 'is ideas about 'imself were nothin' but quignogs."

"Queeg-nogs? Queeg-nogs." Puzzled, the woman rolled the word over in her mouth. "What does this mean?"

"It means that 'e's makin' up things about 'imself." Jack looked over at Nick and discovered that his brother was watching him closely, still smiling slightly, but his eyes had gone cold.

"Am I? Maybe I am." He grinned at the woman and leaned over the bar. "My brother 'ere idden much more than a year older than I am, but 'e left 'ome three years ago t' work on 'is own. The last time 'e really took a good look at me, I was just thirteen, and I don't think 'e paid attention to what 'e was seein'." He finished his drink and gestured to the woman to come a bit closer. "Let me tell you what I 'ave planned for these mountains."

As Jack walked out into the street, he looked back and saw Nick sketch out an invisible diagram on the bar with his finger, and then raise both hands to trace shapes in the air. The woman was listening intently, nodding and watching carefully as Nick began to arrange the used glasses in a pattern before him.

A few days later, Joseph roused the others very early to meet the Pascoes on the edge of town. They walked out of Red Dog on a wagon road that followed the creek for a while and turned to climb a gentle ridge and lead through a series of groves, past clusters of fresh, raw stumps, and around a rocky corner to a field trampled bare and muddy. Across a shallow wash, a dozen men seemed bent on reducing an overhanging bluff to gravel.

Two men stood braced against a canvas hose, one holding the last few feet of its length and the other grasping a brass nozzle nearly three inches across at the tip, aiming it at a point on the hillside at least thirty yards away, where the stream, hardly diffusing at all in spite of the distance, washed away all of the soil and the smaller rocks, sending muddy cascades down to a roiling torrent below. Wherever the operators found a boulder, they directed the stream slowly on each side until they dislodged it, and sometimes, rather than fall away with the runoff, it flew into the air and landed with a splash in the mud beneath, a granite cannon ball. As the Trevennas watched, the stream cleaned all of the loose rock off of one portion of the hillside, leaving what appeared to be a solid face, but the operators persisted, slowly traversing the cliff to wash each portion carefully until parts of it crumbled and disappeared. A man in a red flannel shirt clambered up to shout over the shooting water and crashing rock, and the hose men directed their stream to a darker grey area about halfway down, roaming back and forth, back and forth, until a whole section above their target gave way and collapsed into the runoff. They directed the stream down into the falling portion to break it up into smaller pieces, and shards of rock flew in all directions.

Old Pascoe tapped Joseph on the shoulder and pointed up the ravine to the source of the water: a flume, a wooden aqueduct on a trestle of boards and logs that adjusted to the changing elevation of the terrain and kept the water flowing evenly, always falling, but not too fast. The entire operation followed the path of the water; in the gully below the rock wall, two or three men worked with shovels to divert most of the runoff into the head of a long series of sluice boxes, and four or five others shoveled the released sand and gravel into the trough, where a few more men guided the rubble and water down through the riffles. The last sluice box released the water, forming a stream that ran across a rocky bar and carried most of the mud and silt down the slope and into a creek a half a mile below.

The man in the red flannel shirt walked up to greet old Pascoe, who introduced the visitors. As the man shook hands, he took off his hat and wiped his forehead with a blue bandanna. "If we can get the water, we can get the gold. That flume belongs to a company that has a whole system of canals and ditches higher up; they bring the water down here and charge us 50¢ per inch."

Jesse was puzzled. "Per running inch?"

"No—depth by width, and they promise a certain current. This flume brings in water four inches deep and seven inches wide, so we pay them $14 a day. We're lucky to get it—it's been two years since there was enough rain for everyone to get as much water as they wanted. Now the water men can name their price. The water itself doesn't cost them nothing; but just above that flume, around the bend there, is a ten-mile canal that cost the company $18,000 to engineer."

"Can ye make a profit?"

He grinned. "We're taking almost $600 a day out of this hill. After we pay all of our expenses, that works out to about $40 for each man!" He pointed down to the end of the sluice box. "Every week or so, we bring that gravel back up and send it through again to catch the dust we missed the first time through. After we're done here, the only ones who'll work this bar are the Chinamen!" One of the shovelers called out something, and the man in the red shirt walked and slid back down into the gully.

Jack looked around and realized that they were standing in what had once been a meadow, with rich grass and aspen trees mixed with young oaks. Now it was a field of red mud and grey gravel, and the trees that weren't suitable for supporting the flume had been taken down and thrown to one side. He couldn't tell what the hillside had been like, but he guessed that the crew had started work where he was standing and then, as they washed away the bluff, had moved down into the pit they had created. The runoff from the sluice boxes was heavy with sludge and muck, and he could see, down the slope, where the thick water had stained the granite boulders red.

Old Pascoe had been looking back along the wagon road, and now he beckoned the Trevennas to follow him to where two men were waiting. They retreated from the noise to find some shade under a cluster of oak trees that the hydraulic men hadn't needed, and Pascoe gestured to the strangers. "Joseph — Jesse — this 'ere 'ere is Hannibal Carne, an' 'is brother, Martin. They came from Breage, down near Helston—used t' work at Tregurtha Downs and Wheal Vor."

Jack blurted out, "I was workin' at Wheal Vor just last month." He thought that Hannibal, with his spectacles, thin lips and carefully combed, curly hair, resembled a bookkeeper more than a hard-rock man.

Hannibal turned to Joseph and Jesse. "How d'ye like the hydraulic set-up?"

Joseph brought his lower lip up over his mustache, so Jesse answered. "It looks quick an' easy—no drillin', no powder. But they can't get much below th' surface." Pascoe nodded.

"When they found th' gold 'ere, almost ten years back," explained Martin, pulling at his short tuft of a beard, "all they knew t' do was wash it in pans and rockers. Placer mining. Some got rich right away, but most made just enough t' buy flour and bacon, got tired o' sleepin' in the open and went 'ome, back t' their farms in New York or Ohio." He grinned. "These boys y'see over there are organized; they're professionals compared to th' forty-niners. But ye're right—they're just scratchin' at th' top. It's still nothin' but placer mining, just fancied up."

"Some o' these hydraulic men get lucky," said Hannibal, "They find a rich 'illside and wash it away. Some o' them even know 'ow t' follow a vein, but if it dips too far below th' surface, they get lost. They make more mess than money. There's more inside these mountains than most o' these Yankees know."

Cousin Jack

He turned and led the others back along the wagon trace towards Red Dog. After a mile or so, he stepped down the embankment to follow a faint path through the woods, and they crossed a small creek where a band of four Chinese were crouched over a cradle, barely glancing up at the white men as they shoveled sand over the sideboards. They walked for another half hour and came to a clearing, where the Carnes stopped in front of a hole dug in the side of a gentle, rocky slope.

Nick peered in. The tunnel descended at a twenty-degree angle, just easy enough for a man to walk in or out, but although it extended farther than he could see, there were no tracks for ore cars, no cables for hoists, no lights—there was no equipment at all. He turned to Hannibal. "Did you dig this?"

Old Pascoe snorted, and Martin smiled. "No, we 'ad nothin' to do with this little 'ole until we saw it three weeks ago. It belongs to a company of Americans, from Connecticut they are. They don't know what t' do next, and they've run out o' money anyway."

Hannibal sat down on a rock and wiped off his spectacles. "The men around 'ere don't understand quartz mining, and they don't trust it. Most o' them 'ave never gone underground, and they don't know 'ow. They'd rather wash away 'illsides with their 'oses. Oh, there are mills 'ere—even a couple on Wolf Creek, over in Grass Valley. But people think that quartz mining can't pay for itself."

Martin leaned over to his brother. "Tell 'em about Brennan and th' Rocky Bar." Old Pascoe snorted again, sat down on a fallen log, and took out his pipe and pouch.

Jesse raised his eyebrows. "Who's Brennan?"

Hannibal sighed. "There's not much to tell. Just a couple o' months ago, the Rocky Bar manager killed 'imself, and 'e took 'is wife and children with 'im."

"What 'appened?" asked Jack.

"They found 'em in their 'ouse on a Sunday evenin', Brennan on th' parlor floor an' the others in their beds. They'd all taken acid." Jesse grunted. "'e left a letter—it was all 'is idea. Only God knows 'ow 'e got 'is wife and the little ones t' go along." He stopped, and no one spoke for a moment.

Joseph frowned. "What's the point?"

"Brennan," said Hannibal, "was workin' a quartz mine with its own stamp mill. 'e'd been there two years, and only last fall they sank a new shaft. It was a good idea, but it didn't pay off fast enough, and th' company couldn't get out of debt. Brennan blamed 'imself, but some o' th' miners say that no one can make a quartz mine pay. And since Brennan took 'is life, there are even folks who say that a man who works underground will get in a way an' go off 'is chump, like Brennan surely was."

Martin nodded. "The problem is that most o' the Americans don't know 'ow t' do it right. They don't know 'ow t' find a vein, they don't know 'ow t' follow it, they don't know 'ow to use powder underground, and they'd rather not work at th' bottom anyway. Yet some o' them 'ave tried, so there are coyote 'oles, like this 'ere 'ere, all over th' district."

Old Pascoe took his pipe out of his mouth. "Most o' them won't stick with it long enough. They'll work a claim fer a while, and then move on if it don't look rich. If everyone else thinks it's played out, they'll let th' Chinamen 'ave it—they'll work anything, and make it pay, too."

Joseph glanced at Jesse, and then looked Hannibal full in the eyes. "What d'ye propose?"

Hannibal stood up. "We've been 'ere nearly a year. We 'ave five claims, small ones, but they're 'ardly payin' their way. We need to organize somethin' bigger. We know th' gold is there, we know 'ow t' find it, and we know 'ow t' bring it out. But Martin and I can't do it by ourselves, and we can't use these Americans, even if they were willing. The Irish're worse. We need men from 'ome."

"Why us?"

"William says 'e trusts ye." Hannibal glanced at Pascoe and back at the older Trevenna brothers. "Yer mother was 'is cousin. That's good enough fer us." Martin nodded. "And 'e says ye might 'ave somethin' t' put in." Jesse looked over at Joseph, but he was still staring at Hannibal, listening carefully. "Martin and I could buy this 'ere 'ere, but it ain't worth it. We need somethin' better than we can afford, and then we need enough money to work it properly. After we get down a ways, we'll need a pump an' a hoist, and when we start t' bring out the quartz, we'll need our own mill. It'll be a while before it all pays off. We need someone who'll work with us and be willin' t' wait awhile."

Joseph looked over at the hole next to them. "How d'ye know this 'ere 'ere's no good?"

Hannibal lifted a bull's-eye lantern that he had brought with him. "See fer yerself." The two men looked at each other. For all Hannibal's assurance that he trusted the Trevennas, this was a test. Joseph knew that the Carnes would only want to work with men as experienced as they claimed to be. If they inspected the shaft and made the same assessment as the Carnes, then the men of all three families would feel that they could rely on each other. If not, this would probably be their last meeting.

Joseph took up the lantern and walked into the shaft. The others followed, also carrying lanterns that the Pascoes had provided. The tunnel bored into the hillside no more than a hundred feet in a gentle, irregular curve. Bent down beneath the low, crude ceiling, they studied the layering of the rock, its shifting colors and textures, and they chipped away little chunks, every few feet at different elevations, to look for quartz or other minerals, and to assess its hardness and tendency to fracture. There was a vein about halfway down, but the visible portion was small and its direction indeterminate. They spent nearly an hour exploring and collecting samples, and finally they walked out to the mouth and spread out what they had found. Joseph and Jesse crouched over the collection with Jack and Nick peering over their shoulders. Old Pascoe had lit his pipe again, content to hear the Trevennas' judgement, and his sons were slowly fanning their faces with their hats. No one spoke. Finally, Joseph and Jesse walked away from the others a few steps and conferred quietly. When they returned, Hannibal asked, "What d'ye think?"

Joseph took a deep breath, gazing down at the samples, and then, without warning, said, "You tell 'em, Nicky."

No one was more startled than Nick. The Carnes exchanged glances, wondering if this were some sort of tactic to gain an advantage or to make fun of them, and old Pascoe pulled his pipe out of his mouth, watching the gaping boy. Jack glanced at Jesse and Joseph, but neither face told him anything.

Slowly, Nick began to explicate the shaft. He paused between phrases, glancing at his father as though expecting comment or correction, but as no one interrupted and all seemed to be paying serious attention, he grew more confident. He picked up one of the samples and waved it in the air to illustrate a point as he elaborated his analysis of the hill, the layers of rock, the construction of the shaft, and the vein itself, its apparent dip and angle, its likely direction, and the possibility that it would pay off. He explained how he would sink the shaft farther into the hill, how he would space and vector the drifts, and what equipment he would need for the first six months, but he offered his opinion that the claim probably wasn't worth the effort that nine Cornish hard-rock men could put into it. Finally, he slowed down and stammered, realizing that he had nothing more to say. His voice trailed off into silence.

Jack was amazed. He had never realized that Nick knew anything about the rock, and here he was, talking about a shaft he had just encountered as though he had been working it for years. He looked at his father, who smiled at Nick, checked with Jesse, who nodded almost imperceptibly, and then actually winked at Jack, whose astonishment became complete. Still smiling, Joseph turned to the Carne brothers. "I'll stand by Nick's judgement. What d'ye think?"

Hannibal took off his spectacles and wiped them clean with a handkerchief. "Mr. Trevenna, I like what yer son 'as t' say." He paused, then settled his spectacles back on his nose and grinned. "I believe we'll kidney together very well!"

The men gravely shook hands to confirm their partnership. When any man found a claim, whether for sale or for the taking, he would present it to the others. If they deemed it promising enough to justify their collective effort, they would form a company, share the costs of equipment, and work it together, each family making a fair contribution of time and money. If not, then that man's family would be free to work it on their own or with anyone else they chose. Any man among them was free to add his name to any impromptu association staking a new claim, each man taking his one hundred feet along the ledge, but he would ask the discoverer, the man who found the claim, to consider making room for others in the partnership. There were no papers and no signatures; just an understanding.

Hannibal added one more comment. "We can look all over these hills, and well we might, but th' best quartz veins are near Grass Valley. That's where th' smart men'll get rich, and that's where we should plan t' be."

4
The North Star
1860

Jack Trevenna stood in the shadow of a clump of pines and gazed down into the shaft. Some of the timbers had begun to split or sag, but the tunnel was straight and true and could certainly accommodate tracks for ore cars. The walls and ceiling were still rough and raw, but thousands of footsteps had begun to grind away the floor, wearing down the jagged edges and the bumps, and leaving a residue of earth and gravel. He peered into the gloom but could see no farther than twenty yards, so he turned, took off his hat and lifted his face into the cool breeze.

The Trevennas had spent two years working the pick of an assortment of claims scattered across the hills. They had built a cabin in Red Dog, but where each man slept was a matter of where he happened to be working that day: on the north side of the Bear River in Little York township, on Deer Creek about a mile below Pleasant Valley, at Iowa Hill twenty miles away on a hog's back above the American River, or on Irwin's Ridge, nearly three hours' ride northeast of the town of Nevada. They were doing better than most, but Joseph wanted something more. He had become preoccupied with the conviction that they could find a quartz mine, one whose owners had neglected, probably out of ignorance, whose potential they could reveal and recognize. There was a string of quartz mines clustered south of Grass Valley, so when there was time to spare, Joseph sent his brother and his sons roaming up and down Wolf Creek, investigating prospects from Gold Hill to Weimar Hill.

Today, Jack stood on the southeast slope of Lafayette Hill, looking around at the stamp mill, boiler, steam engine and dry room of the Helvetia Gold Mining Company. The owners had gone into debt and given up, and the mine had sat idle for nearly three years. In honor of the men who had discovered the vein nearly a decade earlier, the miners in the area called the place the "French Lead."

He heard someone call his name, and he looked down the shaft to see Nick emerge from the darkness and stand in the sunlight, there to catch his breath and wipe the sweat off the back of his neck. He was wearing a sage green felt hat with a wide, sweeping brim, and he had stuffed his trousers into the calf-length, soft leather boots that he had kept clean in spite of his trip down the shaft. No one questioned Nick's judgement any more, and only new acquaintances were surprised that so young a man—only just eighteen—knew so much about quartz. Jack had learned that his younger brother's sense of the rock was just as keen as his, but quicker. Jack took his time in a drift, not just collecting samples or tracing layers and veins, but also running his fingertips along the rock, tasting the seepage for minerals, smelling the air of the tunnel, and doing something that he once described—and only once, for Jesse laughed at length and Joseph seemed genuinely concerned with his oldest son's state of mind—as listening to the earth breathe. He liked to stay underground until he had a sense of where he was, as though he could see through the solid masses over to the nearest creek and up to grass. Nick, however, had no time for what he called Jack's "bucca-magic." In truth, Nick had no doubt that the mines harbored piskies and night-riders, and that the rock, at a level no mortal miner could understand, had a will of its own, but he was simply too impatient to contemplate such mysteries, and he knew, beyond any doubt, that most of the men would consider such notions sheer foolishness and clear proof that his mind had gone soft. He walked down a shaft, spent fifteen minutes in the most promising drift, and without apparent effort, emerged knowing everything he needed to know in order to sketch out plans for boring new drifts and adits, to rig a better pump, to redesign the hoisting gear, and to formulate a schedule of work for the next several months, mapping out the progress along the vein and predicting how many men and how many stamps they'd need to put to work. Jack could produce the same results as Nick—in fact, the two brothers nearly always came to the same conclusions—but Nick was driven by the compulsion to bring the gold out of the vein, no matter how many men, how much machinery, how much rock, or how many trees felled to feed the fires of the boilers, and he raced on, obsessed, towards that consummation. The older Trevennas were content to let the younger ones hurry down every new shaft; Joseph and Jesse simply scrutinized their findings and conferred with each other before making a decision. So far, the boys had been right every time.

Nick turned to speak, but then pointed over Jack's shoulder. Two wagons were approaching, Jesse driving the second, with Joseph and old William Pascoe riding on the bench, and the first carried the Carne brothers and two men Jack didn't know.

The driver of the lead wagon was John Sterling, an Englishman that Martin had met at Iowa Hill. He had been raised somewhere near London, arriving in America when only a boy, not yet in his teens, and living back East before coming to California. He called himself a miner, but none of Jack's partners had ever seen him spend a day drilling or digging. He had lived in the gold country for nearly ten years, and now, as his grey wool suit and clean white shirt suggested, he spent his time managing and trading claims rather than working them.

Cousin Jack

Sterling brought his horse to a halt and sprang down to hurry over to Jack and Nick, his hand outstretched. The men shook hands, and Sterling slapped Jack on the shoulder. "So, friend Trevenna—what d'ye think?" He grinned and turned to look down the shaft. "McLaughlin gave up on it—that Irish fool!—but I'm telling you that this is the hole that will make us all rich!" Nick nodded politely, but discreetly raised his eyebrows in Jack's direction.

The others had gathered around, and Sterling took charge. "Jack—Nick—this is Richard Chenoweth and his brother, Mark." The men shook hands all around, and Hannibal explained that the strangers were his cousins from Helston, recently arrived from Wisconsin, where they had worked for two years in the lead mines. Sterling clapped his hands. "They'll do better here, won't they?" He nodded, smiling at the others; Pascoe kept smoking his pipe impassively. "Now let's get down that shaft and take a look!"

Each man lit a candle and put on a helmet. The Chenoweths shouldered three drilling rigs that they lifted out of Joseph's wagon, and Jesse picked up a tightly-buckled canvas sack. Falling in line by pairs, they walked slowly down the shaft, Sterling and Pascoe in the lead, then the Carnes, the Chenoweths close behind, and the Trevennas in the rear. The red earth of the surface quickly gave way to dark rock as Sterling led them past one drift, then another, and then turned into the third, ducking under the heavy timber that served as a lintel. The others followed, finding that the drift was tall enough for even Jesse to stand upright, and they stopped at a niche carved into the wall. Sterling beckoned, and Pascoe and Joseph stepped in to look.

The niche revealed the vein in the rock, a solid quartz river fully two feet thick. There was no way to tell how far to either side or how deep into the rock the vein extended; they might have been looking at a small pocket, a section of a long stream, or even the tiny edge of a vast subterranean lake of quartz, a layer trapped in the rock and extending in all directions. Only months, even years, of drilling and blasting would tell them what the mountain truly held for them.

Sterling had dropped his ebullient manner. Out of a bag slung over his shoulder, he took a hammer and a sharp chisel, then he stared at the vein for a moment before reaching up and, with three quick taps, breaking out a chunk of the quartz. He picked it up, washed it with a few drops of water from a bottle in his bag, and handed it to Pascoe, who held it in one hand and lifted a bull's eye lantern with the other. They all knew that the old man was looking not for the gold itself, for it was rare that even a fleck of color showed itself, but for a certain quality in the rock, a promising way the light might pass through the dense translucence. After a moment, he lowered the lantern and nodded.

The Chenoweths brought the drills up to the vein. Pascoe pointed to two places in the niche and retreated several steps down the drift with Sterling while the others got to work. They worked in pairs—the Carnes, the Chenoweths, and Nick and Jack—one man holding the drill while the other swung the sledge. The quartz was hard and unyielding; each stroke of the hammer sent a jarring shock back through the hands and arms of the man swinging it, while the man holding the drill had to brace himself against the tendency of the steel rod to jump back out of the hole. They worked for over an hour, scarcely stopping to rest, the men of each pair trading places every ten minutes or so. Finally, they stopped, and Pascoe rose from where he had been sitting to come forward and peer into each hole. He nodded, satisfied, and Jesse opened his canvas bag to bring out the black powder. He tamped it down securely in each hole, prepared the charge, and strung a long fuse to each one. The other men walked down the drift and several yards up the shaft before Jesse struck a spark, started each fuse, and hurried to join them. Every man braced himself against the wall of the shaft opposite the drift, covering his ears and closing his eyes against the blast. The two charges detonated almost simultaneously. The concussion rang and rebounded through the confined space, and the men could feel the multiple ricochet inside the rock wall where they were leaning. They remained where they were for several minutes, waiting for the grit and fumes to dissipate, before walking back into the drift.

On the floor of the tunnel was a pile of broken rock, at least forty cubic feet. Out from the shadows, Sterling now rolled an old ore car; it had been designed to run on rails, but some impecunious miner had rigged it with large wheels that could barely roll along the rough floors of the underground workings. The men filled up the car, tossing in the larger pieces and using a shovel to pick up the smaller bits, and then rolled it down the drift, turned it carefully to face up the main shaft, and pushed it slowly up the incline and into the sunlight. Jesse backed up one of the wagons against a ledge that provided a crude loading dock; the men eased the car onto the bed and the Carnes lashed it securely and wedged their sledges underneath the wheels so it could not roll. With the others walking alongside, Sterling drove the wagon back towards town, to a small stamp mill in Boston Ravine.

The mill owner cleaned off the surfaces of the shoes and dies, carefully removing the residue from previous jobs. When he was ready, they rolled the ore car over to the feed inlet of the mill and tipped it halfway over. The owner opened the cocks, letting water flow into the base of the mill, and started the stamps, tall pistons that let loose a deafening, clattering racket. The men tipped the car the rest of the way, and the load of rocks fell down under the stamps. The job took nearly two hours, with the five stamps, each weighing several hundred pounds, slamming down on the rocks and grinding them against the bottom of the mortar box. Presently, a slurry of fine, wet sand began to push through the screen at the bottom of the battery and ooze across the table, leaving an amalgam of gold and mercury. One of the mill hands scraped the mess off the table and into a cast iron kettle about three feet across, set at a tilt. The kettle rotated slowly, sending two cannon-balls whirling around in the bottom and squeezing the mercury out of the gold. The owner heated the mess in a crucible, distilling out the last of the mercury and leaving a small sponge of gold, a lump with tiny pockmarks where bubbles of mercury had evaporated.

Jesse and Pascoe agreed to accompany Sterling down to the assay office, leaving Joseph to drive the other wagon back to the livery stable. Jack was about to climb up next to his father when Nick tapped him on the shoulder and took him aside. "Alonzo Delano is givin' a lecture at th' Congregational Church in about an hour. This is yer chance t' hear what 'e thinks about th' Pony." The two wagons drove off, and the brothers walked back into town. The road in front of the church was lined with buggies, carriages and wag-ons, and when they walked in the door, they discovered that the only re-maining seats were in the back corners. Most of the people in the hall were miners in red shirts and muddy boots, but scattered among them were men who spent their days in town: messengers, hostlers, shopkeepers and even a couple of the town trustees.

Every pair of eyes was fixed on the man standing in the front of the hall, and every face wore an anticipatory smile that seemed incongruous for a lecture on the geology of quartz veins. The speaker waved his long arms at a diagram he had placed upon an easel.

"You see, gentlemen—and ladies—that the quartz vein turns, and turns again. The ledge is there. You will find it. Yet you might just as well take a compass or a dowsing-rod into the hills if you hope to find it without sinking one shaft after another. Yes, you can chase that rascal upstream and into a hillside, but it will turn—it will turn! So you must devote yourself to it—you must live *with* the vein and live *like* the vein. I once went three months without taking a peep in the looking glass, and the first view of my own phiz, at no time very inviting, absolutely made me stare at myself; a beard of three months growth, an old worn-out hat, from which my matted locks were sticking out in all directions, a greasy buckskin coat, wrinkled and dirty, with unmentionables ditto; my toes peeping out into daylight from my old dilapidated shoes, like frogs from the scum of a pond, made about as outlandish an appearance as a wild Arab from the desert of Sahara, and yet, under all this, a small portion of the soul was still left, and an innate sense of decency, so I went to work and cleaned up, and a decent suit of clothes and a sharp razor soon changed the Arab into something like civilization."

Jack found himself grinning idiotically at the man, and when he looked around, embarrassed, he realized that nearly everyone else in the audience was chuckling out loud.

"So you see, my friends, the geology of the quartz vein is nothing more nor less than the geology of a man's life! When you trace the dips, angles, spurs, variations and sinuosities of the vein, you are tracing the shifts in your own life path."

He stepped forward and abruptly bent himself double at the waist, and the audience broke into a roar of applause, rising to their feet and clapping on and on as the speaker walked slowly down the center aisle, smiling and shaking hands with everyone within reach, each of whom seemed to be a dear friend. Nick drew Jack outside. They waited until only three or four people stood with the speaker, and then walked up to shake his hand. The man seemed especially pleased to see Nick. Would he join the Trevennas for a drink? Delighted! As soon as he was able to finish thanking his admirers, the three of them walked down Neal Street, turned the corner at Mill, and in a few minutes were seated at a corner table at the Empire Billiard Saloon.

Alonzo Delano had lived in Grass Valley for nearly a decade, arriving as the local agent for Wells, Fargo, and then setting up his own bank in a small office next to the Exchange Hotel. Now he was in his early fifties, no taller than Jack but so thin and bony, wrapped tightly in a jacket buttoned up to his chin, as to seem six feet tall at least. He never stopped moving; when he spoke, he gestured from shoulder to fingertip, waving his arms in the air or articulating his point with precise movements of his long hands, and when he listened, he twitched and danced in his chair. Only his eyes remained still, wide open under thick, black eyebrows and, from the moment he sat down, fixed firmly on Jack's face. Yet even the eyes were unremarkable compared to the nose. It began its journey somewhere in the middle of the forehead and traveled the considerable distance down between the eyes and cheeks to hover, like a predatory vulture, over the incessant mouth. The bone and cartilage formed a perfectly straight ridge that caught the light and shone from one end to the other. The top was as narrow as could be, but just past the middle, the whole assembly flared out into nostrils placed just above the corners of the mouth and on either side of the great, glistening, perfectly spherical knob.

Delano noticed Jack's gaze slipping helplessly down to his nose, and his entire expression changed. He clenched his fists in front of his body, nearly bringing the twitching under control, hunched his shoulders and lowered his head, bringing his eyebrows down, his lips up and his chin out as he gradually glared at Jack.

"Mr. Trevenna!" Delano growled. "Do you see something that interests you?"

Jack backed away and denied any interest whatsoever in anything at all.

"Are you certain?"

Cousin Jack

Jack was quite certain.

"Yet you keep looking down! I like to look a man straight in the eye, but you keep looking down—just below my gaze! What could you be looking at?"

Jack mumbled something about a spot on the table. Nick's face was beginning to turn purple and he seemed compelled to inspect the inside of his hat. Delano's eyebrows shot up and his mouth fell open in amazed dismay.

"I have it! Could it be . . . could it be that you . . . are . . . looking . . . at . . . my . . . NOSE?"

Jack dissolved into babbled assurances, excuses, denials, protests and wild fictions while Delano listened in apparent fury and Nick, shaking a bit, concentrated on something happening across the room. As Jack ran out of breath, a very small fly buzzed past his ear, hovered for a moment, and settled abruptly on the very tip of Delano's nose. Jack stopped speaking completely, horrified, now completely unable to look away from the nose. After a long moment, he realized that Delano was addressing him. The fly, flouting the behavior of all other flies in all other saloons, remained where it was in spite of the resonance of its host's voice.

"Mr. Trevenna? Jack? Jack!" Jack finally looked up into Delano's eyes, which looked back at him, slid slowly down to the insect, and back up again. "Jack, my boy—Will you kindly brush that fly off the end of my nose? You are nearer to it than I am."

At this, Nick could no longer control himself, and actually fell off of his chair, laughing, tears running down his cheeks, slapping his hands in the sawdust on the floor. Delano himself threw back his head, trumpeted to the ceiling, and slapped both palms down on his thighs. Confused, his face flaming red, Jack finally laughed with the others.

Nick ordered more beer all around, and then told Delano, with little preamble, that he and his brother needed advice. Jack had been reading everything he could find about the future of California, most recently a new book by an Eastern journalist named Greeley, and he had begun to realize that he need not settle for hard-rock mining. There were fortunes to be made in farming and logging, and more opulent ones in shipping. He felt isolated in Grass Valley, too far removed from Sacramento and San Francisco, where, he felt certain, men wearing tailored suits and polished boots sat in leather chairs surrounded by mahogany paneling and polished brass, charting the course of the entire West by directing a million here or there and confirming far-reaching agreements with casual handshakes before pouring old brandy into cut crystal glasses. He yearned to join them, to be one of those who got in at the beginning and whom, in later years, others regarded with envy. After studying the newspapers and listening to the talk in saloons and livery stables, Jack had become convinced that his best opportunity, at the moment, lay in the Pony Express. He knew that the idea would puzzle Jesse and elicit Joseph's stormy scorn, so Nick had arranged for them to meet with Delano in hopes of hearing some useful advice.

Delano spread his arms wide and raised his eyebrows. "The Pony? Ah, yes—the Pony! Just think of it, boys—to bring a letter across the western wastelands in just a week! A mere week! Take it across the Isthmus, best allow a month. On the overland route, perhaps twenty days."

Jack leaned in. "But is there money in it?"

Delano looked up at the ceiling. "He asks if there's money in it!" He slapped his palms down on the table and thrust his nose across so it hovered over Jack's beer. "Just consider, friend Trevenna. I am a banker." He nodded gravely. "Think! . . . of what it would be worth to me to know what is happening in the New York markets only a week after the events actually occur." He sat back dramatically. "Well," with a wave of his hand. "It's incalculable. And what if I were a merchant, like friend Johnston down the street here?" He brought his eyebrows together and nodded portentously. "News is everything. Information. Facts. Elections. Wars. Treaties. It all affects business. Today's ordinary goods can be tomorrow's treasures, or vice versa. What is plentiful tomorrow may be in short supply next week." He leaned forward again and beckoned the brothers to listen closely as he whispered. "The man who *knows* is the man who makes the profit. Well!" He lifted his beer and took a long pull, emptying half of the tall glass at one draft.

Nick looked over his shoulder and lowered his voice. "Alonzo, we 'ave a chance t' buy a share in th' company. D' ye think we should do it?"

"Stock?!?" Delano cried, much to Nick's consternation. Then he spoke so softly that Jack could hardly hear him above the conversations around them. "A share of the Pony. Hmm. A share of the Pony. Fascinating. Intriguing. Y'know, if I weren't so old, I'd ride for them meself."

"What should we do, Alonzo?" Nick pressed him.

"Do? Do?" Delano seemed surprised. "Follow your heart, friend Trevenna, follow your heart. I cannot advise you, but I have always done as my soul bid me, and I cannot say that I regret a single day of my life." He now peered around as though engaged in a dark conspiracy. "I'll tell you this, though— if I had a chance to buy into the Pony, why . . . I'd do it like that!" He snapped his fingers under Jack's nose and sat back to drain his glass.

The next morning, the boys found Joseph and Jesse sitting at a table in the dining room of the Exchange, studying the assayer's report on the Helvetia sample. It claimed nearly an ounce per ton, certainly rich enough to warrant their investment, so now they had only to estimate what it would cost to put the mine on a properly working basis. Joseph reviewed every piece of

Cousin Jack

equipment, estimating its condition, and Jesse made notes on what repairs and additions they would need. After they had gone down the list, Joseph turned to Nick. "And what would you plan for th' next five years?"

Nick smiled and stretched back in his chair. "We 'ave only three stamps; we'll need more. I'd like t' bore the incline shaft deeper, and send out drifts every 'undred feet or so. We'll want a good drain tunnel, and after a while I'd want t' sink a shaft straight down, cuttin' into the incline, so we can hoist th' rock straight up."

Jesse raised his eyebrows. "Would it be worth it?"

Nick grinned. "We won't want to haul th' rock all the way up the incline, an' mounting another 'oist at th' top of th' vertical shaft will save time. And we'll need a stronger pump engine."

Jesse tapped his pencil on the papers in front of him. "'ow many men?"

Joseph looked at Nick. "Eighty?"

Nick nodded. "And another twenty at th' start, just t' get things moving."

Jesse turned to Jack. "What d' you think?"

Jack looked over at the papers. "That's about right, for th' first year or so. At least 'alf o' them will 'ave t' be 'ard-rock men—can we get that many?"

Jesse started making a tally with his pencil. "P'raps ten o' th' partners will work. There must be at least thirty quartz miners, just in Grass Valley, who'd be glad t' 'ave steady wages while they're 'opin' for one o' their own claims t' come in. Even th' placer miners're findin' that it's not like it was ten, even five years ago. A lot o' them came back from th' Comstock empty-'anded and 'ungry. It's goin' t' be big companies from now on, and th' men'll be lookin' to hire on."

Joseph sat staring down at the table, his thumb hooked under his chin and his forefinger scratching his beard, and the others sat back, watching, waiting for him to speak. They had seen virtually every claim and working mine in the area, and although some were richer, they were more expensive and seemed no more promising. Sterling had arranged a fair price with McLaughlin, and most of the prospective partners were men whose skill and judgement he trusted. The capital costs were acceptable if enough partners committed enough money. He looked up at Jesse. "What d'ye think o' Sterling?"

Jesse sighed. "'e's ... well, 'e's English, but ... 'e's almost like an American. 'e surprises me—says things I don't expect. 'e 'asn't actually worked underground fer at least three years. And 'is brother is more of a money man than 'e is."

"'is brother?" asked Jack.

Jesse nodded. "Edward—doesn't get out much—stays at 'is desk. 'e'll be a partner as well; they do everything together."

Joseph leaned in. "D'ye think one o' them'll want t' be superintendent?"

"Iss," said Jesse, whistling the affirmative through his teeth. "They're not men t' sit back and let others make th' decisions."

Joseph considered. "We may need more partners. Men from 'ome."

"I've been talkin' to a family from Redruth," said Jesse. "Their name is Nankervis." Joseph nodded, chewing his lip.

Jack was frowning slightly. "D' ye mistrust Sterling because 'e's from London or because 'e wears a boiled shirt?"

Joseph raised one eyebrow at his son's impertinent tone, but Jesse smiled as he answered. "Both ways, John, both ways. I know what a Cornishman will do, and I know what a miner will do. Sterling and 'is brother're English nobs, or as like t' be."

Jack pressed the point. "But idden that what *we* want? Fayther," he said, turning to Joseph, "didn't we come 'ere t' make our money and then go 'ome and stay out o' th' mines for good and all? If Sterling is farther along that road than we, is that any reason to doubt th' man?"

"Don't get cocky, boy." His father shook his head. "Tidden that alone. John Sterling is too comfortable for me—if ye told 'im th' moon was green, 'e'd agree with ye, slap ye on the back, and then grin about it th' next day. As fer Edward—'e's a close man. We'll never know what's 'e's thinkin'."

There was a brief silence. Then Jesse asked, "What d'ye want, Joseph? Should we drop it?"

Joseph looked into Jack's face, then at Nick, and finally at Jesse. "No. Let's see what we can work out. If there're enough partners, and if all but th' Sterlings are men we can trust, then we're all right." He took a deep breath and pushed his chair back from the table to give his legs more room. "I'll put in fifteen 'undred, or maybe two thousand if need be. What about you?"

Jesse was adding figures on a piece of paper. "About 'alf that, p'raps a bit more."

Joseph looked at his sons. "And you?"

Nick pursed his lips and rolled his eyes over to Jack, who caught the look and turned to Joseph. "We'll work th' mine, Fayther, if ye'll 'ave us. But we're not goin' in." His father's face darkened. "We've somethin' else before us."

"Another mine?" asked Jesse.

"No," said Jack. Joseph's eyebrows were nearly hiding his eyes. "We're goin' t' buy a share in th' Pony Express."

Joseph seemed puzzled. "A share in what?"

"Th' Pony Express—th' new courier service. They'll be carryin' mail from Sacramento t' St. Joseph—right over th' mountains to Carson, and Salt Lake, and down th' Platte. We've a chance to get in on th' beginning."

Cousin Jack

Joseph was incredulous. "Mail service?! You . . . "

Jesse broke in quietly. "Are ye sure? D'ye know anythin' about th' men runnin' it?"

Jack was eager. "They're freight men out o' Missouri—one o' them's been runnin' wagons since 1848, and t'other ran a stage line to Denver after Pike's Peak. They're 'moast ready, but there's a bit o' room fer some more capital." Joseph slammed his fist down on the table, rattling the crockery.

"What will they pay in dividends?" Jesse asked.

Jack paused. "They're not tellin' just yet." Joseph snorted, but Jack went on. "It's bound t' do well—they'll beat the overland mail by two weeks. They'll charge $5 fer each 'alf ounce, and they'll get it—th' bags'll be full. Everyone'll want t' send by Pony."

Joseph could no longer contain himself. "Everyone?! You nogglehead!"

Jesse put his hand on his brother's arm and kept trying to reason with his nephew. "John, this is somethin' entirely new. No one knows whether they'll still be runnin' their ponies a month after they start. It's nigh on t' spring now, but 'ow will they get over th' mountains in th' winter? Some think the Indians'll 'unt th' riders on th' run—take 'em down like deer, just fer sport. An' I've 'eard men say that they're 'irin' boys to ride for 'em—young slocums who just want t' race each other out o' St. Joseph and who'll get drunk on their pay."

Jack flushed. "Tidden so. They're 'irin' only th' best—young they may be, but they're men grew up in the saddle. I met a fellow from Auburn was goin' t' ride. 'e's a fine lad. An' 'e told me that every rider must sign a pledge not t' drink." Joseph snorted again.

Jesse pressed his questions. "John, their own government won't even 'elp 'em out. Doesn't that tell ye somethin'?" Jack had no answer. "Besides, they'll be stringin' telegraph wires any day now."

Jack sighed. "I know the telegraph is goin' in, but it won't be for years. They'll build th' railroad first."

Jesse shook his head. "Either way, th' Pony'll close. Then where's yer money?"

"We'll sell our stock when it's doin' well. Right now, they're 'avin' trouble gettin' men t' come in—everyone's scared. They'll give us a few shares cheap. When they've tripled, we'll sell, and dividends or no, we'll make our money." Neither his father nor his uncle looked even slightly impressed. "It's a one 'undred thousand dollar operation—bigger than anythin' we could manage 'ere! Just look at this!"

Jack handed over a page out of a newspaper, and Jesse read aloud the passage that Jack had circled. "'The prospect of the Pony Express challenges our admiration and startles us with an exultant ambition, which teaches us to believe, justly, that human will, power, device, and intrepidity, surpass in their achievements even the extravagancies of speculation. Even

the most sanguine mind, only a score of years past, could not have entertained that the transit across the Plains could be accomplished at the rate of
nearly TEN miles an hour, night and day, successively, until the Courier Pony,
with the edicts of government and commerce, should stand on the very
shores of the Pacific, with convulsive chest and reeking body, to stimulate to
a still higher pitch the unflagging energy of the great metropolitan city of the
west and further our efforts to build up an empire on the Pacific, the glories
of whose civilization shall be held up as an example to the rest of the
world.'" He cleared his throat and finished. "'This is manifest destiny. Hur-
rah for the PONY EXPRESS!'"

Joseph glared across at Nick. "An' what about you? 'ave ye nothin' t'
say fer yerself?"

Nick shrugged. "Fayther, I've little o' my own—Jack's makin' me a
loan so I can go in with 'im."

Joseph was perplexed. "What 'appened t' what ye've earned th' last two
years?" Nick looked down at the table.

Jesse had been reading farther in the newspaper. "He goes on t' predict
that th' government will approve th' telegraph and then th' railroad within
ten years—'a foregone conclusion.'"

Jack smiled. "Ten years is a long time. I don't think th' Pony'll run that
long, but if it does, th' more money we'll make."

"How much are ye puttin' in, John?" Jesse asked.

Jack paused. "About six 'undred, maybe seven."

"Is that all ye 'ave?"

"No," said Jack quickly. "No, I've more. But that's what I'm puttin' in."

Joseph rose from the table and, without a word, strode out the door. Jesse
followed. Joseph was disgusted and humiliated, ready to give up on the
whole idea of buying the Helvetia mine, but under Jesse's patient coaxing,
he conceded that there was no reason to let his sons' waywardness, if that's
what it was, govern his decision. They consulted with Hannibal and Martin,
and the four agreed that with the Pascoes and the Chenoweths, they had
enough partners to make the company viable and enough Cornishmen to
keep the Sterlings at bay.

A week later, the partners met in the Mill Street office of a young
attorney named Dibble, who drew up papers specifying an initial investment of $15,000, divided into twenty shares. Edward Sterling promptly
confirmed that he would buy four shares, and John took three, although
Jesse later suspected that he was using his brother's money. The rest of the
men bought one or two shares apiece. Edward announced that he would
serve as superintendent, and since he was the largest single shareholder, the
others acquiesced without debate. John proposed that they elect an underground captain and, in the same breath, nominated Joseph. No one objected,
and Joseph was amenable, so the partners signed the papers, and there, on

the first of April in 1860, they formed the North Star Quartz Mining Company.

Jesse contended that the boys' apparent betrayal was temporary, youthful folly, assuring his brother that within the year, they would be looking for a way to buy into the mine. Joseph relented, assigning Nick to hire a crew to clean out the drifts, and appointing Jack to solve a special problem. There had been little chance for Joseph to learn to read and write, so he was one of the many men in Grass Valley who made his mark rather than signed his name. He'd had little reason to regret his lack of learning, but now, as underground captain, he had to work closely with Edward Sterling, a man he did not trust, and whose responsibilities included everything related to contracts and accounts. To make matters worse, John Sterling showed no inclination to get involved in the actual working of the mine other than occasional walks down the incline shaft to smile and cheer the men on; when he came to the mine, he stayed in the office with his brother, and whenever Joseph met with Edward, John was sure to be there, leaning back in a chair set to one side of the broad oak desk. Hannibal and Jesse were the two experienced men best qualified to check Sterling's paperwork, but Joseph realized that the superintendent would probably challenge the necessity for the captain to bring other senior partners with him to routine meetings. Jack, however, wasn't a shareholder at all, and he was Joseph's son. Who more suitable to appear as Joseph's clerk and assistant? Hannibal spent evening after evening teaching Jack how to read ledgers, and soon Jack became a regular, accepted participant in his father's meetings with the Sterlings, taking notes, reading documents, checking figures, and discreetly helping Joseph defer any ticklish questions so that they could take the time to consult with the other Cornishmen. By the middle of July, the grounds were clean, the machinery was repaired and the new buildings were complete. Edward sent out a team of boys to post handbills throughout the district, within three days he had signed on two shifts of men, and the stamp mill set up a shake and a rattle as the first load of rock poured down the chute.

Jack and Nick invested their money in the Pony. The agent hardly gave them a chance to ask questions, drawing up the papers while declaiming on the finest California mustangs, special saddles, dedicated young riders bred to Western trails, and a support system of way stations and well-disciplined crews. They left his office with the certificates they wanted, but his chatter combined with pessimistic saloon gossip and Joseph's exasperation to make them nervous. They decided to go down to Sacramento to welcome the first rider bringing the mail in from Missouri, so the evening of April 13 found them clinging to the roof of a warehouse on J Street, where they could survey a crowd that extended all the way down to the levee. Over the thin percussion of hundreds of excited voices, they heard the clatter of hooves, and as the cheers rose, rolling like a wave down the street, they saw the frantic rider, his hat fallen down behind his shoulders, urging his mount to full gallop, carrying a small American flag in one hand, and sending a small cloud of dust back into the faces of the horsemen who were racing him to the depot. Amidst cannon salutes and pealing of bells from firehouses and church steeples, the rider swung down from the saddle and slung his *mochila,* the leather blanket with the four padlocked *cantinas* that held the mail, into the arms of the waiting agent. The Trevennas ran down to the wharf to watch the *Antelope* pull away towards San Francisco, carrying on its main deck the last courier with a fresh horse, decorated for the occasion, and then marched by torchlight to a large bonfire, where they stood in a crowd of Americans and listened to men in silk top hats speak, to enthusiastic applause, of the new era in California's progress.

Early on the following morning, they climbed into the Colfax stage, settled into their seats, and looked across to find, sitting in a corner, a Chinese man wearing a neat black cap and an iridescent silk suit displaying a pattern of monkeys climbing up the vermilion frogging of the jacket to the upturned collar. The stage company, when they grudgingly agreed to sell a Chinaman a ticket at all, usually insisted that he ride on top, and on the rear at that, so Jack immediately assumed that their fellow passenger must be a man of unusual influence. Then he looked at his face more carefully and recognized Ah Choy, the laundryman from Red Dog. Jack introduced him to Nick and casually mentioned the North Star, hoping to make an impression, but Ah Choy seemed to know all about it. He would reveal little about his own affairs, only that he had moved his business from Red Dog to Grass Valley, and that he no longer ran the laundry himself. Jack quietly guessed that the man must be a merchant of some kind, working with wholesalers in Sacramento, and possibly San Francisco, and selling the goods to the Chinese miners in Grass Valley. As he considered the possibilities, he realized that Ah Choy was speaking to him not in pidgin, but in accurate, although careful, English. He wanted to ask him about that, but Nick was describing the arrival of the Pony Express and explaining that he and Jack had an interest in the company.

"The Pony Express?" Ah Choy raised his eyebrows. "A very . . . American . . . enterprise. Unusual to find two young Englishmen so involved." Jack rehearsed the many reasons why the Pony would bring prosperity to California. The merchant nodded, showing no surprise at anything Jack had to say. "Very fast. Very exciting. But . . . no cargo. No freight. Only messages." Jack presented Delano's position that information could be useful. "Ah, yes. Useful, yes. Also powerful. But soon, very soon, the Americans will bring the telegraph across the mountains."

At that moment, the driver called to the horses and set the coach in motion, and the creaking of the springs and the rumbling of hooves made conversation so difficult that Jack spent the trip into the hills gazing out of the window. They reached Colfax, quickly transferred to the stage for Grass Valley, and before mid-day, they stepped down in front of the Exchange. Before the merchant could walk away, Jack stopped him and drew him aside. "'ow soon? 'ow soon will they finish th' telegraph?"

Ah Choy watched a heavily-laden wagon clatter down Main Street. "No one can know for sure. There is already a survey. But their government, the one in Washington, must decide." He looked back at Jack. "Twenty years ago, this land belonged to Mexico. No Americans, no English, no Chinese." He smiled. "The Americans came. It is theirs now, and they belong here. So they think. And they think that you and I do not belong. We stay only if they choose." Jack began to protest, but Ah Choy shook his head. "You English are like them, so they accept you. But they are very, very suspicious of Chinese. Sometimes I think they are afraid. I find that I must be very careful." He picked up the small bag he had brought with him. "I do not always understand these Americans. So open, but very unexpected. But I will tell you this, as one stranger to another. They never forget that they are American, and that is their pride. That is why they do what they will do. They do not always look for profit. They do not always do what is sensible. A man makes a speech, whistles blow and bells ring, and they shake their fists in the light of many bonfires. If you want to know how quickly they will bring the telegraph, ask yourself . . . if I were an American, would this telegraph make me cheer? Would I wave a flag?" He shook Jack's hand. "Yesterday, they shout for a man riding a horse. But not tomorrow. Not tomorrow." He turned and walked down the hill towards Chinatown, leaving Jack standing in the sunlight.

5
Joseph
1861

Joseph closed his eyes and lifted his face to a passing breath of air, cool on his sweaty eyelids. Within a month after the grass crew had dumped the first load into the mill, he had known that the North Star was the venture he had been seeking, and he had announced that the Trevennas would settle at French Lead. The new cabin was much larger than they needed, with two stories and no fewer than three sleeping rooms, but the mining companies on Lafayette Hill had felled so many of the Ponderosa pines, throwing them aside into gullies and ravines, that lumber was too cheap to resist, so they built the place out of long, white planking and sealed the boards with their own oozing pitch. Jack had wanted to rent out the shack at Red Dog, arguing that they had an easy, sure source of income, but Joseph and Jesse had agreed to lock it up and keep it available as a base for the occasions when one or more of them needed to visit one of their old claims, now lying quiet and waiting for the day when the family would either sell them or, if the North Star faltered, need to return.

Joseph heard a muffled thudding that surged into dull, stuttering drum beats, and he opened his eyes to see a little company of men riding into the clearing: Jack and Nick galloping ahead, racing each other, with Jesse and the Carne brothers trotting behind. Nick cantered back and forth in front of the cabin waving his hat and repeating a lilting "halloo" that sent the agitated jays fluttering, jeering, from branch to branch, while Jack swung out of his saddle and ran up the porch step to where his father sat, waving a sheaf of newspapers in front of him and panting, "It's war, Fayther!"

One "extra" headline, bold and dark, read, "BEAUREGARD FIRES ON FORT SUMPTER," and the breathless paragraphs declared that after months of defiance and siege, the federal commander had refused to surrender, and with the citizens of Charleston cheering from rooftops, the confederate batteries had opened fire on the small garrison in the harbor. There was little else in the way of actual information—the editor of each paper had transcribed, almost verbatim, the terse message that had arrived on the Pony—so the rest of the pages were filled with speculation and patriotic rhetoric. Every one of the local newspapers insisted that the Union must be preserved.

Jack, his fingers smudged with the black ink, read aloud. "'There are some hopeful lovers of what lately was the Great American Republic, who mauger the recent deplorable events at Charleston, will continue to hope for a peaceful solution of the section-vexed questions which threaten the national existence, and who promise themselves a successful reintegration of the Union. That such patriotic hopes may not be blasted ought to be the prayer of every true American. It is true, there are grounds for these hopes—good grounds—and though there is much to lament in the madness of the hour, which is hurling brother against brother in angry strife, there is still enough of calm wisdom, in both sections of the Republic, to check this madness ere it finally accomplish the national ruin. The peaceful and the wise, in both the north and the south, will make themselves heard above the clash of arms and end the fratricidal conflict by restoring the Union in all its pristine strength and excellence. There is still hope for our glorious Republic.'"

Nick laughed derisively. "Does 'e really think they'll settle this 'ere without a fight?"

"'ow many states," asked Joseph, "'ave seceded from this Union o' theirs?"

"Six, I think," replied Jack.

Jesse had been sitting in a sort of crouch, his beard resting on his fist, but now he looked up and shook his head. "Seven. Everythin' from South Carolina to Texas. And more likely t' follow."

Joseph let a smoke ring float up into the still air. "At this rate, Mr. Lincoln'll be President o' nothin', and right soon."

Hannibal read aloud from the *Nevada Journal*. "'In the present crisis of national affairs a large and liberal allowance must be made for diversity of views in regard to the policy to be pursued. A disposition to concede should be prevalent among patriots—to concede to the views of one another. All men of whatever party who love the Union must be aware that the best policy devised by the Administration can be rendered inefficient by a want of support to it by the people. As in all probability the difficulties in the Union will be settled during the four years of Mr. Lincoln's Administration, if settled at all, it behooves us all to stand by the President in all his efforts to preserve the Nation as our fathers made it, yielding our opinions in some cases to those of others that we may present a solid phalanx of determined patriots to the enemies of the country.'" The others waited while he scanned the rest of the page. "'e's tryin' t' cabobble us; 'e's nothin' t' say, but 'e wants us t' follow along t' nowhere."

Jesse shook his head. "Lincoln 'as said that the Union will continue, but 'e 'asn't said what 'e'll do about it."

Joseph kept puffing on his pipe. "P'raps 'e's a smart man—'e waited for the rebels t' fire the first shot. Now there's a war, but not 'is doin'."

"An' what do it mean fer us?" asked Martin.

Joseph, 1861

The men considered the question. Jack suggested that California might raise a militia for its defense, but Hannibal wrinkled his nose over the idea. Over a thousand empty miles, rough country, lay between California and Missouri; Texas was closer, but he couldn't believe that the rebel troops would march across the southwest desert all the way to the Pacific. Jesse agreed, thinking that the southerners would have enough to do just to defend their own territory. Nick stammered that some men in town were already talking about forming a brigade, gathering together companies from the various mining camps and booking passage out of San Francisco.

Joseph snorted. "By th' time they got there, the whole thing'd be finished." He frowned at his son. "An' don't you be thinkin' o' joinin' with 'em." Nick started to answer, but checked himself and looked down at his hands.

Jesse bit his lip. "You may be right. It may be brief."

"What d'ye mean?" asked Martin.

Jesse sighed. "I've been talkin' to men at th' mine and in town. Some o' them can't believe that there'll be a war."

"But they can't stop it!" interjected Nick. "You saw the paper—they attacked th' fort!" The streets of Grass Valley had been full of men cheering defiantly, slapping each other on the back and passing around deep pitchers of beer. Nick had found the momentum irresistible, but when three of his friends had run up, calling his name, Jesse had insisted that he keep riding.

His uncle stared at him. "I 'aven't 'eard anythin' about Lincoln sendin' 'is troops south." He turned back to Martin. "I know men from Tennessee and Kentucky, and Ohio and Pennsylvania and Virginia. They tell me that th' farmers trade back and forth, one state to another. Ye can't see th' borders, y'know, and there's no one askin' ye t' account fer yerself when ye cross. If there's a war, it'll be neighbors fightin' each other, an' there're some think that can't 'appen."

"How'll they settle it?" asked Jack.

"I don't know. But if they don't—if they fight th' war—it won't be soon finished."

Joseph nodded. "And that's what we 'ave t' consider. A long war. What'll 'appen t' th' mines? An' what'll 'appen to Englishmen like us?"

Jack studied his father. Joseph hardly ever referred to himself as an Englishman, reserving the term for men like Sterling, but now the distinctions had shifted. To the Americans, the men from Penwith were just as English as the men from London or Northumberland, and not much different from the Irish. In a war, especially a civil war, a foreigner was a foreigner.

Hannibal ran down a list of possibilities. "They could tell us t' leave, t' get out and go 'ome. If England stands up with th' rebels, then we're all spies and traitors. They could take away what we 'ave—th' mine and all.

Cousin Jack

There are Americans right 'ere in Grass Valley that would be just as 'appy to take over th' North Star."

Martin clucked his tongue. "It's 'ard t' believe. And 'ard t' believe anyone pullin' that on Edward Sterling." Jack nodded. The Sterlings knew all of the important men in town; they were rapidly becoming part of the small group that seemed to run things.

Hannibal smiled thinly. "And d'ye think Edward would object t' seein' us put out and 'im and 'is brother the only share'olders?" Martin scowled. "They'd need men t' work underground, and they'd be worse off without us, but they don't know that." He tossed a pebble down the steps. "An' there's one more possibility. They might press us."

"What d'ye mean?" asked Nick, puzzled.

Hannibal grinned. "I mean a press, jus' like in England, years ago. They came fer my gramfer's brother, took 'im away, jus' like that, an' no one ever saw 'im again. Think about it. If ye need troops t' fight a war, especially a war against yer own, who better t' send than th' foreigners that've been camped out in yer territory, takin' yer gold?"

Joseph slapped his pipe against his cupped palm, scattering bits of burned tobacco in the dirt. "So that's the worst of it, eh? Us off t' war and the Americans takin' what's ours."

"Or," returned Jesse, "it'll be over before midsummer."

Jack had been rolling a long green pine needle between his fingers, crushing it until the sharp scent rose in the air. "The war'll be good for th' North Star. I mean, if we can stay with it."

"Why?" asked Joseph.

Jack shrugged. "They'll 'ave t' pay fer it some'ow. T' fight a war ye need men and arms and transport. Provisions. Freight rates'll rise, an' th' farmers'll get more fer their crops. What if they can't make enough cannons in their own foundries? They'll 'ave t' buy 'em abroad, and the English won't take greenbacks. They'll want gold."

Hannibal nodded slowly. "The price o' gold'll go up."

Jesse shook his head. "An' so will wages. Especially if men leave fer th' war; we'll 'ave t' pay more t' replace 'em."

"True," returned Hannibal, "but I think Jack's right. All in all, th' war'll be good fer us."

Martin looked dubious. "Not if they take away th' mine."

Jack paused for a moment, catching his breath. "They won't if we're Americans."

There was a long silence. Joseph had stopped in the midst of filling his pipe, and now he looked up at the others. Every single man looked away or down at his feet. "What is it? Americans? Are we back t' that again?"

Finally, Jesse told him. "We filed our papers today, Joseph. Martin and

Joseph, 1861

Hannibal an' myself. Over t' th' county courthouse in Nevada. That's why we rode into town."

His brother tamped down the tobacco, struck a match and drew on the stem for a few puffs. He inhaled deeply before turning to Jack. "You and Nick are too young."

"We know. But we're yer sons, and if you declare, then we're safe."

Joseph actually laughed. "Safe from what? D'ye really think they'll send a press gang all th' way up to this 'ere just t' hale ye back t' fight in Virginia?"

"There's a chance."

"What falderal!"

"Then what if they take over th' mines?"

"'e's right, Joseph," said Hannibal. "That's a possibility. I agree with ye—I can't credit that they'd be takin' men against their will. Mill Street was full of volunteers only this afternoon, and no one's yet invited 'em! But if they fight this war, it'll be a dear one, and th' government might be 'appier runnin' th' mines themselves rather than buyin' th' gold from us."

"If they'll take over," retorted Joseph, "then they'll take over from Americans, same as us. No difference at all."

"Maybe not," suggested Martin, but Joseph interrupted him.

"Besides, think o' what yer about. If ye become an American citizen, ye're no longer a British subject. Ye're sayin' that ye won't be goin' 'ome again."

"And what's wrong with that?" demanded Jack.

Joseph glared at his son for a moment, then took a deep breath and another pull on his pipe before turning to Jesse. "What about you? Are ye goin' back t' Camborne?"

Everyone looked at him, waiting for the answer. "I'm not sure," Jesse replied.

"And yet ye've filed th' papers."

"It's only a declaration of intent," explained Hannibal. "'e 'as t' wait two years anyway, and if 'e don't finish, then nothin' comes of it."

"Well, Jesse?" asked Joseph.

Jesse sighed. "I'm thinkin' of askin' Zennora 'ow she feels about it."

"At least you're askin' 'er," said Nick. "No one's askin' my mother."

Joseph growled, "That is none of yer affair, ye young staver, and ye'd best take care o' yer own business before ye start tellin' me 'ow to mind mine!"

"She's my mother—"

"And I'm 'er 'usband." Joseph rose to his feet. "Jesse may do as 'e thinks best, but it's my judgement that Margaret and Charles are better off in Cornwall. So will I be, when I'm ready to leave this place, and so will you, if ye 'ave any sense."

Cousin Jack

Nick lowered his voice a bit. "Fayther, Fayther . . . d'ye really want to go back to Cook's Kitchen or the Dolcoath? Back t' the auction fer th' pitches, and wonderin' whether yer drift will pay anything, and knowin' that you can't go find another 'til the next round? Back t' tippin' your 'at to Billy Arundell whenever 'is coach splashes ye goin' around th' corner?"

Joseph sneered, irritated. "Ye're makin' Camborne into one o' those fairy tales we hear about 'ere whenever these rumbustious Americans celebrate their Independence Day. Ye'd think that King George 'ad ridden 'is 'orse right through George Washington's tobacco patch, and that th' good folks o' Boston were chained t' their shop doors, workin' day and night, and sendin' every penny they earned t' th' lords in London. Ye know—or 'ave ye forgotten?—that we were all doin' right well in Cornwall, not like these dirty Irish that 'adn't a potato fer their dinner or a piece o' sod t' call their own."

Nick shook his head. "But 'ere ye're a mine owner. An adventurer! When would any of us get a chance like that in Penwith? It's Arundell and Pendarves and that lot that own everything. 'ere a man can dig a 'ole, strike a vein, 'ire men to work it, and set 'imself up in the fanciest 'ouse in town, and there's no one t' put 'im down."

"D'ye really think ye can live like a gentleman 'ere? Who runs this country? Who's goin' t' run this town when it settles down? It'll be Americans and the sons of Americans, and th' longer they've been squattin' 'ere and th' more money they 'ave, th' better fer them. Oh, I grant ye, the Sterlings'll buy and sell this town one day, but we won't be standin' next to 'em when they do it, nor will any Cornishman."

"The Sterlings are English, just like us." Nick had begun to sulk.

"English, yes, but not like us, as well ye know." Joseph was no longer angry, and he felt sorry for his son. "Suppose we do become citizens. It won't be Jesse or me that takes charge, nor you, nor John. It might be yer children, but then again it won't because the others'll get there first, and they'll shut th' gate behind 'em. In Camborne, it's Arundell and Pendarves who got there first, and 'ere it'll be these Americans from Ohio and New York and Illinois. But it won't be us. We might as well take our money and go back."

"Back t' work for someone else?"

"No, boy, back t' take our ease." Joseph sat down again, grunting softly. "In just a little while longer, I'll be able t' go 'ome, buy a 'ouse with a bit o' land, a little farm, p'raps, and leave th' minin' t' someone else. You and John can do th' same, and I'd like it if you did."

Nick sighed. "You're settlin' fer so little."

"I'm settlin' fer more than I could 'ave 'ad if I 'adn't come 'ere. Listen to me, Nicholas. Ye never knew yer own gramfer. 'e'd worked in the tin mines from th' time 'e was a boy, and 'e spent fifteen years in Wheal Trewavas, walkin' down under th' sea every day, with th' salt water drippin' on 'is 'ead, and th' tunnels as 'ot and as wet as ye can imagine. After a few years ye 'ave a cough that stays with ye fer th' rest of yer life. 'e was worn out, wheezin' in 'is chair by th' fire, and just as old as I am now. But remember this—'e chose 'is life. It 'ad nothin' t' do with Arundell or Pendarves or any o' th' rest. 'e could 'ave gone out with th' fishin' boats, or gone t' work fer a farmer, and maybe ended up with 'is own fields an' cattle and all. 'e could've worked at grass. 'e chose t' go down in th' mines because it was what 'e knew, and because 'e knew 'e could do well with th' tin and th' copper. I 'ad a chance t' come 'ere, t' bring out th' gold, and when I leave th' mines, I'll leave with my 'ealth and full pockets. I came 'ere, and I'm glad of it, but Camborne is my 'ome." Nick sat quietly, staring down at his feet, and Joseph put his hand on his knee. "Come now, ye apty-cock, don't be gettin' all glumped up. I know ye'll be wantin' to make yer own decisions. But don't be gettin' cocky and tellin' me what I must do."

Martin tossed a small bit of granite into Nick's lap and said, "P'raps ye left Cornwall too young to remember it properly. It's not as woodsy as this, I'll allow, but there's somethin' about th' sea breeze and th' gardens in the towns. Some day we'll go back together and I'll show you my gramfer's farm."

"If ye think it's so fine, then why did ye file th' papers?"

Martin smiled. "Just keepin' th' door open both ways."

Joseph knocked out his pipe. "'ow long do ye think it'll be before France or England sends over an army to knock some sense into their 'eads back East and take over th' lot? California will be on 'er own then, and you'll be citizens of nowhere."

Jesse bit his lip. "What if th' North and th' South tear each other apart? P'raps this is the end o' th' United States. No one'll 'ave any attention t' spare for what's goin' on 'way out 'ere. There were two or three renegade republics after th' Yanks took this land from th' Mexicans, and I think we'll see a few more if things go sour."

Jack read a passage from *The Daily Transcript*. "'Can not a Californian, whether of northern or southern birth, lament the madness that has driven his eastern brethren to the verge of civil war, without hating or insulting his neighbor who happens not to be born in the same quarter of the Republic with himself? Are Californians, who are supposed to be the very *elite,* in mental and physical energy, of the states whence they emigrated, to reproduce on the shores of the Pacific the terrible prejudices and hatred now tinging the waters of the Atlantic with the blood of brothers shed by brothers?'"

Jesse frowned. "It's a lot of pious falderal, nothing but triddling."

Cousin Jack

Nick stood up. "I'm ridin' back t' town. There's t' be a torchlight parade, just t' show that we're behind Mr. Lincoln, even if we are 'way out 'ere in California. Jack, are ye comin'?" Jack looked up and shook his head. Without another word, Nick walked down the stairs, swung up into his saddle, and pulled the horse around to canter off into the trees.

Finally, Jesse spoke. "Well, there's little risk. Let's wait and see. If there is a war, and it goes badly, we'll book passage 'ome."

"I won't be waitin'," said Joseph. "When the autumn comes, I mean t' make that journey. By October, I'll 'ave enough t' go 'ome and buy th' kind o' place I fancy. I'll plant a garden, with flowers fer Margaret, and when th' days are fine, I'll walk up the 'ill and set on a rock and smell the sea breeze and watch the tide bring in th' fishing boats. P'raps young Charles'll get married one day and give me some grandchildren."

Hannibal considered. "Ye'll be sellin' yer share in th' North Star?"

"Iss," grinned Joseph. "I 'ope as none o' ye piljacks is too penny-liggy t' give me a fair price!"

Martin rose to his feet. "Well, I'll be sorry t' see ye go, Joseph, but I wish ye well." He looked down at his brother. "I'm ridin' back t' see that parade—are ye comin'?" Hannibal nodded, and they walked over to their horses. Watching them, Jack thought to himself that in another year he would be old enough to file the papers, no matter what his father might say. No one could make him return to Cornwall; not to stay, anyway. Abruptly, he got up and joined the Carnes, and the three rode single file out of the clearing, back towards town.

Joseph filled his pipe again, tamped the tobacco down into the bowl, and struck a match to light the dried leaves. As he drew on the stem, sucking the tiny flame down and out of sight, he looked over at Jesse, who was gazing out at the sunset. "Ye're stayin' 'ere, aren't ye?"

After a long moment, Jesse turned. "I'm not yet ready t' quit."

"So ye want t' work harder and get richer, is that it?"

"Ye make it sound wrong."

"Not a bit of it. I'm sure Mr. Wesley would 'ave approved."

"And what about you?"

Joseph pulled deeply on the pipe. "We've come a long way from Land's End, 'moast 'alf-way 'round the world. It's too far for one man t' tell another which way t' turn."

Jesse smiled. "I may go back one day. We've been 'ere three years—after another three, or perhaps another, I might be ready."

"What about Zennora?"

Jesse stopped smiling and looked out the window again. "She's still thinkin' it over." He thought for a moment and, without looking at his brother, spoke hesitantly. "D'ye know that she talks to th' piskies?"

Joseph, 1861

Joseph snorted. "Dabbety fay! Give us faith!"

Jesse nodded. "That's what I said, but she believes it. There's somethin' about that woman."

"Hould tha bal! Stop yer chatterin'! There's somethin' about you, too!"

"Maybe so."

Joseph shifted in his chair and considered for a moment. "Jesse, can ye look after th' boys for me?"

His brother stared at him, puzzled. "O' course I will. Why d'ye ask?"

"I worry about Nicholas. Camborne was diff'rent, quieter, some'ow, but 'ere, it's like 'avin' the may-games every week, and whenever I turn 'round, 'e's up to 'is gammuts again."

"Not every man is settled in at nineteen."

Joseph shook his head. "There's somethin' reckless about 'im, as though 'e's runnin' along a drift without lookin' for the winzes beneath 'is feet. I fear one day 'e'll drop through, and that'll be the end of 'im. And then there's John."

"He's quick."

"Iss, 'e's learned more than 'e tells. But 'e's careful. 'e won't dig a drift unless 'e knows what 'e'll find at the end o' th' day, and th' next. 'e sails in all cock-a-hoop, lookin' fer th' gold, but then 'e stops and ye can see 'im addin' it all up."

Jesse patted his brother on the shoulder. "I'll watch them for ye, Joseph. They'll be fine men."

"I pray ye're right. I do pray it."

The men scarcely noticed as the grass turned brown and crunchy in the sizzling heat of summer, for they worked long shifts down in the cool darkness of the North Star, drilling in the most promising drifts and bringing out carloads of the richest ore they had yet seen. His plans made and confirmed, Joseph worked with the freedom of a runner who sees the end of the race and knows he can release his last reserves. He smiled as he swung his sledge, his weight perfectly balanced, his legs and back and shoulders behind each blow, and he hit the drill dead center every time. His movements fell into a symmetrical rhythm that gave each limb and sinew a moment's rest before coming into play again. When the men retreated up the drift to wait for the black powder to blast the quartz out of the wall, Joseph lay in a crevice, feeling the greenstone enfold him like his mother's arms, and accepting the explosion as man in a mountain meadow, drunk with the rain, revels in the thunder. The others covered their faces against falling debris and their ears against the concussion, but Joseph opened himself, gazing into the darkness and embracing the hurly-burly. After twelve or fourteen hours beneath the surface, finally exhausted, he would trudge up the incline into the warm dusk and watch the last flicker of the Sierra sunset. On the darkest nights, when the moon rose late, he took his blankets outside the cabin to lie in a clearing, every muscle spent and relaxed, and marveled at the starry sky during the few moments before he fell completely asleep.

The war hardly touched Grass Valley. A few men left to volunteer, but their company spent the next four years in Arizona marching in drills while back at home, some zealous patriots raised nearly ten thousand dollars for the Sanitary Commission. The Pony brought the news that troops were gathering for what would surely be a decisive confrontation in Virginia, and the price of gold did, indeed, start to rise.

One morning late in July, Joseph and Jesse had finished a shift together and joined several other men for the walk up the incline shaft. By the time they were about halfway up, Joseph had lagged behind, staring at the ground before him, aware of little other than the weight of the tools on his back. He did not usually work all night, and he felt a bit dazed. Suddenly there was a staccato burst of shouts and cries from the head of the tunnel, and the men at the front of the group, trudging up the firm ground along the tracks, looked up to see a fully-laden ore car running straight at them, out of control. The miners leaped to this side and that, and as he vaulted to safety behind a pile of timber, Jesse looked back to see his brother still trudging up the slope. He screamed at him to save himself, but he didn't seem to hear. Just as Jesse was scrambling to his feet to help, he saw Joseph look up. His eyes opened wide in surprise, but there was no more time. The heavy car struck him squarely in the chest and knocked him back at full length so his head came down hard on the unforgiving floor of the shaft. Interrupted, the car wavered to the left and to the right, and finally the wheels lost their grip on the tracks and the car fell over on its side, skidding down the tunnel and scattering rocks everywhere.

Jesse dropped everything and ran. Joseph lay on his back, bleeding from his chest and head. Jesse called his name, but his eyes were rolled back behind the drooping lids, and he didn't answer. The others gathered around and quickly formed a litter made of jackets and ropes. They gently lifted the injured man onto it and carried him up out of the tunnel to lay him down next to the hoisting engine. Old William Pascoe was grass captain that day, and he knelt beside his former helper, involuntarily gasping when he saw the blood dribbling out of his mouth. The nearest doctor was two miles away, in Grass Valley, so the men quickly loaded a wagon with clothing, rags and blankets, laid the litter on the makeshift padding, and one of them drove it into town as fast as he dared, with Jesse riding beside his brother, trying to keep the injured man steady in spite of the lurching. The doctor shook his head as soon as he saw him, and while he was cutting his clothing away to examine him more closely, Joseph shuddered out one last, wheezing breath, and then lay perfectly still. There was no need to close his eyes.

Joseph, 1861

They sent a rider out to Red Dog, where Jack was spending the day inspecting their old claims. Just before noon, Jesse looked out of the doctor's window to see Jack gallop down Mill Street, pull up in front of the hitching post, and slide off the saddle to run up the stairs. He burst into the room and came to a halt, staring down at his father. Jesse watched as Jack reached out to brush a lock of hair away from the dead man's forehead and put his hand on his chest. After a moment, he turned and slammed his fist against the wall so hard that the bottles in the cabinet rattled and the doctor's assistant came running in to see what had happened. Finally, Jack fell into a chair and sat there, leaning forward, working his fingers together and biting the inside of his cheek. Jesse waited for a few minutes, and then rose from the window seat and walked over to him.

"Jack?" His nephew looked up at him. "No one knows where Nick is. Ye must find 'im." Jack stared up into Jesse's face. "Jack?" He nodded, took a deep breath, rose to his feet, and walked out of the room without looking at the man on the table.

The sun was setting by the time Jack rode into the town of Nevada. He left his horse at a livery stable, giving the boy firm instructions to brush the animal down, for he had been riding most of the day, and paid him extra for the best feed. He walked up Broad Street, stopping in each saloon, and within an hour found a man who had seen Nick earlier that evening. Over on Commercial Street, Jack stopped to scan the row of second-story windows of the ramshackle boarding house.

In the upstairs room, the laughing woman had just unbuttoned Nick's vest when there was a sharp knock at the door, three quick raps, and the rough growl of a man's voice. Nick frowned at the rattling door knob and started to shrug to the woman just as the voice petulantly asserted that he knew Trevenna was in there and that the rascal had better come out. The woman, her eyes wide, held a finger to her lips and Nick reached for his boots as she went to the door and asked, in as sleepy a voice as she could manage, who was there.

"I tell you, it's Thomas Sims, and I know that Nick Trevenna is in there with you. That little thief gave me a promise to pay tonight, and I mean to get his gold before he leaves town or wastes it all on a slut like you!" He began to pound on the door, and voices complained from down the hall.

She ran to the window, heaved it open, and ran back to the door. "*Who* is it you want?" Sims was now spluttering with frustration, but managed to articulate Nick's name. "I have a visitor with me, but that's not who it is, and I don't think he'd like it if you came in just now." Sims predicted that everyone in the building would like it even less if he were left waiting in the hallway any longer, and the pounding changed to a slow, steady, heavy thud: he was throwing his weight on the door, trying to break it in with his shoulder. Nick glided to the window and tossed out his hat and coat. He straddled the sill, grinned at the woman, and gestured that she should give him a farewell kiss. She made a face and stabbed her forefinger at the window, all the while assuring Sims that as soon as her guest was dressed, she would open the door and he could see for himself that Nick Trevenna, whoever he might be, wasn't there. Nick swung his other leg over, studied the drop for a moment, then waved before pushing off into the night. She heard him land on the ground below and swear softly, and there was a sudden crescendo of voices from the first floor; apparently Nick had fallen in full view of the men and women drinking in the saloon beneath.

Jack had gone around to the back of the building and now turned the corner just in time to see Nick drop. He helped him up and was brushing him off when they heard a splintery crash. The woman shrieked. A burly, hatless man appeared abruptly at the window, his jowly, grizzled face angry and dazed. He peered out into the night, but the woman appeared, trying to pull him back into the room. He tried to fend her off with one arm, but she began to pummel him and he, startled, set his jaw, swung his arm back, and clouted her just below the right eye. She bounced off of the wardrobe and fell against the burly man, grabbing his lapels with both hands. She found her footing just in time to see him lift his fist again, and as she released him and recoiled, she reached into her bodice. The woman retreated out of view as the burly man backed up against the window frame into a half-crouch, laughing harshly, his hands held out in front of him like a wrestler. He sprang heavily, and there was a shot. The woman shrieked.

"Nick!" Jack hissed. "There was an accident. Fayther is dead." Nick's face stiffened, and the smile slowly faded away, leaving only a look of confused disbelief. "Come on."

They buried Joseph on Cemetery Hill. A hundred men stood in the summer sun while the undertaker's helpers lowered the coffin into the grave. Even the Sterlings had driven up in Edward's buggy; John looked somber in his black suit, and his wife blinked back her tears. The minister read the service, they filled in the grave, and the mourners gradually departed until no one was left but the three Trevennas. Nick was walking slowly around the grave, picking up clods and rocks and laying them carefully on the rusty mound of earth, and Jack stood several yards away, staring west towards the town that lay across the far side of the valley. Jesse gazed down at the headstone, shining white with the letters sharply chiseled into the surface. The top half depicted a woman standing next to a pair of weeping willows, her head bowed in sorrow, reaching out her left hand to support her weight on a font while she held a handkerchief in her right. The artwork was far too sentimental for his brother, but the stonecutter had offered few alternatives. The boys had refused to look at the samples, so Jesse had tried to choose what he thought Margaret would like. Now he would have to write to her, to explain why Joseph would never come home again.

Jack walked back to the grave, and stood looking back and forth at the other two men. "Fayther left no will." He paused. "There's some money, and there's 'is share in th' North Star. And th' property 'is mother left 'im." He brought his lower lip up over his mustache. "I went t' see Dibble yesterday. 'alf goes to Mother, and th' children split the rest." He looked at Nick. "The others'll 'ave no use fer their shares in th' mine. We should buy 'em out."

Nick reached down to pick up another rock, and he weighed it in his hand. "'ow much?"

"About fifteen 'undred." Nick shook his head dubiously. "If ye 'aven't got it, I'll lend it to ye. An' if ye won't do it, I'll buy 'em out on my own. But I know ye 'ave it. And it's time we went in."

Nick dropped the rock down on the grave. "If ye know so much, then buy it and 'ave done with it."

Jesse caught his nephew's eye. "Nicholas."

Nick's eyes narrowed slightly as he appraised his uncle. He stooped to pick up another rock and passed it from hand to hand. "All right—it's th' best thing t' do." He grinned suddenly. "Share'olders! What will Sterling say?"

John Sterling welcomed them effusively to the next partners' meeting, while Edward shook each man's hand without saying a word. There was little to do but confirm that they would continue as before, and to replace Joseph as the underground captain, they elected Hannibal Carne.

6
The Fire
1861-62

Jack sat in the lobby of the Exchange re-reading the letter in his hand. Nehemiah Larkin, Agent, begged to advise that the Congress of the United States had authorized Wells, Fargo & Co. to operate the mail service known as the Pony Express only until such time as the transcontinental telegraph had achieved completion. The company therefore wished to inform him that said service had been discontinued as of October 26, 1861, and to recommend that those parties who had purchased stock in the enterprise from Mssrs. Russell, Majors & Waddell, the original operators of said service, should apply to them for information concerning the disposition of their certificates.

He sighed. He knew that Bill Russell wouldn't offer compensation to the small investors, for the Pony had run at a disastrous loss ever since the first rider left St. Joseph. The telegraph companies had begun stringing their wires much earlier than Jack had anticipated, and he remembered, as clearly as he remembered the cave-in at the Wheal Vor, the afternoon when he walked into a bank on Front Street, in Sacramento, and saw the ambrotype of crews planting poles across the desert. The graceful riders, pounding their relay race across the mountains, would give place to bespectacled clerks wearing eye shades and black oversleeves in stuffy offices. Jack had hoped that the telegraph charges—$6 to send only seven words to New York City—would inspire the public to demand the continuation of the Pony, but the government and Wells, Fargo had lost interest immediately, and all that remained was the newspaper's flowery elegy to "that proud and star-caparisoned charger, the fleet courser of the continent."

Jack walked out of the hotel and stood on the sidewalk for a moment, so preoccupied that he didn't even notice when a passing acquaintance greeted him. He turned and walked down the hill, crossing the street at Loutzenheiser's drug store to head south and then turn off of the busy roadway to enter a warren of shacks and sheds that extended down to the west bank of Wolf Creek. He stopped in front of a three-story wooden building, rather like a haphazard barn with apparently random additions. There were no signs hanging from the eaves, so most of the whites who blundered into the alley assumed that the pile was simply a large tenement, probably on the verge of collapse, but Jack knew it as the preeminent business of the Chinese community and the place he was most likely to find its proprietor, Ah Choy.

The Fire, 1861-1862

Over crude but impeccably clean counters, his brisk clerks sold everything that his Chinese neighbors could possibly need: fresh vegetables grown in small gardens on Alta Hill, clothing sewn from Shanghai fabric in miniature impromptu factories in San Francisco, and a complete assortment of mining tools and equipment. His restaurant, a collection of stools and tiny tables pushed into one corner of the store, was always full of young Chinese men drinking tea and scooping noodles out of bowls with wooden sticks. This was the public Ah Choy, but from occasional fragments of conversation, Jack had begun to suspect that his business was much more complicated than it appeared, that some came to him as a banker, asking him to lend money and finance new ventures, and he had wondered, from time to time, whether he were involved in the gambling houses, opium dens and brothels that the men in the Mill Street saloons assured him were a necessary and prominent part of any Chinese settlement.

Jack walked into the store and a clerk, peering out from behind the burlap bags piled high on the counter, swung his queue around to scurry up the stairs to the mezzanine, where he knocked on the door. Ah Choy appeared on the landing, studied the white man for a moment, then bowed slightly and gestured that he might join him in his private office. As Jack was settling into his chair, a boy set down a tray, poured tea, and vanished. Jack took a sip from his cup, looked across the small, worn desk at his host, and began to feel foolish. He mumbled something about the Pony, but realized that Ah Choy would, of course, know about its demise, so he blurted out that he needed help, and he began to list his remaining assets.

The merchant held up his hand for silence. "Let us suppose that a young Chinese miner came to me and said 'I have some money. What should I do?' Perhaps I would invite this young man to work with me and learn. Perhaps, if he seemed useful, I would suggest that he go into business with me." He took a sip of tea and shook his head. "But you are English."

Jack frowned slightly. "Could we become partners—invest in something together?"

Ah Choy sipped his tea again. "You do not understand. I sell to everyone in what your people call Chinatown. These men come to my store because men like Silvester, Findley and Spencer either do not sell what they need, or they do not welcome them. You see? They want only white customers, and let the Chinese keep to themselves. Very well, then I will buy from Chinese—food, clothing, some other things. I have many regular suppliers, and they are pleased to sell to me. But I need goods that they cannot provide—tools and hardware—so I must also go to the big supply houses in Sacramento and San Francisco. Their agents do not have time for me, and I wait in the street. Finally, they come out to take my order, and then they make me pay more than their other customers. Many special charges. White men own all of the freight companies, and sometimes my shipments are delayed—there is no explanation. Yet they will serve me as long as I pay and do not make trouble. You see, Mr. Trevenna, I travel between these two communities, and the whites take my money even while they spit on my shoes. They would not approve if I went into partnership with an Englishman."

"You seem to accept it so easily."

The merchant lifted his cup to his lips, took a long sip, and set it down, carefully choosing its position on the desk and studying it for a moment. When he lifted his eyes again, his face was completely impassive. "It is not possible for you and me to work together."

"Can ye give me any advice at all?"

Ah Choy sighed and gazed down into his teacup again. Then he looked up at Jack and smiled. "You are now a partner in the North Star?" Jack nodded. "And you are a miner—you go down the shaft with the other men." Jack nodded again. "There lies your fortune. Only a very lucky man can own a business and trust someone else to run it for him. This—" He spread his arms to indicate the building around them. "This is my North Star, and I sit here to tend it very, very closely. This is a rich land, and you can be one of the men who finds the gold and brings it to the rest of us."

Jack leaned forward. "But there is more—much more!—than mining. There're men in San Francisco gettin' rich without ever goin' near a mine. How can I do that?"

The merchant considered for a moment. "I will say only this—dreams do not make a man wealthy. I do not *dream* of selling tea and rice to the Chinese miners, but they buy a great deal of tea and rice, and so I prosper."

"Last year, you told me that the Americans will choose what feeds their pride in being Americans—that they do not always do what is sensible."

Ah Choy raised his eyebrows. "You remember. I must be more careful." Both men smiled. "Yes, they are proud, and yes, what they do may seem foolish. Now they fight a war with each other over who shall be the real Americans. Very foolish, we may say. But although they may feed their pride in public, there is a moment when they become very, very sensible. Very determined. At that moment, it is very American to make money—to negotiate without mercy, to lie, to cheat, even to steal. Even while one man waves his arms and shouts slogans to a cheering crowd, while the bells ring and the fireworks light up the sky, another man sits quietly in an office with a pencil, adding up figures and writing a contract. That is the man to fear and respect."

During the next several months, Jack devoted himself to the North Star, which was paying so well that the partners agreed to improve the works. They expanded the smithy so they could repair their own machinery rather than send it to Boston Ravine, and they rebuilt the old hoisting engine in order to bring the ore cars up more quickly. They overhauled the pump just in time for the wettest winter anyone could remember; by the end of January, nearly a hundred inches had fallen, rain and snow, and some of the smaller mines had to close down while they pumped out their shafts. The North Star, however, remained dry, and the men stayed at work.

Nick had supervised the pump work himself. He had become prominent at the partners' meetings, for he did not hesitate to speak his mind, and the other Cornishmen were inclined to agree with his point of view. His mere presence provided a new and irritating challenge to Edward Sterling, who regarded him as a spendthrift and a carouser, and so found his insight and eloquence startling. Nick persuaded the partnership to extend the drifts so they could attack the vein at many more points, and they agreed to begin work on a new drainage tunnel, half a mile long, that would probably take two years to complete. Edward simply glared at this proposal while John Sterling, smiling broadly, rambled on and on, scoffing at the notion and announcing his confidence that the other partners would of course see the folly of such an expensive, probably pointless endeavor. He was precisely wrong; the Cornish partners knew that the pump could clear the water more efficiently into a tunnel than all the way up to grass, so they quietly insisted on it. Only on the issue of the stamp mill did the Sterlings sway enough support to prevail. Nick felt that six stamps were not enough, but the Sterlings contended that there was no point in crushing more rock with the gold market as unpredictable as it was. Old William Pascoe, who tended to resist expansion, supported the Sterlings, and the proposal failed.

Yet the Sterlings reserved their most determined efforts for the expansion of the mine. Some of the smaller owners in the district had become desperate: they had been losing men to the lure of the Comstock Lode, and the wartime market was tricky to manage, but the flooding pushed them past the breaking point. Yet when they tried to sell their claims, they found that the men who usually had money to invest—merchants, lawyers, bankers— were disinclined to make any new commitments; the high water on the Bear River and the Yuba had isolated the hill towns, delaying not only shipments but also news of the war. The Sterlings stepped into the gap with ostensible indifference, grudgingly indicating to the more anxious owners that they might be able take their burdensome properties for a modest price. A few of the deals were too tempting to refuse, so by early spring, the partners had bought new claims on Weimar Hill and Lafayette Hill, as well as the defunct White Rock Company, all adjacent to the North Star site. Yet in spite of the general satisfaction with the expansion, the partners' meetings remained strained. After one particularly touchy conference, old William Pascoe asked Jesse to meet him at his cabin the next morning.

Cousin Jack

The two walked away from French Lead, traversing a few hundred yards of rocky slope and meadow before entering a small grove of digger pines, where the older man sat down on a granite boulder and took a pipe out of his coat pocket. Jesse waited while Pascoe dipped the pipe in his worn leather pouch, tamped the tobacco down with his thumb, struck a match and methodically pulled the flame into the bowl, sending tiny puffs of smoke up into the still air. His face was pale from years underground, but worn by wind and water as a cliff is worn, with crevices and furrows carving patterns and networks in his forehead and cheeks, and spreading out from the corners of his eyes and mouth. His eyebrows were bushy and white, matching the thick side whiskers that were his only apparent vanity, although when anyone mentioned them he would respond with a long, silent, affronted stare. Jesse realized that William was probably the oldest working quartz miner he had ever known. Most hard-rock men in Cornwall, if they lived to the age of fifty, were either crippled or so worn out that they could no longer work effectively, but William had survived, climbing up out of cave-ins that left others dead and buried, enduring the occasional injuries, and finding well-paying pitches even when the price of tin or copper fell and the adventurers offered only the meanest rewards. He had come to California not to change his life but to pursue one more promising pitch, yet another vein whose wealth his dogged effort would reveal.

His pipe ready, Pascoe began without preamble. "Jesse, us'll be sellin' our shares. Th' boys an' me." He continued to suck at the stem, looking off towards the stamp mill.

"All three of ye?"

"Isssss," William hissed, nodding. "Iss fay. Yes, i' faith. All four shares."

Jesse sat down on a fallen log to look the other man in the face. "Why, William? Be ye leavin'?"

Pascoe blew a smoke ring—a rare frivolity. "No, we're not leavin'. The boys have some claims up past Nevada City, and we'll work 'em."

Jesse considered. "Why be ye sellin'?"

Pascoe picked up a tiny twig and poked it into the bowl of the pipe, stirring up the tobacco. He drew hard two or three times and, satisfied, flicked the twig into the leaves. "This company be 'eaded for trouble. It's a rare pitch, but there'll soon be a putty taer."

"Why? Don't ye think we'll be able to agree?."

Pascoe shook his head slowly. "There'll be dover t' pay, and I've no taste fer it."

Jesse knew better than to ask the old miner to elaborate, for he would act on his instincts and explain them to no one. Jesse could only guess that William was brooding on the petty disagreements between the Sterlings, on the one hand, and Hannibal, Jack and Nick on the other. Yet with so many partners, and with none holding a controlling share, he had always believed that they would find a way to work things out so that the mine would continue to produce and everyone would prosper.

"William, listen to me." The older man looked at him steadily from beneath the bristling eyebrows. "You and yer sons 'old a fifth part o' th' company. Who'll buy?"

Pascoe actually smiled. "Well, Jesse, I'm a man o' business now, a trader like them Americans on Main Street. I'll find a man who's willin' to rise all 'e can, an' I'll be lookin' fer a skuat o' money!"

"William, ye must not sell t' th' Sterlings."

Pascoe lost his smile instantly. "Ye'll not be tellin' me 'ow t' run my affairs, Jesse Trevenna. If ye want t' buy, then douse out yer money, else leave me be."

Jesse bit his lip. "If ye sell t' th' Sterlings, they'll 'old over 'alf o' th' shares. They'll be able t' do whatever they want."

Pascoe kept puffing, looking past the stamp mills to the gravel piles. "Douse 'em out, Jesse, douse 'em out."

"I don't trust 'em, William. They don't understand."

"They're hard-rock men, anan?" Pascoe knocked out his pipe against the hollow of his hand. "They've been down t' th' bottom."

"They're different. Edward won't listen to any of us, and fer all John's chatter, ye know he's made up 'is mind before 'e begins to talk to ye."

Pascoe rubbed his pipe slowly between his hands as though trying to form it into something else. "What is it ye want, Jesse?"

"Just wait, if ye can. Give me two days."

Jesse had no money to spare, and he knew that both Jack and Nick, since the Pony Express had shut down, were trying not to overextend themselves, so that evening, he went to see the Carnes. Martin offered him a chair and Hannibal poured him a cup of coffee as he told them about the Pascoes' decision.

"They'll get a fair price," said Hannibal. He looked out the window and thought for a moment. "Four shares—twenty per cent of the company. It's worth about ten thousand dollars."

"Could you and I raise it?" asked Martin..

Hannibal chewed on his lower lip and frowned. "No. No, I can't see a way. Nearly everything we 'ave is obligated." Jesse suggested that they approach the Chenoweths, but Martin was certain that they had little money to spare. Of all the partners, only Edward Sterling would be able to buy out the Pascoes.

Jesse sighed, and then looked up. "What if we each bought a piece? There're seven of us. I might be able t' buy a share, and if th' two of you could buy one, we'd leave one fer the Chenoweths and one fer Jack and Nick."

Martin tapped his finger on the table. "And if any man lacks th' money, 'e could borrow a bit—'e'd surely make it back within the year. Hannibal?"

Hannibal was bent over the table, drawing circles around figures on a scrap of paper. "It might work, if the others can manage it. I'm sure that th' two of us could buy a share." He stopped and laid the pencil down. "But we must not do it."

Martin was surprised. "Why not?"

"Think of it. We all agree that Sterling will want t' buy out th' Pascoes. If they sell without 'im knowin' what they're about, 'e'll be some vexed. That's only t' be expected. But if 'e finds out that all the other partners got together t' buy the Pascoe shares—without even tellin' 'im about it—'e'll know that we did it just t' shut him out."

Martin shrugged. "An' there'll be nothin' 'e can do about it."

His brother leaned in. "We've been 'avin' trouble with the Sterlings all winter. They're more interested in dividends and land 'oldings than in developin' the mine into somethin' that we'll be workin' twenty years on. If we slap 'em in th' face like this, Edward'll turn ugly."

Jesse considered the prospect. "We can still outvote 'em. They have seven shares; th' rest of us'll 'ave thirteen. There'll be nothin' for 'im t' say. Oh, John may kick up a dido, but we need not pay 'im any mind."

Hannibal pulled at his beard for a moment. "We need the Sterlings." Martin started to expostulate, but Hannibal continued quickly. "They know the men in town better than we. They go t' their 'ouses for tea of a Sunday afternoon. Their wives run the church socials. It's Edward who goes to th' foundry, and it's John who goes to th' bank. If we cross 'em like that, they'll sell their own shares."

Martin snorted. "Let 'em sell!"

"And who would buy? They own seven shares—we know that none of us can buy 'em. They'd sell t' someone we don't know, maybe someone who'd hinder more than help."

Jesse felt stymied, but he remembered when they had, at the start, considered trying to bring in more partners, and he had proposed a family from Redruth, a father and two grown sons named Nankervis. Hannibal knew them slightly, so after breakfast the next morning, he and Jesse went to visit them at their small quartz claim on Gold Hill.

Charles Nankervis returned their greeting with a scowl, and as he waited for them to explain their business, Jesse realized that his face was a mask, deeply lined, wearing an expression that was permanent rather than a response to his visitors. Samuel and Seth were in their late teens, clearly living under the firm authority of their father's toneless, gravelly voice, and they continued working while Hannibal and Jesse explained what they had in mind. The elder Nankervis sat and stared at his visitors, listening carefully while Hannibal described the workings in great detail and mapped out the shafts and drifts in relation to the vein. He kept talking, trying to impress the man, but Nankervis simply kept staring, showing no interest whatsoever, as though simply waiting for him to finish. Finally, Hannibal stopped, convinced that there was no point in continuing. Nankervis turned his mask on Jesse, who only nodded, as though to confirm what Hannibal had said.

"Ye think 'e'll want ten thousand?" Hannibal nodded. Nankervis stared for another long moment. "Well, send 'im around. I'll 'ave th' coin ready tomorrow." He rose, and Jesse and Hannibal looked at each other, perplexed, before standing and offering their hands. Nankervis took each man's hand briefly, scarcely acknowledging their smiles and thanks, nodded curtly, and walked back to where his sons were preparing a charge to take down into the shaft.

As Hannibal had predicted, Edward Sterling was deeply affronted that Pascoe had sold his shares without making the opportunity public. However, there was nothing he could do about it, and Jesse, Hannibal and Martin chose to say nothing about their part in arranging the transaction. Nankervis' manner and attitude never changed; at his first partners' meeting, he matched Edward in reticence and inscrutability, and the superintendent, although he sat formally erect, as always, slowly flushed, the blood mounting angrily to his face as John tried harder than usual to keep the gathering jovial. Much to Jesse's relief, Nankervis proved that he was a true hard-rock man, so he dismissed—no, he simply was unable to hear—any arguments that deflected the partners' efforts away from developing the workings. On such issues, his views exactly matched those of the other Cornish partners, and although he had bought a share for each of his sons, they sat quietly, without contributing a word, and voted as their father instructed them.

With the North Star beginning to declare regular dividends, Jesse faced the decision that he had been postponing: whether to stay in California or return to Cornwall. Most of the men he knew were young, like Jack and Nick, men with neither wives nor children in England, and they had come with vague dreams and no plans, following the scent of adventure to Fraser River, or Washoe, or wherever the next rich strike was reported. Some of the older men had, like Joseph, come with firm, declared intentions of earning enough to return to their families in England, there to live in comfort. Others had given themselves a fixed period of time—three years, or five years, or ten years—and promised that they would go home, rich or poor, at the end of that term; some of those went back empty-handed and tried to pick up their lives where they had left them, bidding for pitches in the big copper mines. A few men had brought their families over to join them; they spoke of building houses in town and of becoming American citizens.

Cousin Jack

Jesse was one of the lucky ones, a shareholder in a large, successful mine. He had considered settling in California, but there were mornings when he longed for the wind in the furze, the smell of the sea when the gales swept across Penwith, and the cries of the vendors in the stone market building in the grey light of dawn. Yet if he chose to go home, he could not leave just now; he would have to stay for at least two or three more years to enjoy the full benefit of his partnership. He kept coming back to this problem, for his children were nearly grown, and he no longer knew them. When he left Camborne, young Joseph had been nine years old, and now he was thirteen, while the girls were almost of age to be married. He did not want to live without his family any longer. He must go home or bring them to him, whether permanently or not.

He mentioned his quandary to Jack and, as he expected, his nephew paraphrased nearly everything about manifest destiny that Jesse had read in the newspapers. Yet where Jesse's family were concerned, Jack's level of conviction was somewhat startling. In his mind, there was no question, no question at all, but that a man of Jesse's prospects should stay in America and should have his family at his side, and, moreover, there was no reason for them to remain in England when they could come to California and enjoy the future as it unfolded. He saw the Civil War as a temporary aberration, one that Lincoln would soon resolve, and certainly no significant obstacle to enterprising Cornishmen pursuing their dreams. Jack went on at such length that Jesse began to smile to himself, and he left the encounter somewhat amused.

The more he pondered the matter, the more he thought of Zennora. He had been gone too long, and he realized that the root of his indecision lay in the impossibility of consulting with his wife. She always knew his own mind more clearly than he did, listening patiently to what he had to say and gently sorting out the contradictions, and he did not know how she felt about leaving England, possibly for good, and about the chance of seeing her grandchildren raised as Americans.

Unable to resolve the question, he wrote a long letter to Zennora and invited her to choose, to decide for all of them. Several weeks later, her response arrived in a letter from Susan: they were packing everything they owned, and would send word from New York when their ship put in on its way to Aspinwall. The letter was brief, and he read it over and over again, looking for more than his daughter had written, some hint of regret or pleasure, of enthusiasm or accommodation. On the very next day, he checked at the telegraph office and found a message: ARRIVING SAN FRANCISCO JUNE NINETEENTH GOLDEN ERA.

He spent the intervening month preparing the cabin for their arrival. Jack and Nick rarely slept there any more, and both cheerfully agreed to remove their things and consign the house to the imminent family. Jesse planned to meet the travelers in San Francisco, but on the eighteenth, Hannibal ran into some trouble opening up a new drift and begged for Jesse's experienced help. Much to Jesse's surprise, Jack volunteered to go to San Francisco, or, rather, almost insisted on going, and left immediately so as to be sure of meeting the family when their ship arrived. Jesse was standing in a pile of rubble the next evening when one of the boys picked his way through the gloom to hand him an envelope: it was a telegram from Jack announcing that the *Golden Era* had docked. On the following afternoon, Jesse donned his best suit to ride into town and wait in front of the Exchange for the Marysville stage.

Young Joseph was the first to disembark, surprisingly tall now, hardly a boy any more, looking timidly, almost furtively, over at his father before turning to help his sisters down the bouncy steps. Then Zennora appeared, pausing in the doorway of the coach to scan the storefronts before settling on her husband, who was standing uneasily in the dust and fingering the brim of his hat. She took her son's hand, descended firmly, and walked over to Jesse. One Sunday afternoon on the rocky shore of St. Ives Bay, he had joked that she had a mermaid's eyes, light grey flecked with green, and now he remembered that day as he looked down into his wife's face. He saw no regret and no remonstrance, only calm pleasure at seeing him and perhaps some weary exhilaration from the journey. They embraced, and only then could he turn to greet his children, first Joseph and then Bessie, but he had to call out Susan's name to get her attention, for Jack had already taken her arm and the two were intent on each other.

Zennora devoted all of the next day unpacking their baggage and then asked that they all drive into town so she could buy provisions. Jack met them outside the livery stable, and they all promenaded up Main and down Mill, past Terrill's wine shop, Spencer's books, McLaughlin's hardware, Johnston's bakery and Dalton's provisions. Jack, with Susan on his arm, served as tour guide, elaborately explaining the architectural distinctions of the Golden Gate Hotel and the new reconstruction of the Exchange, and proudly pointing out the genteel new homes that marched up Main Street.

To Susan, the town seemed awkward and raw, even though the proliferating brick buildings represented the second generation of construction after the hasty wooden shops. It was all new and rough compared with Camborne, Redruth and Penzance, ancient villages of weathered rock rising solemnly above streets of cobblestone and worn brick. Yet she walked beside Jack and let him talk on and on, realizing that something in this new place had somehow engaged him, drawn him in and ignited his imagination. He spoke of the town as though the men on the streets had met that very morning and invented it, fully blown, out of their collective resolution. He could not pass the Exchange without explaining the stage routes, could not point out Delano's bank without referring to the history of Wells, Fargo & Co., could not notice Silvester's hardware store without describing the pattern of the quartz mines that had sprung up around the veins that laced through the town. In Jack's mind, the town was a complex synergy, all urgent activity and eager interaction. They paused on the corner of Main and Mill so Jack could elaborate on his vision of the future, a revelation of energy and hope.

As the Trevennas stood there, they heard a tinny clinking of metal on metal, and they turned to see a strange company proceeding down Main Street. Two black horses drew a wagon carrying a simple pine coffin draped with red and gold fabric. Driving the wagon was a white man wearing a rusty black suit and heavy, dirty boots; he was chewing a cigar and he had pulled his frayed hat low over his eyes. Two Chinese men sat on either side of the coffin, looking very much like bookends, each wearing a black silk skullcap with a tassel falling down on one side, and each facing the cargo with his hands folded and his eyes fixed on it as though trying to see through the cloth and wood to the passenger within. An old horse was tethered to the rear of the wagon, a bony, dusty animal who barely lifted his hooves as he kept pace with the wagon. Completing the cortege was a troop of thirty Chinese men, each wearing a dirty dark blue smock and trousers, and wearing his hair in a single black braid running down from his cap to the center of his back. They chattered to each other, using sounds that Susan had never heard before, each speaker seeming to address not any one of the other men, but the group at large, and even the onlookers. Four of them clapped finger cymbals in an irregular rhythm, and at odd intervals, one man brought a mallet down onto a small drum. The rest of the marchers were twisting and scattering small slips of paper in all directions: out in front of them, over their shoulders to the rear, to either side, and up into the air, to fall like twirling snowflakes. Yet the most remarkable member of the caravan was the lady sitting next to the driver. Like him, she was white, but dressed impeccably in a dark silk gown, parasol trimmed with lace, and dark hair carefully swept up to support a gracefully feathered hat. She stared straight ahead with a certain inexplicable determination, as though unaware not only of her companion and the Chinese behind them, but also of the people staring from the boardwalk.

The wagon made the slow right turn to head south through the shops and saloons, and the customers came to the doorways to join those on the road who had already stopped to watch. One marcher threw a twirling twist of paper in Susan's direction, and it landed on the bottom of her skirt and caught for a moment in the heavy fabric before falling to the planking beneath her. She stared at him, marveling at the butternut complexion, the narrow eyes, apparently free of lids or sockets, the high forehead and the long braid. Each man seemed identical to every other, and in the fading light reflecting off of the upper walls of the storefronts, they all seemed to wear the same serious, impenetrable mask.

Susan turned to Jack. "What was that?"

He grinned. "A funeral. They'll probably bury him somewhere outside o' town." The Trevennas turned to continue their walk down Main Street, but Jesse looked back to realize that Zennora had stepped out into the road, looking after the cortege as though she could still see it. He went to her, bent his face down near hers for a moment, and the two of them turned to join the others. Just as they did so, Susan heard a sudden, sharp cry: "Fire!"

She turned and saw smoke drifting out through the open door of the Center Market. A man wearing shirtsleeves and bushy side whiskers staggered out onto the sidewalk, called "Fire!" and disappeared back into the hazy gloom. On both sides of the road, people stood, galvanized, while others threw open second-story windows to lean out and search for the source of the cry. Four men, their boots pounding heavily on the rough planking, ran down from Haywood's saloon and, without even a pause, rumbled through the door of the market. Susan stared through the storefront windows and saw the flames, already a glaring yellow, leaping up the walls and shelves.

A bell clanged frantically, and Susan began to step out to look up the hill, but Jesse turned and, stretching his arms wide, swept his wife and children back against the brick wall behind them. He stayed there, leaning on them, his arms outstretched and his beard scraping Susan's upturned face. She squirmed and ducked and looked under his arm in time to see a fire engine clatter down Main Street, the horses pulling frantically as the grinning driver, crouched in front of the tank, lashed them on. He brought them to a skidding halt in front of the market and nearly tipped over just as a group of three horses, all in a row, burst out of the livery stable, swerved to make the corner, and galloped down Mill Street, their riders urging them on. Their dust still hung in the air when two more horses clattered through the doorway. Jack was mounted on the first, and he held a long leather lead for the second, checking up and down the hill as he came down the little ramp, and taking them at a quick trot after the others.

A small crowd of men had gathered around the fire engine, most of them yelling and waving their arms while a few, wearing identical jackets and helmets, quickly attached hoses and fittings to the tank and the pumping assembly. One man, wearing a black derby, stood high on the engine, holding onto the tank with one hand, and kept shouting "Gentlemen!! Gentlemen!!" to the others. The driver had jumped off of his bench, run around the front of the team and grabbed their halters; the horses stamped and tossed their heads, rolling their eyes at the shouting and the crackle of the flames. The men who had run into the market had formed a chain and were passing furniture and bundles from hand to hand and out into the road. Susan realized that she had crushed her hat against the wall behind her, and it was slowly pulling away from her hair.

Suddenly, from inside the market, a man started yelling, then another, and a knot of men burst through the front door and out onto the roadway, pushing aside three firemen who were laying out their hose. At the same moment, the roof fell in and sent a cloud of sparks into the air. Burning embers fell on the roof of the dry goods store on one side and on the saloon and clothing store on the other. The shingles smoldered for a moment, then burst into flame. Above the livery stable, a woman threw open a window and began throwing bedding and bundles of clothing out onto the road. Small teams of men were carrying armloads of goods out of two or three of the stores: heavy bolts of canvas, boxes of hardware, and bundles of tools. Two men were carefully carrying crates of bottles out of the saloon and setting them down next to a man who glared fiercely at anyone who came near.

Susan lifted her hand against the glare in her eyes; the sun was setting behind the Golden Gate Hotel on the far corner of Church Street. The deep blue of the sky began to fade as a breeze swept up from Wolf Creek, whipping the flames into a roar and forcing the firemen, who had begun to pour water into the market, to retreat. The man in the derby gathered a few others around him into a little huddle, their heads bent in towards each other, and seemed to be speaking to them with great intensity, driving his point home by slamming his right fist into the open palm of his left hand. One man ran over to the tank, grabbed a hose and ran down to the dry goods store, and, with two men helping him, he began to spray the flames where they had spread in from the market. The rest assaulted the livery stable, four firemen laying the hose in through the front door while a chain of volunteers formed a bucket brigade leading from some unseen cistern up to the windows of the building. The roof had begun to smolder, and the firemen drenched it with the stream from the hose while the bucket brigade doused the walls adjacent to Haywood's saloon. The man in the derby called for more volunteers, and Jesse suddenly ran out into the road to join the others. Susan stood up straight, tried to take a deep breath but choked on the drifting smoke, then pulled off her hat and looked around.

Five buildings were burning. The man in the derby had decided to try to stop the flames at the dry goods store to the east and the livery stable to the west. In between, the market was nearly destroyed and the two saloons, rough affairs built quickly out of raw timber, burned quickly, while the clothing store sent clouds of brown smoke up into the wind as the flames worked their way through the stock. There was a sign hanging from the front rafters that read "J. Cohn, Men's Clothing" until the paint peeled and turned black from the heat. In the middle of the street, the woman from the livery stable confronted the man in the derby, shaking a finger in his face and pointing at the men who were drenching the livery stable and trampling the bundles she had thrown out to safety. As she scolded, a fireman appeared in the upstairs window with an axe, chopped out the window frame, sending shards of glass onto the short roof protecting the boardwalk below, and called to the men with the hose, who sent the stream through the new opening and against the walls. The woman in the road stared, amazed, as the fireman cut the opening, and when the water poured into the second story, she screamed and began to pound her fists on the man with the derby. He held her off with one arm until two other men came and carried her off, still screaming.

Zennora had gathered her children into a doorway. Joseph had taken a step towards the bucket line where his father was working, but his mother had stopped him with one look. Bessie had been crying almost since the beginning, terrified but unable to look away from the flames. Susan could feel a rapid pounding in her ears, but she studied her mother and realized that Zennora, who was wiping Bessie's nose at intervals without looking around, was gazing raptly not at the frenzied effort but into the flames themselves as though searching for something. Susan looked into the heart of the fire, yellow and orange quickening up walls, across roofs and through timbers, raging as the wind blew through the now-skeletal walls, and danc- ing frantically through the air, where there seemed to be nothing left to burn, to form a maelstrom. She peered into the market, now gutted, and the flames there seemed to rise out of some cavity beneath the floor.

The man in the derby stood in the middle of the road, his arms folded, apparently satisfied, but just as the flames in the middle of the block seemed to falter, the saloon next to the livery stable, caved in completely, and the wind sent a swarm of embers hurtling through the sky, now nearly dark, to land on both the Golden Gate Hotel and the new Exchange Hotel, still unfinished and now decorated with sawdust, shavings and fresh paint. Im- mediately, a man in a black suit strode up to the man in the derby, bent in towards his ear and spoke briefly. The man in the derby looked at him, then at the stores his men were dousing, and called one of the firemen to him. He spoke to him and pointed to the hotels up the street. The fireman nodded and ran to the men leading the hoses to the livery stable and the dry goods store. The men at the pump paused while the others dragged the hoses up the hill, and resumed to send water streaming onto the roof and façade of each building.

The line of men bent up the street towards the Exchange, a double rank that passed full buckets up and empty ones back. The man in the derby kept sending more men in, until dim silhouettes appeared on the roof. Susan looked up at them and recognized Jack, balancing on the edge, bareheaded, in his shirtsleeves, taking the bucket from the man behind him and pouring the water on the eastern wall even while the spray from the hoses beneath soaked him. There was a brief hiatus in the stream of buckets—someone halfway up the line had lost their grip, and the pause rippled through the chain of men—and Jack looked down at the street, wiping his forehead, and suddenly, finding Susan, he grinned and waved. She lifted her hand to him, but he was already taking the next bucket and splashing it on the wood siding to keep the flames at bay.

After another hour, the fire had burned itself out. They had been lucky, for the evening breeze had dwindled, and the flames grew listless, as though bored with the game, and acquiesced to the fire-fighters' persistent efforts. Four of the buildings were completely destroyed, and two others so damaged that the owners would probably choose to raze them and rebuild. Yet no one seemed discouraged except the woman from the livery stable, who had finally collapsed onto the boardwalk across the street, her feet in the mud, weeping against a post. The Exchange was only slightly scorched on one side, and the proprietor sent out three men who offered pitchers of beer to all those who had helped. Jesse was just collecting his family to take them back to French Lead when Jack returned, his coat over his shoulder and a tall glass in his hand, smelling of smoke and cinders. Something about him puzzled Susan, for his eyes seemed unusually bright, even in the dim lantern light, but she realized that he wore a layer of soot and his face was as dark as a piece of old furniture.

That night, as Susan lay in her bed, the smell of the sheets distractingly unfamiliar, her nose still twitched with the sting of the smoke, and she still saw the flames flick their ephemeral tips against the night sky. She could not let go of the image, just as she had been unable to look away from the heart of the blaze, but she could not, strangely, imagine the blackened, useless timbers that she knew she would see when next she went into town. Then she saw Jack, standing in his shirtsleeves, unafraid, scanning the flames as though he could chart their course. He grew taller and taller, a centaur, a magnificent chestnut with flashing blue eyes, and as he reared in front of the brightest burning building, she fell asleep.

7
The Match
1862-63

Jack took Susan's hands and danced her around the circle, spinning and turning as they orbited the room to the music of the tiny orchestra. Her cheeks were pink and her forehead shone, but she looked eagerly from side to side, trying to keep up with the unfamiliar steps, and she laughed whenever the pattern changed and caught her unawares.

Near the glistening punch bowl stood the evening's hosts, prosperous men carefully wearing the dignity that they could not quite relinquish even for the Christmas holiday, experimenting with the thrills of prestige and condescension—Findley, the banker; Simpson, the physician; Spencer, the stationer; Loyd and Johnston, the rival hardware dealers; Alonzo Delano, who could not keep his long arms and legs from flapping in time to the music; and the Sterlings, Edward, stern and erect, next to John, whose wife was the only hostess who smiled and greeted everyone who passed by.

The invitation had grandly offered a "musical soiree" with "fancy dancing." Jesse had hesitated, for his mother, following Wesley's example, had censured dancing of any kind, but Zennora had quietly suggested that she, at least, so recently arrived and so warmly welcomed, could not insult her new neighbors by refusing to attend. Jesse had driven Zennora and the girls in his new carriage, with Jack, Nick and the Carnes escorting them on horseback. As they approached Boston Ravine, the girls looked anxiously out from under the canopy at a scattered procession of snowflakes that drifted slowly down past the carriage lanterns, but just as they drew up at Hamilton Hall, the clouds eased aside to reveal a half moon that shone down on the thickly-frosted gallery railing.

Susan could scarcely keep from laughing. There had been few opportunities (and little encouragement) to dance in Camborne, and she felt freed. The music and the steps were completely unfamiliar, but perhaps because she expected so little of herself, she didn't care what happened, and the music seemed to carry her along. Now the orchestra was playing a reel, and Jack pulled her all the way up the length of the clapping ranks and back again, then spun her around, flicked her into the ladies' line, and retreated. Through the music she could hear fragments of unfamiliar phrases spoken in flat, nasal American tones. She looked down the row at Bessie, all red in the face with her hair matting against her temples, but still hopping up and down, and then back to Jack, who didn't bother to conceal the small smile that seemed to convey that he knew what she was thinking.

Cousin Jack

In the months since she had arrived, Jack had been her casual guide. When she rode into town with her mother, he usually appeared outside a shop and, smiling and tipping his hat to Zennora, asked for permission to take his cousin for a walk. He knew everyone and introduced her to men who deferred graciously to her femininity and seemed especially pleased to meet Jesse Trevenna's daughter. The men who ran the shops and hotels and saloons—men with thick thighs, quick fingers and an amazing variety of whiskers—had never, apparently, entertained the notion that the town might not go on forever. In their minds, as in Jack's, Grass Valley was an accomplished fact, and its lack of a past, so strange to her, did not distract them, for they were entirely focused on the future. On one warm evening in September, Jesse, giving in to Jack's insistence, drove the family to town for the celebration of the new gas lighting system. Susan took Jack's arm and promenaded through knots of smugly grinning men and past garishly brilliant storefronts.

Yet Jack's presentation of the town was carefully selective. On a cool afternoon in early November, they were walking along Mill Street when a man staggered out of a saloon just ahead of them and nearly collapsed, hanging onto a lamp post and howling in a shrill, pinched voice. Jack hesitated for an instant, but the street was too deep with mud for them to cross, so he simply hurried past, reaching over to hold the hand that she had tucked above his elbow, and keeping a close watch on the howling man until they were well past him. She stared, fascinated, as they passed by, and the man lifted his face to gaze directly at her, still howling. His face was dark, even darker than the people she had seen in Panama or on the coast of Mexico, and his long, black hair fell down past his collar in a matted tangle. His eyes were black, so utterly opaque that she imagined he could see nothing at all. Jack seemed reluctant to explain the man, but admitted that he was an Indian—a Digger, they called them—and muttered that the saloon keeper had no right to serve liquor to such people. She strained to look back over her shoulder and saw a man douse the howling man with a bucketful of water.

Yet Jack was eager to introduce her to Chinatown, although he insisted that she tell Zennora nothing about it. They walked through the crisp December air past carefully-painted clapboard siding and comfortable porches, and suddenly crossed an invisible threshold. The place was amazingly crowded, worse than anything she had seen as she passed near the docks in Liverpool, with shacks built on top of shacks, doorways and narrow staircases in the most unexpected places, and windows scattered almost at random in the unpainted walls of warping, weathering green lumber. Even more than the men on Main Street, the Chinese hurried everywhere, all marching at the same relentless pace, seldom running, but never strolling, striding through the narrow alleys with their queues swinging beneath their strange black caps. As she walked past the restaurant and between the vegetable stalls, completely unfamiliar smells, carried in clouds of vapor, first caught her interest and then made her gag. She paused next to a counter laid with fish sitting on a bed of ice, remembering similar counters in St. Ives and Penzance, but the gaping mouths and silvery scales belonged to strange varieties, and she realized that they were fresh-water fish, food for people who lived a long day's journey from the ocean. The fishmonger bared his teeth, holding up a specimen eighteen inches long with a rainbow stripe running the length of its side, and challenged her in a loud voice. Susan wondered how he could articulate without bringing his lips together; the strange sounds all seemed to originate somewhere deep in his throat. Jack introduced her to Ah Choy, whose silk smock displayed what she at first took to be rampant flames but then realized were brightly colored birds with feathers that unfurled in all directions. She was surprised to hear him address her in English, quite formal and oddly inflected.

As they walked back up Bank Street, Jack explained Ah Choy's business affairs and then, almost shyly, began describing his own ventures. He had begun lending money, which, he assured Susan, was common practice in the mining towns, for even successful men sometimes discovered that all of their resources were committed to one project or another, so they lacked the ready cash to embrace the next opportunity. In one deal, he had lent over a thousand dollars to a man who promised to pay one per cent each month—some agreements involved as much as two per cent—and offered a share in a mining company as surety; if he failed to pay off the loan, the share would go to Jack. He had been talking to an acquaintance about a lumber mill, which was sure to succeed as prosperous men with families, men like Jesse, built comfortable homes. He spoke of other ideas—of ice brought down from the higher elevations and kept on salt in thick-walled warehouses, of farming in the valleys below Rough and Ready, and of a railroad line from Grass Valley to Colfax. Susan listened politely, but she was thinking that Jesse had never mentioned taking an interest in anything but the mine, and she finally asked Jack why he didn't use his money to buy more shares in the North Star. He smiled and looked off at a bank of clouds nestling on the skyline, then patted her arm and remarked that there was more to California than mining.

They had been dancing for nearly an hour, since the moment she walked in the door, and both of them were panting and ready for a rest. They stood next to a cut holly tree, all candles and scraps of gilt paper, and sipped cups of punch. Susan was so thirsty that she drank one straight off and asked for another. Jack regarded her over the rim of his cup as though approaching a decision.

Cousin Jack

"I'm going to Sacramento next month—they're breakin' ground for the Central Pacific." He paused, looked around, and drew closer. "Would ye like t' come with me?"

"To Sacramento?"

"There'll be speeches, and probably a parade." He grinned. "Maybe ye'll get t' meet the governor!"

She smiled. She hadn't left Grass Valley since she had arrived, and Jack made the idea seem plausible. But she must ask her father, so they walked around the dancers to where Jesse was talking to the Carne brothers under a garland of cedar and moss. "Fayther, Jack wants t' take me t' Sacramento."

Jesse leaned in, trying to hear over the music and the voices in the crowded hall. "Sacramento? What for?" He listened to Jack's explanation, then looked down at Zennora, who wore a bland smile. "I think not. No."

Jack frowned. "Why not, Uncle Jesse? It's just for the day."

"Because I say so, an' there's an end of it."

Jack looked stung, and Susan suddenly felt as though she had blundered into a conversation where she was not wanted and had said something insipid, foolish and irrelevant. She looked down at her mother, who seemed concerned but said nothing. At that moment, Hannibal Carne pushed his spectacles up higher on his nose and asked whether she would be willing to dance with him. She dropped a slight curtsey and allowed him to lead her onto the floor, where they settled into a waltz. He was just a bit shorter than Jack, so she could look into his face without tilting her head back so far, but she found that she could not follow him as easily, and because the steps were no more familiar than before, her shoes kept bumping his; every other moment, she had to mumble an apology, and he unfailingly assured her that there was no cause. She hardly saw Jack for the rest of the evening; at the end of each dance, Hannibal escorted her back to her parents, spent the next song talking with Jesse and Martin, and then invited her out onto the floor for another turn. There was a chair for her, next to her mother's, and as she sat and patted her face with a handkerchief, she could see Jack exchanging stories with Nick and some of the other young men. Whenever they laughed, Jack glanced towards the little group where she sat. She was relieved when Jesse announced that it was time to go home, but only the Carnes rode next to the coach on the way back to French Lead.

Susan saw Jack several times during the rest of the Christmas season—at church, at a hymn-singing party, or when Zennora invited both Jack and Nick to the Trevenna cabin for Sunday dinner—but he made no attempt to find a moment alone with her and even seemed to arrange to stay in the company of others. She didn't speak to him privately again until mid-January, after he had returned, exhilarated, from Sacramento.

The Match, 1862-63

Jack and Nick had arrived early and found places to stand between the levee and the platform. The day was cold and damp, and the grey sky hung low over the river, as though about to descend and enfold everyone. A line of carriages, their brass fixtures brightly polished and American flags draped over the doors and railings, traveled slowly down the street, the drivers reining in their horses to keep them from splattering too much mud. They pulled up, one by one, to a landing, and their passengers disembarked, the women carefully lifting their heavy silk skirts away from the sandy, wet planks. The last coach pulled away from the landing, and at that moment, exactly at noon, a ship at the wharf let loose a long blast on its steam whistle. A large, florid man stepped up to the rostrum, and in a stentorian voice, called for order and attention. He then introduced Leland Stanford.

The governor was dressed in a frock coat that parted in front to reveal a purple velvet vest and a shining gold watch chain; he reminded Jack of the British ministers that he had seen in engravings of Victoria's court. Stanford was probably about Jesse's age, but he seemed older: his beard was beginning to turn grey, he carried his considerable bulk with stately balance, and he presented a solemn face to the crowd, assuring them with his very demeanor that he took his important responsibilities, both as their governor and as the president of the Central Pacific, quite seriously. He placed several sheets of paper on the podium and, without looking up, slowly and deliberately read his speech in a monotone. He assured his listeners that they were witnessing the inauguration of a great highway, one that would connect the Far East with the busy cities of the nation that would surely, one day, stand preeminent in the world. Sacramento, as the western terminus of the railroad, would serve as the meeting place for the powerful and the freight yard for both hemispheres. As soon as the Republican Party led the armies of democracy to quell the rebellion which had interrupted the country's natural progress, the people of the United States would look to their Pacific shore as the vanguard of the future.

He paused as though taking a breath, then folded the papers and looked up at the people arrayed before him. The applause began in the platform party and spread to the listening crowd. Stanford descended, walked out onto a plank that stretched across the mud, and took a shining spade from a man standing with his boots ankle-deep in ooze. Just below the plank sat a freshly-painted wagon draped with red-white-and-blue bunting. The governor set the point of the spade into the earth, carefully placed one foot on the edge, thrust the spade into the soil, planted both feet on the plank, bent over slightly, lifted the wet silt, making a slight smacking noise as he pulled the shovel out of the muck, and flung the sodden dirt into the waiting wagon. The band struck up a quick march, and the florid man led the assembly in nine cheers, insisting that each be louder than the one before.

Cousin Jack

The band played on while Jack and Nick, nearly running through the muddy streets, followed the line of carriages to St. George's Hotel. The lobby was mobbed, but Jack, with Nick close behind him, pushed and slipped through the people until he reached the platform party and the burly man in the velvet vest. He offered his hand. "Congratulations, Governor!" Stanford turned towards him. His face was a complete blank, but Jack kept his hand outstretched and raised his voice over the furor. "I say, congratulations, Governor!" The man still stared. "I'm John Trevenna, from Grass Valley, and this my brother, Nick. The miners all voted for ye in the election." Out of the corner of his eye, Jack noticed the perplexed expression on Nick's face. Actually, most of the miners they knew either hadn't bothered to vote or were still British subjects, and the town had given Stanford no more than a modest plurality in the three-way race. Jack, still holding out his hand, tried to speak in as American an intonation as he could manage, thinking that his Cornish accent might have confused the governor. "Delighted to see the Central Pacific under way!"

Stanford raised his eyebrows ever so slightly, took Jack's hand in a firm, dry grip, and intoned, "Thank you, sir." That said, he turned back to a man who, all during Jack's greeting, had been elucidating the details regarding the composition of the soil between Sacramento and Colfax. Someone pushed Jack aside, and a few moments later, he and Nick were standing in a corner, watching the endless bustle of the railroad men and their well-wishers.

Jack told the story as though it were all something of a joke, but he kept slapping his gloves on his leg and looking off as though he expected someone to come riding through the trees. Susan realized that the encounter had excited him, but it had also made him nervous, even anxious. He chewed on his lip and told her that Stanford and his partners were surely among the more far-seeing men in California. A man at the reception had told him that an engineer had tried to raise the capital for the railroad in both San Francisco and Sacramento, and that most of the merchants and bankers had dismissed the idea. And now Stanford would build the road that would link the Pacific with the Atlantic! The bankers had been fools, he insisted, plain fools, and Susan decided that he was really talking about himself—if only he had been in the right place at the right time, he would have seized the opportunity, and he, too, would be a partner in the Central Pacific.

Jack came to see her more and more during the winter, sitting next to the fireplace to tell her stories or taking her for walks around Lafayette Hill and down through Boston Ravine. Snow fell for three straight days in February, and when the sky receded, spent, into a dull, grey ceiling, he took her over the ridges, through the pine forests, now glazed, glistening even in the diffused light, and down to Wolf Creek, whose current rushed past frozen rocks and beneath bellied droplets of ice that hung from the overhanging branches. She took off one glove and dipped her hand in the water; it was so cold that her fingers swelled red. They climbed up out of the gorge to the crest of the hill and down the other side, and she realized that the forest was absolutely silent. She spoke to him, and they halted, he looking down at her, and she working her fingers in the crook of his arm. The air was perfectly still, the animals slept, and the stamp mills and hoists, still buried in drifts, were motionless. She held her breath, watching, listening, wondering. Finally, she patted his arm, and they walked on.

Jack preferred to take her out because when he visited her at home, Zennora hovered in doorways and floated through rooms, patrolling. She never seemed to listen and even when passing by appeared to be preoccupied with the task of the moment, but she would sometimes offer an interjection as though she had been part of the conversation all along. Occasionally Jack would shift his glance from Susan and, out of the corner of his eye, see her mother watching them from a doorway. Once he was leaning against the mantel when he noticed a polished silver pitcher that revealed a warped reflection of Zennora, standing just of sight in the front hall. When Jesse was home, he sat in his accustomed chair near the fire, an apparently unintentional chaperone, and the conversation became general. If he happened to be out, he usually returned during Jack's visit, stopping in the doorway to release a slightly surprised "Oh!" and raise his eyebrows before pacing out the distance to the kitchen or his bedroom. Zennora seemed to glide through the house, but the wooden floors played like drums under Jesse's feet.

One morning early in March, Zennora decided to air the bedding, and when she and Susan had finished hanging the blankets in the sunshine that spread across the porch, she asked, after a moment's hesitation, whether Jack would be coming to visit that week. Susan never knew when to expect him, but she reminded her mother that he usually stopped by every two or three days. Zennora turned away to gaze up the hillside, until Susan broke the silence.

"What is it, Mother?" At first, Zennora didn't move, then she dropped her eyes, picked a fleck of lint off of her dress, and looked over at her daughter.

"'e's yer cousin, Susan."

"I know that, Mother."

"Yer first cousin." Zennora reached down to pick up a pine needle that the breeze had brought to her porch. "I think, Susan, that it's time ye started to think about what kind o' life ye want to 'ave."

Zennora had never been anxious about her children, trusting that they would survive and endure, but since she had come to California, she had begun to realize that there was little time left, that one by one, they would be leaving her, and the uncertainties and choices began to gather. She had always thought of herself as reckless and brave, a miner's wife who accepted the imminence of calamity with a calm smile, but now she found herself resisting the growing suspicion that her life had been too safe and controlled for her to claim any remarkable degree of audacity. Cornwall offered only so many possible futures, echoes of lives gone by, paths familiar and predictable, but the wealth glittering far beneath the red hillsides was going to offer her children a new kind of freedom and present them with possibilities that she could not fathom. Usually so serene, Zennora awoke early on certain mornings with the feeling that she and her family were hurtling through an indeterminate space where there were no points of reference and no sense of up or down.

While Zennora suspected that her daughter was shutting her out, Susan, for her part, simply felt bewildered. More than once, she had awakened from a dream that she had become a wooden statue sitting in the kitchen, her carved hands folded in her lap, staring straight ahead while her mother and father circled around the room. Their noses had become oddly long and pointed, almost like blue jays' beaks, their eyes had collapsed into slits, and their voices echoed and reverberated off of her hard, painted skin. They chattered and called to each other, utter gibberish, and at unpredictable intervals, abruptly, they fell silent, thrust their noses towards the statue's face, and waited for a response to something they apparently believed that they had just said. All three faces would stare like masks for a moment, and then her parents would nod violently, as though she had made a suggestion or answered a question, and they would continue circling, waving their arms and calling in all directions. Waking to a vision of fading stars, blurred through the window glass, Susan discovered that she was panting and exhausted.

Without warning, Jack brought the entire situation into sharply disturbing focus. He came to visit, but rather than riding his buckskin gelding, he drove a smart buggy drawn by a black mare, and he wore a new suit and hat that Susan had not seen before. He lifted her onto the seat next to him, and they drove through the late winter sunshine, already promising spring, northeast on McCourtney Road and up Boston Ravine into town. He stopped twice to greet men and discuss, in elliptical, allusive phrases, their business affairs; when he introduced Susan, they swept off their hats and nearly bowed. He drove through Chinatown, where the passers-by looked discreetly sidelong at the white people in the crisp buggy, and up to the top of Bennett Hill, where he reined in the horse and helped Susan down to sit on a stump in the shade of a tree.

The morning sun lit up the town as well as if someone had arranged the scene for their gaze. Main Street climbed directly away from them, and they could easily trace the road from Loutzenheiser's drug store, past the shops to the Exchange, and on up to the gabled clapboard houses with their neat yards. The storefronts on the west side of Mill Street, peeking between their opposing counterparts, formed a gentle curve that ran parallel to Wolf Creek and led towards the churches and Gold Hill. Off to their left, beneath Kate Hays and Ophir hills, were the new houses starting to spread south on Auburn Street: tiny, fragile frameworks of bright, unpainted matchsticks. Surrounding the town, the ridge tops alternated between thick marches of pine and fir trees, and bare, scarred stretches where the mining companies had left careless piles of gravel.

Jack looked over the town for a few minutes and then turned back to her. "D' ye know . . . fifteen years ago, there was nothing here, nothin' at all, and San Francisco was just an army camp with a few ships ridin' at anchor. Now all the gold and silver west o' the Rockies comes t' the City's vaults. We're sitting on a keenly lode—it's . . . like a river shining inside the rock. And the gold is only the beginning."

He kept talking about the future and began to stumble from phrase to phrase, proclaiming the bright destiny of the northern mines, scorning the skeptics' warning that the seduction of Washoe silver would soon transform Grass Valley into a ghost town, and speculating on the effect of the transcontinental railroad that would surely pass very close to them, if not right through the valley and on to the Nevada territory. Someday soon, the town would become the business center of the hills, second in California only to San Francisco and Sacramento, rich in lumber and farming as well as mining. Anything was possible.

The breeze freshened and swept across the hill, bearing the chill of the snow still covering the slopes of the higher mountains to the northeast. Susan shivered and tried to settle herself more comfortably on the stump. She sensed where Jack was leading, so she shut out what he was saying and studied him, trying to think. She could not fathom the connection between this man and the gangly boy who gravely pondered all of her confidences in the Gwennap Pit. For all his enthusiasm and apparent reluctance to come to the point, there was something confident about him that she did not remember from before. He also seemed taller, especially in his polished, calf-length boots, and as he went on and on about the prospects that galvanized him so, his voice grew stronger. She looked away from him to gaze out over the town, trying to imagine the future that he saw so clearly. Then she realized that he had stopped talking and was, instead, sitting next to her, holding his hat in his lap. He seemed to be waiting for something. "What? What is it, Jack?"

He smiled and laid his hand gently on her arm. "Susan, I asked ye t' marry me. Will ye?"

She stared at him for a moment, and then reached down to lay her hand on his, and he dropped his hat on the damp pine needles to clasp her fingers with his gloves. They sat like that for a long moment, and then another. Then she withdrew her hand and rose to her feet, walking away a few steps. Jack picked up his hat and stood there, looking at the back of her head.

"Susan?" She neither turned nor spoke. He waited, spoke her name again, and walked over and turned her gently by the shoulders. She was crying, her face strained and distorted as the tears ran down her flushed cheeks and fell onto her coat. "Susan?! Please . . . I'm sorry. I'm sorry." He let her go and moved away. "I thought . . . never mind. Never mind." She made no sound at all, and hardly seemed to be breathing. The silence unnerved him. "Please stop. I'll take ye 'ome. We won't tell anyone."

At that, Susan erupted. "No!" she cried, and again and again as she broke into furious, uncontrollable sobbing. She tottered to Jack and reached for him with both hands, pulling herself into him so she could fasten her face to his shirt front, still weeping and, at odd intervals, moaning, "No! No!"

Jack was completely lost. Susan seemed unable or unwilling to stop crying, so he helped her into the buggy and drove her back to French Lead, choosing back paths in order to avoid seeing anyone. After a mile or two, she subsided, but she sat obdurately mute, refusing to answer his questions or accept his apologies. When they finally reached the cabin, she descended from the buggy to walk right past her alarmed mother and into the house. Jack looked at Zennora, opened his mouth to speak, but shook his head and drove off.

Zennora found Susan in the girls' bedroom, crouched in a chair, weeping violently. She tried to put her arms around her, but the girl pushed her away and retreated to the corner, hiding her face against the wall. Zennora sat down in the chair and waited patiently, and after several minutes, Susan became less hysterical, wearily sinking onto the bed and accepting the handkerchief that her mother offered.

"'e asked me t' marry 'im." She sat on the mattress, disconsolate, folding and re-folding the handkerchief.

Zennora sighed. "I know that yer fayther and I 'aven't . . . well, we 'aven't . . . " She realized that Susan had stopped crying completely and was looking at her with an annoyed expression.

"It's not that, Mother. It's . . . 'e wants t' stay 'ere." All at once, she unleashed everything she was feeling. California wasn't what she thought, not at all, the Americans treated the English like fools, and living with all these foreigners—the Chinese, the Mexicans and even the Irish—wasn't exciting, it was just difficult. She never seemed to do the right thing or say the right thing, and when she visited the town or went to church, she felt as though people were laughing at her. The summer had been hot, and would be again, and she missed the sea breezes. She even missed the sea; she hadn't paid it much attention when they lived there, but she would when she returned, and she wanted so much to go home. Everything was changing here, everything was new, and you couldn't rely on anything. Camborne had been so much more peaceful. Even Father was different here, and she didn't understand Bessie any more, and Joseph was just in the way. But Jack . . . Jack had written the entire history of California even before it had happened. He was building stamp mills and farmhouses and railroads in his head, and his greatest ambition was to set up an office on Mill Street to act as the broker for the entire world as the town got bigger and bigger. She just couldn't do it, couldn't do it. Uncle Joseph had been planning to return to England before he was killed; couldn't Father do that and take the family back? Couldn't they go home?

As Zennora listened, she suddenly remembered the night when Susan, little more than a baby, had developed a deep chest cough, and when Zennora had tried to hold her under a wet towel over a vat of steam, she had gone wild, struggling to get away and toddling into a corner where she coughed and screamed, and coughed and screamed, crouched at bay, demanding that her mother stop the coughing, but adamantly refusing comfort for over an hour.

Susan subsided and paused to wipe her eyes and blow her nose. Zennora looked at her for a moment, then decided to take a chance. "If you want t' go and Jack wants t' stay, then it's simple. Refuse 'im."

Susan looked at her mother incredulously, took a deep breath, and another, and then, when she began to cry again, unable to stop herself, she slammed her fist against the wall next to her. "Oh, Mother, ye don't understand at all." She gasped. "Don't ye see? I love 'im! Oh, th' fool!" With that, she gave herself to the tears, and Zennora moved to sit next to her on the bed and hold her. She waited, staring across the room and occasionally lifting one hand to push back a strand of clinging hair from her daughter's damp, red cheek. After a while, Susan wore herself out and sat limp in her mother's arms, exhausted, and Zennora began to talk.

There was Jack, and there was Cornwall. If Jack was set on staying here, then she couldn't have both. Yet what could she expect if she went back? She would surely have to go alone, for Jesse showed no inclination to leave California; sometimes he spoke of Cornwall as though it were an enchanted land where he had once lived and which now had drifted away into the mists of the western sea. Susan would return to live with her aunt, most likely, marry a miner from Camborne, and live as her mother had lived, which was cause for neither regret nor delight. And what might she expect in Grass Valley? She might learn to like the place. True, the people were strange, but more and more of their friends and relatives were making the journey from England, and surely, very soon, most of the congregation at the church would be Cornish, even if the minister was an American. And then there was Jack. He was a man of some ambition, not likely to spend the rest of his life going down a shaft. He might make something of himself; his wife might be able to live comfortably. If there was a choice to be made, and if Susan had a chance to marry the man of her heart, and a man of promise and prospects at that, then giving up Cornwall for California seemed a fair trade.

By this time, Susan had recovered herself completely, and now sat folding her handkerchief in her lap. "I thought ye warned me away from Jack because 'e's my cousin. I thought ye disapproved."

"It's not what I would've chosen for ye, but if 'e's a good man an' ye love him, I can't see that it's wrong enough to walk away."

"Then it is wrong?"

Zennora sighed. "My great-grandmother used t' say that all the people in Penwith were cousins. When I was a little girl, she used t' sit by th' fire an' trace th' marriages an' th' children back and around, farther than I could follow."

Susan resumed folding her handkerchief. "Maybe we'd better ask Reverend Putnam."

Zennora looked around at her and rose to her feet. "No. We'll ask your fayther." With that, she left the bedroom and walked back to the kitchen.

Jesse's response was direct, simple and devastating. On the following morning, he left the house before breakfast. Around noon, he returned and he walked into the kitchen to inform Susan that he would not consent to her marrying anyone in the family, and that he had invited Hannibal Carne to come for Sunday dinner. He hadn't asked Martin, nor any of the Pascoes, nor the Chenoweths. No one else was coming, no one involved in the North Star or their church—only Hannibal.

Susan spent the next few days in a strange isolation. She and her father hardly spoke to each other, and Bessie suddenly became quite confidential with Joseph, who seemed impressed that either of his sisters was willing to pay any serious attention to him, and who, with Bessie, watched Susan furtively whenever she came into the room. She saw nothing of Jack; she didn't leave the house, and he didn't come visit. Zennora was the only one who really spoke to her, and the two women spent most of their time cleaning the house as though, Zennora once remarked, the queen herself was coming to tea. The tension grew until Sunday, when Susan and Zennora rose at dawn to get everything as ready as possible before the entire family dressed in their very best clothes and rode into town for morning services. While leaving the church, Susan saw Jesse walk over to exchange a few words with the Carne brothers; she stayed close to Zennora and turned her face away when she realized that Jesse, Hannibal and Martin had all looked over at her.

The dinner was worse than a disaster. Susan thought later that she would have been relieved if her father had lost his temper, or if she herself had sat, as silent as a stone, all through the meal, or if Hannibal had failed to compliment Zennora's cooking. Nothing of the sort happened. Everyone was polite, even cordial, and the conversation continued unabated, dealing with everything that was completely irrelevant to the occasion and, to Susan's mind, utterly inconsequential. They discussed the growth of the North Star, the question of whether or not to hire Chinese miners or even to allow them to live in the county, Governor Stanford's administration and the progress of the Central Pacific Rail Road, the growing number of amusing and trivial stories that the local newspapers now gleaned from the transcontinental telegraph in order to fill their pages, whether it was an English or an American clipper that had broken the record for passage around the Horn, the rough clientele of the new livery stable down past Loutzenheiser's, the proposed plan to elevate all of the buildings in downtown Sacramento in order to avoid the periodic flooding at the confluence of the American and Sacramento rivers, the problem of drunken Indians accosting decent citizens on Main Street, and, as always, the progress of the war, so remote, but always fascinating, and all the more so for the rumors, which Jesse and Hannibal scornfully dismissed, that President Lincoln would take over the western gold and silver mines in order to pay the costs of saving the Union. Late that night, while lying in bed and staring up into the shadows, Susan wished that she had snubbed everyone, that she had not passed the potatoes to Hannibal when he deferentially asked for them, and that she had not smiled when her father complimented the cake that she, at her mother's insistence, had baked. From Jesse's point of view, the afternoon had been a flawless success, but Susan regarded the entire episode with exasperated, bitter remorse.

Hannibal started visiting the family every two or three days, usually staying for supper and always joining them for Sunday dinner. His arrival never ruffled her parents, who nearly always managed to give the two young people considerable time alone, and she began to wonder if they had been arranging the appointments without telling her. Late one afternoon, with Zennora in the kitchen and Jesse off to check on something at the mine, Susan and Hannibal sat on the porch, she in a chair and he on the steps, and as he described a new harness shop that had opened on Mill Street, she stared at him and wondered how he could play, so unselfconsciously, his assigned role in Jesse's contrivance. There was something comical but also excruciatingly sincere about him. He looked rather like a schoolmaster, with spectacles sitting on a narrow nose, thin lips with no mustache, a beard scarcely hiding a neat, orderly chin, and brown curls unfolding beneath his hat brim and belying the thinning locks on his crown. His eyes looked exactly like Jack's; not only were they the same perfect blue, but they conveyed the same open wonder. Yet to Hannibal, El Dorado had little to do with railroads and farming empires and cities of the future, but rather with dividends, rents, assessments and commissions. Susan found his vision neither shocking nor repugnant, but merely dreary, and all the worse for that.

By April, Hannibal had become so routine a part of the family that Susan confronted Zennora with her desperation. Her mother had only sympathy to offer, and not much of that. Jesse would not let her marry Jack. She did not have to marry Hannibal; in fact, she didn't have to marry anyone. She had said that she wanted to return to England—had she asked Hannibal about that?

Susan had made the westward journey eagerly, not because she wanted to leave Cornwall, but partly because there had been too many times when she had longed for her absent father, and more because she coveted the excitement, the sheer exhilaration of exploration, of sailing beyond Land's End to introduce herself into a place she had never seen. Only when the leaves had begun to drift down from the black oaks did she realize that she and this new land seemed to resist each other. The Sierra foothills did not wait pliantly and hospitably, ready to reveal their secrets, but instead presented a series of riddles and pitfalls that fooled Susan and left her apprehensive. One afternoon in October, she and Bessie had gone for a short walk around the edge of Devil's Punchbowl, a gentle inverted dish of a hill. Her sister pushed aside a pine branch and then, preoccupied with her footing, let it spring back into Susan's following face. She stopped, startled, stung, and as she caught her breath, she decided that her progress through her new home was a matter of stumbling onto slightly unpleasant surprises. People did not behave quite as she expected, and the customs and habits seemed odd to her. The more experience slipped away from expectation, the more Susan became estranged, and she occasionally felt as though she were reading about herself in a book, watching without becoming truly involved. Yet she could not shake the perplexing impression that she and this place were somehow wooing, each making overtures and then retreating, hurt, when the other misinterpreted an advance.

Camborne had little to offer her. At first, she would have to live with her aunt Elizabeth, even though she did not like her. She would clean Elizabeth's house and supervise Elizabeth's children while their mother thumbed through her hymnal and her prayer book. She would be yet another unmarried woman who lived off of her family's sense of obligation. Such women had little status of their own: they cared for children and the elderly, usually orphaned nieces and nephews and feeble parents, and they went to church. The Methodist ministers had learned to regard such women as the only truly reliable people in their congregations, for they attended every service and prayer meeting, worked tirelessly on the endless series of tea treats and charity hymn gatherings, and always behaved according to strictest interpretation of principle, wearing modest dresses of muddy colors with neither flowers nor ribbons. As they grew older, their relatives died and they either lived alone, eventually dependent for company and help upon other lonely women from the congregation, or they moved in with unwilling cousins whose hospitality became even more grudging as the permanent guest grew old and frail. The ready alternative to such a life was to become a bal maiden, swinging a long-handled mallet to break up the rocks before they went to the stamp mills, and earning a shilling a day—much less than the three pounds each month that the average miner brought home. Until the work wore her out and destroyed her looks, she had to contend with the leering smiles and peremptory hands of the grass captain's assistants, men who regarded her as theirs by right. Susan had known such women only slightly as acquaintances at church; they were from the poorer families in the parish, some with husbands, fathers and brothers who had been disabled in mining accidents, and they usually sat in the back pews and left quickly at the end of the service, not staying to talk with the other women. A few embraced their work, boasting of how much rock they could crush in a day, much like the men who contended, just for sport, to see who could swing the heaviest sledge or climb up a ladder faster than the others. Susan could not imagine becoming one of them.

Zennora's question kept repeating in her ears: "What kind o' life d' ye want to 'ave?" In the weeks since Jack's proposal, she had realized how few women she actually knew. When she accompanied her mother downtown, except for the few other female shoppers, nearly everyone they saw was a man; even at church, for every woman who sat in the pews, there were four men. As in Camborne, nearly all of the other women she met—American, English, Irish or German—seemed to be housebound, and only the married women enjoyed any prestige at all. A wife ran the household and raised the children, and because her husband was probably gone most of the time, working long hours on a six-day week, she was her own mistress. About half of the miners' wives took in boarders, usually only one or two men, frequently someone their husbands knew, but there was little difference, in terms of both the work itself and the regard of the community, between keeping house for the immediate family and, in addition, providing for the needs of a paying guest, as long as the arrangement was impeccably respectable. Some wives and widows earned small incomes by selling fancy goods out of their homes, and others, as well as some single women living in rented rooms, worked as seamstresses. A Mrs. Janes had actually opened a milliner's shop on Main Street, but the women in church whispered that she had never really been married at all. The only other option that was accepted, although not admired, was to work as a servant in someone else's home, either living with the employer, usually sleeping in a small outbuilding or on a cot off of the kitchen, or boarding with yet another housewife. Then there were alternatives that, for Susan, were too remote even to imagine. She had heard a rumor of a woman in Nevada City who had opened a practice as a physician, but even if the story were true, she had no idea how one trained for that profession. She had read of the actresses who dazzled San Francisco, reciting Shakespeare or dancing in scandalous lacy gowns, but because they frequented saloons and poker parlors, failed to marry and attend church regularly, and generally flouted everyone's conception of decency, they were no better than common prostitutes, who lived a life that Susan did not even attempt to imagine.

Susan felt stymied. Zennora's question seemed pointless, for all of the conceivable choices kept coming back to the same thing, that she must have a husband and a home, but she vaguely yearned for more. She began to realize that she had yet to discover not only what she wanted, but also how to find it out. Of two things she felt certain: she wanted to go home to Cornwall, but she could not bear living under Elizabeth's glare and becoming a nonentity, hardly to be noticed except with condescension and scant tolerance. The only answer to her dilemma, as disappointingly ordinary as it seemed, was to live in Cornwall as a married woman. She must therefore return and marry, or marry a man and return.

On the following Sunday, the family had returned from church services and Bessie was helping Zennora prepare dinner. Hannibal was coming, as usual, and Susan had slipped away from the kitchen to sit on the porch and think. The afternoon was relatively quiet; the only noises were the hoisting machinery in the distance and an occasional staccato rhythm of an axe as a neighbor chopped wood for his stove. Susan gazed through the pine trees, so preoccupied that she didn't really see the hills beyond and didn't notice when Jesse walked up to lean on a porch post. He cleared his throat, and she started. He smiled at her.

"It's a fair afternoon."

"Yes, it is." He was still wearing his Sunday best, except that he had changed his good boots for the ones he customarily wore to the mine.

"I've been over t' th' main shaft t' see t' th' men. They're a fine crew, as good as any at Dolcoath." Susan looked up warily; he seldom referred to Cornwall—what was on his mind? He took his foot from between the balusters and trudged slowly up the porch steps to take the chair next to hers. He sat silently for a moment, his eyes scanning through the trees and back and forth across the horizon. Then he spoke, very calmly, and without looking at her. "I know that ye're in love with Jack Trevenna." She flushed immediately, feeling the heat all through her body. "And I know that ye're not much interested in Hannibal Carne." He sighed. "Yer uncle once told me that I spoiled ye. Bessie and little Joseph, too, but you most of all. 'e told me that I might have trouble."

Susan tried to get her breathing under control. She couldn't remember the last time she and her father had talked to each other, just the two of them, and there was something in his tone and attitude that was completely different, as though he was conceding her womanhood and speaking to her not as a child, but more as another adult. "D' ye think 'e was right?"

Jesse smiled. "I told 'im to mind 'is own business. Joseph was always too sure of 'imself." He shifted in his chair. "But there are some things I cannot allow. Ye may not marry yer cousin, Susan. I'm sorry, because I think 'e'll be a good man fer some woman, and because I know th' two of ye were friends, an' now that ye're grown, it's all become somethin' more than that. But ye may not do it, and there's an end. If ye truly love 'im, then my 'eart aches for ye, but this 'ere is finished." Now he turned to her and took her hands in his, as though he were a suitor rather than a father. "I love ye, girl, and I want ye t' be 'appy. Ye're eighteen now, and ye may marry if ye wish, but there's no need t' be hasty. Yer mother was five years older when she married, an' my mother five years older than that. Ye can wait. But think o' this, an' I'll tell ye down souce, as plainly as I can." He looked down into their hands, then back into her face. "Hannibal Carne is a decent man. 'e'll not be runnin' off t' th' Comstock, and 'e'll not be takin' chances. 'e owns part o' th' North Star, and I think 'e'll own other mines one day. 'e won't be spendin' his life swingin' a sledge in a drift and hidin' from th' blast. 'e'll be workin' at grass. The woman who marries 'im will 'ave a fine 'ome and children who're safe. I think she'll 'ave an easier time than yer mother 'as. There are few men 'ere that I'd want for ye, Susan. Ye can certainly have yer pick—ye know as well as I that th' towns and camps are full o' men, with only a few respectable girls like yerself. But most o' those men're cracky or caudlers—they'll spend their money an' waste yer life. Hannibal is different. I know 'e's not exactly a slappin' fellow and 'e's not much for tinkerin' after a girl—I don't know what th' two o' ye have to say t' each other when ye're alone—but 'e's a good man."

He paused, still looking full into her face. She tried to hold his gaze, took a breath, and told him the truth. "I want to go back to Camborne, Fayther."

He sat up straight. "Anan? What d'ye say?"

She tried to speak evenly. "I don't like it 'ere. I want to go 'ome."

Jesse stared at her for a moment, then sat back in his chair. "Well. I'll confess, I'm fair mazed. Back to Camborne. Why d'ye want to leave 'ere?"

She tried to explain how she felt, but after a few minutes, there were tears running down her face, and Jesse reached over to pat her shoulder. When she subsided, he shook his head. "If what ye want is to live in Cornwall, then ask Hannibal about it. I don't know that 'e's plannin' to stay 'ere." He rose and looked down at her. "And Susan, remember—don't marry th' man if ye don't wish to." The tears welled up in her eyes, but Jesse cleared his throat and walked into the house.

Susan raised the question with Hannibal after dinner that afternoon. She felt as though she were prying, but he seemed to regard the matter as inconsequential, casually assuring her that he and Martin both planned to return home when they had earned enough in the gold fields to be able to live comfortably and perhaps set up as adventurers in the mines near Helston. The Carne family had, for longer than he knew, owned a farm in Breage, and although their uncle lived there now, the old man had no children, so when he died, he would surely leave it to Martin, the oldest of his nephews, and there was ample room on the property for Hannibal to build a house if he wished. Susan pressed him, wanting to know how long he would remain in California, and he took off his spectacles to wipe them clean before answering. There was no way to tell, he mused, but he thought he would surely return to England before five more years had passed.

Two days later, Jesse walked out on the porch to find Susan sitting on the bench, bolt upright with her hands folded in her lap and her face firmly set, staring down the slope towards the mine. He stopped, looking down at her, but she seemed not to notice him. "Susan?" She didn't move. "Susan?"

"Fayther, I'll marry Hannibal Carne if ye wish."

"Susan. Susan, look at me." She looked up at him. Her face was perfectly calm. "Are ye sure this is what ye want?"

"Yes."

"Ye look none too happy about it."

"This is what I want."

"What about Hannibal?"

"'e 'asn't asked me."

Jesse considered. "I think 'e will."

On the very next evening, Hannibal came to supper and proposed to her in the twilight. Yet as she consented, she felt as though she were falling, falling from nowhere to nowhere. It was all so ordinary, so disappointingly mundane. She looked into Hannibal's face, searching for heat, or need, or magic, but his lips were pressed primly together and just as she began to answer him, he reached up to wave his fingers at a persistent mosquito. There was no suspense when he left her on the porch to walk into the house and ask Jesse's permission, but she made herself sit still and wait until Bessie came to fetch her so she could try to smile as she walked into the parlor. Zennora served fairings, her favorite cookies, and clotted cream, and Hannibal left as soon as he could manage it. Late that night, Zennora tiptoed to Susan's doorway, thinking that she had heard the girl crying, but when she looked in, her daughter was sleeping soundly.

The spring flowers faded as the days grew warmer and the plans for the wedding proceeded inexorably, piling on top of one another like bricks in mortar. Hannibal managed to buy a piece of property next to Jesse's, and he and Martin began building a house in a grove of pine trees, far enough from her parents so that both families would have some privacy, but close enough that Susan could run to Zennora in less than a minute. It was nicer than any of the miners' cabins, with a large kitchen and two extra rooms just for children. Hannibal chose the floorboards carefully and sanded them smooth, promising Susan that he would finish the parlor with any rug she chose. He was becoming the perfect husband, so solicitous and so inclined to antici-pate what he thought would be her needs that she felt, more and more, surrounded. In June, the minister announced their engagement before the congregation, as was the custom, and she and Hannibal stood as witnesses to a little boy's christening. Alrcady, the people they knew expected to see them together.

She hardly saw Jack. On a Sunday nearly two weeks after the betrothal, she walked out of the church door and almost bumped into him where he stood talking to Nick and two other men. He stepped out of her way, swept off his hat, and offered his congratulations. She thanked him, not knowing where to look, fearing the curious faces arrayed before her, but finally glanced up into his eyes, finding them as blue and open as ever, and so telling her nothing at all. The moment seemed merely formal; he might be congratulating his sister, or his brother's fiancée. The churchyard became a blur, and she placed her fingers discreetly on Bessie's hip so that she could follow her out to the coach.

On the first of July, with neither invitation nor warning, Jack rode up to the house. He announced that the town was getting ready to celebrate the Americans' Independence Day, and because the war against the southern rebels was now in its third year, the local people were determined to demon-strate their loyalty as never before. He described the plans in tempting detail until Zennora, laughing, threw up her hands and exclaimed that they really must go. On the morning of the fourth, Jack met them on the Auburn road to escort them into town and usher them to a bench that a friend of his had reserved. They were raised up on a small scaffolding, and so would be able to see over the heads of the people standing on the boardwalk, and there was an awning to protect them from the sun. Susan obediently watched the parade that passed before her—coaches full of town officials, ranks of the local militia, and two brass bands—and joined the rest to walk up to Hamilton

Hall to hear the speeches. In the hubbub of the crowd, Jack drew her aside and said something about a wrestling match. Disoriented by the noise and the pushing, Susan let him pull her away from her family, and as they turned a corner to walk down behind the row of shops, she looked back and caught a glimpse of Zennora straining to see over the heads around her.

They walked up the hill, down an alley, up another, and into a crowd of aggressive male voices. She recognized some of the miners from around French Lead, and several called out greetings when they saw Jack. Susan thought that there had to be at least five or six hundred people gathered there, and their feet kicked up a haze of dust so thick that her eyes began to burn and she could taste the grit in her mouth. Jack led her to a bench, one of many arranged in rows that formed a rough square, all facing a dirt arena surrounded with a low wall of planks and covered with straw. A man wearing a straw hat walked out into the middle of the arena, put his fingers to his mouth, and gave a sudden shriek of a whistle. The noise rose briefly and subsided. All around the ring, men were finding places to sit, crowding onto the benches so that there were nearly fifty sitting in each of the four front rows. The man next to Susan bumped her before he noticed her, then tipped his hat, apologized, and turned and yelled something down the line before shoving the man next to him in order to regain his original place and leave Susan a bit more room. She looked out into the ring, where the man in the straw hat was waiting with his hands on his hips. Beyond him, on the edge of the ring, she could see boys running back and forth carrying pints and pitchers of beer. Susan was just leaning over to ask Jack why they were there when the man in the straw hat began to speak in a rasping tenor voice.

"And now, gentlemen—round four!" The crowd cheered, and across the ring, men grinned and waved their hats. The man in the straw hat raised his arms, and when the cheering dwindled, he called out, "Edgar Penallack and William Crowgey!" There were more cheers as two men stepped out onto the straw. Each wore a loose canvas jacket, tight trousers down to his calves, and no shoes. The man in the straw hat clapped his hands once and climbed over the wooden partition to stand outside one corner. At each of the other corners stood a man who peered intently in at the men in the ring. The contestants spat in their hands and approached the center, each crouching slightly and carefully studying the other's movements. Suddenly, one man grabbed for the other, and they came together in a sort of bear hug, pushing with their feet against the straw as though they were walking slowly uphill. Then the heavier man got one arm free, reached up to pry the other's face away from his shoulder, and spun him around so that he fell flat on his back. The three men in the corners raised their arms in a sort of signal.

The two men rose and circled. The smaller man kept rotating his shoulders and wincing, but then shifted his feet quickly and dove for the other.

They locked together again, straining and striving, and for a moment each had an arm free, looking for a new hold on his opponent. Then—Susan could not see how it was done—the heavier man once again took the other off his feet and dumped him on his back. The crowd raised a din as the victor helped the loser to his feet and they walked off together.

Susan began to feel sick. The canvas canopy blocked the sun, but the air was hot and stifling, and the smells of spilled beer, cheap tobacco and sweating men were starting to make her gag. She turned to Jack, but he pointed across the ring and said, "There 'e is!"

Two more men in canvas jackets were climbing over the partition. One of them was Nick. The man in the straw hat stood in the center with his arms raised, and as soon as he could make himself heard, he called out, "Samuel Scawn and Nicholas Trevenna!" Jack shouted Nick's name, so close to Susan's ear that she jumped. The men around her were cheering and calling out suggestions, and someone behind her was reaching over to slap Jack on the shoulder over and over again. Nick and the other man grabbed for each other, pedalling and turning, reaching and sliding, and the noise increased. Susan drew a handkerchief out of her sleeve and bent down to wipe the sweat and grit off of her face. Suddenly, the man next to her bellowed, and she looked up just in time to see Nick throw his adversary. Jack was standing now, clapping his hands, shaking his fists and yelling at his brother in the ring. The wrestlers circled again, and came together again, and this time it was Nick who fell down in the straw. Susan no longer felt nauseated, but her mouth was terribly dry and she wished she could go somewhere to find a breath of fresh air. Her back began to ache, and she planted her palms on the bench, trying to lift herself slightly to take the pressure off of her corset. She wondered whether Zennora were concerned; by this time the speeches in Hamilton Hall must be well under way. Suddenly, there was another general shout, and she looked into the ring to see Nick down again, and then standing up to shake the victor's hand and climb over the partition. Jack yelled into her ear to follow him. They squeezed past the row of men's knees and into the dusty aisle, where Jack led her to a space behind a small shack. Nick was standing there wearing nothing but his trousers, and he was wiping himself off with a dirty rag. Jack congratulated him and said something about there being a chance for fourth place. Nick smiled and suggested that Jack go into the ring himself, and the brothers laughed. Nick took Susan's hand and thanked her for coming before picking his duck jacket up off the grass and walking away.

Jack led Susan over to a little tent where a man stood behind a plank stretched across a couple of crates. He poured beer for Jack and lemonade for Susan, and they went to stand in the shade of a sycamore tree to drink. The lemonade was warm and tasted faintly rank, but she rinsed out her mouth and drank the rest of it down. She wiped her face all over with her handkerchief and turned to discover that Jack was staring at her.

"Marry me, Susan." It must be a joke, a strange and callous joke. "Please marry me."

"I'm marrying Hannibal in two weeks." Her answer sounded ridiculously obvious and irrelevant even as she gave it.

"I know that. Don't do it. I'll talk to Jesse again. I'll explain. Ye must marry me."

She looked up at him. He had taken off his hat, and across his forehead was a crease that cut through the dust and sweat. She stared into his eyes, those innocent, wondering blue eyes, trying to find something solid, a reliable foothold. Then the eyes remained but the face became Hannibal's, thin-lipped, polite, with the spectacles slipping down his nose. She looked away.

"I can't. You know I can't. Please take me back t' my parents." He didn't move, so she turned and walked, as quickly as she could, in the direction of Main Street. He caught up with her, and she tucked her fingers in the crook of his elbow as they hurried down Church and up the steps of the hall. A man on the stage was waving his arms and declaiming something about the war against the rebels.

Zennora looked up when Susan tapped her shoulder. "Yer fayther's out lookin' for ye."

Jack flushed under his layer of grime, then leaned over and whispered to Zennora, "I'll find 'im." Then he was gone.

On the drive back to French Lead, Susan could not think of how to answer her father's annoyed questions, so she hid behind the ambiguous explanation that Jack had wanted to show her something. Jesse tried to press the matter when they reached the cabin, but after Zennora took him aside for a moment, he walked out to sit on the porch by himself.

During the next two weeks, the wedding preparations dominated the household, but Susan felt removed from the entire event, as though it were really happening to someone else. She was seldom alone. When she came to breakfast one morning and found the entire family looking up from the table with careful faces, she had a sudden impulse to run out of the house and scream, or to tear off her clothes and splash through Wolf Creek—anything to break the composure of the event that was surrounding her. Zennora took her to town to buy her dress, a severe but regal arrangement of carved bone buttons and dark green silk, ordered especially from San Francisco, but when they came out of the store to find that young Joseph had already brought the coach around and was sitting, bolt upright, with the reins in his hands, Susan felt as though he were her guard, come to escort her back to her confinement. She was the bride, but she did what she was told. Everyone seemed to ask her what she wanted, but she could not shake the impression that the questions had been as carefully arranged as flowers in a crystal vase. Zennora gave her only the simplest tasks and stayed close to her while she worked at them.

On the morning of the wedding, Susan awoke in a houseful of strangers. Zennora had become brisk and curt, pinching a handful of pins between her lips while she ordered Susan to turn this way and that so she could adjust the seamstress' work, and Bessie, who looked as though she were bursting to tell some secret, had parted her hair on the wrong side and tried to hold the curls in a bunch with a cloisonné clasp. Joseph stood by the coach with his hair slicked down, shifting his shoulders in a new charcoal grey suit and trying not to scuff dust onto his shining boots. When they arrived at the church, Jesse dismounted to help her down, but she looked past him towards a score of unfamiliar faces, all staring at her, some smiling and whispering to each other, and when she reached to take his hand, his had become one of the faces, not her father but a man she had never known. She allowed him to take her into the little anteroom, and as they stood, waiting, she watched the people file in. She thought she saw Jack and Nick, but Jack's face was turned away from her. Jesse escorted her up the aisle, so slowly that she wondered whether the altar were receding and rising before them, forcing them to climb up a slope that would never end. Finally, she was standing in front of Father Putnam, whose face was even redder than usual in the summer heat, his neck bulging over the tight white collar. Hannibal was there, too, but he, incongruently, looked so familiar that she furtively checked him from head to foot to make sure he was wearing his best black suit and not his work clothes. He smiled, but she felt certain that he was worried about something. The minister read the service, and she answered automatically, reciting the ritual phrases. There was a pause, and she realized that the ceremony was over. She turned to look for Zennora, but could not find her, and Hannibal took her back down the aisle and into the churchyard, where people she did not remember embraced her and loudly presented their congratulations before gathering at the curbside to wave as Martin drove the couple off in Hannibal's new carriage.

Jack stood leaning against a tree, off to one side, watching the guests pour out into the yard, mill about, talking and laughing, and dissipate in Susan's wake. Nick, who had been making the rounds in the crowd, walked up to him and grinned.

"I know where we can find a bit o' fun."

"Where?"

"Come with me."

They rode to Nevada City and left their horses outside the Union Hotel, and Jack followed Nick along the boardwalk and into the lobby of the Metropolitan Theatre. A large, gaudy placard announced that Lotta Crabtree would be performing that night. The little hall was full of men, mostly miners, it seemed, who laughed and called to each other and stomped their feet, eager for the show to begin.

They applauded, and Jack looked up on the stage to see a young woman standing in the light of a chandelier. She was hardly more than a child, with a round face, a mischievous smile, and russet ringlets bouncing across the back of her head. The piano player rummaged through an introduction while Lotta assumed a pensive attitude and began to sing, "Dear Mother, I'll Come Home Again," gazing up at the corner of the ceiling and clasping her hands in front of her bosom. When she was finished, the men in the hall clapped, whistled and shouted for more. Her next song was more cheerful, and on the choruses she danced a jig, kicking her feet out to show her little ankles under the fringe of her hoop skirt. There was more applause, and then Lotta danced. Jack had never imagined such variety, for as the piano jumped from tune to tune, changing tempo capriciously, Lotta danced a hornpipe, then a fling, then a soft shoe, and finished with a fandango and a polka with a man with shining black hair who stepped out. Then she disappeared, dancing out from behind the curtain only to blow a round of kisses at the stomping men. After a few minutes, the curtain drew back to reveal a backscene and a collection of tattered furniture, with Lotta standing in a pose next to a mirror. Jack could not quite follow the story, but the men around him laughed and whooped as Lotta impersonated Jenny Lind, even mocking her trills and her facial expressions. The curtain fell into place, only to draw back again to reveal Lotta in blackface, playing the banjo and tapping her feet to a song like nothing Jack had ever heard, but which pleased the men so much that they would not stop cheering when it was over.

Nick rose and pulled Jack out of the room, pushing past men who were climbing up on benches and waving their arms, through the hotel lobby and a series of rooms and corridors, finally stopping in front of a door where a man stood with his arms folded. Nick spoke quietly to him, and after a moment, he opened the door and said something to someone inside. A woman with piercing black eyes appeared and seemed pleased to see Nick. He asked her a question. She laughed, made some remark that set Nick to laughing, but then nodded and indicated that he wait. After a few minutes, Lotta emerged, with her dancing partner behind her, and took Nick's arm. The little party walked up the hill to Broad Street and into the Bed Rock Saloon, where a man with a drooping mustache showed them to a table.

Nick immediately engaged Lotta in an intense conversation that left little room for anyone else. Her dance partner sat aloof, hardly nodding when anyone addressed him, so Jack contemplated the young woman who had attracted so much adulation. She looked older than she did on stage, but he decided, after a few minutes, that she was probably about Bessie's age, and that both the innocence on stage and the sophistication at this table were carefully studied, each presented for the situation at hand. He wondered what she was really like. At that moment, she turned to look at him, smiled, and said something to Nick, who grinned.

Jack was trying to think of a clever remark when a man planted his hands on the table right between Jack and Lotta, leaning down to say something to the girl. Nick asked him to leave. The man stared at Nick, then glared at the dance partner, who was leaning farther back into the shadows, and glanced at Jack. His breath reeked of cheap whiskey and cigars, and he stank. He turned back to Nick.

"I'll take yer head off, ye English bastard."

Nick stood up, so suddenly that his chair fell over, and pulled Lotta around behind him. The Irishman set his feet and swung his arm back, but Jack reached up to lock his elbow and throw him off balance. He fell to the floor with a thud. Nick yelled a warning, but Jack had no time to look around before someone crashed into him and began pummeling him in the ribs. He tried to catch his balance but slipped and landed on the floor, and for a strangely long moment, he realized that he could smell the spilled beer and whiskey. Someone pulled him to his feet, and he looked around for Lotta, but a short, red-haired man swung his fist at him, so he ducked the blow and knocked the man down. He found Nick wrestling with the Irishman, who kept trying to push away so he could swing a punch. The Irishman slipped and fell, and Jack pulled Nick over to the front door. Half of the men in the saloon were pushing, grabbing, swinging and falling, and the man behind the bar was putting away decanters and glasses as fast as he could. The brothers looked for Lotta, but she and her dance partner had vanished.

8
The Live Yankee
1864

Under the blanket that Susan had draped over the arms of the rocker, Jack could easily see that she had let her knees fall apart to accommodate her swollen belly. Hannibal turned around to offer a cup and saucer, new bone china, and Jack let the warmth of the coffee rise into his face as Hannibal began to explain his plan. "I'm proposin' that we start a new company out near Red Dog. You an' Nick 'ave a couple o' claims there; so do Martin and I. The Pascoes, too. They're all quartz claims, an' they look promisin', but none of us 'ave spent much time with 'em. They're all near to each other; if we bought just three more claims, they'd all be connected, one alongside another. The company would own 'em all, make 'em into one, and work the ledge wherever it seems most likely."

"What about those three claims—are they for sale?"

"Iss fay. The biggest belongs to a group of Americans from Connecticut, and they've decided t' go 'ome an' get rich makin' uniforms for Mr. Lincoln's army. They call theirs the Live Yankee, and that seems like a fair enough name for the company."

"You and Martin, Nick and me, and the Pascoes. Who else?"

"Jesse, of course. That makes eight. I'll ask Chenoweth and Nankervis; if all of 'em come in, that's thirteen."

"What about the Sterlings?"

Hannibal's face was a bland mask as he looked into the fire. "All they have to offer is money, and what we're doin' won't cost much."

"It's all Cornishmen."

Hannibal smiled and took off his spectacles. "That's right. At least we'll be sure that every man knows 'is business. And for them as are 'omesick, we can get together and trade stories about market day in Redruth." He glanced over at Susan, but she didn't look up from her knitting. "What d'ye say, Jack?"

Jack decided that Hannibal had made up his mind. He was going to start the company, and that was that; if a man wanted to pick through every detail of the plan, then Hannibal would quietly find someone else. "How much for a share?"

Hannibal put his spectacles back on and stared up at the stone chimney. "Say five 'undred each. That'll leave enough t' buy th' claims and set up some equipment. If we find somethin', then we can talk about puttin' more in." He looked back at his guest. "D'ye have five 'undred, Jack?"

Both men grinned, and at that moment, there was a loud knock on the door. A boy from the North Star stood panting in the wind. "Can ye come, Mr. Carne? Th' men on th' second level ran into a bit o' bother."

"Is anyone hurt?"

"Nay, sur, they just found some shale they weren't expectin', and they want you t' see before they go on."

"Are they waitin'?"

"Iss, sur."

"I'll be there as soon as may be." The boy ran off, and Hannibal took his coat and hat from a peg. "Sorry, Jack. Susan—I may be 'alf an hour, or all day." He paused in the doorway, looked at the two of them, took a breath as though to say something, but stopped, nodded his head, and walked out, shutting the door behind him.

Susan kept knitting. "Ye need not stay, Jack. If I need somethin', I'll walk down t' Mother's."

"D' ye want me t' fetch 'er for you?"

"There's no need."

He rose and stood with his back to the fire. She looked up at him, and he moved to one side so she could feel the heat of the flames.

"Are ye cold?"

She smiled. "Just my feet. An' my hands, too, but I can't get them close enough t' th' fire without standin' there all day. The rest of me is warm."

"Surely this cold will break."

"I don't mind it. Anyway, it'll be warm when th' baby comes."

"And when will that be?"

"Towards the end of April, I think. P'raps a bit earlier."

Jack suddenly wanted to take off his jacket, unbutton his collar and open a window to breathe the clear, sharp air. Through the glass, he could see a small patch on the northern slope of a knoll where the snow, protected from the sun, had refused to melt. "Susan . . . Susan, d' ye think of me?"

She kept knitting, turning the needles and twisting them, back and forth, clicking down one row and up the next. "Did ye know that Bessie is gettin' married? And to Martin!" She looked up at him standing next to the window, staring at her. "I told her that Father Putnam might not approve of 'er marryin' 'er own sister's brother-in-law, and I promise ye, th' girl blushed."

Suddenly, a log snapped, and a bright spark sprang out and landed on the blanket where it draped over her feet. She reached to brush it off, but he was there first, kneeling, bending over her ankles, flicking the glowing speck away with a finger. He rubbed the wool, exploring it. "I don't think it's singed."

"Thank you."

Cousin Jack

"Susan . . . "

"It was kind of ye t' come visit, Jack, but ye need not stay. Hannibal will be 'ome soon, and I can get around just fine."

"Susan . . . "

She laid down her knitting and looked full into his face. His hands had found her feet and now he held them through the layers of wool, pressing them. Finally she spoke. "Please, Jack. Please."

He winced, let go of her feet, and staggered up to stand over her. "I'm . . . sorry." He shook his head, turned, took his hat and coat off the peg where Hannibal had hung them, and let himself out. She sat gazing into the fire, her eyes shining.

On the last day of February, the twelve partners of the North Star gathered for their monthly meeting. John Sterling had arranged for them to use a comfortable room at Findley's bank, and although the Chenoweths had complained about having to ride into town when they could just as easily meet in Edward's office at French Lead, no else felt inclined to argue, so John had his way. Jack enjoyed the genteel surroundings almost as much as the sight of the Chenoweths and the Nankervises, dressed in their customary work clothes, sitting uneasily in Findley's leather arm chairs.

As Jesse listened to the strained, irritable voices around him, he thought of William Pascoe's warning. The irony, he thought, was that the mine was doing well, even better than they had hoped, and they were showing a net profit of about four thousand dollars each month. The disputes involved not how to make a success out of the mine, but how to manage their prosperity. No one sought to return every penny of the profit in dividends, but the partners did not agree on how to improve the mine. As always, Edward Sterling sat silently, his face betraying nothing, while John spoke for both of them.

"We've developed the underground works as far as we can. Even the new drainage tunnel"—he nodded towards Nick—"is nearly finished, at the cost, I might add, of nearly fifteen thousand dollars. The pump and the engines are more than adequate."

Hannibal folded his hands on the table. "What d'ye suggest?"

John smiled and leaned in as though presenting a great and wonderful secret. "I propose that we expand." Mark Chenoweth let his breath out through his nose with a long hissing sound, and Hannibal frowned at him across the table. "We can afford to buy more claims, and there's one on Wolf Creek, not far from us, that might be available."

Hannibal asked, "Is there equipment on the site?"

John shrugged. "There's a small stamp mill. I can't speak for the pump or the hoist. We can handle the ironwork in our own smithy."

Nick shook his head. "I know th' claim. There's nearly as much t' be done as at th' North Star four years ago. It wouldn't be easy, John. And it wouldn't be cheap."

John laughed. "Gentlemen, these are trivial problems! If the machinery isn't quite up to Nicholas' standards, we'll repair it as far as need be, and if the stamp mill isn't satisfactory, we'll cart the rock over to our own."

Nick winced. "Our mill 'as only six stamps. We can't even 'andle th' rock we 'ave now."

Jesse laid his hand on Nick's arm. "Is that so, Edward? Are we running behind?"

The men around the table waited while Edward turned his black, un-blinking eyes on his questioner; even John chose to remain silent. Finally, he answered. "We are running up to capacity."

Hannibal slammed his hand on the table. "Jimmery chry! What ye mean is that th' stamps're runnin' day an' night an' th' rock is waiting t' be crushed." Jesse frowned at Martin, but before he could intervene, Hannibal continued. "I'm tellin' ye, Edward, if ye can't run the operation better than that, let someone else take charge!"

In an instant, the room fell silent. Edward stared down the table at Hannibal, and even John, no longer smiling, seemed lost for something to say. No one had ever challenged Edward's judgement so boldly in an open meeting, and the partners were exchanging furtive glances. Nick had his hand over his mouth, apparently trying to appear thoughtful but probably covering a smile. Jack thought quickly. If Hannibal forced a vote, the major-ity would probably challenge Edward's supervision, but that would leave the question of who would replace him.

Finally, Charles Nankervis asked, in his monotone rasp, "What d'ye suggest?"

Hannibal took a deep breath. He was furious with himself for finally allowing the Sterlings to provoke him: Edward with his aloof manner, John with his soirée chatter, and both of them with their disregard for the under-ground workings that were the heart of the mine. "I've been talkin' to Nick. Let 'im explain."

While Edward kept his blank stare focused on Hannibal, the others turned to Nick, who outlined his ideas in broad terms. "There's enough gold down there t' keep us busy for the next ten years or more; all we 'ave t' do is plan how we'll bring it out. We can take the incline shaft down a bit farther and open up a new level. As for stamps, we need more now, and we'll certainly need more yet if we drive new tunnels." He looked at Hannibal, and then at the Sterlings. "I've no objection to buying new claims, but we must be able t' work 'em properly. I want to expand, but I want to expand underground."

Hannibal's provocation went unanswered, but most of the tension had dissipated, and the conversation became general as the partners, with Jesse gently mediating between Hannibal and the Sterlings, explored the various possibilities. Jack listened to the others discuss the placement of a new level and the maintenance of the pump, and he wondered why Nick had not mentioned an idea that had tantalized him ever since he had proposed it to their father in 1860: to sink a vertical shaft down to intersect the incline, and so reduce the distance that they had to hoist the ore. In the end, the partners agreed to defer the question of buying new claims but to add three stamps to the existing six.

Jesse walked out of the door on Main Street and was just turning towards the livery stable when Hannibal stepped out of a shadow. "D'ye have time fer a walk, Jesse?" The two men headed south on Mill Street, waving at Nick and Jack as they rode through the light rain towards Boston Ravine. Jesse glanced over at his son-in-law, but his face told him nothing. He was always difficult to read, for while he spoke his mind freely and clearly about business matters, he seldom expressed his feelings about anything else, no matter whether trivial or momentous, typically conversing with brief comments or questions, maintaining an expression of polite interest that betrayed neither enthusiasm, boredom, impatience, censure nor agreement. His outburst tonight had been completely out of character.

As they turned the corner to walk down Bank Alley, Hannibal raised the subject of the Live Yankee, but the rain was falling harder now, so Jesse turned aside into a doorway with an overhang.

"This may be a bad time for th' North Star."

Hannibal raised his eyebrows. "Each share brings home $200 tonight. Nothin' bad about that."

"We're producin' just fine, an' I'm not talkin' about dividends. Ye all but called Edward Sterling a bufflehead with every man there t' listen."

"I know." Hannibal's lips tightened and he winced has a gust blew a handful of droplets into his face. "I can't figure what the man's about, and if we listen to 'im, the mine'll back up like an old cow."

"I wish ye'd 'eld yer tongue." Hannibal glanced up quickly, and Jesse smiled at him. "But what 'as me thinkin' is that no one at that table took ye on. None o' these men liked th' Sterlings from th' start, but while most of 'em think John is a regular staver—always 'as somethin' t' say about every man's business—they've respected Edward. 'e's a cold man—and he sets up as a gentleman, no miner—but 'e's tough, tough and hard." Jesse sighed. "Ye told Edward off—nearly asked him to resign—and no one stood up with 'im, so I must think that they've been askin' th' same questions as you. They must realize that Nick is right about th' stamps, an' that Edward idden runnin' things as well as might be."

"What does this have to do with the Live Yankee?"

"Only this. If this 'ere 'ere will take 'em away from th' North Star, then I won't go along. And I'll tell that t' the others."

"Why?"

"Ye're invitin' all the partners except th' Sterlings. That's well an' good, an' I understand why ye leave 'em out. But if th' rest of us start spendin' our time out at Red Dog, we'll lose th' North Star. The Sterlings will do what they will, and we'll be left behind. We might be chasin' a vein that looks keenly but may be no more than a broil, and then we'll be standin' there empty-handed while the Sterlings ride to San Francisco in their own coach."

Hannibal grinned. "Jesse, I do believe ye're worried about not gettin' rich."

"That's not it at all, not for me. But we have a responsibility t' th' mine—t' the other partners, and t' th' men who work it. Ye may not take away th' men—yerself included—who can keep it successful. We made th' North Star what it is, and we can't leave it now."

Hannibal considered. He could not explain to Jesse how desperately he ached to create something substantial, impressive, and especially outside of the oppressive authority of Edward Sterling and the effusive blather of his brother. Even though he had suggested his remorse over his outburst, he was just now realizing how much he had enjoyed it. For a moment, just a moment, he thought he had seen something in Edward's face, some sort of response, some recognition that Hannibal was a man who deserved attention. Yet Jesse was right; he should not seduce the partners away from the North Star. Even if he chose to risk Jesse's regard to undermine the partnership deliberately, Susan would remain loyal to her father and would scorn him. Then there was the money. Jesse had just claimed that his own dividends were not his primary concern, and Hannibal wondered if he really believed that, or if he thought Hannibal would believe it. For him, the money had always been all there was, until that moment when he called Edward Sterling a fool. Now, in the soft rain, he returned to the money. The Live Yankee might not pay at all, but the North Star had become the envy of the district. With that thought in mind, he shook Jesse's hand and assured him that the Live Yankee would never run to the detriment of the North Star, and the two men walked back to the livery stable, their collars turned up against the blowing droplets.

When Hannibal reached home, he let himself in as quietly as he could, sat down in the parlor to take off his boots, and walked softly up the stairs to where Susan lay sleeping. She was lying flat on her back, and he could see, under the blankets, the arching curve of her belly rising and falling slowly with each breath. She had left the window open a crack and pulled the counterpane up so it just covered her chin. He studied her face, intrigued, as always, at how much younger she seemed when asleep.

Cousin Jack

The wife he saw in the daylight was a grown woman, running the house as though it were a telegraph office, keeping everything so ready and so carefully arranged that no matter how often Hannibal had to spend odd or long hours at the mine, meals and clean clothes appeared when they were needed. Whenever Hannibal had tried to compliment her, she had smiled and lightly remarked that the piskies would provide. Once Zennora was there to hear her daughter say that, and the older woman just smiled, a secret, knowing smile that Hannibal realized was not really meant for him to see. In that moment, he felt as though it were Susan's house, not his, even though he had built it with his own hands, and that she, her mother and the piskies would satisfy his needs only as long as their whimsy lasted, or until he, the guest, committed some transgression against the household that he would probably not even understand.

Yet the wife who slept in his bed seemed, in the shadows, to be a child. Her face, relaxed, took on a fullness that reminded him of a little girl who had dozed off in her mother's arms, and when he gently pulled back the covers to climb in beside her, she licked her lips, smacked them softly and turned her head. He remembered the morning when he, awaking first, had watched the transformation as she fluttered her eyelids, gasped, and, in recognition of the day, rearranged the pattern of her face.

After supper a few days later, Hannibal was checking his notes on the Live Yankee when a shattering crash punched a hole in the stillness. He looked up to see Susan bent over the table, her knuckles white and her eyes astonished, and on the floorboards, the slivers of a china pitcher sparkling among splashed puddles of cream. As soon as she could catch her breath, she sent him for her mother, refusing to explain, refusing to insist, simply stating that he must and would go. Zennora lifted her skirts and ran the hundred yards between the two houses, not bothering to stop to put on a shawl or pick up a lantern, but letting her feet find the path. By the time Hannibal and Jesse caught up with her, she was already helping Susan up the stairs towards her bedroom. The men waited in the parlor, standing quietly and straining to hear what was happening upstairs. Finally, they fell asleep hunched in the two more comfortable chairs, and awoke just before dawn to discover that Zennora had spent the night watching at her daughter's bedside. She descended only to brew some tea and send Hannibal to town to fetch Dr. Simpson. By the time he brought the man back, Zennora had drawn the upstairs curtains against the sun that had risen well above the trees on the crest of hill. She insisted on staying in the room while he examined her daughter, just as she insisted that Hannibal and Jesse remain downstairs. They could hear his mumbling drone as he spoke to Susan, and a few minutes later, Zennora drew him to the corner near the top of the stairs, where they conferred in whispers. He accepted a cup of coffee from Jesse and informed Hannibal that Susan must stay in bed until the baby came, which should be in about a month or so. Any exertion, he advised, would bring the baby too early, which could lead to complications. That last remark was so open that Hannibal wanted to ask a dozen questions, wanted to define and limit the possibilities, but Simpson offered no explanation and marched methodically out the door. Zennora now consented to let the men come upstairs, and Hannibal walked into the bedroom to find Susan sleeping, her mouth slackly open and dark circles under her eyes.

That very afternoon, Zennora moved her things into Susan's bedroom and banished Hannibal to a makeshift mattress in front of the fireplace. He wanted to stay at home, ready for whatever might happen, but she ordered him off to the mine, even arranging, for the first few days, for Jesse to walk him down to the mouth of the incline shaft. During the following weeks, he saw his wife only briefly, usually once in the morning and once in the evening, until he offered to read to her, and she, tired in spite of lying in bed all day, persuaded her mother to consent. She lay quietly, her head propped up on a pile of down pillows, and gazed out the window as he read the brief news items and anecdotes from the newspapers. Once he looked up from the page to find her staring straight at him with a strange expression—dismay? concern? curiosity?—before shifting her eyes down to the coverlet that Zennora had brought to lay across the bedclothes.

Their home became Zennora's headquarters for planning her younger daughter's wedding. Hannibal returned one afternoon to find Bessie standing in the parlor with Zennora on her knees, pinning up the hem of a new dress that the girl would wear on the day after her wedding. When Hannibal greeted them, both women looked up, annoyed, and Zennora hissed at him to keep his voice down for fear of waking Susan. Martin came to talk not with him but with Zennora, and the two of them intently discussed details regarding the ceremony and the festivities, leaving little room for him in the conversation. His brother had been more than usually reticent ever since the partners' meeting when Hannibal had challenged Edward; when Hannibal finally asked him if there was something on his mind, he raised his eyebrows, protesting his perplexity. He had bought a house in Grass Valley, just below the cemetery on a slope facing the town to the west, and Hannibal had been trying to help him get the place ready, but with Susan in bed, he felt obligated to stay at French Lead, even though Zennora insisted, repeatedly, that there was nothing he could do.

Early on the day of Martin's wedding, Hannibal was patrolling the drifts when one of the boys, flouting the safety rules, sprinted down the incline shaft to announce, breathlessly, that he must come home at once. He covered the distance in less than ten minutes, still in his underground clothes, caked with sand and clay, but as he started up the stairs, Bessie met him halfway and delivered Zennora's decree that he stay below. He stood next to the front door, loath to sit in any of the furniture, but not wanting to leave in order to clean himself. Finally, lost, he sat down on the floor and leaned against the wall. For the next three hours, he listened to the mystifying sounds from above: Zennora's even tones, occasional quick footsteps, the delicate splash of pouring water, but most conspicuously, Susan's whimpering.

She lay in the bed, hating it now, tired of feeling so heavy, exhausted from not walking, and met the pains with surprised outrage. Zennora had shut the window and drawn the curtains, so Susan felt even more stifled than during the past weeks. The cramps were worse than anything she had imagined—even Zennora's careful advice had not prepared her for this—and made her want to curl up and clasp her hands around her shins even while she felt compelled to spread her arms and legs, arch her back and give—what? By early afternoon, she had forgotten what day it was, how long she had been there, and even where she was and what she was doing. Zennora had given her a clean rag to twist in her fists and, if she chose, to dip into cool water and chew, and there were moments when, lying there with her eyes tightly shut, all she knew was the soggy cotton that she clenched between her teeth. Once Bessie bent over her just as a cramp stabbed her, and she swung her open hand around to grab her belly, slapping her sister across the face on the way. The girl retreated to a corner and sat there, sniveling, while Zennora tried to comfort them both. The cramps seem to build one on another, without giving her a rest, and she gave up trying to be brave, as her mother had urged, and simply screamed, not so much in pain, but in fury at her helplessness. Then, abruptly, she felt completely calm, even relaxed, so she shut her eyes for a moment, feeling the moist warmth of the lids against the cool, damp cloth that Zennora had laid across her forehead, and opened them to look around the room. Bessie was slumped against the side of a chair and Zennora was peeking past the window shade to look out at the trees standing outside. Susan took a deep breath and thought, It must be over soon, I must finish this, I can do this. The cramps took her again, so suddenly and so hard that she could hardly cry out, but Zennora smiled, patted Bessie to rouse her, and rearranged the bed clothes. Susan bit down on her rag and pulled with all her strength on the ends, pinning herself back on the pillow. Then, suddenly, she felt as if she must push, could not do anything but push as hard as she could, and her insides stretched unimaginably so that she was quite sure she would burst, and she slid through space, as though down a slick embankment into a deep, quiet stream, and she began to tingle all over. Zennora was rummaging around near her ankles, there was a strange, tiny cry, and Susan opened her eyes just as her mother laid the baby on her breast. His face was red and his eyes were a deep grey, almost black, soft but opaque, and she stared down at him as he began to suckle. She hardly noticed when Hannibal crept into the room to greet his son.

Late that afternoon, the spires of the Emmanuel Episcopal Church slowly turned ruddy as the wedding guests gathered, bringing their wagons slowly up Walsh Street to turn the corner and come to rest in front of the chapel, where the men tethered their horses and paused near the gate to brush the dust off of their best hats and coats. Hannibal made a great show of escorting Martin to the doorway and checking his coat, hat, tie and—new for the occasion—ruffled shirt, while Will Pascoe offered a bottle to his brother and the other younger men before bringing it over to insist that Martin take a drink. They all laughed, and Mark Chenoweth whispered something to Hannibal, who smiled and glanced over at Mark's wife, waiting with the other women, a bouquet of bonnets. At that moment, a black mare drew a smart buggy around the corner, and the men looked over to see the Sterlings: John driving, Mary sitting next to him, and Edward on her other side. John helped Mary down, and Edward escorted her into the church, barely nodding to the men near the door, while John stopped to exchange a joke and a drink with Will. Most of the men drifted over to them, leaving the Carnes in front of the church and old William Pascoe standing alone under a tree. The Trevennas arrived in Jesse's carriage, with Jack riding behind on a bay stallion that pranced and gummed his bit impatiently while waiting for his place at the hitching post. Jesse and Zennora escorted Bessie down to the doorway, where Martin doffed his hat, and into the church. The Carnes followed, and, after Will Pascoe had offered Jack and Nick a taste of his bottle, so did the rest.

Through the stained glass windows passed just enough of the fading light to create a dull glow in the chapel, and in spite of the constant murmur of the minister's voice, every guest became suspended in the bottomless quiet of the place. People might ride up Church Street on their way home at the end of the day, and wagons and drays on Mill Street might rumble and squeak back and forth between Boston Ravine and Grass Valley, but the apparently fragile timbers of the little church did, implausibly and reassuringly, create a sanctuary. They sat in little groups: Charles Nankervis and his sons with the Chenoweths, the Pascoes across the aisle, and the Sterlings two rows behind them, with Edward just slightly separated from John and Mary. Yet when the time came to sing a hymn, they rose as one:

> The power to bless my house
> Belongs to God alone;
> Yet rend'ring him my constant vows,
> He sends his blessings down.
> Me and my house receive,
> Thy fam'ly to increase;
> And let us in thy favour live,
> And let us die in peace.

Cousin Jack

Father Putnam continued the ritual, and Zennora moved her lips silently, unconsciously mouthing the words and barely remembering to speak aloud at those moments when the service required the congregation to answer the pastor. As she gazed up towards the altar, the glow from the windows divided, like a beam through a prism, into a thousand shades and hues, some brilliant and some soft, and the particles of dust passing through the beams glistened, seeming not to drift, but to dart here and there, swarming in one corner, then scattering across the altar to form up again in half a dozen little groups before ranging, randomly and languidly, through the air. She glanced surreptitiously at Jesse and Jack, sitting on either side of her, but both seemed oblivious to the dance that bewildered her. One particularly brilliant collection hovered for a moment directly over Bessie, and Zennora gasped as the little cloud of specks suddenly released and fell lightly on the bride's head and shoulders like a veil, there to twinkle and glimmer. Jesse glanced discreetly down at his wife, puzzled, and turned his gaze back to the minister. Zennora took a deep breath and smiled.

The service complete, the new couple walked back down the aisle, the guests in their wake, and everyone paused in front of the church, under the reflected flush of the sunset. Jack watched Zennora as she kissed the bride and groom, shook hands with most of the guests, and collected Joseph, who would drive her back to French Lead to sit with Susan. Edward mounted his buggy and sat impatiently, staring at John until Mary finally walked over to the knot of laughing men to persuade her husband to come away, and the Sterlings rode around the corner and down towards the creek. The rest of the party finally got into their wagons, Hannibal now driving Martin and Bessie, and headed north on Church Street to proceed through town and on to the couple's new home. Jack led the way, galloping his stallion ahead and back again, waving his hat at the passers-by.

Hannibal insisted that the bride and groom sit on either side of the fireplace like visiting royalty, and served cups of punch to the guests, parading around the room with an enormous silver tray. As soon as the rush of arrivals subsided, he took Jesse aside. "Will ye help me talk to William Pascoe about the Live Yankee?"

Jesse smiled incredulously. "'aven't ye enough t' busy yerself—a baby an' a weddin'?"

The younger man pursed his lips. "Every man we need is 'ere tonight. There'll not be a better chance."

Shaking his head, Jesse permitted Hannibal to take him by the elbow, and they found old William Pascoe out at the far corner of the porch, smoking his pipe. He had drunk two or three cups of Hannibal's punch, and his eye bore an uncharacteristic twinkle, but he showed no surprise at discussing business on such an occasion. Hannibal came to the point. "Them that are partners in the North Star need t' keep workin' there. We need someone else to take charge of the Live Yankee. Will ye do it?"

The old man looked over his shoulder and bellowed suddenly. "Will! Fetch yer brother!" When his sons walked out onto the porch, William asked Hannibal to repeat his proposal, and then he asked them, "What d'ye think?"

Will looked at James, folded his arms and raised his eyebrows. James stared down at his boots for a moment, then drained his cup and handed it to Hannibal. "We can do it."

William nodded. "There's yer answer."

Within five minutes, Hannibal had assembled all of the men on the porch, each with a full glass, even his brother, leaving the wives inside, clustered around the chattering Bessie. "Gentlemen: to the Live Yankee!" Nick, with the Chenoweths, gave a little cheer, and as the little ceremony dissolved, Hannibal took Martin aside. "Congratulations."

Martin grinned. "Thanks. And thanks for everythin'."

"I'm sorry I didn't 'elp more with the 'ouse, but . . . " Hannibal clapped a hand on his brother's shoulder. "Thanks for joinin' in on the Live Yankee."

Martin's smile faded and he studied Hannibal's face. They had not really talked since the acrimonious partners' meeting, and for a moment, each waited for the other to speak, to unbend. Then Martin lifted his chin slightly, and the corners of his mouth turned down. "Ye're welcome. But I doubt it'll come t' anythin'." Martin turned and walked into the house, leaving Hannibal there, stung. He took a deep breath and leaned on the porch railing, and out in the shadows, he thought he saw a horse and rider walking quietly away towards town.

As soon as he was out of earshot, Jack urged his horse to an easy canter along Wolf Creek, following it all the way down into Boston Ravine and up the slope towards French Lead. Soon he could see Susan's house through the trees, and the light of a bright fire shone through the downstairs windows. He swung down off of the saddle, walked up onto the porch, and knocked gently on the front door.

Zennora opened it. She had let her hair down and brushed it out, and it framed her face softly, making her look much younger than usual and, Jack thought, much more like Susan. "Jack."

He took off his hat. "Is Susan awake?"

Zennora stared full into his face, and Jack found that he could not look away. Her gaze held his, and he waited, wondering. Then Zennora's hair seemed to float away from her shoulders, the brown strands catching the firelight, but it was her eyes that held him, the green flecks glowing and now spinning like a flywheel, burning in her face. Jack tried to smile, but found that his face would not move, and he realized that he had stopped breathing. He wanted to reach out, to balance himself against the porch post, but he could not lift his arm.

Finally, Zennora spoke. "She's with th' baby. Go 'ome, Jack." And she shut the door. He stood on the porch, transfixed, breathing now, but cold. After a moment, he wondered whether anyone had answered the door at all. Perhaps he had knocked, and no one had opened, so he would, as he did now, mount his horse and ride back into the cool night.

9
The Menken
1864-65

Jack felt as though he were looking in a mirror. He had walked in the door of Findley's conference room to find his accustomed chair taken. Hannibal was sitting in it, so he sat down across from him, with Martin on his left and Samuel Nankervis on his right. The unfamiliar vantage inverted his perspective, so no one looked quite the same. Edward's head, he now noticed, tilted slightly to one side, and John's smile, now in profile, was so wide that the tip of his nose pulled down slightly every time he grinned.

The meeting was not going to be an easy one. After Edward finished his superintendent's report—all contracts met, stamps running to full capacity, net monthly profit still over four thousand dollars—Hannibal reviewed the situation beneath the surface, quickly covering the routine matters—how many men, how much powder, how much rock—and emphatically declared the new drainage tunnel to be a great success before leaning forward to urge the partners to bore the incline shaft deeper and open up another level. As soon as the thrust of his remarks became clear, Samuel and Seth began to glance at their father, and the Chenoweths shifted restlessly in their chairs. Mark looked around as though he wanted to put his feet up on something but then, remembering where he was, arranged himself rigidly against the leather upholstery.

The central issue—at least, apparently—was whether to expand underground or at the surface, and Jack knew how each man would take up position. John would argue in favor of expanding the territory that the company owned and controlled, and he would mention at least one claim, quite close to their mills, that was available. The Chenoweths would object, insisting that the grass crews would have to waste time roaming from site to site. Charles would speak little, if at all, but he and his sons would favor the underground expansion, for he condoned only those parts of the surface operation that were directly and clearly necessary for the miners to do their work—the pump, the hoist, and the stamp mill—and regarded the offices and even the smithy with sullen suspicion. Nick, if given a chance, would trace diagrams in the air above the table, mapping out the simple grace of the subterranean complex that he imagined so much clearly than anyone else. Martin would say nothing and defer to Hannibal, and through it all, Jesse would sit at his corner of the table and try to mediate.

Cousin Jack

The real problem, thought Jack, was Edward. More and more, he let John speak for him, and so sat silently at the head of the table, staring down its length at Charles, who returned his impassive, sinister gaze; a nearly matched pair of stone masks. Edward seemed firmly fixed in his position, but ever since Hannibal's outburst at the February meeting, the partners had begun to regard the superintendent warily, as though watching for signs of weakness, and Jack had been waiting for the next challenge, wondering who would bring it and who would step forward to take Edward's place.

Without warning, Edward leaned forward and rapped his knuckles on the table. The startled partners subsided. He looked from face to face, his own expression as unreadable as ever. He finished with Jesse, but turned his gaze back to Hannibal, and while he looked him in the eye, said, "It seems that some here disagree with my views on the future of the company." Richard Chenoweth sighed; Edward always referred to the North Star as "the company," while most of the others called it "the mine." "That being the case, I now call for a vote of confidence."

The quiet remark pre-empted all of the scenarios that Jack had imagined. He had thought that the crisis, when it came, if it came, would tumble, helter-skelter, from grievance and recrimination, the accusations crowding on each other until the belligerents ran out of ideas and the more reticent men were able to guide the meeting to some sort of resolution. He glanced around the room: Hannibal was nonplussed, the Chenoweths were looking at each other and the Nankervis boys to their father, while Martin had begun to drum his fingers on the table, a galloping riff, over and over again. Jack wondered if Edward's initiative would be enough, by itself, to sustain the partners' support.

Jesse folded his hands and leaned forward. "Is this truly needful, Edward?" He scanned the table. "Surely we may disagree among ourselves, but is there any man 'ere would take yer place?"

No one spoke for a long moment. Then Hannibal lifted his chin. "I would not, but I would 'ave another superintendent."

John opened his mouth to speak, but Edward lifted a hand and he froze. "And why would you not, Mr. Carne? You have spoken out against me for nearly a year. At every turn, you question me. Why not run the company yourself?"

Hannibal frowned uncomfortably, feeling the others' eyes on him. "My place is down below. But I won't deny I'd be 'appier with a different man in the office."

Jesse chewed on his lip and looked across the table. "Jack—how d'ye stand on this?"

Only last week, he had shared a pot of tea with Ah Choy, and the merchant had warned Jack against planning the next venture without paying proper attention to the one at hand. Jesse's question, so apparently casual, served to remind him that he, too, was a partner in the North Star, and that he must, at some point, take a position. But not now. "Edward is the superintendent. If he wishes to call for a vote of confidence, then we must respect that wish."

Edward nodded. "Jesse, since it is my work that is under scrutiny, will you manage the discussion?"

Reluctantly, Jesse turned to invite Nick to comment. When his nephew declined, he moved on to Hannibal, and so around the table, receiving a shake of the head from this man and an awkward cough from that, until he reached Martin. Hannibal raised his eyebrows as his brother, usually so taciturn, explained his position. "I don't see that th' partnership must agree with th' superintendent, or 'e with the rest. 'e runs th' mine as th' partners wish, just as you do, Hannibal. I favor sinkin' th' shaft deeper, and I'll vote against buyin' new property right now." He looked around the table. "But which of ye's ready to replace Edward? Which of ye's able? We're 'ard rock men. Adventurers now, it may be, but each man 'ere goes down th' shaft nearly every day." Jack noticed that he had swiveled slightly in his chair, giving the back of his shoulder to the Sterlings, and so addressed only the Cornishmen. "We need someone at grass t' do what we're unable or unwillin' t' do." From across the table, Hannibal was glaring at his brother, so angrily that Jack, sitting next to Martin, felt uncomfortable. "I know there may be a few 'ere who would stand fer superintendent, but none I'd accept."

Finished, he sat back in his chair. His last remark had nettled nearly every man at the table. Hannibal, his brow knit tightly, was about to say something, but Jesse spoke first. "Each man 'as 'ad 'is chance. Now we vote. Which of ye're willin' t' give Edward Sterling yer vote o' confidence?"

John raised his hand immediately, and then Martin. The Chenoweths sat with their arms folded, and the Nankervis boys looked over at their father, who sat staring down the length of the table as though nothing at all were happening. Jesse raised his own hand and looked at Jack, who hesitated. Finally, Jesse lowered his arm. "If ye're votin' fer yerself, Edward, that's four out o' twelve men, and barely 'alf th' shares. Now what is yer wish?"

Sterling rose and thrust a finger into his fob. "I will not continue without the support of the partners, so I ask you to select someone else. John has my proxy for the remainder of this meeting." With that, he turned and walked out of the room.

At first, Martin's warning seemed all too insightful, for no one volunteered for the position now vacant. In spite of Hannibal's disclaimer, Jesse asked him to consider accepting nomination, thinking, Jack guessed, to give him a clear chance so there would be no confusion later. Hannibal refused and, in turn, nominated Jesse. Everyone seemed to like the idea, even expect it. Jesse knew as much about hard-rock mining as anyone there, and everyone respected him. Yet Jesse declined, and refused to elaborate except to maintain that he was the wrong man for the job. The partners were disappointed and dismayed; even Charles Nankervis snorted in disgust when it became clear that Jesse would not budge. At that point, John assumed an unusually pious expression to suggest, obliquely and at considerable length, that he might be willing to serve, only for the good of the company. When he had finished speaking, no one answered him. Finally, Hannibal, not even acknowledging John's offer, looked across the table. "What about you, Jack?"

Jack stared into Hannibal's face. As superintendent, he would know no peace, none at all. Nankervis and the Chenoweths would almost certainly support Hannibal's views, and the Sterlings would oppose them. That would leave Jesse and, apparently, Martin in ambiguous positions. Nick would agree with Hannibal as long as they were extending tunnels, but he knew that his brother didn't really take any of this seriously. Besides, the job would tie him to the mine; he'd have little attention to spare for anything else. Still, the man who ran the North Star was a man that the community would respect, a man who would, as a matter of course, be included at the beginning of every important new venture. Conflicted and uncertain, he looked around the room, and what he saw made his decision. The partners might accept him as superintendent, but they had doubts; even Charles looked slightly suspicious and troubled. Yet the most disquieting face was Hannibal's. He was clearly trying to hide what he was thinking, but Jack saw something in his expression that was incongruously amused, even contemptuous. Suddenly, Jack realized that Hannibal had offered the suggestion only because he was confident that no one would support him. Why? Was Hannibal setting him up to lose a vote of confidence? Or was he stripping away the options in order to guide the meeting to some other conclusion?

"No . . . no, thank you. We must choose someone else."

Jesse shrugged. "Where does that leave us? Is there no man 'ere who's willin' and who the rest'll support?"

There was yet another silence, and Jack watched Hannibal scan the table before quietly announcing, "I'll nominate Nick." Nick looked at Hannibal, and the entire table looked at Nick. "No one knows the underground workings better than Nick, not even me. And 'e knows people in town. If 'e needs 'elp with th' books, then Jack can step in, or I can. With Nick as superintendent, we can work th' North Star the way she should be worked."

Jack wanted to laugh out loud. The notion was ludicrous; Nick never kept regular hours, even when he was needed, and there would be days, perhaps two or three at a time, when the mine would have to run without him. Yet the others seemed to be taking the proposal seriously; Mark Chenoweth was whispering to Richard, and Samuel had leaned over to ask his father a question. Then Charles spoke. "I'll favor Nick. The boys an' me."

The Chenoweths were still whispering when John announced, "Edward and I will also support him." Jesse simply stared, and Nick laughed aloud. Everyone at the table looked at John incredulously, but he seemed to be serious, even though he looked back at the others with his eyebrows raised slightly, as though protesting his sincerity.

With the Sterling and Nankervis shares added to those of Hannibal and Nick, the vote of confidence came to fourteen of twenty shares, and seven of twelve partners. The Chenoweths looked uncertain, and Martin sat with his arms folded. Jack was so dumfounded that he simply forgot to vote for his brother. When Jesse asked Nick whether he would accept the appointment, he grinned at Jack and said, "Iss fay!"

Hannibal and the Nankervis boys pounded their fists softly on the table, and Jesse, smiling now, asked whether the new superintendent had anything to say to the partners. Nick considered for a moment. "We'll start extendin' the incline shaft as soon as may be. And I'll ask Hannibal t' let me know 'ow soon we can support sixteen stamps." He grinned. "And if there's no more business, I declare this meetin' adjourned, and I'll buy a caulk for any man who'll join me next door t' crook an elbow!"

The men rose and followed Nick out. Jesse held the door for the others, but when he turned to scan the room, he found that Martin had stayed in his chair and was carefully watching Hannibal, who stood at the head of the table, hat in hand, interrupted. Jesse opened his mouth to speak, thought better of it, and turned to go. As his footsteps receded down the staircase, Martin shook his head. "Well, I hope ye're satisfied."

"Me?! What about you? Votin' fer Edward!"

"An' what 'ave we got now? Nick Trevenna!"

"Nick knows th' mine like no one else."

"And 'e's almost the youngest o' th' partners."

"What 'as that t' do with it?"

"The man is wild, Hannibal, and ye know it."

"'e's not."

"'e is. You wait—there'll be days when 'e won't show up at th' mine, an' no man will know where t' find 'im, not even Jack."

"'e'll be there."

"P'raps not." Martin's eyes narrowed. "Is that what ye wanted? A superintendent who's not there?"

"Of course not." Hannibal began pacing back and forth across the end of the room.

"Hannibal, if ye wanted t' be superintendent, why didn't ye just say so? They would have voted ye in with no trouble at all."

"I told you, and the rest, that I don't want th' job."

"Then who'll run it when Nicky goes missing? Ye're the underground captain; they'll all look to you."

"Nick'll be there."

"Think of it. Can ye imagine Nick comin' 'ere t' th' bank t' see Findley? Or askin' Dibble t' draw up a contract?"

"Nick knows everyone in town, an' they all like 'im."

"Iss fay, they like 'im—who wouldn't like 'im? 'e laughs with 'em, 'e drinks with 'em, 'e wrestles 'em an' then thanks th' man who brings 'im down. Of course they like 'im, but they won't take 'im seriously."

"'e's the superintendent of the North Star—they'll 'ave t' give 'im that."

"Oh, they'll do business, all right, but they'll find it different from workin' with Edward. 'alf o' th' men in town are afraid of Edward—they give 'im what 'e wants, when 'e wants it, and at th' price 'e offers."

"I can't work with 'im any more."

"What's th' man done but give us th' best advice 'e knew 'ow?"

"An' what kind of advice was that?"

"What does it matter? Don't ye see? The superintendent must do what th' partners wish. 'e didn't want t' put through that drainage tunnel ye're so fond of, but we did it anyway. 'e an' John 'ave been wantin' t' buy these neighborin' claims, but we 'aven't bought 'em. Where's the 'arm in Edward speakin' 'is mind?"

"Listen to ye!"

"Iss, listen to me."

"Martin—ye don't have t' work with th' man like I do."

"An' what 'as 'e done to you? P'raps ye don't like the way 'e looks at ye. Well, neither do I. But 'e's no worse than Nankervis, an' I don't hear ye complainin' about 'im."

"Nankervis idden superintendent."

"I know Edward's not like the rest of us."

"The man has no respect. 'e thinks 'e's better. Look at th' clothes 'e wears."

"There's nothin' wrong with wearin' a fine suit."

"Of course not, but 'e's makin' a point. 'e's settin' 'imself up as a gentleman, and I didn't come all th' way to this place just t' tip my 'at to a man like that."

"What's the matter, Hannibal? Aren't ye satisfied with th' way things are turnin' out? Idden it enough?"

"We're doin' better 'ere an' ye know it."

"Are we? I'm not so sure."

Hannibal threw up his hands, exasperated. "Then go back to Breage if ye like it so much!"

"I will!"

"What?"

"I will. I will go back t' Cornwall."

Hannibal stopped pacing. "Martin. What're ye talkin' about?"

Martin sighed. He had said it; he was committed now. "I had a letter from Mother last week."

"Is she all right?"

"Oh, she's hearty, but Uncle James is startin' to complain about the farm bein' so much work."

"What does that 'ave t' do with you?"

"Ye know 'e was talkin' about leavin' Penbro to one of us."

"Iss, but 'e's other nephews. I recall 'e was wantin' the Mitchells to 'ave the place."

"Well, now Mother thinks 'e wants one of us, or both of us, to 'ave it."

"Martin, th' man's 'ardly sixty. It'll be ten years before 'e gives it up. Fifteen."

"Mother thinks 'e's gettin' tired."

"So ye're goin' back t' milk 'is cows 'til 'e decides t' die."

Martin frowned. "There's no need for ye t' get so piffed about it. What's it t' you?"

Hannibal sat down next to his brother. "Martin, we're doin' so well here. The mine'll do better an' better. The Live Yankee might strike a vein. And ye just got married—what does Bessie say about it?"

"She'd as soon go 'ome as stay. Besides, ye know we never meant t' stop here."

"P'raps not, but now's not th' time t' leave."

Martin smiled slightly. "Hannibal, when will th' time come? I'm startin' t' think ye'll raise yer grandchildren 'ere."

"And what if I do?"

"Are ye serious? Stay 'ere? Never see Cornwall again?"

"Martin, I'm tellin' ye that we can do well 'ere, better than we're doin' now."

"Does Susan know ye want t' stay?"

"I 'aven't said I want t' stay. All I'm sayin' is that there's no call t' go back just yet."

Martin shook his head. "Well, p'raps not, but I'm goin' anyway. Penbro or no, I've enough to buy a 'ouse and garden and set up as an adventurer at one o' th' copper mines near Helston."

Hannibal laughed, a short bark. "Ye're a regular pattick, Martin Carne. Ye're walkin' away from a fortune."

Martin rose. "Look to yerself—ye've been fightin' with Edward, and just because 'e's no longer superintendent doesn't mean 'e'll vanish. And then there's Nick—one o' these days, ye'll come to the mine and find 'im missin' and somethin' not done, and ye'll kick up a chivvy."

"That's not so."

"No? An' what about the Live Yankee? Ye know that Jesse signed only because 'e couldn't figure out how t' say no t' ye."

"If ye won't take a chance, ye'll end up with nothin'. I think ye're goin' back because ye're scared."

Martin sucked at his lower lip and stared at the ornate brass sconce glaring from the velvet-papered wall. "I didn't want t' leave like this. I'm sorry, Hannibal—I 'ope ye're 'appy 'ere." With that, he turned and walked out of the room, leaving his brother sitting at the table.

Inside the saloon next door, Jack and the Chenoweths were trying to sing a hymn in harmony, but Nick kept interjecting mischievous changes to the lyrics, and the others were laughing too hard to stay with the beat. Martin let Nick order him a beer but managed to take him over to a table in a corner. No matter what anyone said, Nick laughed in response, and Martin wondered whether he were really drunk or simply putting on a show. "Listen to me, Nick. I'm goin' back t' Cornwall." Nick laughed and turned around to wave at the others, but Martin stopped him. "I'm not ready t' tell everyone yet. But I need t' tell you."

"Why?"

"I'm goin' t' sell my shares in th' North Star."

Nick stopped smiling. "Well, then ye'll sell 'em to Hannibal, won't ye? What d'ye mean, ye're goin' back to Cornwall? For good?"

"Iss, for good. An' I don't want t' sell t' Hannibal."

"Martin—ye just got married." Nick began to giggle. "Ye just bought a 'ouse. How can ye be leavin'?"

"I can. Listen, Nicky—I want t' sell my shares t' you."

Nick sat back in his chair and looked at Martin. "T' me?"

"T' you."

"Why?" Nick had dropped his playful manner and was looking intently across the table.

"Ye're th' superintendent now, but ye 'ave only one share in th' mine. I've two. If I sell t' you, ye'll 'ave three, an' I think ye'll need 'em."

"What for?"

"Part o' th' reason we made Edward superintendent was that 'e 'ad four shares on 'is own, an' John 'ad three more. Ye need t' be a major partner. If ye buy mine, and ye can count on Jack and Jesse, that's five shares goin' yer way."

"What about Hannibal?"

"What about 'im?"

"Can't I count on 'im, too?" Nick was watching Martin carefully, waiting for the answer.

Martin looked down into his beer glass. "I can't say. But if 'e does vote with ye, that's two more."

Nick thought for a moment. "Ye know I 'aven't the money." Martin had not known that, but he wasn't surprised. "I'll 'ave to borrow it. Jack's right over there—can I tell 'im?"

Still grinning from the foolery at the bar, Jack heard the news without surprise. "Can ye raise th' money, Nick?"

"I don't think so."

"Martin," said Jack, "can ye take Nick's note?"

Martin shook his head. "I trust ye, Nicky, but I'll be needin' th' money t' set up at 'ome. Jack—can ye 'elp us out?"

Jack sat back and stared up at the ceiling for a moment. Then he looked at the two men again. "I think so." He grinned and punched Nick in the arm. "What d'ye 'ave to put up for the money, lad?"

Nick gestured for the other two to lean in over the table, and he whispered, "I've two shares o' th' best mine in Grass Valley!"

The others laughed, and Jack said, "Ye've three shares, you noggy, but I'll take your note on two." The three men shook hands on the arrangement and got up to leave. Nick stopped to buy another drink for the Chenoweths, but Jack followed Martin out to the street. "What does Bessie think about it?"

"She may miss 'er mother, but I think she'll be all right."

"D'ye think Jesse'll stop 'ere?"

"I don't know. What d' you think?"

Jesse asked that question himself when he heard Martin's news, but he had no answer, and he found that he was preoccupied with losing Bessie. The girl promised him that they would see each other, perhaps every other year or so, and Jack assured him that the railroad would go through before too long, and that the trip back to England would be no more than a train to New York and a ship to Liverpool, but Jesse found little comfort in the prospect. He had felt lonely when each of the girls married, even though Susan was only a step away. He had thought that with his daughters gone, he might grow closer to Joseph, but the boy had little to say, and there was something strange about him. Two or three times each week, Jesse would look up from his chair to see his son standing awkwardly in the doorway, not wanting anything in particular, but simply there, a pointless presence. Zennora seemed to understand him, but although she had accepted the news of Bessie's departure with her usual aplomb, she now drove herself into town every single day to visit her younger daughter.

Cousin Jack

When Hannibal told Susan of Martin's decision, she sat in her chair, staring, and he realized that her color was mounting, sending a flush all through her face. He tried to tell her that surely she and Bessie would see each other now and then, but as soon as the gist of his remark became evident, she rose, snatched up the baby, and walked out the door, heading for her mother's house.

She was seething; she felt hot all over, and she hardly realized that tears were spilling out of her eyes and falling onto her dress. That Bessie should be going home! Bessie, who giggled, Bessie who had to be shown the simplest task three times, and most of all, Bessie, who cared nothing about where she was. She would escape from these dry hills and go home. Even if she had to live in Breage or Helston, near Martin's family, that was less than ten miles from Camborne, scarcely two hours' ride. Susan marched into her mother's house, outraged, but found little sympathy. Zennora was caught between her own disappointment and her pleasure at Martin and Bessie getting what, she assumed, they wanted. When Susan tried to explain that she felt pre-empted, robbed, Zennora patted her on the hand and took the baby, looking down at his little nose and suggesting mildly that, after all, Susan's duty lay with her husband. Susan took that thought home again, and, that evening, asked Hannibal whether he, too, might decide that the time had come to draw his American stay to a close, but his lips tightened and he answered shortly, almost rudely, remarking only that there was no need to leave California just yet, and sat down behind a newspaper he had just received from San Francisco.

For several days, Susan could hardly sit still, so she started to have trouble nursing the baby. She was beginning to wonder how long she could go on so when Zennora invited the entire family over for supper. Restless, Susan left Bertie in her mother's arms, hissing strict instructions not to trust him with Bessie, and walked outside to sit on a granite boulder and watch the last light fade from the sky. She heard a footstep, and turned to see Jack lighting a cigar. He puffed on it, carefully drawing the flame into the rolled leaves, and pinched the match between two wet fingers before letting it fall onto the pine needles. He looked down at her, and when she could not read his expression, she decided that he was examining her in some strange, intrusive way. Just as she was about to snap at him, he turned his head and blew a stream of smoke up into the branches.

"It must be 'ard for you, 'avin' Bessie go back." She didn't answer, but after a long moment, he spoke again. "I've been thinkin' about goin' with 'em—with Bessie an' Martin."

She frowned. "For how long?"

"I'm not sure. P'raps for a while, p'raps not."

"Ye mean ye might stay?"

He rolled the cigar gently between his teeth so that the tip waggled up and down. "I might. I 'aven't been back for six years—I might not like it. I'd 'ave to find out what there is for me to do."

She remembered the time Jack had taken her up to Bennett Hill and convinced her that he would stay in California, and she wondered if he had been fooling with her then, or was fooling with her now. For Bessie to return to England was bad enough, but for Jack to go . . . For days now, she had felt as though she were about to explode, and she wondered how long she could go on feeling like that. She looked up and saw Jack gazing down at her, concerned, the cigar down at his side.

"Do you want me to stay 'ere, Susan?" She stared at him, incredulous. He waited for an answer, but she didn't speak. "Would you like me to stay?"

For a strange, dizzy moment, she remembered an afternoon back in the Gwennap Pit when Jack had asked whether she wanted him to come with her family on a picnic to the rocks near St. Ives. She closed her eyes, trying to settle her mind, and then opened them again to look into Jack's face. His features seemed to blur and shift, as though in a nightmare, alternating between the boy she remembered and the man she had been so convinced that she loved, but at the last, he was a stranger, someone who understood nothing about her, an intruder with probing questions, an invader. She took a deep breath, placed her hands on her thighs and rose, trying to stand as firmly as she could, hoping that her voice would sound as serene as Zennora's.

"That's your decision, Jack. What difference could it make t' me?" She walked back to the house, up onto the porch, and in through the front door to check on the baby.

Like Jack, Hannibal found Susan inaccessible. He sensed the anger and hurt, but she hid those feelings behind her impatient, annoyed eyes. Whenever he tried to talk to her, she would stop him in mid-phrase to tend to the baby, cuddling Bertie in her arms and bending her face down to his, or wiping the shining spittle off of his chin, or changing him. She was crisp and efficient, as though she and her husband were mere acquaintances or men arranging a matter of business, usually turning to him with raised eyebrows, as to a tiresome, uninvited visitor, whenever he asked a question or walked into the room. After a few days of this, Hannibal gave up trying to converse with her about anything but the simplest, most routine matters, and he began spending more and more time at the mine.

As the grass, already brown, turned crisp, and the pine needles released their scent into the hot, still afternoons, Hannibal became increasingly preoccupied with his brother. Martin was the elder by a year, but he had always stood slightly in the background, content to follow Hannibal's lead and let him speak for both of them. So well did they agree that when they were negotiating a deal, they almost never had to step aside in order to consult with each other. The difference of opinion over Edward and Nick, and the way in which it had unfolded, had defined a gap between them, and they, unaccustomed to the distance, did not know how to traverse it.

In September, after a meeting at the mine office, Nick told Hannibal that Martin had accepted an offer to buy his home on Bennett Street, and he was making specific plans for the move back to Cornwall. Hannibal stood next to the hoisting engine, oblivious to the noise, as other men marched past him, each intent on some task or other. He took off his hat and lifted his face to sun, shutting his eyes to feel the heat stretch his skin and dry the sweat on his forehead. He thought of Breage, of the cold wind freshening up from Mount's Bay, spreading trembling patterns across the water of Loe Pool and laying flat the grass around the old stone church, its battlements standing so secure against the storm that even the bells in the tower barely shivered in the heaviest gales, and its gargoyles grimacing, forever frozen against the grey sky. He held the image for a long moment, put on his hat, and walked over to the stable to saddle his horse for the ride into town.

He found Martin standing on a ladder, nailing a piece of trim onto the edge of the porch. His brother glanced down at him as he drew near, but he finished driving the nail and checked the wood for splits before climbing down the ladder and inviting Hannibal to join him in the shade of the overhang. Below them lay Wolf Creek, the water crowded with blackberry brambles, and beyond it the shacks and cobbled towers of Chinatown.

Martin wiped his face and the back of his neck with a dirty handkerchief, then folded up the cloth into a neat square, lining up the corners and pushing at the wrinkles with his fingers. "Hannibal . . . I'm sorry I didn't offer ye th' chance to buy my shares in the North Star." Hannibal was surprised. Martin's quiet sale to Nick had stung, but he had said nothing to anyone. "I know I should 'ave. I was fair cagged with ye, an' I truly thought Nick would need the extra votes."

Hannibal took off his hat and picked a bit of a stick out of the brim. "I know ye think I made a mistake, pushin' Edward out like that. But I tell ye, th' man was gettin' me in a way. Ye don't know what he can be like."

"Well, p'raps not. Anyway, you'll be 'ere, not me."

"Martin."

"Yes."

"What about yer share in the Live Yankee?"

Martin stretched his legs out as far as they would go and sat regarding the toes of his boots. "Ye're convinced that ye'll find a vein, aren't ye?"

"There's a fair chance."

"Could be. What would ye rather? That I keep th' share or sell it t' you?"

"Whatever ye wish."

"Truly?" Hannibal nodded, and Martin considered. "Well, I'll keep it, then. But I'll assign my vote t' you."

"Thank'ee, Martin."

And so the two brothers reconciled, finishing the quarrel as they began it, almost casually, as though nothing had happened. Gazing out over the valley, they spoke of home. The letters from Keziah, their mother, had been growing more and more pious of late; she was walking to the churchyard nearly every day to weep in front of the little row of four gravestones, all lined up next to the tall one that bore their father's name. Hannibal had finally written to their aunt to ask whether Keziah were still able to take care of herself. Hester assured him that she was well and capable—after all, she was not yet fifty—but lonely in the empty cottage at Pellar Row, and she lightly reproached the boys for leaving so soon after their sister died of diphtheria, such a helpful girl, so attached to her mother, staying at home even though grown, so sad to watch her join the others in the churchyard. The men imagined Martin's homecoming—who would be there to greet him and Bessie? Keziah, of course, and Hester and her husband, and Uncle James. That was all. Bessie would want to go to Camborne, to introduce Martin to Jesse's sisters and their children. Hannibal wondered whether all the families in Penwith had lost so many men; so many miners had gone to Australia and America, and some never returned, leaving mothers and children at home to sing hymns in the little chapels.

Martin rose abruptly. "Well, there'll be one man at least! And Uncle James idden as old as he might think. We'll see about Penbro—there may be somethin' there."

Martin and Bessie left Grass Valley in early October, and Jack went with them. He had dallied with the idea for weeks and seemed to be looking for someone to help him decide what to do or, more likely, assure him that his preference, whatever it might be, was the right one. One evening, he walked Jesse home from the mine, talking casually about this and that, but then mentioned that he might go, and let the remark hang in the ensuing silence, as though he were waiting for Jesse to ask him to stay, perhaps to tend to business at the North Star, or to confer on him an important errand in Cornwall, something that would validate the journey. Jesse later discovered that Jack had tried the same tactic on Zennora, who only smiled and patted his arm, and on Nick, who laughed and wished him luck. Hannibal, when he realized what Jack wanted, lost his temper and told him to go or stay, but to get on with it. Yet he kept playing with the idea, hinting that he might return to Cornwall permanently, but in the next breath mentioning business he would undertake on his return. Susan had no patience with him; when he brought up his ostensible dilemma at a family supper, she snorted, rose from the table, and stalked out of the room.

The family gathered in the lobby of the Exchange to wait for the stage to Marysville. Martin had already shipped most of their belongings, so they were carrying only the clothes they would want on the voyage, and the trunks and bundles formed a mound next to the swinging double doors. Nick had taken Martin and Jack to the saloon for a last drink, while Susan sat on a velvet cushion and tried to comfort the baby, who persisted in crying and squirming fretfully. He kept trying to crawl off of her lap, but whenever she put him down on the carpet, he howled and reached up for her, so she lifted him back up again, there to struggle. Hannibal sat with her, asking what he could do to help, but she released him, knowing that he would rather drink with his brother than sit with a woman and a complaining infant. She looked for Zennora, wishing for her help, but she was sitting in a corner talking intently to Bessie. Then she heard a team of horses draw up in front of the hotel, and Jesse stepped in to call out that the stage had arrived.

The leave-taking seemed almost casual and effortless at first: firm handshakes and brief embraces, and only a few words. The mound of luggage vanished from the lobby and reappeared on top of the coach, where the freight man covered it with a tarp and lashed it down tightly. The driver called for the passengers to board, and Martin helped Bessie up and through the door to her seat. She settled herself down, patted her skirts, looked out the open window to wave at her mother, and then, abruptly, her face crumpled. She gulped for air as the tears actually sprang from her eyes, wetting the sill next to her. Susan, striving to get little Bertie under control, even if only for a moment, looked up towards her sister, but just at that moment, Jack stepped in front of her. He put his hands on her shoulders, but she had to shrug him off to adjust the baby. He leaned down to kiss her, so she turned her head, presenting her cheek. She tucked Bertie's blanket around his chin and looked furtively up at Jack. The innocent blue eyes looked wounded, strangely out of proportion, she thought, and she could not decide how to read his expression: disappointment? concern? regret? Bertie kicked and struggled, so she bent down to him, and when she looked up again, Jack was swinging himself up into the compartment. The freight man shut the door behind him, the driver called to the team, and the coach rolled slowly up the hill, with Bessie still sobbing inconsolably in the window.

In the days that followed, Susan found that she was marking the journey in her mind, even while she cleaned the house, tended to the baby, and visited her mother. Now they were in San Francisco, now stopping on the coast of Mexico, now crossing the Isthmus, and on towards England. Martin sent Jesse a telegram from New York, another from Liverpool, and a final message when they reached Helston, and on that evening, Susan felt drained and dull.

Throughout the autumn, Susan and Hannibal walked carefully through the house as though they were strangers and guests, each loath to disturb the other, each careful to replace things—a chair, a book, a pillow—as they had been, so that there would be no sign that anyone had disturbed the arrangement. At meals, they were polite, and when Bertie needed attention, Hannibal would ask, courteously, whether he could help in some way, and Susan would respond, with equal formality and restraint, that there was no need. Only the baby's unpredictability prevented their daily routine from becoming a ritual, as symmetrical and precise as a piece of needlepoint. Susan never went anywhere except to her mother's house, and at Christmas, she looked up from slicing a saffron cake to see Zennora studying her, concerned and troubled.

This precarious promenade continued into mid-January, until the evening that Nick knocked on the door to say that he had received a letter from Penzance. Jack had gotten married. The girl was the daughter of a builder, a man Jack had met through a banker, and they had arranged the wedding scarcely a month after Jack's return. Clara, wrote Jack, was very excited about living in California, so they would be sailing from Liverpool immediately after the New Year.

Listening to Nick read the letter, Susan felt completely dislocated. Not only did this abrupt marriage leave her stunned, as though someone had punched her in the belly and set her gasping, she realized that Jack was already at sea, and would, in a month or so, be escorting his new wife around the streets of Grass Valley. She could hardly manage the idea; somehow, she had not expected Jack to return, at least not so soon, and she could not quite envision him bringing this strange woman to dinner at Zennora's house. Suddenly, she felt as though she were about to stifle, so she rose to her feet, handed Bertie to Hannibal, wrapped her shawl around her shoulders and, without a word, walked out the door and beyond the porch to stand next to a tall pine tree and try to breathe in the cold, dry air. The moon, only a few days short of full, shone through the branches of the trees on the crest of the saddle that separated her from Wolf Creek. Somewhere over her head, there was a faint flutter of wings, a night hunter, and beyond her mother's house, she could hear the grinding of the hoisting engine as it lifted the ore cars up out of the shaft. She closed her eyes and sighed. Then she opened them to study the little house where, implausibly, she lived. The bare trunk of the trumpet vine traced a wandering line up one of the porch posts and lay spraddled on the orderly cedar shingles of the simple shed roof. The firelight flickered through the window pane, and she could see Nick sitting in a chair and gesturing with one hand. She walked down the slope and back in the front door. The men looked up at her as she took off her shawl and draped it over a peg on the wall. "Nick," she said, "Can I get ye somethin' hot t' drink?" On her way back with the tray, she passed behind Hannibal and ran her fingers lightly from the point of his shoulder up to the hair at the nape of his neck. He looked up at her, his eyebrows raised, the beginning of a smile on his lips.

Cousin Jack

Jack discovered that Clara's presence in San Francisco was a repeated surprise. He had learned the city on his own, so his wife seemed an interloper, and more than once, when he paused on the street to look at a landmark, he forgot, for a moment, that she was there, and so turned and stumbled into her. He could not imagine how she felt about visiting this strange place with a man she had known for only three months, but he gave up trying to discern her feelings from her perfectly round face, calm hazel eyes, and impenetrable smile. They had planned to stay in the city for five days before going on to Grass Valley, and he had promised to take her to see at least one of the theatrical exhibitions. She left the choice to him, so he bought tickets to *Mazeppa*, not bothering to explain that he could not resist a chance to see Adah Isaacs Menken, the notorious actress, whose exploits he had heard described at length by a man in the hotel saloon.

The Menken had arrived from Panama on the *Palace Queen,* disembarking to a cheering crowd who applauded her traveling costume, a flamboyant confection of yellow chiffon, feathers and lace. Tom Maguire had escorted her to a reception at the Opera House, where she met everyone in San Francisco; that is, everyone who counted, from Mayor Coon and his belching wife to the mad, infatuated writers of *The Golden Era.* The Menken charmed them all so that each fascinated guest went home convinced that the actress was the epitome of gentility—so elegant and cultivated, so refined and sophisticated. They did not realize that their regard for her was pure narcissism, for she had succeeded in incarnating San Francisco's own aspirations, becoming the emblem of the style that the city wanted the rest of the world to admire behind the Golden Gate. Unconsciously and subliminally flattered, the citizens found the Menken so dazzling and convincing that when she presented them with a scene normally relegated to the saloons and brothels of the Barbary Coast, they accepted the performance as High Art. The Menken had seduced the city.

Jack and Clara had just settled into their seats when the curtain rose, bugles blared, and a collection of actors in extravagant costumes marched on, more and more until the stage was full of them. The Menken and several of the men pretended to fight with swords and rode back and forth on broken-down horses who lurched into stiff, reluctant trots only when the actors whipped them and yelled ferociously. A beautiful young woman sobbed because she could not marry the man she loved. There was another gaudy procession, and the Menken, wearing a helmet with nodding black plumes, pretended to fight and defeat a man in a gold doublet. A group of soldiers ran on stage, stripped off her outer costume, and carried her to a horse surrounded by a dozen torches that flared wildly, casting distorted shadows on the back scene.

As they strapped her to the horse, it stamped and snorted, shying away from the flames, and in the process, her shift pulled, as if by accident, away from her shoulders. Music played, and the horse began walking up the series of cantilevered ramps that represented the mountainside of Casimir's precipitous climb, and with each turn and stumble, the Menken's shift pulled away a little farther until it fell off completely and revealed her, apparently naked except for a small white loin cloth. All over the theatre, sweating men studied the spectacle through their opera glasses, trying to see in the uneven gaslight exactly where the tights left off and the Menken began. She twisted on the back of the horse, writhing her arms, straining with her thighs and calves, reaching for the horse's flanks with her bare toes, arching her back to raise her pelvis, and throwing her dark curls back and forth over her anguished face. There was enough play in the ropes so that she could roll to one side far enough to caress the horse's back luxuriously with one breast, and then roll back to offer the other. There was a slight sheen of sweat on her brow and bosom, and her cheeks flushed red over her parted lips. Jack sat a little forward in his seat, his mouth fallen slightly agape, while Clara, next to him, had apparently turned to stone, her eyes amazed and unblinking, her breath coming in short rasps, and her color mounting as high as the Menken's. The horse climbed farther and farther up on the scenery, once nearly losing its footing and tottering off the precipice as the agitated body on its back strained at the ropes and the audience gasped in unison. The Menken cried out, and the beautiful young woman tried to run to her, but two men held her by the arms, so she wailed and wept. The music reached a climax as the horse disappeared beyond the highest corner of the scenery and the curtain fell to the stage.

Jack took a deep breath and looked at Clara, who had brought out her handkerchief and was patting her face. She seemed dazed, and did not answer when he asked whether she wanted to go for a walk, so he left her there and pushed his way into the lobby, where a fat man in shirtsleeves served him a tall glass of beer. He stood next to a marble statuette and took a long draft; the beer was warm. At every moment, he heard the name of the Menken from a dozen excited voices. Someone rang a bell, and Jack returned to his seat. There were two more acts, but he hardly understood what was happening, carrying away only confused impressions of shepherds dancing in a frenzy, men in sheepskin vests walking about under canvas awnings, actors shouting and crying, more brightly-colored costumes, and sudden bursts of gunfire like firecrackers popping in the night air.

When the curtain fell for the last time, the audience rose to its feet, and everyone seemed to be cheering as the stage filled with actors, bowing and striking poses for the audience. They all walked off, and the Menken appeared alone, standing in the center of the stage with the footlights shining up under her chin. She bowed, and yellow roses flew from all parts of the theatre to land on the stage. She bowed again, her head low and her arms outstretched, and a small leather sack landed near her with a firm thump. Another followed, and another. The Menken lifted her face and kissed both hands to the crowd. From a box hanging over the corner of the stage, a burly man in a tailored suit rose to his feet, waited until the Menken looked over at him, and tossed her a shining bar of silver the size of a thick pencil. It spun through the air, twirling, twinkling in the lights. The Menken smiled, lifted one hand slowly, languidly, and caught it easily. She laughed. The applause turned to an overwhelming roar.

As soon as they reached the lobby, Clara nearly ran to the ladies' lounge, so Jack waited for her, and as the crowd dispersed, he noticed a thin man, probably younger than his full mustache made him seem, standing on a landing, waving a cigar decoratively in the air and addressing a little knot of smiling men and women. "Graceful? I can't say. She moves like a dancing-jack, cavorting to this side and that, bending herself back like a bow, and rolling over like a pack mule at the end of the trail. A fine equestrienne? Perhaps. That brute she was riding seemed more concerned with the fiddlers in the orchestra than with the wild Poles who were grabbing his bridle. One of those fellows looked downright exercised when he thought that animal was going to decline to ramble up those painted mountains. I once saw a circus horse stop to chew some new grass at the edge of the ring and pay no mind at all to the fellow in the tall silk hat; could be this is his brother-in-law." His listeners chuckled, and he placed the cigar between his lips, inhaling until the tip glowed brightly and sending a stream of smoke out from under his ginger-colored mustache. He noticed Jack watching him. "Here's a fresh face—p'raps a fresh opinion. And you, sir—how might you describe the fiery steed that provided the Menken with such a challenge!"

Jack swallowed, stammered and shrugged slightly.

"Now, sir, don't be shy—this ain't Washoe, you know—folks here are civilized—a man can speak his mind without fear of a pistol shot in the morning!" His admirers laughed again, watching Jack, waiting to see what he would do. Jack finally managed to suggest that the horse was, perhaps, not quite so wild as the proprietor seemed to want everyone to believe. As he spoke, the man's eyebrows shot up, then came together over his gleaming eyes. "Now, sir, could it be—am I addressing an Englishman—a subject of our friend the Queen?" Jack admitted that he was English, and the man stepped down off of the landing to offer his hand. "Welcome to America, sir, that is, if we can properly claim this remote hamlet to be part of America. I have always wanted to visit your green island, but my horse took a wrong turn somewhere back in Missouri, so here you find me." The others laughed again, and started to move off as the man drew Jack aside.

"Twain is my name. Mark Twain." Jack introduced himself, and Twain puffed on his cigar again. "So—how does John Bull regard our lady of the stage? Hmm?" Jack began to wonder whether the man was mocking him, but he replied that he found the performance astonishing in every way. Twain's eyebrows rose again. "Astonishing? Hmm. Yes, well perhaps you in London are better versed in such matters." Jack assured him that he had never visited London. Twain seemed mildly surprised, and took another puff on his cigar. "Well, surely after a man has seen San Francisco, all else pales. But tell me—" He appraised Jack from under his eyebrows, never losing the smile at the corners of his mouth. "—would you care to meet the Menken? I assure you, sir, that I can arrange it."

Just at that moment, Clara joined them, and Jack explained Twain's offer. She looked at the stranger for a moment, and then at Jack. Her face seemed different, and for a moment he had the absurd notion that she was not really his wife, but someone posing as her. She considered him for a moment, and then tucked her fingers into the crook of his arm. "You go," she said calmly, "but first take me back to the hotel."

Twain accompanied them down the street and waited in a tall leather chair while Jack escorted Clara to their suite, where she retreated to the bedroom with barely a word. He returned to the lobby, and the American led him up the street, around the corner and into a block of shadows where lone men slipped along the sidewalk without looking up. They stopped in front of a stone building. The windows were perfectly dark, but as they approached the door, Jack thought he could hear voices within.

Twain lifted his stick and knocked on the door, which opened immediately to release a cloud of heat and noise. Inside was a suite of rooms, all hung in vermilion velvet and laid in thick cobalt rugs, adorned with crystal chandeliers that cascaded across the ceiling, and a liberal sprinkling of gas fixtures, each with its own pristine reflector. To the left was a saloon with an enormous, etched mirror, a long counter of dark, polished walnut, and a brass footrail gleaming impeccably in spite of the many boots now placed upon it. To the right were green baize tables where groups of men were playing poker, the chips competing with nuggets and bags of dust, all under little clouds of smoke from fine cigars; in the midst of the tables, a dozen men and women crowded around a raucous game of craps. The center room looked like the lobby of a fine hotel, furnished with comfortable chairs and small carved tables, where men conversed in knots of two and three, sometimes with women hanging on prosperous arms and laughing. Each man wore a rich, dark suit with elegant boots; each woman wore a gaudy gown that left her arms and bosom bare. As Jack and Twain handed their hats and coats to the butler in the foyer, one man left his friends and climbed the stairs with a woman who kept a firm grip on his elbow and a careful eye on his face. Twain beckoned to Jack, and they walked over to join the group at the craps table.

Rattling the dice from the head of the table was the Menken. Her hair was slicked back close to her skull, and instead of her stage makeup, she wore only the slightest hint of rouge, a subtle plum outline around her lips, and charcoal drawn dark and clear across each full eyebrow. Her suit was as fine as any man in the room, but it was made of closely-woven lavender linen, with a vest displaying a pattern of Chinese dragons embroidered in orchid silk. She clenched a long, brown cigar between her grinning teeth, leaving both hands free to shake the dice, hurl them down the table, and spread her arms in supplication, or perhaps incantation. As she threw them down, nearly everyone at the table leaned in and cheered. Only two seemed not to notice the play, for they seemed hypnotized with the Menken. One was a tall man wearing a diamond stick pin and a bushy grey mustache, and the other was one of the women of the brothel, spellbound and vulnerable beneath her garish paint and nodding feathers.

Jack felt a hand on his arm, and turned to see Twain looking at him with a small smile. "'Age cannot wither her, nor custom stale her infinite variety.' Just when the public think they know who the Menken is, she re-invents herself. Who is she? The women you saw riding naked at the theatre? The gambler you see before you? The lady of fashion that arrived from Panama last year? You can be sure of only two things: that she will remain in the public eye, and that she will surprise you."

Twain lit a cigar as the onlookers roared, and Jack looked down to discover that the Menken had thrown a deuce—crapped out. She laughed and threw a few bills down towards the croupier, who nodded his thanks. The Menken moved away from the table, still smoking, and the man with the diamond stick pin followed her, taking her arm and murmuring something in her ear. She laughed again and shook her head. He persisted, finally reaching into his pocket and bringing out a roll of bills. The Menken looked at the money and began to frown, but two uproarious couples arrived at that moment to pull away towards the saloon, so she smiled and waved at her admirer, who set his jaw, put away his money, and vanished into a faro game in a dark corner of the casino.

Jack turned to say something to Twain, but found that his companion was leaning over a marble-topped table and carrying on a vehement conversation with two men Jack had not noticed before. He stood there for a moment, watching Twain, and turned and looked into the saloon where the Menken was sitting. She had one knee crossed over the other, and she smoked a new cigar as she tilted her chin at the men sitting on either side. Jack noticed the woman of the brothel, the one he had seen at the craps table, standing far to one side of the wide archway that led to the saloon from the sitting room. She was still staring at the Menken. Her mouth hung open slightly, and she was panting, so her bare bosom, pushed up by her stays, billowed and collapsed in hasty jerks. When a man walked up and leaned down to say something in her ear, she turned and snarled at him. Finally, Jack found his hat and coat, let himself out into the street, and walked back to his hotel.

Jack entered the bedroom to find one of the gas fixtures still burning very low, its dim light casting faint shadows on the embossed wallpaper and over Clara's sleeping form. He could hear the cries of late-night revelers passing on the street beneath his window. Quickly and quietly, he changed into his night shirt, turned the covers back, and reached for the gas.

"Leave it alone." He looked down, surprised. Clara had rolled over onto her back and was looking at him, fully awake. The coverlet had fallen away and her shoulders were bare. "Get in." He obeyed. Under the bedclothes, she was completely naked.

She pulled him to her and wrapped her arms and legs tightly around him, opening her mouth for a long kiss. She ran her hands up and down his body, exploring, probing, experimenting, and finally ripping his night shirt in her determination. She took his hand and guided it, now on her face, now on her breasts, now on her belly, now on her thighs, and finally on her vulva. With her arms entwined around his neck and her lips and tongue finding his, her pelvis began to rock like a ship at sea. Her skin scalded him, but he welcomed the heat and her, her and the heat, lost in the dim light and the confusion of sheets and blankets and coverlets. She ran her hand down his flanks, reached, lifted her thigh, and guided him in. She was slick and wet, and immediately they found a rhythm, steady, not too fast, but urgent. After a few minutes, she pushed off of the mattress and rolled so that he lay on his back and she sat astride, now leaning on his chest with both hands, now stretching backwards, never losing the rhythm. He looked up at the absolutely unfamiliar, alien vision of his wife romping above him, naked in the soft light, claiming her husband. He could not stop himself; whimpering, he came and came. Yet she would not stop. She rode him faster and faster, and he, now tender, could only bite his lip against the pain. She began to hiss something to herself, chanting a word that he could not understand at first. "Mazeppa! Mazeppa! Mazeppa!" Finally, she gave a gagging shriek, virtually danced over him for a moment, flailing her arms and running her fingers wildly through her hair, and fell, sated, on the bed. They slept.

Towards noon the next day, John and Clara descended the stairs to the lobby. She stood quietly next to a window while he made arrangements for their luggage and summoned a carriage that would take them to meet the eastbound stage. Nick met them at the Exchange, so it was he that spread the word that Jack had returned. Hannibal walked in his front door that evening to find Susan on the floor with Bertie, who had just learned to pull himself to a standing position. When he reported the arrival, she looked up, nodded, and turned back to offer the baby her arm.

10
The Shooting
1865

Jack had just dismounted in front of the Exchange when his horse shied at a sudden burst of shouts from inside the telegraph office. Two men ran out, hatless and in shirtsleeves, yelling, "Lee has surrendered! Lee has surrendered!" Within ten minutes all of the shops up and down Main and Mill had emptied, and the sidewalks and streets were full of men and women talking, laughing, whooping and cheering. By late afternoon, drivers on Main Street had to slow their teams to a bare walk and call out to the revelers to make way. Everyone seemed to be carrying an American flag; there were even tiny ones for the children, who held them high in the air and danced the stars and stripes against the sky. Now and then, there was a chattering volley of firecrackers, and women, lifting their skirts and reaching up to hold on to their hats, scurried out of range, shrieking.

From a window table in the Exchange saloon, Jack watched a cluster of hilarious clerks parading up the hill singing "Tramp, Tramp, Tramp, The Boys are Marching" in what they apparently intended to be four-part harmony. When their howling receded, Jesse continued reading aloud from a newspaper. "'The Lincoln Administration requires the Southern States to yield up all those rights for which they contended equally with the North in the War of the Revolution, with which they stood invested when they entered the Union. Is this the way to bring peace? Is this the way to win people to lay down their arms? No, sir, it is the way to madden, exasperate and arouse to the last pitch of indignation and wrath, a people not trained to submit to despots, and not educated in the base school of cowardly subserviency. The day of reckoning will one day come, immediate or remote, when those who have sowed the wind will reap the whirlwind, and when the crime against Constitutional Liberty will visit with its due rewards the heads of those who have deliberately and brazenly committed it. If the pillars of the Constitution are to be torn down, it is not alone the Southern people who are to be buried in the ruins.'" He laid down the page and picked up another. "They published that two weeks ago, and then, just last week, this is what they had t' say. 'The war being over, it will be the duty of the Democrats to oppose any reconstruction of the United States, having for its object the destruction of that form of government which was bequeathed to us by the founders of this great Nation. It will then be more truly seen than now who are the patriots, venerating what is sacred in the traditions and the principles of the Revolutionary Fathers, and who are the secret traitors planning new empire on the ruins of a government which they themselves helped to tear down and destroy.'"

Nick snorted, "Damned copperheads!" and took another pull at his beer. At French Lead, the Americans on the shift had demanded a holiday, so he had laughed and sent them on their way. Two men remained to mind the pump, but the rest of the crews, both at grass and below, had run off, and the North Star was as quiet as on Easter morning.

"Uncle Jesse," said Jack, "that's the *National*. It's a Democratic newspaper, and now that the Republicans have won the war, they're lookin' for a safe place to stand."

Jesse looked worried. "Copperheads they may be, but are they right?"

Jack frowned, puzzled. "Are you askin' whether the nation will fall apart?" His uncle nodded. "Who knows? But I doubt it."

Jesse tapped his forefinger on the table. "This 'ere 'ere says that th' Constitution will collapse an' th' Republicans will make an empire."

"It's all politics," said Jack. "If ye believe everythin' ye read, then both parties are about to cave in for having no reason to continue."

"I know that, I know that," said Jesse. "But is it safe?"

"Is what safe?" asked Nick.

"Is it safe fer us t' stay on?"

Outside, the singing and cheering continued unabated. "Jesse," said Hannibal, "d'ye remember—oh, almost two years back—when the Republicans were talkin' about takin' over the mines? That would have been the sensible thing to do."

Nick laughed incredulously. "What're ye talkin' about?"

"Fighting a war is expensive. There's no profit in it, at least not right away. If ye're a man o' business, d'ye cart everything ye produce out into a field and then destroy it?"

Jack shook his head. "There are men back East who got rich off that war."

"If Lincoln 'ad taken over the mines in California and Nevada, 'e'd've been able to pay all his bills with no trouble at all. So why didn't 'e do it?" No one answered. "Because the last thing they want 'ere is for the government to run the country. If Washington even hints about it, someone makes a speech about liberty and the rest reach for their rifles."

Nick grinned and lifted his glass. "'ere's to 'em!"

"They'll make sure," continued Hannibal, "that we can keep operating the mine the way we want."

Jack leaned in towards Jesse, who still seemed skeptical. "Hannibal's right. These people will fight to keep anybody from telling them what to do. That's why we're safe here."

Jesse shook his head. "They've been nose to nose with each other ever since we arrived. Look at the Americans right 'ere—we're more'n a thousand miles away from th' nearest fightin', but ye'd never know it to 'ear 'em argue."

Hannibal shrugged. "These men come from back East. They'd brothers and uncles and such fightin' in the army, and some o' th' battles were fought near their 'omes."

Nick smirked. "I didn't notice any of 'em volunteerin' to go back and fight."

Jesse would not be put off. "They're a contentious lot. Who'll they go for next?"

Nick reached over and slapped him on the shoulder. "What're ye afraid of?"

"I'm not afeared, Nicky, but it's somethin' we must consider. Look at the way they treat th' Chinese, and th' Mexicans. We're British subjects. Who's t' say they'll leave us be?"

Jack sighed. "What d'ye want—a surety?" Jesse stared at him without speaking. "We took a chance in coming here, but it's paid off."

Hannibal took off his spectacles to wipe the lenses with a napkin. "Jesse— I think ye're right about the Chinese and the Mexicans—they'll never be welcome 'ere, and that's fine with me." He looked around carefully and lowered his voice. "But most o' these men think that we left England for the same reasons as their own grandfathers. Never mind that they can't tell the difference between a Cornish hard-rock man and a Yorkshire pig farmer. Besides, they need us, and the Germans, and even the Irish." Nick laughed and drained his glass. "There's the surety. We're makin' money for 'em."

"Besides," said Jack, "they'll not be going after American citizens, will they?"

Jesse frowned slightly. "What d'ye mean?"

"The war's over. Why should we wait any longer?" The men at the next table got up and ran out into the street to join a group of drunken teamsters and set up a raucous cheer.

Jack's question reminded them that there was a bridge lying before them, one that defined the distance from the idea of California as a temporary place, where a man could make his fortune, to the notion of California as a home. Martin had chosen not to cross that bridge, affirming quietly that Cornwall was still where he belonged, where he would raise his children and, God willing, watch his grandchildren play. He was like a gambler who counted his chips, took a deep breath, and rose from the table, making his peace with his luck, leaving the winning and losing to others, and recognizing that the game was, for him, something that did not go on and on, but had an ending.

The Shooting, 1865

For seven years, they had lived and worked with all of their options open, free to dig deeper or to move on in search of the richer claim that lay in the next valley. Yet with each passing year, each man had made choices that seemed to settle him in California—to invest in a mine, to build a house, to bring a family here, to marry a woman there and bring her here, to marry a woman here, to start a family. Yet to become an American citizen implied a renunciation of almost palpable violence. Among their grandmothers' random memories of cottage, parish and mine, none could find a recollection or tradition that even hinted that their families had lived anywhere but in Cornwall, stubbornly fixed on the rocky moors between England to the east and the open sea to the west. For a man to become a citizen was to admit—to announce—that he would not go back.

"So," said Jesse, "ye'll be askin' fer citizenship 'ere."

"And why not?" asked Jack. "I'm staying on. Anything can happen here, Uncle Jesse—anything. Mining is just a beginning. Now that the war is over, they're sure to finish the railroad, and the whole country'll look our way."

Jesse shook his head dubiously. "There's a great desert between us an' the rest, and more mountains than you can imagine."

"It doesn't matter. I'm tellin' ye that San Francisco will be as big as New York someday, and Sacramento—just think of it!—a port sittin' a hundred miles inland!"

Nick chuckled. "Ye're dreamin', Jack—ye're all cock-a-hoop."

"Maybe I am, but Jesse knows what I'm talkin' about. Columbus sailed out to find China, didn't he? Well, we're going to finish the job!"

Jesse smiled. "Great plans."

Hannibal drummed his fingers on the table. "Jack may be right. They'll finish the railroad, I'm certain. What comes after that, I'm not so sure. But I'll tell ye this—even if the mines play out—and I can't think that they will, not in our lifetime—but even if they did—there's enough farming and lumbering here to keep everyone busy for a long time. Ye can't say that about Cornwall, and even if ye could, the land is taken."

"Are you stayin' as well?" asked Jesse.

"Iss fay. Martin will surely take over Penbro when our uncle passes on, and welcome to it."

Jesse looked sad. "Don't ye miss it at all?"

Hannibal shook his head firmly, but Jack reached over to put his hand on his uncle's arm. "I don't mean to scorn it, Jesse, but we came here to do something that we couldn't do at home. I'm far from finished."

"So ye'll become a citizen."

Jack nodded. "The Americans are more interested in Americans than in anyone else. When a man becomes a citizen, it's like joining the Odd Fellows—they take it as a compliment, and they welcome you in. If I'm a citizen, they'll look at me as one of 'em."

"And you too, Hannibal?" His son-in-law nodded. "Does Susan know?"

Hannibal withdrew slightly. "I'll decide what's best."

Jesse started to ask him another question, thought better of it, and turned to Nick. "And you?"

Nick grinned. All three of them were looking at him, and finally he shrugged his shoulders. "Why not?" The others laughed.

"And what about you, Uncle?" asked Jack. "If you're stayin' on, why not make it official?"

Jesse sat back in his chair and thought of his brother. Joseph had always harbored a careful and usually private disdain for the Americans, and it was as well that he was not sitting at the table now to hear what Jack had to say, for what his son seemed to admire in these people was precisely what had galled him. Jesse remembered one cool autumn evening in Red Dog, when the two of them were sitting by a fire. Jesse had been reading a piece out of a San Francisco newspaper, an effusive polemic about manifest destiny, and Joseph had listened, smoking his pipe peacefully. Finally he shook his head. "These people 'ave no feelin' for who they are." He had declined to explain, but Jesse had decided that Joseph regarded the Americans as having no respect for tradition and no sense of the past. Joseph had nothing but contempt for the speeches the Americans made on their political holidays, for they ranted as if their nation had been thriving for a thousand years and was about to expand, inexorably, to encompass the whole of the known world. To stay on, and especially to become a citizen, would be to join a kind of rabble.

But Joseph was dead, and Jesse had others to consider. Just a week ago, he had asked Zennora how she felt about staying. For several moments, his wife had, in some strange way, retreated into herself, the soft grey eyes gazing beyond the cluster of cedar trees rising above the carriage turn in front of their house. Finally, she had returned and looked at him, saying only, "I think we'll be stayin'." The answer had puzzled him, for she had expressed neither a wish nor an imperative, but rather stated her perception of a fact, something barely discernible but unmistakably before her. He was disappointed, for he had hoped that she would resolve his own confusion; after seven years, he had yet to find a ground from which to assert himself.

He looked at the younger men around the table. "Well, I'll turn citizen if Zennora agrees. But I'm tellin' ye—I've 'ad enough o' their party politics, and I'll not be votin' in their elections."

They laughed and shook hands all around, and at that moment, they heard the distant, insistent thud of a drum and then the blaring of sour music, and they ran out onto the sidewalk to look down the hill. Approaching them was a small parade, first a brass band playing a fast march, and then at least a hundred men, spread into ranks, all carrying muskets and wearing, variously, the uniforms of the Nevada Light Guard and the Grass Valley Union Guard. They tramped up the hill and turned the corner with a small retinue of boys and dogs trailing after them in the twilight.

The four men joined the crowd that surged and stumbled down Mill Street. Nick stopped at Newman's to buy an American flag, but the clerk there assured him that they had been sold out since before noon. Everyone on the street seemed to be carrying a banner, and flags and bunting hung from the storefronts and balconies as though the owners had been keeping them ready to display in an instant. Every store was open, but no one did any business except the saloon keepers, who had set up small counters near their front doors to pour glasses of cold beer at five cents each. Boys carried the pitchers back and forth, never stopping, running with the empties and walking flatfooted, eyes front, with the full ones.

Jack led the others up Bank Alley and across to Hamilton Hall, where a speaker was lifting his chin and stretching his mouth into a grimace, declaiming over the constant rumble of restless people milling in and out, and shaking his fist to give emphasis to each point. "Actions are inadequate to give evidence of the unbounded exuberance of joy that thrills the whole soul of the Union patriot to-day. Four years ago, those fiendish traitors swore to high Heaven that the Star-Spangled Banner should never mount the battlements of Fort Sumter, and treason belched forth its hellish tempest of shot and shell upon our flag then, as now, waving proudly over those very battlements. America, the land of the free and the home of the brave, has been redeemed from treason." Rhythmic cheers and chants punctuated the speeches until a man in a grey silk hat announced that the entire community was invited to join in a triumphant procession through the town. As the throng reached the sidewalk, Jesse and Hannibal shouted over the din that they would be riding back to French Lead. Jack turned towards Nick, but saw him smile and wave as the mob pulled him away.

The torches flared so brightly that Jack could see as clearly as if it were day. He followed the crowd around the corner and down to Main and Auburn, where the guardsmen were once again forming into ranks. Lights burned in every window of the Wisconsin Hotel, and Will Mitchell stood before the entrance, a torch lifted high in each hand, the smoke drifting past the red, white and blue draperies that hung from the portico. Someone was passing out candles to the people in the street, and a man selling cheap lanterns emptied his box in less than fifteen minutes. A man on a horse, wearing a uniform full of brass buttons and a cocked hat with a red plume, paced up and down, up and down, sitting perfectly erect as he called orders to the people below, but no one paid him any attention. Jack took a candle from a miner dressed in smears of silt and clay, and after him, with a burning match, came a clerk, still in his shirtsleeves and eyeshade. Jack saw Simpson, the physician, talking to Findley, the banker; miners standing in threes and fours; women wearing fancy hats, grabbing their hoop skirts to step quickly after their unruly, ecstatic children; clerks and shopkeepers craning their necks to see whether the vanguard of the procession was ready to move; and even a pair of prostitutes, laughing and chattering, on holiday from a brothel near Chinatown. The shuffling feet kicked up a light haze of dust that floated in the firelight.

The townspeople and the fire wagons followed the militia up Main Street to the crest of the hill, where Alonzo Delano's home was a mass of shining lights that set off the eccentric banker's silhouette as he stood on his porch and hailed the revelers. They turned, and turned, and turned again, marching around three sides of each block, but always then turning the other way to outline the next, mapping out the town like a patchwork quilt. As they rounded the corner from Neal to Mill, Pope, the undertaker, climbed up onto a crate in front of his store and threw up a sponge. He was an Englishman born, and a Copperhead, but now he acknowledged the Union victory, so the procession stopped to offer him three cheers. The parade continued on into the night, back and forth, around the town, until finally Jack simply could not walk any more, so he found his horse and rode home.

When Hannibal announced his decision to become a citizen, Susan stopped dead still in the middle of the kitchen, holding an iron frying pan with soap suds dripping from its lip onto the floor. For a moment, he thought she might hurl the pan or let it fall, but she simply stared at him as he kept on talking, explaining, sorting out all the reasons why staying in America made sense for them and their children. When, finally, he stopped, she still stood there, the pan in her hand. After a long moment, she took a deep breath and let it out with "Oh, Hannibal!" She laid the pan in the sink, snatched Bertie out of his father's lap, and marched up the stairs.

Susan lay awake most of the night, measuring the shadows that stretched across the floor and vanished as the moon rose above the trees and arched over the roof. She could insist that he take her home, or she could go home herself, daring him to follow, or daring him not to follow. Her father would disapprove, but he wouldn't stop her, not if she explained to Zennora how she felt. But they were staying, too, and her father—Jesse, of all people!— was a conspirator in this citizenship scheme. And she was going to have another baby, probably just before Christmas, so she couldn't leave just yet. Hannibal had trapped her and then betrayed her. She felt that she would do almost anything to erase the wedding. She rolled over and looked at him, asleep next to her, lying flat on his back with his head thrown back on the pillow, the thin lips parted and the beard curling on the sheet. The breath rasped through his throat, and she hated him, hated the sound, hated the fact that he could sleep, that he had the insolence to sleep, and hated his stubbornness.

She rolled over again to stare through the translucent curtains. Jack had tantalized her with his trip to Cornwall, which had turned out to be only that, not a true return, even though he had come back to California with that wife, that aloof stranger with the round face, now always there when Zennora invited the family over for dinner. She had relinquished Jack in search of a way home, but now he had enticed Hannibal into this citizenship nonsense, and so still stood in her way. She thought of his innocent, open blue eyes, and tears rolled down her cheek. Bertie stirred in his cradle, and she got up to sit in the darkness and cuddle him, holding him against her neck until he slept soundly again.

A few days later, Susan and Hannibal were riding to church in her parents' wagon when a man rode up from Boston Ravine waving a newspaper, and Jesse pulled over to read that Lincoln had been assassinated. Father Putnam delivered a sermon on the text, "Know ye not that there is a prince and a great man fallen this day in Israel?" and closed with an exhortation to the congregation. "I urge you by all that was glorious in the career of the martyred dead—by all that was grand in his devotion to the public welfare—by all that was sublime in his character and teachings—to swear as you bend over his bleeding corpse to-day, that inspired by his industrious example, you will ever be loyal and true to that country for which he lived and for which he died. Now, by the glorious grave of the great patriot, let all renew their vows of allegiance to country and loyalty to law. Now, let the countrymen of the second Washington, as did the countrymen of the first Washington, appealing to God to witness the sincerity of their declarations, give themselves to their country, pledging to her their lives, their fortunes, and their sacred honor."

Women wept and men displayed generous white handkerchiefs. After the service, Jesse asked Findley how the government could continue, now that the President had fallen, but the banker remarked that Johnson had surely taken the oath of office by now—the news was two days old—and the government would proceed as before, although, of course, bereft and sorrowing. Jesse pressed him, asking if there would be order in the cities, and Findley, perplexed, assured him that there would be no trouble, although surely the army would hunt down the murderer and his accomplices, though their trail led around the world. Susan realized that her father was reconsidering his decision, anticipating chaos and anarchy and so looking to Cornwall as a safe haven, but on the way home, when she eagerly tried to draw him out, he would only say that the reverend's call for vows of allegiance seemed well-placed. Snubbed, she folded her hands and slumped in her seat, not caring that the corset pinched her flesh.

Susan saw Jack and Nick only on those monthly evenings when Zennora invited the entire family to French Lead for Sunday dinner. Nick regaled the women with stories of his travels all over the hills in search of promising claims, of tracing the rivers—American, the Bear and the Yuba—up to their headwaters, where shining granite mounds thrust up above unexpected clusters of lakes, hidden in alpine vales and fed by fields of slowly melting pink snow. He had even purchased a claim on a quartz ledge beyond the Sierra crest, near Donner Lake, and he had persuaded Jack to file the papers with him and call the enterprise the "Trevenna Company."

Jack smiled at his brother but offered very little news about his own affairs, although Hannibal had confided to Susan that he was heavily involved in lending money to those who had farm land and mining claims to offer as collateral. Jack did tell them that he was negotiating to buy the house on Bennett Street that had, briefly, belonged to Martin, and that he and Clara hoped to move in shortly. Zennora cut into the pasty, the steam carrying the scent of potatoes and salt pork, and declared that the house was perfect for children; Clara smiled blandly.

Jack did not bother to mention that the house was convenient not only to downtown Grass Valley but also to Chinatown. He had resumed his old habit of going to Ah Choy for advice, but the merchant continued to refuse, quietly but adamantly, to accept Jack as his partner. He was now contracting laborers, Chinese men, to work on the Central Pacific Rail Road, and Jack felt, once again, that he was standing just outside of something that was not only a lucrative opportunity but also part of what was going to make California's future. He smiled at his relatives around the table, but as he helped himself to Zennora's rice, liberally laced with black currants, he was preoccupied with his search for a way to get closer to the source of the excitement that was, he felt sure, developing all around him.

As the weeks passed, Susan found a place for this notion of citizenship, putting it on a sort of shelf in her mind, like an awkward gift that ends up gathering dust in a closet. She had come to regard this naturalization—odd word!—as something that men did for no sensible reason, like drink in saloons, wrestle in the amphitheatre, or fasten hopes on mining claims in dry gullies; she had so lost patience with the Live Yankee that Hannibal stopped telling her about his progress with it, even though he and Pascoe had found a piece of a vein that inspired them to hire four men to work it for a while.

On July 4th, the Americans gathered to celebrate their Independence Day, and Hannibal persuaded Jesse to ride into town, where they would meet Jack and Nick and join in the festival. Partly to define her own independence, to declare that she would live her life in spite of the nonsense of the men around her, she asked Zennora to arrange for Joseph to drive them both into town with little Bertie. They waited until after noon, planning to reach Main Street during the lull between festivities, and rode in to shop at the market. They left Joseph to load the wagon and walked over to the drug store.

Susan sat near the doorway while Zennora bought some castor oil and asked Loutzenheiser to show her his selection of paint colors. Bertie climbed down from his mother's lap to hold her knee and practice standing, and Susan gazed past him, the doorway and the brick surround carefully framing her field of vision. On the sidewalk underneath the awning, a couple stood with their backs to her; facing them was a small, stout man wearing a round hat and round spectacles. He was Henry Silvester, a friend of Nick's who owned a general store just up the street. He laughed at something the couple said, then shook hands with the man and tipped his hat. The couple crossed the street and walked up the hill and out of her frame, and just at that moment, a burly, red-faced man wearing a white coat jumped in from the left and struck Silvester in the face. He went down at once, sprawling with his head in the street and his spectacles flying off into the dust. The white-coated man reached down to grab him, but Silvester kicked out with his feet. Suddenly, Nick appeared on the right side of the frame, breathing hard, and grabbed the white-coated man by the shoulder, shouting at him, "Don't hurt a man that's down!" Silvester rose to a half-crouch, glaring at his assailant, panting a little, and slowly reached up to feel his cheek. He held out his hand and looked at it, and Susan could see the blood glistening on the fingertips. His brow furrowed as he looked up at the white-coated man, who was trying to shrug himself out of Nick's grip, and he slowly reached into his coat pocket and pulled out a shiny pistol.

The white-coated man threw Nick towards Silvester, and the two entangled for a moment while the other ran out of the frame to the left. Susan grabbed Bertie and held him tightly to her, wanting to run out of the store, wanting to run in to the back, but she stayed frozen to her chair. Now Nick and Silvester were arguing and pacing back and forth; Silvester kept insisting, in a surprisingly quiet voice, "I didn't provoke him. I didn't provoke him." Susan heard Nick tell the storekeeper that if he waited there, the other man would have the advantage when he came back, and besides, his pistol was too small to do the job. Silvester kept looking past Nick's shoulder, trying to move towards the left side of the frame, but Nick kept pushing him to the right, finally moving him up the street and out of Susan's field of view. She heard a footstep in the store, and she looked over to see Silvester standing inside the other doorway, holding his pistol and peering out. Nick ran through the frame from right to left, calling for someone. A small boy squatted in the gutter, picked up Silvester's spectacles, handed them in to him, and scrambled away again.

Susan could hear Nick arguing, and the back of his shoulder inched into the frame. He was pushing against someone, for every moment or two, he would dig in his feet and lean so that his head disappeared, then recover to wave his arms and get ready to push again. She heard him say, "For God's sake, John, don't go back—there are too many people in the store! There are women and children! Go up in the hills where there's plenty of room!" As they kept arguing and pushing, Nick lost ground, and Susan could see the other man. It was the white-coated man, but this time he had his right hand in his coat pocket. He was grunting at Nick, "Now, you'd better let me go!"

Susan felt a tight grip on her upper right arm and turned to see Silvester standing there. He pulled her to a standing position, she still holding Bertie, who was beginning to whimper, and told her, "Stand back—there might be trouble." He drew her farther into the store and released her; she lost her balance and half fell against the cabinet in the corner. Silvester closed the door and stood with his chest against the brick wall of the entry way, a pistol still in his right hand. He was breathing hard and fast, and the sweat was running down his face. He kept his eye on Nick and the white-coated man, and he pulled a handkerchief out of his pocket to wipe the blood off of his cheek and the mist off of the lenses of his spectacles. The back of his coat was covered with dust, and his sour odor nearly gagged her.

She could not help staring over Silvester's shoulder and through the frame, smaller now that she was farther inside. A third man walked into view, and while Nick restrained the white-coated man with one hand, he began to argue with the new man, who seemed puzzled. After a moment, he took the white-coated man by the elbow and tried to walk him up the street, with Nick following. The white-coated man still had his hand in his pocket, and as they passed, he looked through the window, trying to peer into the darkness of the store. His eyes were wide open, the brows up, and his jaw hung slack so that Susan could see his teeth, stained and uneven.

At that moment, Silvester fired right through the door, shattering one of the lights. The white-coated man grimaced and cried out suddenly, doubling over and grabbing at his crotch, where Susan could see a small red stain. Nick and the third man recoiled for a moment, then grabbed for the white-coated man just as Silvester fired again and hit him in the chest. Nick and the third man pulled the white-coated man to a standing position, but he broke away and burst through the door. Silvester stepped back suddenly, and as he turned, his pistol at the ready, he whipped Susan across the temple with the barrel. Still clutching the screaming Bertie, she lost her footing completely and fell across the cabinet.

The Shooting, 1865

Silvester and the white-coated man were struggling, and the pistol went off again. The white-coated man threw Silvester to one side, staggered toward the rear of the store, and fell to his knees in front of a horrified Zennora. Loutzenheiser, behind her, was pointing at Susan and Bertie, insisting that the white-coated man was all right but calling for Nick and the third man to come in to help that woman on the cabinet. As they reached for her, she could see the white-coated man fall heavily against Zennora, who gasped, and slide to the floor and roll over. Blood covered his chest and dripped down onto the floor.

The sheriff walked in and stopped to look around. Loutzenheiser was crouched over the man in a white coat, who was lying motionless in a puddle of blood. Susan was still sprawled on the cabinet, hanging on to Bertie, but Nick was helping her up, and the third man had found a chair for Zennora, who was staring at the dead man. Silvester hugged his gun and insisted, again and again in a shrill staccato voice, "He was going to kill me! He was going to kill me!"

Nick helped Susan to a bench behind the counter and led Zennora over to sit with her. Bertie stood between the two women, sucking his thumb and staring at the blood stains on his grandmother's shoulder. There were several men in the store by now, some in hats and some in shirtsleeves, and two of them stood over Silvester, who was sitting in a chair, wiping his face with a handkerchief and muttering to himself. The sheriff stood a few feet away from the dead man, calmly asking questions of each man who had seen some part of the altercation. Nick walked over to him and spoke quietly into his ear, pointing over towards Susan and Zennora. The sheriff looked at him for a moment and walked over to where the women were sitting. He was a tall man with a big belly and drooping eyelids, and he looked down at Susan without speaking. Nick whispered in his ear, and he looked at Zennora, then down at Bertie, who had buried his face in his mother's lap. "Right," said the sheriff, and he walked over towards Silvester.

Nick had somehow hired a carriage, and he drove the women and the boy back out to French Lead. On the way, a man on a horse caught up with them. Nick reined in his team to speak to him, and he looked hard at the women before spurring his horse up the hill and far ahead. By the time they reached Susan's house, Hannibal was waiting on the porch. He lifted Bertie down out of the carriage and took Susan's hands as she slowly made her way down the narrow, bouncing steps. Nick clucked to the horses and turned the carriage down the path to Jesse's house, with Zennora swaying in the seat behind him.

Susan could barely stand. Hannibal found a toy for Bertie and helped his wife upstairs. She sat on the bed, dazed, while he took off her cloak, unlaced her shoes to pull them off with the stockings, unbuttoned her dress, and removed her stays, leaving only her shift, so wet it clung to her. She lay back on the pillow and he pulled the sheet up to her chin, leaving the blankets folded at her feet. He walked quietly back downstairs, leaving her in bed alone, her eyes closed and her chest rising and falling slowly. Yet before she fell asleep, she could hear the sound of firecrackers in the distance, so like the firing of Silvester's pistol, and men cheering for the independence of America from England. She reached down to her belly, but she could feel nothing there, nothing that would comfort her. Cut adrift, she floated, slept.

11
The East Star Shaft
1866-67

Charles Nankervis stood close against the wall of Pope's furniture store and tucked his chin into his coat collar to shield himself from the wind that swept down Neal and across from Mill, meeting at the intersection like two runaway horses. He had grown up with the wind, in a stone cottage near Trewinard, where the hills channeled the blast straight across the narrow neck from Mount's Bay to St. Ives. Yet this Sierra wind was different, hard and dry where the seaborne gales had been soft and moist. He shivered. If he had endured fifteen years here, it was because he had spent most of his time underground, for only thirty fathoms down did these strange mountains feel right.

Two men approached, bent against the gusts, leaning into the incline as they climbed the hill, their faces so muffled that he could not be sure they were his sons until they had crossed the street and stood next to him. Together, they walked the last two blocks up to Edward Sterling's home. The elegant white house was stripped for winter: the caretaker had pruned back the vines, emptied the encircling verandah of its summer furniture, and closed the shutters on the upstairs windows. As they walked up the steps to the front door, they saw warm lights and heard low voices in conversation. Seth knocked at the door, and after a brief moment, it swung open.

John Sterling stood in the foyer, his teeth flashing and his eyes crinkling as he welcomed them in with a laugh, shaking each man's hand, looking him straight in the eye and clapping him on the shoulder. The door swung shut behind them and a Chinese manservant stepped out of the shadows to take their coats and hats and then vanish silently. John kept talking and laughing as he swept them into the sitting room, where Edward stood in front of a crackling fire, his left hand tucked behind the small of his back while he extended the right just far enough for each visitor to grasp it.

The furniture was all carved oak with velvet upholstery in deep, muted greens and blues, set against embossed wallpaper with a burgundy pattern flecked in gold. The rugs beneath their feet were thick but impeccably clean, and felt soft even through hard boots. Gilt frames displayed paintings of Edward and his wife, and of two older couples whom Charles supposed to be their parents, and large plate-glass mirrors faced each other from the walls perpendicular to the fireplace. There were only a few ornaments on the various side tables; Mrs. Sterling apparently displayed her prized Oriental curios elsewhere, outside of Edward's domain.

Cousin Jack

Another Chinese manservant appeared with hot rum, serving quietly and efficiently, his formally polite eyes carefully watching each man as he reached towards the steaming tray. Finally, every guest was seated in a comfortable wingback chair with his hands folded around the warmth of his cup. Edward cleared his throat and nodded towards John, who stepped forward.

"The North Star is doing well, better than we'd hoped. We've dug the main shaft down over 500 feet on the incline, almost 150 feet below the surface. We've extended the three old drifts, and we're starting on a fourth." He began pacing around the room, moving from man to man. "In the past five years, we've shown a net profit of three hundred thousand dollars, and we've put about half of that back into the mine. Each month, the mill produces $20,000 in ore, and we pay out $8,000 in dividends, or $400 per share. That is the present condition of the company."

He paused as though waiting for something, and after a beat, Seth asked, "If the mine's doin' so well, what's the problem?"

John clapped his hands together and waved a finger at his guest. "Yes—absolutely true—we *are* doing well! So what *is* the problem?" He sat down and lowered his voice confidentially. "The problem is that we could be doing even better. We've hardly begun to find the extent of the vein." He began to diagram the mine with his hands, creating a three-dimensional picture in the air. "The incline shaft comes down like this, and the drifts extend out here—here—and here. The new drift is pushing out this way. We have all of this space, from the bottom to the surface, between the drifts, that we haven't touched."

Seth shifted in his chair, and said, "If ye start diggin' in all directions, the whole thing'll fall in on ye. What ye call 'space' is what's holdin' up those drifts an' keepin' the men alive."

John regarded the younger man with a serious, completely sympathetic expression. "You're absolutely right, Seth—we can't turn the mine into a warren. But look here: we can drift out to the west and the north at different levels, and we can take the main shaft deeper, all without weakening the system. Edward hired a geologist last month to go down and investigate. He's told us that we have plenty of room to expand and that we have perhaps thirty thousand tons of ore sitting in our reserves, just waiting for us to blast it out."

Samuel gnawed on his lip. "Ye take that main shaft deeper, ye'll 'ave to extend the pump rod, and ye'll 'ave a fair way to haul the ore."

John grinned at him. "Exactly right, exactly right. What would you say to sinking a new shaft, straight down, right here?" The Nankervises stared at the space that John was shaping with his hands. "A vertical shaft for hoisting the ore. We don't take it up the incline any more at all. We install a new hoisting engine at the new shaft, and take the ore right up to the surface."

Samuel shook his head. "You'll need a good hoist fer that." He glanced deferentially at his father. "You take care, Sterling, that you're not getting this business all backsy-forsy. We're in this t' make money, not t' spend it."

John had dropped his grin and assumed an expression of concern. "I agree, I agree. But the new hoist will pay for itself easily."

Edward cleared his throat, and the other four looked up at him. "This company is part of the community, and our position in this town is excellent. We're employing more and more men, and we keep them working. We don't send to San Francisco for our machinery. The local foundry manufactured all the parts for our new stamps; they'll give us a reasonable price on the new hoist."

John leaned in and lowered his voice again. "We have a valuable mine, gentlemen, but we've only begun to bring out the gold. We owe it to ourselves, to our partners, and to the people of this town to do our best to take out what God put in. We can hardly lose."

He sat back in his chair, waiting. Edward had hardly moved from his place at the fire, while Samuel continued to nibble at his upper lip. Seth looked over at his father, who suddenly sat up, set down his drink, and fixed his gaze on John.

"Ye're quite a dab at this, aren't ye, Sterling? Sure, we'd like to open up th' mine. Sure, we'd like t' bring out more o' the ore. Sure, we'd like t' make a skuat o' money an' go 'ome t' Cornwall t' set up as squire. But why did ye call us in 'ere tonight? Where are th' Trevennas and th' Chenoweths? Where's Hannibal Carne? Is this a partners' meetin' or idden it? What's got ye so nag-ridden?"

Charles sat back in his chair while his sons stared at him and John waited. Edward still stood with his hands clasped behind his back, but he lifted his chin and his brow began to fold into a frown. "The problem is Nicholas Trevenna."

"Nick?!" exclaimed Samuel incredulously.

Edward stared at Samuel, and John turned to Charles to explain. "He's a fine man and a fine miner. But he won't listen to reason, and as long as he's the superintendent, of course we do things his way. He can't see the potential in the North Star, and he wants to keep going as we are. As long as Nick is in charge, the mine can't expand the way it should."

Edward looked down at Charles. "The man is unreliable."

John nodded, still studying Charles' face. "He'll work a shift, or maybe two, and then he'll be gone for two days, three days, leaving the foremen to keep things moving."

"And that's a captain's job," exclaimed Samuel. "Name a mine where the super's there all the time! We'd do well t' find better captains than Mark Chenoweth and Hannibal Carne. Who should keep things moving if not them?"

"The superintendent makes the major decisions," explained John. "We can't be having partner's meetings every week to decide how far to dig a drift or whether we should be stamping more rock. Nick goes his own way, and his way doesn't always lead to the mine."

Seth crossed his legs. "I think Nick's cracky. The man sings walkin' down the shaft, and 'e talks to 'imself while 'e's drilling. P'raps 'e's pisky-led." He noticed his father staring at him, and abruptly fell silent.

"It's time," said John, "that we had a superintendent who can get the mine moving."

"Who d'ye 'ave in mind?" asked Samuel. Edward stared out across the room as John came to the point of the meeting.

"Edward." Seth and Samuel looked up at the man standing at the fire, not knowing what to say. "He doesn't want to do it—he's done it before, and he has a great deal of other business at hand—but we need him."

"So what d'ye want from us?" asked Charles.

John sat down next to him, his expression grave. "You know what's best for the mine—you know that we can't continue with Nick Trevenna as superintendent. But how to make the change? That's the question." Charles stared at him expressionlessly, and after a moment, John continued. "Nick won't resign—we know that. He's too caught up with the idea of running the place. We can't expect Jesse or Jack or Hannibal to vote against him—he's part of their family. And the Chenoweths probably feel the same way; after all, they're Hannibal's cousins. We can't ask a man to deny his own family, can we?" He smiled and slapped a hand down on Charles' shoulder. Charles did not move. "With your votes—all of your votes—"He looked around to include Samuel and Seth. "—we control 55% of the shares. We don't have quite half of the partners, but I know that Jesse and Jack, and probably Hannibal, will understand. They might even approve, though we can't expect them to say so."

Charles still stared at John, and finally Samuel spoke. "I'm wonderin'—with all respect to Edward—" The elder Sterling continued to stare, apparently at a painting hanging on the opposite wall. "—whether this might be the time to ask Jesse to take over."

John nodded his head emphatically. "An excellent choice. He's one of the most experienced men in the company, with almost as many years underground as yourself, Charles. But I doubt that Jesse would agree to do it."

"Why not ask 'im?" Samuel wanted to know.

"Why not indeed? We can certainly do that. But consider—Jesse is a fine man, always thinking of his responsibilities to others, and hardly ever thinking of himself. If we go to Jesse and explain the problem, I think he'll take the job and regret it later. No, no—he's a good man, and we must not take advantage of him."

"If ye want one o' the older men," suggested Seth, "then why not Fayther?"

"We couldn't do better, could we?" John nodded at all three of the visitors and rubbed his hands together. "Certainly there's no one more reliable, more knowledgeable, than you, Charles. And the men respect you, oh, yes, no doubt about that. But we couldn't ask you to do it."

"Why not?" asked Seth.

John shook his head regretfully. "You men still have that quartz claim on Gold Hill. You work it every day that you can spare. We can't ask you, Charles, to spend even more time at the North Star and neglect your own interests. It's a fine claim, it's paying a bit, and—who knows?—perhaps, some day, you'll hit a rich vein and put us all to shame." He laughed. "No, no, it wouldn't be fair. It wouldn't be right."

"If Fayther wants t' say 'no,' tidden up to 'im?"

John paused for a moment and glanced up at Edward. "Well . . . Well, yes, of course. Thank you, Seth." He cleared his throat. "Well, Charles, what do you say? Would you . . . Would you be willing to serve as superintendent?"

Charles looked into the fire, and he remembered a day at Dolcoath when he had just started working as a tributer, no longer a boy helping his father, and the adventurers had gathered the men together to auction off the pitches. The prices were low, and the miners left unsatisfied, but Charles had noticed that the adventurers, in their tailored suits and clean, polished boots, exchanged discreetly pleased glances with each other. There were, he had decided, two kinds of men in the world: the men that worked in the earth, and the men that stood on its surface. In Cornwall, those below worked at the pleasure of those above, so he had come to California for a chance to get free of the adventurers, and had become one himself, even though he kept descending into the subterranean gloom. Edward Sterling had begun as a miner out in Placer County when he was about the same age as Seth, but now he lived in a tall white house with Chinese servants. Charles knew who would ultimately control the North Star.

He rose to his feet. "Do what ye wish, Edward. Ye've got my vote." He turned and strode through the room to the foyer, where the manservant, anticipating him, appeared with his hat and coat. Samuel and Seth stared at their father for a moment and then scrambled to their feet, barely nodding to Edward as they eased out of the room. John escorted them every step of the way, thanking them and promising great things for the future of the mine, and as the three visitors walked down through the frosty garden, they could hear him calling after them from the open doorway.

When the partners gathered in Findley's conference room, John took Charles aside to assure him of Edward's respect and gratitude. Charles turned his stone face on the younger man, fixing him with his unwavering eyes until he subsided, and then walked past him to take his seat. Nick said nothing when John called for a vote of confidence, but he was openly surprised and puzzled when the Nankervises declined to back him. When Jesse, once again reluctantly taking charge of the meeting, asked whether he wished to continue as superintendent, given that he had less than half of the shares behind him, he simply shook his head. He showed no inclination to leave the room, but remained in his seat at the head of the table, making slow, careful cross-hatched patterns on a scrap of paper. When John nominated Edward, Hannibal slouched down in his chair, his brow furrowed, but when Jesse asked him, directly, whether he would accept nomination himself, he refused without elaboration and declined to propose anyone else. From the moment that Nick conceded his removal, Jack had been listing and adding columns of figures on a sheet of paper, and when Jesse, methodically progressing around the table to give each man a chance to stand for election, spoke his name, he looked up, nearly smiled as he took a breath, but stopped short as he turned to survey the partnership. After looking at each man carefully, he shrugged at Jesse, shook his head, and crumpled up the paper into a tight ball. No one would volunteer and no one would nominate anyone else, so Jesse, after an awkward pause, called the question. Only the Sterlings and the Nankervises voted to approve Edward, but they represented eleven out of twenty shares, just enough to justify election. Yet before he formally asked the candidate whether he would accept, Jesse raised his own hand and so gave Edward a majority of the partners. As soon as the new superintendent agreed to serve, Hannibal, his face perfectly blank, collected his papers, rose to his feet, and quietly left the room. The Chenoweths followed him, leaving the remaining eight partners sitting in an uncomfortable silence. After a moment, Nick stood up, and Jesse reached up as though to hold him in the room, but his nephew merely gestured to the chair, indicating that Edward might sit there, and took the seat that Hannibal had left. The meeting adjourned a few minutes later.

At the bottom of the stairs, Jack took Nick by the elbow and pulled him down the street to a saloon where they were unlikely to see the other partners. He ordered a beer for each of them and turned to his brother. Nick's face was an enigma; he showed no reaction to what had just happened. "What'll you do now?"

At that, Nick actually grinned. "What won't I do?! I've so many claims, I 'aven't time for 'em all."

"I know that, but what'll ye do for money?"

Nick's face changed. "I've paid ye what I owed."

"I know, and thank you, but what'll ye live on?"

"I told ye, I've claims all over the 'ills."

"And which of them is paying?"

"They'll pay soon enough."

"And until then, you'll be buying tools, equipment, p'raps hiring men. Where's th' money t' come from?"

"I don't need much."

"Don't you be borrowing from anyone else—if you need money, come to me!"

"I can take care of myself!"

"I mean it."

"Iss fay—I heard ye sued that fellow in Auburn."

"That's the business, Nicky—don't expect anything different."

"I won't."

"Zennora told me you've been seein' a girl in Nevada City. A good girl."

"And what if I 'ave?"

"Well, if ye're thinkin' of gettin' married, you need t' be able t' support her."

"Dabbety fay, Jack—who d'ye think ye are? My mother?"

"Don't you?"

"I'm not marryin' anyone, not today, and if I do, what business is it of yours?"

"All right—all right—I'll leave it to you."

"Well, thank'ee, Mr. Trevenna."

"Look, Nick . . . I'm sorry that Nankervis didn't back you up—I didn't know."

Nick looked at Jack for moment, then relaxed slightly and smiled ruefully into his beer. "'e's a regular duffan, ain't 'e? I didn't see it comin'. Ah . . . Let's forget about it. Let Nankervis 'ave 'is way, and pray fer 'is sons." He chuckled bitterly, and Jack smiled. "Poor Hannibal. Edward again. I give 'em three months, and then I don't know what." Nick took a long pull on his beer and wiped the foam off of his mustache. "Jack—if it makes ye feel any better, I can go down t' th' Norambagua if I want."

"Doing what?"

Nick grinned and thumped his own chest with his fist. "Superintendent, of course! They can't get along without me." He thought for a moment. "Do ye never wonder why th' North Star don't 'ire a super from outside?"

Jack shook his head. "It doesn't make sense—we're all miners. Things'd be in a way if we couldn't run the place ourselves."

Nick nodded. "P'raps ye're right. The Norambagua owners are all from Sacramento—they ride up twice a year, walk 'alfway down the main shaft, and then brush the dust off their boots and 'ead for 'ome. But p'raps th' North Star'd be better off with someone else."

Jack looked down into his beer and smiled. "P'raps you're right. But is there any man in these hills antic enough to work for us?" The brothers laughed and finished their drinks.

The Sterlings moved quickly. Within a month, they filed to extend the company's claims a thousand feet farther to the east, and they paid Jules Fricot six thousand dollars for his interests on Weimar Hill, a collection of two dozen claims enclosed on three sides by North Star property. Soon after that, they bought out an Irishman, satisfied with his success and dreaming of home, who had been working on their southern boundary. As Nick and Hannibal had warned, the machinery at the new sites needed rebuilding, and the stamp mills were inadequate, so Edward hired a crew that spent all of each day just hauling rock from the new claims back to the North Star shops, and the stamp mill fell farther and farther behind. Hannibal grew more and more exasperated and complained so much and so often that Susan finally banned the mine as a subject of conversation.

Then the Sterlings offered two surprises in quick succession. At the regular meeting at the end of June, Edward formally recommended that they install a new mill with sixteen stamps. He calmly explained that such a mill, with an engine generating fifty horsepower, would be able to crush a ton of quartz every hour and run virtually around the clock; with time allowed for maintenance, they would be able to process 150 tons each week. Hannibal's mouth hung open until Nick caught his eye from across the table and grinned, shaking his head helplessly. The Chenoweths began to shift restlessly in their seats and Jesse, sensing that the meeting was about to degenerate, quietly asked Edward about the cost. He assured the partners that the foundry in Boston Ravine could cast the parts and deliver the equipment on schedule, all with fair terms. When he finally confided that the price, installed, would be just under thirty thousand dollars—less than two months' anticipated profit—he actually smiled. The figures mollified everyone; even the men who had long wanted the new mill felt no inclination to carp at the Sterlings for waiting so long.

Edward offered his second surprise at the July meeting. After the routine reports, he stood to unroll two drawings on the table. The first was a map of the mine, showing all of its new acquisitions and precisely locating the shaft and all of the buildings. The second was a cross-section, showing the contour of the terrain on top and tracing the extent of the incline shaft below, with notations showing the four working levels. He brought out two sheets of translucent paper and laid one on each drawing. The partners leaned over the table, and even before Edward explained what he had in mind, every man there realized that he was looking at the vertical shaft that Nick had been proposing since the day they formed the company.

"We open the shaft here, about five hundred feet from the mouth of the main shaft. It will run straight down and meet the incline about a hundred and forty feet below the surface, right about at the fourth level."

Charles Nankervis studied the cross section. "What kind o' hoist d'ye plan?"

"Twenty-five horsepower," said John. "Stronger than the hoist we have now, because of course we'll be lifting the rock straight up, not on tracks."

Nankervis looked dubious. "This shaft o' yers'll serve only th' fourth level."

"Not at all, not at all!" John looked at Edward, who seemed secretly pleased about something. "We'll take the main shaft down deeper, probably to seven hundred feet on the incline, and open up new levels, most likely three more in the next two years or so."

Richard Chenoweth looked at his brother. "Can the pump 'andle the extra depth?"

Mark nodded. "Blame me if it don't. The engine'll do fine, an' there should be no problem runnin' the rod down and addin' another station."

John slapped Mark on the shoulder. "Hannibal—if we hired another crew, do you think you could handle another drift starting in January?"

Hannibal's chin jerked up as if he had been slapped. "Of course I can handle it, you . . . "

Jesse broke in. "When would we start on th' vertical shaft?"

John stood back from the table, deferring to Edward, who waited until everyone in the room was paying attention, and then said, "We should begin soon and get as far down as we can before winter. I think we can open it up next month."

"Can we afford it?" Mark wanted to know.

Edward regarded him for a moment before answering, "The new stamp mill will be running two weeks from today. We can afford it."

John broke in, "And we'll still be paying dividends to every man here."

Jack looked at Hannibal, whose face had turned a mottled red but who seemed determined to remain silent, and then at Nick, who was looking down at the drawings, fascinated, hardly listening to the conversation. He ran his finger along the map from the stamp mill to the mouth of the new shaft, and then, on the cross section, traced down the incline to the sump and beyond, down into the greenstone, where the quartz vein ran. "Nicky—what d'ye think?"

Nick looked up from the table, his eyes shining, and chewed the inside of his cheek before answering. "I think it's a fine idea." He took a breath as if to go on, but shook his head and looked down at the drawing again.

The partners approved the plans without a dissenting vote, and Jesse, at Edward's invitation, suggested that they call the new shaft the "East Star."

Jack lingered to study the drawings with Jesse, and by the time he reached the saloon, he found Nick sitting alone. Before him, on the gleaming oak bar, stood a bottle of whiskey, not quite half full. The bar man was polishing glasses a few yards away, but he kept glancing at Nick, and when

Jack caught his eye, he winced and shrugged.

"Nicky," said Jack, "what is it?" Nick didn't answer. "Nick?" He reached over and slid the bottle away, but Nick quietly brought it back to where it had been standing. "Is it the East Star?"

Nick smiled. "The East Star. Sounds like . . . I don't know. Like Christmas, p'raps. The East Star." He finished his drink and picked up the bottle to splash a little more whisky into his glass. Jack leaned in, ready to catch the bottle if it fell, but Nick's hands were perfectly steady and he poured accurately, even deliberately. "The East Star."

"Let me take you home."

Nick took another swallow. "Why now? Tell me that. Why now?"

"Why the shaft?"

Nick nodded. "Th' shaft. An' th' stamps." He frowned. "How long was I super? More'n a year?"

"Yes."

"So why now? 'e's been runnin' th' place fer . . . What? Three months?"

"Four."

"Four. Four months. What's so now that wasn't so four months ago? I've been wantin' more stamps, and that shaft, since . . . I don't remember. I don't remember." He turned and looked Jack straight in the face. He didn't look drunk except that his face seemed oddly stretched over his bones. "That shaft was my idea. You remember."

"I know, Nicky."

"You remember." He sighed. "I don't mind, y'know. Really—I don't. We should've dug th' shaft three years ago at least. It's well that we're doin' it now." He took another swallow. "I just wish I could be there t' see it go down."

"Nick, you're a partner. You have three shares in the mine. If you want to supervise the digging, just say so. We'll get Hannibal and Jesse to agree, and the Chenoweths. Even if Nankervis won't go along, Sterling'd be a fool t' say no. No one would do it better, and he knows that."

Nick looked mildly surprised. "Does 'e? Hmm. Strange man. Strange, strange, strange man. I don't like it when 'e smiles."

"Let me take you home, Nicky."

"Tell me somethin', Jack. Tell me."

"What?"

"Did 'e do it just t' slap me in th' face? Was that it?"

Jack bit his lip. In Nick's mind, the men who went below contended with the rock on its own terms, proving its strength and theirs in the struggle. To Nick, the underground workings held a certain purity, as though the tunnels were dug to honor the earth itself, and the rising California hill country had importance only as the site for a vast, interrelated structure of shafts, drifts and adits. He had never been able to understand how two men could turn their progress through the rock into a personal grudge or competition. For his part, Jack had become convinced that the Sterlings had made their plans well in advance, and that every move they had made in the past four months—buying new claims, installing the stamp mill, and now sinking the vertical shaft—was part of a well-conceived program to develop the mine to its fullest extent but without conceding a scrap of Edward's authority. He had also realized that the Sterlings might have more plans in mind, ideas leading to some conclusion that he could not predict. But Nick would understand none of that. "P'raps 'e did. But Nicky—that's bad on him, not on you. Let it go by."

The North Star flowered under the Sterlings' rule. The new stamp mill ran even more efficiently than Edward had promised, and the mound of raw ore that had been accumulating for months steadily dwindled. By January, they had extended the main shaft to nearly 750 feet on the incline, reaching almost thirty-five fathoms below the surface. Hannibal and the Chenoweths opened up three new drifts, running them out to the east, and by March, the crews were working on seven levels. The East Star was completed well before Christmas, the hoist was installed and tested just after New Year's, and just as Nick had always known, the new arrangement brought out the rock more quickly and cheaply than ever before. Even Hannibal stopped complaining about the Sterlings, for Edward had surprised him by consulting with him closely on anything involving the underground workings, and had accepted his advice several times on questions regarding the timing of jobs and the assignment of crews. Through all the changes, the company continued to declare dividends, and when Edward had finished paying for the new excavations and machinery, the profits rose higher than anyone had dared anticipate.

After Nick's humiliation, Jack had resolved to stay away from the mine, but he made an exception for the sinking of the East Star Shaft. Hannibal recommended Nick as the man most qualified to supervise the job, but because Nick adamantly refused, Hannibal turned to Jesse, who surprised both the captain and the superintendent by quietly informing them that securing Jack's assistance would be a condition of his accepting the job. Jesse took his nephew up to a granite outcropping on Weimar Hill, where they could look down at the proposed site for the shaft, and he slowly convinced him to set everything else aside for the two months they would need to complete the major part of the work. Jack, he said, was one of the best hard-rock men in California, a match for Cornishmen of even more experience, no matter that he had hardly worked as a miner for nearly two years. Moreover, Jesse needed someone he could trust, a Trevenna, a man who would respect the rock and use everything he knew, to work beside him on what would most likely be his last big job. That remark puzzled Jack, for his uncle was barely more than forty, and fit, but when he pressed the point, Jesse refused to elaborate. Finally, Jack agreed, and in late August, with the thunderheads looming on the Sierra crest and the hissing of insects slicing through the hot, still afternoon air, the two men set to work.

Jesse bored in from above and Jack excavated from below, each running his own crew, drilling and blasting, drilling and blasting, the whole hill shaking from the thudding force of the black powder, set in charges much larger than the ones they would have used for cutting a drift or working a vein. Jesse's crew piled the tailings in a mound that grew higher and higher, and Jack assigned two teams just to haul his rubble up to grass. As the work progressed, they set up a winch to lower the men down from above, and cobbled together a series of ladders and platforms to raise them up from below. Each morning and each evening, Jack and Jesse met to inspect both ends of the shaft, carefully measuring their progress and surveying the angles to make sure that they would eventually meet in the middle.

With Jesse's consent, Jack appointed young Joseph as his assistant, and he studied him during those brief respites, the moments when they huddled in the drift to wait for an explosion and the crashing roar of falling rock. By the light of the flickering candles, the boy's pale grey eyes seemed docile and unsurprised, hardly flinching with each detonation. He reminded Jack of Susan, but only from a certain angle; when he turned, the illusion melted, for he showed nothing of his sister's temper. He was fully grown now, but he deferred so readily to Jesse and Jack, accepting their authority and expertise without question, as though his subordinate role were part of an immutable order, that Jack found it difficult to think of him as one of the men, even though he was as strong and able as any of them. When they paused for lunch, each man taking a heavy, folded pasty out of his can, Joseph crouched alone in a dark corner, speaking only when someone asked him a direct question, content to eat his food quietly and stare blankly at the wall of the tunnel.

Near the end of October, Jesse calculated that they were close to breaking through, so Jack led his men up to grass and directed both crews while Jesse stood aside to watch. For three days, they set double charges, and after each blast, Jack sent in a small team of the most experienced men to clear away the rubble before he dismissed everyone to the surface and, under Jesse's concerned eye, traversed the floor of the shaft himself, tapping with his hammer here and there to gauge the thickness of the rock still separating them from the dark cavern below. As they moved lower and lower, the men worked more and more carefully, sometimes winching themselves down to hang above the greenstone and drive in their drill bits to make room for the charges. At the end of the third day, Jack's tapping and Jesse's measurements convinced them that the rock surface was quite thin, and the crew set half again the usual number of charges precisely where Jack had marked the weakest points. They strung a long fuse up the surface, cleared the men away from above and below, and Jesse himself struck the match. They waited, scarcely breathing, while the flame trickled down into the shadows, and each man huddled, well away from the mouth, his arms over his ears. Then the blast came, but instead of sending a geyser of dust and fragments aloft, it produced nothing more than a few wisps of smoke. Jesse and Jack crept to the brink and looked in. They could see nothing in the gloom, so they winched themselves down, farther and farther, until they came to the jagged edges of a great hole that led deeper into the impenetrable blackness. They had smashed through the membrane, marrying the two ends perfectly, and the East Star Shaft reached a full twenty-three fathoms down.

There was much left to do—crews would sling platforms down the shaft to chip away at outcroppings and rig for the hoist, which would itself demand careful installation—but Jack had finished his part of the job, and he packed his things to move back into town, where Clara was waiting for him. He was on his way to the stable when he found Nick standing at the mouth of the new shaft. He walked around the lip to peer in from all directions, then took off his hat and crouched down, still gazing down into the darkness. When Jack approached him, he looked up and grinned. "Looks like lousterin' work, Jack. Been keepin' busy?"

"What d' ye think of it?"

Nick looked down for a long moment, then reached up and pinched his nose hard between his finger and thumb. When he looked up again, Jack realized that his eyes were wet. "It's a nation fine job."

"Do you want to go down?" Jack asked him.

Nick shook his head. "Already been. I was just gettin' ready to leave. Goin' to town?"

For the next six months, Jack hardly visited the North Star. The smooth operation and the rising dividends produced partners' meetings so congenial that even Charles Nankervis managed a smile, though cracked and contorted from disuse, as he rose from one gathering to invite the rest out for a beer. Jack was glad to let the mine run without him, for he was investing every penny he could spare, speculating in stocks and lending money at high interest on short terms. He found the foreclosures more interesting and profitable than the routine payments; early in the spring, he sued one of his delinquents and the judge awarded him shares in two different mines in Placer County. He was becoming a man of some property, with an increasingly comfortable income.

Cousin Jack

But it wasn't enough. He began searching for investments outside of Nevada County. He spent nearly a week trying to talk his way into partnership with a contractor who had bid to elevate several city blocks in Sacramento, dredging out the bed of the American River and hauling wagon loads of sand and gravel to dump in the downtown streets. Another outfit was engaged in lifting entire buildings, inch by inch, with screw jacks, raising them up to the new street level and waiting while the fill gangs boosted the city above flood level. Neither man seemed willing to come to terms, and Jack began to lose interest, so he moved on to San Francisco. In the saloon of the Cosmopolitan Hotel, he met a man, a friend of a friend, who had been involved in the formation of the Odd Fellows Savings Bank; Jack thought ruefully that the company had been arranged while he was helping Jesse sink the East Star Shaft. The man told him that a consortium of financiers and investors was, at that very moment, negotiating the terms of something they would call the Bank of California, which promised to be one of the biggest concerns on the Pacific Coast. Jack found someone to introduce him to one of the principals, but although everyone professed to appreciate his interest, no one offered him a chance to join in the enterprise. Weary, he returned to Grass Valley, and stopped in Chinatown to consult with Ah Choy, but the merchant was absent; he had become one of the more important hiring agents for the Central Pacific, meeting with Charles Crocker every month in Colfax, scouring the settlements to offer six-month contracts, and traveling up the line to check on the workers and witness the extension of the shining steel bars that were connecting the coasts. When Jack finally opened the door to his own parlor, Clara greeted him with the decree that he must stay close to home, at least until the baby arrived. That evening, he walked out onto the porch to smoke a cigar and consider how easy it had been to forget about the imminent child while sitting next to a gilt mirror in a San Francisco saloon.

At the end of May, Edward Sterling made an announcement that jolted Jack's full attention back to the North Star. He informed the partners that he was calling a special meeting for the sole purpose of discussing an offer to purchase the company. The room fell completely silent as the partners stared at the superintendent and then at each other. John clearly knew all about it; he could not hide his delighted grin and could scarcely sit still in his chair. Finally, Charles Nankervis spread his hands on the table and asked about the terms, and Edward nodded to John, who rose and walked around the room, handing each partner three sheets of paper penned in a fair, round hand by one of Findley's clerks. Most of the proposal was quite straightforward: a group of investors from San Francisco proposed to buy everything—the claims, the mill, the hoisting works, and all of the machinery and equipment—for $450,000; a quarter of a million when the documents were signed, and the rest, with ten per cent interest, out of the projected profits.

On the following evening, Jack rode out to French Lead to discuss the offer. He walked into Jesse's house to find Hannibal's two boys chasing each other around the kitchen, and Susan, cuddling the baby, looked up and smiled so warmly that he felt uncomfortable, as though there was something happening between them that had slipped his mind.

In the parlor, Hannibal was gnawing on his lower lip, and as soon as the men drew their chairs up to the table where Jesse had laid out the proposed contract, he waved a page in the air and stabbed his finger at it. "They promise to continue working the mine. We can count on that; they'd be fools not to. But look at all this clap about 'ow they'll do their business—'with energy, diligence, skill and economy'—'continuously worked and economically and energetically managed.' Who's t' decide?"

Jesse smiled. "Did they slack off, we'd find out soon enough."

"Issss," said Hannibal, letting his breath whistle through his teeth. "And then what? Do you and I 'ave t' go down there every day t' keep 'em at it?"

"Why wouldn't they work it as well as they could?" Jack asked.

Hannibal leaned in. "Do you know these men? Do you know anything about 'em?" Jack shook his head. "Nor do I. All we know is that they're money men from San Francisco. They won't be 'ere t' run th' place themselves, and wouldn't know 'ow anyway. They'll 'ave t' bring in someone. And who'll that be?"

"P'raps they'll hire you, Hannibal," said Jack, smiling, "and then we can rest easy."

Hannibal almost glared at him. "Iss, ye'd like that, wouldn't ye, Jack—to 'ave me do the work for ye?" Jack sat back in his chair, startled at the man's anger. A movement in the next room caught his eye, and he glanced through the doorway to see that Susan had draped a shawl over her shoulders to nurse the baby.

Jesse put his hand on Hannibal's arm. "Easy, Hannibal, easy. Ye're right—it's a fair concern. But there should be no trouble findin' a man who can do th' job."

Hannibal would not be put off. "It says 'ere they'll be payin' their superintendent three 'undred a month—that's as much as we're payin' Edward, but who knows if th' new man'll be worth it? And 'ere's this scaval-an-gow about wages and supplies—'shall not be in excess of current prices.' Who's t' decide what's current?"

"At least they're not payin' th' President of their board," Jesse observed.

Jack sighed. "If they run up wages, then they're making nothing themselves. They take half; we take half. And why would they pay more than they had to?"

"How do I know?" Hannibal retorted. "P'raps to bring in the best men from the other mines. P'raps because they're hirin' their own. P'raps they'll bring in a smart clerk who'll draw up the books t' make it look like they're payin' out more than they really are."

"Ah, hold your bal," said Jack. "You're seein' piskies in th' rafters."

Hannibal went on, using the stub of a pencil to slash furious circles around the passages that offended him. "And look at this bit about payin' th' legitimate expenses each month before they divide out our share. 'Such expenses as are necessary for th' judicious and prudent working and development of said mining property.' They're includin' the incline shaft there— what if they decide to run it down to a thousand feet an' they put every penny into hirin' crews to do it? Or that t' work the place 'prudently' they'll need a new engine or two, shipped in from San Francisco?"

Jack started to speak, but Jesse cut him off. "They're givin' us a mortgage on th' mine—if they don't pay on th' note, it comes due, and if they can't raise th' money to pay it off, we take it all back."

"Iss fay—wouldn't that be fine? We'd spend months in court, and no one workin' th' mine. We'd be lucky if th' place didn't flood."

Jack slammed his fist down on the table. "So what d'ye want?" In the other room, the boys stopped playing and Zennora looked up, startled and apprehensive. The baby began to cry. "Is it the terms that ye don't like, or don't ye want t' sell at all?"

"D' you?" Hannibal's lips were pressed together so tightly that they had disappeared, and his spectacles had slid so far down his nose that he was looking across the tops of them.

"If the terms are fair—yes. Yes, I do want to sell. Why not?"

"Why not? I'll tell ye. We've been runnin' th' mine for nearly seven years now. We finally 'ave the shafts and the stamps that we need, so for a good while, all we'll 'ave to do is bring out the rock and crush it. We can count on twelve thousand a month in net profits—that's six 'undred a share."

Jesse intervened. "Let's set th' terms aside. Sellin' th' mine means a change. P'raps not for you, Jack, but for me, and most of all, for you, Hannibal. Ye're the underground captain. What'll ye do if we sell?"

Hannibal considered. "I'm not sure. Nick's workin' down at Norambagua." He looked over at Jesse. "Why idden 'e 'ere t'night?"

"I invited 'im," said Jesse, "but 'e said 'e'd vote 'is shares with mine."

Hannibal looked down at the table and tapped his pencil. "I might go work for another mine. Or I might take th' money and use it for somethin'. Get into somethin' different."

"There's the Live Yankee," suggested Jack.

"Iss fay, but I'd 'ardly expect you t' be puttin' it forward."

Jack's eyebrows rose, but Jesse cut in again. "We need t' decide 'ow we really feel about sellin'. Each man on 'is own. Jack?"

"I say we sell."

Hannibal looked down at the papers and resumed tapping his pencil on the table. "They're offering four-fifty. We'd see that much in dividends in three years, or likely less. So after three years, we'd be bringin' in more money than we're lookin' at now. Do we want four-fifty now, or more than that later on?"

"What do you want to do?" Jesse asked gently.

Hannibal clapped his pencil down on the table and looked up. "I say we stay. I stand t' make more with the North Star, partner and captain, than I could by movin' on to somethin' else."

Jack shifted in his chair. "But what about the Live Yankee?"

Hannibal bared his teeth. "Jack, I know ye think I'm a great fool over that mine. But I know it's not payin', and it may not pay."

"Then why d'ye stick with it?"

"Because I promised the Pascoes. And because it was my idea." He looked down at the table, refusing to say more.

"If we sell th' North Star," suggested Jesse, "ye'll be quit of Edward Sterling."

Hannibal grinned. "I've thought o' that. But 'e's easier than 'e was, and the money makes it worth while."

"Jesse," said Jack, "what do you want to do?"

Jesse folded his hands. "I'm for sellin'." Hannibal's face lost its smile. "I know, Hannibal, I know. But I'm just not . . . interested . . . any more." He stopped, knowing that he could not explain. He had spent his life underground, as at home below as other men were at grass, and he had always thought that he would go down in the mines as long as he was able. But while he and Jack were working on the East Star, there had been several moments, usually early in the morning before the crews arrived, when he had climbed down into the hole and felt like an interloper, as though he did not belong there. He kept having the impulse to look behind him, as though there were some danger that he had noticed only subconsciously, but there was never anything amiss that he could discern. The experience had left him apprehensive and exhausted. "I'll build a 'ouse in town and live easy."

And so the sale went through. Only the Chenoweths joined Hannibal in resisting the plan, but they formed so small a minority that they, disappointed, acceded to the others. Even Hannibal couldn't challenge Edward's ability to enforce the intent as well as the letter of the agreement; no one could imagine a more obdurate overseer. And besides, as Jack observed, $450,000 was somewhat more than a fair price for the company. They'd have a quarter of a million in their pockets, and if, for some unlikely reason, the rest of the money was slow in arriving, they'd have the interest, and all in all, they'd do well out of it.

Cousin Jack

The next two weeks were given over to lawyers and documents, clerks and county officials, but during the interim, the men working the shifts at French Lead, already apprehensive because of the change of management, discovered that the partners seemed to be finding reasons for paying visits to the mine. The captains started arriving early and staying late—Hannibal once appeared at the incline shaft just before the early June dawn, and stayed below until well after midnight—and the others found excuses for visiting the lower levels. Even John Sterling walked down to the seventh gallery with the morning shift, and then, with Hannibal's amused permission, he stayed all day to work with a man whose partner had taken sick, careless of his clothes, swinging a borrowed sledge and setting his charges with the rest. The others in the tunnel were younger men, hired recently, who had grown accustomed to viewing some of the partners as true miners and the others as men of business; they were baffled to see that a man they had come to regard as a grass fool was as good a hard-rock man as any of them.

Jack visited the mine as often as he could, but Clara pestered him into staying home most of the time. She spent each day lying in bed, where she complained of the heat, no matter how cool the breeze was, and insisted that he come to her room every half hour to bring her fresh ice wrapped in a rag to lay over her closed eyes. Just after midnight on the first of July, her pains began, and as soon as the sun rose, Jack sent a boy out to French Lead to fetch Zennora, who had promised to help her niece, so far from her own mother, when the time came. A few hours later, Jesse pulled up in front of the house to drop off Zennora and to bring the news that Dibble had finished drawing up the papers. Zennora checked Clara and assured Jack that there was plenty of time, so he climbed into Jesse's carriage for the short ride into town. The air was hot and heavy, and tall clouds mounted in the sky as they pushed up through the foothills towards the Sierra crest. They found most of the partners already sitting in Dibble's office, and Edward had just finished reading the documents. The attorney produced a pen and a bottle of deep blue ink, and offered them to Edward. He approached the desk, dipped the pen, bent over to sign in his neat, small hand, and passed the pen to John, who wrote his name with extra flourishes. Each of the other partners took his place, leaned over the papers, dipped the pen, and signed. Hannibal hesitated for just an instant, staring down at the paper, but he, too, signed. Finally, Dibble witnessed Charles Nankervis's mark and called in his notary to verify the signatures.

As Jesse drove back towards Bennett Hill, a peal of thunder rolled across the valley, and then another. The thunderheads floating up from the south had gathered, linked up and formed a broad, dappled grey ceiling that loomed above them. Large, warm raindrops began to fall, and a fickle breeze kicked up the dust and lifted their hats, so that each man had to keep one hand on his brim. As the horse climbed the hill up from Wolf Creek, lightning flashed to the north, and the sudden, tearing crack of thunder frightened the animal, but Jesse held him in check. They pulled up in front of Jack's house and ran up to the porch just as the shower began in earnest, and they stood there, stamping the damp dust off of their feet and slapping the droplets off of their hats. Then, suddenly, there was a tremendous clatter on the roof above them, and bits of ice drummed into the carriage, dancing off the canopy and onto the roadbed below. Just as abruptly, the hail turned to rain again, but softer now, and the thunder rolled, muffled, from the mountains to the northeast. As the shower diminished and the rumbling dwindled, the men could hear, from upstairs, the sound of a baby crying.

12
The Idaho
1867-69

Dibble offered Hannibal a pen, but he shook his head and picked up the top sheet again, poring over the phrasing, searching for something, anything that would convince him that the agreement wasn't a disastrous mistake. The former partnership of the North Star "for value received," did sell, grant, assign and transfer the "agreement and indenture of mortgage" to Archibald Peachy, President, North Star Gold Mining Company, a corporation. After only three months, the Sterlings and their partners were excusing the debt: the entire two hundred thousand dollars.

The new owners had taken over without losing a day, but after several weeks, the new superintendent—a good hard-rock man whom Jack had known in Red Dog—had informed Peachy that production was falling far short of what the previous owners had predicted. The company clerk calculated that retiring the debt, given the apparent rate of earnings, would take at least ten years, far more than the three years that all parties had expected. Skeptical, Hannibal had insisted that Jesse visit the mine with him. Everything was running as before, with the same men working the same jobs in the same shifts, and the new underground captain, a Cornishman, seemed to know his business. As they walked back to Jesse's house, Hannibal could scarcely contain himself. If the mine was producing as much ore as before, he argued, then Peachy was lying about his net profits. The only other conceivable explanation was that Edward Sterling had been paying dividends out of his own pocket and cooking the ledgers in order to claim high profits that would make the mine attractive to potential buyers, and that, Hannibal snorted, was far-fetched even for that scalawag. Jesse listened silently, shaking his head and pulling at his beard.

On the polished table in Findley's conference room, they opened Peachy's ledgers for inspection. The expenses were all appropriate and well within the bounds of the agreement, and the production of ore had fallen off by less than three per cent, a margin that everyone excused as a predictable consequence of the transition, and certainly not large enough to explain the disappointing profits. The only answer lay in the reports from the stamp mill and the captain's daily inspections of ore samples: the vein simply wasn't as rich as it had been before, so a ton of rock yielded less gold for Peachy's men than it had for the old partners. As soon as this point became clear, nearly everyone around the table sat back, waiting for Edward or Peachy to suggest a resolution. Only Hannibal persisted in the investigation, flipping pages in the ledger and asking questions about the most minor details related to wages, arrangement of crews, maintenance schedules for the engines, and so on. He ran on so incessantly that Jesse finally asked him to let someone else speak, and when Hannibal kept interrupting, jabbing a forefinger at some petty anomaly in the ledger, Charles Nankervis lost his temper, rose half way out of his chair and growled at Hannibal to hold his tongue.

It was at that moment, as Hannibal and Charles glared at each other, that Edward proposed excusing the remainder of the debt. No one liked the idea, but John, who had responded to the crisis with uncharacteristic gravity, suggested that the mine had fallen so far short of advertised expectations that the new owners would have grounds to sue. When he turned to Peachy for confirmation, the president, who had sat through the discussion with his arms quietly folded, simply nodded. That being the case, said John, they would do best to protect themselves by accepting the current level of production as the basis for revising their agreement. By the end of September, they would have received approximately ten thousand dollars from the new owners, which they could, in effect, regard as having increased the price by that amount. Jack observed that excusing the debt altogether was scarcely warranted by the reported profits, and he suggested that they, instead, revise the sale agreement to reflect a lower price and reduce the note accordingly. Edward reminded him that no one had expected the note to last longer than three years; Jack shrugged his shoulders and challenged him to suggest a figure and a term. If he wanted the debt retired in only two years, for example, they could hold note down to fifty or sixty thousand dollars. The Sterlings exchanged glances, and Edward asked Peachy if he would be willing to let the partners discuss options among themselves. The new president nodded, rose, and left the room.

Edward waited for the door to shut and the footsteps to fade down the staircase. He then turned to Jack and, in an even tone, informed him that Peachy and his partners would surely sue unless the debt were excused in its entirety. The Sterlings had gone to San Francisco to meet with the directors, and they, he assured the men around the table, had been outraged. Two of them accused the former owners of deliberately lying about their profits and threatened to bring an action no matter how the situation was resolved.

Hannibal denounced Edward's proposal as completely unacceptable. As far as he knew—here he paused and looked around the table—the reports of their profits had been impeccably accurate, and if the only plausible explanation of the current dilemma was that the ore wasn't as rich as it had been, why, that was part of the risk of mining. Moreover, he interpreted the failure of the vein, if that's what it was, as only temporary, and predicted that at some point, not too far off, the mine would pay as well as it had, if not better.

Cousin Jack

They would be fools to resign so large a debt—nearly half of the negotiated price! His argument rang true in his own ears, but he saw no support in the other men's faces. Beset and incredulous, he asked Jack how large a note the current profits would justify.

Jack shook his head. "It doesn't matter. If they take us to court, we'll spend more fighting 'em than we'll lose by letting 'em go. Remember, Dibble would be arguin' in front of a judge who can read a balance sheet but knows little about mines. He'd most likely find against us."

Hannibal turned and looked at Jesse, who simply said, "There's no use."

Nick, who had contributed nothing to the debate, now leaned over to Hannibal. "Th' men who own the Norambagua run t' their lawyer whenever someone sneezes, an' this lot from San Francisco know less about mining than Jack's judge. I say we move on."

Hannibal felt the blood rising in his face, and his hands began to shake. "But we made a fair deal."

Jack smiled ruefully. "So we did, but it doesn't matter. It won't look fair to anyone else now."

Even the Chenoweths had given up, and Charles sat at the foot of the table releasing long breaths through his nose every time someone asked a question that delayed the end of the meeting. When Edward called for a vote, only Hannibal dissented, so John trudged down the stairs to call Peachy back to discuss the exact terms of the new agreement.

Now Hannibal sat in Dibble's office and stared at the papers. He could not believe that such a keenly lode had dwindled so. He wondered if he and his partners had seen most of the wealth of the mine, selling just as the vein became exhausted and left nothing but "raffain" ore—rock of too little value to warrant the work of bringing it out. If that were so, then Peachy would certainly send his lawyers with accusations, demands for restitution, and more papers, always more papers. Hannibal could not stop thinking about the money. Allowing for the three months of payments, his share of the forgiven debt came to nineteen thousand dollars—enough to buy a business on Mill Street, five or six of the finer homes in town, or a major interest in one of the better mines in the county. He felt as though he had lost ground somehow and would need to find a way to recoup the missing dollars.

Jack had already begun investing his share; only a week after they closed the deal, he bought the narrow brick storefront building on Mill Street where John Johnston kept his grocery. He had complacently described it as a long-term venture, but a sure one: he wouldn't recoup his initial investment for at least six years, but there would always be a tenant paying a regular rent. Hannibal reflected that the move was somehow typical of Jack: he talked a lot about great enterprises and marching in the vanguard of the inevitable progress of the great state of California, but when the time came to make a decision, he invariably found a solid and reliable place to put his money. Jack was becoming tiresome; he had invited Hannibal and Susan to join him and Clara to see *Romeo and Juliet*, and he spent the entire evening bragging and telling amusing stories to the two laughing women. Hannibal found the play contrived and over-wrought, and when he and Susan returned home, she, apparently annoyed with a silence that she took to be judgmental, changed for bed with crisp efficiency, answering him with a cold, raised eyebrow whenever he spoke to her.

He sighed, took the pen from Dibble's fingers, and signed the document. He laid the pen down on the paper and looked up at the attorney, who was studying him. "What?" asked Hannibal.

Dibble hesitated as he picked up the pen and the document. "Did you know that the Sterlings are negotiating to capitalize the Idaho Mine?" He watched Hannibal's face change. "They're going to incorporate and sell stock."

"How much?"

"One share for each foot on the ledge—thirty-one hundred shares at a hundred dollars each."

Hannibal knew the claim, a new one on Wolf Creek, just east of town, that had yet to show any promise. The partners had worked it haphazardly, but even after sinking a shaft down to the ledge, they'd found nothing, and when a few partners refused to pay their shares of the expenses, the company shut down. Over a year had passed since then, and everyone had assumed that the claim was worthless. Hannibal had heard rumors that the partners had wasted at least twenty thousand dollars, or perhaps upwards of thirty thousand, on the venture. But now, if they raised the capital Dibble was describing, they would have over three hundred thousand dollars behind them. If there was gold down there, they would surely find it. "How much are the Sterlings puttin' in?"

Dibble smiled and checked his watch. "I don't know that, and if I did, I couldn't tell you."

Dibble himself had been one of the original partners in the claim, along with his law partner and several of the storekeepers in town. "What about you?" asked Hannibal.

Dibble smiled again and now reached up to stroke his sandy mustache. "Well, I'm not really a miner. I think I can do better right here."

Hannibal nodded. Most of the men in town came to Dibble's firm, so in his own way, he was involved in the mines, the mills, the foundries, the farms, the livery stables, the lumber yard, and most of the stores. Hannibal envied a profession that imposed no risks or dangers, but offered a steady stream of clients who had no choice but to request his services. He found his hat, thanked the lawyer, and walked down to the street level. By the time he reached the sidewalk, he had made up his mind to talk to the Sterlings.

On Sunday after church, he hurried Susan and the children out towards the street in order to intercept John Sterling, as if by chance, as his family walked through the churchyard. Mary and Susan complimented each other's children as Hannibal drew John aside. "I hear the Idaho may be startin' up again."

John raised his eyebrows and smiled. "Do you? Well, well, yes, we hope so."

Hannibal pursed his lips as though weighing the possibilities. "If ye need anything, John, I just might be able to 'elp." John kept smiling, but now looked baffled. "If ye'd like, I could meet with you and Edward—p'raps on Tuesday?" Sterling, still mystified, suggested that he come to Edward's home after breakfast.

On the appointed morning, the Chinese servant answered the door and showed Hannibal into the sitting room. John rose to greet him, shaking his hand and slapping him on the shoulder, but Edward remained where he was, sitting like a statue in a large chair next to the window. As soon as he could, Hannibal mentioned the Idaho Mine and asked about the state of the works. John looked at Edward, who took a patient breath and explained that the original partnership had sunk a vertical shaft down to a depth of 120 feet and a drift out about 60 feet to a small ledge that showed no gold at all. There was nothing at the claim but a small pump and a smaller hoist.

Hannibal smiled. "Now, I think I heard that th' two of ye were takin'— what was it?—'alf th' shares?"

The Sterlings looked at each other, and John replied, "Not quite half."

"Ah, yes," said Hannibal. "Still a good portion. Now, I know ye wouldn't be takin' the risk unless ye knew somethin' was down there." Edward frowned, and John leaned in to assure Hannibal that there were no other prospects beyond what they had told him. "Well, p'raps ye need t' get a good hard-rock man t' go down and 'ave a look. Nankervis is one o' th' best— 'ave ye asked 'im?"

John shook his head. "It's reasonable to expect that there's a rich ledge down there, but we don't know. You're right that we're taking a risk, but it's just that."

"What'll ye do if it doesn't pay?" asked Hannibal.

John shrugged slightly. "If we determine that we've gone far enough, we'll liquidate the shares—each man will take his portion of what's left of the capital."

Hannibal guessed that they were committing over a hundred thousand dollars, and he could not believe that they would venture so much—possibly all they had realized from the sale of the North Star—without good reason. They must know something about the mine, something they weren't willing to tell. "Sounds like ye may need a few more men. I might be able t' buy some shares." He tried to present the suggestion as though he were doing them a favor, but without condescending.

Edward folded his arms and looked out the window, and John sat back with a concerned expression on his face. "I'm sorry Hannibal—we're fully subscribed. If we had known you might be interested, we could have included you, but now there's nothing left." Hannibal tried to keep his face under control, but he knew that he must have betrayed something, because John leaned in, his brow wrinkling. "We had to offer the opportunity to the original partners—you understand—and about half of them took up the idea."

"Of course, of course." said Hannibal. "Well, I wish ye luck." He rose to his feet, and as the servant handed him his hat, he turned, as if remembering something, and asked, "If th' two of you are th' major stockholders, ye'll surely be runnin' th' place?"

"We'll have to wait and see."

A moment later, Hannibal was walking down towards Mill Street, hardly feeling the ground beneath his boots. He had made a fool of himself, and to no purpose. The Sterlings were surely laughing at his feeble attempt to appear that he had approached them only out of good fellowship. Now they would think that he was desperate, able to find neither a project nor a partner. They might even speculate that he had already lost the money he had taken from the North Star, and they would wonder how he had done it.

He stopped at the saloon next to the livery stable and called for a beer. Here he was, a hard-rock miner, still a young man, who had, until recently, owned a share in one of the best mines in the most prosperous and productive gold mining town in California, and he felt completely shut out. As he stood at the bar, his foot wedged into the brass rail, John Johnston, the grocer, walked in. After making a commonplace remark about the weather, Johnston mentioned the sale of his building to Jack.

"He's your cousin, ain't he? Well, he gave us a fair price, a fair price indeed. A fine man of business. And you know—" He leaned in to speak quietly so that the bar man could not hear him. "We knew we'd want the cash for something, and now we've found it. We're buying into the Idaho Mine. The Sterlings are forming a corporation, and so many of the old partners wanted to get out that they've been looking all over town for new investors." Hannibal set his beer down carefully and stared at the man. "There are still some shares left, so Peter and I are going up to see them this evening."

After supper, Hannibal sat next to the fire, so oblivious to the boys that Susan scooped them up and took them upstairs. He felt numb, paralyzed. When he thought about the way he had handled Edward, from the day he met the man, he kept hearing his mother's voice saying "foochy," as she had on the morning when he spilled an entire pail of fresh milk. There was the day in the mine office when he had lost his temper and accused him of having forgotten everything he knew about working underground. Surely he still resented his deliberate exclusion from the Live Yankee—no matter that he had once told Martin, in a rare moment of candor, that he thought the project worthless—and now he was paying Hannibal back in kind. Either Edward hated him or he thought him a fool, and either way, Hannibal had brought this on himself. When would he learn? He had always scorned John Sterling's manner, but even though the man went too far, there was no denying that he had the right idea—you treated every man as your friend, for you never knew when you would need him. Hannibal realized now, uncomfortably, that Jack Trevenna knew how to handle himself; he made his opportunities and he kept every contact alive.

A few weeks later, the family gathered at Zennora's house for dinner. Hannibal found the conversation oppressive and, seeking solitude, walked out onto the porch for a quiet smoke in the brisk autumn air. He had shut the door and reached for his pouch before he realized that Jack was leaning against a post at the corner. Jack asked, quite casually, about his current interests, so Hannibal offered a long, evasive answer about mining claims, various stocks and even some land down near the Bear River. He thought quickly as he spoke, and he realized that this was the kind of encounter that other men used to his advantage, so he indicated, as clearly as he could without being absolutely direct, that there was room for someone to join him on any of his various endeavors. Rather than acknowledging the implied offer, Jack changed the subject.

"I need some help, Hannibal, and I think you're the man I'd trust more than any other."

"What is it?"

"I can't stay in town all the time, and I have more t' do than I can manage. Johnston's store is more complicated than I'd realized. There are taxes t' be paid, and insurance. When th' place needs paint or repairs, I have t' take care of it, and if I'm not here, then I don't know, and it doesn't get done. Then there are my stocks and claims. If they levy an assessment, they want t' be paid right away, and if they send out a dividend, I like t' take it t' th' bank the day it arrives. I just can't quite keep up."

"What d'ye want me t' do?"

Jack smiled. "It's simple, really. I want you t' keep my books for me. When the bills come due, you pay them. When the checks arrive, you deposit them. And you keep records of everything."

"So I'd be yer accountant."

"Well, more than that, really. You'd manage everything. And I'd pay you a salary. I really need you, Hannibal. I don't know anyone else that could handle this as well as you."

Although Jack seemed to be presenting the proposal as a compliment to his probity and skill, Hannibal suspected that he was using it to deflect the idea of them becoming partners. Jack, he inferred, had plenty of opportunities, so many that he did not have time to mind them all. He would make the money, and he would hire Hannibal to do the day-to-day work for him. Hannibal was trying to find a way to refuse and tell Jack what he thought of the implied rebuff, but he realized that he wanted to do something, wanted to be involved. He might as well keep Jack's books as sit at home. And, he had to admit, he might learn something by tracking all of Jack's investments. He accepted the offer.

As winter settled in, Hannibal did not have enough to do, so by early afternoon each day, he found himself wandering aimlessly around the house. Keeping Jack's books had turned out to be quite routine, not even requiring his daily attention. Each time he rode out to the Live Yankee, there was nothing new to see or learn; the Pascoes were sinking a shaft towards the ledge, but very slowly, since they had agreed not to hire anyone outside the partnership, and without apparent success. For a week or so, he threw himself into a small list of repairs and chores that Susan had drawn up for him, but he found the work tedious and unsatisfying. After a two-day snowstorm in January, he went for a long walk down French Ravine, carrying a stick to knock the bare oak branches and watch their loads of snow fall in unpredictable patterns. Even the acrimony with Edward Sterling, he decided, was preferable to this isolated idleness.

With that thought in mind, he went to see Jesse. He knew of several claims, promising but small, just right for two experienced men to explore at their own pace, enough to keep them busy without becoming burdensome. Jesse sat in his kitchen, occasionally rubbing his fingers through his beard. Hannibal kept talking, trying to pitch his proposal so it would sound interesting without being overwhelming, and he realized that from time to time, Jesse was looking past him, over his shoulder to where Zennora stood at the sink. He realized that he was beginning to repeat himself, so he stopped.

Jesse looked out the window for a moment, and then down at the floor. "All right, Hannibal. You find a couple o' claims, and I'll look 'em over with ye." He waved off Hannibal's thanks and then, exchanging another look with Zennora, asked, "'as Susan told ye that we're movin' in t' town?" She had not. Jesse was negotiating to buy a lot on Auburn Street, about a third of a mile south of Wolf Creek. He planned to spend the spring and summer building their new home, and they hoped to be living there by Christmas.

Cousin Jack

Hannibal walked home, back to the house he had built because Susan wanted to live near her parents, and he wondered whether she would now demand that they move. He found her in the kitchen, dicing meat for a pie, and he mentioned, casually, that Jesse had told him about their plans. Susan's face was unreadable; he could not even be sure that she acknowledged keeping the news from him. She made no comment about living a half an hour's ride from her mother, and anyway the boys were clamoring for her attention, so Hannibal let the subject, if it was a subject, fade away.

Now that Jesse had agreed to work with him, Hannibal devoted himself to hunting for claims. On some days, he saddled his horse and rode out before dawn, not to return until dusk, and occasionally he rode far to the northeast, staying overnight near the prospects he was checking. Susan didn't seem to care whether he went or not; when he left the house, she returned his farewell briskly and continued with the housework. When he returned home, he looked for a welcome not from his wife but from Bertie and James, who ran to the door, calling for him and reaching their arms to be picked up.

Returning from one excursion, he stopped in town and happened to see the Chenoweths, who asked if he could spare a few minutes. As soon as they were settled at a table in Cryer's Saloon, Mark announced that they had decided to sell their shares in the Live Yankee, but that they would give Hannibal the first chance to buy them. They were reluctant to explain their decision, but they grudgingly confided that they didn't really believe that the Pascoes would ever find a ledge, much less one that paid. They had waited for four years, they had paid their share of the assessments to hire labor and purchase equipment, and they saw no point in waiting any longer. Hannibal asked for two days' grace, and he rode back to French Lead trying to decide what to do. Mark and Richard each owned a share, an undivided twentieth of the mine, and the fair price was three thousand dollars apiece. Hannibal had the money, but he had hoped to use it to find some new ventures; if he set aside six thousand now, he would diminish his freedom and his options by that much. He couldn't, somehow, discuss the situation with Jack, and Nick would probably agree to help out only if Hannibal lent him the money, so he decided to talk to Jesse. His father-in-law listened gravely, the dark blue eyes fastened so steadily on Hannibal's face that he had to keep looking away as he spoke. If Jesse would buy a share, then Hannibal would buy a share, and they would keep the Live Yankee among the close circle of men whom they trusted. Moreover, Hannibal still controlled Martin's two shares, and the three men together would have half of the company. If, someday, it paid well, then . . . But that was only speculation.

Jesse sighed and looked out at the spring flowers, splashes of orange in the sunny spots between the groves of trees. He offered Hannibal a choice:

either he would buy one of the shares, or he would join Hannibal on a claim. He could not do both. He would have little time to spare from building the new house, and he thought it best he keep his money close until they were moved in. Weary, Hannibal chose the share. On the following day, he went to Dibble's office, and when they had finished instructing the lawyer, Mark drew him aside.

"I'm sorry, Hannibal. I know this means a lot to ye, but it's time for us to find somethin' else."

"It's all right."

"It'll pay one o' these days, and then you'll be winkin' at me for a fool."

"P'raps ye're right."

Mark looked away and ran his tongue back and forth across the inside of his lower lip. "Listen, Hannibal . . . There's trouble comin'."

"What d'ye mean?"

"I don't want t' tell ye everythin' just now. But the mine owners are goin' to be wantin' t' make some changes that the men won't like."

"What kind o' changes?"

"Ye'll be hearin' about it soon enough. But I wanted to ask ye . . . When it comes to it, we'll 'ave t' stand together."

"I'm not workin' anymore."

"I know that, but ye're still a hard-rock man."

The changes that preoccupied Mark were rooted in the advent of dynamite to the northern mines. The men called it "giant powder," for it was far more powerful than the traditional black powder, but the owners' temptation was the miners' fear: that the mines would be able to operate with fewer men. Black powder had to be set deep into the rock, packed into the holes that only a two-man rig could drill, but just one man, working alone, could drill the shallower holes for giant powder, so there was no need for a miner to work with a partner. Curious, Hannibal attended a meeting at Hamilton Hall. Most of the men he knew were there. Mark was one of the leaders, and midway through the program he thrust out an arm and introduced Jesse as the next speaker. Susan's father had little to say, but by the time he was finished, the men in the hall were applauding and yelling their support up to the rostrum. Hannibal left shaking his head over the excitement.

The miners established something they called the Miners' League and voted to strike until the owners promised to ban giant powder, but although Mark once again asked for his help, Hannibal had neither time nor attention to spare, for he was, once again, roaming the county in search of likely claims. He had resigned himself to the idea of working alone, and as he rode up and down the hills, he tried not to dwell on the notion that he was, for some reason he could not fathom, a pariah. Finally, he found a claim on Massachusetts Hill whose owners, two Cornishmen who had decided to go home, were willing to sell at a reasonable price. The claim was five hundred feet long and the owners had built a blacksmith's shop, so Hannibal agreed to pay them a thousand dollars.

Yet as he sat at the table in the parlor, sketching out a map of the claim, he contemplated the work he was planning for himself and considered the fact that Jack Trevenna was making his money without lifting a pick or a sledge. Perhaps, he thought, he should be looking for different kinds of opportunities, and with that in mind, he began to explore not the hills but the streets of downtown Grass Valley, where he bought men drinks and asked them questions. Each man had a different vision, a different strategy, but after several days, Hannibal became convinced he would do better not as a working partner, involved in the daily management of the mine, as he had been in the North Star, but as a stockholder, one of many, insulated from the day-to-day decisions, relying on the directors to run the company, and making his money on dividends and on the rising value of his shares.

He bought thirty shares in the Eureka Mine, which had been paying well for over two years, and, as a sort of a game with himself, he chose not to even visit the site. His confidence rising, he bought a hundred shares in the Spring Valley Water Company, which had, since 1861, been pumping water out of the Sierra streams and across the Sacramento Valley to fill a reservoir that served San Francisco. He began to wonder whether he should buy some farm land, or perhaps a commercial building like the one Jack owned on Mill Street, and lease it out.

The newspaper announced that there would be another meeting regarding the giant powder issue, but this was to be a gathering not only of miners or strikers, but of all citizens. Hannibal sat in the crowd and watched Mark present the miners' case. Findley, the banker, took the rostrum to argue that the strikers were attempting to pervert normal business relations and would, in the end, destroy the town. The meeting disintegrated until men were shouting angrily at each other from opposite corners of the hall.

Hannibal got up and slowly pushed his way through the throng, but when he reached the lobby, Jack Trevenna beckoned him over to where he was conferring intently with several men. Jack explained quickly, quietly, that they had to take action. Mark was losing control of the situation; the miners might follow him out of loyalty, but the townspeople didn't trust him. Hannibal could not think of a way to sidestep Jack's pressure and urgency, and as soon as he agreed to help, Jack plunged back into the hall, returning a few minutes later with Jesse. He sat his uncle down and quickly persuaded him to convince Mark to displace the League with a new association, one pledged to forgo violence and to recognize the owners' right to run the mines. Jack had clearly thought this out in advance; in his hand, he held a list of resolutions, and he had an answer for each of Jesse's objections.

With Jesse firmly recruited, Jack turned to Hannibal and asked him to bring Mark out.

Carville Conaway, the lumber man, was standing at the rostrum, holding a gavel in his hand and listening to a man who had stood up in the middle of the audience, while Mark whispered vehemently to a man who stood crouched next to his chair on the platform. Hannibal caught his attention and beckoned him. Mark looked over, puzzled, and lifted his palms and shrugged his shoulders, so Hannibal walked over to the side of the platform and hissed that Jesse wanted to see him. Mark muttered something to the crouching man and climbed down to join Hannibal, who took him by the arm and walked him out to the lobby. As they pushed their way past the men in the aisles, Mark kept asking, "What is it? What do you want?" They walked through the door into the comparative quiet where Jack and the others were waiting. Hannibal stood to one side while Jack and Jesse explained the list of resolutions. Mark read it over twice and then brandished it as he paced this way and that, arguing. Finally, his face bitter, he agreed to go along with them. He walked back towards the hall, but turned to snap at Jack before he disappeared through the door. Hannibal stood in the doorway with the others to watch Mark turn the meeting, but as soon as it seemed clear that he would succeed, he quietly slipped out the front and mounted his horse for the ride home.

The strike dragged on for some weeks, but Hannibal's attention turned elsewhere. Before they sold the North Star, he had lent a thousand dollars to a man named Jacob Hivner, accepting as surety a mortgage on a place known as the Kentucky Ranch, nearly five hundred acres in French Ravine, a couple of miles south of the mine. Hivner had made the first annual interest payment, but at the end of the second year, he drove up to the Carnes' house with a wagonload of cordwood. Hannibal refused to accept it, but after listening to the man whine, he relented, although he insisted that he pay the balance due in cash. Hivner promised to comply, but Hannibal saw nothing of him for months. He turned up a year later, this time with another stack of cordwood but also with a small bag of gold coins. Hannibal pointed out that the payment wasn't enough to cover one year's interest, let alone what was left over from the year before, and again the man grumbled and complained, promising to do the best he could and implying that the interest rate was too high. Hannibal sent him on his way, and a year later, the date for payment came and went without any word from Hivner. He showed up two months later riding a broken-down mare and offering a sum that covered barely half of the interest due for that year. Now, with another payment coming due, Hannibal began to ask questions of his friends on Mill Street. Several of them knew Hivner, and while they weren't at all surprised to hear that he had failed to pay on his note, they were quite intrigued with the idea that he actually owned a ranch securely enough to present it as collateral. One merchant actually laughed when he learned that Hannibal had provided the man with a loan. Anxious and humiliated, Hannibal studied the records in the courthouse and decided that Hivner and his wife did, indeed, hold clear title. When, exasperated, he told his story to Jack and asked his advice, Susan's cousin grinned and thumped a fist on the table. "Sue 'im!"

While Hannibal fretted over the Hivner affair, the Idaho Mine announced that their workmen had found the ledge they had been seeking. The vein lay three hundred feet below the surface, a hundred feet west of the shaft, and it was so rich that the owners decided to install a fifteen-stamp mill to crush the ore that they would be bringing up. Within a month, the mine was fully-equipped and working two full shifts. Hannibal spent many evenings sitting in his parlor brooding: if only he had included the Sterlings in the Live Yankee, if only he had been able to avoid offending Edward, if only . . . Restless, he took pointless walks along the Auburn road, continuing until he once again wanted to sit and gaze out the window, and then facing the trudge home as an added grievance. He had tried to talk to Susan, to explain how he felt and what he was trying to do, but she would listen for a few minutes, her face wooden, her eyes cold, and offer a curt, impatient solution and return to the children, who were, more and more, regarding their father warily from behind door jambs and furniture.

Hannibal pondered and vacillated into the heat of mid-August, interrupting his isolation only to attend Nick's wedding. The mining community had chuckled over the news; they had become convinced that Nick would always live as he had when he was twenty, spending more on his horse than his home, always in debt, and never attached to anyone, but now he had decided to marry the daughter of a quartz miner, a Cornishman, who had opened a small store on Main Street and become very friendly with the other merchants, even spending a weekly evening at the meetings of the local Republican Party. Jack joked that his brother was making a new kind of business deal, but when Susan didn't laugh, he abruptly remarked that he had to go see Jesse, and let himself out the door.

The wedding was a rowdy one, for Nick's friends from all over the county came to "see him off," as one of them put it. They were single men, some young, and some not so young any more, but all men without families whom Hannibal had seen at the wrestling matches, marching in the Guard, and shouting to each other outside various saloons on Saturday nights. They sat reverently through the service and sang the hymns in heavy, hoarse voices, but when the church emptied out into the dooryard, they let themselves go, giving the new couple one rousing cheer after another until Nick's wife began to look a little scared.

Jack had hired the dining room at the Exchange to give a supper for the family and a few close friends, but the two places at the head of the table sat empty until well into the main course, when Nick finally showed up, his face flushed and his wife biting her lip. As soon as the plates were cleared, Jack rose to offer a toast to his brother, and then, without any warning, announced that he and Clara were returning to Cornwall. Hannibal was completely surprised, and as he looked around the table, he decided that no one else had known anything about Jack's plans. Zennora was smiling and patting Clara on the hand, and Nick had thrown one arm around Jack to hold him in place so he could give him little punches in the belly. Hannibal turned to look at Susan, sitting next to him. She was trying to smile, but her face had gone completely white. He was about to lean over to ask her what was the matter, but she pulled a handkerchief out of her sleeve and turned away to do something to her face. Little Jane began to fret, frightened at all the noise, and Susan took her away from the table, turning to Hannibal only to direct him to keep the boys in their seats and prevent them from tipping over the water pitcher.

A few weeks later, Jack invited the Carnes to dine with him and Clara at their home, a last gathering before the Trevennas left the country. After dinner, while the women sat in the parlor watching the children play, Jack took Hannibal into the small room where he kept his papers. There was a brief contract assigning Hannibal a two per cent commission on all income from the store and the other investments, and he had drawn up a document assigning Hannibal his power of attorney for all of his business in the United States. As he sat there reading and listening, Hannibal remembered the day he had come to this same house to settle his affairs with Martin.

"How long will ye stay?" he asked.

Jack smiled. "We don't know. Clara wants to see her family, and I'd like to see what there is for me t' do."

"Will ye be comin' back at all?"

Jack laughed. "You can be sure o' that!" He clapped a hand on Hannibal's shoulder and steered him back out into the parlor. When the time came for the Carnes to leave, Susan picked up Jane and somehow marched the boys out to the wagon so that Hannibal, standing with one foot on the porch as he thanked Clara for the dinner, felt that he was keeping his family waiting.

In mid-October, Jack took his family to San Francisco for the trip to England, and Hannibal was left with his ledgers and the unfinished business of the Kentucky Ranch. Hivner, true to form, had not made the annual interest payment and Hannibal was not even sure where to find the man. He reviewed the whole story with Susan one evening after dinner and found her unusually willing to listen, although she seemed to regard the whole affair as somewhat tedious. She offered no opinion as to whether he should go to court, but on the following morning, he rode into town to ask Dibble to help him swear out a complaint.

The sheriff could not find Hivner to serve him the papers; there were rumors that he was prospecting in Placer County, driving a freight wagon in Sacramento, or working in a saloon in a camp near Truckee. In the meantime, the Idaho began to pay dividends, and Hannibal heard from a friend in town that each stockholder stood to earn, in only one year, as much as his shares were worth. Then Dibble brought word that the sheriff had located Hivner. The defendant stood in the courtroom, holding his hat to hide the dirty knees of his trousers, and whined that he was doing the best he could. The judge listened to both sides, his eyes flickering down to his pocket watch, and curtly found for the plaintiff. When Hivner made it clear that he no money to pay his debt, much less the costs and fees, the judge instructed the sheriff, after the customary six-month grace period, to sell the property at auction.

Hannibal rode back out to French Lead and hitched his horse to the wagon. "Susan!" he called. His wife appeared at the front door. He smiled and waved his hat. "Get the children!" A few minutes later, the Carne family was riding up the slope of Massachusetts Hill, headed towards town. Susan kept looking at Hannibal, who was humming to himself, and finally she asked where they were going. "You'll see!" was all he said, so she turned back to keep James from climbing out of the wagon. When they reached Boston Ravine, Hannibal drove across the bridge and up Ophir Street. He noticed Susan looking at him, but he said nothing. He turned the corner and drove north on Auburn Street, past Jesse's new house, nearly finished, and kept going for another hundred yards before pulling up in front of an empty lot.

He turned to Susan with a pleased smile. "What d'ye think?"

She looked at him, and then up and down the street. "What do I think o' what?"

"This!" He waved an arm at the property sloping gently up from the road. There were a few small trees, and the upper half was overgrown with poison oak and blackberry brambles.

"D'ye mean we should buy it?"

"Yes."

Susan got down out of the wagon, still holding Jane in her arms, and stood at the edge of the road. James and Bertie were crawling around in the back of the wagon, growling at each other and apparently pretending to be bears. Towards Wolf Creek was a lumber yard, and on the east side of the street were a few scattered new houses. "Why can't we buy that?"

Hannibal looked where she was pointing. Next to Jesse's construction stood a cross-gabled, two-story house painted white, with wisteria climbing up the porch posts. "It's not for sale."

"Have you asked 'em?"

"I don't need to ask 'em." Hannibal's good mood was beginning to go sour. "I know it's not available."

Susan's mouth was set and her eyes had gone wary. "I want t' live next door t' Mother."

Hannibal took off his hat and dug his heel into the dirt, digging a small hole. "I know that, Susan, but ye can't. This is only one door down. Idden that close enough?" She said nothing. Bertie had pushed James, who began to howl. "I thought ye'd be pleased."

She looked at the lot again. "What made ye decide t' do somethin' about it today?"

Hannibal put his hat on and grinned. "I won the suit against Hivner." She looked at him blankly. "That ranch down on the Auburn road." She offered no reaction at all. "Listen, Susan." He reached out and took both of her hands. James had subsided, and the boys were chasing a beetle around the back of the wagon. "I'm goin' t' buy that ranch. I think I can make somethin' of it. And I've other interests as well. I know ye want t' live near yer parents, and that's fine with me." He did not say what he had been thinking, more and more, that he would rest more easily if he weren't living so close to the North Star. "We can build a house 'ere—bigger than the other one. This time, I'll hire someone t' do it."

She looked up and down the street again. "How much will the ranch cost?"

"I'm not sure."

"How d'ye know we can afford it?"

"Oh, I know we've the money."

"Don't ye know th' price?"

He started chewing on the inside of his cheek. "The sheriff'll sell it at auction. I'd say p'raps two thousand dollars, and if I'm right, I won't have t' put up much cash at all."

"Then how will ye pay for it?"

"I'll use th' settlement—the twelve hundred Hivner owed me, and some interest and costs."

Susan thought for a moment, frowning. "Ye make it sound like we're gettin' the ranch for nothin', but th' twelve hundred is money ye gave 'im, and ye paid th' costs."

Hannibal started to snap at her, then thought better of it. She didn't understand. Of course it came at a price, but it felt easier if he didn't have to pay out of pocket. "All right. 'ere it is. After ye add it all up, it'll cost me about seven hundred."

"I thought ye said ye gave him twelve hundred."

"He paid me some interest."

"'ow much land?"

"About five 'undred acres."

"Is there even a road?"

"Iss fay, the Auburn road goes right along it." She said nothing. "We might plant fruit trees down there, Susan—start a farm."

"But we'll be livin' 'ere."

"Idden that what ye want?"

She looked at the empty slope again. "'ow much will this cost? This 'ere?"

"Twelve 'undred. I can borrow a bit from Jack if need be."

She pushed that idea away. "Fayther paid only seven 'undred for theirs."

He sighed. "I know, but people are movin' out 'ere now. It's worth more." She walked away a few steps, looking up at the white, cross-gabled house. "Look, if ye don't want it . . . "

She turned back to him. "I didn't say that."

"Well, ye don't seem . . . "

"Hannibal, give me chance. Bertie!" The boys were pounding on the sides of the wagon. "Bertie! Stop it!." They looked up at her, poised.

"D'ye want me to get 'em down?"

"It doesn't matter now." She drifted away again, moving onto the property, looking up at the brambles. From down the street, the gritty scream of the big sawblade sliced through the cold winter air.

Hannibal thrust his hands into his pockets. "Listen. There're some other places nearby." She was standing with the back of her shoulder turned towards him, so when he looked for her face, he could see only the line of her jaw and cheekbone. "There's a house up Kate Hays Hill that might be all right; then we wouldn't 'ave t' build."

"Hannibal!" She walked a few yards farther onto the property. "Could we put the house over there, so we're not too close t' that one?"

"Yes. Wherever ye want."

She moved along the front of the lot, staring up the slope. Jane had fallen asleep and now lay with her head flopped over to one side, her mouth distorted against her mother's shoulder. Abruptly, Susan turned and walked back to toward the wagon. "We must get back." She stopped and looked at him, slowly disengaging the baby from her shoulder. He took the child and held out his free arm so she could lean on him to climb up to her seat. As she raised her boot, he could see the swelling of her pregnancy.

He handed Jane up to her before walking around, climbing up to take his place, and draw in the reins. "Well?"

"What?"

"D'ye want t' take it?"

"If ye want to."

"Susan." He stopped for a moment, looked up the road, and took a breath. "I thought this is what you wanted."

"Well, then, take it."

"Would ye rather look at somethin' else?"

"Can we go home now? I still 'ave t' get dinner, and the boys'll need baths tonight."

"What d'ye want t' do?"

"I said ye could take it, didn't I?"

Hannibal started to say something else, but changed his mind, clucked to the horse, and drove the wagon back to French Lead.

The judgement had somehow released Hannibal from his paralysis. He rode into town nearly every afternoon, and he soon formed a regular route of offices, stores and saloons, where he exchanged news and advice with the men he found there. They discussed the progress on the new state Capitol in Sacramento, the anti-coolie clubs in San Francisco, the race to finish the Central Pacific, and, always, the work in the mines in the district. He discovered that he was now able to hear about the startling success of the Idaho without feeling, a moment later, trickles of sweat run down from his armpits, but whenever one of his cronies marveled at the lavish dividends the mine was paying to the Sterlings and their partners, Hannibal would usually nod blandly and look away.

He gave up hoping for Susan's approval of the lot on Auburn Street, so he bought it and hired a builder. After working with the man for a while, he brought home some rough drawings. Susan seemed interested, even enthusiastic, and he, charmed when she smiled at him, answered all of her questions and then, feeling encouraged, pointed out every feature on the drawing. He realized, after several minutes, that he had exhausted her curiosity and that she was now humoring him, but even that little show of patience and forbearance beguiled and reassured him. A few days later, he walked into Zennora's kitchen to hear Susan explaining the advantages of the house that he had designed, and both women smiled at him. He now left the house earlier each day so he could make his round in town and still have time to spend a few hours checking the construction and working with the carpenters.

Susan had her baby in the spring. Hannibal had gone to town, as usual, but found the streets and saloons full of men celebrating the driving of the Golden Spike. Everyone was toasting the Central Pacific partners, and they were predicting a new era for California. The *Union* had printed a special edition, so he bought a copy and took it home to read to Susan while she played with the children. He was half-way through an unusually extravagant set of predictions regarding overland travel—the rhetoric reminded him of Jack Trevenna—when she gasped and slowly lowered herself to her knees. She was all right after a moment or two, but he helped her upstairs and ran to a nearby house to ask the neighbor to ride into town for Zennora, who swept upstairs while Jesse unloaded bundles of blankets and clothes. By dawn, it was over, and Zennora came down into the parlor holding a little boy with a red face and thin lips drawn up in a knot. Jesse suggested naming him "Crocker," in honor of the man who had built the railroad, but Zennora scoffed at the idea as a joke. They climbed the stairs to where Susan lay, drowsy, and she accepted Hannibal's suggestion that they name the child after his brother.

The new house was ready late in June, and Hannibal spent the long first day of summer, from dawn to dusk, working with young Joseph and two of his friends to take wagon loads of furniture and belongings across Wolf Creek. Zennora had decided that her daughter and the baby should stay where they were until the bed absolutely had to be moved, so she had, in spite of Susan's protests, assigned herself and the other children the task of putting away the new kitchen, where even little Jane worked, sorting out the wooden spoons. Finally, the men carefully loaded the bed into the back of Jesse's wagon, Susan lay down on it with tiny Martin in her arms, and Hannibal slowly drove her to the new home, silhouetted against the setting sun.

As soon as Susan was strong enough to banish her mother, Hannibal began to think about the Kentucky Ranch. He had considered orchards and timber, but Hivner had planted vineyards, and the idea appealed to him. He had heard that some men in the valleys north of San Francisco had begun to raise grapes, and one of the fruit farmers in Marysville thought that the vines might thrive if they didn't get too much snow. With that in mind, he went to see Alonzo Delano.

The eccentric banker seemed taller and more angular than ever. They sat at a table in a window, watching the traffic pass to and fro on Mill Street, and Delano smiled and twitched, offering sprightly interjections as Hannibal explained about the ranch and his plans. When he suggested forming a partnership to develop the property—Delano would contribute capital, Hannibal would bring in the land—the banker smiled, wheezed, pulled his long nose, cackled, and began to tell a story about a farm his father had owned in New York. Hannibal listened, trying to smile, but when he started to urge the question, Delano assured him that the resources of his bank would always be at the ready disposal of so reliable a fellow citizen, and—he leaned in, lowered his voice to a wary whisper, and winked several times—at an unusually favorable rate of interest. Then he drained his glass, thanked Hannibal effusively for his company, and scuttled out the door, looking rather like an excited crane.

Finally, the day came when the sheriff stood on the steps of the court-house in Nevada City, his assistant declaiming the property description in round tones, to accept bids from all and sundry. There were two or three other buyers, but no one was willing or able to put up enough cash to beat Hannibal's position or to persuade him to let the property go and liquidate the debt. He rode back to Grass Valley and hitched up the wagon to drive Susan and the children out to French Ravine to look over their new land. A light breeze set the trees quivering around them, and they could hear the water in the ditch gurgling towards the flume that led to Wolf Creek.

Susan pushed a lock of hair out of her face. She seemed calmer than Hannibal could remember, almost since they were married. "It's quiet 'ere."

"Yes."

"What will ye do with it?"

He took off his hat to wipe the sweat off of his forehead, and looked around at the trees and underbrush. "I don't know, not exactly. But it'll be all right."

She nodded, and he clucked to the horses, turning the wagon back to the road and towards town.

13
Giant Powder
1868

Two men waited in the gathering dusk, standing in the shadows near the main headframe of the North Star. Out of the mouth of the shaft, they heard a distant, muted explosion, no more than a thump, and a moment later, they could feel the soft concussion in the soles of their feet. Still they waited, gazing down into the endless darkness of the shaft. The engineer set the hoist in motion, and presently a mining car rose out of the gloom and into view, carrying four men. Only one looked a miner; his clothes were wet and stained with mud, and he cradled a drill in his arms. He left the car first and walked towards the shed where he had left his gear, keeping his eyes carefully on the ground in front of him as he passed. The other three headed towards the company office, but the two waiting men stepped into their path. The leader stopped short and looked at them, his brow furrowing slightly.

"Chenoweth!" He looked from one face to the other. "And your brother, too." The brothers didn't speak. "What is it?"

Mark Chenoweth pointed to the canvas bag that the leader was carrying in one hand. "What's this 'ere?"

The leader stood stock still, looking straight into Mark's eyes, and smiled slowly. "And what business is it of yours?"

Richard stepped forward. "We've a right t' know."

"You've no right at all." The leader still smiled at them, but there was nothing friendly about his eyes. The other two men, standing behind him and to one side, waited, watching to see what would happen. Finally, the leader reached into the canvas bag and drew out a solid cardboard cylinder, nearly a foot long and over an inch thick. He held it up for all to see. "Giant powder." He waited for a brief moment, then stuffed the cylinder back into his bag and walked on to the office with the other two men following close behind. The brothers looked at each other, then turned and disappeared into the night.

On Auburn Street the next morning, Jesse Trevenna sat in the shade of a tree, studying his construction plans and checking off on a list the stacks of lumber that surrounded him. He looked up to rub the sweat off of his eyelids, and he noticed that two men had stopped on path at the front of the lot. He beckoned, and the Chenoweth brothers walked up the gentle slope to shake Jesse's hand and sit down with him.

Mark looked around at the lumber and over at the level clearing. "Ye seem to 'ave a bit of a job, Jesse."

Jesse grinned and nodded. "I've just been sitting' 'ere waitin' for you two t' show up and get t' work." The brothers smiled. "I've 'ardly seen ye. I 'eard you were workin' down at Norambagua."

"We're back at th' North Star." said Richard. "An' that's why we're 'ere."

"We need yer 'elp, Jesse," said Mark.

Jesse grinned again. "'ave ye got a twister down there—somethin' too kicklish for ye?"

Mark shook his head. "The captain wants t' start usin' giant powder."

Jesse's face stiffened, and he turned away to consider the news. Like his father and grandfather, he had always used black powder to blast away the rock. Giant powder—dynamite—was new, and those who favored it claimed that black powder was crude and inefficient by comparison. Yet Jesse, like all the other hard-rock miners, understood its ways and felt safe with it. Giant powder was tricky and even dangerous. There were risks with black powder, but giant powder raised the stakes. If a charge of black powder, badly placed, could bring down the wall of a drift, then the same charge of giant powder could collapse the whole tunnel. If bad luck with black powder could leave a man without a hand, the same folly with giant powder would simply kill him.

"What're they sayin' about it?"

Richard rubbed a clod back and forth between his hands until it crumbled. "It's what they're not sayin'."

Mark moved over to sit closer to Jesse. "After ye set it off, the air in th' drift is no good for an hour or more, but th' men want t' go back in, get th' rock out, an' keep movin'. I've seen men come t' grass coughin' an' turnin' green. Sometimes they're sick for a few days an' can't work at all."

"And what do the owners say t' that?"

Richard snorted. "They don't care."

Jesse looked at him. "We've been owners ourselves."

Mark shook his head. "It's different now. Look at th' North Star—the owners don't even come t' Grass Valley; they just send orders t' th' captain. The Sterlings're runnin' the Idaho, and ye'd think they'd never gone down a shaft in their lives, for all they care about what 'appens outside o' the assay office. We 'ave to look after ourselves."

"We're havin' a miners' meetin' on Sunday," said Richard, "and we're goin' to organize. The owners can pin one man, or two, or three, but they can't take on the whole lot of us."

Mark looked at Jesse intently. "We'd like you t' be there."

Jesse looked away from the brothers and stared at the stack of four-by-six timbers. "I'm not a miner any more. I 'aven't been down a shaft in over a year, and I pray I never go down again."

"We know that," said Mark, "but we want ye to come anyway."

"Why?" Jesse turned. "Why d'ye want me?"

"Most of us who're callin' this meetin' weren't much more'n boys when we left England. All we know is what we've done 'ere. You know 'ow they ran th' mines in Cornwall, and 'ow we've run 'em 'ere, and the best o' both. And you've been an owner. Not like Richard and me—we did what we were told, but we all listened t' you."

"Why don't ye ask William Pascoe t' go t' this meetin'? 'e's older than I am—'e knows more about the mines than I ever did, and 'e's still workin'."

Richard threw a rock across the clearing, and it bounced off of a tree trunk. "The old gommock won't even talk to us. Told us t' clear out."

"He did?" Jesse was puzzled.

Mark glanced at Richard and back at Jesse. "I don't think 'e likes giant powder any more than the rest, but 'e can't take in the idea that th' miners should tell the owners 'ow t' run things."

"With giant powder," explained Richard, "they can bring out more rock and spend less doin' it."

"A man can work alone, drillin' shallow 'oles, an' get out more rock than two men before. There'd be no need for partners." Mark paused to let Jesse consider the situation. "Just last week, at the Empire, one man used a seven-eighths bit to drill a 'ole twenty-six inches deep, charge it and fire it, all in only ninety minutes."

"How much rock did he get out?"

"They filled two cars. Jesse—it's not just th' bad air, nor th' danger. It's goin' t' put men out o' work."

Jesse looked up at him. "If I were Edward Sterling, I'd send down just as many men as before. They'd bring out twice as much quartz, or better, and we'd all get rich."

Mark shook his head. "'is stamp mill is runnin' day and night as it is; if 'e doubled 'is quartz, th' mill wouldn't be able t' keep up. All 'e'll do is hire fewer men, maybe bring out a bit more rock, and then add on as 'e's able. 'e'll offer those men less per ton than before, and they'll take it, because each man'll be bringin' out so much more rock that 'e'll still come out ahead. But the rest o' th' miners'll be out o' work."

The prospect of hundreds of miners losing their jobs troubled Jesse, but not as much as the disappearance of double-handed drilling. Cornish miners had always worked in pairs: one man holding the drill while the other swung the sledge hammer that drove the drill point into the rock. They took turns so that the man swinging the hammer was always fresh, but the important thing was that no man worked alone. You always had a partner with you in case something happened.

Richard had stopped tossing rocks. "It'll 'appen all over these 'ills, Jesse, and there'll be no place to go."

Jesse sighed. "Who else feels as you do?"

Mark shook his head. "No one outside o' th' mines. And not all o' th' miners. Some o' them are scared, and some don't understand. We need you to show them that it's all right."

On Sunday afternoon, Jesse walked downtown to find two hundred men gathered outside of the Wisconsin Hotel. They formed a ragged parade and marched up Main Street past the shuttered shops and the few families out for promenades. Hamilton Hall was filled with miners, most sitting on benches and some slouching against the side walls surveying the crowd. Mark gestured to Jesse that he should take a seat on the dais. From there, he could see many men he knew, mostly miners from Cornwall, but a surprising number of the faces were strange to him: men from other parts of England as well as Irishmen, Frenchmen and even Americans. One of the men on the platform, a miner named Taylor, was trying to call the meeting to order as Jesse noticed Jack Trevenna standing in a back corner next to a doorway, wearing a new grey suit with a hat to match. He grinned, lifted his chin and waved.

Taylor was trying to make himself heard over the rumble of voices, but there was a sudden burst of excitement in one of the rows. Everyone turned to look, and in the lull, Taylor was able to get their attention. "What's the matter back there? What's the matter?" One of the men on the floor called back that Edwin Bean had come to the meeting. The crowd nearly fell silent and Taylor stepped to the edge of the platform. "What can we do for you, Mr. Bean?"

The editor of the *Gazette* took out a large, fine white handkerchief to wipe the sweat off of his face. "I'm simply here to report the news, sir, to the people of Grass Valley. Surely you have no objection?"

Taylor looked around the room. "This is a miners' meeting. Let the miners decide!" He let the sudden clamor build for several moments and raised his arms for attention. "How say you, gentlemen? Shall we invite the press to our meeting?" There were shouts of "yes" and "no," and a variety of suggestions. Taylor raised his arms again. "All those in favor of welcoming Mr. Bean to our gathering, let me hear you say 'Yea.'" A scattering of men throughout the hall responded. "All those opposed?" There was a rolling shout of "Nay," and then several cheers. Taylor once again asked for quiet. "I'm sorry, Mr. Bean. I assure you that we'll provide a full report."

The editor rose to his feet and put away his handkerchief. "You do that, sir. But be warned, sir, that I have an obligation to my readers to tell them what's going on here. This is a secret meeting, open only to those you deign to admit." The rumble in the room began to rise. "What's next, sir? A password? A rite of initiation?"

From the other side of the room, a voice called out, "Just like the Masons!" The crowd broke out into laughter, for Bean was a prominent member of the lodge. They kept laughing as he pushed his way out through the center door. Jesse could see Jack, an anxious expression on his face, watching Bean leave.

Mark rose to speak. "We're 'ere to agree on three resolutions that we'll present to the owners. First: we won't use giant powder." The men cheered. Jesse kept watching Jack, who was looking not at the platform party but at the men around him. "Second: we won't use th' single-'anded drill. We'll work with partners, as we always 'ave." There were more cheers. "Third: No man will go underground for less than three dollars a day." Some of the men cheered while others called out suggestions; some voices called for three-and-a-quarter, or even three-and-a-half, while others insisted that there be a new schedule of shifts, or that the owners pay more for digging drifts. Mark stood at the rostrum, his arms folded, while the miners shouted back and forth to each other. Taylor and Richard rose from their chairs to stand on either side of Mark and try to calm down the crowd. After several moments, the noise subsided enough for Mark to make himself heard. "I've brought a friend with me—a man ye all know. 'e's worked th' mines 'ere and in Cornwall. 'e's drilled more 'oles, blasted more powder and taken more rock than any six of ye. Jesse Trevenna!"

Some of the men cheered; others turned to those nearby to ask who the new speaker was. Jesse sat in his chair, startled, until Richard walked over, pulled him up by the elbow and brought him down to the edge of the platform. The men started to applaud. Jesse looked out at them, realizing that his heart was beating as though he were about to light a fuse. There were more familiar faces than he had realized. The younger Pascoes were there, probably defying their father, and the Nankervis brothers were clapping and whistling. Hannibal Carne was sitting on a side aisle, his hat tipped back on his head and his spectacles hanging on the tip of his nose. Nick Trevenna was laughing and cheering. He checked the back corner, and Jack was still there, but rather than scanning the men in the room, he was staring full into his uncle's face, waiting to hear what he would say. Jesse discovered that his mouth was dry, and at the same moment, he realized that the room was quiet. Everyone was waiting for him to speak. He tried to swallow.

"I'm not a miner now." Some of the men groaned. "But I was a miner for many years." A few men clapped their hands. "I was a share'older in th' North Star." This remark produced some cheers but also a few cat-calls. "But I'm not any more." He took a deep breath. "I went down in th' copper mines, an' th' tin mines, when I was a boy, back in Camborne. I went down in Dolcoath." A few men murmured quietly to each other. "I went down in Cook's Kitchen." More murmurs and comments. "I went down in Tin Croft, and Wheal Gons, and Binner Downs, and Godolphin Bridge." The voices grew louder. "I went down in th' Wheal Vor, and sent th' black tin up t' grass." Several men cheered. Jesse looked to the back of the room and saw Jack, his mouth slightly agape, staring up at the platform. "I worked in th' mines for thirty years, man and boy, but I never crawled into a drift without a partner." More men cheered, and Jesse had to raise his voice. "I never drilled a 'ole, nor set a charge, without another man next t' me." The clamor grew, and Jesse felt his heart pounding. "We won't go down alone!"

The meeting broke into bedlam. Taylor, the Chenoweths, and the other men on the platform were applauding him. Jack was shaking his head as though amazed, and Nick had his fingers to his mouth and was making a series of shrieking whistles. Mark ushered Jesse back to his seat. Taylor brought the crowd under control, and they passed Mark's three resolutions by acclamation; they had established the Miners' League of the Grass Valley district.

On the following morning, Jesse walked over to the North Star with the Chenoweths as the men were gathering at the headframe for the first shift of the day. Monday mornings were typically drowsy, but today, the miners were wide awake and alert. The engineer warmed up the hoist mechanism, and finally Mitchell, the superintendent, arrived to check off the crews as they went down. Mark stepped forward.

"Before ye start work, Captain, I'd like ye to read this."

Mitchell's black mustache was carefully combed, and his chin and cheeks were smoothly shaven. He read the handbill and returned it. "Thank you, Mr. Chenoweth." He paused. "So?"

Mark held up the paper. "Most o' th' men 'ere are members o' th' League, and we ask ye to honor our resolutions."

Mitchell looked around at the men. "You will work for what we're offering, or you'll not work here at all. You will work in whatever crews I assign. And you'll use whatever powder I provide." There was a long moment of silence.

Richard stepped forward. "Captain Mitchell, these men 'ave agreed to abide by those resolutions. If ye won't honor 'em, we won't work 'ere."

"Mr. Chenoweth, I am the superintendent of the North Star, and I am responsible not to you, nor to your League, but to the men who own the company. I will run this mine as I see fit."

The gathered miners were getting restless, and Mark heard someone, just a few yards to his left, mutter that Mitchell had a right to run the mine without anyone else telling him how to do it. "Captain, these men 'ave a right t' work in safe conditions. We all know th' risks, but there's no need t' use giant powder, and it's not right t' send a man t' drill alone."

Mitchell set his jaw. "As long as you men are working here, you'll work under my supervision. If you don't like it, you can quit."

Richard turned to the men and raised his hands. "No one will quit. We work 'ere, and we want t' work 'ere, but we want t' work under fair conditions."

Mitchell snapped at him. "You'll work under the conditions I set, or you'll not work at all."

Mark shook his head. "No one will quit, but no man 'ere will work with giant powder or a single-'anded drill."

The captain pointed an accusatory finger at Mark. "You have no right to form a combination in order to dictate policy or practice. This League has no validity—your demands mean nothing."

"'ere are yer miners, Captain," said Mark. "They're ready t' work."

Mitchell scanned the crowd, a hundred and fifty men, silent, watching, waiting. "How many of you are members of this League he's talking about?" Most raised their hands. "All right, then, you're fired! Ask your League to pay your wages! Any man who wants to work on my terms is welcome to go down and get started." Fifteen or twenty men sidled away from the others and climbed into the waiting skip.

Mark turned to Mitchell with a smile. "You 'aven't enough fer a shift there, Captain. Ye'll 'ave t' shut down."

Mitchell's eyebrows shot up. He turned to consider the men lined up at the headframe. "All right, there'll be no work today, and no wages. And if any of you don't like it, you can talk to this fellow."

Mitchell turned to walk away, but Mark called after him. "We'll be back tomorrow, Captain. Ye can't ignore the League forever." Mitchell never broke stride, took the office stairs three at a time, and slammed the door behind him.

Two days later, Jesse and the Chenoweths were standing on the corner of Main and Mill waiting to meet with the other League officers when Jack Trevenna walked across the street to greet them. In addition to the confrontation at the North Star, there had been trouble at the Empire and the Norambagua as well. Mark assured him that the men would stand fast. Jack listened, watching Mark carefully, and then gazed down the hill at a series of three heavy wagons shipping out a load from the foundry. He sighed. "I've heard that some o' the men threatened Ned Lee at the Eureka. Is that so?"

Mark folded his arms. "And what if it is? The men're angry."

"It won't do any good."

Richard let out a short bark of a laugh. "And what'll bring 'em around? Give us the answer t' that, and we'll make ye president o' the League."

Jack smiled. "I mean that they're stubborn men, and they won't let you intimidate them."

"And just whose side're you on?" asked Richard. "They've already shown us that they won't see reason. All we can do is threaten t' shut down th' mines."

Jack shook his head. "Someone told Lee that he'd better watch his back when he goes home at night."

"Get out of it, Jack!" cried Richard, starting to pace, his feet thumping on the boards of the walk. "The owners want a war and we'll hold up our end!"

Mark stepped in to speak quietly. "I 'eard about that, too, Jack, and I'm sorry for Ned Lee. But th' miners're some vexed—I've never seen 'em in such a way. They fear for their lives an' their livelihood."

Jack spoke quite deliberately. "The threats will do no good. The strike will do no good."

Mark drew back a step. "Well, if that's how ye see it, Mr. Trevenna, then I'm afraid we can't agree. Perhaps ye'd be more comfortable talkin' t' the owners, not to us 'ere." Mark turned and walked up the hill, with Richard following, to meet Taylor and two other men.

Jack turned to Jesse. "You have little to say."

"I don't like everythin' that's 'appenin', Jack, but p'raps I can 'elp."

"Then keep 'em quiet. If they hurt someone like Ned Lee, the owners will never back down."

"And aren't ye sayin' they'll not back down in any case?" Jack looked away, and Jesse put his hand on his shoulder. "Think, Jack. When 'ave a group o' Cornishmen ever gotten together on anythin' outside o' Sunday services or a wrestlin' match? Most o' these men'll stay in this country, but even if they ask to be citizens, 'alf o' them'll never vote."

Jack smiled slightly. "Like you, Uncle Jesse?"

Jesse smiled back. "Like me. I mean t' say that these are men that stay out o' such things, but this time—this one time—they're takin' an interest." The Chenoweths called over to Jesse, beckoning him to join them, and started up the stairs to the office of the *Union*.

Jack bit his lip. "Are you going up to see Deal?"

"That's right," said Jesse.

"I wish you luck. But consider this, Uncle Jesse. Giant powder will come to the mines. It will happen. The only questions are when it will happen and how men like you and Mark can help the miners get used to it."

A clerk ushered Jesse into a room where the other League leaders were sitting in a semi-circle facing an immense, polished mahogany desk. Behind it, leaning back in a carved, rolling armchair, sat Marcellus S. Deal, editor-in-chief of the *Daily Union*. He wore luxuriant grey whiskers that curled down past his ears but stopped short of his chin, which jutted out towards his guests. He had two fingers of his left hand thrust into a tiny pocket in his silk vest, and with his right hand, he toyed idly with the gold chain that hung across his round belly. At his shoulder stood William Byrne, his partner, whose equally luxuriant whiskers were a flaming red, just like the bushy eyebrows that set off his cold blue eyes.

Deal stared at Jesse, and then seemed to make a specific decision to smile. "Welcome, Mr. Trevenna, welcome. Always a pleasure." To the best of his recollection, Jesse had met Deal only once before, a brief encounter in a saloon while he was still involved with the North Star. "Now, gentlemen, you were explaining your concerns."

Mark cleared his throat, shifted his feet, and referred to a sheet of paper that he had taken from his coat pocket. "There're really only two issues, Mr. Deal. First, the League opposes the use o' giant powder. The blasts poison the air underground and make th' men ill. Second, the League wants every underground worker to earn at least $3 each day." Byrne's eyebrows arched and he started to speak, but Deal, without looking around, silenced him by raising a finger. Mark continued. "I 'ave 'ere a list o' th' resolutions that th' men passed on Sunday. All we ask is that you print them in th' *Union* and explain t' yer readers that we want only what's right."

Deal picked up a pair of spectacles, adjusted them on his face, and read the sheet carefully. No one spoke. Then he took off the spectacles and looked around the room at his visitors. "Only two issues? No, no, my friends, I see a great many more." Byrne snorted and folded his arms. "This is a very interesting situation, very interesting indeed. Will you concede, Mr. Chenoweth, that this is my watch? That it belongs to me?" He pulled on the gold chain and drew out a large, ornate watch from his vest pocket.

"Yes, of course," replied Mark, slightly puzzled.

"And you, Mr. Taylor, will you concede as much?" Taylor mumbled that he would. "And what about you, my dear Mr. Trevenna—will you concede?" Jesse nodded warily. "Excellent. Now, if this is my watch—my property—then surely I may dispose of it as I wish, may I not? I may have it cleaned and regulated according to my whim. I may carry it or not carry it. I may set it any way I please. And I may give it to whomever I please, either while I remain in this life or after I have proceeded to the next. Will you, gentlemen, concede that this is so?" The men around the room nodded their agreement, now completely baffled. "Excellent, excellent. So we all agree— and you, too, I trust, Mr. Byrne?—that I am the owner of this watch, and I may maintain it, keep it, run it, and dispose of it without interference from anyone else. Ah—but what of my jeweler?" Byrne was tapping his foot and staring out of the window at the storefronts across the street. "May Mr. Lundquist tell me how to care for this watch? He is, after all, the expert. He knows its workings better than I. Perhaps he might wish to direct me to wear it in this pocket or that, or to wind it twice a day instead of once. Must I do what he commands?" No one responded. "Of course not. I may take his advice, or not, as I please. It is my watch."

"Mr. Deal . . . " began Mark.

"Yes, yes, I know," Deal assured him. "These little illustrations can become tedious, but I am ready, Mr. Chenoweth, to strike to the heart of the matter. What you propose to do, gentlemen, is to dictate to me what to do with my watch—my property. That is, you have formed a combination of laborers who intend to dictate to the owners how to run their mines. And that we cannot have."

Richard could not contain himself. "But if we don't stop 'em from usin' giant powder, who will?"

"Who, indeed?" asked the editor, shaking his head regretfully. "Who, indeed? Not you. Not I. The point, my friend, is that no one has the right to tell those men how to run their business."

"Listen to me, Mr. Deal," said Richard, leaning forward in his chair. "Giant powder gives a man a 'eadache that lasts for three days. If we let it into th' mines, after a month there won't be enough 'ealthy men to make one shift for th' smallest company in the district."

Deal patted his comfortable belly. "Surely a man's health is his own business? I certainly don't expect you to look after mine, and I assure you," he smiled, "that I have neither the time nor the interest to look after yours. If you believe that giant powder will give you a headache"—he smiled again—"then you are free, according to the laws of the land, to decline to work under such conditions. That is entirely up to you. Besides, my friend, the owners are well aware that they need strong men to go down in the mines. They know that a sick man won't work as hard as a well man, so you can rely on them to act in your best interests."

Richard jumped to his feet. "What a crammer! They don't care . . . "

Mark interrupted him. "Thank ye fer yer time, Mr. Deal—Mr. Byrne. I 'ope you'll find th' space t' publish our resolutions so th' people o' Grass Valley know where we stand." Deal rose magisterially and intoned courtesies as the men filed out, through the outer office and down the stairs.

An hour later, the clerk knocked on the door of the inner office to present a card. Deal read it, showed it to Byrne, and nodded to the clerk, who stood to one side and beckoned Jack Trevenna into the room. Deal rose and offered his hand. "Welcome, Mr. Trevenna. You know Mr. Byrne, of course." Jack shook hands with both men, and all three settled into their chairs.

"I'm here because of the Miners' League, Mr. Deal." Byrne made a sudden, suppressed choking noise and went into a coughing fit that lasted long enough for Deal to lose his complacent expression and glare at his partner. "I believe their committee came to see you."

Deal nodded and leaned forward a bit. "Why, yes, yes, they did. Are you involved with this League, Mr. Trevenna?"

"No, but I know many of the men involved. I've come to ask for your help."

Deal brought the tips of his fingers together and began tapping them lightly against each other. "And what might I be able to do for you?"

"The miners are angry, Mr. Deal, and most o' them aren't thinkin' too clearly right now. They're saying things and doing things that they'll regret in a few weeks."

"I imagine so."

"Giant powder is here to stay, Mr. Deal. I know that, and I think you know that. It's goin' t' change the mines. The miners will have to give up double-handed drilling, and some o' them will be out o' work for a while. Do you think it's fair to say that the businessmen in town will stand with the mine owners?"

Deal gazed at Jack, his eyes narrowing. "I think that's a fair estimation, young man."

"The miners are out o' their depth. These are men that don't trust associations; most of 'em don't join political parties, or even clubs. They're dealing with something they can't manage, but they don't know it yet. All anyone can do, Mr. Deal, is to try to forestall a war and to help the miners and the owners work out the future. That's where the *Union* could help."

Deal's hands were folded across his belly. "Very interesting, Mr. Trevenna. Very interesting." He spoke in measured tones. "What we have here is a mob of miners trying to dictate terms to their employers."

Jack took a deep breath. "How will you handle the story?"

Byrne actually sneered at him. "Read the paper, Mr. Trevenna—read the paper!"

Jack rose to leave, but Deal raised a hand. "Before you leave . . . I have the impression that most of the men in the League are English—is that so?"

"Most o' the quartz miners in this county are from Cornwall, Mr. Deal, as you well know. Without them, there'd only be a handful o' men who understand how to work the deep mines."

Deal barely smiled. "Consider: I see in this unfortunate action a strike against American interests led by English immigrants. Foreigners. Intruders."

Jack stiffened. "These are honest men, Mr. Deal, and they care about th' mines as much as any investor from San Francisco."

"What position would you take, I wonder, if the Chinese formed such a League?"

"It's not the same."

"How many of these men have families here? How many have become citizens?"

"I'm not sure."

"My point is that you cannot expect the American people, even here in the friendly foothills of the Sierra Nevada, to befriend a mob of foreigners who threaten the American way of life. I suggest to you, sir, that there lies the root of the problem." Jack turned to go, but Deal cleared his throat, and he stopped. "And one last thing, Mr. Trevenna. If your miner friends want the newspapers to stand with them, they might find a way to improve their manners. I think they owe Mr. Bean an apology."

In the next edition of the *Union*, Deal and Byrne published not Mark's list of resolutions, but their own whimsical, biting version:

> 1. All Mining Superintendents are nuisances in mines and should at once be discharged by mine owners. These Superintendents in some cases interfere with the ease and comfort of men while working.

> 2. Three men to every drill, and Black Powder, of the weakest description, for charging the holes and firing the blasts.

> 3. Abolition and demolition of all dry houses, and an immediate discharge of all "Specimen Bosses."

> 4. The men to run the mine and mill as they may think best and according to the rules followed by their fathers, and all gold left over to go to the mine owners.

> 5. The owners must pay out of their own pockets all the ordinary and extraordinary expenses of the mine, furnishing all the material used therein, and paying for all the labor employed.

> 6. Owners generally being capitalists have no right to put on airs in saying how the mine shall be worked.

> 7. Neither Giant Powder, nor any Chinaman, shall come within a quarter of a mile of any mine, whether that mine will pay or not, under "our forefathers' system."

> 8. Steam engines and Railroads are not of advantage, as they work too fast, and prevent many men from being employed in pumping out mines, and they bring other miners to the country.

Jesse read Deal's parody aloud to the Chenoweths. Richard stormed out of the cabin halfway through, but Mark sat through the entire list, and when it was finished, he smiled ruefully. "Th' man 'as a sense o' 'umor, don't 'e? That piece about specimen bosses—'e's callin' us all thieves."

Jesse folded the paper and refolded it, smoothing out the crumpled corners on his thighs. "I 'eard some men talkin' last evenin', Mark. A couple of 'em wanted to go back to work, giant powder or no, but one o' th' others told 'em t' think about what's good for 'em. Some o' th' men are scared."

"And some of 'em are angry," returned Mark.

Jesse kept rubbing the newspaper as though he would iron it. "I don't like it. Someone may get 'urt."

The younger man rose. "That may be. But if we don't 'old fast on this, they'll put giant powder into the mines, and men will get 'urt in blasts and cave-ins, or go sick from th' fumes. An' they'll be th' lucky ones, for th' rest'll 'ave no work at all. I pray no one suffers, Jesse, but it's the owners can stop it." He walked out of the cabin.

The strike spread throughout the district from the Norambagua to Banner Mountain. Each captain kept his stamp mills running as long as there was rock to crush, but one by one, each mine exhausted its supply until even the amalgamation was finished and the refined gold had been shipped out. Finally, even the Empire and the North Star were silent, and the only men at work were those tending the pumps, which kept throbbing, day and night, to keep the works dry for the day when the crews would descend again.

Only the Idaho remained open, for Edward Sterling had, true to form, quietly decided to keep using black powder and let the other owners work out the crisis. He hired only the men who had been working for him before the trouble began, and at the gates opening into the Idaho's grounds, he placed armed guards to bar anyone involved in the controversy.

Jesse intended to devote himself to the construction of his new home, but on most days, by mid-afternoon he was wandering through the streets of Grass Valley, listening and watching. Many of the miners, bored with sitting idly in their cabins, were spending their time standing on street corners or drinking in saloons. The town seemed crowded, and the shopkeepers were restless, quick to attend anyone who walked in the door and inclined to hover near any customers until they left. The bankers, lawyers and clerks found their customary lunch tables pre-empted by miners, edgy and strangely clean. As the days passed and some of the miners began to run short of cash, they left the saloons to sit on the steps of Hamilton Hall, lounge outside Woodward's livery stable to watch the horses and carriages, or wander through the lobby of the Exchange.

After two weeks, the town heard a rumor that Mitchell was going to re-open the North Star, but none of the League men knew anything about it, and none had been notified to return to work. Mark called the other strike leaders to his cabin to tell them that the news was confirmed; Mitchell would send down a shift on Monday morning.

In a warm, clear dawn, Jesse met the Chenoweths at their cabin and walked over to the main shaft, where they found nearly a hundred men. Most of them were League members, men they knew, but a score were strangers, standing off to one side, dressed for work. Jesse walked up to one to ask his name, and the man answered in broken English; he was German, and as far as Jesse could make out, he had arrived in the district only two days earlier. The men standing near him nodded their heads at what he had to say, their eyes wide and apprehensive. As the sun rose higher, more men arrived, until there were forty newcomers and over a hundred League men. The strangers were silent, each standing alone, glancing furtively at the others near him and at the strikers, who stared across resentfully.

Mitchell stepped out of his office with two assistants behind him. He walked over to the headframe and stood between the two groups of men with his hands on his hips, scanning the faces and letting his gaze rest for a moment on the Chenoweth brothers. His jaw set. "The North Star will resume underground operations today. I'm hiring a hundred men for the day shift, and I'll hire a hundred more for the night shift. You men line up, experienced quartz men on this side, and the rest on that side."

Before anyone else could move, Mark stepped out from the group of strikers. "Captain Mitchell, I'm 'ere t' represent the Miners' League of Grass Valley. Th' men want t' know what kind o' powder ye're usin'."

Mitchell folded his arms. "Mr. Chenoweth, I will use whatever powder suits the job. That is my responsibility."

"So it is, Captain," replied Mark, "but these men 'ave a right t' know and t' make their own decisions. What powder will ye use?"

"Any man here will work the drift I assign and he'll use whatever means I deem fit and necessary."

Richard called out, "Will ye be usin' giant powder, Captain?" Taylor pulled him back into line, but Mitchell turned to glare at him.

"I'll use whatever I please, Mr. Chenoweth. If it's my judgement that giant powder will do the job best, then giant powder it is. And what have you to say to that?"

Jesse was standing in the front of the strikers. Several feet over his right shoulder, he heard a pistol cocking. He turned just as someone cried "Damn you, Mitchell!" There was a brief scuffle involving four or five men and some quick, hissing whispers. Jesse looked back at Mitchell, who regarded the crowd and then looked over at Mark with his lips drawn back to show his teeth under his mustache.

Mark hadn't moved. "The miners o' Grass Valley're concerned fer their safety, Captain. D'ye share their concern?"

Mitchell spat into the dust. "No man can accuse me of sending a crew down to face unnecessary risks. The North Star is as safe as it always was."

Some of the strikers had begun to talk among themselves, and now they began to call out challenges, their words piling up like the first clatter of a hailstorm; first a few sparse, tentative taps, and then little clusters that quickly bunch up into a constant drumming. "We won't work with giant powder! Mitchell, ye fool! Ye're starvin' us! Ye'll take th' mine to ruin! And th' district with it! Let's break th' pump and let it drown!"

As the angry voices hammered away, punching through the rising air like drum beats, Jesse noticed that several of the Germans had disappeared and a few more were slipping away. Mitchell was trying to stand firm, but Jesse could tell that he had not expected this kind of confrontation. Mark stood with his arms folded, perfectly calm, looking into Mitchell's eyes.

Under the noise, Jesse heard two pistols cock—no, three—and he looked over to see one man, quite near him, aiming directly at the mine captain. He jumped out in front of the group of strikers, holding up his hands and asking to be heard. Out of the corner of his eye, he saw Mark break his pose, startled, and look over at Taylor. Richard began to move towards Jesse, but as he did, the noise subsided enough for Jesse to call out, "We must not 'arm this man!" Most of the men fell silent, and Richard stopped in mid-stride, waiting to see what Jesse would do. Now some of the strikers realized that others were carrying weapons, and they drew away from them. The armed men, exposed, tucked their guns away. Jesse didn't know what to do next.

Suddenly Mark pointed a finger towards the headframe. "Look, Captain! Yer crew is gone!" Mitchell turned to look, and swore bitterly. Only a dozen Germans stood near the shaft, far too few, as everyone there knew, to make up a shift. The captain scowled at Mark, but he had already turned to the strikers. "We're finished 'ere, but we're not finished fer today. We'll go down t' th' Norambagua and work our way up th' creek t' Rocky Bar an' Stockbridge, and up t' the Empire and on t' Banner Mountain!" The men cheered and started off, chattering and kicking up the dust as they went.

Jesse grabbed Mark by the elbow and stopped him. "What're ye trying' t' do, Mark? Ye've got men with pistols there—who'll get shot at th' next mine?" Mark smiled, and after a moment, Jesse released him and watched him follow the others out of the grounds.

Mitchell was staring at the headframe, but he felt Jesse's eyes on him and turned to meet his gaze. He opened his mouth as if to speak, then changed his mind and turned away. "Captain," called Jesse. The man stopped, looking over his shoulder to listen. "If ye can run the mine th' way ye always 'ave—with black powder—th' men'll come back to work and there'll be no more trouble."

Mitchell turned to face him. "Black powder? Looks like I'm not using any powder at all." He walked up the slope and into the office, leaving Jesse standing in the sun.

By late afternoon, word began to spread that there would be another meeting at Hamilton Hall, not a miners' meeting, but rather a gathering for all citizens. Reluctantly deciding that he must attend, Jesse walked into town and found the place so crowded that he could hardly get in, much less find a place to sit. He judged about half of the men to be miners; the rest were merchants, hotel keepers, teamsters, clerks, messenger boys, manufacturers, doctors and a couple of lawyers. There was even a small group of women, four schoolteachers sitting together in a back corner and waving their handkerchiefs against the cigar smoke and strong smell of sweat. At the podium stood Carville Conaway, one of the town trustees. Taylor and Richard stood with a few other strikers on the main floor at the right end of the platform, and near the left end, sitting in a chair with his legs crossed carelessly, was Jack Trevenna.

Conaway called the meeting to order, and Mark took the rostrum to review the League's position—no giant powder, fair wages for all underground men, and the right to organize. The crowd listened politely, and Findley stepped up to the podium. Everyone knew that he held shares in the Idaho, and there were rumors that he had ongoing business with the investors from San Francisco, so for the first time since the strike began, a speaker would present the owners' position. He took off his spectacles, folded them, inserted them carefully into his breast pocket, and surveyed the crowd before him.

"The issues before us are clear. The Constitution of the United States assures each man—every American citizen—the right to dispose of his property as he sees fit. In fact, the purpose of government—the true purpose, for which it was established and for which we maintain it—is to protect that right. This so-called Miners' League"—there were surly mutterings from a few of the miners—"proposes to dictate to the mine owners. They would tell these men, these leaders of our community, how to run their business. This they have no right to do. On this point alone, we cannot accept the League's demands or, as they call them, resolutions. On this point alone, they violate the laws and the customs of this nation."

The muttering increased, and Findley waited. When the hall fell silent, he placed his palms flat on the podium. "Yet there is a deeper issue. The League proposes to interfere—pointlessly and inappropriately—with the natural laws of political economy. They propose to meddle with the relationship between labor and capital. A working man sells his labor, and capital will always hire that labor as cheaply as possible. The laborer and his employer each enjoy the right—a right that no man and no government can take from them—to enter into any contract that provides mutual agreement and satisfaction. No man can tell another what to pay for labor, and no man can tell another what wages to accept. If the League proposes to set wages for the mines, they are not only interfering in decisions that are primarily the concern of the owners, they are also denying their own members the right to make any agreements they wish."

The hall had been growing warmer, and men began to shift in their seats and comment to those near them. Mark was crouching down at the right end of the platform, whispering heatedly to the men standing there. Conaway rose to ask for quiet, then gestured for Findley to continue.

"I regret to suggest, my fellow citizens, that the men who have goaded our friends, the miners, into forming this League do not have the best interests of our community at heart. Consider. The League is preventing honest men from working. By doing so, they are forcing businesses to the brink of ruin; not only the mines but the foundries and draymen and lumber companies that serve them, not to mention the mercantile concerns that many in this very hall own and operate. In effect, they will damage the community and drive away the capital that could help us grow and thrive. This strike is a war against capital!" He paused in deference to a sudden storm of catcalls and hoots. Jesse looked around the room and discovered that Nick was standing on a chair, grinning and whooping.

"Consider further. This League has threatened to use force if persuasion will not suffice; that is, if we will not do what they wish"—he paused, looking around the room—"then they will destroy our property and perhaps even harm our families. This is tyranny. Moreover, this League is a secret society, one that meets behind closed doors to conspire against the public at large." Angry voices began to fill the room. "This League would break the laws of the land, scorn them and hurl them into the dust. I put it to you, citizens of Grass Valley, that no American, raised to cherish and revere the hallowed principles on which this nation was founded, could possibly find it in his heart to form a combination that would promote such vile purposes." Belligerent outcries sounded from all corners of the room, and Findley raised one hand for leave to speak and be heard. "I realize that there are many honest Englishmen here tonight, and I want it clearly understood that I do not mean to cast aspersions on them. We value our Cornish miners, and we respect both their generations of experience and their admirable industry. Yet there are those among them that scorn our laws and traditions, and who would destroy what we have built simply so they can take power—power that is not rightfully theirs—into their own hands."

Mark had returned to his seat; he and Conaway were whispering at each other furiously, neither man stopping to hear what the other had to say. Taylor had been trying to get their attention, but now, frustrated, he jumped up on the platform and shouted over the crescendo. "The miners of Grass Valley do *not* propose to dictate to the mine owners. They simply want to work in safe conditions. Giant powder is not safe!"

A man in the crowd stood and pointed a finger at Taylor. "I heard that they're using giant powder in Placer County and they're having no problems at all."

Taylor shook his head. "Giant powder makes a man sick, and we'll do whatever we must to keep it out of our mines!"

Several men hissed, and one shouted, "They're not *your* mines, mister!"

A miner in the crowd yelled, "Ye're puttin' good men out o' work, Findley." Several more cheered.

Jesse could see the sweat running down Findley's temples and into his whiskers. "It is true that to bring out the same quantity of rock, the owners need hire only half as many to drill. But they will hire just as many men as before to run the pumps and the mills, and to shovel the rock."

A score of men jeered, and one shouted above the din. "What about th' quartz miners—th' trained hands? What about us?"

Findley raised his hands, and Conaway stood next to him, begging for quiet. "Consider, good people—consider. If the owners can bring out more rock with fewer men, the mines will become more profitable. The owners will expand! They will dig more shafts, open new mines, and hire more men."

A man with a derby pointed an accusing finger. "You damned Englishmen! You're standing in the way of progress!"

Another man stood and shouted, "I heard that if the owners can't cut costs by using giant powder, they'll start hiring Chinese!"

At that, the room erupted. Findley stood serenely at the rostrum as Mark and Taylor argued heatedly with a group of men standing below the edge of the platform. All over the room, men were shouting at each other, and Jesse saw Nick cheering and waving his hat in the air as a miner shoved a clerk over a bench and down onto the floor. At that moment, he felt a hand on his shoulder, and he turned to see Jack Trevenna beckoning him out into the lobby.

The place was empty except for several men waiting in a corner. Jesse recognized a few of them: James and Will Pascoe, and Hannibal Carne. Jack checked around the room, and began to talk in an undertone. "Listen. If there was ever a chance for Mark t' get the people of this town t' back the League, he's lost it now. We have t' find something for the miners t' take with 'em tonight, or they'll lose any influence they ever had."

Jesse stared at him. "What d'ye want me t' do?"

Jack steered his uncle to a bench and sat down with him while the others gathered around. "I think that there's a chance—a good chance—to form a new association for the miners."

"Here? Now?!"

"Yes, Uncle Jesse, right now."

"What for?"

"Findley did everything he could to break up the League, and he knew how to do it. The shopkeepers don't give a penny for all that blather about labor and capital. They don't really believe that the mines'll fail. They're upset because he's convinced 'em that the League wants t' tell 'em what to do. Remember that the people we're dealing with, the men who control the town, are Americans. Do what you will, but don't threaten their idea of freedom." Jesse looked around at the circle; everyone there was a Cornishman.

"What d' ye want me t' do?"

Jack pulled in closer. "Many of the men still listen to Mark. And I think he trusts you. Will you help me persuade him t' propose a new list of resolutions—t' replace the one they published two weeks ago?"

He handed Jesse a sheet of paper. In effect, it announced the establishment of the Miners' Union of Grass Valley, dedicated to the mutual aid and protection of miners. There was a statement that disavowed any threats or violence attributed to the League, and a new list of resolutions that denounced giant powder, promised to use only moral suasion and respect the law, and recognized the right of the mine owners to run their business as well as the right of the each miner to work under whatever terms he wished to accept.

Jesse looked up at Jack. "When men like Findley and Deal see this, they'll claim that Mark and Richard coerced men t' strike against their will."

He saw no sympathy in Jack's face, and the other men were equally impassive. "I'm sorry for Mark, Uncle Jesse, but he let this get out of control."

Jesse shook his head. "Mark never told th' men to 'urt anyone."

Jack nodded. "I'm sure he didn't. But that doesn't matter any more. What matters is that the people of the town believe that he did, and that the League will do anything they have t' do t' get what they want. Will you talk to Mark?"

Jesse looked around at the anxious, sweating faces and sighed. "Yes."

Jack stood up. "Hannibal—could you bring him in?"

Hannibal nodded. He had been standing slightly apart from the others, listening carefully, but now he leaned in. "It's th' best thing for th' town, Jesse, an' for business." He turned and walked back into the hall.

A few small groups of men, talking tensely, walked through the lobby and out the doors. From inside, Jesse could hear a voice proposing loudly that each miner should make his own free and independent choice whether or not to work with giant powder, and that if the men of the League felt so strongly about it, they should form a co-operative and open their own mine. He felt very tired.

Hannibal returned to the lobby with Mark, who kept asking, "What is it? What d'ye want?"

Mark quickly read over Jack's document and gave it back, openly annoyed. He opened his mouth to speak, but Jack stopped him. "Uncle Jesse, what d' you think o' this?"

Jesse looked up at Mark. "We're not givin' up anything important. All that's new is that we're promisin' not t' break th' law and t' let each man, miner and captain alike, make up 'is own mind."

Mark bit his lip. "And what d'ye think will persuade the owners t' change their minds about giant powder?"

"I don't know. But I won't shoot a man just fer not comin' around t' my way o' thinkin'. You know that I didn't like th' threats from th' first."

Mark looked down at the sheet of paper. "And who wrote this?" No one answered, but a couple of the men glanced involuntarily at Jack. "I thought so." He turned away to think for a moment, and looked at Jesse. "Ye realize, don't ye, that I'll look a proper fool? I'll be sayin' that th' League was wrong."

Jesse folded his hands in his lap. "Ye'll get nowhere with this meetin', Mark, not the way it's goin'. The best ye can hope for is t' get back in there and get somethin' out of it before Findley finishes the job."

Mark kept gnawing on his lip. "I guess ye're right." He took the sheet of paper and read it over again. "Says nothin' about th' wages." No one spoke. "We can still refuse t' work with giant powder, can't we?" Jesse nodded. "Well, maybe that'll be enough." He turned towards the hall, but paused at the doorway to look back at Jack. "Congratulations, Mr. Trevenna."

Jack and Hannibal and the others walked back into the hall, but Jesse stayed on the bench in the lobby, listening. Mark proposed the Union over Taylor's indignant protests and Richard's puzzled questions. He called for a vote by the miners present, and while the response sounded weak, Conaway, as president of the meeting, declared the resolutions approved and quickly framed a statement of support from the townspeople.

The strike persisted for two more months. The mines—all except the Idaho—remained closed, but there was no violence other than an occasional scuffle outside a saloon. By the end of June, most of the miners had run out of cash. The town butchers announced that they would cut off credit after thirty days and then publish the names of those who hadn't paid their bills. Outraged and hungry, a group of miners, most of them men with families, declared that they would start a co-operative grocery and boycott the shops in town.

Mitchell tried to re-open the North Star, offering to use giant powder only when the ground was too wet for black powder. He hired enough men to make up two small shifts, but before the week was out, some men claiming to be from the Union warned some of the working miners not to co-operate as long as Mitchell persisted in using giant powder. On that Saturday night, four men who were never identified ambushed two miners as they were walking back to their cabin after their shift, leaving one with a broken arm. The newspaper and several community leaders accused the Union of engaging, once more, in threats, intimidation and violence, but the Union disavowed the incident, suggesting instead that someone else had beaten the men to make the Union look bad. The North Star closed again.

At the end of July, Archibald Peachy rode up from San Francisco to instruct Mitchell to re-open the North Star under any reasonable terms. In effect, the miners had won the strike, even though Marcellus Deal ran a lofty column proclaiming that none of the superintendents and owners had given up their right to run the mines according to their best judgement.

Jesse had stayed clear of the Union, and the new leaders—men he did not know—did not seek him out. He spent most days working on his new house with three young miners, men just arrived from Cornwall, who were eager for employment and found the strike bewildering.

The Chenoweths had left town. Jesse never saw them again after the citizens' meeting. They stopped to say farewell to Hannibal, but Susan chose not to repeat to her father Mark's most bitter assertions: that Jesse had betrayed them and that Jack was not to be trusted.

When Jack heard the news of the mines re-opening, he went to see Jesse and found him working fast, trying to get the roof and the heavy timbers into place before his three assistants went to look for work in one of the mines. He sat down heavily in the shade and wiped his forehead with a dirty kerchief. Jack thought he looked exhausted, bent. "You did the right thing, Jesse."

The older man looked at him thoughtfully and turned to watch two of the men start nailing long pine planks onto the posts to form one of the walls. "Did I?" He shook his head.

"Remember what I said: giant powder is coming. Now it'll come more easily, more peaceably. When the captains bring it back, in two or three years, the miners'll think they've always been using it."

Jesse stared at him. "Ye're very sure o' yerself."

Jack grinned. "Wait and see."

14
Summer's Lease
1867-70

The man in tights ran across the floor, then back again, and across, and back, over and over. The woman in the loose white gown reached her arms out over the railing, and withdrew, and reached, and withdrew. Finally she raised her fingers to her lips, tilted her head to one side, and, drifting slowly backwards, out of sight, unfurled her arm so that at the last, her fingertips still bent towards him. He clasped his hands at his chest, raised his face up into the light, his features strained, and ran off. The curtain fell into place, and the audience applauded.

Susan would always remember *Romeo and Juliet* as a ravishing welter of bright colors and passionate poetry, oddly like the roiling sea below the cliffs near Camborne, so surrounding her that by the end, when the actress wept on her dead lover's bosom, Susan, too, felt tears running down her cheeks. During the intermissions, Jack amused her by speculating on how each performer might fare in a Cornish mine. She could not imagine Miss Kingsbury, so graceful and tiny, as a bal-maiden, and her partner, a man named McCullough, didn't look as though he could swing a sledge for more than an hour. After the play, while the men walked down to the livery stable, she stood in a corner of the lobby with Clara, each woman helping the other fix her face with a handkerchief. Jack embraced her—suddenly, unexpectedly—before lifting Clara up into his phaeton, and Susan settled into the front seat of Hannibal's wagon for the silent ride back to French Lead. Jack, she thought, was trimming his mustache in a new way, and his face looked leaner.

After breakfast the following morning, while the boys played outside and Jane methodically tore a scrap of paper into tiny bits, Susan closed her eyes against the glow passing through the drawn curtains and considered the two actresses she had seen on stage. The company was touring all over California, so the women were, like the men, sleeping in hotels and traveling from town to town in coaches. She wondered whether they were married, and whether they had children. She could hardly imagine taking children on such a trip—who would look after them?—but neither could she suppose that they were staying at home, perhaps in San Francisco, without their mothers. Her own children were always near her, even when they visited Zennora. Jack had confided that the woman who played the nurse was married, but not to a man in the tour. If that were so, then they were separated for weeks at a time. She tried to imagine how Hannibal would react if she proposed going off without him.

She had spent a series of evenings quietly listening to Hannibal angrily rehearse bitter complaints about the sale of the North Star, pointless diatribes that he later confessed he could not repeat to the other partners. When he no longer had to go to the mine every day, she thought that she might enjoy having his company and watching him spend time with the children, but he spent hours sitting in the parlor, staring out the window, and scarcely looking up when someone approached him. He had come home one evening and mumbled something about seeing the Sterlings, but refused to explain what they had said to him, answered all of her questions in monosyllables, and pushed the boys away when they came to climb up in his lap, so she took the children upstairs and left him to sulk by himself. She hoped that he would enjoy the evening out with Jack and Clara, but he had acted resentful or offended most of the time, as though someone had deliberately spilled something in his lap, and she finally gave up trying to include him. There was, apparently, nothing she could do to bring Hannibal out of his doldrums, and when she accepted that resolution, that temporary closure that was itself the discovery of a breach, she realized how lonely she truly was.

The only person with whom she felt intimate was Zennora. After the first exhilaration of marriage had ebbed and the sense of adult autonomy had become routine, she and her mother had become re-acquainted, less as a woman and her daughter, and more as two women of different ages, the younger exploring paths that the elder had already traced. Around the time Bertie took his first steps, they had fallen into the habit of passing the more pleasant afternoons on Zennora's porch, and when the conversation flagged, Susan read aloud to her mother. At first, she read only the newspaper that Jesse usually had left from the day before, skipping from events back East, the brief elaborations of the briefer telegraphed dispatches, to the more amusing anecdotes about local affairs. Then Zennora discovered that a woman in the congregation owned an unusually large personal library and was willing to lend volumes, carefully wrapped in soft muslin for the ride between French Lead and the church. Susan began with *The Song of Hiawatha* and then tried *The Courtship of Miles Standish,* but found the topic vaguely uncomfortable and moved on to *Ivanhoe,* which seemed pleasantly remote. Irving's stories about life along the Hudson were charming and, somehow, not too American. They spent a whole series of afternoons on the verge of tears over a worn copy of *Uncle Tom's Cabin*, so alarming Bertie on one occasion that he began to wail while trying to climb up into both laps at once. After that, they discovered Mrs. Southworth's novels, and Susan read quickly through *Self-Raised, The Hidden Hand,* and *The Fatal Marriage.* As she worked her way through a stack of novels by Charles Dickens, Zennora sat fascinated with the tales of bereft children and looming pasts.

Yet while Susan enjoyed the stories and found her mother's rapt attention endearing, she had come to regard their sessions as yet another way in which she was tending to someone else's needs and leaving her own neglected. She routinely solicited Zennora's advice regarding the children, but whenever she mentioned her difficulties with Hannibal, her mother seemed strangely tentative, as though traversing unfamiliar, unexpected ground whose unanticipated appearance dismayed her. Susan considered approaching Jesse, but could not find a way to begin.

She decided to break her solitude. Clara had lightly teased her about being so reclusive and had invited her to bring the children for a picnic, so on a summery morning a few days after the play, Jesse, her accommodating coachman, brought his wagon to a halt in front of Jack's house, waited for Susan to unload the little ones, and handed down the basket of rolls and fresh fruit that she had brought as her contribution. The women sat on the porch trading Clara's baby back and forth and keeping Jane supplied with little toys and trinkets while the two boys wandered among the rose bushes. When James discovered the sharp points of the thorns that guarded the fragrant blooms, he toddled over, howling with outrage, his face a blotchy red, to climb the stairs and present his hurt finger not to his own mother but to Clara, who drew him into her lap, nestled him in her arms, and licked the smarting tip. Susan, holding the sleeping infant on her shoulder, pushed from her imagination the image of Clara not with the sniveling child, but with Jack.

For the rest of the summer and into the fall, Susan went to visit Clara as often as she could. She had never attempted a formal garden at French Lead, so she followed Clara among the vines and bushes, asking questions and admiring the splashes of color against the shining green leaves. Clara's curiosity about raising children was sincerely insatiable, and they spent hours foraging in the hundreds of moments that Susan could glean from the past four years, and she, who had always turned to Zennora for an attentive ear, discovered a new kind of reassurance in comparing experiences with a woman her own age. The mothers soon reached a tacit, mutual trust; on the third visit, when the baby began to fret, Susan took her inside to change her diaper while Clara watched the boys to make sure they didn't climb too high on the rocky embankment. Clara finally felt comfortable enough to nurse tiny Florence without retreating to an upstairs bedroom, so at each visit, the women looked forward to that quiet time of the day when they would sit in the gentle breeze, Clara discreetly draped and Susan sitting with one of her children drowsing in her lap, while the infant peacefully sucked her fill.

At the end of Susan's fifth visit, Jack rode up just as she was lifting Bertie into the wagon. He and Jesse moved just out of hearing, the pair of them standing in the dusty roadway with feet planted and hands on hips, conferring as they gazed out at the town spread beneath them. On the next occasion, it was not Jesse but Jack who collected her for the ride back to French Lead. He returned in time to walk part way up the porch steps and smile up at the women, one knee bent, lightly brushing his hat from side to side to keep the flies from settling on his trousers. He managed to fit them all into his phaeton, giving Bertie and James turns sitting in his lap and pretending to hold the reins. Susan, feeling more sheltered than she liked, crisply pointed out that she was quite capable of driving herself in Hannibal's wagon. Jack grinned at her, his mustache framing his teeth, and said, "That's fine! You drive and I'll hold the little ones." She settled Jane into her lap and looked away, disdaining to answer, but she found that she was smiling in spite of herself.

Even when an unusually cold September breeze skidded down from the high mountains, she kept her engagement with Clara because to break it would mean waiting another three days to see Jack. On their first rides together, their conversation wandered among harmless topics—town gossip and Jack's trips to Sacramento and San Francisco—but as the weeks passed, they shared confidences as though they were once again children watching the clouds race across the cup of Gwennap Pit. One day, Susan realized that she was telling him all about her problems with Hannibal, and just when she caught herself and was about to feel ashamed, as though she had revealed a humiliating secret to a mere acquaintance, she realized that he was listening quite gravely. She decided to let herself talk, and Jack surprised her, for he, who always teased, offered no advice and didn't dismiss her frustration; instead, he simply listened and nodded. On their next ride, she eased into the topic again, this time fully aware of what she was doing, and with the intention of testing him. Enthralled by his sympathy, she asked him to help Hannibal. The idea so intrigued him that he pulled the carriage to a stop at the side of the road. She had no specific suggestions, but sought something that would engage her husband's abilities, attention and especially his burdensomely free time. Soon afterwards, Jack approached Hannibal on Zennora's porch and made the offer that left him puzzled but irresistibly tempted. Hannibal never found out that it was Susan who had set the idea in motion.

More and more, on those visiting days, Susan turned to her yearning for Cornwall, trading with Clara recollections of recent events and re-living childhood incidents with Jack. Once, halfway back to French Lead, she broke into tears, and Jack stopped the carriage, lifted the boys down to explore a pair of granite boulders, and took the sleeping Jane onto his shoulder. When her sobbing subsided, he asked her why she missed Cornwall so keenly, but she found that she could not explain. He sighed and looked up the slope, where a grove of pines stood against the deep blue sky, and very cautiously offered a facetious but accurate description of Camborne, with its cinders and bitter water, and the wind, the endless wind that sent grit from the crushed ore sailing from village to village but at the same time swept the peninsula clean, leaving most places bare of everything but the stubborn furze. Susan finally laughed, but then she slapped his hand and told him that he did not really understand. The place was home, she said, and she wanted to return.

When next he drove her down from Cemetery Hill, Susan directed him into town, past the shops of Main and Mill, and along the houses on the slope above. Grass Valley, she said, was just like she imagined most of America to be; that is, too new. Twenty years ago, there had been nothing there but a meadow, but now there were hasty frame houses, knocked together from plain sugar pine boards covered in whitewash, and raw brick stores that had risen as fast as the masons could set up the lines of mortar. Everyone rode helter-skelter, as though there were something momentous going on that they might miss, and the whole community was too convinced of its own importance. Jack grinned, reminding her that the freshness and bustle were exactly what he liked about the place, so she accused him of becoming more American than he was willing to admit, and she teased him about his careful imitation of American speech and pronunciation. Besides, she insisted, the stands of pine were all very well, but in another ten years, the miners, the farmers and the lumbermen would have scraped the hills clean, and there would be nothing left but red dust whirling in the wind.

She began to poke him playfully in the ribs as she made one point after another, and as the children giggled, enjoying their mother's game, he smiled, but he realized that she was using the joke to hide a loneliness that he could not address. She had confided that Hannibal had no patience for her longing and that while he would make no commitments one way or another, he had never—she had realized too late—seriously entertained the idea of returning to Cornwall.

With the rain and snow, Susan's visits to Clara dwindled and then ceased, but Jack found excuses to ride out to French Lead, invariably stopping for a cup of tea at the Carnes' house, usually when Hannibal was out roaming the hills in search of a claim. On one particularly bitter day, he knocked the snow off of his boots and turned to find Susan on the verge of tears, slamming pots and pans down so hard he thought she must dent them.

"Susan, what is it? What's wrong?" She picked up a bucket of filthy water, carried it to the back door and dumped it out so it splashed on the stoop. She slammed the door shut and strode back into the kitchen. "Can't you tell me?"

She glared at him. "Fayther an' mother're movin' t' town."

"Not for some months yet."

Cousin Jack

"Oh, Jack!" She brought the kettle over to the stove and set it down to heat. "What difference does that make? They're movin' into town. Fayther's already picked out th' lot, and 'e's talkin' about buildin' a new 'ouse."

"Where's the harm?"

"The 'arm? Hannibal built this place so we could be nearby, an' now they're leavin'."

"Susan, the ride's only half an hour even if you dawdle."

"I like 'avin' Mother near. And what'll I do with myself out 'ere, all alone? None of ye come around any more since ye sold th' North Star, and Hannibal is out Lord knows where, lookin' for somethin' he can't even tell me."

"I come around all the time."

"Iss fay, of course ye do, Jack. But tidden th' same. I'll be lost out 'ere. And besides . . ." She looked away.

"What?"

She took a deep breath. "I always thought they would go back. I thought Mother would want t' go back, even if Fayther couldn't make up 'is mind. Now that Fayther's not workin' any more, there's no real reason for 'em t' stay on, except fer me and th' children. They could go 'ome. But now they won't."

"Because they're building a new house?" She nodded. "But how could they go back with you here?"

"Bessie's livin' in Helston—she's two little boys now—grandsons they've never seen. They'd go back t' be with them."

"I mean they wouldn't leave you here, not with you wanting go back."

"They're leavin' me t' go t' town, aren't they?"

Jack shook his head. "Susan, that's only two miles away. You'll see them."

"Ye don't understand."

The weather turned, and on a flowery spring morning after church, Clara suggested that Susan bring the children over for a visit. Susan accepted the invitation but avoided setting a date, and after a week, she became intrigued with her own hesitation, wondering if she were reluctant, for some reason she could not fathom, or simply lazy. As a sort of experiment, she mentioned her indecision to Hannibal, who paid attention just long enough to ask, impatiently, "Why don't ye go?" before taking his hat and walking out to go on one of his long rides. Finally, she asked Jesse to take her into town, and she spent the middle part of the day with Clara as she had before, talking of teething and lilies, but she felt ill at ease, and she thought Clara spoke less freely than she remembered. Jack came home as he had during the autumn, standing halfway up the stairs, leaning on the railing as though he were a gentleman caller and not the owner of the house, and as she looked down at him from her seat on the porch, Susan realized what had changed. Her enthusiasm had flagged because Jack had continued to visit her all during the winter, and she no longer felt compelled to visit Clara in order to palliate her loneliness. As Jack drove them back out to French Lead, she caught herself chattering away like a little girl at her sixth birthday party, released and uninhibited. She fell into a chair, exhausted and breathless, reached up to find that her cheeks were hot and pink, and wondered if she were about to be ill.

So Susan took the children into town, but only once a week or so, while she organized each day around the chance of hearing Jack's mare whicker outside her door. If he came, he came early in the afternoon, and by that time, she had done her cleaning and her laundry, given the children their noonday meal, sent them out to play, and stolen a moment to take off her apron and pat her hair into place. Then she would wait, but pretend not to wait, dusting the sideboard again, or checking the woollens for moths, or browsing through the next chapter of the novel she was reading to Zennora— all trivial matters that she could defer if she heard his horse's footfall. If he did not come, she slowly allowed herself to ease into a task that needed her full attention, or she went to play with the children, or, taking a deep breath to dispel her disappointment, she sent Bertie to invite Zennora to join them. Yet if he did come, she checked herself in the mirror and opened the front door, smiling, welcoming him in, but trying to appear relaxed, as though the visit were pleasant but not truly of any consequence.

They began each afternoon sitting on the porch, where he told her the news of the town, reporting when the carpenters set the posts for a new house, or when the hardware store received a shipment of gleaming stoves from Marysville, or when the police had to finish a brawl in one of the livery stables. Then they searched out the children, hunting upstairs or among the granite outcroppings and pine needle flats beyond the porch. Clara had occasionally complained that Jack showed little interest in Florence, and Susan had assured her that Hannibal's attitude was just the same, but Jack now confounded and charmed her. He swung Jane up to ride on his shoulders, where she giggled and screamed, urging him to trot in a circle, faster and faster, until she insisted that she was scared and must be held instead. Then, with his forearm tucked securely under her rump, she clinging to him like a monkey, he addressed the boys gravely, as though they were men, asking after the progress of the "shaft," as he called it, that they were digging behind the house. Bertie, now four years old, became quite solemn with Jack, resolutely explaining to him a rock, a pine cone, or the corner of the house, while James clamored for him to look, look, please look, so they could make faces at each other. When the children grew impatient with adult company, Susan fixed a pot of tea, and they sat and talked of Cornwall. Jack had given up trying to understand her longing, so he simply listened to her daydream about the gulls wheeling over the surf that crashed around Crane Islands, the music of the congregation singing hymns in the little chapel, the shape of the long spring grass when the wind bent it over in irregular waves, the clatter of horses along the cobblestones that divided the neat shops of Camborne, the smell of fresh milk at a friend's dairy, and the day that the entire family had driven out towards Land's End to roam among the druidical stones.

Susan welcomed Jack partly because his company was so soothing, but also because no one else seemed to have time or attention to spare for her. Jesse had begun building his house, and when she visited the site so that her father, proud of his new project, could show her the arrangement of the rooms, she snapped at him peevishly. She went to see Zennora one morning and found her sketching out a picture of the garden she hoped to plant at the new house, so she felt surrounded by what she still regarded as their departure. She could not turn to Hannibal, for he had made it clear that he had no patience for her "creening," as he put it, about her parents. He spent hours at his desk, measuring levels and extending imaginary shafts, and he had started buying stock in strange companies. When she asked about one of them, feeling obligated to show some enthusiasm and hoping that he would return the gesture, he would only explain that someone was taking water out of the mountains and running it through a canal to San Francisco. She asked why the people in the City couldn't use the water from the hills nearer to them, and when he brusquely informed her that she simply didn't understand, she retorted that there was no sense in drying up the Sierra just to fill a sink in a fancy hotel. He stood there, exasperated and spluttering, as she climbed the stairs to check on the children. Hannibal, she thought to herself, could just as well talk to the bricks in the chimney, for all he wanted anyone to respond. He had been fretting over some money he had lent to a man who sounded like a fair caudler, a man who couldn't hang on to a single gold coin to save himself, and when she said as much to Hannibal, he flared up and proposed that if she had neither encouragement nor sound advice to offer, then she could just listen, and if she didn't care to do that, why, then, he wouldn't bother her with it at all.

Yet Jack made no demands on her. He made his affairs sound amusing and never expected her to solve his problems or, worse, reassure him after he had already made up his mind about something. Talking to him was a relief after trying to pick her way through Hannibal's peeves and anxieties, and once, on a sudden impulse, she wrapped her arms around his neck and kissed him on the cheek. He accepted the embrace, smiling down at her when she stepped back, and swung up into his saddle. From then on, she kissed him when he arrived and again when he left, simply as a matter of routine, as though she had always done so, and after a few days, she noticed that when she reached up to his shoulders, he rested his hands lightly on her waist. These little gestures of greeting became part of their custom, like her habit of taking his hat and hanging it on a certain peg, which she had, earlier, taken care to make vacant, and his preference to be the one to pour the tea.

So as the scent of the Ponderosa pines rose from the melting pitch, Jack and Susan became as intimate as lovers to whom everyday moments are no longer matters of invention, and the rituals of their apparently innocent encounters formed a mosaic against which the flowering of a new intimacy seemed, at first, to be almost inconsequential, nothing more than a missing piece that would inevitably nestle into place.

Susan later realized that a randomness infused the course of events; the sense of chance nearly persuaded her that something she could neither perceive nor understand was pressing her on. On a warm morning in July, Zennora came to the house, fretful because it was not yet time to pack for the move, and insisted on taking the children with her for a long walk and perhaps a picnic in the woods. Susan had protested that Jane could not possibly manage and that she would have to accompany them so that Zennora and the boys could enjoy themselves, but her mother simply smiled and scooped the baby up into the air and down onto her hip. The boys had already gone fifty yards down the path towards Nana's house, scarcely able to wait to see the fresh blackberry pie that she had promised would sit in the top of the picnic basket, so Susan gave in, and stood in the doorway watching the little group flicker in and out of the sunlit patches beneath the cedar trees.

The house was so quiet that Jack remarked on how strange it felt to visit her without the children running in and out, and because the little ones were not there to demand their attention, he suggested that they, too, go for a walk. They climbed up the gentle slope of the saddle and down the other side, bearing a little to the left to stay as far as they could from the noise and intrusion of the North Star, and down to Wolf Creek. In spite of the fresh rush of the water, the air was hot, hotter than she had realized, and as she stood in the shade, she took off her hat and, almost unconsciously, unfastened the top four buttons of her dress. She ran the back of her hand along her hairline, bringing it away wet, and she patted her cheeks, feeling their heat. All around her, insects sang ecstatically. She heard Jack take a breath, and she turned. He was standing quite close, and she looked up into his face, wondering, as always, at those incongruously childlike blue eyes, so clear, so open. He bent down to her, and her own eyes closed as their lips met, and met again. She could scarcely breathe, but she didn't care. She reached up to find his face with her fingers, marking the contour of his mustache, mapping his cheekbones and, even as they kissed again, threading a curious fingertip in between his lips. She could feel him running his hands up and down, from her shoulders to her hips, and he was breathing quickly, almost gasping.

She stopped and stepped back. He was looking full into her face, still panting a little, one eyebrow raised as though in question. She picked up her hat and moved into him, placing one palm on the center of his chest and lifted her face to be kissed again. She turned to the stream, crouched to dip her fingers into the water, and rose, her fingers in her mouth, sucking her knuckles clean, careless of the wet sand smeared on the hem of her dress. A jay called from the tree above. Susan stepped up onto the embankment and walked back up the hill, steadily, never hurrying, with Jack a half a pace behind her the whole way. He stayed there, just in her shadow, as they approached her house, stepped up onto the porch, passed through the door and climbed the stairs to her bedroom, their bedroom, hers and Hannibal's, but now hers, only hers.

She turned to face him. He took off his jacket and draped it carefully across the back of a chair. He reached out and undid her buttons, slowly, quite gently, until she was able to step out of the dress. He unhooked her stays, lifted them away, and pulled delicately, with his fingertips, to coax the warm, damp fabric of her chemise away from her skin, where the whalebone had left a pattern. She sat down on the edge of the bed, still looking at him, and he unlaced each of her boots, laid it on the floor, and reached up to pull off her stockings. She stood, and he slid down the drawers with the bits of lace at the cuffs. Grunting softly, he rose to his full height, and she reached her arms up to him. He kissed her, picked her up, and laid her on the bed. She watched him undress, so leisurely, and welcomed him with both hands when he lay down beside her.

She later remembered, intrigued, how familiar he had seemed to her, even in those moments when she could scarcely think, scarcely breathe. Even when he had cried out suddenly, even when she realized that she was wailing and moaning with every breath, there was nothing strange, nothing clumsy. They rose and fell on the soft coverlet, with the warm breeze drifting in past the curtains, caressing them with the scent of honeysuckle mixed with hot pine needles. When it was over, Jack lay as though a giant hand had flung him onto the bed, his arms and legs limp and arranged at random. She traced patterns on his face and chest with the tip of her little finger. He opened his eyes, scanned the ceiling, then turned and smiled at her.

Jack did not come to visit her the next day, or the day after that. On the third day, she was walking out to check on the boys when she saw his horse picking its way slowly down the slope, and she stood on the porch, waiting. He dismounted, threw the reins over the railing, and strode over to her, taking off his hat and bending down to kiss her all in one motion. Sitting in the parlor, she listened for a few minutes to the news of the town and then broke in.

"Jack." He paused, his eyebrows raised. "Jack." She took a breath and let it go. "I can't see ye any more."

He frowned. "What do you mean?"

She looked down at her hands, folded in her lap. "I don't mean I can't ever see ye—I mean I can't see ye 'ere, like this."

He walked over to the window and stared out. She had rehearsed this conversation over and over again, while playing with the children, while cleaning the house, while serving Hannibal's supper, while lying awake in her bed, their bed, at night, but even though she had imagined—hoped— that they could do it calmly, even politely, Jack's composure set her nerves on edge. She wanted to run out the door, to throw something, to scream, to fasten her arms around his neck and refuse to let go. She realized that he was looking at her again.

"Susan—" His voice shook. "Susan. I love you."

"Yes."

He took a step towards her. "I love you."

She felt tears well up in her eyes and start to spill down her cheeks. Her nose began to burn inside and she had to gasp for air. "What am I supposed t' do?" He reached out towards her. "No! No!!" She turned in her chair, trying to control herself. "I won't be yer mistress."

"I wouldn't ask that of you."

"And what else is there?"

He knelt down in front of her, and she shied back, skittish, but he held up his palms; he would not touch her. "Susan, ye don't know 'ow much it means t' me to see ye. T' talk with ye."

"Talk t' Clara!"

He flinched. "I do. But ye're different."

"How?"

"I've known ye longer than almost anyone. We were children together."

"And does that make it right?"

"What?"

"The two of us bein' 'ere!"

He rose and began to pace aimlessly about the room. She could hear the children on the porch, and she hoped Bertie could keep Jane amused until Jack left. "Listen, Susan . . . I'm sorry about what happened."

She actually laughed, surprising herself. "Oh, Jack, don't ye dare take th' responsibility all on yerself."

"Well . . . "

"No. Must I say it? Ye didn't take advantage of me. All right?"

"If ye chose, then . . . "

"It was th' wrong choice." She took a deep breath. "I didn't know it then, didn't want t' know it. But I know it now. And I can't go back, can't change it."

He had stopped pacing and was standing in the middle of the room with his arms folded. "I want t' keep seeing you, even if it's not easy."

"Ye ride in 'ere an' ride out, well, it's up t' me whether to open my door."

"If you decide, all by yerself, that we can't see each other, then ye're decidin' fer me as well, and ye're takin' away somethin' I want."

"I can't help ye wantin' it. Wantin' me. I'm . . . I'm not my own t' give, not th' way ye want."

"We can keep seein' each other, just as we 'ave been. What 'appened won't 'appen again."

She sighed and pressed her handkerchief against her eyes. "No, no, no, no. I won't do it. I can't. Ye don't understand."

"I want t' try."

"Please go, Jack." She felt completely exhausted. "Please."

He walked to the door and lifted his hat down from the peg. He stood there for a moment, his back to her, and then turned.

"Clara's been asking if we could go back to Cornwall." He paused as she stared at him. "I told her I'd think it over. I didn't want to leave you. But if you won't see me . . . "

She felt like every nerve was on fire. "I *can't* see you! Don't ye understand? Ye can threaten t' leave, but still I can't see you!"

"That's not what I meant!" He had nearly shouted at her, and he stopped, startled. Out on the porch, they heard Jane beginning to whimper.

"The children need me, please . . . "

"Susan, wait just a moment. If ye can't see me, then ye can't. But all I'm sayin' is that I don't see enough reason t' stay 'ere. I'm not sayin' that t' get ye t' do somethin' ye don't want. I'm just sayin' what's so. I'm goin' back to Cornwall."

She felt bewildered. "Fer 'ow long?"

"I don't know. P'raps t' stay."

She wanted to reach up to the rafters, tear the house off of its piers and hurl it up to the sky, leaving the two of them standing there in the void, her rage towering over him like a cliff. But she kept hearing Jane whimpering, and she thought she saw Bertie peeking in through a window, so she bit her lip, feeling herself flush all over, and hissed at him. "Don't ye understand? I married Hannibal because you were stayin' 'ere and 'e was goin' back!"

The clear blue eyes opened wide, finally purified by genuine surprise. "Jesse told me that 'e'd never let ye marry yer cousin. 'e told me t' give it up."

She began to feel dizzy, as though the floor were tilting beneath her feet. "And you believed him?! Ye didn't ask me?" Now she let go and cried out from her very bottom. "'e would've if I'd wanted to! Mother would've made 'im! 'e would've let me! But ye told me you were stayin' 'ere! Oh,

Jack, I want t' go home!"

She dropped down on the floor, crouched over her skirts, sobbing freely now. He started towards her, but the door opened and the boys ran in, Bertie crying a little, his face red, and James with his thumb stuck in his mouth. After them toddled Jane, still whimpering, and when she saw her mother on the floor, weeping, she opened her mouth and began to howl. All three of the children crowded around Susan, who tried to put her arms around them. Jack stood there looking at the family. Susan had no attention to spare for him, but kept kissing and soothing the children. Finally, he walked out the door and left them there on the floor.

During the next two months, Susan felt, every moment, as though she were scarcely holding herself together. She could not tell anyone about Jack's decision to leave California, and she could not even ask him—for she successfully avoided seeing him alone—whether he were actually going through with it. She continued to visit Clara, suffering under the other woman's careful scrutiny, whether genuine or imagined, but Jack's wife never mentioned their possible departure. Finally, at the dinner following Nick's wedding, Jack got up to speak, and even while he was offering the traditional toast to the bridal couple, Susan knew, somehow, that he was about to announce his plans. She twisted her handkerchief into a knot under the drape of the table cloth and hoped that her face would not give her away, but when Jack had finished and everyone was offering their good wishes, she realized that Hannibal was staring at her curiously—how much, she wondered, did he know?—so she took refuge in Jane, murmuring that she had to take the child out of the room.

She saw Jack alone just one more time before he left, and only by chance. She was leaving Johnston's grocery, reaching up to hold her hat against the breeze, and nearly bumped into him, just descending the stairs from Dibble's office. As he apologized, they heard the tinny cacophony of a brass band. Marching down Main Street were about two dozen men in rough ranks; two policemen escorted them on horseback while three more sat in a wagon, and the band followed. The marchers grinned at each other, waved at the onlookers, and sang in hoarse grunts. They wore red flannel shirts, broad-brimmed hats and heavy boots, with burly shoulders, thick necks, half-grown beards and red, calloused hands that closed into fists as they tramped along. Jack turned to a man next to him and asked who the marchers could be.

"They're the miners from French Corral." Nearly a hundred drunken men had invaded a Chinese camp, driving off the residents, pulling down their cabins and scattering their belongings in a ravine. The newspapers and local officials had offered pious remarks about the "outrage" even while assuring the public that the Chinese, as one of the "colored races," were, of course, "inferior." Now the police were escorting the rioters to Nevada City, but rumor held that the trial was to be for show only, that Judge Kendall might levy a small fine on the ringleaders, but would release the others and declare justice served.

Cheerful and confident, the marchers called sarcastic advice back to the musicians, hailed acquaintances among those who lined the streets, and grinned in the warm spring sunshine. Two boys in white aprons trotted out of a saloon with wooden buckets of beer that slopped and spilled over the sides. The marchers stopped to drink, and while they passed the buckets among them, Susan noticed that Jack was waving across the street at someone, a man, a Chinese man.

He was standing in a shadow. His face was absolutely blank under a black silk hat, but he missed nothing, marking the boy who ran back for more beer, the saloon keeper who came out to the sidewalk to exchange jokes with the sergeant, and the two burly marchers who found a female acquaintance and followed her into Spencer's book store without arousing more than casual attention from their supposed guards. All around the intersection of Main and Mill, Americans, English and Irish chattered and laughed while the man watched silently.

Susan asked Jack who the man was. He looked down at her with an oddly guarded expression. "Ah Choy. Don't you remember? Come on!" Without giving her a chance to demur, he took her by the arm and walked across the street, threading a path through the crowd. He greeted the man quietly, but as the merchant turned, one of the marchers suddenly raised his voice from the middle of the street.

"Hey! Look a' that!" He had a bucket of beer in one hand, holding it high against his shoulder as though he were just about to tip it over and get a drink, and with the other hand he was pointing straight at Ah Choy. "Hey! Hop Sing! You washee washee? Mebbe you catchee dolla', maybe not!" The men near him broke into raucous laughter. Ah Choy didn't move. "Hey, you heathen! I'm talkin' to you!" He seemed to remember the beer bucket on his shoulder. "Hey, maybe he wants a drink. Whaddya say, Hop Sing— drinkee? No? Mebbe brandee, eh?" Ah Choy stood motionless, his face a mask and his eyes fixed on the burly white man standing in the street. "Whatsa matter? You deaf?" Four or five more of the marchers had gathered next to him, so he handed the beer bucket to one and grabbed another by the shoulder. "I say we take him with us to Nevada—show him to the judge!"

The men near him laughed and several started to approach. Jack turned, but Ah Choy was already twenty yards away, striding down Main Street towards Chinatown, his pigtail slapping his back with each step. He disappeared into the crowd so quickly that by the time his antagonists reached the spot where he had stood, they could not even tell where he had gone. The sergeant, who had found the incident tremendously amusing, signaled his constables, who gathered the marchers and sent them on down the street. The band struck up a new tune, and the onlookers laughed at the cornet player who could barely hit one note in five as he staggered along with his fellows.

Susan wanted to ask Jack why he looked so disappointed, but she stopped herself, apprehensive that he, if she gave him a chance, would once again try to persuade her to change her mind. At that moment, Joseph drove up in Jesse's wagon. She told Jack good-bye, and before he could protest, she stepped off the sidewalk, reached up for Joseph's hand, and pulled herself up onto the seat. They drove away down Mill Street, and she looked back over her shoulder to see Jack still standing there, his hat in his hand, watching the wagon until the curve of the store fronts interposed between them.

A few days later, Hannibal returned home to report that Jack and Clara had left for San Francisco, there to take ship to Panama for the crossing and the voyage home. As she put the children to bed that night, she marveled that she had no more tears, but when she lay under her blankets, with Hannibal breathing heavily next to her, she found that she could not sleep, for whenever she closed her eyes, she saw Jack—riding up to the house, grinning down at her from his phaeton, pouring her a cup of tea, and bending over to brush his mustache across her cheek. As the stars wheeled outside her window, the images of Jack became blurred with glimpses of Hannibal, her mother, the children, and impossibly tall Ponderosa pines reaching up into the blue sky like sharp towers. The figures coalesced into a breathtakingly clear memory of the waves crashing below the cliffs at Hell's Mouth, a tiny, rocky cove that she and Zennora had visited when she was just a little girl. She stood there, five years old again, staring down into the turmoil, fascinated to see Jack, a grown man, standing on a rock surrounded by angry water, laughing as he stretched out his arms to the storm. She drifted, exhausted, confused.

Within a week, Susan discovered that she was pregnant again. She counted the days and suddenly felt foolish, realizing that she must have missed a month without noticing it, and counted them again, feeling the blood mount in her cheeks, the flush spreading across her chest and out along her arms, making her fingers tingle. She felt so dizzy that she staggered, light-headed and careful, to the nearest chair and sank into it. She counted on her fingers, backwards and forwards, again and again. If the baby came in June . . . But if it came in May . . . She couldn't be certain, and she sat in her chair, counting and counting again. There was no way to know for sure. She got up and went about her housework, dazed, hardly paying attention to what she was doing. The weight in her belly seemed to pull her down.

Cousin Jack

On a chilly afternoon in mid-winter, Hannibal arrived home and called to Susan to bring out the children and put them in the wagon. Without a word, he drove them into town, and she began to think that she was taking them to Jesse's new house, nearly finished, but he passed it and pulled up in front of a vacant lot. He seemed unusually pleased with himself and wanted to play some sort of game about explaining what he was about, but she got him to tell her that he wanted to buy the property and live there. It looked barren, much more desolate than the woods around their home at French Lead. Hannibal had occasionally talked of moving, of building another house, and he had promised that she could ask for whatever she wanted. She had never taken him seriously, hearing just another of his pointless notions, but now here he was, apparently ready to start work. The prospect of Hannibal trying to please her, of asking what she wanted and then, with his lips in a thin, tight line, trying to convince her to want something else, wearied her. She looked towards her father's new home; there was a perfectly nice house next door. "Why can't we buy that?" she asked. He brought his lips together and, in an irritated tone, told her that it wasn't for sale. He admitted that he hadn't even approached the owners, but he insisted that there was no use. He started talking about buying a ranch in French Ravine, but he seemed to have no clear idea about how he was going to pay for it or what he would do with it. He might, it seemed, borrow the money from Jack. She kept asking him questions, trying to find out what he could be thinking, but the boys began to roll around in the wagon right next to where he was standing. She realized that he wasn't going to do anything about it, so she called to them, in a voice sharper than she intended. "Bertie! Stop it!"

The boys froze, and Hannibal seemed to notice them for the first time. "D'ye want me to get 'em down?"

She shook her head and walked away. Behind her, he started talking about buying a different house, and she asked him to stop. She was trying to think. He was trying to please her—she knew that—but it was so typical of him not to realize what it all meant. All he remembered was that she was upset at her parents moving away from French Lead. He thought he could fix that by moving her out to be near them, but of course, he wasn't able to find a place next door, so there would be another house, another family, between her and Zennora. If she wanted to go visit, she would have to put on her hat for the walk up the street. It wouldn't be the same.

Yet as Susan stood there looking up at the blackberry brambles, she felt trapped. Living near the mine was simply expedient, something that she could accept as long as her husband was working there. Moving into town, independent of whatever Hannibal was doing—or not doing—to earn a living, represented a commitment that made her stomach turn over. She had given up asking Hannibal about returning to Cornwall; every time she tried, he pressed his lips together and looked down at his fingernails while telling her, in effect, that he knew what was best for the family. When she asked him, directly, whether he wanted to stay in California, he rambled on about opportunities and investments. Now he wanted to settle here, but as she looked around at the half-built neighborhood, she realized that she really had little choice: living near Zennora was better than staying at French Lead, alone. She suddenly realized that her feet and hands were cold, terribly cold, so she walked over to the wagon, took Hannibal's hand, and climbed up to the seat. He kept at her, kept asking questions, even though she told him to go ahead and buy the place. As the wagon swayed and jerked back down Ophir Road, she closed her eyes, trying not to think about what she was doing.

Susan's belly blossomed until Hannibal, without consulting her, hired a maid to do the housework. She spent hours sitting on the porch in the spring breeze, and she would, at unpredictable intervals, find her heart pounding and her breath coming in short gasps. Hannibal tried to entertain her with reports on the progress of the new house, but she could not concentrate on what he was saying, and, many times, their conversations would end when Hannibal abruptly dropped his solicitous manner and walked away, and she would realize that she must have said something to make him feel unwanted.

She awoke early one morning in the middle of May feeling strangely nervous, as though something had happened without her noticing it. She was so distracted at breakfast that Hannibal asked if she wanted to see Dr. Simpson, but she focused long enough to dismiss the idea and assure him that he could, as usual, ride into town. Bertie, with a solemn face, took charge of the little ones and marched them outside, in spite of James' protests, to dig holes. Late in the morning, well before his customary hour, Hannibal returned to announce, cheerily, that Stanford had driven the golden spike, and the transcontinental railroad was complete. He seemed exhilarated, and she wondered if he had been drinking, so early in the day. He gathered the children in the parlor to read the commentary in the special edition of the *Union*.

Suddenly, Susan crumpled in her chair, the contraction so sharp and powerful that it doubled her up. She slowly let herself down to her knees, trusting only the solidity of the floor, and when the pain subsided, she let Hannibal take her upstairs. When Zennora arrived, Susan was huddled under the blankets, her cheeks smeared with tears and a dribble of blood running down her chin from where she had bit her lip. Zennora looked concerned, obviously anticipating that the labor would be unusually difficult, but not realizing that her daughter was preoccupied with a different anxiety. By the time the night began to wane, Susan, frantic from exhaustion, had become convinced that the baby would never come out, that it would refuse to emerge into the light of day, but would instead struggle inside of her, resisting, until she died. She mumbled incoherently, and Zennora, apparently thinking her feverish, began to lay wet rags on her face. As the sun rose, Susan felt herself spread and open, and her body convulsed, wrenching and pushing. All in a rush, she felt her insides turn out as something enormous fled, and she heard a whimper. Her eyes closed, too heavy to stay open, and she felt as though she must sleep, but a small weight settled onto her arm. She looked up and saw Zennora laying down the baby, already wiped clean and wrapped in a blanket. For a moment, Susan resolved not to look, not to see, not to know, but she could not resist, and she turned her head to gaze at the tiny face next to hers. The thin lips and narrow nose were so like Hannibal that she laughed aloud, subsiding into giggles and splutters so uncontrollably that Zennora leaned over her, apprehensive. Susan began to cry and did not stop even when her mother turned back the covers and helped the nuzzling infant fasten himself to her breast. When the men came into the room several minutes later, she had composed herself enough to acquiesce, calmly, to Hannibal's suggestion that they name the little boy after his brother, Martin. She did not care, she thought, she did not care at all.

Now, when she thought of Jack, she did not fret, but rather wondered what he was doing, as though thinking of a casual friend who was visiting a place she had once seen. She nearly wrote him a letter about the town's reaction to the railroad, knowing he would be interested, but after trying to begin two or three times, she put her pen away and burned the smeared pages in the fireplace. Hannibal continued to come home with reports on the new house, and now she nodded, trying to encourage him, but she told herself that a house is a house, and she could live in one as well as in another. By June, she was still spending most of her time in bed, so Hannibal assigned the maid to watch the children while he, Jesse, Zennora and Joseph spent three days packing everything into crates. Susan spent a strange day lying in bed listening to the cycles of the moving: an hour of thumps and bumps and curt orders while the men loaded the wagon, the sound of the wheels grinding up the slope towards the road, then an hour of absolute stillness, and then their return to do it all again. Even the children were gone, taken to the new house, so she lay in bed, her only responsibility nestling in her arms, listening to the distant thumping and grinding of the mine. In mid-afternoon, the men cleared out the upstairs, leaving nothing but Susan and Martin lying in the bed, now set in an empty, echoing room, even bare of window curtains, and at the end of the day, she walked slowly down the stairs, clutching the baby carefully, and waited while the men loaded the bed into the back of the wagon and lifted her into it, and she lay there, under a light blanket, watching the sky fade from blue to pale gold to grey as

Summer's Lease, 1867-70

Hannibal slowly guided the team into town, where they found Zennora and the children waving from the porch.

She felt stronger every day, and soon took over the house from her mother. In August, Hannibal bought the Kentucky Ranch. He drove the wagon up to a knoll overlooking the ravine, and because the children were unusually quiet, gazing around at the new surroundings, Susan had a chance to realize how peaceful the place was, with its stands of black oaks and digger pines, and the brook running cheerfully down through the undergrowth. Hannibal still had no clear idea of what he would do with the property, and as she hugged little Martin and felt Jane's hand resting lightly on her shoulder, she realized that she did not mind. Hannibal would go his own way, spending his time wandering through the town or hunching over the account books at his desk, pursuing this or that scheme, always explaining it to her at tedious length, but making his own decisions. She settled herself in her seat as he turned the horses around and drove back into town.

Susan had hoped that she and her mother would resume their habit of spending the afternoons together, reading and watching the children, but she found that Zennora was gone from home more days than not, for she had begun to go for long walks, even in the chill of autumn. She seemed reluctant to tell Susan about her little excursions and even avoided revealing where she went. As the winter gave way to warmer weather, Zennora approached her daughter, impelled by her anxiety over Jesse, who had, without consulting her, decided to build an addition onto their house.

He had been restless ever since they moved in, especially during the long winter evenings, prowling around the rooms, testing windows and trying doors until Zennora, more than once, had simply left the house rather than ask him what was the matter and have him simply stare at her. Several times, when Susan walked up the street to visit, she found her father walking around and around the house, now peering at the walls, as though trying to discover some hidden mystery, now walking with his hands clasped behind his hips, his eyes on the ground in front of him. As she sat in the parlor with Zennora and the children, she could see her father passing outside the window at regular intervals. He had let his beard grow longer than usual, and the whiskers, turning grey now, curled all the way down his chest. Once in a while, he would stop in front of the house, lifting his chin and cocking his head as though listening for something. Shaking his head, he would walk on, like a man trying to resolve a profoundly troubling problem.

He built most of the addition himself, reluctant to let anyone else lay hands on the lumber. He spent several days preparing to set the posts and beams into place, meticulously whittling the tenons and carefully chiseling out the mortises for an exact fit. He grudgingly hired a boy to help him for one day, firmly directing him to hold each joint in place while he checked it for fit and gently tapped the pieces together with a hard leather mallet. When the women peeked around the side of the house, they saw him carefully planing planks, checking and re-checking them for true, hammering boards into place, setting each nail with painstaking precision, or simply standing there, staring at the corner of a wall amidst stacks of raw lumber and little piles of curley-cue shavings. Susan, wanting her father, tried many times to get him to tell her what he was doing, but he answered in short, sometimes cryptic, phrases, and gazed at her from underneath his eyebrows, which had grown strangely bushy.

So for two months, the family spied on Jesse as he worked. Hannibal came to see the project once, responding with surprisingly warm concern for Susan's apprehensions, and told her that it seemed to be only one room, but there was, as far as he could tell, no door leading into the main part of the house. Jesse had become so disinclined to explain his plans that Susan was afraid to ask him about the anomaly, so she took Joseph aside, thinking that Jesse might have confided in him, but her brother shrugged his shoulders. Yet he, usually so apathetic, actually seemed anxious, and when she came to visit her mother on a Sunday, she found him sitting in a corner window, biting his lip as he watched his father bend to his work.

The affair reached a crisis that left everyone in the family gasping for breath as though they all, at the same moment, had stepped on something apparently firm that had given way and dropped them through. Jesse had begun to enclose the walls, working his way around the three sides of the room as it jutted out from the rear of the house. The first proved to be a seamless row of sugar pine boards, each a uniform twelve inches wide, each meeting the adjoining boards smoothly in testimonial to Jesse's rigorous, patient skill with eye and plane. The second wall was just as featureless, just as flawlessly catenated, and the family waited to see what the third would look like. Susan answered a knock at her back door to find her mother standing there without her hat.

"Susan, 'e's finished it."

"Mother, what's th' matter?"

"Ye must see fer yerself."

Zennora pulled her out of the kitchen, still in her apron, leaving the children behind, and led her up the street. Jesse had finished the last wall, and it was just like the other two. He had enclosed the entire room, leaving neither door nor window. He had long since laid the rough floor and nailed boards across the rafters, so the room was a completely enclosed box. Susan stood there, wondering, but then something happened that made her struggle for breath. From inside the box, she could hear her father's voice. He was singing a hymn.

> With this cold stony heart of mine,
> Jesus, to thee I flee;
> And to thy grace my soul resign,
> To be renew'd by thee.

The women listened, amazed, and the voice changed melodies.

> Far from the world, O Lord, I flee,
> From strife and tumult far;
> From scenes where Satan wages still
> His most successful war.

Zennora was shivering. The two women huddled together for the rest of the afternoon, fascinated, horrified, afraid to approach the mysterious room where Jesse's voice sang hymns with scarcely a pause. Late in the day, Joseph arrived and joined the women where they crouched under a tree. He hardly seemed to hear Zennora's explanation, and as he stared at the singing room, Susan looked into his face and felt as if she were watching a wound tear deeper and deeper. When Zennora insisted that he find out what his father was doing, Susan had to turn away from the pain in his eyes; he looked just like a fawn they had once found bleeding to death, the casual prey of a careless hunter, in the woods near French Lead. Still, he said not a word, but walked slowly up to the raw, blank wall, waited for the end of a verse, and tapped with his knuckles. A muffled voice came from within. Joseph asked a question, listened, and walked around to the other side, where the women could not see him. They waited, and after a moment, they could hear two voices from inside, but they couldn't make out the words. As they listened, Susan felt a hand on her shoulder, and she turned to find Hannibal, who had come home and found the maid in charge of the children. Joseph appeared, walking back around the corner of the room to join them, looking down at the dry earth as he tried to decide what to say.

"'e says 'e idden comin' out 'til the end of 'is core." Susan felt Hannibal release a long breath. "But 'e says we'll 'ave t' clear away the cave-in, first." He looked up at his mother. "'e'll be singin' 'ymns so the men know where t' look. When the way is clear, 'e'll come t' grass." Spent, Joseph squatted down and buried his face in one hand, covering first his eyes, then his mouth.

Hannibal took charge. He sent Joseph off to find Dr. Simpson, and all three men entered the room, lifting out the board on the far side that Jesse had nailed only on one end, allowing it to pivot. After several minutes of listening to men's murmurs, the women watched as a little procession inched its way around the corner: first Hannibal, walking ahead a ways and stopping to look back, and then the others, the doctor on one side and Joseph on the other, with Jesse in the middle, wearing the mining clothes that had hung in the stable ever since they had moved in. He carried his lunch pail in one hand and a sledge in the other, and the candle on his hat was still flickering. The men held his upper arms gently and guided him slowly, carefully, up the porch steps and into the house.

Simpson proposed to keep him in bed for a while, but on the second day, Zennora climbed the stairs to find the sheets thrown back from the empty mattress. She searched the house and was on her way out to the privy when she heard, once again, Jesse's voice singing from inside the new room. She took a deep breath, considered, and walked down the street to bring Susan back with her. The two women walked around to the side of the room and stood before the loose board.

> Expand thy wings, Celestial Dove;
> Brood o'er our nature's night;
> On our disorder'd spirits move,
> And let there now be light.

Susan lifted the board out so Zennora could enter, then bent down to follow. They stood blinking in the darkness, and they could hear someone breathing heavily just a few feet away. After a moment, Susan realized that there were a few flecks of light scattered about what had at first seemed like a perfectly sealed chamber; even Jesse's carpentry could not persuade the fresh planking to hold its shape in the sunshine. Her eyes adjusted, and she could see her father sitting in a corner, his knees drawn up under his chin and his face strangely calm. He was talking to himself.

"They'll find us soon. Joseph, and William, an' th' others. They'll dig down and clear th' rab away. They'll blast it out if they must, an' then th' walls will shake!" He nodded and smiled. "We'll wait 'ere. No matter that th' candles're gone. God will send all th' light we need." He clapped his hands together. "Joseph wants t' go t' California. Wants t' bring out th' gold. Ah, well, a thousand feet down, it's all th' same, all th' same."

Zennora walked over and crouched down in front of her husband, looking full into his face. Susan stood behind her and spoke in hardly more than a whisper. "Fayther?"

Jesse paid them no attention at all. Zennora patted him on the cheek gently and said, "Jesse, wake up," but still he gave no sign that he knew them or even realized that they were there. He seemed perfectly reasonable, thought Susan, and she almost wished he would rave or cry out.

Jesse lifted up his chin, his face serene, as though listening. "We were trapped in Carn Brea fer three days once. We waited, sat there in th' dark, savin' our candles, and after just one day, we could 'ear 'em comin'. We knew. Ye can 'ear through th' rock, better'n the air. Joseph could feel th' sounds with 'is fingertips." He twisted and reached for the wall with his hand, spreading the fingers gently on the fresh boards. Then he smiled and relaxed. "I never could. Well, boys, we'll wait. They'll be 'ere soon."

Summer's Lease, 1867-70

He began to sing again, and the women picked their way through the dim light and out through the tilting board. When the doctor came again, he took Zennora aside and told her that Jesse would have to go to the hospital. No one in Grass Valley could do anything for him, but in Stockton, there was a place where he might be all right. He should go, and he should go soon, right away, for there was no telling when he might become violent.

When Hannibal heard Simpson's advice, he took out a small pad and began making notes. "Joseph, we'll 'ave to take him. There's a coach that leaves for Sacramento tomorrow morning."

Susan looked at her brother, who was staring at the floor. "Joseph?" He looked up at her. "Will ye be all right?" His eyes were full of tears, but he nodded.

Jesse boarded the coach with neither objection nor protest, but he hardly seemed aware of what was happening; when Zennora threw her arms around his neck and held her cheek to his, the attention seemed to puzzle him. He started up the steps, but stopped to turn and look around at the façade of the Exchange and the men and women bustling up and down the street. Hannibal reached up, ready to seize his arm if he tried to jump off, but Jesse ignored him, taking in the scene with mild interest, as though it were a stop on a long journey. He stepped inside, Hannibal and Joseph followed, and the coach pulled away, leaving Susan and Zennora weeping in the dust.

Every Friday for the next few weeks, Dr. Simpson telegraphed Stockton for a report on Jesse's progress. There was little change; he seemed to see nothing around him, but continued to sing hymns and offer calm encouragement to the other miners that he imagined to be sealed into the drift with him. The attending physician wrote to assure the family that Jesse was quite peaceful; in fact, surprisingly so, for most of his patients grew agitated and even dangerous. His only concern was that Jesse was refusing his meals, choosing to eat only tiny morsels and take small sips of water as he assured his illusory companions that they would be wise to ration their small store. Then the telegrams became more frequent, for Jesse had taken to his bed, still singing and talking, but weak now, for lack of food, and he had lapsed into a fever. Zennora listened to these more disturbing bulletins for three days and directed Joseph to buy a ticket for the two of them to go to Stockton. He returned from town not with the tickets but with a new telegram, just arrived at the Western Union office. Jesse Trevenna was dead.

Hannibal walked into Zennora's parlor with his pad and pencil as the others sat there with handkerchiefs held to their eyes. Joseph, he decided, would have to go to Stockton and bring his father's remains home. He, Hannibal, would send a message ahead to arrange for a casket. At most, Joseph would have to stay overnight, but there should be little delay. Hannibal was finishing his plans as neatly as if he had drawn up a contract when Susan announced that she would go. He started to expostulate, but she cut him off, not angrily, but firmly. "No, Hannibal. I must go. Joseph needs me." They looked at Joseph, leaning forward on the edge of a chair, his head bent over his clasped hands, praying. He looked up at his sister, his eyes red and shining, and nodded. "Mother can 'elp Josephine look after th' children."

Susan later remembered little of the journey. They rattled down out of the hills, swaying and lurching, and on down the valley to Stockton, where there were papers to sign and a team of officials who wanted to convince her of their sympathy but had little time to spare for her. There was a shaky moment when she had to confirm her father's identity; they had laid him out as though sleeping, and but for the shocking pallor, she expected him to open his eyes and smile at her. She and Joseph had little to say to each other, and she felt as though she were traveling not with her grown brother, a working miner, but a young boy, lost and alone. As she had anticipated, he relied on her to manage the situation; she paused once, in the middle of a detail regarding the delivery of the casket, to reflect that she was doing just the sort of thing that Hannibal and Jack did so well. Finally, they were on the last leg of the journey, the horses pulling up from the Bear River towards Grass Valley.

The coach reached the top of the saddle and the driver flicked the horses into a brisk trot down the last, long slope into town. Joseph shifted his feet on the casket, pulled the window open, and thrust his face into the fresh, warm air outside. They passed the cabins on the outskirts, and then the first few clusters of houses and gardens. As the coach approached the center of town, they heard a ringing that grew louder and louder; deep church bells, insistent fire bells, and jingling coach bells all mingled into a wild, dissonant crashing that hurt Susan's ears and made her wince involuntarily. She looked at her brother; he had thrust his fingers into his ears and was squinting against the dust and noise. She started violently at a sudden, clipped crack. The battery continued to fire, alternating with the more ragged sound of a collection of rifles firing together as if in a salvo. The coach seemed to plunge into the din as the driver took the last turn onto Main Street and into the freight depot. Joseph stepped out, his cramped legs scarcely able to carry him, and reached up to offer his hand to Susan. He shouted something over the noise and walked off, leaving her dazed and disoriented in the commotion.

Every walkway, every porch, every window and every roof was crammed with people, all dressed in their best and waving tiny American flags. Susan had never seen so many packed so tightly together in one place—there had to be four or five thousand—and she noticed, in a strange sort of delayed perception, that every single one was smiling broadly and cheering; the multitude shared one grotesque face. Red, white and blue bunting hung from windows, balconies and cornices, transforming the dusty brick façades into party decorations. The bells kept ringing and the salutes kept firing; Susan could not see the artillery, but the explosions seemed to come from just on the other side of the coach. She looked about and realized that the horses were standing quietly, unconcerned, and the coachman and his assistant were calmly unloading Jesse's casket and laying it in the dirt nearby.

A brass band struck up a march, and the blaring, squealing and beating generated a procession which streamed out from beside the armory. Bewildered, Susan stepped up onto the casket itself in order to see. There, standing in a tall open coach hung with bunting, drawn by a matched pair of white horses, was William Pope, the undertaker. She wanted him to take the responsibility now, to transport the casket to his store, to the church, or to Jesse's home. She wanted to know what to do. Oblivious to the din, she asked, in an ordinary tone of voice, as though they were standing together in a quiet room, that he help her, but she could not even hear herself speak in the overpowering noise. She shouted something incoherent and pointed down at the casket beneath her feet. Pope's smile grew wider, a mask stretched out of proportion, and as he lifted his far arm to wave his hat, Susan could see pinned to his lapel the oversized, gaudy rosette of the Grand Marshal of the Independence Day Parade.

Pope's coach moved out of sight, and the procession continued with Dewey's Band, stepping out in time to discordant music that echoed unevenly off of the store fronts, the Grass Valley Union Guard, in smart white tunics with red braid and brass buttons, and the Howell Zouaves, their tight jackets, baggy trousers and little cylindrical caps making them look like a displaced company of Turks. Susan still stood and gawked as a series of carriages passed by, each carrying two or three leading citizens, the men dressed in striped cutaway coats with tall, silk hats, and the ladies apparelled in white chiffon and lace, balancing stately hats with wide brims and carrying ribboned parasols. Following them was a tableau on a flat wagon: Liberty, draped in bunting and gazing heroically off in the direction of Boston Ravine, and her court, all in poetic attitudes. The music faded as the procession turned south on Mill Street, but now another band, following the tableau, thundered into a protracted roll-off and began a new march. Susan finally stepped off of her father's casket, sat down on it, and wept.

She sobbed and gulped, wiping her eyes and nose on the sleeve of her dusty coat. The band passed up the street, leading an interminable convoy of fire trucks, and finally all of the onlookers joined the parade, marching in cohorts: miners, craftsmen, clerks, tradesmen, and finally the professionals, riding in carriages, with the occasional dandy strutting his favorite horse. Susan's eyes streamed, not only from her weeping, but from the thick dust that filled the air as the streets and buildings emptied. The parade formed a river that flowed up the hill and around the corner, draining Main Street of people and noise, leaving only the dust and the thick smells of horse sweat and manure. Susan crouched on the coffin, choking.

Her sobbing slowly subsided, and she noticed that she had dropped her hat in the dust. She reached down to pick it up and brush it off (the sleeve of her coat was hopeless by now), and she realized that the distant noise of the parade had fallen off to nothing. The town seemed to be holding its breath. Susan stood, wondering, and then she heard the seraphic voices of a children's choir, floating to her from somewhere up the hill.

> My native country, thee,
> Land of the noble free,
> Thy name I love.

The tune sounded familiar, but the words were all wrong. Main Street was completely empty; even the coach horses had abandoned her. She glanced down and discovered that she was sitting on the coffin itself. She knelt in the dust, dropping her hat once again, and her eyes filled as she called to Jesse, who, like the others, had abandoned her. In the distance, the children's voices, clear and true, ravished the pure, crystalline air.

> Let mortal tongues awake;
> Let all that breathe partake;
> Let rocks their silence break,
> The sound prolong.

15
Nick
1872-73

Annie hesitated for a moment, patting the child that had fastened itself to her skirt, then smiled brightly. "He's prospecting up in the high country."

Hannibal considered. "D'ye know when 'e'll be back?" She did not, so he tipped his hat and nudged his horse towards town. In the two weeks he had spent searching for Nick, he'd found no one who had actually talked with him since winter; there were only second-hand rumors that he had been seen anywhere from Truckee to San Francisco. He rode past the shop boys sweeping walks and dumping wash buckets, wondering whether Susan's cousin had come to some unexpected end, and then he saw him leaning against a post outside the Exchange.

Nick had been roaming the mountains. Over a table in the hotel café, he described the mining operations along the Comstock and as far south as Mariposa, and he related how, one day early in the spring, he had crossed the Sierra crest over Sonora Pass, well above the timberline, with the horses shivering in the wind that swept over the vast tilted planes of striated granite. "But what is it, Hannibal? Ye said ye needed me."

Hannibal was determined to incorporate the Live Yankee, persisting even though the Pascoes saw no advantage. Susan had listened to the idea for a few minutes, cradling Ernest while Martin tugged at her skirts, and then, turning back to a pot of potatoes, remarked in an impatient, petulant tone that she didn't see the point. Eagerly seeking approval, he cornered Joseph in his coach house, where he was re-stacking the lumber, now warped and weathered, that he had scavenged from Jesse's final project. Hannibal elaborated his hopes for the mine and how a more formal organizational structure would protect everyone's interests in the future. Joseph listened, receptive and noncommittal as ever, his light grey eyes blank in the diffused light. He had acquiesced; now Hannibal needed Nick's consent.

Nick stirred his coffee and stared down into the brown spiral. "Remind me now—who're th' partners?"

"The Pascoes. You. Martin and Bessie. Zennora. Joseph. Susan and me. That makes ten. And there'll be one new man."

"What about Nankervis?"

Hannibal had found Charles looking much older than he had remembered. He agreed to let Hannibal buy him a beer, so they walked down to a shabby saloon in Boston Ravine, where they sat drinking to the rush of water in Wolf Creek. Charles seemed weary, and his gaze was strangely mild, as though he was actually seeing the man before him rather than staring through the back of his head. Hannibal wanted to clear away old enmities by arranging for the new corporation to buy out the Nankervis shares, and he was prepared to meet strength with strength in order to push him out, even to the point of reminding Charles that the Pascoes still mistrusted him for his treacherous alliance with the Sterlings against Nick. But there was pain in his eyes, so full and clear that Hannibal wondered if he were ailing. As he listened to the fragments that Charles reluctantly disclosed about his claims, Hannibal realized that the man had never felt comfortable as a partner in the North Star. His dogged hunger for complete independence made him a loner, a hard-rock man who could be neither captain nor cobber, for he could neither muster other men, except his intimidated sons, nor accept someone else's orders. There had been no place for him in the entrenched, stratified mining community in Cornwall, and the California hills had provided a congenial home for only a short while; big companies like the Idaho were turning mavericks like Charles into anachronisms. As they carefully avoided the subject of the meeting, Hannibal remembered that Nick, the one who had most reason to hate Charles for what he had done, had never expressed the least rancor. Hannibal gently raised the question of the Live Yankee, and to his relief, there was no resistance, so they agreed quickly and easily on a price. Charles finished his beer, shook Hannibal's hand, and walked up the hill back toward his old claim.

Nick gazed down into his coffee again. "And who's th' new man?"

The eleventh partner was Zebulon Day, a young New Yorker who had earned old William Pascoe's reluctant trust. Hannibal had come to expect, whenever he rode out to Red Dog, to find Day's pale, clean-shaven face looking at him gravely from beneath the perfectly straight brim of his brown hat. The man treated him with distant deference, answering questions in his flat, nasal Yankee tones and listening to advice with what Hannibal, perhaps too sensitive to possible slight, interpreted as reluctant courtesy. In spite of the Pascoes' promise to run the works, Hannibal realized that it was Day who was making the decisions. Knowing that he no longer had the resolve to take over the operation himself, he accepted the arrangement but permitted himself, as the principal proprietor, at least one visit each month to express his opinions. Once or twice he thought he noticed Day raising his eyebrows at a Cornish expression, and those moments made him feel self-conscious not only about his automatic use of the old phrases, but also because he seemed to be growing more touchy.

Nick smiled. There was something about all of this paperwork and lawyer's confloption that pleased Hannibal; perhaps it made him feel more like one of the American businessmen in town. "Well, it makes no matter t' me, one way or the other. Just tell me where t' sign."

Relieved, Hannibal let the conversation wander. Two years had passed since Nick quit his job at the Norambagua, but when Hannibal asked a question that discreetly invited him to reveal his current employment, he began to explain a new method of propping up a drift, and as he spoke, Hannibal realized that something about Nick reminded him of Charles. Each man, in some way that Hannibal could not fathom and felt incapable of investigating, was wounded. Nick was still fascinated with the world beneath the surface, but now, thought Hannibal, he presented his smile as camouflage for a deep, overwhelming disappointment that flickered whenever he dropped his guard.

"Nicky—listen. I've been lookin' at buyin' a store down to Marysville. A hardware store. It's a good location."

Nick seemed mildly interested. "Why Marysville? Why not 'ere?"

Hannibal shifted in his chair. "Well, there's not much for sale 'ere, nothin' that I want, anyway. And besides, Marysville's a busy town. They get all the freight goin' through from Sacramento up t' th' north, and to 'ere as well."

Nick grinned. "So ye'll be spending yer time traipsin' down t' th' valley, will ye? What'll Susan think o' that?"

"I wouldn't run it—I'd just own the building. There's a fellow there, a man named Jenkins, a good man, 'e's been there for six or seven years now. The stock is all 'is—I'd just keep the place up and 'e'd pay me the rent."

"Sounds like ye're fadgin' along, Hannibal. Ye'll make a skuat o' money."

"Nick—I want ye t' buy it with me."

"What?" Nick looked up from his coffee, now giving Hannibal his full attention.

"I want ye t' buy it with me. We'd be partners."

"Hannibal . . . "

"I'd take care of everything. All ye do is put up yer money—buy any share ye want—and take yer share o' th' rent."

"I'm not a shopkeeper."

"Ye wouldn't be a shopkeeper—ye'd be an owner." He realized that he had raised his voice slightly, and he tried to relax.

Nick looked down the street again and shook his head. "You be the owner, Hannibal—ye'll do well."

"Why won't ye come in with me?"

"Why d'ye want me to? Can't ye go it alone?"

"Of course I can."

"Then what d'ye want me for?"

"I thought ye'd want to, ye . . . "

"Are ye tryin' t' do me a favor, Hannibal? Is that it?"

Hannibal caught his breath. Nick was looking at him straight in the eyes.

"And what if I am? Why shouldn't I want to do business with ye, ye're my cousin."

"Susan's cousin."

"Where's the difference?"

"If ye can't see it, I can't show it to ye."

"Don't ye want to go partners with me?"

"I didn't say that."

"All right, all right—forget it, then."

"I will!"

Nick was sitting with his palms flat on the table, his jaw set. Hannibal started to say something, thought better of it, scraped his chair back, rose, and walked out of the room. For several minutes, Nick gazed out the window and occasionally tapped his fingers in a little dance. He rose, drained his cup, took his hat and left the hotel.

About an hour later, Nick walked down the steps from the porch of John Sterling's house, pausing at the vine-covered archway to fold some papers into a leather wallet and tuck it inside his coat pocket. He rode out of town, heading east and south, following dry creekbeds and skirting the stands of cedar and groves of pine, until he reached Red Dog, and kept riding until he could see the small shacks that marked the shaft of the Live Yankee. He reined in his horse beneath the shade of an oak tree, and stayed in the saddle to watch the men working there. He waited patiently, letting the horse walk slowly around the tree to crop the grass near the trunk. When the sun stood high overhead, the men laid down their tools, and two others walked up out of the shaft into the daylight. One walked off into the woods, and Nick guided his horse over to him, taking care to stay in the cover of the trees, keep them between him and the sheds. When he crossed a patch of rocky ground, the clop of his horse's hooves drew the man's attention. It was Will Pascoe.

"Nick!"

"Hello, Will."

"Come an' eat with us."

"Thanks, no."

"Is somethin' the matter?"

"I want t' talk to ye alone."

Nick swung down and explained what he wanted. Will listened without comment and looked away, his lips pursed. "All right, Nick. But I don't 'ave it 'ere. Can ye meet me in town tomorrow?"

"Iss fay."

"How about Findley's bank?"

Nick winced. "Can we meet at the Exchange? No—'ow about the Empire?"

"The Empire it is. An' I'll buy ye a beer."

"Thanks, Will." The two men shook hands, and Will walked back to the clearing while Nick rode up the slope and back towards Grass Valley, hoping to find Zennora at home.

No one in the family had noticed Nick's visits with Zennora. She did not investigate the impulse, and he could not have explained it, but if she had paused to consider the matter, she might have decided that he came to talk with her as with his own mother, if only he could shatter distance with a wish and sit in her parlor in Camborne. They became friends, the middle-aged miner's widow and her reckless nephew, and with every pot of tea, he grew more comfortable with her, so although she never pressed or pried, he began to offer the answers to the questions that Hannibal dared not ask. After the sale of the North Star, he had paid off some of his debts, but he used most of the money to buy more claims and equip them. Some of them looked keenly, so he gave them hopeful names: the Mammoth Company, the Savage Ledge, and the Columbus Lode. He was the sole owner of the smaller ones, and where the mining regulations allowed each partner only so much distance along a ledge, he had enlisted his family and friends, so all over the district there were people who were partners in name only, for Nick was paying all of the expenses and doing all the work. He gradually acquired so many claims that he quit his job at the Norambagua in order to work them, but none paid as well as he had hoped; the rock, it seemed, had become inscrutable to him. He felt drawn to Zennora partly because he sensed in her an intuition, an understanding that he remembered and craved.

Only Nick knew that Zennora had been taking long, solitary walks through the hills and valleys around the town. When Jesse had been spending most of his time building the new house, and Susan had frequently seemed preoccupied and impatient with her, Zennora had realized that she had time to herself, sometimes most of a day without enough to keep her busy. Restless, she began to walk. At first, she left her cabin for only fifteen or twenty minutes at a time, just long enough to pass a few neighboring houses and exchange greetings with the other wives. Once she walked over to the North Star mill, but the men had completely stripped the hillsides of trees, leaving only gravel and red dust, and the percussion of the stamps was loud enough to set the blood pounding in her ears so that she almost lost her balance. She began to wander through the hills, usually staying within a few miles of home, until she knew every grove, meadow, creek and flume in the area. The walking dwindled after they moved to town, for there was much to do with the new house, and more to do when Susan moved as well, and more yet when Jesse fell ill. After he died, she had, for a month or two, spent her idle hours sitting in the parlor, just sitting, and she began to feel stale. Then came a morning when she awoke very early, with the sky barely grey in the east and the darkness thinning almost imperceptibly, and remembered the ravines south of town. She rose, laced up her strongest pair of boots, and set off down the road in the dawn, turning to follow a gully until she found Wolf Creek.

The grass and gravel gave way to thick manzanita with copper bark peeling from every branch. Farther downstream, she discovered pine trees, at first short and scrubby, but then tall and straight, as if they had risen out of the ground one night and reached for the moon. Among them stood black oaks with curly, lobed leaves and friendly limbs. Wherever the manzanita left the ground clear, the pines had laid down an ankle-deep inland sea of brown needles. She found a break in the underbrush and walked away from the trace into a tiny clearing, where she stopped, waiting, listening, feeling the absolute stillness, feeling her feet take root in the red earth.

She looked up into the completely blue sky and raised her arms, and at that moment, a breath of air brushed against the bough of a pine and embraced an oak, setting its leaves shivering as though it were a quaking aspen. No other tree moved, but the leaves kept quivering, as though in ecstasy, until finally, as Zennora stared, amazed, her mouth open, one by one, the leaves spun right off of the smallest branches, but did not, as she expected, fall to earth. They kept twirling in the air, weaving themselves into a dance, as delicate as the finest music. Finally, each leaf took its sustained pirouette in a long, slow arc down around Zennora and to the waiting brown needles, there to lie perfectly still. She stood there, fascinated, hardly breathing, until a jay flew into the clearing and broke the moment with a sudden jeer. Zennora walked back to the trace and continued down the ravine.

She had walked for nearly two hours when she reached a ford overhung by oaks and willows, with wild blackberries growing high on the banks, and she found a granite boulder where she sat in the shade. The brook was in full flood. Over the grey sand, the water ran red with silt, and the rocks higher up on the banks were stained red. The Norambagua lay just a mile above where she was sitting; when the men released excess water, it must have brought the red silt down the gulch and engulfed the channel.

Zennora heard a sudden plop! and looked into the deeper water to see a tiny frog swimming across the current and climbing up on a small, black rock near where she was sitting. His shiny skin was a transparent olive green, but the red silt had glazed his back and the bumps and ridges on his head and eye sockets. There was another plop! and another frog, identical to the first, swam to join the first. Through the rushing of the water, Zennora heard frog after frog jump into the tiny swimming hole. She hadn't noticed any frogs sitting on the rocks, banks or moss surrounding the hole, and no matter where she looked or how carefully she kept scanning the area, she was never turned the right direction to see where the frogs came from. After a few minutes, the frogs had filled the first rock and had begun to populate those nearby, climbing on top of each other to form random amphibian piles and pyramids, and soon as each found firm footing, it waited, hanging on with its toes, for any newcomers to climb aboard. Soon there were hundreds of frogs, and they covered the cluster of rocks in the shade at Zennora's feet, until suddenly, the gathering ceased. Every frog looked exactly like the first two, each carrying its light finish of red, and every pair of eyes was turned on Zennora.

She stared back at the frogs, hardly daring to move. Even the creek seemed to fall silent as they gazed at each other.

She smiled.

At once, the piles melted, the pieces falling and rolling into the water like an embankment when the heavy winter rains wash away the soil that holds it together. There were little splashes everywhere, and when Zennora peered into the rippling green heart of the creek, she could see tiny legs pulling mightily. After a few minutes, there were no frogs at all, and she could hear, once again, the sound of the water rushing down towards the Bear River. Exhausted, she walked back to town.

She spent several days pondering the frogs. Ever since she was a little girl, she had been able to see the piskies scampering in the rafters of the house and chattering in the dusty corners of the eaves. One day her mother walked into the room to find her chuckling and clapping her hands for no apparent reason, and when she pointed up at the little elves making faces and tossing back flips in the shadows, her mother became suddenly angry. She took her by the wrist and commanded her never to speak of such things, for if they were real at all, they were the devil's work and God would surely punish her. Surprised and horrified that her mother, always so gentle and kind, would treat her harshly, Zennora had cried all day. After that, she tried not to see the sprites, but in the evenings, when she lay with the sheets tucked up under her chin, they came softly down from the rafters to sit on her bedposts and ask, in hurt tones, why she longer paid any attention to them. One was a kindly old woman with bunched-up skirts and a funny little cap who sat on Zennora's pillow and sang lullabies until she fell asleep. Gradually, Zennora decided that she could not help seeing the piskies and she could not believe that they were wicked. She passed her childhood accepting that she was, simply, different from everyone else, for to her, the piskies were as real as the front door, while the rest of her family seemed blandly oblivious to them. Then, at the age of fourteen, she realized that she might be mad, and she spent an entire day walking on the moor, keeping to the open spaces in an attempt to clear her mind, but when she returned in the evening, she looked up to see smiling faces and waving arms offering friendly welcome. Once again, she passed through confusion to acquiescence, yielding to her vision peacefully, for she could no more change what she saw than she could change the constellations that wheeled outside her window at night. She did not know whether the imps were the result of magic or sorcery, or the afterthought of some divine hand, and she spent no energy trying to sort out the question; they were simply there. Yet she knew that she could not share her knowledge with anyone else. After she married Jesse, the piskies became more elusive; late in the evenings she would hear vague scuffling sounds and see tiny shadows flickering in corners and up in the eaves. Once in a while, they would show themselves, and once Jesse surprised her in the kitchen while talking to a little group perched on the cupboard. Although he made light of it—he, of course, assumed she was talking to herself—from then on he treated her with a hint of wariness. She had come to California wondering whether the encounters would cease, but as soon as she settled into the cabin at French Lead, she looked up to find the mischievous, inquisitive faces peering down at her.

Yet although she had resigned herself to seeing piskies dancing in the rafters, the prospect of finding sentient frogs in every pond was downright daunting. She wanted to get out of the house and enjoy the feeling of the ground beneath her feet, but she feared what she might find as she roamed. After several days, restless, she decided to take her chances, and as she walked through a meadow towards a hillside of cedar trees, the wind lifted a harvest of dandelion seeds, glistening white and fluffy, and sent them twirling in the air above her head. She paused to enjoy the array but caught her breath when she realized that the puffs were arranging themselves in rows and choruses, their lines and companies meshing and dissolving in ways that no breeze could manage. When she confronted the piskies that evening, they giggled and raced about the rafters whooping. That did it; Zennora now knew that her unique vision had flowered. She did not know whether the hills had changed, perhaps in response to her presence, or if they had always been enchanted. On some afternoons, she saw nothing out of the ordinary, but on others, she was ravished by a grove of pine trees whose needles sang piercing harmonies in the mountain breezes, or a falling feather that changed colors at it swirled to earth, or a parade of squirrels playing leap-frog across a shimmering flat.

Nick came to Zennora for the very reason that she was apart from the rest of the family, removed from the politics and competition that seemed to embroil the others, even his own Annie, as they grappled with marriage, children and, always, the investing and the trading, turning even the rock into a medium of hard dealing. Yet Zennora's very distance, not only from the others but also from the patterns of everyday life, rendered her powerless to extricate Nick from the currents that threatened to pull him under.

They sat on Zennora's porch through the early autumn, he looking out at the horizon and she dazzled by the dancing russet leaves that trembled in the light airs and traced graceful pirouettes in sarabandes that floated across her yard. She tried to think of what Jesse might have said, or Nick's own father, Joseph. She remembered something Susan had read in the newspaper, that mining all over the district had fallen off in the last few years, but Nick shrugged at the idea that his problems might be only part of a larger situation. She asked him whether he had tried investing in established companies with other men. He sighed and admitted that he had, five years earlier, paid $1500 to Dennis McGrath for a 5% share in the Stockbridge company on the east side of Massachusetts Hill. He and Annie had been trying to live off of the dividends, but the income wasn't enough; not enough to keep house and raise children, and not enough to engage his interest.

As he spoke, Zennora remembered Jesse ruminating on Nick's strange ability to tell which way a vein would dip, but he had regarded his nephew's intuition as a matter of luck and experience, perhaps the natural consequence of so many generations of men going down in the mines to run their fingers along the jagged walls. Yet perhaps in some way that even he would not be able to explain, the rock spoke to him, just as the piskies spoke to her. She anticipated that Nick would laugh at such a notion, but on the other hand, he seemed bereft, as though the voices in the rock had fallen still, either because they were reluctant to reveal their secrets or because they had no good news to tell. Whatever the truth, Nick seemed to her like a small boy who had lost his way. He was innocent, she thought, so innocent. Jesse had told her of the conspiracy to replace Nick as superintendent of the North Star, but whenever she mentioned the men involved, she discovered that he bore them no ill will and could not, apparently, even imagine that they had resented him.

Yet even though she understood him, she could find no way to help him. She knew something of business—more than she was inclined to reveal to Hannibal—but she did not have enough money to give Nick the help he needed. Late in October, Nick arrived with news of a financial panic in New York City. The details seemed vague and far removed from Grass Valley—there was something involving railroads, although not the Central Pacific—but one result was that the bankers and investors in town had suddenly become very anxious. Nick now confessed that he had been borrowing money, some from Findley and some from men he knew, and he had fallen behind on paying the interest. So far, Annie knew nothing about it, but if these men pressed him, he might have to sell everything, even his house, in order to meet his obligations. He talked almost with stopping for over an hour, listing his debts, reviewing his shaky assets, and assessing the attitude of the men who had helped him and who now, fearful of the maelstrom that

New York had become, would do whatever they felt necessary in order to shore up their own positions. When he stopped, spent, all she could think of was to suggest that he write to his brother in Penzance. Jack had always been the one to see an opportunity and make a deal. Perhaps Jack would know what to do; perhaps he would pay off Nick's debts. Perhaps he would return to Grass Valley. Desperate and helpless, Nick wrote the letter.

Jack's answer arrived after Christmas. He avoided actually refusing Nick's plea for help and expatiated on the disaster in New York and the folly of men like Jay Cooke, who acted with complete disregard for the future of the country and the welfare of the ordinary people. Yet when Nick sifted out the rhetoric, he discovered that Jack's only suggestion was to approach his creditors and work out an agreement to pay them on a regular basis, even if he could only give them small amounts at first with the prospect of larger ones later. Nick closed his eyes and, for the hundredth time, reckoned his liabilities and his assets, all of the notes with their varying principals and interest rates, and the various claims and companies scattered across the county. Nothing was paying well; he could not see when he would recover. He chose to do nothing.

He returned to his old habit, from before he married Annie, of visiting the saloons in Nevada City. There was usually someone willing to buy him a drink and then overlook the discourtesy if he neglected to buy one in return. None of the men seemed unduly concerned about the mines, or the banks, or the markets in San Francisco. They told stories about the Comstock, or horses they owned, or wrestling matches they had seen, or women in the dockside dance halls in Sacramento. If they mentioned serious matters, they displaced all culpability to men outside that particular saloon, usually men of public standing who, they affirmed, should know better, and they offered clear and forthright solutions that they would present if they had the authority. They finished such conversations by turning the subject into a joke.

Late one afternoon in March, he was sitting at a table when a man called in from the doorway for everyone to come and look. He walked out and stood in the shadow of the awning, squinting into the setting sun that shone straight down Broad Street. There were ten or twelve Chinese standing on the corner above him, most with their arms folded, and a few pacing back and forth, waving their arms and exhorting the others in twangs and coughs, occasionally wandering out into the dusty street and into the paths of the passing carts and buggies, whose drivers called sharp warnings and cracked their whips as they swerved out of the way. One man leaned against a street lamp, smoking a long pipe. All wore blue smocks and trousers, black slippers, and long queues, a few with the familiar coolie hat, but most with black skullcaps. Nick shaded his eyes against the glare just as one of the pacing men stopped, scowled down the hill and called to the others. Nick looked to his left, and saw, marching up the hill from Deer Creek, a company of forty or fifty men, also Chinese. Some carried clubs or rough two-by-fours cut to lengths of three or four feet, while others held short iron bars, castoffs from smithies and foundries, some mounted with rivets or broken fittings. None spoke as they strode up the hill, the sun tinting their faces orange.

The group at the corner stared down at the arrivals, and the nervous ones raised their voices, calling up the hill, over to Commercial Street and down the other way, towards the bridge. As the larger group came to a ragged halt about ten yards from the others, more men began to appear, walking or trotting in small groups to join the faction at the corner. Most of them carried clubs.

All up and down Broad Street, white men peered out of doors and windows, some with beer or whiskey in hand, laughing and pointing. Near the top of the hill, the sheriff stood in front of the theatre, slowly lighting a cigar while one of his deputies scowled down at the confrontation and another took a quick pull out of a silver flask. A smartly-dressed man and woman in a buggy tap-tapped down the street until the man realized what was happening in front of him and turned the horse so quickly that one wheel tilted off of the road bed for a moment. The woman stared back over her shoulder as the buggy disappeared up a side alley.

Now there were more than fifty men in each group. They began to mutter among themselves and make sharp remarks across the gap, until a leader stood forth from each band. The white men in the doorways quieted each other so they could listen, but they laughed and hooted when they realized that the two antagonists were challenging each other in Chinese. The spokesmen cackled and wailed at each other, stringing together vowels with nasals and glides, all swallowed in a way that turned their harangues into gibberish in the white men's ears. One grinning miner wearing a black beard, an extravagantly muddy pair of old boots and a brand-new derby called out, "You tell him, John!" and set the whole block laughing. The men in the street ignored the onlookers completely, staring intently at each other, their lips pressed tightly together and their mouths distorted, their faces drawn and their eyes apparently unblinking. The leaders clattered on, waving their arms and pointing vigorously at some remote, unseen injustice. The sun settled lower in the sky, and the light slowly turned into a smoky russet, tinting the blue smocks black and sending even longer shadows down the street.

Suddenly, one of the leaders strode right up to the other to stand so close that the two men were breathing on each other. The second man held his ground for a moment, then took a half-step back and pushed his challenger. As he turned to point out this new insult to his followers, the first man swung his fist and caught the other behind the ear, knocking him into the dust. With that, the two mobs screamed and rushed into each other. The men on the sidewalk cheered in delight; some called for the bartenders in the saloons to bring out more whiskey, more beer, more smoked fish and fresh crackers. The sheriff watched from above, smoking calmly, but his deputies began to shift their feet restlessly.

There was a gagging, gutteral shriek from the street. The mass of wrestling bodies rolled away on all sides to reveal two men, one sagging, a stream of red dribbling from his mouth, and the other, his mouth curled in a vicious grimace and his eyes wide open and staring, holding him up with a knife in his chest. As the drinking miners watched, he wrenched the knife out from the victim's ribs and plunged it in again, this time lower, and seemed to try to lift his opponent on the blade. The gagging man rolled his head back and coughed blood heedlessly down his shoulder and into the dust.

Three men howled insanely and ran full tilt into the thickest part of the opposing mob. Clubs appeared everywhere, each swung with the full force of a strong laborer's arm, and each blow that landed produced a deep, solid thud and an uninhibited cry of pain and anger. Some men carrying two-by-fours met with those carrying iron bars, and as they parried frantically, splinters flew into the air. Other men fought with pikes, each a long staff with a blade fixed to the end, that no one had noticed them carrying to the confrontation. The rest rolled in the street, gouging eyeballs and kicking testicles. One man huddled in the gutter, vomiting and grasping insensibly one of his hands that had two fingers sticking out at impossible angles; he hardly noticed that his tormentor was still kicking him in the ribs. The barflies retreated back against the walls of the buildings and farther into doorways, but when the sheriff, his cigar still in his mouth, led his men and five or six town policemen into the battle, the rowdier miners, cheering, jumped into the street.

Nick handed off his beer mug, settled his hat on his head and ran into the flying dust. Almost as soon as he sprang off the boardwalk, he bumped into a Chinese man who was spinning from side to side, screaming a mad defiance, his hands clenched against anyone who might come against him. Nick waited for the right moment, swung his fist and caught him in the temple as he shifted directions. The man fell like a carful of rubble. Nick turned to see another Chinese man brandishing an iron bar at a red-faced miner wearing an old straw hat. His target ducked, and Nick pushed the man over and down, the momentum of his swing carrying him into the dust, where the policeman starting beating him with a club. Nick grabbed the iron bar and held it in front of him, quickly checking in all directions. Two men in blue smocks came at him, their lips curled back from their clenched teeth. He held his ground and swung the bar like a battering ram into the first man's belly, guiding him into his partner's path. As Nick wrenched the bar out of the frenzied grip of his falling adversary, someone jumped on him from behind. He dropped the bar as he fell back on top of his attacker, and he felt the man's fingers take him around the throat. He tried to pry them loose, but the man's grip was too strong, so he reached up and behind, feeling the man's face, and dug his thumbs into the soft eye sockets as deeply as he could. The man howled and let go, so Nick rolled over and tried to stand up, but someone pulled his arms back and held him in a crouch while someone else slugged him in the belly and clubbed him on the back of the head. Dazed, he could barely see, but he blinked his eyes and they cleared long enough for him to see a face like a gargoyle laughing at him. He took a deep breath, found his footing, and jerked himself down and forward, throwing the man behind him over his shoulder. He slipped and fell, and he felt someone apparently trying to drag him away. He kicked as hard as he could, and felt his foot land solidly. The other man grunted, let go of Nick, and swore in an unmistakably American voice. Nick rubbed the sweaty dust out of his eyes and tried to focus in spite of the throbbing in the back of his skull. The policeman glared down at him, spat into the street, and turned to club a pig-tailed head behind him. The street seemed less crowded than a moment before, so Nick sat still for a moment, trying to catch his breath.

The sheriff and his men gradually took control. Most of the gang members disappeared down streets and alleys, but the police arrested two dozen, principally those with wounds that prevented them from escaping, and dragged them off to jail. Two of the deputies found a crude stretcher to take away the knifing victim. He was dead.

As the crowd dispersed, one of the policemen walked over to Nick, who was sitting against a lamp post brushing himself off. "And you! The next time I try to save yer worthless skin, ye tarnation Englishman, ye keep yer feet to yerself!" Satisfied, he marched off after his fellows, but one of the sheriff's deputies lingered.

"What's yer name?" His tone of voice and the look on his face allowed for little discussion.

"Trevenna. Nick Trevenna." Nick rubbed the back of his head and spat another mouthful of grit onto the street.

"Well, Nick Trevenna. We have enough trouble with these Chinee without you and yer drunken friends barging in where yer not invited. If you get in my way again, ye Cornish bastard, I'll bash yer head in with yer own club and I won't bother to tell yer friends about it. Unnerstand?"

Nick nodded, and the man rose, glared at Nick from underneath thick black eyebrows, and walked away into the dusk.

When Nick returned home that evening, Annie offered no sympathy at all for his bruises when she found out how he got them. He slept poorly and didn't rise until mid-morning. Feeling restless, he walked downtown and found Henry Silvester sweeping the walk outside his store. He grinned when Nick told him about the policeman and the sheriff. "Yer lucky ye didn't make the paper!"

"What do you mean?" said Nick.

The *Union* had run an editorial on the subject of the Chinese.

> Not long ago, John Chinaman was held up as the coming man who would, by patience, diligence and obedience, break up those combinations made by white laborers, and would set things all right by doing a great deal of work for very little pay. His late actions, however, show that he wants to rule in the labor market in spite of the forbearance wasted on him by soft-hearted American men.
>
> What shall be done with John Chinaman? We may abide his presence, and hire him to do dirty work; but we never could endure an assimilation with him. We wish him to keep where he is and not to introduce any of his abominable ideas into the civilized system. But John Chinaman is here; he is coming every day; he is getting stronger in numbers; his coming and his right to remain are guaranteed by the treaty-making power of the nation. Then what is to be done with him? We can not answer; who can?

Silvester grinned again. "Ye watch yerself, Trevenna. As soon as we git rid o' the Chinee, we'll do fer you Cornishmen."

"Don't be ridiculous."

"We'll git ye outa the mines and put American boys t' work." He winked. "We'll even use that giant powder yer so scared of, and we'll take more outa the mines with half the men!" Silvester roared with laughter and resumed sweeping. Nick knew that he scorned the big mine owners, especially the San Francisco nabobs, but the joke was depressing. Silvester turned to him again. "Seriously, Nicky—stay outa trouble. There are men in this town who don't like you, and they'd just as soon find a reason to do something about it. If you fight with the Chinee, someone's bound to say that you were fightin' on their side. Be careful."

Yet Nick still drifted. He worked his claims in a sort of rotation, spending a day or two on one, and then moving on to the next. Several were far up in the hills to the north and east, so he fell into the habit of spending a week or more away from home, rising before dawn to pack his horse and tip-toe back into the house to kiss Annie and the children good-bye as they lay asleep in their beds. One claim lay out in the Meadow Lake district, beyond the Sierra crest, so he slept under the cold, still stars, a rounded lump of granite under his head for a pillow.

Neither of the other two men in the family seemed able to focus on Nick's decline. Hannibal had bought the store and was now surprised and charmed to discover that he, an unimportant outsider in Grass Valley, was regarded in Marysville as a man of consequence, the Englishman who had made his money in gold and was now investing it sagaciously. Joseph was willing to listen, but that was all. He asked no questions and offered no comment; he simply continued working, an unprotesting, passive echo chamber for Nick's confusion. Sometimes, when Nick could not find the words to convey what he was feeling, the two men sat silently together, lost.

Susan alone remained to guide Nick away from the uncertainty that loomed before him, but she was so preoccupied with keeping house and looking after her six children that even with Josephine's help, the days slid by like water through her fingers, so that every night, when she let her head sink into her pillow, exhausted, she felt as though her life were falling away from her. She had never felt close to Nick; as a child, he was merely Jack's little brother, and as a man, there was something wanton about him that inspired a mistrust so deep that she was hardly aware of it. He rarely came to her house except for a family gathering, and she had scarcely set foot in his home. She was leaving church one Sunday when she met Annie in the entry way. The two women smiled and then laughed; each was carrying a baby, each was trying, with feet and hips and elliptical commands, to keep her children moving out towards the yard, and each was there without her husband. They paused under an elm tree to watch the children collect leaves. Annie asked after Hannibal; Susan told her that he had spent the night in Sacramento. Turn about, she asked about Nick. Annie's friendly smile became studied, and then wooden. Nick had bought a second-hand drill to replace one that had broken, and he had ridden out to a claim near Goodyear's Bar to test it. Susan, for a brief moment, turned her attention away from her children and looked carefully at the other woman. She saw neither anxiety nor petulance in Annie's face, but fear. Whatever was happening with Nick had left her gasping, and the easy congeniality of the previous moment was only a pose. Annie's baby began to whimper, and Susan realized that she was holding her too tightly, pressing her into the hard buttons that ran up the front of her dress. James pulled at Susan's skirts, and she turned to load the children into the wagon for the ride home.

Relentlessly, the landslide began. Nick answered the door one evening to find a man holding two packets of papers; each was a summons to respond to a suit for payment of debt. One bore the name of John Sterling. Nick wasn't at all surprised; he had expected Edward to goad his brother into taking action long before this. When he read the other packet, however, he was dismayed to find that the plaintiff was Will Pascoe.

Nick reached the Live Yankee the next morning just as the men were preparing to go down into the shaft, and as he approached, he saw Will and waved. His friend nodded to the others to continue and, alone, waited next to the tool shed. Nick swung down and turned to face him.

"Ye're suin' me, Will." Pascoe did not answer. "I thought p'raps there might be a mistake, somethin' we could work out."

Will shook his head. "There's no mistake, Nick. Ye owe me five hundred dollars, and ye 'aven't paid any interest. Can ye pay it now?"

"I'll pay ye, Will."

"Then ye 'aven't got it."

"No."

"There it is, then."

"But why are ye takin' me t' court?"

"T' get th' money back."

"I told ye, Will—I'll pay it."

"When?" Nick did not answer. "I'm sorry, Nicky. It's business. Remember—you came to me. Now I'm out."

"I thought we were friends."

"So we be, I hope."

"An' still ye're servin' me papers."

"I'm tellin' ye, Nicky, I've no choice."

"Will, if I 'ad th' money, I'd pay ye. The judge can't make me more willin' than I am right now. 'e can't find somethin' in an empty purse."

"I know that." Will looked around and drew closer, lowering his voice. "Don't ye get it? Ye owe money to Sterling, and Findley, and Granger, and George. And Conaway. And Pope." Nick was startled. Will had listed most of his creditors. How did he know so much? "These are the men that run the town, Nick. I 'ave t' work with 'em. If they know that you owe me money, and that I do nothin' about it, then I'll be just another Cornish 'ammer'ead, an' they'll 'ave nothin' t' do with me."

Nick snorted. "What'll they do? Publish yer name in the *Union*? Run ye out o' town?"

"Don't talk like a timdoodle—tidden like that. They'd give me no respect. I'd go to do business with 'em, an' they wouldn't treat me seriously. I'd go to borrow money myself, an' if I could get it at all, the interest would be high."

"And all because I owe ye five 'undred dollars?"

Will sighed. "Nick, I'm not the one t' tell ye yer business. But ye don't seem t' unnerstand that ye live with what ye do. They're cuttin' ye off, and anyone that stands with ye."

Nick felt suddenly cold. "It's not right. For God's sake, Will, it's only money."

"'Tis and tidden. This is a strange country, Nicky. When they're not winnin', they think they're losin'. No one wants to stand still, no one wants to wait an' bide 'is time. When things're goin' well, they're glad to 'ave us. Now they're lookin' out fer their own."

Nick, 1872-73

Will would not be moved, and so, hurt and bewildered, Nick rode back into town. Over the next month, more packets of papers arrived at his door; once a man knocked late in the evening while Nick was encamped by the South Yuba, and Annie, frightened, refused to open, so the next day, three men came, one wearing a metal star, and sternly told her to find her husband and bid him answer. When he came home, he found the children crying and Annie's face red, swollen and streaked with tears and dirt. She refused to let him leave her there alone again, so he took her and the children with him that evening when he went to ask Hannibal for help.

Hannibal listened with wary eyes, occasionally glancing at Susan or Zennora. He took a deep breath and let it out through his nose. "Ye're makin' it all more important than it is. They're just suin' ye for payment o' debt." He looked over at Susan. "Jack used to do it all the time, for mining stock, mostly."

Susan looked at him evenly. "That's how you picked up the ranch." Hannibal hawked slightly to clear his throat.

Nick shifted in his chair. "Hannibal, I've no cash left."

"What about yer claims?"

"What about 'em?"

"The judge can assign 'em to plaintiff, or tell the sheriff to put 'em up for auction."

Nick looked puzzled. "Those claims are all I 'ave. An' one of 'em's bound to hit a vein soon."

Hannibal would not be deflected. "How much are they worth?"

"What d'ye mean?"

"I mean if ye sold 'em, what would they bring?"

"I don't want t' sell 'em."

"Nick, if the court takes 'em, ye've no choice in the matter. What are they worth?"

Nick looked over at Annie, who was nuzzling the baby. "I don't know."

"'ave they paid at all?"

"No."

"Then all ye really 'ave is the equipment that's out there."

"There isn't much."

"Then ye don't 'ave much."

Susan flared. "Why are ye so angry at Nicky? Ye're talkin' like 'e's done somethin' wrong and ye're judge and jury."

Hannibal's face was a stone mask. "'e came 'ere for 'elp, an' I'm givin' 'im what I can. There's no point in lyin' to 'im." Susan looked at her mother, but Zennora had nothing to say.

Annie looked up suddenly. "What about the Stockbridge mine?" Nick looked at her and frowned slightly. "Aren't they doing all right? Your share must be worth two thousand now."

Hannibal nodded. "Ye could sell that and pay some of what ye owe."

Nick shook his head. "I sold it already." He looked at Annie, whose surprise was plain. "Last year. I didn't tell ye." She bent down to the baby.

Hannibal leaned forward. "Look, Nick. If ye sell all yer claims, all yer equipment, all yer stock, and yer 'ouse, would ye 'ave enough to pay off yer debts?"

Zennora reached out a hand. "Hannibal, don't make 'im sell 'is house."

"It's not up to me. Would ye 'ave enough?"

Nick looked down into his lap, biting his lip. Both of the babies had fallen asleep, and Susan could hear Bertie's voice upstairs, calm and even, reading a story to the younger ones.

Finally he looked up. "I don't think so, no."

Hannibal brought his hands together. "Then it's fairly simple. The court will take yer assets, and yer creditors will get as much as may be. Ye'll be bankrupt, but ye'll be out o' debt."

Susan hissed at him, not wanting to wake the baby. "How can ye suggest that? They'll 'ave nothin', not even a home."

Hannibal pursed his lips. "Ye're makin' this into somethin' it's not. It's not some sad story, not one o' yer novels. The man's in debt, and 'e can't pay. Th' court takes care of it all, and everyone goes on."

"But 'e'll 'ave nothin'!"

"There are men all over town that 'ave nothin', and they manage."

"But what will 'e do?"

"'e can go to work. Not on 'is own claims, no, but in one o' th' mines. The Idaho'd be glad to 'ave 'im."

Nick smiled ruefully. "I wonder if the Sterlings'd give me a job, seein' as I owe John."

Susan rose to her feet, still holding the baby. "Ye can't do that, Hannibal."

"Can't do what."

"Ye can't leave 'im like that. Ye must help 'im."

"'ow can I 'elp? 'e's in debt, isn't 'e?"

"You can pay off 'is debts. Call it a loan if ye like, an' work it out any way ye please. At least it'd be in the family. Ye can stop all this."

Hannibal did not answer. Annie was holding her baby up to her cheek, but her eyes were on Hannibal, waiting. Zennora was gazing out the window as though seeing something in the gathering dusk, and Joseph sat in a corner, watching the scene from a great distance. Nick stared down at his folded hands, so tightly clenched that the knuckles were white. Susan towered over them all, looking down at her husband and cradling the baby in one arm, leaving the other free. The silence extended like a long note that keeps ringing and reverberating through an empty cavern.

Finally, Nick spoke. "Susan, it's all right . . . "

"No, Nicky." She cut him off with a glance. "Let 'im answer."

Hannibal looked up at her, intrigued, almost smiling. Husband and wife took measure while the others watched, feeling the shift in the air, wanting to be gone. Hannibal settled back in his chair. "I'll not give 'im the money."

Susan looked at Zennora and back at Hannibal. "And why not?"

At this, Hannibal rose to face her. "I will not give 'im the money. I will not lend 'im the money. And I will not explain why I will not." Still looking into Susan's face, he continued. "I'm sorry for yer trouble, Nick. But I've given you what 'elp I can."

Susan gasped slightly, and then, without looking at anyone, swept out of the room and up the stairs.

Within two weeks, Nick had left Grass Valley. The first of the lawsuits came to trial, but the county sheriff reported that he was unable to locate the defendant in order to serve the papers. There was a rumor that Nick had gone to San Francisco, but no one could find him there. As far as anyone knew or was willing to let on, he and his family had vanished.

A month later, Zennora received a letter from Australia, and she sat gazing at the hills while Susan read it aloud. Nick wrote that he hoped to find a friend of his, a man from Camborne who had worked in the mines near North San Juan during the sixties. He assured her that there were colonies of Cornishmen in the outback, and that a man with skill could always do well. With any luck, he'd find a rich claim and maybe locate his brother, Frederick, and his sister, Louisa. The letter was full of hopes and great expectations. He made no mention of his last encounter with Hannibal, nor of the trouble that had driven him away. A stranger reading the letter would have concluded that Nick had, all on his own, set off on a great adventure that was certain to end successfully.

Early the next morning, Hannibal rode off to Marysville to inspect the store and then head down to Sacramento to learn what he could in the dockside saloons.

16
Hannibal
1875

Hannibal Carne stared out at the falling rain. Two weeks earlier, tiny rivulets of clear, chattering water had formed on either side of Auburn Street, trickling down past Leach's lumber yard and into Wolf Creek. Now the whole roadway seemed to be oozing downhill, carrying rocks and the dried stalks of spent flowers along with the cold, dull mud. There was neither wind, nor lightning, nor thunder; the rain fell calmly, without any variation in intensity, from morning to evening and around again. Even the grass cowered beneath the weight of the relentless shower, and the roofs of the houses sagged under the water dripping off of the eaves. Only the bare tree branches seemed unbowed, although their bark had turned black from the soaking and the crooks of the larger elms had begun to sprout colonies of moss.

The Yuba River had overflowed and inundated Marysville. Even the higher portions of the downtown area were submerged under six feet of water, and the slow, muddy current had carried fragments of boardwalks, fences, furniture, and debris out from stores and houses, spreading the mess all over town. There were rumors that hundreds had drowned. Hannibal had hoped that the *Union* had, as usual, overstated the event, but while patrolling Main Street, he had met a man who had ridden out of Marysville just after the riverbanks had broken, and he confirmed everything.

He folded the newspaper and stared out the window, seeing not his sodden front yard but rather the hardware store to which he had committed so much capital. He could easily imagine what it looked like. Like most such shops, the one he owned was raised only a step above street level, so the interior was surely flooded up to eye level. Jenkins would declare a total loss of his stock and abandon the business, so Hannibal would be left to clean up the mess and restore the building. All of the wooden floors, walls and cabinets would be ruined beyond reclamation, for the cold soaking would cause the timbers to swell and split. Worse, the storage was all in the cellar, a spacious, cool brick cave that had seemed quite secure. He would have to pump out the water in order to bring up what by then would be rusty tools, corroded pots and pans, and worthless window frames, and he might have to rebuild the staircase. Of all the goods, only the sheets of glass would have any value, unless he could somehow scour the crockery and convince someone to buy it. After all the cleanup, he would have little more than a brick shell, and to attract a new tenant, he'd have to offer to restore the floor, provide new shelves and cabinets, and probably reduce the rent.

The women had responded with outrage, but not at Hannibal's misfortune. He had found Susan in the kitchen pouring a cup of tea for Zennora, and she had stood, pot in one hand and quilted cozy in the other, as he blurted out that the river had burst its banks and ruined the store. He had waited for sympathy or regret, prepared to console her and so console himself, but Zennora sipped grimly at her tea while Susan set the pot on the table, slipped the cozy over it, parked her fists on her hips and raised her eyebrows at her mother before turning to him with her lips pursed.

"It's the mining, Hannibal. They've ruined the river."

He was puzzled. "The mining?"

Zennora poured a drop of milk into her cup and stirred the tea, the silver spoon tapping musically against the bone china. "They've filled up th' river—there's no more room fer th' water."

Hannibal turned away. He knew where all this started. Susan had been reading to her mother a series of articles about hydraulic mining. A few farmers had complained that the slickings—the fine gravel, and especially the sand and silt, that washed downstream—were diverting the creeks that should have run through their fields, leaving them with no way to irrigate their crops or water their stock. A crackpot newspaperman, hungry for scandal, had grabbed the story, and his editor, reluctant to sanction the nonsense but unable to resist selling a few more papers to the fools who would read the drivel, had assigned him a sporadic niche in the inside pages. The more frantic articles called for the complete abolition of hydraulic mining, a position that left Hannibal groping for a way to express the childishness of the idea and then, under the remonstrative gaze of his wife and her mother, subsiding into a helpless, idiotic smile at the absurdity of it all. The women were concerned not only over the plight of the farmers, but also about the damage done to the hillsides; one company had moved into a valley where Zennora used to go for walks, and now both her path and the bluff it traversed had been washed away. Hannibal shook his head at the presumption that a man could take rock out of a mountainside and leave it as clean and fresh as a lady's flower garden in springtime. God had put the gold in the rock for the miner to find, and surely he knew that no mortal man could restore the rock to its former condition. The women might as well argue that pumping out the deep mines meant robbing the earth of its water, or that the hard-rock men should dig out a shaft without leaving a pile of rab and row at grass! Every mine produced refuse, and if the tailings from the hydraulic operations were clogging up the farmers' troughs, then someone would find a way to dispose of the mess somewhere else. But to abolish the big nozzles entirely? Only a fool—or a woman—would even frame such a thought.

Cousin Jack

Yet even the newspaper in his hand accused the mines of contributing to the flood. In stentorian tones, the editor asserted that the sand and silt had filled the riverbed, raising the level so high that there was little room to accommodate the winter rains. Moreover, there was too much water; the hydraulickers had tapped into sources at higher elevations, bringing it down in networks of flumes and ditches that siphoned the flow over the intervening ridges, and whenever the spraying and washing was at its height, they dumped torrents into the Yuba. Had the channel been as deep as in 1850, and had the greedy hydraulic men not taxed the current so recklessly, the town of Marysville would have been safe. How long, asked the editor, would the farmers of the Sacramento Valley submit to slavery and poverty at the hands of the vandals in the hills? Hannibal read the paragraph again and sighed.

No longer able to support what he imagined, he rode to Marysville, alone and wet, to see the actuality. He knew that his horse would never be able to negotiate the muck in the flooded downtown area, so he stopped to hire an old buckboard wagon with exceptionally high wheels and a pair of draft horses. For what he paid, he could have engaged a fancy buggy in Sacramento, and the farmer that owned the rig took his money with a bitter smile, standing in filthy boots above a field that the river had invaded. The look in the farmer's eyes was wary and strangely recriminatory, as though Hannibal were responsible for the calamity and would, at any moment, manifest in some alarming and dangerous way his innate irrationality and recklessness. His expression reminded Hannibal of someone else, and as he settled himself on the wagon's hard, wet seat, he caught the image: Susan, standing in the kitchen door, watching him ride off. She had looked at him exactly as the farmer was looking at him now. He pulled his hat down so that the brim reached his upturned coat collar behind his neck, then clucked to the horses and drove off into the monotonous shower.

As he approached the town, he saw the remains of sheds and barns that the river had torn from their footings and scattered, leaving the timbers so saturated with silt as to be useless, even as firewood. The floodwaters had receded, but the central district was covered with a smooth, stinking muck that forced the horses first to step high and then to wade through, reaching with their great hoofs for firm ground. When he reached Jenkins' hardware store, he reined in the team, pulled on a pair of hip-length boots, and eased himself over the side and into the sludge.

The rain had already started to wash the mess off of the façade, but he could easily see how high the flood had run, for there was a dividing line about six feet up from the walkway. Above, all was as before, although wet, but below, the slime had stained the brickwork and leached the color out of the painted signs and woodwork. All of the windows had broken, leaving only an occasional tiny jagged fragment pointlessly marking where the edge of a pane had been, and the door had pulled away from its hinges and crumpled against the nearby wall. The inside walls were as discolored as those outside, and there were a few places where the flood had taken advantage of dry, flaking mortar to drag out a cluster of bricks. Where partitions, cabinets and shelves remained, they were swollen and warped. A surprising amount of the stock was gone, and because Hannibal doubted that anyone had waded through the streets to steal it, he decided that the river, leaving the town, had taken the goods with it. The remaining iron pots and steel tools were already rusting; when he picked up a shovel and swung it against the wall, the metal spade and the wooden handle cracked at the same time. As he stood there, gazing around the room, he realized that he had walked right by the staircase without knowing it, for the entire floor was covered with mud up to his ankles, and the basement was full to the brim. No pump could handle the viscous mass; he would need a crew with shovels to dig it out before it dried and set like a vast adobe brick.

As he stood there, he began to feel dizzy, and he realized, even as the cold sweat came and his knees began to shake, that the mire was giving off a foul, nauseating stench, and he remembered that the implacable flood would have carried not only sediment but also filth from the cesspools in the town and manure from every nearby stable, corral and pasture. Marysville now lay under a fermenting layer of silt and offal, and while the rain outside cleared the air somewhat, here in the confines of the brick shell, even with empty window and door openings, the frowst was unbearable. Hannibal had no time to reach the doorway, for his belly wrenched at him and his knees buckled. He crouched in the mess, heaving helplessly and adding his vomit to the foulness before him. He heaved again, the spasms contorting his frame and bringing tears to his eyes. Finally, he could heave no more, but the sweat had left him completely chilled and trembling, so he stumbled to his feet, using his sodden coat sleeve to wipe the bile from his beard, struggled to the door, waded out into the street, and climbed up into the buckboard to hold his face up to the rain and catch his breath. Finally, he turned the horses and guided them out of town.

His interview with Jenkins was brief. He had no family, and now no store, so he was on his way, heading back to San Francisco. Hannibal did not even try to argue with him. Neither said good-bye; neither offered to shake the other's hand. As Hannibal left the room of Jenkins' boarding house, the shopkeeper was wrapping some supplies in a tarp and reaching for a length of rope.

He turned his horse east, back into the hills, knowing that he could not face the process of restoring his property, and that he would have to find an agent who would sell it. All that was certain; he wondered only how long he would have to wait to find a buyer and how great a loss he would have to swallow. He camped for the night under an oak tree near Brown's Valley, not caring that someone might try to rob him, not sleeping, just apathetically listening to the rain.

He reached home in mid-afternoon, opened the front door and nearly tripped over a wooden doll that lay sprawled on the floor. Then he shrank against the hall tree, making way as Zennora marched out of the kitchen, carrying Sarah on her hip and flourishing a pan at the older boys. Bertie was nearly eleven now, and he had become adept at luring James into one sort of mischief or another, always setting him up to take the scolding, and their grandmother, usually so serenely capable with children, had, more than once, declared that she simply could not manage those two. Hannibal watched the boys run up the stairs and wondered whether he should sit them down for a serious talk, but he remembered that the last time he had done that, Susan had made a sharp remark about him not being there most of the time. Now, he guessed, she was upstairs with the baby. He walked into the parlor, lifted a basket of laundry down from his favorite chair, and sat down to watch Jane reading from a picture book to Martin, who sat huddled on the floor, sucking his thumb.

He remembered the day, not quite two years back, when he had come home to find Susan, tears running down her cheeks, sitting next to the stove with Martin held tightly in her lap. His son had looked up, his face strangely like a little old man, serious and troubled. Slowly, painfully, she had managed to explain that Dr. Simpson had come to examine the boy and had pronounced that there was nothing more he could do. Soon after he was born, they had noticed that the left leg was a bit thinner than the other, and as he grew, it started to turn in slightly, not much, but enough for Simpson to put him in a brace for several months. The boy had tried to learn to walk, resolutely pulling himself up on the window seat and stumping along, his rhythm uneven. When they removed the brace, he kept falling until he learned how to balance the sound leg against the weak one. Although the turn-in wasn't as noticeable as before, it gave him an odd gait that became more pronounced when he tried to run after his older brothers. The physician's dismal prognosis so engulfed Susan that she rejected any comfort, scorning Hannibal's suggestions that Simpson might be wrong, that the boy might outgrow the problem, or that Martin could learn a trade where a gammy leg wouldn't matter. She saw only the limping child, an object of ridicule, standing with one knee bent in order to level himself, or with joints locked, submitting to the tilt. From that day on, Jane had gravely made Martin her special charge, and the two of them held hands whenever they went for a walk.

The rain finally wore itself out, but Hannibal took no pleasure in the cold, sunny afternoons and the occasional flurries of snow that glazed the houses across the street. He spent entire days sitting in the front window pretending to read the newspaper or one of Jesse's books. Susan tried offering him a cup of tea or a bit of conversation, but she found him so unresponsive that she gave up. The children quickly learned that there was no point in visiting their father in his chair, so they changed their habits to avoid the parlor altogether, passing the doorway, when necessary, with carefully impassive faces, their eyes on him as though he might at any moment leap up and pursue them. Even little Sarah, who had loved to climb up in his lap and cuddle, now shunned him.

At odd intervals, he felt suddenly restless, and on such mornings he saddled his horse before breakfast and rode down to the Kentucky Ranch to trudge all over the property and let his fancy run. He imagined clearing out the undergrowth, pruning the healthy vines, replacing the spent ones, and making wine. Surely the hotels in San Francisco would welcome a steady supply of reasonably-priced wine of reliable quality. There might even be a certain cachet to a wine made in California, especially one bottled near the mines that had made so many fortunes in the City, and he would succeed where Hivner had failed. Then again, he could rip out the entire vineyard and plant trees, row after row of apples and pears that would require little care but would produce fruit that he could easily ship to the markets in Sacramento; perhaps he could secure the contract to supply the Central Pacific Rail Road and the river boats connecting Sacramento to the Bay. Perhaps the best idea of all was to plant the entire ranch in pines and harvest them for timber, hiring Leach to mill the logs until he could afford to build a sawmill of his own. After a day of such speculation, Hannibal would review each idea and find it too risky or too optimistic, the sort of thing that would have engaged Nick Trevenna and inspired the scorn of the other men in the family. He would then return home to spend another three or four days sitting in the parlor.

Late in April, he received a letter from Martin. Their mother had died. A neighbor had knocked on her cottage door, hoping to accompany her to church, and found her lying peacefully in her bed, a lonely woman just short of her sixtieth birthday. Martin offered little other news, except that she had been laid to rest in the Breage parish cemetery and that Penbro was doing well.

Hannibal stared at the wallpaper before him, the felt designs blurring into confusion against the textured backing. He had not seen his mother for nearly twenty years, and he could not quite remember what she looked like. Keziah Tregembo had been delicate, with large eyes, high cheekbones, and narrow lips over a neat chin, the long hair always pulled carefully down and back across the ears to a swirling, compact knot at the nape of her neck. He closed his eyes and tried to see Pellar Cottage as it was when he was a boy, with the sun shining in the dooryard on those days when the breeze had whipped the clouds out into the Atlantic. His mother seemed always to be wearing black, and for three straight years, spring was the appointed season for burials. First there was John, only five months old, then Mary, no older, and finally James, the father that Hannibal barely knew. He could just see his mother looking down at him in the church pew, whispering that a boy of six was old enough to sit up straight and hold his hymnal high. He remembered the next black dress well enough, for he was nearly a man and already working in a copper mine when he picked up little Mary James, only ten years old, named after a dead sister and a dead father, and laid her into the half-sized coffin before driving the cart to the cemetery with his mother sitting silently beside him. After that, Keziah spent more and more time with her prayer book while Hester, now the only daughter, ran the house, and Hannibal and Martin went away to the mines, and then farther away to California. Hester herself eventually died of scarlet fever, but Keziah had ignored Martin's repeated invitations to join him and Bessie and the children at Penbro. Now she had joined the others instead. Hannibal reached up to wipe his eyes with the back of his hand.

Ever since the flood, Susan had fallen into the habit of regarding Hannibal with mild impatience, deciding that he had shut himself off from any help that she might feel inclined to offer, and declining to notice him until the day when he might choose to return to the family. Now Martin's letter engaged her attention; she looked in the envelope for some note from Bessie, and finding none, turned on her distant sister some of the impatience and resentment she had been focusing on her husband. When she saw him covertly blotting his tears, she realized that he might be able to use one calamity to drag himself out of another. She changed her tactics, looking up to smile whenever he came into a room, listening carefully to his long ramblings on what he might do with the ranch, and even asking questions about his investments. After a few days, he seemed to realize that she was paying more attention to him, and he began to follow her through the house, craving this new sympathy. He even spent less time on his daily visits to town, and when he sat in the front window, the smaller children were welcome in his lap as long as Susan was close enough to hear what he had to say, needed to say. He talked compulsively, on and on about the flood and the ranch and the mine, telling the same stories and parsing the same anxieties and dreams over and over again. At the end of each day, as soon as the children were in bed, Hannibal, too, crawled under the covers, exhausted, while Susan retreated to the most comfortable chair in the parlor, sitting in the quiet darkness before the last embers of the fire, and closing her eyes against the dull headache that had grown steadily since breakfast.

After a couple of weeks of this, Hannibal, encouraged, suddenly decided to ride out to Red Dog to visit the Live Yankee and check on Zebulon Day. He rode his horse into town, hired a rig, and invited Alonzo Delano to join him.

The old banker was thinner than ever, so his coat flapped around him even more redundantly than before, but when he pulled back the lapels, he revealed a new silk waistcoat, embroidered in vermilion lions rampant, that fitted him so tightly that the buttons strained and he could scarcely pry his watch out of the fob. The skin of his face seemed to be stretched over his skull, so the cheekbones and chin protruded and shone, and the nose, that improbable, astonishing nose, preceded the rest of the man with unabashed pride. His hair now grew in wild, grey clumps that sprang out between his hat and his ears and riffled in the breeze.

Hannibal intended to suggest to Delano that he consider investing in the mine. The banker seemed to intuit the agenda, for he scarcely stopped chattering during the hour's journey, providing an unsolicited gazette to the more eccentric news of the week. Ballooning was the latest fad among the idle rich, and several of them had nearly perished when the *America* had descended considerably faster than anyone had intended. A group of enthusiasts in Nevada City were discussing the formation of a base ball club, and the saloon keepers on Broad Street had agreed to back the venture. The new Capitol was so popular that a company had applied to the governor for permission to conduct guided tours through the building. The newfangled cable car was clearly the best solution for sparing both men and horses the weary trudge up and down Nob Hill, so there was no doubt that crews would soon be digging ditches all over San Francisco. And he, Delano, had dined just the other night at the Exchange—no, the Holbrooke, recently renamed after its new proprietor—feasting on fresh Chesapeake oysters that had traveled, nestled in beds of ice, via the transcontinental railroad. "Indubitably, friend Carne, the gentlemen of the Central Pacific would better serve the greater good of the community if they would sell off their luxurious passenger cars and devote themselves to the transportation of oysters, clams, mussels, shrimp, quahogs and crawdads. Leave the nabobs to grow fat and fester in their Eastern piles! Bring us the bivalve and his cronies!"

Yet the news that seemed to preoccupy him, although he joked about it, smacking his lips and laughing with a wheezy squeak, was the imminent opening of the Pacific Stock Exchange. The financiers of San Francisco had been pouring money into mining stocks, and he knew of at least one mine that had closed simply because its owners had speculated themselves into bankruptcy. He, as an authentic '49er, held that if a consortium of money men proposed to invest in a mine, then at least one of the partners should take the trouble to visit the workings and see what it was all about. As it was, the publicly-traded mines had become mere names on artistically penned stock certificates. The opening of the Exchange might introduce a modicum of control into the trading frenzy, but it would also insert one more layer between the miners and the owners. After the banker improvised on this theme for ten minutes straight, Hannibal realized that there would be no better time to mention the Live Yankee, but as soon as he brought up the subject, Delano overwhelmed him with a lengthy oration on the idiosyncrasies of harnessmakers in Grass Valley. As he moved on to a disquisition on stable boys and farriers, they passed through the village of Red Dog and turned down the road that led to the mine.

Day's report was much as Hannibal had expected: they had not yet found the vein on which their hopes were fastened. He was working the claim with a crew of only two, both young Pascoe cousins recently arrived from Cornwall and willing to work for modest wages, and nearly every day they found a bit of ore that seemed to promise a rich source. He wanted to drive another shaft, but he would need more equipment. He also informed Hannibal that his ledger was approaching a zero balance, and in order to keep the men at work, they would have to assess the partners again.

While Day and Hannibal conferred, Delano scuttled about the site, peering into the tiny smithy, gazing down the main shaft, and pacing off the tunnel's extent as though tracing a map on the surface. Hannibal tried to give Day his careful attention, but he could not keep from glancing over at his guest, who, with his spindly shanks and long beak, looked like a strange cross between an eagle and a flamingo. Yet although he explored the site thoroughly, the banker showed no inclination to discuss the mine and was clearly determined to regard the conversation as a private business matter between partners, in which there was no room for an outsider like himself.

Discouraged, Hannibal shook Day's hand and climbed up into the buggy, with Delano perched next to him, and turned the rig up the road, back towards Red Dog and Grass Valley. He hardly spoke during the ensuing hour, not even rising to the moment when Delano interrupted a lecture on the skulduggery of local politics to explain, in great detail, the geology of a vein that ran near the road and then regale his companion with the complete history of the Last Chance Lead, an allegedly desperate venture in which he had been the primary owner. When they reached the town, Hannibal politely declined Delano's enthusiastic invitation to join him "for a stirrup cup," returned the rig to the stable, and mounted his horse. As he headed down Main Street, he glanced back over his shoulder to see the old banker lurching up to the Holbrooke, surrounded by a little swarm of petitioning men in silk top hats.

A few days later, Hannibal was clearing the brush behind the stable when Jane came running around the corner to tell him that Mother had fallen down. He burst through the back door to find Susan sitting on the floor, clutching her belly, with a pool of vomit splattered next to her. He sent Jane for Zennora, and by the time he had helped his wife into a chair, wiped off her face and found her a glass of water, the older woman had arrived. She took charge immediately, ordering Hannibal to carry Susan upstairs and then banishing him to the parlor. When Simpson examined her, he confirmed their suspicion: typhoid fever.

Hannibal scarcely saw Susan for the two weeks she lay in bed, for Zennora took over the household completely. She heated a vast pot of water and washed every dish and utensil in the kitchen, carefully instructing the children to dry each item carefully, using clean towels she had brought down from her own linen closet, and put it away without dropping it on the floor. She heated another cauldron full and washed all of the clothes in the house, hanging them carefully on a line that swung in the spring breeze, and then washed the baby's diapers and all the dish towels again. Jane and the two older boys served as her unwilling but resigned assistants, scrubbing the floors, helping to prepare meals, and running endless errands to Loutzenheiser's drug store, but she adamantly refused to let them see their mother or go near her room. She worked around the clock as nurse and housekeeper; no one knew when she slept.

Zennora found a neighbor girl to take care of the baby, but she placed Sarah and Martin in Hannibal's charge. He had never spent so much time with his children, and he soon learned that they were not at all content to amuse themselves while he studied his newspaper or sifted through his accounts. They were satisfied if he read stories to them out of a little worn picture book, a gift from Jesse, and they were happy to play outside as long as their father sat on the porch, ready to serve as audience on request. After three days, Hannibal felt restless, compelled to go to town to buy the newspapers and hear what the men on the street had to tell. Zennora was upstairs with Susan, so he instructed Bertie to tell Nana, when she came down, that Father and Martin and Sarah had gone to town and would be back well before supper.

The three of them walked hand in hand out of the dooryard and down towards Wolf Creek. As they reached the bottom of the slope, a pair of women passed them going the other way, and they smiled first at the children, then at Hannibal, and then at the children again, whispering to each other and looking back over their shoulders as they continued up the hill. Hannibal strolled along Mill Street and down Main, stopping to talk to the tradesmen in the doorways, but also pausing whenever a woman, usually someone from church, turned to study the children and congratulate their father. He realized that everyone they met, man and woman alike, seemed genuinely pleased and impressed that he had brought his children to town with him. The unexpected attention and approval warmed him, and he caught a glimpse of his reflection in a plate glass window: he was grinning like an idiot. The children began to tire, so he stopped at the Holbrooke to buy each of them a strawberry ice cream soda, a new concoction that the waiter served with an extra flourish. Martin finished his in two minutes, but little Sarah sat quietly on the wooden stool, sipping the sweetness up through a straw, letting it slide back down again, and then bringing it up into her mouth, where she rolled it around thoughtfully on her tongue. Finally, they headed for home, Hannibal carrying Sarah, who wrapped her legs around his waist and rested her head on his shoulder, and Martin hanging onto his right hand, tugging slightly with each limping pace. As soon as they entered the house, each child curled up on the parlor rug and fell asleep, too exhausted to climb the stairs.

When Susan recovered, the household seemed to return to normal. Hannibal spent far less time musing in the parlor window and even worked for several days at the Idaho Mine. Then, late in July, he awoke in the middle of the night soaking wet, struggling out of a dream that he was smothering in the hottest tunnel in the deepest mine on earth, reaching full consciousness with a terrified shudder just as the spectral drift began to collapse on him. Just as he realized that he was aching all over, an astonishing cramp doubled him over and he cried out involuntarily. Susan helped him use the chamber pot and climb back into bed, and she sent Bertie to bring Zennora, who examined her son-in-law and announced that typhoid fever was visiting the Carne family once again.

The sickness lingered for weeks. He ran a high fever that scarcely wavered or abated, day and night, no matter whether Susan was able to persuade his stomach to hold broth or even water. Her alcohol sponge provided some relief, but he began to shiver, and as soon as his skin dried, the fever returned. His bowels shriveled up within a day, and he felt as though someone had left a rock embedded in his gut. Under Zennora's tutelage, Susan dosed him with spoonfuls of castor oil, and not half an hour later, his frantic cries brought her running up the stairs and into the sickroom to brace him over a slop bucket while he shivered and gasped with the convulsions. He begged for an antidote to the oil, so she gave him citrate magnesia, which blocked him again, but he was eating so little it hardly mattered.

The fever set every joint to aching, and his legs cramped up more and more with every day he spent in bed, so Susan gave him quinine, the bitter taste forcing a spasm that nearly made him vomit. After that, the fever and its aches bothered him less than the acute, convulsive cramping in his belly, and there were hours when all he could do was lie curled on his side, moaning and whimpering. As the weeks passed, he came to depend on brandy, for it dulled the pain and helped his mind drift, and the only way he could sleep was to take laudanum in spite of the dreams that terrified him and set him to brooding during the daylight hours. On the better days, he was able to read the newspapers and even try to write letters to his brother, but most of the time, the fever was so high that he could scarcely concentrate and found himself mumbling about nothing at all. The headache made it difficult for him to think, but when it subsided, he felt lonely, for the women had banished the children and visited his room only to care for him, not simply to keep him company.

After three weeks, Susan sent again for the doctor, who examined the patient carefully, shook his head, and quietly advised the women that they could only persist and hope for recovery. After he left, Susan sat in the parlor and stared out at the children playing in the yard. As far as she knew, her husband had written no will, and she remembered the confusion that had ensued after her father had died intestate. She might have to spend two or three years sorting out Hannibal's affairs and paying his bills. She decided to call on Dibble, the lawyer, as soon as she could arrange to go to town.

Yet on the very next day, Hannibal seemed to improve. His fever subsided and he was able to eat a little. After a week, he was able to manage the stairs if he leaned on Susan's shoulder, and to visit the privy. Zennora still refused to let him play with the children, so he sat in the window, wrapped in a blanket in spite of the August heat, and watched them run under the trees and call to the birds perched over their heads. On the last day of August, he spent the morning reading the newspaper, and by nightfall, he was delirious with fever.

The Bank of California had failed. Findley shut his doors, contributing to the panic but protecting himself against the kind of run that brought pandemonium to the Bank of Nevada. The *Union* assured its readers that Findley's firm was reliably solvent because the proprietor himself had "ample resources, outside of his banking business, to make good all demands." Even so, merchants who tried to call in their debts had little success, for no one in town had any cash. The Idaho and the Empire continued to pay dividends, but only in certificates, not in gold coin.

Hannibal had no attention to spare for the local inconvenience, for his share of the collapse lay farther afield. Since the Pacific Stock Exchange opened, he had been buying stock in mining companies located along the Comstock Lode. Rather than buy a few expensive shares in established mines that were paying dividends, he bought blocks of cheaper shares in smaller claims that had yet to show reliable returns. He had never visited the sites, and so knew nothing about the concerns at first hand. The investments were pure speculation: he had paid bargain prices with the intention of holding the shares for a few months, hoping for at least one company to strike a lode, and planning to sell the lot by Christmas, dollar for dollar, if nothing came through. Now, with the panic, the market value of his shares had fallen to nothing, and he would have to wait for the bottom feeders to decide that the worst had come and to start paying pittances to those who lacked the patience to nurse their holdings back to health. The banks themselves had become heavily involved in mining stocks, and their directors were just as anxious as Hannibal. Worst of all, the editorials declared that California was following the rest of the nation into the depression, which meant that the prospect of finding new investors for the Live Yankee had grown appreciably dimmer. Hannibal felt irretrievably trapped.

He spent the night raving, and by morning, Susan was exhausted and the children huddled in the kitchen, glancing fearfully up at the random thumps and wailings resonating in the ceiling. Zennora took charge, and Susan put on her hat to walk to town and meet with Dibble. He promised to draw up a simple will and to come to the house the very next morning with two witnesses. Zennora gave Hannibal enough laudanum to put him to sleep, but his fever was higher than ever before. When he awoke in the gathering dusk, he refused the drug, babbling about appalling hallucinations, so the women offered him drams of brandy to quiet him down until, once again, they were able to give him enough laudanum to get him to sleep so that the entire household could rest.

After breakfast, Dibble appeared on the porch with two men standing behind him. Susan led them upstairs, where Hannibal lay with his eyes half closed and his mouth hanging open, dribbling a rivulet of spittle down towards his neck. The lawyer leaned over the sick man and showed him the document, asking for his signature so that the others might witness it, but Hannibal seemed puzzled. Dibble asked him three times to affirm that Susan should, indeed, enjoy the full benefit of his property so that she might care for their children, but Hannibal did not answer. Finally, he dragged the back of his hand across his cracked lips, stared out the window, and in a rattling, wheezing whisper, asked Susan for brandy. Dibble stood up straight, bit his lip, and settled his spectacles firmly on his nose before bringing a pen and ink well out of his coat pocket. Susan gave Hannibal his drink while the lawyer made his preparations, then the men helped the sick man to a sitting position and Susan wrapped his fingers around the pen while Dibble offered him the document. The lawyer moved the paper one way while Susan guided her husband's hand the other, and then they reversed the dance. Dibble stood erect again and held the will to the light: there, next to Hannibal's name, was a straggling "X." The two witnesses signed their names, Dibble signed as the attorney of record, and he nodded to Susan before leading the others out of the room, down the stairs, and out of the house.

There was no change for the next three days. If the women waited too long between doses of brandy, he ranted and complained, and only laudanum put him to sleep at night. He used the slop bucket only once a day, for there was little left in his system, and to Susan, standing in the doorway and trying to keep her gorge from rising against the stink, he seemed to be shriveling. The children had become strangely apprehensive, the smaller ones clinging to the nearest apron while James and Bertie kept watch at the foot of the stairs, their faces like masks as they listened to their father's muffled moans. Sarah wept constantly. Everyone but the baby knew that Hannibal could not last much longer. Everyone waited.

On the fourth day, Susan awoke to find that the sun had already climbed above the roof of the house across the street, and she walked slowly down the hall to find Hannibal's bed empty, a twisted mess of dirty linen and stained blankets. Her sudden cry awoke Zennora, and the two women searched the house for him, finally sending James and Bertie and Jane to ask the neighbors whether they had seen him. No one had any news to offer, and the family gathered on the porch in the warming September morning, looking up and down the street as though Hannibal might ride up on his horse at any moment.

He had awakened before dawn, feeling unusually well rested. The stars were just beginning to fade, so he rose, went to the closet to find a suit of work clothes, and dressed himself, resolving as he buttoned his pants to visit Mill Street very soon to buy something that would fit him better. He nearly lost his footing at the head of the stairs, so he took them one at a time, step-together, very carefully, keeping one hand on the bannister all the way, and laying each foot down as quietly as possible so as not to disturb his family. He took his hat, settled it on his head and walked up the street. His knees felt strangely wobbly—in fact, he felt giddy and out-of-balance all over—but by the time he reached the top of the hill, he felt stronger, so he turned the corner to head west.

Several days passed before Susan learned what had happened. At the mouth of the main shaft of the North Star, the day crew was sharing a pot of coffee when Hannibal staggered up to them, nearly tripping on the scattered gravel, his mouth sagging open. One of the men greeted him by name, but Hannibal scarcely nodded before heading down into the gloom. His breath was rank, his coat had nearly fallen off of one shoulder, and his head was bare. The men traded jokes on what might provoke a prosperous family man to drink himself into such a state at that hour of the morning, but the man who knew Hannibal persuaded two of the others to follow him.

At the second level, a team of three men and a boy were drilling in preparation for a blast and didn't notice Hannibal come up behind them. Their leader turned to reach for a packet of powder and saw the stranger, gaunt, his eyes shining, picking up a sledge. Puzzled but annoyed, he demanded to know what he might be thinking about to borrow a man's tools without asking leave. Hannibal shouldered the sledge and walked right past the leader to where one of the others was still holding a drill in place. All four watched him, fascinated, as he took his position, struggled to find firm footing, and addressed the drill. For a moment, he stood poised, weighing the hammer, grasping the tapered wooden handle in one hand and cradling the heavy steel head in the other. He looked as though he might topple over at any moment. Then he seemed to grow taller, and with perfect balance and flawless rhythm, he shifted his grip, brought the sledge back, and swung it in a flat, even arc, bringing to bear the full weight of his body, hitting the drill squarely on the head and driving the bit at least an inch deeper into the greenstone. The men from the surface arrived just in time to see Hannibal strike the sledge home and freeze as though he had himself turned to stone, not recoiling from the blow at all. Every man in the drift held his breath, then the sledge fell from the miner's fingers, and he collapsed against the rock wall and slid into a dent in the floor, shaped like a long cradle, where he lay staring witlessly up into the blackness. The man who knew him walked over, knelt down, and closed his eyes. Hannibal Carne was dead.

The funeral procession set out from the church, heading towards Greenwood Cemetery, but when they reached Main Street, there was a sudden blaring of horns, and the coach carrying Susan and the coffin stopped in the middle of the intersection. She looked down the hill to see another cavalcade climbing up from Auburn Street and turning south on Mill. There was a shining hearse, draped in black, with silk bunting tied to every available railing and sprays of flowers laid in every corner. At least two dozen coaches followed, some driven by bearded men in livery and others by solemn Chinese wearing formal brocaded silks; inside, the passengers wore brushed top hats, diamond stick pins, and fashionable gowns with meticulous lace trimmings. A brass band paced slowly along behind the last buggy, the drums beating a dead march even while the horns and bugles scattered their broken notes off of the storefronts, and behind them straggled a hundred men, some in formal mourning and others wearing dirty working clothes, but each carrying a bunch of golden poppies. A small group in the center was singing in spite of the band, and at the end of each verse, they cheered and waved their bottles over their heads before lowering them to their lips.

The driver leaned back towards Susan to explain. Alonzo Delano had died, and this was his cortege. Every flag flew at half-staff, and all businesses were closed in his honor. Only the saloons remained open, and each one was full of men drinking solemnly to the memory of their beloved, eccentric banker, storyteller and fellow miner.

Susan looked over her shoulder at the three wagons and carriages that held Hannibal's small party of mourners. No one cheered, no one sang, and no one offered to lower a flag or display a bouquet. The picture seemed familiar, and after a moment, she realized that she was remembering the funeral procession for her grandmother, back in Camborne. Now, as then, the faces turned towards her were rock, just like the cliffs at St. Ives, just like the boulders scattered near Dolcoath and the North Star. She turned her head to watch the last of Delano's followers disappear around the corner, and then she called to the driver to continue, to take Hannibal Carne to the grave that awaited him.

17
The Narrow Gauge
1876

The cold winter light sifted through the parlor curtains as Susan read the letter again. Although Jack had done well in Penzance and his prospects seemed more promising each day, he could no longer deny that the best opportunities lay in California, and he had resolved to raise his children there so that they could share in the inevitable prosperity of America. The current business troubles, he assured her, could not last much longer, and the country would once again move forward to fulfill its destiny. He would begin the journey as soon as he had finished building a row of houses with his father-in-law, a firm commitment and a sure investment from which he could not so precipitously turn.

She laid the letter down and stared at the opposite wall, counting. Jack had been gone for over seven years. What would he find when he returned? A widow with six children and her eccentric mother; that was all. Then she clucked her tongue, mildly exasperated at herself, because, as always, she had forgotten about Joseph. He had grown even quieter since Jesse's death, and she had, more than once, seen him stagger up the walk and fumble at the latch on the side gate. She wondered what Jack would say about that. Through the ceiling, she could hear the children's feet pounding from room to room, and she shivered. The house seemed colder than usual, even for January.

Jack looked across the polished desk at the pen that was scratching figures in neat columns. He waited. Finally, his father-in-law peered at him over the spectacles that sat on the tip of his nose.

"I cannot spare you."

"You can't keep me, Tobias."

"Can't I?" He screwed up his face into a lopsided knot, lips and nose and brow all grotesquely crinkled in an expression that would look puzzled to most, but which Jack knew to indicate that he was calculating, not merely numbers, as usual, but leverage. "Leave now, and I declare our contract broken. I'll not pay you, and I'll sue you for damages."

"How would you explain that to Clara?"

"You are over-extended, are you not?" He smiled. "I doubt you have enough to pay your passage."

"Damn you."

His father-in-law's face reversed itself completely, losing its furrows, the eyes and mouth opening in mock surprise. "And how would you explain *that* to Clara?"

"If we'd run this business my way, we'd have twice as much income by now."

"If we had run this business your way, we should be sharing a pallet in the workhouse."

"You're an old fool."

Harris sat back in his chair and laced his fingers across his vest. "Ah, yes. That would explain everything."

Jack leaned forward. "We don't get on, Tobias. We both know it. Let me go."

Harris stared at him, his face wooden. "After you finish the row. And you'll do them properly. And you'll stay until we sign the contracts with the tenants."

Jack tried to breathe calmly. "Will you buy out my share?"

The other man's eyes went blank for a moment, then focused again. "I'll pay you what you paid me."

"The business is worth more than that now!"

His father-in-law frowned. "This is not California!" He shut his eyes as though wincing, and when he opened them again, he looked strangely resentful. "Very well. I'll add five per cent, but not for you. For my daughter and my grandchildren." Jack rose to his feet and began to speak, but Harris lifted an admonitory finger. "Will I see them again?"

Jack looked down at him, his eyes veiled, and turned towards the door.

He drove the crews as fast as he dared, and there were two occasions when Harris, inspecting the work, directed him to tear out a section and re-do it. Jack was impatient; they were building the row for tenants; what did it matter if the quality was merely acceptable? Finally, in April, the row was finished and the leases filled. The last tenant was a distant cousin, a young man named Stephens who had just married and hoped to find a position as a clerk; Jack persuaded him that there were more opportunities in Penzance than in Camborne or Redruth.

He was eager to leave, so rather than sell their house, he consented to let Clara ask her father to manage the property. He suspected that she harbored a secret hope that they would someday return, even though he had firmly declared his resolution to the contrary, so the arrangement both suited his convenience and provided her a small consolation, however delusive, for the move. He hired an auctioneer to dispose of his horse and buggy, the wagon, and the furniture they had decided not to ship. Harris raised his eyebrows when he saw Jack's tools put out for bids, but Jack was determined that while he might one day own a construction company, he would never again work alongside of the men. They packed everything into crates and took the train to Liverpool for the passage to New York, where they boarded another train that would carry them across the continent. When Jack set down his traveling-case on the floor of their compartment, he took in the comfort of Pullman's appointments and smiled as he remembered his trips across the Isthmus.

Their passage through the East was a collage of cinder-blackened stone arches mixed with riots of green foliage. The train roared inexorably past embankments and through tunnels, along the back sides of tall, sooty brick tenements and across entwining railroad yards that led to platforms set under arching ironwork. The children grew touchy and anxious because the view kept changing so abruptly as barriers sprang up, apparently only inches from the window glass, and vanished again, revealing prospects entirely different from what they had seen just moments earlier. After they left Chicago, the walls subsided and the view expanded, offering farms and broad green fields. Out in the open, the sound of the train dissipated, and the passengers found that they could converse more easily. The children began to relax, and the girl fell asleep in Clara's lap. They crossed the Mississippi and continued west, leaving the cities behind, and for Jack, the journey seemed to begin as they headed across the plains of Nebraska.

West of Omaha, the grass was dry, crackling brown like the California hills in summer, and the setting sun tinted the plains a dusky gold as the train steamed on. Jack had just settled down in his bunk when he noticed a glow seeping through the windows, and he sat up to raise the shade. The prairie was on fire, a ragged line of flames licking calmly along the sea of grass and sending a lazy curtain of smoke up to vanish into the night sky. The train drew closer, and Jack could see the sparks floating up in the breeze and falling, still red-hot, on the dry fields ahead of the fire line, like scouts making an advance sortie. No man blocked the fire's advance, and no animal fled before it. Jack wondered whether the engine would halt, whether a band of men would jump out to stop the flames, but the train continued.

They arrived at the fork of the Platte River just as they were finishing breakfast, and Clara was reaching over to help one of the children when she happened to glance out of the window and dropped her spoon, splitting a china cup into three pieces. Covering the gently rolling plains, as far as they could see, was a herd of buffalo. The train lurched and then slowed until it was barely moving. Everyone in the dining car had crowded over to the windows, and Jack helped the children stand up on the benches so they could see. Suddenly, the boy gave a little squeak, for there, right outside the window, close enough to touch, stood an enormous bull, stock still, staring with placid, opaque eyes. His coat looked like a rough, worn rug, wrapped evenly over the contours of his body. Two stubby horns curved out above his ears, and he lifted his soft, wet nose to catch the scent of the locomotive as the car moved ahead and left him behind.

The Narrow Gauge, 1876

A sharp report sounded up ahead, and another. A moment later, the window revealed another buffalo, but this one was lying on the ground gasping, his tongue pulsing out of his mouth. Blood bubbled up from holes in his flanks. As the family stared, they heard more shots, an irregular, stuttering fusillade, like a string of firecrackers scrambling the air. Jack reached across, tripped the latches, and threw up the window so he could lean outside and look up the line. The train bristled with rifle and shotgun barrels that jerked as they fired, and with each volley, several buffalo went down, some heaving and rolling, and others simply collapsing into motionless heaps. In the next car, a man swung his leg over the window sill and braced his foot against a rivet. He lifted a Springfield rifle, all dark metal and polished wood, took careful aim, fired, and laughed and pointed to a bull tossing and kicking on a knoll a hundred yards away. Jack looked back into the dining car. The children were crying; the boy was staring out the window, his face red and his mouth distorted into a grimace, while his sister had fastened herself onto Clara, who was trying to wipe her cheeks with a crumpled handkerchief. The buffalo waited calmly for the barrage. Jack looked up towards the locomotive and flinched when he saw a man in the next car swing his rifle around towards the rear, apparently aiming right at him. The train accelerated and passed through a shallow cutting, and when they emerged, the herd was far away and mostly hidden behind a series of shallow knolls. There were a few more shots by laggards frustrated at having missed the hunt, then the rifle barrels withdrew. The train did not stop to pick up the slaughtered animals. When Jack escorted his family back to their car, he had to push through clumps of laughing men cleaning their guns and grinning at each other.

They crossed the divide that night, and awoke the next morning in the western foothills of the Rockies. The train eased down through a series of canyons, and the green conifers gradually gave way to aspens and clumps of grass. At a coaling station, Jack took the children out for a walk, halting at the end of the platform to study the measly collection of run-down shacks that formed the settlement. About thirty yards from where they stood was a pile of refuse composed principally of broken pieces of hardware and rotting food that had attracted a swarm of flies, two or three gaunt dogs, and a pair of Indians who squatted in the dust, systematically picking through the garbage for scraps to eat. Their hair was long and tangled, their feet were bare, and they wore ragged, torn remnants of dark wool suits. One man shaded his head from the sun with a shining straw skimmer that sat at a perky tilt. The wind shifted and brought the stench down to the platform, so Jack hurried the children back to their car.

The train continued on through canyons and gullies that looked as though they had been washed by great rivers, but there was no water in sight. Near the end of the day, they passed a cluster of rock obelisks, titanic fingers stretching long, thin shadows across the dry, rocky fields and pointing straight up into the vast, empty sky, so emphatic that the children, compelled, laid their faces on the window sill to stare upwards. Beneath the setting sun, the desert of white salt shimmered in the heat that rose from its surface into the cooling air, and Clara drew the shades against the glare that turned her white blouse the color of singed, wilted marigolds. In the morning, the desert was dingy, studded with scraggly bushes, and now and then the track swung closer to the Humboldt River, where groves of thirsty green trees hugged the water.

Finally, they climbed into the Sierra Nevada, slowly up the steep eastern slope, past the barren rocks and into the thick pine forests. The locomotive traced its way along the edge of granite cliffs, seemed to hesitate and stumble as it took a turn over Donner Lake, but steamed on into the safety of the snow sheds that curved above the gorge. The children screwed up their faces against the brightness of the polished granite slopes and tried to estimate the height of the trees. As the train ran down towards the Sacramento Valley, the passengers began to sort through their luggage, and even the men who had played cards for most of the journey now looked out of the window, some seeing California for the first time, some returning for business, and some coming home. Jack and his family disembarked at Colfax and found a room at a hotel next to the station.

They had intended to take the stage into Grass Valley, but they learned that the very next day marked the opening of the railroad line from Colfax to Nevada City. Jack could scarcely sit still after he heard the news, and halfway through the meal, he tossed his crumpled napkin on the table and strode out of the room. Nearly an hour later, just as Clara was beginning to think she must go upstairs without him, he re-appeared to announce that he had found them seats on the official train that would steam the length of the line to mark the completion of the Nevada County Narrow Gauge Rail Road.

Early the next morning, their car was so crowded that Clara sat on a bench seat with the girl in her lap and the boy sitting next to her while Jack stood in the aisle next to them. Some of the ladies had worn their new spring gowns, all light and puffy, even though the air was unseasonably cold and the sky loomed grey above the trees. The little train lurched away from the station, puffed down a slope, away from the town, ran alongside of the main line for nearly two miles, and turned away to pass through groves of trees wearing bright green leaves. They crossed the Bear River on a trestle bridge so tall that Clara pulled the boy back from the window; they could see the ties flicking past close beneath them and, much farther down, the slow unreeling of the rocky riverbed. A tunnel caught the fumes from the stack and sent them swirling around the cars, but the train emerged to cross Greenhorn Creek over another bridge. The line made a sharp hairpin turn,

The Narrow Gauge, 1876

doubled back for a while, and looped around again to climb towards Grass Valley past the gently-waving green fronds of cedar trees. Jack, crouching down to look out the windows on both sides, noticed more and more onlookers watching them from below the embankment, and one fellow on a horse kept pace with the train for nearly two miles. As they pulled into the station, something about the view seemed familiar, and as he helped Clara and the children climb down onto the platform, he lingered for a moment on the steps and suddenly realized where he was. Their old home stood no longer; the railroad company had torn it down and taken over the property for the depot.

The station was draped in tricolor bunting, and the passengers gathered near the locomotive, where the mayor waited on a platform, but Jack hurried his family down to the street and hired a carriage to take them into town. He directed the driver to wait while they checked in at the Holbrooke—he kept repeating the new name, gazing at the brightly-painted lettering as though memorizing it—and he took Clara and the children upstairs. He ran out again, jumped into the carriage and told the driver to take him to the house on Auburn Street.

Susan opened the door. She was wearing a black silk dress, buttoned tightly up the front, and she had pulled her brown hair away from her face into a knot at the nape of her neck. A little boy peered around her skirts to stare up at the visitor.

Jack knelt down to look at the child, who ran off, with an uneven gait, into the house. Jack rose. "May I come in?"

She looked at him with a strange expression, almost as if she was not sure who he was. Then she stood aside and gestured towards the parlor. "Mother's 'ere." Jack started to say something, but paused when he heard footfalls on the staircase. Zennora descended, carefully holding hands with a tow-headed toddler who took the steps with grim concentration, one at a time, leading with his right foot and planting the left next to it on each level. Safe at the bottom, Zennora looked up, recognized her nephew, and held out her arms for an embrace. The children gathered around, curious about the stranger; only Bertie claimed to remember his cousin, although Susan shook her head skeptically. Zennora asked whether he could bring Clara and the children for supper.

"Thank you———I'm sure they'll want to come———they're resting now———but Susan———Today's the celebration for the Narrow Gauge, over in Nevada City. I've a carriage waiting—won't you come with me?"

Susan laughed incredulously. Of course she wouldn't come, couldn't come. It was almost time for the children to eat, and she had a full afternoon planned. Zennora laid a soft hand on her arm. "Ye've not been out o' the 'ouse fer three weeks, except fer shopping. Not even t' church."

Cousin Jack

"Mother!" Then it all became a game; Bertie and James brought her coat, and Jane tied her hat ribbon under her chin. Not wanting to go, she was going, and before she could muster herself, she was sitting in the carriage next to Jack, who was calling orders up to the driver.

The official train had long since left, but Jack told the driver to take them straight to Nevada City and paid him extra to flog the horses into a gallop at every opportunity. The coach swayed and jerked as it staggered around turns and sailed through the dips in the road. Jack and Susan hung on to the leather straps, he looking towards the railroad tracks, and she concentrating on keeping her stomach quiet. As they sped down the last slope from Town Talk into Nevada City, they could hear the low, roaring murmur of a vast crowd. The driver stopped at the foot of Sacramento Street, and they disembarked to join the people standing there.

The Nevada Light Guard was marching down Boulder Street to the blare of a brass band, the men accompanying the tramp of their heavy boots with a fancy rifle drill in response to harshly shouted commands that sounded to Susan like complete gibberish. Each spinning rifle seemed ready to fly into the air, and the gold braid on the men's shoulders flapped extravagantly. There was scarcely room on the narrow road, and the onlookers pressed back, pushing Susan into Jack, who had braced himself against the stone wall behind them. She could feel him breathing hard, and his face was set in an amazed grin, like a child at a circus. The militia, with its incomprehensible shouts and flashing insignia, had arrived at the new railroad station, but the band, which seemed to be composed of strangely deformed trumpets, was parading past them, the music, if there was any, lost in the raucous howl of whichever instrument happened to be pointing, momentarily, in her direction. Two ranks of drums brought up the rear, and she wanted to cover her ears with her hands, but found she could not raise her arms, for one was pinned by the woman standing next to her, and Jack had, unconsciously, grabbed the other above the elbow. The noise reminded her of standing inside a large, enclosed stamp mill, with the rock pouring down the chutes and the stamps hammering away.

As soon as the band passed, the people on the roadside surged forward, and Jack pulled her, stumbling, through the mess to the station. The pushing and pulling stopped, and she was able catch her breath and straighten her hat. She noticed that she was cold, and she looked up just as the first tiny flakes of snow fell, sticking on her eyelashes and momentarily blinding her.

The Completion Day train was sitting on the tracks: the engine "Nevada," still with steam up, leading its string of gleaming passenger cars, each painted with the slogan, "Nevada County Narrow Gauge" and decorated as though for Independence Day. On either side of the boiler, a cluster of American flags fanned out, the banners hanging limp in the cold air. The railway coaches were crammed: hats and faces showed at every window, people perched on the platforms between the cars, and a few of the more reckless men balanced on the roofs, pretending to be nonchalant but surreptitiously looking through the crowd to see which young women might be noticing and admiring their daring. Abruptly, the train bell began to clang, and Susan looked back at the cab to see a man in a derby, certainly not the engineer, wildly jerking the cord and laughing as he looked out at the crowd. Nevada City answered him with fire bells, machine shop whistles, and mill horns. There was a rifle shot, and the whistles and bells slowly straggled away as everyone looked towards the Guard to see the captain striding furiously up and down the ranks of impassive soldiers, standing frozen to attention, demanding to know which man had disgraced them all.

The snow fell more heavily as a speaker mounted a rostrum set across the tracks. Susan could barely see past the hats and shoulders, and she began to feel not only cold but tired, and could scarcely pay attention. It all sounded wearily familiar: "the good people of Nevada County," "this great nation of ours," "our destiny before God," and "Progress." After a few minutes of this, the people around her began to applaud, and she looked up to see two workmen carrying in a railroad tie, holding it high above their heads so everyone could see that it was painted blue, blue like the American flag, with gold leaf running up and down the corners. They set it into place, and the speaker called for "Mr. John C. Sterling, one of our most prominent citizens, and President of the Nevada County Narrow Gauge" to approach and drive the last spike.

Sterling was smiling and waving, and alternately clapping his hands and clasping them above his head. He took a sledge hammer from one of the workmen, nearly dropped it, and so made a burlesque of its weight, to the great amusement of the onlookers. The other workman handed him a spike, polished so that it shone even in the dull, grey light that filtered through the snowflakes, now falling more thickly and even beginning to accumulate on the track bed and on hats and shoulders. The Narrow Gauge, proclaimed Sterling, had reached completion not as a consequence of the tireless efforts of men like himself (he nodded at the scattered cheers), but because of God, Progress, and the ordained destiny of the great American nation, whose people marched in the vanguard of the future. He finished to wild applause, then knelt on the tracks to drive in the last spike, carefully inserting the sharp tip into the hole, lifting the sledge up above his head, and driving it down, hitting the spike squarely. Bells rang, whistles blew, people cheered and screamed, and just as Susan bit her lip at this new din, there was an explosion so loud and low that it vibrated through her chest, almost throwing her to the pavement. Someone had dragged a cannon to Sugar Loaf Hill, and it was firing a salute in honor of the new railroad. Galvanized by this new assault, she turned on Jack.

"Why did ye bring me 'ere? Why did ye come back at all?"

He turned to her, astonished. "What's the matter?"

"'What's the matter?' Isn't that just like you? Ye never see what's the matter, ye never think that somethin' might be wrong. Ye just go along on yer way, never mind about the rest."

Although everyone near them seemed to be listening to Judge Searls, who was speaking from the cab of the "Nevada," he drew her away from the crowd and around the corner of the station house. "What is it you want of me?"

"What do I want? Why is it so 'ard for ye to know what someone else wants, Jack Trevenna? What can ye be thinkin' about?"

"Susan, what have I done? I went back to England because you didn't want me near you."

"Iss, and now ye're 'ere again. What d'ye expect of me?"

"I don't expect anything of you. I came on my own account."

"When did ye arrive in town, Jack? Just this morning, wasn't it? And yer first thought is to drag me out o' my 'ouse t' stand in th' snow and listen t' John Sterling."

"I did not drag you."

"Why did ye think I'd go with ye?"

He pursed his lips. "You came, didn't you?"

"Iss, well, ye can thank my mother for that."

"Listen, Susan, I wanted you to come to the celebration because . . . Well, I'm not sure why, but I wanted you to come."

"Ah, Jack, ye never know what ye want."

"That's not true."

"Of course it is. If ye were doin' so well in Penzance, then why did ye leave? Will ye be goin' back in a few years? 'ave ye asked Clara 'ow she feels about yer goin' forth an' tooey?"

"I'm here to stay."

"Well, I'm sure she'll be glad t' know that."

"Why are you so angry with me?"

"What're ye doin' 'ere?"

Judge Searls had opened his arms to the depot, presenting it as an emblem of the national centennial. Jack took a breath and coughed a little from the chilled air. "I came to see you because I wanted to see you. Whatever else we've been to each other, we're cousins, and we were children together."

"That was a long time ago."

"I came to see you because I thought you might need my help."

"Your 'elp?"

The Narrow Gauge, 1876

"That's right. I know it must be harder for you with Hannibal gone, even with Zennora so close by." He stopped because she was clearly furious now.

"Oh, Jack! So that's it! Ye think ye'll be . . . what? My big brother? My guardian angel? Or will ye be my gentleman friend, like some o' those ladies in San Francisco? Does Clara know?"

He tried to keep his voice under control. "I told you, I expect nothing. I just want to help."

"Oh, that's grand! Do you 'ave any idea what it's been like? Fayther gone, Hannibal gone, but I'm still 'ere."

"I know it must have been difficult."

"Jack if ye wanted to 'elp someone, ye should've 'elped yer own brother. Poor Nicky 'ad t' go to Australia; 'e can't come back or they'll put 'im in jail. Hannibal wouldn't 'elp 'im either; th' two of ye's a pair."

"It was more complicated than you understand."

"Ye don't think much of me, do ye?"

"That's not true."

"Oh, so ye say, but ye don't give me credit for 'avin' good sense."

"Susan, I'm here to help you."

"Well, ye're too late. Hannibal's been dead for eight months, Jack, and the court is still fiddlin' with 'is will. Where've ye been all that time?"

"I'm sorry. I didn't know."

"Ye 'ave a knack for knowin' what ye want t' know. Shall I tell ye what ye've been missin'? D'ye know who's been 'elpin' me?"

"Who?"

"That man right over there." She gestured towards the rostrum.

"Judge Searls?"

"No, not 'im. John Sterling."

"Sterling?"

"Iss, Sterling. Hannibal left the 'ouse, a worthless ranch, and some minin' stock. Most of 'is money was in th' Live Yankee, and I couldn't pay the assessments. Can ye guess who paid 'em for me?" He stared down at her without speaking. "John Sterling. He's paid, oh, six or seven hundred. If I can't get some cash, and soon, I'll 'ave to sell th' stock to pay 'im what I owe 'im."

"I'm sorry, Susan."

"And not t' mention all the fal-the-ral with this an' that. Hannibal never told me enough about 'is business, Jack, or 'is dealin's with you, and I suspect that ye're back 'ere because now no one's been keepin' up on yer affairs."

With a grandiose sweep of his top hat, Searls presented the Narrow Gauge to the people of Nevada County. The noise began to swell.

"I'll take care of everything for you, Susan."

Cousin Jack

"Ye will not. I'll live my own life, and I'll do it without yer 'elp."

All at once, the town collapsed into a bedlam of steam whistles, church bells and cannon fire. Everyone on the platform was cheering and waving their arms, heedless of the wet snow that kept falling around them. Jack reached down to take Susan by the shoulders, but she pulled away and disappeared into the crowd. He called after her and tried to follow, but he could hardly hear himself shouting, and he could not push his way fast enough through the packed bodies. Ten minutes later, when the throng began to dissipate, he could not find her.

When Clara took the children to pay a call on Zennora and Susan, Jack told her, with manifest regret, that he simply had to meet with a lawyer in Nevada City that day, and so would have to forego the pleasure of a visit with his relatives. At the end of the week they took the train back to Colfax and made the connection to San Francisco, where Jack booked them into the Palace Hotel and began looking for a comfortable residence, immediately available, convenient to church, school and streetcar line.

18
The Highwayman
1879

Jack shifted in the pew and tried to concentrate on Father Hill's sermon.

"It is written by a Jew, and the Catholics have given it their approval. Yes! The bishops and priests of this city not only condone this disgrace, they have blessed it and the archbishop himself has written one of the scenes!"

Jack glanced down at his daughter. She was sitting exactly as her mother had taught her, with ankles crossed and gloved hands folded neatly in her lap.

"If you would join with Jews and Catholics in sacrilege, then attend this play! If you would have your children watch a mere actor—without a doubt a man of profane and dissolute habits—desecrate the Son of God by presuming to impersonate him on stage, then attend this play! If you would trample on your very faith, then attend this play!" Hill lowered his voice and leaned over the pulpit confidentially. "We are decent people. We turn away from impiety and apostasy. We know that to bring our Lord Jesus Christ into a theatre—a theatre!—is more than a mistake, it is clearly a sin!"

Hill was not normally inclined to rant—Jack had brought his daughter to church hoping for a quiet, kindly talk on charity to others—but this play had, obviously, provoked his outrage. Jack sat bemused for the rest of the service, and as he was leaving, he paused while shaking the minister's hand and asked him, if he didn't mind, to repeat the name of the play that had brought sacrilege to San Francisco and jeopardized the morality of their community. Hill's routine smile folded into a dire frown and his grip tightened. "*The Passion Play*, Mr. Trevenna. That Irish impresario, Maguire, would toy with Christ's passion and mock our faith."

All the way home, the girl continued to play the grown-up lady, tucking her fingers into the crook of Jack's arm and making genteel conversation about the pigeons and brightly-painted gingerbread that gleamed in the March sunshine, but he could not stop thinking about Hill's sermon. He took for granted San Francisco's juxtaposition of piety and license, the church and the Barbary Coast each remaining within accepted boundaries and discreetly unaware of one another. The clergyman must have somehow strayed outside of his sanctuary and stubbed his moral toe, but Jack could hardly believe that Tom Maguire had plumbed undiscovered depths in the City's notorious depravity. Even so, Hill's indignation—so marked and so genuine—had whetted Jack's curiosity. He was trying to imagine what *The*

Passion Play might be like when the girl tugged at his elbow; they had begun to walk right past their own front door.

The air inside was stale, carrying a faint but importunate odor that made Jack as restless as a dog who feels compelled to sniff out the source. As he hung his hat on the hall tree, the Irish servant girl whisked by, barely bobbing to him before scurrying upstairs with a pitcher of something. Clara was feeling ill again, and with less than two months before the expected arrival of the new baby, she was spending more and more time in bed. He found her distracted and petulant, unwilling or unable to come down, but convinced that the household could not manage without her. He listened to her fret, nodding at her anxieties and promising to execute her various edicts, and left the room as soon as he could manage. He had no intention of acting as Clara's steward; Mary might not run the house just the way his wife would wish, but she ran it adequately all the same.

Three days later, Jack finished his supper quickly, entrusted the children to Mary's care, and quietly slipped out of the house to catch the streetcar. At the Opera House, he found a long line at the box office, animated parties disembarking from carriages, and knots of onlookers, some babbling at the passers-by, some offering handbills, and others simply staring, their faces set hard. Jack followed the throng through the lobby and into the hall. As he settled into his seat, the clatter of voices rose suddenly, and the wall sconces dimmed until they cast flickering shadows on the red velvet and gilt fixtures. The curtain rose.

Jack later remembered *The Passion Play* as a clamor of crowds, fragments and discontinuous images that rendered the story obscure and elusive. The action began in a temple filled with men wearing hats and long beards who waved their arms, argued, and abruptly fell silent and stared as a woman walked on stage carrying a baby who squirmed in her arms, tugged at her gold earrings and finally beat its fists on her neck. One of the men pointed at the baby and delivered a long harangue to the others, frantically raising his voice higher and higher as the baby began to fret, then cry, and finally squall so loudly that Jack could not help wincing. The temple rolled away, and the stage filled with women, each carrying a baby, some trying to assume what someone supposed to be reverent attitudes. One infant kicked and cried while its "mother" held it at arms' length, her face averted and her teeth clenched. A man with a long beard and a striped cloak jumped on stage waving a long sword, and all of the women shrieked as they ran up against a wall, knocking each other down and dropping the screaming babies. The man fell to his knees before one of the infants, who was driving his fist into the mouth of the woman carrying him, and the stage became a green canvas mountainside covered with sheep that bumped and bustled past a man and a woman before stampeding into the wings with the "shepherds" close behind them. In a throne room hung with gold and amethyst, a king and queen scolded each other while a mob of rowdy courtiers stared at a short, plump woman who danced and flung pieces of her clothing into the crowd until a servant ran in with a silver tray carrying a crudely sculptured bust dabbled with red paint and loosely wrapped in a dirty napkin.

The courtiers rumbled off, and the stage filled with singers arrayed in rows, chanting exultantly as a man wearing a white robe walked towards them, his eyes fixed on the upper balcony, a halo around his head, and his right hand held up as if in benediction. The woman sitting next to Jack gave a little gasp, collapsed out of her seat into a kneeling position, sobbing, and reached out towards the stage, flailing her arms about the ears of the man sitting in front of her. Jack looked around and realized that in every part of the audience, men and women were kneeling, praying aloud, and even singing with the performers. The man with the halo sat at the center of a long table with other men, all wearing beards, caps and flowing robes. He tore a loaf of bread into pieces and poured drinks from a chipped ceramic pitcher. They prayed. They all went to a garden, soldiers came, one of the robed men pointed to the man with the halo, and the soldiers dragged him away. The others prayed. A horde of shouting men swarmed onto the stage from all sides and shook their fists at the man with the halo while another man washed his hands in a brass basin. Women prayed. Finally, a band of soldiers pretended to nail the man with the halo to a wooden cross, and they raised it up as hundreds of people filled the stage, wailing and praying.

In the audience, women fainted and men bellowed. Nearly everyone stood or knelt; only the decrepit remained in their seats, buried in the forest of suppliants. Jack felt someone grasp his shoulder; it was the man standing next to him, who was shouting angrily at the stage while tears dripped from his eyes and mucus oozed from his nose. He released Jack's shoulder and began pounding on it with his fist. The pandemonium turned into applause and cheers as the performers came down to the footlights, lifting their open palms and nodding with satisfaction. Several minutes later, the audience poured out onto the street, carrying Jack with them.

On his way downtown the next morning, he bought a copy of the *Argonaut*, and he was surprised to read that the editor condemned the play as "an absurd and irreverent money-making spectacle," and dismissed the text—that is, anything not taken directly from the Bible—as "a lot of meaningless drivel." Jack stood on the sidewalk scanning the column, puzzled, and walked back to buy another newspaper, and another. He had never seen such unanimity in the press; every article and commentary reported what the journalists characterized as an irrepressible and stormy wave of righteously censorious public opinion. The editor of the *Bulletin* complained that the play turned "the holiest traditions of Christianity" into "the vulgar sensation of the hour," while his counterpart at the *Chronicle* demanded to know how long the people of the city would tolerate "a spectacle so sacrilegious, blasphemous and unholy," and called for retribution against those who would perpetrate such a desecration. Jack walked slowly to his office as he read and re-read the inky pages, occasionally bumping into annoyed men who were hurrying to work.

The challenge was soon answered; on that very Friday evening, a mob of angry workingmen—composed entirely, declared the conservative *Call*, of Irish Catholics—stormed two or three blocks downtown and destroyed several Jewish pawnshops and jewelry stores. The newspapers dutifully reported that the "laddies" had, regrettably, also done considerable damage to neighboring stores owned by Protestants and Catholics, but this information simply fanned the public ire against Maguire and his profane spectacle. The City Council passed a new ordinance:

> It shall be unlawful for any person to exhibit, or take part in exhibiting, in any theatre, or other place where money is charged for admission, any play or performance or representation displaying or intended to display, the life or death of Jesus Christ, or any play, performance or representation, calculated or tending to debase or degrade religion.

Maguire had already closed the play. The manager had received several threats against his life, including one wrapped around a large stone that shattered a window in his office and landed on his desk before his stunned eyes. The playwright was nowhere to be found; when a reporter knocked on the door of his synagogue, the rabbi unlocked it just long enough to insist that he knew nothing of his whereabouts, didn't expect to see him again, and in fact had never met the man.

Jack followed the controversy obsessively, littering the parlor with newspapers and forbidding Mary to throw them away or even rearrange them. Clara, who had begun to feel a little better, finally demanded that he drop the subject at least while they were dining. He rearranged his routine so that he walked by the Opera House on his way to his office, always pausing in front of the edifice to stand for a moment as if in contemplation. One afternoon early in April, he approached to find two men pasting up large playbills while a third watched. He was young, probably in his mid-twenties, but the dark suit, carefully polished shoes, generous gold watch chain and confidently folded arms made him seem older. His round face framed full lips and dark eyes, and he wore his thick, dark, curly hair cut low over his forehead. Jack approached slowly as one of the workmen turned and addressed his supervisor as "Mr. Belasco."

Jack recognized the name; David Belasco was Maguire's assistant and, more to the point, was currently notorious as the producer of *The Passion Play*, which, the playbill announced in large black letters, would re-open on

April 15. Jack clapped his hands in delight and amazement, and Belasco turned to look at him. Jack now realized that the man's salient feature was his nose: not unusually large, but definitely full and arched autocratically over his face. Belasco stared at Jack, whose mouth had sagged open but who showed no signs of speech, and his thick, dark eyebrows rose.

"Yes?"

Jack managed to mumble an introduction and inquire if, indeed, the play would once again grace the magnificent stage of Maguire's Opera House. Belasco assured him that it would; had he seen it already? Yes, Jack had enjoyed the privilege of attending an earlier performance and had found the spectacle splendid, majestic, sublime and altogether unforgettable. Belasco thanked him for his kind words. Encouraged, Jack gabbled on. The play was a monument, an affirmation of faith, a celebration of Christian civilization and a pinnacle of theatrical achievement. And was he in the presence of the man responsible for—if he might so describe it—this miracle? "You . . . " Jack groped for something adequate. "You . . . are an artist!"

Belasco's eyebrows rose again as he lifted his chin slightly, but he also smiled. "Yes. Yes, of course."

Jack was taking a breath to begin another irrepressible encomium when he noticed a man emerging from the door of the Opera House. He moved slowly towards them, as though he were leading a solemn procession, and although he paced right through the little group of men, he acknowledged no one, keeping his troubled but visionary gaze fixed on a point far beyond the horizon. There was something strangely troubling about the shape of his mouth. The two workmen took off their caps as he passed, and Jack followed their example as he pondered the man's impenetrable eyes. He continued slowly up the street and turned the corner as a few passers-by stopped to stare.

Jack turned to Belasco in time to see on his face a small, enigmatic smile, which vanished as soon as he noticed Jack's eyes upon him. "Was that . . . "

Belasco nodded reverently. "Yes. That was O'Neill." It was the actor who had played Jesus, the man with the halo, the man for whom scores of women had fainted and to whose image still more had prayed.

Jack stammered a pleasantry and set off down the street to stop at the nearest saloon. He took one shot of whiskey in a single gulp and regarded a second while sorting out the episode. He had encountered two of the greatest artists in San Francisco, possibly in the world. He had also, most likely, made a plain fool of himself. At their next meeting, Jack would show Belasco that he, too, was a man, and a man of accomplishments. Belasco might have mounted the production of the century, or perhaps of the Christian era, but that was no reason why Jack should not speak to him as an equal. So resolved, he went to his office.

Cousin Jack

On the Tuesday before Easter, *The Passion Play* re-opened as promised. Once again, the Opera House was packed, and once again, Jack was sitting in the orchestra. This performance was even more highly charged than the first, partly due to the vociferous public debate over the play, but specifically because a band of four policemen, led by a tall, gangling sergeant, had taken four seats in the center of the front row with the intention of arresting anyone who violated the new city ordinance. Jack looked in the lobby and around the auditorium, but could not see Belasco anywhere.

The play began. As before, the stage was peopled by clamoring mobs. As before, people cried out, wept and prayed. As before, Jack felt overwhelmed by the mounting images and tumult, but he kept watching the police in the front row and checking behind him for Belasco. Yet the manager didn't appear, and the four policemen sat motionless, their arms folded and their faces tilted up towards the lights and commotion on the stage.

As the soldiers began to nail Jesus to the cross, the tall sergeant nodded to his officers, rose, donned his helmet, and marched his men through the door that led backstage. The audience was already standing and spilling out into the side aisles, so Jack had to push his way past the hysterical spectators to follow the policemen. Once through the door, he ran up a little flight of stairs and past a small knot of stage hands who were nonchalantly smoking cigars. They stared as Jack bustled past them but seemed disinclined to intervene. He stopped in the wings and looked across to the other side to see the four policemen watching the final exit: the dead Jesus sprawled on the shoulders of the faithful who were carrying him off. He ran around the back scene, tripped on a cleat and fell headlong, found his footing again and staggered around to where the police were waiting. O'Neill had cast aside his halo and wig. "Damn you, sir! You might let me go to my dressing room and change into clothes fit for a gentleman!" One of the officers reached out and clapped one hand on each of O'Neill's shoulders. "And tell this damned Englishman to put his dirty hands somewhere else!"

The little scene so bewildered Jack that he grabbed a rope to keep from losing his balance. Then, remembering his errand, he turned and ran down a short flight of steps, through a door, and into a hallway. He could hear two men arguing, and he threw open a door. There was Belasco pounding a desk furiously. "I won't go! That's final!"

The other man turned and beckoned to Jack. "Come here, you—help me with him. He wants to stay and get himself arrested, and it's up to us to get him out of here."

Jack walked around to the other side of the desk and took one of Belasco's arms. He and the other man dragged the protesting manager out of his office, down the corridor and out of the back of the building, where a carriage was waiting. Belasco kept looking over his shoulder and calling, "Police!" but

The Highwayman, 1879

Jack and the other man thrust him into the carriage—Jack had to pry one of his hands off of the door jamb—and slammed the door. The other man hopped on the back and ordered the coachman to drive on. While the carriage accelerated, Jack trotted alongside and reminded Belasco that he was an artist, a great artist, and surely should not be allowed to languish in a common jail. Belasco became incensed. "An artist?! My God! Damn your art! If I'm arrested, we'll be sold out for a month. Get me out of this!" He pounded on the window and reached for the latch as the other man pulled him back into his seat and the coachman lashed the horses into a gallop. The manager threw open the window and stuck out his head. "At least tell them where to find O'Neill!" he wailed. Left behind, Jack stood in the street and watched the carriage turn the corner, leaving only a haze of dust behind it. The back door of the Opera House was locked from the inside, so Jack walked around to the front. The police had done their work quickly; only a few idlers and passers-by were left to get in the way of the man who swept the walk after the performance.

Exhausted, Jack walked home, hardly noticing where he was or who he met. He finally reached Sacramento Street at dusk and trudged up the stairs. The front door opened before he reached it, and Mary peeked through the opening, her dark eyes open wide above her flushed cheeks.

"Oh! Maister Trevenna! I thought ye was th' doctor, sur." She shut the door behind him and took his hat and coat.

"The doctor? What's wrong?"

"Why, th' missus is 'avin' 'er baby! We sent fer th' doctor 'alf an hour ago!"

Jack ran up the stairs and into Clara's bedroom. She was lying on her back moaning, her face green and dripping with sweat. "Where have you been?" she gasped. She turned away from him. "Get out. Get out."

He stood there, uncertain, and at that moment the doctor pushed past him, set down his bag, and began to examine the groaning woman. Jack turned and walked out into the hall just as Mary arrived with a large basin of hot water, her arms and shoulders draped with towels and rags. The girl and the boy were sitting on the stairs to the attic; they must have been there before, but he had not noticed them. He walked down to wait in the parlor, and sat there leafing through the clippings that littered his desk and spilled onto the floor.

Jack looked out the window at the leaves blowing across the pavement. Behind him, Clara shifted in her bed. "I don't see why you must take Kathleen with you. I need her."

He took a deep breath and tried to keep his voice calm and reasonable.

Cousin Jack

"We hired her as a . . . er . . . nursemaid. You know that, Clara. She must stay with Frederick."

His wife turned the edge of the coverlet over and smoothed it in place. "Then leave him here. I can't think why you would take a baby so far. He's only six months old. Really, Jack!"

Her hair was carefully brushed to lie neatly on the pillow beside her head, and her nightgown was clean, but her skin looked rough and she had been biting her lip. "I have to go to the wedding, Clara—they'd be disappointed if I didn't. And I'm sure Susan and her children would like to see him. And Zennora. You know they'll never come to San Francisco. Listen." He stepped closer, smiled carefully, and laid a hand gently on her shoulder. "He'll be fine. I'll hire the best coaches so he won't be bounced about too much, and Kathleen will stay with him every minute. He's a fine baby."

"Jack . . . " she whined, and he leaned down to pat her pillow.

"It's all settled, Clara. We'll be fine, and Mary will take care of you and the children. I'll be back soon." He kissed her on the forehead and turned away before the tear had time to well out of her eye and trickle down her cheek. Even so, as he pulled the door shut, he could hear her give a long, shuddering sigh.

Jack spent the trip engrossed with Kathleen's management of his son, accepting her deft expertise as vindication of his own judgement. She seemed to know what the infant needed even before he cried, and she kept him amused when the coach jolted over rough patches in the road. More than once, Jack caught her looking at him, but as soon as he met her eyes, they flicked away and her full lips curled into a surreptitious smile. She was anxious only when the stage stopped at a depot; as soon as the horses came to a halt, she reached for the lever and flung open the door, carefully but quickly stepping down and disappearing into the station house. At the third stop, when the driver gruffly asked him where the young woman might be, Jack realized that she must be changing and feeding the baby. The intimacy excited him as part of the adventure of the trip, and he became even more impressed with the masterful daring that he was displaying by taking his tiny son away from the comfortable, established routine in the Sacramento Street house. As the coach pulled away, he leaned over, feeling bravely unconventional, and assured Kathleen that because they were the only passengers, she might, discreetly of course, offer the baby nourishment whenever he seemed to want it. Her eyes grew wide and her cheeks flushed as she nodded. Two hours later, she buttoned her cloak all the way up to her neck, drew in her arms, leaving the sleeves hanging empty, brought Frederick into the dark shelter she had created, and, after some quick, efficient fumbling, settled back into her seat, her eyes fixed firmly on the passing view. Jack conspired with the little drama, glancing from window to window as he had done since they left San Francisco, and giving no sign that he had noticed anything the least bit unusual.

As they pulled into Colfax, Jack noticed that the stores and stables were gaily decorated; red, white and blue bunting hung from every cornice, post and archway, and the roof top corners sported clusters of American flags. The coach drew up next to the railroad station, where a crowd was surging toward the Central Pacific platform. Jack helped Kathleen descend and hurried her down the walkway.

A small train, only four cars, the engine with steam up, was waiting in front of the station. Another train sat on the spur that led to the Narrow Gauge line, and people were climbing down from the cars to walk across the tracks towards the main platform. Jack found someone he knew, a dry goods merchant who owned a shop on Mill Street, and he asked what the occasion might be.

The man raised his eyebrows. "You don't know? General Grant is on his way to Sacramento. He's going to meet the Governor, and they'll light up the Capitol for him. Four hundred of us came over from Grass Valley to get a look." A thundering tattoo cut him off, and the Nevada Light Guard marched around the corner in rigid lines, approaching so relentlessly that the people on the platform swayed back to give them room. Jack, still pulling Kathleen behind him, managed to work his way to the front of the crowd, and just as he got there, a door opened onto the tiny observation platform at the rear of the last Pullman.

A burly man stepped out into the sunlight. He was wearing a severe suit, a broad-brimmed hat and a grizzled beard, and he saluted as the Light Guard passed in formation. Their captain barked, and they marched in place. He barked again, and again, until they had stopped, turned to face the train, come to attention and presented arms. The drums ceased, leaving a dead silence. A woman next to Jack was asking her escort where the President was when someone shouted "Three cheers for General Grant!" The people responded willingly, and the men waved their hats at the weary, sagging man looking down at them.

He descended from his car and walked up and down the ranks so the delighted captain could introduce him to each man. Some saluted, some offered their hands, and some simply stood at attention, paralyzed. He passed along the front of the crowd of well-wishers, shaking hands, acknowledging curtseys, and accepting greetings. As he drew nearer, Jack noticed that he was nodding almost mechanically, wearing a slight smile that was incongruous with a concerned expression in his eyes that Jack decided must be ingrained or habitual. He spoke quietly to anyone who addressed him, but he seemed not to hear the specifics; when one man grabbed his hand and implored him to run for President again in 1880, the General responded,

"Ah, yes, yes." Then he was before them. Kathleen curtseyed and displayed Frederick, who brought up a wet bubble; the General said, "Thank you, thank you." Jack shook his hand and made some commonplace remark about welcoming him to California. For that brief moment of contact, he looked into the General's eyes. They were completely black, the iris blending into the pupil and creating an impenetrable opacity like an abandoned shaft on a dark night. Jack tried to see the whole face, but in spite of the quiet murmur, he felt as though there was no one standing in front of him.

When their train pulled into the yard on Cemetery Hill, Jack hired a carriage to take them into town. He left Kathleen and the baby in a comfortable room at the Holbrooke and went to rent a horse at the livery stable. Susan's house seemed deserted, so he continued up the slope to Zennora's home, climbed the porch steps and knocked on the door.

Joseph answered. He wore a beard now, so full and long that he reminded Jack of some of the prospectors he had known twenty years earlier. The eyes were the same, though, shy and wary, as though looking for what might come around the corner. Jack shook his hand and made some remark about the old bachelor finally getting married, but his cousin hesitated, apparently uncertain as to whether he was hearing a joke or a warning. Then he smiled and suggested that Jack come inside.

Zennora and Susan were sitting on footstools in the parlor and sewing on either side of a man's dress coat draped over a dress form. Zennora rose and went to him, holding her needle and thread carefully to one side as she returned his embrace with her free arm and offered him a cheek to kiss. He looked down at Susan, still taking neat, even stitches to join the lining to the inside of the coat.

"Hello, Susan."

She looked up at him and smiled. "Hello, Jack." She glanced past him to the entry way and returned to her work. "Where's Clara?"

"She's still not well enough to travel. But I brought Frederick with me."

Susan stopped and sat up straight. "The baby?" Jack nodded. "To bring a baby all this way! And who'll take care of 'im? Where 'ave ye left 'im now?"

"He's at the Holbrooke with Kathleen."

"Kathleen?"

"The nursemaid." Susan shook her head and checked a row of pins. "She's fine with him, Susan. She's been looking after him since he was born."

Susan spoke through two pins that she had placed between her lips. "'e should be with 'is mother."

Zennora put a gentle hand on Jack's shoulder. "I'm sure she's a fine girl.

Ye must bring 'er and th' baby t' supper tonight." Susan glanced up at her mother, but said nothing.

That evening, Jack engaged the wary curiosity of Susan's children by pulling up in front of Zennora's house in an old-fashioned, closed landau with the top up. James and Bertie, now thirteen and fifteen, ran down the walk to hold the front horses, standing nonchalantly while Jack unfolded the steps for Kathleen and reached into the front seat for a hoop-handled basket full of bags of raisins. Everyone took turns with Frederick while Kathleen sat quietly in a corner watching carefully, always ready with a rattle or a clean rag. When he began to fret, she retrieved him from one of his young cousins and followed Zennora upstairs. Jack noticed Susan standing in the kitchen doorway and following Kathleen with a strange expression on her face, but when she realized that Jack was watching her, she pursed her lips and returned to the kitchen, where she had adamantly spent most of the evening. He followed her, but the room seemed full of children hanging on her skirts or carrying dishes from cupboard to table and back again.

The wedding was a small one. Aside from the immediate families, there was no one there that Jack knew; the only other guests were a few awkward young men, wage-earning miners that Joseph had met at the Idaho. The bride, Katie Pengelly, was hardly more than a girl, scarcely eighteen, with a perfectly round face encircling two round eyes that seemed to pop out from under her brows until she laughed, shutting her eyelids tightly and throwing her head back to squeal in delight. Jack watched her huddling and giggling with her two younger sisters, and he tried not to imagine how Joseph, just thirty but always so willing to be led, would adjust to living with so childish a wife. As he accepted a glass of punch from Zennora, he asked blandly where the young couple would live, and she replied that they would stay on with her. The house was so big, and she would be alone without them, so the arrangement seemed ideal. Jack looked over at the tittering bride, then down into his aunt's face, snagged for a moment by her mermaid's eyes, the colors shifting and blurring like the sea, and he had to blink twice to pull back, look more cautiously, and realize that Zennora knew perfectly well that Joseph and Katie could never manage on their own.

Susan stood in the kitchen doorway, watching the little party with her mouth set in a thin, straight line. She had given herself to the wedding preparations, and whenever he mentioned Hannibal, or Jesse, or Nick, she had found a garland to hang or a child's dress to iron. Now, as he approached, she stood her ground, neither retreating nor finding something pressing to do, and looked up at him with one eyebrow raised.

"You must be tired," he said.

She smiled ruefully and shook her head. "'ow else could I be?"

Cousin Jack

They looked back towards the parlor, and Jack tried again. "They look like a happy couple."

She gave the smallest possible laugh, or perhaps a snicker: just a wisp of air through her nose. "Isn't everyone on th' day they marry?" Then, ambiguously: "I'm sorry." She sighed. "I 'ope they'll be all right."

"Why wouldn't they be?"

She appraised him. "I sometimes wonder if ye're as foolish as ye let on. They're children, the pair of 'em."

"You were eighteen when you married Hannibal." She shrugged. "You're but thirty-four now."

She seemed genuinely startled. "Is that all?" she asked quietly, and he thought her eyes began to fill with tears.

"Anyway, Joseph's a grown man. A miner."

She shook her head again. "'e's 'ardly a boy. 'e'd be lost without Mother." She cleared her throat. "Did ye know that Fayther threatened t' kill 'im?"

"No."

She nodded. "It was just before they took 'im away. I'd never seen 'im like that. Wild. 'e told Joseph that 'e knew 'e was tryin' t' poison 'im, and 'e took 'is axe an' smashed the water bucket all t' pieces. Joseph thought 'e would come for 'im next, and so did I, but 'e threw the axe down and went out t' th' shed. Joseph was always nag-ridden when 'e was little, after Fayther left us back in Camborne, but I've never seen 'im creemin' the way 'e did that day. Shakin' all over. And th' look on 'is face when 'e and Hannibal took Fayther into th' coach for th' ride t' Stockton. There 'e was, sittin' right between 'em, and I could see the sweat runnin' down Joseph's face."

"Well, raising a family settles most people."

She bit her lip. "Katie may bear th' children, but Mother'll be raisin' 'em."

"You've been through a lot."

She looked at Jack as though just realizing that he had been standing there. "And what d' you care about it?" She walked out into the parlor to gather empty cups on a tray and tie up the ribbon that was falling out of little Sarah's hair.

Jack returned to Zennora's house the next morning. His aunt cuddled Frederick while Jack tried to make conversation with the newlyweds. Joseph sat as if dazed, his pale grey eyes focusing on nothing and his face hidden behind the dark beard. Katie's cheeks were so pink that Jack wondered whether she might be using a bit of rouge. She seemed obscurely annoyed and resentful, and when Joseph rose to pour himself a cup of tea, she scolded him sharply for not asking her to do it for him. He settled back into his chair, his head nodding so that he seemed to be studying his knees.

The Highwayman, 1879

Jack left the baby with Kathleen and Zennora, and walked down the street to say good-bye to Susan. Out in the yard, Bertie was sitting on a tree branch and taunting James and Martin, who were trying to collect acorns. Susan answered the door, a broom in her hand, pausing just long enough to concede that Jack might come in. She continued with her house cleaning, Jane following her with a bucket and Sarah with a dust rag. She showed no inclination to sit and talk, and when Jack tried to apologize for having annoyed her the day before, she asked him what he had said, as though she could not quite hear him, and when he repeated it, she insisted that she didn't know what he was talking about. After ten minutes, Jack gave up.

Impatient to leave, Jack collected Kathleen and Frederick from Zennora's, drove back to town, and checked out of the Holbrooke. The clerk informed him that he was too late for the last train to Colfax, so he bought tickets on the next stage, a line connecting through Auburn to Sacramento. The coach didn't leave until after sundown, a night "special," and as they drove down towards Wolf Creek, the first stars were twinkling in the eastern sky, and the full moon shone just above the horizon.

They had just started to climb up from the Bear River when the stage slowed and lurched to a stop. Jack looked out the window and saw, standing in the moonlight, the muffled figure of a man. He was wearing a dirty linen duster with only two or three buttons fastened so that the hem fell carelessly about his ankles, but instead of a hat, he wore a flour sack that completely covered his face and head except for the two small eye holes. He cradled a double-barreled shotgun, steadily aiming it straight at the driver.

"Throw down the box!"

His voice was hoarse but deep, as though resounding lazily down an abandoned shaft, but he spoke quietly, almost gently. Jack looked around eagerly but saw neither accomplices surrounding the stage nor a horse tethered nearby to aid the bandit's escape. The man must have simply waited for them behind a ledge and stepped out at the appropriate moment, standing there with full confidence that the driver would stop and, under the calm menace of the shotgun, do what he was told.

The driver hesitated for a moment, but the highwayman lifted his shotgun to settle the stock into his shoulder, the better to take accurate aim. At once, the driver twisted around on his seat to fumble with the ropes holding the Wells, Fargo box onto the shelf behind him. The bandit turned his head slightly and called, "If he dares to shoot, give him a volley, boys!" The driver started and crouched down, scanning the hillside. Jack followed his gaze into the clumps of manzanita, indeterminate dark shapes in the soft, cold light. He began to breathe faster, for he was certain that he saw three or four rifle barrels trained at the coach. The driver scuffled, hurrying now, and a moment later, he dropped the metal box over the side and into the soft earth

Cousin Jack

below. He reached for the mail bags and tossed them out as well. The bandit walked forward and crouched down next to the box, keeping his shotgun aimed at the driver, who sat quite still on his bench.

Jack felt Kathleen's cheek next to his, and he heard her whisper, right next to his ear and so softly that he could barely hear her, "What's wrong with 'is feet?" He peered through the gloom at the oversized, heavy socks pulled over his boots. For a moment, he puzzled over the strange footwear, but then he realized what it must mean, so he turned his head and whispered back, "He's trying to hide his footprints." The wrapped boots would leave no identifying heel or toe marks, and all a lawman would find would be implausibly large, vague impressions in the damp earth.

With his free hand, the bandit was sorting through the box. He set aside two canvas bags that seemed heavier than their small size would indicate, and Jack guessed that they must contain gold coins from one of the banks, or possibly gold dust from an assay office in Nevada City. He took out a hunting knife, slashed each leather mail bag with two quick cuts, pushed through their contents, and took a parcel from one of them.

Jack suddenly realized that the highwayman would surely demand the passengers' valuables. For a moment, he considered resistance, but decided that he could not afford that luxury. He reached into his inner coat pocket and withdrew his wallet, a finely-tooled fold made of soft cowhide. He whispered to Kathleen that she should give him her purse. Her mouth fell open slightly, then her lips set petulantly, as though annoyed with him. Frederick stirred in her arms. She looked down at him for a moment, and fumbled to find a simple little rag with a drawstring; Jack guessed that it probably held only a few silver coins. He dropped his wallet into it, drew the cords tight, and handed it back to Kathleen, indicating with a glance the open window. She leaned over and pushed it over the edge.

The bandit rose, still holding the shotgun in his right hand, his coat pockets now sagging heavily. He turned and noticed the bedraggled purse sitting in the mud next to the stage. He stepped over and picked it up, held it in the palm of his gloved hand as though weighing it, and looked up to the window, where both Jack and Kathleen were peering out at him, fascinated, afraid. He extended his arm, offering the purse to Kathleen. "I don't wish your money, ma'am." She took the little bag, too frightened to respond.

The bandit moved back from the stage and waved his shotgun up at the seat in front. "Drive on," he rasped. Immediately, the driver flicked his whip and the horses, startled from their doze, broke into a brief trot, slowing to a plodding walk when they discovered the angle of the slope they were climbing. Jack looked back; the muffled man waited until the stage had passed, then turned and disappeared into the shadows of the chaparral.

The Highwayman, 1879

The stage continued for about a hundred yards and stopped again. There was no sound except for the breathing of the horses. After a long moment, the driver climbed down from his seat and walked slowly and warily back to where they had stopped before. In the dim light, Jack could barely see him bending over the metal box; he seemed to be filling it with the bags and parcels that the bandit had disdained. The driver looked up suddenly and made as if to run back to the stage, but hesitated. He stared into the underbrush for a full sixty seconds, then crept forward, moving in the direction that the highwayman had taken, and disappeared behind a broad clump of manzanita. Jack held his breath, waiting. He heard an ejaculation, and the driver returned to the wagon trace and shouldered the box. When he reached the window, he stopped. "Look a' that!" He held up a long, straight stick, stripped of its bark so it shone in the moonlight. "There's one o' his confed'rates!" The robber had apparently wedged the sticks into rocks and bushes to fool the driver into thinking he had a band of men supporting him. "And here—see what you can make o' that! I found it layin' in the box!" Jack took the piece of dirty paper and unfolded it. There were words scrawled on it in letters dark enough that he could just decipher it if he held it at the right angle. The writing was eccentric, leaning to the left in the first line and to the right in the second. Jack read the words aloud.

> here I lay me down to Sleep
> to wait the coming morrow
> perhaps Success, perhaps defeat
> And everlasting sorrow
>
> I've labored long and hard for bred
> for honor and for riches
> But on my corns too long you've tred
> You fine haired Sons of Bitches
>
> let come what will, I'll try it on
> My condition can't be worse
> and if there's money in that Box
> tis munny in my purse.

The doggerel was signed, "Black Bart, Po8."

The driver snorted, shook his head, and spat into the mud at his feet. "Two thousand, easy! And him crack-brained!" With that, he climbed back up to the front of the stage and called to the horses. The stage lurched and slipped, and dragged up the hill.

They arrived in the capital late at night, slept for a few hours in a waterfront hotel, and continued on to San Francisco by steamship. It was mid-afternoon when they finally reached the house on Sacramento Street. The cabbie brought their bags in as Jack stood in the hallway taking off his traveling coat and staring at his tired, dirty face in the mirror. He heard a sniffle, and he turned to find Mary standing at the base of the stairs. "Oh, Maister Trevenna!"

"What is it?"

"It's the missus, sur. She's not well, sur, not at all. The doctor just left."

Jack took the stairs two at a time, strode down the hall and threw open the door to Clara's room. The air was so fetid that his gorge rose, but he controlled himself and walked over to the bed, piled high with blankets and quilts. Clara's cheeks were red and her sunken face was mottled as though she had a rash lying beneath the surface. Her lips hung slightly open, her breath came in small gasps, and a dribble of saliva ran down from the corner of her mouth into the pillow. Jack heard a footstep behind him, and he turned his head to see Kathleen standing the doorway with Frederick in her arms. He reached with his little hands and began to cry.

"Take him to the nursery."

He looked down at Clara, drew a chair to her bedside, and sat down. After a few minutes, he reached into his coat pocket, brought out a handkerchief, and held it over his nose and mouth like a loose mask. He shut his eyes, feeling the warm, moist lids and watching the patterns of light in the darkness. He waited.

19
The Hydraulickers
1882-84

Susan walked down the dirt path that ran between the empty street and the still houses. Bare branches stretched out overhead, motionless in the silent air, and a layer of grey hung low in the sky, a soft, inscrutable ceiling with neither shape nor texture. Wolf Creek ran quietly, deep in its channel beneath the footbridge, the thin stream waiting for the rain that should begin any day now. The morning was cold for late November, and she drew her scarf up over her chin and mouth.

At the drug store, Loutzenheiser himself was standing behind the counter, his mustaches and eyebrows bristling and his thinning hair combed slick across his head. He wrapped up a book and a bundle of stationery for a man in a brown suit, saw him to the door, and turned to greet Susan. She had come for a cough mixture for Jane, and while the apothecary blended it, she wandered aimlessly through the narrow room. The jars of medicines and pills sat in neat rows on small shelves high above and behind the proprietor's counter, while beneath them were collections of bottles: alcohol, camphor, castor oil and glycerine. Another cabinet displayed assortments of patent medicines: Jaynes' elixir, Hoffman's anodyne and Kennedy's medical discovery. The brown bottles with their florid labels reminded her of Hannibal, so she turned and walked to the other side of the room, to deep shelves holding cans of varnish and tubs of paint base, with packets of ochre, umber, sienna, viridian, chromium and charcoal sorted in tiny bins. There were brushes of all sizes, some wide enough to paint a wall, and others small enough for fine detail work on porch decorations. At the far end of the store were boxes of paper and stationery cut in various sizes and ranging from pure white to buff to various shades of pale lavender, rose and faded green. Some of the envelopes had an extra layer inside, shiny paper with tiny repeating patterns printed in saturated colors. Near the paper boxes were small bottles of ink—black, blue, purple and green—and an assortment of pens. In the corner, she found a small arrangement of books: manuals of etiquette, advice on housekeeping, and studies of the geology of the mining region. She scanned the titles absent-mindedly until one held her attention: *A History of England.* She stood on her tiptoes, reached, and eased it down from the shelf. Scattered throughout the text was a series of engravings, mostly of historical landmarks in London, but as she riffled through the pages, the book fell open to an image of St. Michael's Mount. The artist had let his fancy run, for it was a view that only an adventuresome seagull could have enjoyed as she sailed high in the air several hundred yards off the coast, looking past the Mount to Mousehole and Penzance in the encircling bay. Susan stared down at the picture for several minutes. "Mrs. Carne!" She started, closed the book, replaced it on the shelf, walked back to the apothecary's counter, paid him, put the bottle in her bag, and walked out onto Main Street.

The planking was splintered and warped; the green lumber had dried in the hot summers, contracted in the winter cold and swollen with the rain and snow. Brittle in the cold air, the boards felt hard and fickle under Susan's shoes. She walked past Terrill's liquors and Silvester's general store, then paused to wait for a horse and buggy to pass. The brick storefronts on the south side of the street had lost the raw quality that had nettled her twenty years before; the signs had weathered and the doors had settled into their frames. She gazed across at the façades and realized that the more they aged, the more they reminded her of Camborne, even though most of the downtown shops would have been built of grey stone rather than red clay. Comforted, she stepped out onto the cold, red dust to cross over to Watt & Granger's market.

The clerk greeted her deferentially, closing the door behind her and escorting her through the store as she selected provisions for the coming week. There were large sacks: coarse burlap full of potatoes for baking and roasting (she checked them carefully for soft spots and sprouting eyes), and fine muslin holding flour for baking bread. There were smaller sacks: rice (to vary with the potatoes, in spite of her mother's cavilling), sugar for flavoring pies, biscuits and sauces, and salt for curing meat and doing the baking. She indicated different kinds of soap for washing clothes, dishes and people, and settled on a large tub of lard, for making crust, and a smaller one of butter. She paused at the bins of citron, raisins, and currants, but decided that the holiday season was still too far away and took, instead, a few packets of tea.

The clerk stayed at Mrs. Carne's elbow, directing his stock boy to collect her goods and sometimes anticipating her pointing finger. Then he ushered her to the counter, scribbled a quick tally and presented it for her approval. She scanned the list, added the figures in her head, and took the proffered pen to sign her name. The clerk scurried around the counter, waited while she adjusted her gloves and scarf, then opened the door and bowed her out. She had not given him instructions concerning delivery, but he knew that she would expect to receive her purchases that very afternoon, and his employers, who had done business with the late Mr. Carne, regarded the service as merely routine.

The Hydraulickers, 1882-84

Susan knew that she should go home, but she could not, would not return just yet. The house was stifling in these late autumn days, with all the doors and windows shut against the cold. Bertie and James had gone to work and the younger children were all at school, leaving only the maid. She felt, for a moment, free, with no immediate responsibilities or obligations, so she turned left on Mill Street and walked along the east side until she could stop to look across at Johnston's hardware store in the building that Jack owned.

Jack had visited Grass Valley only a few weeks earlier, and they had quarreled. She had asked him why he kept the store, and he had answered facetiously, assuring her that when all of his business interests in San Francisco had failed and his family had lost patience with him, he would move into the back room and become one of those old men that amble down the street at odd hours, stopping to stare at the sky and shake a stick at passers-by, who seem to live only to provide local amusement and topics for saloon conversations. Susan had lost her temper, demanding to know why he never took her seriously, and he had withdrawn, refusing to leave her house and end the visit, but declining to address her questions, his face going sullenly blank. The conversation finally became merely formal, as between two acquaintances, and after a suitable interval, he took his hat and said good-bye. The store annoyed her, although she could not say why; it was just another brick storefront crowned with brash, pointless battlements.

She walked on, crossing the street to avoid Cryer's Billiards Saloon even though it was too early for any of the men to be standing in the doorway. She stopped at the corner of Neal to gaze up at Edward Sterling's white verandah, then turned to continue south into Boston Ravine. When she reached the bridge across Wolf Creek, she paused to consider the slope of Massachusetts Hill. A breath of chilly air drifted down from the crest and freshened, making her eyes water. French Lead was at least a mile away, and most of the path ran up hill. She turned the other way, crossed the bridge, and walked home.

She closed the door heavily behind her, pushing it past the point where it always stuck in the cold weather, and stood in the entry hall. Above, she could hear footsteps, a short series of taps, then a pause, and around again; the maid was changing the bed linens. Susan walked into the parlor, still wearing her hat and coat, and stared out the window. She closed her eyes, listening to the light, capricious wind whispering past the eaves. When the grocer's wagon arrived that afternoon, she would have to sort out the food and supplies, but until then, she had little to do. On other idle days, she had considered dismissing the maid, but she had become accustomed to having someone else do the cleaning, and although running the house by herself would save a little money, she really had no ideas on how to spend it. She slowly unpinned her hat, considering the hours that lay before her. She could walk up to her mother's house, but she sighed at the idea of watching Katie snap at her crying babies. She thought that she might read one of Jesse's books. Joseph had brought them down in a crate, and it remained where he had left it, a heavy obstacle that prevented the kitchen door from opening all the way. Even the unpacking would occupy the rest of the morning, but then she would have to find a shelf for the dusty volumes. She unbuttoned her coat, meticulously patting each buttonhole back into place.

Jack came to visit again in December, arriving on the second Sunday of Advent. Susan hadn't planned to fix supper for the entire family, but by evening, they had all accumulated in her house, and while she, grumbling, lifted her larger soup pot onto the stove, Zennora assigned a task to each child. At the end of the evening, Jack paused in the entry hall, settling his hat on his head while Kathleen took Frederick down the walk to the buggy.

"I'd like to take you to dinner tomorrow night."

"Take me t' dinner?"

"Iss fay." He grinned. "Down at the Holbrooke. When was the last time you didn't have to cook for everyone else?"

"What about th' children?"

"Zennora says she'll take care of yours, and Kathleen can take care of Fred in their room at the hotel."

The invitation seemed nonsensical, but she could not articulate a reason why she should not accept, so late the following afternoon, she rode off in Jack's buggy, waving at the family clustered in the doorway, Jane holding Ernest's hand and Sarah leaning on her grandmother.

The dining room at the Holbrooke seemed entirely foreign to her: the table linens, the silver service, the polite waiter, and the other guests, calmly and effortlessly eating and talking as if completely unaware that Susan did not belong there. As though they were only newly acquainted, Jack gently encouraged her to tell about her children: how old they were, the names of their teachers, Martin's first pair of long trousers. By the time they were halfway through dinner, Susan realized that she was chattering freely about Ernest's broken arm and Sarah's triumph in the spelling bee, and she stopped in mid-sentence, certain that she must be boring him, but he was smiling and nodding, his eyes on hers, taking in every word. She gave up trying to be careful and talked on, now asking Jack about his own children, growing up without their mother. He made light of their situation, depicting himself neither as a bereft widower nor as the head of the household, but as a sort of awkwardly permanent guest in a home run for his three children by three servant women. He insisted on ordering her a large square of gingerbread, and when it arrived, hot from the oven, the scent of molasses stung her nose. She laughed, and Jack smiled at her as he poured the coffee.

He drove her home, letting the horses amble, and when they had pulled up in front of her gate, he turned to her. "I'm driving out to the South Yuba tomorrow. Would you like to come?"

"What for?"

"There's a dam out there I'd like to see. We can be back before your children finish school."

This time, she did not even grope for a reason to refuse, and when she walked into her warm house to find Zennora sitting by the fire reading to Ernest and Sarah, she realized that it was all right.

They left soon after breakfast the next day and reached the dam in just over an hour, parking above a slope that inclined, steeper and steeper, down into the rocky gorge. Susan stayed in her seat, warm in her heavy coat, with the coach blanket tucked around her hips and piled up on her feet, while Jack climbed down and walked a few paces away to stand and gaze down at the river below and the dam that sought to control it.

"What's it for?" she asked.

He looked back over his shoulder. "Tailings. Some of the farmers in the valley sued the mining companies for dumping their overflow into the rivers."

"What's wrong with that?"

He walked back and stood next to the buggy. "The farmers say that the slickens, the silt and slurry, carry all the way down to the valley, especially after the winter rains and the spring snowmelt. The slickens fill up the riverbeds, they overflow, and the fields flood."

"Is that true?"

Jack shrugged. "The hydraulic men say that the riverbeds have been filling up since before white men started farming down there."

"Why don't they try leavin' the river alone for a few years t' find out what would 'appen?"

He smiled. "That means shutting down the hydraulic mines."

"Let 'em dump their slickens somewhere else."

"Where?"

"I don't know. There must be 'undreds of abandoned mine shafts up in the 'ills. They could fill 'em up."

"You've seen a monitor at work. They wash down a whole hillside in a matter of weeks, and everything carries downstream. They'd have to catch the dirt and the rock, load it into cars, and haul it to these shafts of yours. They'd never do it."

"I remember what Hannibal told me about th' flood in Marysville."

"That was one of the worst winters we've ever had."

"But what if the riverbed 'ad been deeper?"

Jack nodded. "That's one idea—to dredge out the river."

"And where would they dump th' silt? Aren't there fields runnin' right up t' th' river?"

He sighed. "That's the problem. The farmers don't want anyone to unload the sand on their fields, and they don't want to pay for the dredging anyway."

"And why should they? They'd be payin' to haul away the miners' mess."

He grinned at her. "Let the men in Grass Valley hear you talk, they'll say you've betrayed them. Why are you so worried about the farmers?"

"Don't you laugh at me. The miners want someone else t' clean up after 'em. Are you sayin' that's all right?"

He looked at her, seriously now, for a long moment. "Well, if these debris dams work, then the tailings'll stop here." He looked down at the dam again, and back at her. "Let's drive back for lunch."

Jack stayed in San Francisco for Christmas. Susan attended church services, pulled hot saffron loaves out of the oven, and kept excited children entertained, and although it seemed that she scarcely finished one task before the next crowded upon her, she found that there were moments of pause, precious intervals as she leaned back to let the steam rise out of a pasty or waited for a child to button a coat, when she glanced at the front door, thinking that Jack might knock.

On New Year's Day, the temperature dropped below freezing and stayed there. Joseph went all over Susan's house and Zennora's, wrapping exposed water pipes and tapping the fittings for soundness, but early one morning after a week of relentless cold, Susan went to fill a pan and only a few drops fell from the tap. She walked up to Zennora's house, but her mother had no water either. The flumes had frozen, and one, bringing water into town from the hills near Red Dog, had cracked and broken. When the water pressure returned that afternoon, Susan and Zennora filled every bottle, jar, pot and pan they could find, and on the next morning they were glad, because once again, the water supply had failed. Two days later, a piercing wind swept down through the valleys from the Sierra crest, carrying the chill of the deep snow pack. A whole row of telegraph poles fell before the blast, cutting the line, and across the street from the lumber yard, an old willow collapsed, providing a makeshift bridge for squirrels if any dared to come out of their holes and try to cross the creek. Susan kept the children home from school, and they huddled before the fire in the parlor, reading stories to each other and trying to stay warm.

A new storm blew in from the northwest, and the temperature rose, but just barely enough so that the heavy, dark clouds released not a blizzard but torrents of icy rain. The house seemed even colder than before, and the family sat around the parlor fire, sometimes gazing raptly out the front window at the sheets of rain that attacked the porch and slashed across the street. On the fifth day, the rain fell even harder than before, so furiously that they could hear it pounding the roof. She sent the older boys up to the attic to check for leaks, and when little Ernest insisted on helping, his brothers wrapped him in a cloak and carried him across the rafters, lowering him down to crawl into the corners where only he was small enough to fit. They returned, with dusty elbows and red knuckles, to report that the attic was surprisingly dry, and Susan silently thought of Hannibal, who had supervised the carpenters so closely that two of them actually walked off the job. She had offered no encouragement then; now she wanted to thank him.

The boys had just finished cleaning up when there was a knock at the door. It was a man, muffled in coat and cloak, and apparently wet clear through, for as he stood in the entry hall stamping his feet, he left a puddle on the floor. He unwrapped his muffler, and there was Jack grinning at her. She sent him upstairs with the boys to change out of his wet things, and fifteen minutes later, he was settled in front of the fire, wearing an old suit of Hannibal's, a blanket around his shoulders and a mug of chicken broth in his hands, his hair slicked back on his head and his mustache bristling as it dried.

Susan asked him why he had come in such a storm.

He actually chuckled. "Only a fool, eh? Well, I have an excuse. I came *because* of the storm."

"Why?"

"I'm here to inspect the debris dams on the South Yuba, and I'll check the ones on the Bear River on my way back. Remember that dam we saw up near Purdon's Bridge? Well, it's overflowing, and it's breached in at least four different places."

"Oh, Jack. So it's no good."

He took another sip of broth. "Oh, I don't know about that. Even the older men, the ones who came in '49, don't remember a storm like this. If this is the worst we'll ever see, the dams aren't doing too badly. The men'll mend them in the summer." He saw the wary skepticism in her face. "Besides, Susan, dams or no dams, Marysville'd still be taking the runoff."

James cleared his throat. "Is th' valley flooded?"

Jack nodded. "Iss fay. It is indeed." He looked concerned. "The farmers have moved their stock to higher ground, but I'm afraid some of the animals won't survive the cold and wet."

Bertie spoke up. "How is it that you come up to inspect the dams?"

"You mean, why me?" He grinned at the boy, enjoying his awkward gravity. "Well, some of the men in San Francisco seem to think I know something about mining. The dams were built to catch the tailings from the hydraulic companies, so I must know something about dams, too. Never mind that I'm a hard-rock man—the bankers don't know a sledge from a monitor. Anyway, they sent me up to see what's what."

"What about the slickens?" asked Susan.

Jack shook his head. "There'll be a good layer of silt left in the fields near the riverbed."

"Then the dams didn't 'elp at all."

"No, that's what I'm saying. There's just too much water. Dams or no dams, the Yuba would have brought the slickens down."

Susan thought for a moment. "Well, that's that, then. They'll have t' shut down the mines."

Jack turned his head to gaze into the fire. "Well, p'raps you're right. But it's a tricky choice—the farms or the mines. Either way, you're looking at a skuat o' money, and some important men."

Susan hesitated, frowning. "What about the river?"

"What about it?" He was genuinely puzzled. "The water's there for us to use. It's just a question of who uses it, and what for."

"But what if the tailin's fill it up? What if there's no more river?"

He chuckled. "Bring her a cup o' broth! 'as yer 'ead gone crum wi' th' cold? The rain will fall, the snow will melt, and the water will find its way out of the mountains and down to the valley. There'll always be a river."

She stared into the fire, troubled. "Mother's seen whole 'illsides washin' down because the miners and the lumber men 'ave taken out the trees."

Jack shrugged. "I don't know what you're talking about."

They made a bed for him in the parlor. Susan lay awake, exhausted but preoccupied with the image of the turbulent brown torrent pouring over the broken dam and carrying its load down the gorge to the waiting valley. Towards midnight, she dozed, but she awoke suddenly, feeling sure that she had heard something. She lifted her head and listened, and she heard it again: a cough. The cough came again and again, until she rose, wrapped her robe around her, lit a candle, and walked down the hall to where her daughters slept. Jane's eyes caught the flickering light and turned away as she coughed again. Susan took her down to her own room, away from Sarah, and listened to the cough grow deeper as the dawn approached.

Jane had had the whooping cough before, when she was younger, but she was sixteen now, nearly grown, too old for a child's disease. The women sequestered her in Susan's bedroom, keeping the younger children away, and for two weeks, the girl lay there, uncomplaining, her cheeks pink with the fever, and convulsed with the coughing fits. Her mother and grandmother took turns sitting with her, sometimes all night, wringing out warm, damp rags to wipe her mouth and chin. She had no appetite and was scarcely thirsty, but she obediently ate biscuits and drank hot broth. Just when Susan was beginning to think that her daughter would always be this ill, never thriving, never declining, the coughing slackened and the fever disappeared, and a few days later, Jane was on her feet again, quietly helping with the younger children, a little thinner than before, but otherwise the same.

In the spring, Jack's status as an expert mining consultant became official, for he was one of a dozen men appointed to serve on a committee that would study and assess the controversy over hydraulic mining and make recommendations to the state legislature. He still made light of the governor's judgement in asking a hard-rock man to present advice on hydraulic matters, but he was clearly proud of the honor. The other committee members were mostly bankers, a few of the governor's political allies, and a Frenchman who had once been involved with the North Bloomfield company.

"Are there no farmers?" asked Susan.

"Well, not really. But no real miners, either—just me and the Frenchman." He was not sure how many, if any, of his associates, had interests in mining or farming. "I wouldn't be surprised if some of them hold stock in the mines. It's all traded in San Francisco now, and I believe one man made his pile when Crown Point went sky high. What difference does it make?"

"Jack—if they 'old stock in th' mines, then they own th' mines."

"Well, yes, in a way, but they don't manage them. These men hold stock in all sorts of things."

"In farming?"

"Farms aren't companies; you can't buy stock in them."

"What about farm land?"

"I know a few men who own farm land and rent it out, but it's not very profitable."

"What ye're tellin' me is that this committee o' yours is more likely t' look after th' mines than th' farms."

"Listen, Susan. The momentum is all on the farmers' side. In the last two months alone, the legislature has looked at four bills on the hydraulic problem, and each and every one of them proposes to shut down the mines. The farmers have found a couple of judges that will issue injunctions against the hydraulic men, telling them they can't dump their tailings in the Bear or the Yuba."

"And why should they? Why should they ruin the river for everyone else? If only bills and injunctions will make 'em stop, then that's as well."

"You don't know they're ruining it."

"Look at th' flooding. Look at th' fields that 'ave gone under."

"Even if they stopped hydraulic operations today, the tailings would keep washing down into the valley for years."

"All th' more reason t' stop it now."

"Why are you so concerned about the river?"

Cousin Jack

"And why are ye so niffed about th' mines? D'ye own stock in North Bloomfield?"

"No."

"Then why are ye doing this?"

He took a breath, paused, and looked away. "It's a big business, Susan. A lot of money. If you shut down companies like North Bloomfield, you'll hurt the whole state. You'll certainly hurt Nevada County. There's a newspaper in Sacramento that calls the farmers the 'Architects of Ruin.'"

"Jack, don't ye think that if th' companies can't dump their slop into the Yuba, they'll find somethin' else t' do with it? They'll keep goin'."

He looked at her for a long moment. "I'm going to a meeting tomorrow night. I'd like you to come with me."

Late the following afternoon, Jack drove up in a small wagon. She settled into her seat and asked what had happened to the buggy he usually rented from the livery stable. He clucked to the horses and remarked that where they were going, it would be better not to show off. He had changed his carefully-tailored city suit for a much shabbier outfit in plain black, with a noticeably worn hat to finish it off. She looked down at her best grey gloves and tucked her hands into the sleeves of her coat.

At the Nevada Theatre, Jack pushed a path through the lobby and into the hall. He led her up and down the aisles and finally found a man who was willing to give up his place. Susan sat down, but reached up to grasp the hem of Jack's coat. "Don't leave me 'ere," she said. He nodded and backed up a pace so he could lean against the wall just a few feet away. Everywhere she looked, men were talking, pointing fingers and shaking fists. There were only a few other women, their faces hard under their cheap hats. No one was smiling. Up on the platform, a burly man with a bristling black beard began to pound a gavel, and gradually, the men subsided. Susan suddenly realized how stuffy and warm the room was, and she began to feel nauseated from the smells around her. She discreetly brought out her handkerchief and held it to her nose.

There were four men on the platform. The first had just ridden in from San Juan Ridge, which was, he announced, practically deserted, for the injunctions had closed so many mines that the men had come to town in search of work, any work, just to feed themselves and their families. When he asked how many of those present had come from the Ridge, half of the men in the hall raised their hands, then applauded themselves. The second man offered a report on the debris dams, which, he assured them, had helped control the usual spring floods in Marysville and had certainly reduced the flow of silt and gravel down into the valley. He argued that the mining companies had met the farming interests more than half way by building the dams, so now the farmers should let the miners get on with their work. The men in the hall stamped their feet and cheered, and Susan looked up to see Jack nodding his head in approval.

The third man spoke very quietly, describing women and children who were going hungry because the mines had closed and their men had no work. "These are honest men, working men. I see many of them here to-night." He let his voice build a slow crescendo. "They're not lazy. They're not strikers. They want to work, but there is no work. The companies want to hire them, but they can't. And why is that?" The men near Susan had been muttering comments to each other, and now they began to call out encouragement to the speaker, whose voice rang out to the corners of the hall. "Because a judge in Marysville—a man the farmers have in their pockets—has issued an injunction. An injunction!" The men began to boo. "It ain't a law—the legislature had nothin' t' do with it—it's just one judge who's lookin' out fer his own!" He sat down, and all through the hall, men jumped to their feet, cheering, whistling, and clapping their hands.

The fourth speaker was the burly dark man. He walked down to the edge of the platform, his jaw set, listening to the roar of angry men and nodding his head. He raised his clenched fist and clapped his hands together, letting the noise go on and on until Susan thought she would have to leave. Then the clamor began to fade, and when it was merely loud, the man on stage cried out in a surprisingly powerful voice, "What are we going to do about it?" They answered with an angry shout. He waited until he could, once again, make himself heard, and bellowed, "Are we going to let them do this to us?" Once again, the men whooped and yelled in reply, and once again he paused, keeping them just below a boil, waiting for his chance. "There's one thing we can do—must do!" The men cheered briefly, listening, anticipating. "We must boycott!" Another cheer. "Everyone in the hills must boycott!" The cheering and stamping built like a wave, rising and falling. Then, almost in a normal tone of voice, he said, "Marysville is more than farmers. If the courts won't listen to us, they'll listen to the merchants and suppliers whose warehouses are full, and whose wagons sit empty at the loading docks." The crowd shouted out their approval. "We can beat 'em!"

With that, the hall broke out into a wild commotion. The men on the platform descended, shaking hands with those near to them, and other men appeared all over the hall to pass out leaflets. Someone thrust one into Susan's hand, and she stared down at the black letters smeared across the top: "BOYCOTT!!!" She wanted to read the rest, but a man pushed past her, nearly knocking her down. She tried to catch her balance, felt a strong hand grab her arm above the elbow, and looked up to see Jack guiding her towards the side door. As soon as she felt the evening air on her cheek, she wanted to stop and breathe, just breathe. They walked back to Jack's wagon and rode back to Grass Valley, neither saying a word.

Cousin Jack

The boycott spread throughout the northern mining towns. Even Grass Valley, where few men were directly involved in hydraulic mining, displayed handbills and placards in shop windows and on brick walls. Chanting men marched in a torchlight rally up and down Mill Street. Everyone Susan met supported the mining companies; no one took any interest in the rivers. In June, she began to hear rumors that the North Bloomfield had put its men back to work, turning their monitors on the hillsides in spite of the injunctions. Soon after that, the *Union* reported triumphantly that the state Supreme Court had dismissed the injunction, finding that the Marysville judge had a personal interest that predisposed him in favor of the farmers. Yet on the very next day, his successor directed the Yuba County sheriff to shut off the hydraulickers' water supply and to serve papers against the mine owners, demanding that they answer charges of acting in contempt of court.

Jack visited Grass Valley at unpredictable intervals, sometimes stopping at Susan's house for less than an hour, sometimes staying for supper, but he had become uncharacteristically discreet, and whenever Susan asked him about the controversy, he managed to change the subject. On one occasion, she didn't know he had come to town at all until she saw him, quite by chance, bent over a table in the Holbrooke's saloon, intent on a heated conversation with a grizzled, shabby man who was smoking a long cigar. She stood on the sidewalk, watching them through the window and feeling like a child spying on a secretive parent.

Susan usually spent Independence Day quietly at home, but this year, Martin and Ernest clamored to go to watch their uncle Joseph compete in the Cornish wrestling match. She appealed to Bertie and James, but they protested prior, pressing commitments, and slipped out of the house before breakfast. By early afternoon, Susan was sitting on a hard wooden bench under the canvas fly of the wrestling ring. Ernest, too short to see over the heads of the men sitting in front of him, was actually jumping up and down in frustration and excitement when the man in the ring announced Joseph's match. Just at that moment, a man swung a leg over the railing and sat down next to her. It was Jack. He grinned and called out something to Joseph, who didn't seem to hear; he was crouched low, his canvas jacket hanging on him, his quiet eyes intent on his opponent. They circled, circled, and reached for each other, and the spectators roared. Jack leaned in close to Susan and shouted, "Half the miners in town are here!" She smiled and nodded. He leaned in again. "Tomorrow they'll really have something to celebrate!"

She looked at him. He seemed to be waiting for a response, so she yelled at him, "What about?"

He smiled and put his mouth right next to her ear so he could speak without bellowing. "Judge Caldwell is going to issue a restraining order against the Yuba County sheriff. He won't let him shut off the water!"

The Hydraulickers, 1882-84

Down in the ring, Joseph hooked his foot behind the other man's ankle and brought him down, but only to a sort of sitting position, and as he bent down to take the advantage, his opponent reached up, grabbed his shoulder, and pulled himself into a crouch. The two broke apart and circled.

Susan turned to Jack. "But the other court told 'im t' do it."

Jack shook his head. "It doesn't matter. This is Nevada County, a different jurisdiction. They'll have to go to the state court in Sacramento."

"So now what happens?"

"Nothing." He grinned, almost mischievously.

The men under the fly roared, and Susan looked in time to see Joseph going down, down, all the way, until he was flat on his back in the sawdust. His opponent helped him up, and the two stood for a moment to acknowledge the applause before Joseph turned abruptly and walked off to where the wrestlers waited their turns. Ernest was now leaning on his mother, burying his face in her shoulder, and Martin was sitting sullenly, slumped on the bench and staring straight ahead. Susan yelled to Jack over the din, "Help me!" He reached across and lifted Ernest, cradling him in his arms as he picked his way down to the end of the section, with Susan following, holding firmly to Martin's hand. Jack kept walking until he found a relatively quiet place between two buildings, then turned and set Ernest down on the ground.

She pulled the wrinkles out of the child's rumpled coat. "It isn't right."

"What?"

"The mining companies can do whatever they please. They didn't like it when th' farmers 'ad a judge 'elpin' 'em out, and now they've one o' their own."

"That's the way it works."

"Where's th' sense in it?"

He nodded gravely. "P'raps none. But both sides will do what they must."

She looked at him carefully. "And which side're you on, Jack?"

His eyes grew wary. "The committee report'll be out in a few months. Then we'll see."

"Ye 'aven't answered my question." She waited, Ernest leaning against her hip.

He shook his head. "It's not simple, Susan, not simple at all." He turned and walked back into the floating dust of the wrestling ring.

The summer swelled, each day hotter than the one before, and the thriving flies became a constant, maddening nuisance. At the end of a particularly torrid day, as Susan and Zennora sat on the porch, their top buttons undone in hopes of catching a breath of evening air, Sarah brought them a pine cone that, as if in a forest fire, had burst. The women probed its recesses with the moist tips of their fingers, searching the empty niches where the nuts had once lain hidden and safe; forlorn cradles. Susan closed her eyes, feeling the sweat and fine dust on her lids, and wondered whether she cared that Jack had not come since the day of the wrestling match. The heat broke with a series of thunderstorms that washed the dust from the fenceposts and awnings, and cool breezes spilled off of the fields of alpine snow that lay peacefully beside sheets of granite, far up in the high country. Still they saw nothing of Jack. Susan hardly noticed the change of the days, and so paused one morning, while helping Jane unpack the woollen blankets, transfixed by the sight—merely ordinary, really—of cold mist drifting over the tops of the houses on Kate Hays Hill. She was stirring a pot of lentil soup that evening when James walked in with the *Union* to announce that Jack's committee had published its findings.

They recommended that the mining companies pay for debris dams in order to protect "agricultural interests," but they urged that all parties suspend litigation, for the competing injunctions, the countervailing lawsuits, and the general interference by attorneys, judges and sheriffs all conspired to prevent the hydraulic men from getting on with their business. While her pot bubbled gently, Susan read the paragraphs again, realizing that the miners were getting exactly what they wanted. True, they would have to build the dams, but the committee had sidestepped the questions of how many dams, and where, and what would constitute acceptable flow of slickings and water. Once the dams were in place, the hydraulickers would get back to washing down the hillsides, self-righteously assuring the public that they had done their duty.

Jack did not come for Christmas, even though Susan, irritably yielding to Zennora's coaxing, had written to invite him. They celebrated quietly— even Katie's new baby nestled comfortably into anyone's arms—but as they were washing the pots and pans, Susan heard Jane cough once, then again, and again. By the following evening, she lay, again, in Susan's bed, restless with fever and coughing uncontrollably. After only a few days, she refused food, so Zennora made a small pot of chicken broth that Susan then spooned into her daughter's mouth, but an hour later, the girl brought it all back up again. Paraphernalia invaded the room: a chamber pot in the corner, an old tin bowl sitting on the floor just below the girl's head, a stack of extra blankets, a pile of clean towels, a basket for soiled ones, an extra pitcher of water, and a rocking chair so Susan and Zennora could take turns, all day and all night, trying to doze while keeping watch. Zennora became so weary that Katie, much to Susan's grateful surprise, quietly insisted that Martin, Sarah and Ernest come to stay with her. She collected their things—changes of clothes, the more cherished toys—and led them in a little parade up the hill, her baby sleeping in her arms and her little boy holding Ernest's hand.

Bertie and James had already found a room in town, so Susan's house was empty except for the maid, the sick girl, and the two women who now lost track of the hours, fighting the scourge with damp cloths and cool fingers. Susan awoke again and again to the sound of her daughter coughing and trying to fill her lungs with air, like a bellows that will not open, and she could no longer remember when any of them had really rested.

Late one morning, Zennora went to answer a knock on the door, and Susan heard her give a surprised little cry. She kept stirring the pot of broth on the stove, listening to the approaching footsteps and voices, and looked up to see Jack standing there, and behind his shoulder, a young woman she had never seen. He leaned in to kiss her on the cheek. "Susan, I'd like you meet Annie Penrose, or rather, Annie Trevenna." He was smiling, but he seemed almost shy and uncertain. "We got married in Truckee yesterday." As soon as she could, Susan retreated upstairs to see to Jane, but she found her sleeping quietly, so, reluctantly, she returned to the parlor. Jack looked worried. "Have you brought Simpson in?"

"There's no need," Susan assured him. "She's 'ad it before, we know what it is, we know what t' do."

Zennora laid a hand on Susan's knee. "P'raps we should send fer 'im."

Susan glanced over at Jack's new wife. She looked to be about eighteen, just Susan's age when she married Hannibal, but Jack was past forty now. The girl seemed quite composed, scanning the room with clear dark eyes. "As ye wish, Mother."

Jack left at once to fetch Simpson, and when the physician finished his examination, he came down the stairs wearing a perturbed expression. "I don't like it, Mrs. Carne, not at all. She shouldn't be having the whooping cough, not again, not at her age, and she's lost too much weight. You must feed her. And I don't like the state of her throat; she could be coming down with diphtheria."

They tried everything they could imagine—broth, biscuits, bits of stewed beef, even a slice of saffron bread and a special pasty that Zennora prepared without any salt pork, thinking that Jane might gag on the succulent fat. Sometimes she would keep a little down, but usually, struggle though she might, she began to bite her lip, perspiration shone at her hairline, and then, helpless, she strained her face over the edge of the mattress to vomit into the tin bowl while Susan or Zennora held her head and wiped her lips with a clean, damp cloth. Her fever rose slightly, and even in the coldest part of the night, just an hour before dawn, Susan found that she had to check to see whether she had kicked off the bedclothes.

Jack and Annie moved into the Holbrooke but spent most of their time at Susan's house, unobtrusively on call. Susan had expected Annie to be an incompetent annoyance, an uninvited interloper posing as a guest, but she trudged down the stairs one afternoon to find her returning from a trip to town, Zennora's grocery list in her hand and Jack following her, his arms loaded with sacks and parcels destined for the kitchen. The girl could cook, and she even took the maid in hand when Susan could not spare the attention. Jack kept his horse hitched to the buggy, always ready to run errands to Loutzenheiser's or the grocer's, or to go for Simpson.

Late one afternoon, Susan plodded downstairs with a pail of soiled towels and surprised Jack muttering to himself and slapping something against his hip. He turned suddenly to look at her, and she gasped a little, for he was glaring angrily. "What is it?"

He lifted his clenched fist; he was holding a tightly-rolled newspaper. "There's news."

"What sort of news?"

He stared out the window, biting the inside of his cheek. "Some farmers sued the North Bloomfield company . . . Oh, last year sometime, or maybe the year before. Most of us had forgotten all about it. But there's a decision now." Susan waited. "Lorenzo Sawyer—his honor, Lorenzo Sawyer—has ruled that hydraulic mining is a public nuisance. A public nuisance!" Jack slammed the newspaper down on the mantel.

"What does it mean?"

He looked over at her. "He's issued an injunction. Another injunction, but this one carries authority. No one can wash slickens downstream. Silt, sand, mud, gravel—it's all the same to Sawyer. Dams or no dams, he wants the rivers clear. North Bloomfield has to keep their tailings out of the streams and channels, and even their own canals and flumes, because they all empty into the rivers. My God!"

"Is that all?"

"All?" Jack laughed. "Not likely. His decision is nearly a thousand pages long. Pity his poor clerks."

"What else did 'e say?"

"Well, he allows that there might be another way to get rid of the debris. Oh, he's a fair man, fair indeed! He's no objection to hydraulic mining as long as the mess disappears!"

Susan set down her pail. "Well, it's about time someone did somethin' t' keep th' companies in line."

Jack stopped pacing, genuinely startled. "What d'you mean?"

"Jack, they're tearin' down the 'illsides and fillin' up the rivers. Leave them be, they'll not stop until the whole district is nothin' but tailin's."

"You're exaggerating."

"Am I?"

"You know as well as I that hydraulic mining doesn't work everywhere. There isn't a monitor running within ten miles of where you're standing right now."

"Give 'em time."

Jack sat down in the window seat and laughed. "Dabbety fay! So you think that if we live long enough, we'll see the hydraulickers wash away the whole state?"

"Now you're the one who's exaggeratin'."

He leaned back, appraising her. "Is it a question, then, of just how much they're allowed? Then should we let the hard rock men dig their shafts?"

"It's not the same."

"No, but if you're after the water, then look to the deep mines. What d'you think the pumps are bringin' up, day and night? And where does the water go? When the North Star went deeper and we pumped it out, the wells went dry."

"Why didn't anyone complain?"

"Oh, they did. But there were only a few of them."

"I never 'eard that Grass Valley 'ad trouble findin' water."

"No, they've always taken it out of Wolf Creek."

"Then if we let your hydraulic men take it farther up or fill up th' creek bed, then th' town will run dry."

"So you're going to stand with Sawyer just in case someone, years from now, finds a gravel bed up past Banner Mountain."

"Yes. Banner Mountain, and the San Juan Ridge, and all the others. If ye wash away a mountain or dry up a river, ye'll not get it back again."

"A man can't make a living staring at a mountain or listening to a river run."

She snorted. "I'm not sayin' we 'ave t' shut everythin' down. I'm sayin' we can't let one group o' men ruin it all for everyone else."

"That's what I've been trying to tell you. Mining, farming, lumber— who has the right to use the land? We can't put the hydraulic men down at the end of the line."

The blood pounded in her ears. She was tired, so tired, but she wanted Jack to take her seriously. "Let 'em wash their gravel. But let 'em figure out what t' do with it. Why should we let 'em fill the rivers?"

"Susan, listen." He lowered his voice. "There's over a hundred million dollars invested in hydraulic companies, and what they do is worth eighteen million each year."

"Eighteen million for who? For your friends in San Francisco?"

"For all of us."

"Are ye sayin' that if we don't let 'em dump their rubble in the Yuba that they can't afford to go on?"

"That's it. They're living on the edge."

"Then we'll 'ave t' do without that eighteen million a year."

Cousin Jack

He looked at her for a long moment. "It's the river, isn't it? Why the river?"

She stood there next to the bucket of rags, wisps of hair straying from the knot at the nape of her neck, her sleeves pulled up above her elbows, and the apron, stained and wrinkled, tied on over her dress. For a moment, he remembered his own mother as she was on the days when she did the washing or scrubbed the floors. There was something about her, something both patient and determined that brooked no contest, something as stubborn as rock. She drew herself up and looked at him full in the face, and for a brief moment, incongruously, Jack remembered, quite vividly, the spectral fox that had found him at the bottom of the Wheal Vor so long ago. Susan spoke, but it was Zennora's voice that rang in Jack's ears. "I can't tell ye why. But the river must be left to run as it will."

The Sawyer decision released havoc. The North Bloomfield Company dismissed their crews and threw open their waste gates, leaving 157 miles of canals and flumes untended in spite of the winter rains and imminent spring runoff. The Eureka Lake company opened its circuit, another 163 miles, and the other hydraulickers followed their example. When the Sacramento newspapers accused the North Bloomfield owners of threatening to flood the valley, they responded by shutting off the water supply to the Derbec Drift Mine, insisting that the court had made them liable for any debris that their water might carry, no matter who controlled it. In Marysville, joyous farmers marched in torchlight parades, declaring a victory and insisting that the rule of law had finally prevailed, but within a week, there was a bitter reaction. Late one night, the Excelsior Foundry, a shop that had once specialized in monitors but had since turned to supplying the farmers with plows, harrows, mills and grinders, collapsed in a volcano of sparks and incinerated in a two-hour inferno while the Marysville fire companies worked frantically to clear three large trees and a load of boulders that blocked their path. In San Francisco, furious bidding sent the prices of mining stock on a rampant roller-coaster that left some men reeling and broke. Through it all, the legislators in Sacramento debated, and debated, and did nothing.

Susan heard little of these events, for on the very evening after she and Jack quarreled, she found Jane writhing in her bed; her fever had risen sharply. Simpson confirmed that the girl had developed diphtheria. Zennora and Susan hardly slept now and scarcely left the sick room. Annie cooked the meals, saw to it that the maid did the cleaning and washing, and soothed the children when they, feeling rootless, wandered in from their temporary quarters with Katie and the babies. Jack quietly ranged through the house and yard, fastening shutters that had broken loose in the winter storms, chopping and stacking cordwood under shelter, and keeping the path to his buggy clear of snow and ice. Susan saw him only when she shuffled downstairs for a stack of clean towels or a pot of steaming water; he seemed always to be wearing his hat and drying his boots before the parlor fire. She no longer knew the time of day, for very little light passed through the drawn curtains from the leaden winter skies, so she could not tell whether she saw Jack at intervals or she was, somehow, repeating the same encounter over and over again, as if in an empty, labyrinthine dream.

Suddenly, the misery ended. Susan was sitting next to Jane's bed, holding her hand while Zennora reached over from the other side to bathe her face with a cool, damp cloth. The girl slept. She was pale, except for the red flush in her cheeks, and the coverlet hardly rose and fell with her shallow breaths. Then Zennora stopped and stared down at the face on the pillow. Susan held her own breath, listening, watching. She dared not move. A minute passed by, and Zennora dropped the rag into the pan and took a handkerchief out of her sleeve. Susan reached up with her free hand and laid it on Jane's chest. For weeks, whenever she had done that, she had felt a faint rasp as the girl forced the air in and out. Now there was nothing. Zennora began to keen very softly, rocking gently to and fro with her handkerchief held to her face. Susan kissed her daughter's hand, laid it down on the coverlet, and rose and walked out of the room.

Jack was sitting in front of the parlor fire, surrounded by newspapers scattered as though someone had stood on the staircase and flung them into the air. Susan sank into the nearest chair. She gazed into the fire, her eyes shining. He took his feet off of the ottoman and leaned forward to take her hand in his. They sat without moving for several minutes. Finally she took out a handkerchief, wiped her eyes, blew her nose, and took a deep breath.

She looked around at the scattered sheets of newsprint and managed to smile. "I've forgotten what day it is."

He smiled back at her. "It doesn't matter."

"What's all this?" She indicated the mess.

"Nothing."

"Tell me what's been 'app'ning."

He started to refuse, but thought better of it. "The *Union* predicts that by July, the merchants in Marysville will demand that the courts release the hydraulic companies and let them get back to work."

"Why?"

He shrugged. "A good bit of their trade comes from supplying the miners in the hills. If the miners aren't working, some of the men in the valley will fail. At least, that's the idea."

She took a deep breath and looked around the room. "I think . . . Well . . . I suppose it's all very important." She folded her handkerchief into a neat square and patted it flat in her lap. "Jack . . . " He reached over and put his hand over hers. "Thank ye for all ye've done. And Annie, too." She slowly stood up, turned, and walked into the kitchen, her back straight and her head level.

Jack returned in May, arriving during a shower that freed the perfume of the flowers to drift across the town. At Susan's house, he found no one but the maid, who claimed to know nothing of her mistress's whereabouts and suggested that she might have gone for a walk with her mother. Katie had all of the children under her charge, but when he asked after Zennora, she answered evasively. Puzzled and troubled, he sat down to wait on Susan's porch. The afternoon passed and the sun set behind him, casting long shadows on the houses across the street. The light faded until the neighborhood became monochromatic, shadows blending into shadows, and the first stars appeared over the dim eastern skyline. Surely even Zennora would not stay out so long, no matter where she was tramping, and Jack began to consider going for the sheriff. He was just climbing into the buggy when he noticed two figures walking slowly down the street from the south. He peered through the gloom, puzzling at their odd gaits and at their hats pulled low over their faces. When they turned into Susan's dooryard, he stepped quickly around the buggy to confront them. The first one, startled, looked up, and Jack saw his face. It was Susan. He reached over to lift the other's hat brim and found Zennora. Both women had tucked their hair under their hats and were dressed in worn, dirty men's clothes. Their faces were smeared with mud, and Susan bore an angry red scratch across her left check, as though something had whipped her. He gasped.

Susan checked up and down the street, then leaned in to speak, almost inaudibly, into his ear. "Don't just stand there. Come into the 'ouse. But do it quietly." She led the way up the walk and across the porch, holding the door open for Zennora and Jack before she closed it carefully. Jack reached up to light the lamp, but Susan took his wrist and stopped him. She walked all around the parlor and the dining room, checking to be sure the curtains were closed completely, and only then did she nod that he might strike a match. In the dim light, the women looked even more bedraggled than ever, and when they took off their hats, Jack saw that their hair was filthy. Susan's face seemed thinner than he remembered, almost gaunt. He was incredulous, so amazed that he could hardly speak. "What have you been doing?"

Susan turned to her mother. "Best change 'ere." Zennora nodded, and the two of them started up the stairs. Jack followed, asking again and again why they were dressed like that, where they had been, why . . . He could not find a way to ask why they were so dirty. Zennora disappeared into one of the bedrooms, but Susan stopped at her own doorway. "Are ye goin' to 'elp me change? Or d' ye just want to watch?" Aghast as well as perplexed, he backed off, speechless, and she grinned, shocking him again, and closed the door. He walked slowly back down the stairs, trying to imagine what could be happening, and sat down in the cold parlor. The maid seemed to have left; except for the faint sounds from the upstairs bedrooms, the house was quiet.

He heard the front door open, and James walked in. The youth was obviously startled to find his cousin waiting for him; he stammered at Jack's questions and, without any explanation, ran up the stairs. Jack followed, but when they got to Susan's room, and she walked out, dressed properly now, her face clean, and her hair, although still dirty, pinned back neatly. She handed an envelope to her son, who turned and clattered down the stairs. Jack followed him far enough to watch him leave, marking that he was careful to turn off the entry way lamp before slipping out the front door. Susan and Zennora stood looking down at him from the head of the stairs. Suddenly, he knew what they had been doing.

"My God! You're not spying against the hydraulickers! Tell me I'm wrong!"

In spite of the Sawyer decision, many of the companies, especially the smaller ones, had tried to keep working. Although they claimed to be dumping their tailings on waste ground, the works were usually so far up in the hills, hidden behind miles of rutted wagon trails, that no one knew for sure what they were doing. Convinced that the hydraulickers could not avoid producing runoff, the suspicious farmers had hired men to travel cross-country, evading the patrols that guarded the mining grounds, to where they could observe undetected. Some of the spies were old prospectors, relics from the early 1850s who were accustomed to traveling through the hills for months at a time with only a mule for company and support, and who were glad to have a chance to get back at the big companies that had made their lonely style of mining obsolete. Some were younger miners, men thrown out of work by the Sawyer decision, desperate enough to turn against their former employers and commensurately eager to maintain total secrecy. Some were adventurers from the farming valleys, young men drawn to the danger of eluding mine owners who, it was rumored, shot intruders on sight, with no challenge given.

Susan shook her head. "The less ye know, th' better."

"What do you mean?"

"Suppose ye're right, Jack. Suppose we're spyin' on the minin' companies. Ye'd 'ave few friends left 'ere if anyone found out."

"Do you think I'd tell?"

Zennora smiled. "P'raps not, but Susan's right. It's best ye not know."

The women descended to the parlor, where Susan began laying a fire. Jack followed, expostulating. "D'ye think I'm a fool? Why else would ye be sneakin' back into town wearin' men's rags? Why else would ye be sendin'

James t' deliver secret envelopes? Why else wouldn't ye tell me what ye're doin'?"

Susan rose. "All right, all right. We're spyin' on the hydraulic companies down near th' Bear River."

Zennora settled into a chair, her face calm. "I've walked all over that area fer years. But Susan can see better, so I'm th' guide and she's th' scout."

Jack was beside himself. "D'ye know what would 'appen if someone caught you? They've posted sentries, and some of 'em are marksmen. And even if they didn't get ye, how would you explain yourselves if someone saw ye strollin' through town lookin' like tutmen from twenty years ago?"

Zennora smiled, and Susan actually laughed, long and loud, until her mother joined in. The two women subsided, and Susan shook her head at Jack. "Ye're exactly right. Mother 'as Fayther's clothes, and I 'ave Hannibal's. The very clothes they used t' wear t' go down below when ye all worked at th' North Star. Don't ye think they fit us well?" The women laughed again as Jack stood there, not knowing whether to scold them or simply storm out of the house.

"Zennora—Susan—what business is it of yours? You could be caught, or hurt, or killed. Does Joseph know? Or Bertie?"

Susan bit her lip, trying not to chuckle at him. "Only James knows. Bertie doesn't live 'ere any more, and Joseph doesn't notice."

"What about Katie, and the maid?"

Zennora shrugged. "Well, I think they're all right, don't you?" Susan nodded.

"I don't understand," said Jack. "Why are you doing this?"

Susan took a deep breath. "Did ye know that at least a dozen mines're dumpin' tailin's into th' Bear River? Almost thirteen thousand cubic yards each day."

"Let the sheriff deal with 'em."

"Oh, yes, so you say, but 'e won't, 'e doesn't. It's up t' people like us t' make sure th' companies obey th' law."

Jack sat down next to her. "Maybe a dozen companies are dumping debris, but twenty more have shut down. Haven't you noticed how many men are out of work? How empty the stores have become?"

Zennora nodded. "We know. But if the only way t' keep th' men at work is t' destroy th' rivers, then th' men will 'ave t' find work somewhere else, doin' somethin' else."

Jack looked at his aunt. "What would Jesse say if he were here today?"

At that, Zennora's eyes became as green as St. Ives Bay during a gale. "I don't know what Jesse would say, and neither do you, Jack. But I'll tell ye this." She rose to her feet. "Since before Jesse died, I've been walkin' these 'ills. We can ruin this land, or we can care fer it. Ye may think Sawyer a fool, an' p'raps 'e is. Ye may think th' farmers own 'im, an' p'raps they do. Ye may think that Susan and I can't make a diff'rence, an' p'raps ye're right. P'raps only th' lawyers're gettin' rich. But I'm not doin' it fer the farmers, or fer Sawyer, or fer any o' th' men in San Francisco. I'm doin' it fer the rivers. Fer th' deer that wait fer me in th' woods. Fer th' wildflowers that dust across the 'illsides in th' spring. Call me a jinny-ninny, if ye wish, but that's what I care about."

She turned on her heel and walked into the kitchen. Jack looked at Susan, whose eyes shone in the firelight. "I hear in San Francisco that some of the spies are lying so the lawyers will keep paying them."

Susan lifted her chin. "I'm sure that's true. But not us."

He sank back into his chair. "I just don't think you understand what's happening here."

Susan sighed. "Ye've never given me credit, 'ave ye, Jack? Of course I understand. I know that companies are goin' out o' business, an' that men are out o' work, an' that stores're closin' from Nevada City t' Sacramento. I even know that th' county assessor's raisin' the alarm because everyone's property is fallin' in value. But I also know what Edward Sterling told me just the other day—that the Idaho is 'avin' one of its best years."

"What does that have to do with it?"

"It means that ye don't have to use a monitor and foul a river t' bring out th' gold."

"You know as well as I do that you can't run a hard-rock mine in North Bloomfield."

"Iss fay, and ye can't run a gold mine of any kind in San Francisco, but I hear no one complainin' about that. Let th' men on th' Ridge try drift minin', if they're so eager to stay there."

Jack let out a breath. "Derbec Gravel is only drift mine in the state that's paying dividends. North Bloomfield has been trying it, but they've been doing so poorly that they'll have to close up the operation and lay off the men."

"Then let th' men move on. We came 'ere, thousands o' miles from 'ome, so men like you and Fayther and Hannibal could work th' way ye wanted."

"It's not that easy."

"P'raps not. Comin' 'ere wasn't easy. But I came, and 'ere I stay." She rose. "I've always 'oped that ye were doin' what ye thought was right, Jack. I just wish ye'd remember that Mother and I can make up our own minds." She left him warming his feet before the fire.

20
Chicago Park
1887

Bertie flicked the whip over the lead horse's ears, and as the team hurried into a trot, he looked back over his shoulder, squinting down from the single coachman's seat, and winked. He had insisted on going to hire the rig for his brother's wedding, returning with this barouche, an unusually formal sort of carriage that Susan had seen before only in San Francisco. She and Zennora sat in the rear seat watching James try to keep his balance without crumpling the tails of his new dress coat.

Susan had liked Eleanor Hosken from the start, but she was puzzled that so cheerful a girl could have grown up in so gloomy a family. Zennora had invited them all to Sunday dinner in honor of the engagement, and Eleanor's brothers and sisters had stood in the parlor as though about to sneak out of the house, shifting their weight and shuffling their feet, offering maladroit smiles whenever someone presented a plate of cakes or tried to begin a conversation. They seemed unusually tall to Susan, with dark hair and deep-set eyes, so she felt as though she were passing among looming trees in a shadowy forest. Mary was gaunt, her lips pressed into a thin, straight line and her hands constantly working on each other as she rolled each knuckle through the opposite thumb and forefinger. Will and Nettie were all spidery arms and needle noses, while Henry, the elder son, wore a patch over one eye. When Susan discreetly inquired, Eleanor sighed and let fragments fall: her mother's new hat, a runaway wagon, the flailing hooves of the startled team. She apparently regarded the mishap a matter of course, and Susan remembered overhearing James amuse Bertie with the tale of the Hoskens' childhood, set as a clumsy chronicle of cut fingers, scraped knees, smashed thumbs, bruised heads and sprained ankles.

Eleanor's father wore his full, dark beard like a screen. Smiling desperately, James assured his brothers that William had traveled all over the West, working in a silver claim near Pike's Peak, the lead mines of southwestern Montana, and even the Sutro Tunnel in Nevada. William arranged for his mouth to be full whenever anyone asked him a direct question, chewing methodically with his blank gaze aimed up the length of crockery and crystal and steaming dishes. When James revealed that he had actually spent several years prospecting in Nevada County back in the 1850s and asked the older man to describe his camp in Rattlesnake Ravine, there was a long silence, and then Sarah and Katie rose to clear the table, so the moment dissipated. Susan glanced furtively at William, searching for a reaction, but for all she could see, he was hardly aware that he had been the subject of the conversation. Susan wondered whether he had dwindled, over the years, before the onslaught of his wife.

Lavinia sat as straight as a stick, as though her corset ran from her hips to her ears, and when she turned her head, she swiveled her shoulders and torso as well. She never laid her arms to rest, but kept her elbows slightly elevated, reminding Susan of a man she had once seen conducting an orchestra. When she pointed, she stabbed with a long, bony finger, and when she passed a dish, she presented it crisply; Sarah nearly upset her water glass when a basket of biscuits abruptly appeared under her chin. She talked rapidly and incessantly, taking tiny bites and sips between phrases, and whenever someone else managed to wedge a remark into the conversation, she leaned back in her chair slightly, tilting rigidly from the base of her spine, and watched her competitor with bleak eyes and arid mouth. Her husband might be reticent, but she was more than willing to tell all about her childhood in her uncle's hotel in Galena, a very refined and exclusive establishment; her years in a boarding school outside London, where she learned to paint and embroider from a woman whose work had inspired compliments from Victoria herself; her older brother, who began as a mere miner (here Bertie and James exchanged glances with Joseph) but rose to open a hotel even more genteel than his uncle's; and that day when Eleanor, dear little Eleanor, not quite two years old, sat in the lap of General Grant, the hero of the Union, clearly an admirable soldier but, truth to tell, a little too inclined to muddy the carpets with his boots and not quite hit the spittoon when one most wanted him to. She left no question forlorn; when Bertie asked William whether he had visited the Odd Fellows Hall, Lavinia, not even waiting for her husband to favor the table with his customary silence, announced that the Women's Christian Temperance Union—as she spoke, she fixed Zennora, Susan and Katie, in sequence, with upraised eyebrows, conveying somehow that she assumed and demanded their membership, in fact or in intention—also met on Broad Street, there better to have access to the scandalous number of saloons for which Nevada City was, regrettably, so notorious. She then delivered herself of a few remarks on the horrors of ardent spirits, alluding to a Galena women whose husband had, in a fit of delirium, employed the fireplace poker to dispatch all eight of their children, and finished the topic with her remonstrative stare resting firmly on Joseph, who paused in the midst of reaching for the decanter of port, and chose, for the time being, to return his hands to his lap, there to keep them folded until a safer moment.

Lavinia had insisted on hosting the wedding, actually snorting in disdain when Susan mentioned holding the ceremony at church, and promptly marching out of the house to drive straight to the rectory, where she apparently intimidated Father Lewis, for when Susan greeted him after services the following

Sunday, his cheeks and neck flushed such a deep red that his purple stole seemed suddenly garish. Lavinia assumed complete control, scorning even the smallest suggestions, and when Susan managed to invite Eleanor to lunch, just the two of them, she found that the girl accepted her mother's dominion as a matter of course. She assured Susan that Lavinia had picked out a lovely gown for her, and it needed only a few alterations, which Mary could handle with no trouble at all.

Bertie reined in the team in front of the Hosken home, a large, rambling affair on Prospect Street that looked as though a previous owner had found the upstairs far too small and so added three rooms whose looming windows overhung the azaleas so far that the gables threatened to shear off. The yard, usually littered with trash and forgotten tools, was quite clean under the bare branches, and Susan wondered how many hours Will and Henry had spent to satisfy their mother's imperious caprice. She walked in through the front door, open in spite of the late winter chill, and felt strangely dislocated. She tried to think of the Hoskens as Cornish, remembering Camborne neighbors no less dark and gloomy, but both William and Lavinia had come to America when still very small children, and if she could hear little of Penwith in their speech, she could see less of it in their habits. When she had first visited their home, she had sensed something missing, and only later realized that every stick of furniture, every framed print, every dish and every knick-knack was brand new. There was nothing from England—no clocks, no cherished side tables, no old silver. Lavinia had spent the better part of a month traveling back and forth between a furniture store on Broad Street and one on Mill, arguing with each proprietor and citing his competitor's offers and treatment in order to goad him into giving her a better deal. Finally, one man had told her that he could do no more for her, and she had bought the entire household, from the bedrooms to the parlor, from his rival, but all in the cheapest pine with the most flimsy upholstery, so that whenever Susan sat down, she wondered whether the springs would finally struggle free to stab her through the cloth, or the whole chair would collapse altogether. Everything matched, but the uniformity made the place seem as though no one could or should actually live there. The house seemed quite American.

The two families and their handful of guests were barely able to cram themselves into the parlor as long as Katie's disappointed children, with Sarah assigned to be their sulky guardian, were relegated to the entry way. They had clamored to sit on the stairs, where they could peek through the balusters at the grown-ups below, but Lavinia had gathered them up and pushed them aside, loudly declaring that the staircase was reserved for the bride's entrance and announcing, ostensibly to herself, that no responsible person would bring small children to a wedding anyway. Father Lewis stood waiting near the fireplace while Lavinia explained, in an aggressively argumentative tone, to Joseph, who happened to be standing within range, that if her daughter were getting married in England, the bishop would surely have presided. Susan, knew, because of Eleanor's one indiscreet moment during their lunch together, that the woman was alluding, possibly without even realizing it, to a celebration she had attended in 1852, invited only because she had happened to be visiting the family of a school friend, where the second daughter of the fifth son of a baronet had married a young cleric, but she closed her eyes and tried not to listen. When Eleanor did make her way down the stairs, her dress seemed oddly off-kilter, and Susan decided that it had been intended for a much larger woman, so that even Mary's reputed skill could not, in the time Lavinia had allocated, transform it sufficiently.

After the ceremony and a few mumbled toasts, Bertie escorted Susan and Zennora to the barouche and proudly led out the bridal couple, winking at James as he took Eleanor's hand to help her into the carriage. Hat thrust squarely upon his crown, he flicked the whip over the team to set them trotting down the street. They had traveled less than a mile when James looked back and turned to whisper to Eleanor, who shook her head ruefully. Susan twisted so she could look over her shoulder, and there was Lavinia, bolt upright, following in her rickety buggy, with Henry driving. At the cottage James had rented in Grass Valley, she marched through all four rooms and gave Henry brisk orders regarding the altering the position of this chair or that table. After ten minutes of hearing Lavinia's steps verge on driving holes through the floorboards, Susan felt that she must go home. Eleanor's patient expression was beginning to show the strain, and James had clearly stopped regarding her mother's behavior as comically eccentric, but, Susan told herself, they were married now, and they would have to deal with the situation themselves.

Susan and Zennora saw little of the Hoskens after that, although they did have to endure monthly suppers that Eleanor, sweetly determined to bring the families together, arranged at her house. Her table sat eight, so to fill the two extra seats, she took turns inviting the various brothers and sisters. She asked Martin only once, for he silently spent the entire evening smoking a series of cigars so strong that even William began to cough and decided that he must go check on the horses. Katie declined Eleanor's invitations, describing at length why she simply had to stay home with the children.

Very early one summer morning, Susan was about to brew a pot of tea to share with Zennora when she answered a knock on her door to find Lavinia, dressed as if for church, with Henry leaning on the post behind her.

"Mrs. Carne!" A sharp nod. "Mrs. Trevenna! Fine morning!"

Susan agreed that it was and, after a moment, asked if Mrs. Hosken would like to come in. She swept into the parlor, hovered until Susan indicated a chair, and then lit, only the base of her spine touching the seat, her gloved hands pinching the purse in her lap, and her chin lifted fastidiously away from her collar button. Henry stood in the entry way arch, his one eye gazing vaguely out the front window and his hat still on his head.

"Mrs. Carne." Lavinia fixed Susan with a stare. "Mrs. Carne, I've come to talk to you about Chicago Park."

Susan had read in the *Union* that the Sterling brothers had sold the old Storms Ranch, over six thousand acres right on the Narrow Gauge line, to a syndicate of investors from Chicago who proposed to sell small farming plots—ten, twenty and forty acres—to people from the midwest. The town center would feature a three-story hotel whose modern conveniences and appointments would, the developers claimed, put the Holbrooke to shame. The newspaper had gone on to describe the "phenomenal success" of the capitalists' last venture, a community called Redlands, far to the south, and predicted that this new addition to Nevada County would become the show-piece of the region. When Susan read Zennora the passage acclaiming Chicago Park as the first genuine colony in northern California on the grounds that its residents would all come from out of state, her mother laughed incredulously, asking, "Where do they think everyone else came from?" The project had become a family joke.

Lavinia leaned forward ever so slightly. "I'm going to buy land out there. Oh, yes!" She laughed, a short bark. "Oh, it took me a good long while to convince my husband, but he finally saw the reason in the thing. Just imagine! People with a purpose! People with some gumption! Why, forty years from now, no one will pay any attention to Grass Valley. And Nevada City? They might as well shut the place up and leave it to the drunkards and the firemen." James had just joined the Reliance Hose Company as a volunteer, but Lavinia persisted in using "fireman" as a catch-all cipher for idleness and dissipation. "Mark my words, Mrs. Carne—Mrs. Trevenna—Chicago Park will lead this county into the next century. All we have to do is decide whether to join in or be left behind."

"Are ye buyin' a lot in town?" asked Zennora.

"A small one, for building a house, and twenty acres not a mile away, a good piece, fine for orchards. Why, they'll be able to grow pears and peaches out there that'll be the envy of the entire state and command prices that no one's ever dreamed of before!"

"Are you an' Mr. Hosken goin' t' move out there?"

Lavinia seemed slightly ruffled. "Well, no. At least, not yet. In time, perhaps. In time." She sniffed and lowered her voice, apparently attempting to sound confidential, but achieving only an oddly condescending tone. "We're renting our house, you know." She sat straight up again. "But that's all right! I wouldn't own it! Oh, no! Not in that neighborhood. Do you know that the man living next to us hasn't painted his place since the day it was built? Why, ten years from now, that whole street will be nothing but shacks.

Oh, no."

Susan felt as though she were listening to three conversations at once. "So I suppose ye'll 'old the land until ye're ready."

"Hold it?" Lavinia seemed offended. "Hold it? Not at all. What I'd really like to do—" She leaned in again. "—is build a house on the town lot and then rent both parcels to the same party. Oh, yes!"

"Would ye like some tea, Mrs. Hosken?" Susan began to rise as if to make for the kitchen.

"Tea! No. Worst thing for the stomach, you know. Dyspepsia." Susan subsided into her chair as Lavinia flicked a gloved hand to dismiss the idea. "Besides, we have business to discuss."

Susan glanced at Zennora, who looked discreetly baffled. "Business?"

"Why, yes, Mrs. Carne! We must get you into Chicago Park while there's still time!"

"What d'ye mean?"

"I mean that the only sensible thing to do is to buy now! To get in at the beginning! The prices can only go up."

"You want us t' buy a lot?"

Lavinia's eyebrows rose. "Why, I'm here because I'm certain, as certain as I can be, that you *want* to buy a lot. I'm just here to help. We really can't wait. What do you think will happen to property values once people actually move in from Illinois and start building houses? Oh, and fine houses they'll be, too, not like the ones they're putting up around here." She waved scornfully out the front window. "And just wait until they build the academy." She paused, holding her breath, waiting for a cue.

"The academy?" asked Zennora.

"Why, yes, Mrs. Trevenna." She barked again. "It will surely be one of the finest schools in the West. Why, it will offer not only the usual instruction proper for young gentlemen, but also a finishing course for young ladies. I wouldn't be a bit surprised if the better families from San Francisco sent their children here before packing them off to Yale. I told the man at the development office that I would be more than happy to give them the benefit of my experience. He was only too glad to hear it, too glad to hear it. Most of the women in California, you know, haven't had the advantages I had." As she rattled on, Susan looked over at Zennora, who shook her head slightly. "We are a bit off the beaten track, of course," Lavinia conceded, "but that will change—that will change. The world will come to us. Why, I wouldn't be surprised if they moved the capital here; all they need is an excuse to get out of that swampy rat-hole."

"Mrs. Hosken . . . " Susan began.

"Oh, I know, I know." Lavinia raised a hand to cut her off. "Where to buy? That's the main thing. Well, the town lots are all right, one's much the same as the next as long as you're not too close to the station or the hotel. You just know—" She leaned in again and almost whispered. "—that they'll have a saloon there, and I don't have to tell you what that means." She drew back and barked again. "As for the farming plots, well, I have Henry here right now, and we can just drive out there to look them over. There's one right next to mine, just below it, good drainage, I'm sure, that would suit you, no doubt about it."

"Mrs. Hosken," said Susan, hurrying a little for fear her guest might begin again. "I don't think we're really interested in buyin' a lot."

"No?" Lavinia's mouth dropped open and she looked back and forth like a startled ostrich. "Why ever not?"

"Well . . . " said Zennora.

"Ah!" Lavinia interrupted. "I understand." She nodded several times. "No need to explain. Well, then, perhaps a partnership!" Neither Susan nor Zennora could think of a response to this new idea. "Yes. A partnership. You see, I really would like to build a house on my town lot. I can do it myself of course—" She nodded again, smiling as though the house were already under construction. "—but just think of what we could do together! No point in building something small or ordinary. Why, you might as well build in Grass Valley!" She barked again, her eyes flickering back and forth. "I tell you, the houses in Chicago Park will be only the finest. Only the finest. Why, we could name James and Eleanor in the partnership papers, not that they would have to invest, you understand, not that they're in a position, with James . . . Well, but only because the property would certainly go to them in the end."

Susan could not decide whether to be annoyed at Lavinia's passing over her other children or to be puzzled at the woman dismissing, in a phrase, Eleanor's brothers and sisters. "Mrs. Hosken, I don't think we're interested in the idea." When Lavinia's jaw dropped again, Susan glanced at Zennora and went on in conciliatory a tone as she could manage at the moment. "Not just now. P'raps next year?"

Lavinia pressed her lips together and shook her head firmly. "Next year? Who knows what'll be left next year? Or what it might cost?" She took a deep breath. "Are you certain? Quite certain?"

Susan nodded, and Zennora answered. "It was very kind of you to ask us."

"Not at all, not at all," replied Lavinia, rising to her feet. "I realize that one isn't always in a position . . . I did, think, however . . . " The bleak eyes seemed puzzled for a moment, but they recovered. "Well!" She marched out the door to her buggy, with Henry hurrying ahead to open the garden gate.

Within two weeks, Lavinia bought her lots. There was no road leading to her "farm," but she insisted that Henry drive her out there, and she shrieked at him every time a mound or gully threatened to trap or tip the buggy. She disembarked and picked her way through the manzanita, heading down a steep grade towards a dry creek bed, but a branch snagged her skirt, and after tugging for a moment, she stood and brayed at her son to come at once in order to extricate her from this arboreal treachery.

When Susan heard the story from Eleanor, she shook her head, unsurprised. She had been walking up Main Street when she stopped, startled by the sound of an angry woman's voice ringing through the windows of Findley's bank. "You call yourself a banker? This is a sure thing, a sure thing! Why, if Jay Gould had as much sense as you, he'd still be digging canals!" The door burst open and Lavinia stormed past, not even noticing Susan standing there, and marched out into the street, where she paid no attention at all to a heavy farm wagon whose driver had to pull up suddenly, and across to her buggy, where Henry sat slumped over the reins. The farmer ran through his repertoire of epithets and expletives, descending to bring one of his team under control, and people stared from the sidewalk and the shop windows as Henry leisurely guided his apathetic horse away from the curb and down the hill, with Lavinia glaring straight ahead. She had already spent at least two thousand dollars on the land alone, no bank in town would consider her application for a loan, and Eleanor believed that William had long since relinquished control over his money, unless he had some hidden away. The girl flushed as she spoke; she was expecting her first child, and her mother, obsessed with her own affairs, had shown no interest at all.

As stories about Chicago Park took up more and more space in the pages of the *Union,* Jack came for a brief visit, his first in three years. He leaned back in his chair, smiled at Susan, and tapped his mustache with a fingertip. "The Redlands colony is doing all right, but it's a good bit warmer down there, more like what those people from Illinois seem to want. Storms Ranch is a nice place if you like manzanita and madrone trees, and cattle, but the last time someone made a town out of nothing around here was during the gold rush."

Although Lavinia seemed to think that the colony could hardly proceed until she resolved her difficulties, the syndicate laid out a public square, designated sites for two churches and a school, and let contracts for clearing several hundred acres of future orchard land. When she attended a meeting of property owners, she discovered that she was one of only a small handful of local people; most of the lots had gone to merchants and tradesmen from the original Chicago, men who hoped to escape the harsh midwestern winter. The president of the company, a man named Hale, welcomed the colonists, and the vice president, one William Gunthorp, described the bright future that surely awaited them. The general manager announced that the syndicate had hired a crew to put the Sterlings' old saw mill back into operation, providing plenty of lumber at fair prices and without the need to haul the materials the eight miles out from Grass Valley, and introduced Quon Hay, a brick manufacturer from San Francisco who had agreed to set up a shop right there in George's Valley. Lavinia drove home somewhat reassured.

Feeling sorry for Eleanor, Susan offered to sew a christening gown for her baby, now only two months off, and she asked Zennora to help her pick out the lace. Joseph drove them into town so they could spend an hour at the dry goods store, then he dropped them off at Susan's house. Susan laid out the samples on the parlor table but looked up to find her mother gazing out at the dried elm leaves drifting down from the branches. "What," asked the older woman, "are we goin' t' do about Joseph?"

Susan sighed. They had thought that marrying Katie might open him up somehow, free him from the brooding, if that's what it was, but having a family seemed to drive him farther into himself. Katie, for all her squealing and her petulant mouth, had become a surprisingly competent mother, which was, as Zennora observed, fortunate, seeing that she had four little ones and another on the way. Yet she scolded Joseph as though he were one of the children, even yammering after him as he calmly took his hat and walked out to the stable. He seemed to be drinking more and more, but the whiskey had little effect; at the end of an evening, he walked more carefully than usual, reaching up to pat a door jamb before passing through the opening. At several family gatherings, Susan had considered that Joseph and William were much alike, quiet men who sat like stoic rocks beneath the tempests of their wives, sitting with heads bowed slightly and faces bland and vacant, the eyes gazing not at the floor but somehow through the room, as though they weren't really there at all.

Yet the problem that Zennora had never discussed with Susan was the fact that Joseph had not been working. He still introduced himself as a miner, on those few occasions that required an introduction, but he worked rarely. He was always welcome at the Idaho, but he went down for only a few days at a time, maybe two weeks at the most, and then simply did not report for the beginning of his shift. The grass captain, a man who had worked at the North Star when he was just starting out, kept his name in his book in spite of the rows and rows of empty check boxes that sliced through the pages. Susan had guessed that his family was living off of Zennora's generosity, and she had wondered how long the arrangement would last.

"D'ye think ye can get 'im t' start workin' steady?" asked Susan, but Zennora's face was a study in confusion. There had been no other man in their family that had simply declined to provide for his wife and children. Men were injured, men fell ill, men were killed. All of that was ordinary, to be expected, but as long as a man was able, he went down in the mines and made his living. Susan still hoped, as Hannibal had hoped, that her sons would find something better, something safer, but the principle was the same. She understood Zennora's perplexity: how to explain to Joseph what was so obvious?

Zennora shook her head. "'e'll do what 'e must. When Jesse was 'is age, th' North Star was th' finest deep mine in th' district, and 'e'd worked all 'is life t' get there. Joseph . . . " Her voice trailed off and she gazed out the window, troubled.

Susan waited, and then: "What are ye askin' me?"

Her mother broke out of her reverie and smiled. "I suppose I need yer advice." She folded her hands in her lap. "I've been thinkin' p'raps 'e'd do a bit better with a 'ome of 'is own."

"'ow can 'e afford it?"

"'e can't. But I think it'd be better. A man needs 'is own place. So does a woman. And they've another child comin'." She sighed ruefully. "I like 'avin' them around, but they're startin' t' wear on me."

"Ye're gettin' older, Mother."

Zennora smiled again. "Well, p'raps that's it, but I think I'd like a bit more quiet."

"D'ye plan t' turn 'em out?"

"No, of course not. But I thought I might get 'em a place."

Susan hesitated, not sure how much Zennora knew, not sure how far to push. "Joseph . . . 'e seems t' be drinkin' more than 'e used to."

Zennora patted her knee. "Ye needn't be so gingerly with me. 'e drinks a lot, more than 'e should. I know it, I don't like it, but I doubt there's anythin' I can do t' change it. P'raps 'e can't 'elp it."

Susan took her mother's hand and held it gently. "What I mean is . . . d'ye think ye can trust 'im t' keep th' place?"

Zennora nodded. "That's what I wanted t' ask ye about. I went t' see Dibble last week. 'e told me that I can put th' place in my name, so it would be safe fer Katie and th' children, but I don't want t' do that. Joseph's a gentle man; it would 'urt 'im."

"What else can ye do?"

"Dibble says 'e can draw up a deed o' gift so that neither Katie nor Joseph may sell until th' children're grown. I think that's long enough. What I really want is fer th' children t' be safe. Later, if Joseph wants t' sell th' place, well, I suppose that's up to 'im."

Susan nodded. "I think it's the right thing." She thought for a moment. "D'ye think they'll move far away?"

Zennora actually chuckled. "I've already picked out a place. It's right around th' corner, on Quartz Street. A fine old 'ouse, enough room fer all of 'em, even a few more. It won't be five minutes' walk even in th' snow."

Cousin Jack

Zennora spoke to Katie and Joseph that very evening. Her daughter-in-law nodded eagerly, her cheeks grew pinker and pinker, until, in tears, she threw her arms around Zennora's neck and thanked her again and again. When they went to see the house, she ran from room to room, heedless of her swelling belly, carrying the baby, with the rest of the children trailing after her and calling out of each new window so loudly that the neighbors stepped out onto their porches to look up for the cause of the commotion.

Joseph sat in Zennora's parlor and bent his face down to the paper she had handed him. Dibble had framed the conditions in his usual style, meticulously thorough and dispassionate, but Joseph read the implications clearly. While Katie bubbled and squeaked, he lifted his face to his mother, and she looked into the grey eyes and read everything: the gratitude, the resentment, the pain. She wished that she could find another way, but she knew that she could never trust him.

As soon as the deal was closed, Joseph took possession with a degree of enthusiasm that surprised everyone. He went through the entire house with level, square, hammer, saw, bit brace and a box full of chisels and planes, checking every door and window, post and trim, replacing this and reinforcing that until the house was ready for painting. He hired Martin and Ernest to mend the plaster and assigned Zennora to paint the woodwork, assuring her that no other hand would be as careful as hers. When she paused to massage her tired fingers, she looked out a window or down the staircase to see her son gazing up at the carpentry, running his eye along the geometry of the intersecting lines, focused on the work rather than his inchoate apprehensions, and she thought of Jesse. Finally, one week before Christmas, he pronounced the place ready.

Eleanor had her baby on Christmas Day, a little girl. When the family trickled through to welcome the new arrival, they found Lavinia towering over the cradle, glaring at each visitor, so the celebration that might have graced James' parlor instead coalesced in Susan's kitchen, where even Eleanor's brothers and sisters gratefully accepted cups of cider syllabub and toasted their new niece. Bertie, winking uncontrollably, was just beginning a speech about Zennora becoming a great-grandmother when the front door burst open, hammering footsteps cut through the parlor, and Lavinia appropriated the doorway. She scanned the room quickly and found Henry, who actually cringed and reached up as if to shield his good eye, realizing that without him to drive her, his mother must have walked the half mile from Eleanor's bedside.

"Well!" She barked, that hoax of a laugh, then turned her glower on Zennora, standing over the stove. "James tells me that you've bought Joseph a house!" Zennora simply nodded, wondering what about this news was so compelling as to drag Lavinia away from the grandmotherly prerogatives she had claimed so forcefully. "You paid six hundred dollars!" Susan set her cup down on the table. She regarded Zennora's arrangement for Joseph, especially the underlying intentions, as private family business, and certainly no concern of Lavinia's. "Six hundred dollars?! Why with just a bit more, only a bit more, mind you, you could have had ten acres in Chicago Park. Or your pick of the lots in town!"

So that was it. Lavinia had scant interest in Zennora's intervention into her married son's responsibilities; she was concerned only with her schemes and what she apparently regarded as Zennora's stubborn refusal to accede to her will. She had believed that neither Zennora nor Susan had money to invest in her pet project, but now that she saw their response, all too clearly, as an outright snub, she was there to demand satisfaction. For a wild moment, Susan wondered whether Lavinia would slap Zennora with one of her gloves, or pick up a cup of syllabub and splash it in the other woman's face. She looked quickly around the room; everyone, from tight-lipped Mary down to the gangly Ernest and Will, was standing in a sort of a crouch, each bent slightly at the hips with at least one hand raised as if for protection.

Then Bertie stepped forward. "Tell me, Mrs. Hosken." She turned, her eyebrows arched up to her hairline, clearly amazed at the effrontery of the interruption. "Tell me—we had a pretty heavy frost yesterday morning. Man downtown told me his storm glass fell to twenty degrees." Now everyone was staring at Bertie, who was winking like mad and skipping one foot back and forth in front of him. "How'd those folks out at Chicago Park like it? I heard that one family packed up by mid-afternoon—said they hadn't come to California to freeze their toes!" He chuckled slightly as though trying to clear a dry place in this throat.

Every pair of eyes slid towards Lavinia. Her eyebrows came down like a fire curtain, and Susan later assured James that her eyes glowed red. She brought her feet together with a stomp and lifted her handbag up to her chest. "Not at all!" She lifted her chin even higher. "Not at all!" Then, without shifting her gaze from Bertie, who had stopped winking and seemed almost paralyzed, she rasped, "Henry!" and turned to march out of the house. Henry waited only a split second, then scrambled, bouncing off of the door jamb on his way out of the room, to follow his mother out to where he had parked the buggy.

Katie had crept halfway down the stairs, the rest of her children peeking out from behind her skirts at the strange woman who was making so much noise. No one spoke for a long moment. Then Martin took his pipe out of his mouth long enough to twist his mouth into its customary wry smile and lift a cup of syllabub. "To my new niece, Ethel." They all echoed the salute and took sips from their drinks. Martin shook his head and finished, "And a very merry Christmas to you all!"

21
Zennora
1888-90

Zennora sat in the parlor window watching the snow fall. She tried to discern the delicate geometry of each crystal as it floated past the glass, but when the daylight faded and the world turned grey, the flakes lost their individuality and became motion itself, the pure phenomenon of falling. In spite of the fire in the hearth and the voices throughout the house, Zennora felt as if the falling sky were infiltrating the walls and windows with an unremitting cold that would surround her. She shivered.

Susan had invited the entire family to Christmas dinner, and she cheerfully turned her mother out of the kitchen, insisting that she hold court in the parlor. Katie's older girl and boy, now six and seven, ran from room to room while the two younger ones stumped along in pursuit. Joseph had tried to play a game with them, but when they shrank into obstinate passivity, he found his sister's brandy and retreated, panting and glancing furtively around him, to the corner where Martin silently smoked and stared through the wall. Katie and Eleanor sat together near the fireplace, taking turn and turn about with their own one-year-olds and with Lucy, the baby. James tried to entertain Bertie, telling him amusing and even risqué stories, and Ernest punctuated them with boisterous laughter. The fire crackled in counterpoint to the rattles and murmurs from the kitchen as Susan and Sarah mixed and chopped and baked and carved.

Zennora wondered what would become of Bertie. Like most of the other boys he knew, he had gone to work in the mines, earning weekly wages from big companies like the Idaho and the Empire. The boys weren't quite tributers, like their great-grandfathers, for their pay depended only partly on what they brought out, and the owners controlled the arrangements carefully so that even a crew working a rich vein derived only small extra reward. Sometimes they worked as tutmen, sinking shafts and driving adits, earning so much per foot, and then the owners were less close-fisted . . . less "cropin," Zennora said to herself, letting the old word form on her lips. Yet Bertie took no interest in the mines; he went to the Idaho like any man going to any job, and whenever Zennora asked him about his work, he shrugged and winked. Zennora decided that if he found neither magic nor challenge in the mines, then he'd be better off doing something else; besides, both his father and his grandfather had imagined for the boys a future without going underground.

Zennora had been pondering Bertie's situation when Jack came up for a brief visit. She took him aside and he listened, smiling a little but apparently taking her seriously, and he promised that he would look into it. Two weeks later, a letter arrived, and Zennora asked Sarah to read it to her. A man named Bennett had a small boot and shoe business on Mill Street and would be glad to take on a younger man who would help him expand his store and, if he devoted himself, become his partner. If Bertie would go see Bennett, and mention Jack's name, they would most likely be able to reach an agreement. Zennora decided not to tell Susan; instead, she quietly invited Bertie to tea. She watched him wink and chuckle and dance his irrepressible feet on the hearth rug, and she sighed, wondering if Bennett would waste even five minutes on him. Yet as she described the opportunity, the twitching diminished until he sat almost still, his tea cooling in the cup. She waited nearly a week, wondering apprehensively whether he had actually gone to the meeting or had flagrantly embarrassed himself, providing Bennett with an amusing story to tell his saloon cronies. Just when she had decided to assume the worst, Bertie knocked on her door, wearing a new black suit, to announce that he would start with Bennett the very next morning and that in six weeks' time he would be getting married to a girl named Emma Rowe, the daughter of a Cornish quartz miner.

All through the following year, Zennora felt as though the center of the family were shifting, leaving her off to one side, like a bird who, following the wind, lifts her wings into a chance eddy and realizes, too late, that the rest of the flock has sailed off in a different direction. At family gatherings, Katie, Eleanor, and Emma—the young wives—clustered in one corner, while Bertie and James shuffled their feet near the doorway, usually with Ernest, trying to claim a place with the men and glancing up defensively whenever anyone approached. Bertie was doing well at the shoe store; when Zennora stopped in, he treated her with gracious deference, as though she were a mine owner's wife whose good will he sought to cultivate, but with whom he would never presume familiarity, and carried off the sale with brisk competence and only a few involuntary winks.

Then the thread unraveled. Emma died only three weeks after the delivering her baby, surviving a difficult birth only to develop pneumonia. Bertie was so bewildered that he could scarcely answer the simplest questions; he could not grasp that his wife was gone, and he stared at little Lucy as though he could not fathom who she was or where she had come from. After several days, he seemed to recover, but the winking and the chuckling were now constant, sometimes suiting the moment, if extravagantly so, but more often at random. His feet were more than nervous now; he actually danced as he walked, hopping up and down so violently that Susan insisted that he never take the baby out of the safety of her nurse's arms. The family tried to enfold him, but there were unpredictable moments, just when he seemed to be enjoying the warm company around him, when he would stop in the middle of a sentence, gaze vacantly around the room, and put up one hand to cover the eye that had begun to wink and twitch uncontrollably. Now, on Christmas Day, he had impulsively agreed to give Lucy's nurse the afternoon off that she might be with her own family, so he had brought the baby and, with great relief, entrusted her to the women. He could scarcely keep his baffled eyes off of his daughter, dressed in a fantastic black concoction resembling a sinister christening gown, and the two young mothers who, without evident effort, kept three tiny children warm, dry, fed and cuddled, all the while carrying on a steady conversation in serene isolation from everyone else in the room.

Still the snow fell. Zennora felt suddenly restless, annoyed with the slow, relentless invasion, and she wished for a storm that would set the house to creaking and stir the ashes in the hearth.

Two weeks later, a gale blew in from Alaska, sweeping down through the Bitterroot Range and across the Columbia Plateau, skimming south from peak to peak along the crest of the high Sierra before wheeling abruptly and turning its full fury on western Nevada County. For six days and nights, the storm hurled snow on homes and stores, roads and tracks, and groves and fields. Grass Valley slowly vanished as the snow piled higher, banking against windward walls and pressing down on roofs and awnings. Zennora barricaded herself in her house, safe with a vast pile of kindling and logs that Joseph had stacked on the enclosed back porch. She hardly slept, feeding the fire in her parlor and tingling as the wind whistled past her chimney and cast icy pellets, like handfuls of pebbles from a clandestine lover, against her window. The snow mounted up to the eaves on the north wall, but the east and south remained clear, and she peered out at the blizzard bearing down on her. She could see nothing beyond her own dooryard; she had become isolated.

On the seventh morning, Zennora awoke to silence. She drew her curtains to gaze out at the calm, white field where muffled gables and exhausted pine trees endured in the pale light of the winter dawn. The air was perfectly still, and the black branches hung motionless above the even, featureless false floor where her garden had been. She watched as her neighbors slowly freed themselves, driving channels out from their doorways. There was no thaw, so the snow froze into a crisp crust, and only those with sleighs could travel. Joseph carved his way to Zennora's door and knocked to find out if she were well. As he was leaving, he hesitated, then bit his lip and beckoned her to watch from the warmth of her entry way. He slowly unwrapped a dirty blanket to reveal a red fox, completely frozen, its eyes closed but its brush full and bright, and its paws perfectly aligned in pairs. An old placer miner, struggling out of the woods and back to the comparative safety of the town, had found the animal in a thicket, a scrimpy shelter. Zennora gasped and stared at the delicate creature who seemed to be waiting only for an invitation so that she might shake herself into order, check the scent on the wind, and trot back to her den in the mountains.

The snow ruined Chicago Park. The colony had been sliding towards disaster anyway; angry owners were threatening to sue over defective property titles and neglected construction contracts, and the company manager had developed the habit of answering each complaint by lowering his head so that his eyeshade veiled his face and droning a litany to the effect that the directors would surely address and resolve each and every case. Right after New Year's, the temperature sank below freezing and obstinately stayed there. Several days later, a colonist named Harper awoke to hear a queer cracking sound and found his house settling beneath him. All over the colony, Quon Hay's bricks were disintegrating in the cold; the courses of masonry subsided, crushed under the loads they were supporting, and left rows of crumbs and dust at the bases of walls and foundations. When Harper and his neighbors visited the company office, they found the door locked and the blinds drawn. On their way back to their tilting houses, they passed lumberjacks bringing in newly-felled pines to Briot's sawmill, where the foreman and his crew were producing stack upon stack of fresh lumber, and because the storage barn was full to the brim, they had begun to pile the clean, white boards in the neighboring field. No one knew who would use the lumber, for no one was building, and the contractors had long since disappeared.

Lavinia was furious. Submitting to her summons, Henry shuffled off to the livery stable and returned with an old cart and an older horse. Lavinia ground her teeth as they drove past Harper's house; one of the side walls had sagged, leaving the roof slightly askew and pulling the rest of the house out of line. At her own lot, she stepped briskly down to inspect the bricks that Quon Hay's men had left in a neat, massive stack. Most of them looked all right, but some on the bottom looked as though someone had crushed them. She lifted a brick from the top layer and tapped it gently against another. It split into three pieces. She picked up a third and dropped it on a small piece of granite embedded in the ground. It shattered completely. She took off her gloves and reached for a fourth, holding it in both hands, her face bent down as though to an unruly child. Her knuckles turned white as she pressed on the clay, and suddenly there were two pieces, one in each hand, and shards fell from the fracture. She stood there for a moment, then climbed back up onto the buckboard. She stared straight ahead, abruptly opened her mouth as widely as possible, dropping her jaw and stretching her lips back over her teeth, and shut it again, the seams below her cheeks running ever deeper.

Cousin Jack

Later that afternoon, Lavinia marched through Susan's door, barely pausing to knock, and, sparing everyone her customary cackle, sat down in front of the fire, as straight as a pole, to make clear exactly what she thought of Quon Hay and his bricks, how she knew all along the man was a charlatan, and how she would have him up before the circuit court, if necessary, not only to recover her money but also to demand that he provide her, free of cost and trouble, a new supply of bricks, this time properly made and probably from someone else's factory. Zennora and Susan sat quietly, pretending to listen, while James gazed across the room and out of the window. The angry lecture upset Eleanor; she was now six months pregnant—if her mother stopped to notice, she would surely scold her for going out visiting in such a condition—and she was having more and more difficulty holding little Ethel in her lap. Now, with Lavinia hectoring the absent manager, her voice cutting through the walls, Ethel became restive and irritable, clambering across her mother's thighs while Eleanor glanced anxiously from face to face.

The damage from the freeze soon seemed paltry, for the snowstorm simply buried the colony. Level fields lay under twenty feet of well-packed crystals, and stands of cedar groaned against windblown drifts thirty feet deep. Telegrams began to arrive from Illinois, Wisconsin and Iowa, a trickle that became a flood, entreaties from people who had taken lots in the original drawing in hopes of escaping the oppressive winters of the midwest. They pleaded for someone to tell them that the record snowfall was a lie and that the colony was still the pleasant valley of their fantasies, the haven where they might raise fruit and sit peacefully in the shade. The colony office remained closed, but a few messages got through to friends who wired back dire confirmation: the colony was engulfed in drifts as high as a house. A series of responses arrived over the transcontinental wire: I ain't coming, sell my land, give me back my deposit, I've sold my farm and now I have nowhere to go, how could this happen? The clerks at Western Union tossed the slips of paper into a carton in the corner of their office. The residents, a forlorn group who had imagined themselves the brave vanguard of the new hope, hired sleighs and wagons to move their belongings out of their crumbling houses and into barns and stables in Grass Valley, where most of them took rooms at the Wisconsin Hotel.

Lavinia regarded the snow as a personal affront. When the blizzard finally abated, she browbeat Henry into hiring a sleigh, and they found the landscape so changed that they lost their way twice. Arriving at her property, she climbed down, intending, as usual, to walk around the perimeter, and immediately broke through the fragile crust and sank up to her waist, calling shrilly for her son to pull her out. The directors, she ranted, were obviously shysters who knew all along that the colony would never succeed, that the property was worthless, and that the courts, indubitably corrupt, would never bring them to a just accounting for their fraud. She drove to town in search of a listener, and found one in the dismayed Zennora, who could not figure out a way to avoid inviting in the old tongue-tabbas for a cup of hot cider.

Zennora sat long before her fire that evening, hoping that the snowy roads might bring her at least a few days' respite from unwelcome visitors, but just as she decided not to fetch one more log, there was a knock on her door. Susan had sent Ernest to bring her to James' house, where little Ethel was running a high fever. Not fifteen minutes later, grandmother and great-grandmother stood looking down into the little bed where the tiny girl, her face flushed, thrashed in her blankets and cried bitterly. They sent Ernest for the doctor, but when he returned, he brought the news that Lucy, too, was ill, and Bertie was frantic.

The diphtheria consumed the babies like a wildfire. Both Susan and Zennora felt compelled to tend to both girls, and one murmured to the other, while wringing out a damp towel, the wish to put both children in the same sickroom, an impossible notion that entailed carrying one halfway across town in the freezing wind. They had begun with Ethel, so they stayed with her, dispatching Katie and Sarah in their stead, one to nurse Lucy and the other to comfort her distraught father, who was pacing up and down the upstairs hallway dancing little jigs and chuckling to himself. On the second night, Martin packed his largest pouch full of tobacco, thrust it into his coat pocket, and walked over to Bertie's house, indifferent to the sleet that enveloped him. He firmly took his older brother by the elbow to lead him downstairs, where he fixed him a hot whiskey and finally coaxed him into an easy chair, there to fall asleep, oblivious to the anxious watch that the women were keeping over his daughter's crib. At James' house, Zennora, Susan and Eleanor took turns, two tending to the child and one napping fitfully, and when the two older women looked at each other across the mound of quilts, the dim light cutting their wrinkles deep into their faces, each knew that the other was remembering the long nights, ten years ago, when Jane lay quietly dying.

When Lavinia heard the news, she screamed at Henry to hitch up the horse and goaded him through the drifts. She walked in the front door just as Zennora trudged slowly downstairs, and the older woman paused at the newel post to regard the erect figure that had brought the breath of winter with her. Lavinia opened her mouth to speak, but checked herself, brought her lips together, and waited silently. Zennora beckoned, and the two women walked slowly upstairs to the sick room so that Lavinia could look down at the flushed face of her only granddaughter. She took in the piles of towels, the pitchers of water, the various basins, and Susan's raw, red eyes. She looked down at Ethel once more, then turned on her heel, descended the stairs and took a chair in an out-of-the-way corner, there to wait and listen, but not to interfere. When James walked through early the next morning, he found his mother-in-law slumped with her head resting against the upholstered wing, sleeping, still fully dressed, coat and all, except for the hat she had laid on the table next to her.

On the morning of the sixth day, it was over. Zennora walked downstairs to wake Lavinia and stood there, numb, too tired to be surprised, when Eleanor's mother retreated to the pantry to sob, not for effect, as anyone in the family might have predicted, but out of sheer grief. She emerged just in time to open the door for Ernest, that wretched messenger, slipping in the room as though the Furies were searching for him, and to hear that Lucy, too, had left them. Now Lavinia, the inconsolable, put her arm around Zennora's shoulders as the older woman sank into a chair, too spent to mourn. Through the ceiling, they could hear Susan and Eleanor keening.

Spring arrived gently that year, almost imperceptibly. The morning frosts dwindled by degrees until just a hint of white glistened in the darker crannies outside the houses, secret shinings that melted away with each dawn. The winter winds faded into warm breezes that floated up Wolf Creek and brought the scent of flowers from the low-lying valleys. Tiny red and brown buds filled the trees all over town, and on Easter Sunday, every bud opened so that the churchgoers drove and walked with wondering eyes through alamedas of arching, translucent pink and white.

After the babies died, Zennora spent each day huddled before the fire, neither complaining nor accepting any comfort. With the waning of winter, she moved out onto the porch, and there, sitting in the dappled shade, her sorrow began to ease. Each morning, the sun found a space between the branches and shone down on her face, and she closed her eyes against the light, holding the warmth on her lids and in her open mouth. While the daffodils flared yellow, clumps and rows of playful bugles, Zennora watched the perfect white clouds sail slowly across the cornflower sky like friendly armadas, she marked each change of the trees as the blossoms fell to reveal ravishing green leaves, and she thought of Cornwall.

She conjured up pictures as vivid as though she was seeing them for the first time, images caught in a moment: her mother and father each holding one of her upstretched hands, the long arc of a bright pebble falling into the roiling salt waves, the muddled music of the congregation singing a hymn, the startling eyes of a forgotten potato, the brush of Jesse's beard, the coolness of Susan's toes on the day after she was born, the aroma of fish at the market, and the damp clod that she dropped onto her father's coffin. One day the scudding white clouds carried her back to the time when she, only a little girl, Zennora Curnow, had visited Men-an-tol, the great stone ring that the druids had set in the ground. It was as tall as she had been, but embedded in the earth, and she wondered whether some titan had dropped it there or it had risen out of the ground, but not far enough to roll away and travel freely. On either side stood a menhir, a stone pillar tilted up towards the sky, and she had run figures around the three totems, looping back and forth as though weaving a spell. Happily out of breath, she fell down on the moor, with the grass and sedge cool beneath her back, and gazed up at the stone and the sky, the sky and the stone, feeling the earth wheel eternally beneath her.

On the first Sunday in April, Susan brought word that Eleanor's baby would surely come by nightfall. Zennora surprised her, choosing not to supervise the birth, but to sit on her porch and wait for the news. For the rest of the day, she watched the finches and chickadees play tag with the squirrels in the green branches while her children and grandchildren brought her breathless reports of Eleanor's progress. Each face reminded her of another, of uncles and aunts long since passed on, or of Bessie's children, the ones she would never see. When Ernest reported that Eleanor was doing well, Zennora looked into the serious blue eyes and wondered how much he might resemble his cousin at Penbro, the boy just his age, just seventeen. When Martin came to check on his grandmother, the expression on his face reminded her less of Hannibal, his father, and more of Martin, his uncle, the man who took Bessie back to Cornwall. Even Katie stopped on her way to bring a basket of bread to Eleanor's house, bringing all five children, from the eight-year-old girl down to the toddler who perched on his mother's hip as though he had grown there. Joseph straggled behind, never quite involved with the conversation, apparently puzzled by the brood that swarmed around his wife, but raising his eyebrows and smiling ingratiatingly whenever Zennora addressed him. As the setting sun stained the houses across the street the color of an overripe apricot, Sarah trudged through the gate, exhausted but gratified, for she had assisted at the birth and earned Susan's praise. The child was a girl, and they had named her Alma. Zennora smiled, imagining the baby sleeping in a nest of white blankets, and stayed on the porch, holding the vision, until the sky lost its light and the chill drove her indoors.

The baby looked much like every other that Zennora had held, but there was something about her mouth that reminded her of someone, a face she couldn't place; there were so many now. At first she was apprehensive, feeling sure that the child would be wet or hungry, but little Alma seemed content, gurgling and waving her arms aimlessly until she found her great-grandmother's fingers exploring her face, and Zennora began to chuckle incredulously, for the little thing had begun to suck on her little finger, just like a kitten she remembered from Camborne. No baby had ever done that before, so she sat with her arm in a rather awkward position, looking down at the tiny arrival who was asserting herself so unexpectedly.

Cousin Jack

Zennora awoke one morning in June to find the air already warm and the fragrance of flowers floating in her window. For the first time in months, she felt like going for a walk, so without even stopping for breakfast, she put on her heaviest boots and set off away from the town, following Wolf Creek. She kept steadily on, not quickly, but without slackening, as the sun rose higher in the sky and the shadows receded to small pools beneath the trees. The heat excited the scent of the pine needles and the mountain misery, and the combined aroma filled her nose. At noon, she stopped in a tiny meadow to rest. She sat with her back against a tall Jeffrey pine, and after she caught her breath, she turned to press her face into a fissure in the bark so she could take in the warm vanilla odor, like cookies out of the oven. A jay called from overhead, and hidden insects kept up a steady, endless slicing sound that seemed to come from everywhere. The meadow was ready to burst like a pine cone in the midday sun. Settling into the rough bark behind her back, Zennora shut her eyes.

When she opened them, a tiny red fox, no bigger than a large house cat, was sitting on the grass not ten feet away from her. The fox and the woman sat motionless, each staring at the other. The animal's eyes were as large as those of a doe, and her ears seemed as long as a rabbit's, but wider and more gracefully curved. Long whiskers spread from either side of her perfect brown nose. Zennora blinked, and the fox shifted position to lift a hind leg and scratch under her chin. Then she yawned, dropping her jaw so far it seemed to come unhinged, and let it snap shut again. Zennora slowly reached out her hand. The fox looked carefully at the hand and rose to her feet, pacing to and fro, always watching the hand and the woman, at first maintaining her distance, but then coming closer and closer until she stood with her whiskers barely drooping over the woman's fingers. Zennora realized that the entire meadow had become absolutely silent; even the breeze had subsided so that there was no rustling of leaves or swaying of boughs overhead. The moment held, and Zennora hardly took a breath as the eyes of the fox enveloped her.

The fox slowly lowered her head and licked Zennora's hand, her tongue rough and smooth and warm and wet as it slid across her knuckles. She looked up into the woman's face one more time, then turned to trot off into the manzanita. Zennora sat dazed, listening to the meadow come to life again.

She hardly slept that night. She lingered on the porch until the last daylight faded from the sky and the first stars pierced the black canopy. Settling into bed, she saw that the full moon had risen above the neighbors' trees and was casting evanescent shadows across her room. She closed her eyes for a moment, and opened them to find that every lighted surface was shimmering, and she realized that the house was filled with a ceaseless, nearly subliminal clamor. She climbed out of bed and crept out of her room to sit on the stairs and peer through the banister.

The house was filled with piskies. They danced on the chairs, organized parades from room to room, and scurried from corner to corner, sometimes skittering up the walls and through the ceiling, which had become calmly transparent, to reach the rafters, where they played tag, called to their fellows below, and chattered back and forth to each other. There were piskies sliding down the lampshades to swing on the fringe, piskies rolling in the ashes between the andirons, piskies running little races through the patterns in the rugs, and piskies sorting through the tiny jars of spices and herbs that Zennora kept in the kitchen. A small band of them had discovered the big armchair in the living room; half rappelled up the carved legs while the rest explored the seams in the upholstery and discovered that they could pull back the lining under the frame and actually enter. They smiled and laughed and chanted and sang.

Zennora sat with her mouth open, hardly able to blink. Never, not even when she was a little girl, had the little people revealed themselves with such abandon. The tiny footfalls were crisp, the murmur of wee voices was clear, and she could see the sprites as easily as the balusters that she grasped in her hands. She lost all sense of the passing of the night, not noticing the moonbeams pulling back towards the windows as the moon rose outside.

She realized that someone was standing quite close to her. She looked down on the oaken floor of the staircase landing, and there, next to her, was a pisky woman. She wore a dress buttoned up to her neck, with a long full skirt and an apron, and a white cap that helped pin back her hair. The network of wrinkles in her face made her look quite old, but she stood perfectly erect, her cheeks were pink and her eyes were bright. She smiled, and Zennora smiled in return before suddenly recognizing her: the pisky woman was a precise miniature of her great-grandmother, from the dress she wore to the expression on her face. Zennora remembered seeing her years ago, when she was just a little girl, standing in the doorway of her stone cottage with her hands on her hips, waiting for Zennora to run to her. The two women gazed into each other's eyes for a long moment, and another, and another, until finally, the pisky turned and skipped down the stairs to join the others.

Zennora watched until the first light of dawn set the front curtains glistening, and the piskies seemed to fade with the night until they had vanished completely. Zennora could not tell where they had gone, but each little group turned to smile and wave as they left the room.

Later that morning, Eleanor and Susan arrived with Alma; Zennora had agreed to watch the baby for an hour so they could take some fresh bread to a woman from church whose family was ill. Zennora nodded at Eleanor's last few instructions, then held the baby up to watch her mother and grand-mother walk down the street.

She wasn't at all tired, but she didn't feel like moving, and she hoped that Alma would be content with cuddling until Eleanor returned. The sun sent warm green shadows flickering across the porch and the flowerbeds, and the scent of cut grass floated past Zennora's face. A jay flew down to perch on the branch that hung near her porch steps; it turned its head to stare at her with one eye, then jeered and fluttered away. Zennora looked down at Alma to find the baby gazing up at her. The old woman smiled, then noticed that the infant's stare was neither aimless nor fumbling—she looked as though she were about to say something, and her hands, usually exploring the air, lay still on her blanket. Zennora raised her eyebrows, pretending to ask the baby what was on her mind, and Alma smiled—a small, secret, knowledgeable smile. At that moment, Zennora realized that the look on the child's face was an exact mimicry of the pisky she had met in the night, and that in Alma, she was, once again, seeing her great-grandmother.

An hour later, Eleanor and Susan opened the garden gate and looked up to the house to see Zennora sitting in her favorite chair with Alma nestled in her lap. Susan called a greeting, but her mother didn't answer. Alma was asleep, sucking happily on her great-grandmother's little finger. Zennora's hands were firmly clasped around the bundle and her face was bent down towards the baby's, but her eyes, unblinking, looked not at the child, but through her and beyond.

22
Warfare
1896-98

I beg to inform the partners of the Live Yankee Quartz Mining Company that I have struck a vein just below the sixty-fathom level on the incline, about thirty yards south by southeast of the main shaft. Judging the vein to be promising, I engaged a crew of five men to further open up the drift, and I am now convinced that this vein may pay well. I therefore propose that we hire a crew to work the vein as fully as possible.

> *Yours Truly,*
> *Zebulon Day*

> *15th Oct. 1896*

Susan considered. Day was a careful man, not at all inclined to exaggerate. If he wanted to hire a working crew, then the vein was probably richer than he admitted. On the other hand, after working the mine, frequently alone, for over twenty years, he might have reached a point of quiet desperation. The vein might be a chance deposit, so small that Day's exploratory crew may have seen most of what it had to offer. Then again, perhaps Day's persistence and Hannibal's optimistic conviction were now, finally, vindicated.

There were fewer partners now. Zennora was dead. Hannibal was dead. Martin had passed away at Penbro just a few years back, leaving Bessie with the farm and two half-grown boys still living at home. Old William Pascoe, after surviving blasts and cave-ins for over sixty years, spent his last day making his monthly inspection of the Live Yankee, and died in his bed. His sons were old men now, James bent over since a heavy timber fell on his back, and Will coughing, always coughing. They hardly ever left their room at the Wisconsin Hotel, and they hadn't visited Red Dog in nearly ten years. Nick was still living in Australia, writing occasional letters from a place called Kalgoorie. No one had tried to sell any of the Live Yankee shares—after so many years without returns, a share was more of a liability than an asset—so Hannibal's mine had dwindled to brief entries in wills and probates as the lawyers meticulously reduced the remains of people's lives to fragments divided among those left behind, fractions of fractions. Susan reckoned that she and Bessie and Joseph controlled more than half of the company, but unless Joseph surprised her, Day would be the one to advise the other

355

partners and direct the operation. The mine would be his. Susan suddenly felt apprehensive about trusting him, a virtual stranger, with Hannibal's enterprise.

Jack had come to Grass Valley for Zennora's funeral and had stayed long enough to help her arrange the sale of the house that Jesse built. No one wanted it. Bertie stammered something about "Gramfer's room" and chuckled and winked when she pressed him, but James, after some persuasion, finally admitted that the two of them had walked up to the house one day when they thought everyone was gone, pried open a board on the windowless room, and surprised their grandfather sleeping in the dusty shadows. Their fumbling awakened him, and he had given a great yell, leapt to his feet and retreated, howling in alarm, to a corner, where he stood at bay, shaking and shivering among the slivers of glass from a bottle that he had knocked over and shattered. The little boys ran home as fast as they could, but they promised each other never to tell what they had seen. After that, neither of them had felt completely comfortable there, and although Joseph had torn down the addition, James could still see the bolt holes where his grandfather had fastened the posts and sills to the main house, now the edifice of Jesse's dementia. Susan offered the house to Joseph, but Katie was comfortable on Quartz Street. Jack suggested that they rent out the place, but she knew that she would have to manage it on her own, possibly not even being able to rely on Joseph for repairs. Jack then found a buyer, and he returned to the hills every month until they completed the sale and the superior court closed the probate. As though sustaining a rhythm, Jack kept making the trip to Grass Valley, and seldom did Susan pass two months without opening her door to find him there, ready to sit and talk with her in the drifting afternoon.

Neither mentioned the Sawyer decision and its consequences. They spoke of their children. He laughed at her exasperated stories about Lavinia and her odd family, and in return, he told her all about San Francisco, about the slow construction of the sea wall that would lead to the reclamation of salt flats, of President Harrison's visit—Jack and Annie had attended the ball in his honor—and of the Midwinter Fair in Golden Gate Park, with the Electric Tower standing in the center of the Grand Court, the grounds all terraced and planted in heavy tropical greenery, and the colorful, startling costumes of the exhibitors from such strange, remote countries as Brazil, Siam and the Ottoman Empire. Jack moved through their encounters almost tentatively, as though groping through a drift without a candle, but with no need to hurry, never pushing himself forward, but rather listening to what she had to say, answering or nodding quietly, as appropriate to the moment.

She asked him to go to Red Dog with her and descend the main shaft to look at Day's vein. She had never been down in a mine before, and when she reached the one hundred foot level, the damp warmth surprised her and she wished she had left her jacket in the buggy. She could not tell whether Day resented Jack's presence—his smooth, white face was as inscrutable as the stone wall of the tunnel—but he seemed willing to defer to Mrs. Carne's cousin, respecting him by reputation. He stood to one side while Jack, wearing a shabby outfit that made Susan smile when she thought of the carefully-tailored suits he usually wore, took out a small hammer and chisel, and chipped away a few fragments that he stowed away in a small leather bag that hung from his belt. He reached up with his fingers and traced his hand slowly along the rock face above his head, following some path she could not see, and stopped, pressing his finger against the mountain. He conferred with Day in what Susan heard as a sort of foreign language, composed of brief phrases about greenstone, and pitch, and dip, and sulphurets, and virgin ground, a compressed vernacular that each man used sparingly, amplifying his thoughts by pointing to places in the wall or offering a subtle tilt of the head that the other comprehended immediately. When they reached the surface, the bright sunshine dazzled Susan for several moments before she could see the lump of rock that Jack offered for her inspection. It was a piece of quartz, a clump of white crystals that some subterranean force had fused helter-skelter. She looked up, puzzled, and he grinned. "Iss fay, there's gold in there. I'll take these samples into the assayer, but I think it's a keenly lode."

When the partners met—a small gathering, just the five of them with Dibble sitting off to one side, ready with pen and paper for whatever his clients might request—Susan supported Day's proposal. As she was speaking, she realized that she controlled the company, for even if Joseph chose, much against his custom, to disagree with her, she held proxies from Bessie and Nick, and so voted just over half of the shares. Her voice faltered, but there was no debate, for Joseph and the Pascoes accepted Day's representations and Susan's report of Jack's visit, so there was hardly any need to call a vote on the question. Day hired a crew and began work the following week, using what remained of the company's cash on hand and taking a short-term loan against their prospects. In December, he installed rails and tram cars for bringing the rock up to grass; a month later, he purchased a small stamp mill so he could prepare the ore on site; and by late spring, he had paid off the loan. In May, Susan tore open an envelope from Dibble, and a bank draft for $212 fluttered down to the floor. Another draft arrived a month later, and then another, and in August, Day solemnly reported that although he was not yet able to assess the extent of the Live Yankee's reserves, he believed that the partners could rest assured of steady production for the foreseeable future. Susan would be receiving nearly eight hundred dollars each month. Jack insisted that they dine at the Holbrooke to celebrate.

Cousin Jack

As the waiters ducked and whirled about them, Susan looked across at Jack and suddenly laughed out loud. He raised his eyebrows, wondering what joke he had missed, but she shook her head and nodded to the waiter who was deferentially offering a decanter of sherry. There was no joke; she had simply discovered, sitting in the leather chair, with the silver and china and linen spread before her, that she had become a woman of means, a partner in a profitable mine. Her fortune would never compare with the wealth of the Sterlings, who had moved to San Francisco, leaving an agent to manage their local affairs, but she would be comfortable and even, within the world that mattered to her, powerful, if power was the ability to change things for the better. She began to interrogate Jack about business opportunities in Grass Valley. Caught off guard, he answered her questions with tentative generalities, but finally could not restrain his curiosity and asked what she was planning.

She laid down her fork and knife. "I want to 'elp my sons. Bertie's workin' in Bennett's shoe store, and that's all right, but James is still workin' underground at the Idaho."

"And what would he like to do?"

Susan sighed. "'e'd like t' spend all day at th' fire'ouse, but it's time 'e grew up. I'd like t' set 'im up on Mill Street."

"What about Martin and Ernest?"

"I'm not sure. I think I'll take care o' the older boys first."

Jack carefully offered advice. Don't look for something that you think will make the owner rich in a month, or a year, or even five years. Look for the sure, steady business, one that will pay regularly and reliably, month after month, year after year. Better to pay a good price for a solid, established concern in a good location than to take over a place that the owner has neglected, or to pick up a bargain a mile away. If you want to start up something new, look around town to see which shops are too crowded to handle the demand. Find out what people need. It doesn't matter what interests you—men sell nails and potatoes not because they're exciting, but because everyone needs them. Besides, if a man who likes his liquor too much opens a brewery or a saloon, he'll go broke within six months.

Bertie and James respected their mother's acumen, but they had forgotten how precise and resolute she could be. She had firmly requested that their wives hear what she had to say, and the younger women listened, their eyes wide, to the opportunities that their mother-in-law outlined so clearly. When she left, Eleanor asked James whether Susan might be going the way of Lavinia, foisting ill-conceived schemes on the rest of the family, but he shook his head. Susan was different.

Ever since James turned sixteen, his mother had treated him with scarcely-concealed impatience that seemed to increase each year and became tolerable only because they no longer lived in the same house. He had often

358

wondered, fretfully, why she found him so lacking, and he brooded over the day when they had quarreled over his job at the Idaho and she had dismissed him as having neither ambition nor gumption. As a boy, he had enjoyed Zennora's stories about the men who built the North Star—Jesse, Hannibal, Nick and Jack, and the elder Joseph, killed in the mine so long ago—but he learned to resent the consequent standard that his mother apparently expected him to meet. He grumbled to himself that Grass Valley had been different in the sixties and there had been room for a man to make something of himself. Now men like his grandfather—the smarter ones, the ones who survived, old men—owned the town and ran it like a little club, leaving little room for men his own age. He poured himself a whiskey and thought that if Jesse were a young man today, he, too, would feel stymied. Besides, everything he considered was too dull; if there had been adventure and opportunity in Grass Valley, there was precious little of it now. Look at Jack; he might have been a giant thirty years ago, but he seemed pretty ordinary now.

Still, his mother was offering to set him up in a shop, and that would be a way out of the mines. Probably more money, and certainly easier work, and he didn't know when he'd have another opportunity. He liked running with the fire company, but that was no way to make a living. Typically, his mother had claimed to be leaving his life in his own hands, but she had organized the options to give him very little leeway. She would not insist on her point of view, but she would dole out her approval in careful measures. She judged that he had failed to make a future for himself and his family, so she would—just this once—do it for him. He was as annoyed as he was grateful, but he decided to welcome her proposition, and for lack of any strong preference in the matter, to rely on her to choose the nature of the business.

Bertie, true to form, chuckled and winked, then jigged across the floor to embrace Susan and promise to do whatever she wanted. Susan looked over his shoulder to see Hettie, his new wife, release a relieved sigh.

On the first of October, Susan signed a lease for a storefront building on Mill Street. When Jack walked down from the Holbrooke to look it over, he smiled, for she had followed his advice to the letter. The location couldn't be better, about halfway between Main and Neal, adjacent to Bank Alley. The place had been a dry goods store since the sixties, and Bertie and James would re-open it as the New York Racket Store, purveyors of fabric, patterns, table linens, chenille covers, portieres, lace curtains, fancy goods, novelties, and a small corner with an assortment of toys. The two men would be equal partners in the business, but because Bertie had considerable experience in such matters, he would supervise the operation, keeping his job as manager of the boot and shoe department at the People's Cash Store, just across the alley, while James did the day-to-day work, managing the two clerks that Susan instructed him to hire, seeing to the stock, opening the building in the morning, locking it in the evening, and greeting the customers as they arrived. James soon learned that running a store could be far more work than drilling quartz. He kept such long hours that Eleanor, for the first time since they were married, began to wonder whether he were lingering in the downtown saloons, but her friends at church reported seeing him in the store at all hours, and when he came home for supper, usually late, he wanted only to collapse into a comfortable chair and sit there with his eyes closed.

Susan made little progess with her younger sons. Martin had taken two rooms above a jewelers' on Mill Street; he slept in one and used the other as his shop, where he rolled cigars and sold pipes and tobacco that he purchased from an agent in Sacramento. Susan proposed to find him a larger location, something more accessible; as it was, a potential customer had to find the small brass plate bolted to the brick wall next to the discreet door leading to the staircase. Martin scowled and limped across the crowded room to pick out one of his own cigars, scorning the imported ones, and stood staring down through the window at the traffic, filling the room with smoke so dry and thick that Susan's nose began to close up. Finally, he grudgingly agreed that she might publish his card in the *Union,* and the very next week, the paper displayed the following notice:

ARE YOU A SMOKER?
Finest Imported and Domestic Cigars.
Also Home Manufactured.
Martin Carne, Mill Street

Susan's questions seemed to baffle Ernest. He shifted his feet and shrugged his shoulders, smiling as though embarrassed. He and Lavinia's younger son, Will, were sharing a miner's cottage in Nevada City with two other young men, all of them working at the Champion Mine on William's shift, and as Susan tried to get the boy to focus on her offer, she could hear laughter and the clinking of glassware in the next room. They were young voices, still thin and light, and she realized that Ernest was listening to her as a small boy might attend to a minister or a schoolteacher: tolerant and obedient as long as the moment lasted, his fidgeting just barely under control, but waiting for release. She was suddenly aware of the distance between her and her son, a gulf composed of time and experience that she could not negotiate, and she tried not to think of what Jack and Nick had accomplished at his age. There was a veil behind Ernest's eyes, a patient, wary look on his face that convinced her that he could not understand, perhaps could not even hear, what she was trying to say. As she walked up the path to her buggy, she could hear them laughing, free.

Several weeks later, Susan walked into the Racket Store to find James in an uncharacteristically ebullient mood. He wrapped up a small collection of notions for a plump woman wearing an impossible hat, bowed her to the door, and turned to his mother, grinning.

She could not help smiling in return. "What is it?"

He drew her over to a chair next to the counter and struck a pose in front of a glass display case. "I've decided to buy a house!" She raised a gloved hand to her mouth, and he continued. "It's new, one of the row along Race Street, behind the Conaway place."

She reached up and took his hand. "James, I'm so 'appy for ye."

"Thank you, Mother."

She considered for a moment, then decided to say what she was thinking without trying to lead up to it. "I'd like to 'elp ye buy it."

He paused. There was something in his eyes, just a hint of what she had seen when she went to speak to Ernest, but it dissipated and she discovered that he was looking straight at her without blinking, his mouth set in a firm smile. "That's very generous of you, Mother. I know Eleanor—both of us, of course—will be very grateful."

By way of housewarming, Eleanor insisted on asking everyone over for scrumpy and fairings, so on the last Saturday before Christmas, Susan sat wedged into a corner between Henry Hosken and Joseph's eldest daughter, sipping hot cider while the young women squeezed through the crush with plates of cookies, usually failing to reach the foot of the stairs before having to return to the kitchen for more. The children, exhilarated with the crowd and the holiday, tried to run back and forth from one end of the little house to the other—Martin was stolidly guarding the staircase so no one could run up and then tumble down—but most of them, with their parents' encouragement, fled to the porch, there to walk along the broad cap of the low wall that was the modern answer to the railing. The noise hammered at Susan's ears.

Lavinia's voice cut through the tumult. She had raised one hand and was lifting her chin to look around the room, trying to smile, but bouncing her jaw up and down to press her lips together nervously. She pushed her way to the staircase, waved Martin aside, and lifted her skirts to walk up high enough so that she could see everyone. She kept calling for quiet until Mary began to shush the people near her with a loud, aggressive hiss. Joseph, Will and Ernest, clustered around the kitchen doorway, regarded the woman on the stairs with slightly silly expressions; Susan was sure that they had been sharing a bottle on the back landing.

Lavinia smiled, then barked. "Well!" The men near the kitchen called out "Hear, hear!" and laughed; Mary turned to glare at them. "Ah . . . I just wanted to say . . . Well, here we are!" She barked again. "I just wanted you all to know that I've bought a lot and I'm going to build a house." Two of the boys ran in from the porch, slamming the front door behind them, and Katie caught them, pointing a finger to convince them to stand still. Susan thought for a moment and remembered that Lavinia had, very quietly, sold her property in Chicago Park and probably taken a considerable loss. She scanned the room and saw Eleanor pouting as she whispered something to Nettie; no doubt she was annoyed with her mother for stealing the occasion from her.

James, a wary half-smile on his lips, called out, "Where?"

Lavinia lifted her nose. "Piety Hill." This was a new neighborhood on the south side of Deer Creek, across the ravine from Nevada City, and Susan had heard her sons mock the pretentious street names—Zion, Cross, Calvary, Gethsemane and Jordan—and suggest that the denizens of the Broad Street saloons would have to make regular forays across the creek just to keep the residents from putting on airs. "And it will be a fine house, I can tell you!" Susan looked over at William, nearly hidden by the enormous carved oak hall tree that Lavinia had picked up cheap and given to her daughter, but she could read nothing in his face.

Lavinia hired a builder early in January, and she escorted him, considerably nonplussed, to the courthouse to have their contract notarized and recorded. In spite of the bitter weather and the likelihood of storms and snow, she insisted that he begin construction immediately, and when he suggested that they might want to spend some time considering various plans and designs, she reached into her bag and brought out a set of drawings that she had, apparently, been working on for some time. It was a compact but elegant two-story home, cross-gabled, with two sets of bay windows and a coach house in the rear. The sketches reminded Eleanor of homes in the nicer neighborhoods in Galena: wide enough to accommodate two large rooms running across, but narrow enough for someone to walk up one side of the house and drive a carriage down the other, and featuring a small porch, with railings below, gingerbread above, and the front stairs descending sideways in front of the dining room. When Eleanor proposed that Henry drive them around town to inspect some of the more interesting new homes—shingle houses, with overlapping scales; Colonial revivals, like elaborations of miners' cabins, with their symmetrical bays; and Queen Annes with porches rambling around the front half of the building, and some with Palladian windows or tall, round towers—Lavinia snorted and glared. She would have her house, and she knew what a fine house looked like.

The builder promised to send men to grade the site and dig out the cellar, but when he arrived with stakes and twine, he found Lavinia waiting, and she lifted her skirts to follow him wherever he went, marching all over the lot in the cold mud and frowning whenever he placed a corner even an inch away from where she thought it should rest. When he mentioned ordering the lumber, Lavinia told him that she had been to every sawmill and supplier in the area, and she knew exactly where to go and what to buy. At the lumber yard—a new enterprise west of Nevada City—she questioned virtually every selection he made, accusing him first of inflating his bid by planning to buy expensive materials and so take a larger profit margin, and then of buying supplies less costly than his bid justified. They very nearly quarreled when she, standing before a great stack of massive posts, demanded that he accept a grade below what he had proposed and then renegotiate the price of the entire contract.

On the day that the builder had designated to begin framing the walls, torrents of rain drenched the town. Before most people had begun their breakfasts, Lavinia was knocking on the builder's door, demanding to know why his men were not working. When the weather cleared and the carpenters did begin their labors, they discovered that Lavinia planned to supervise every notch and nail, and the men began to make jokes, very quietly, about giving her their rulers and squares, and entrusting her with the task of marking each cut. She climbed ladders, traversed joists and rafters, and roamed all over the site, always with Henry close at hand.

When the finish work began, Lavinia's scrutiny became even more exacting. She did, indeed, have her own steel square and even a plumb bob, calling to Henry to bring them out of the leather case he was carrying so that she could check each door and window frame for true, and when two of the men had a mild disagreement about the planing of a sill, she brought out a set of calipers and measured it herself. When they returned to hang the windows, she followed them from room to room, thrusting a knife blade between each sash and casing, hectoring them when the sliding surfaces showed a tendency to bind, and spinning each sash pulley to see that it ran smoothly. She had insisted on the best of wash basins and bath tubs, so she followed the plumber throughout the house, complaining when his assistant was about to settle for less-than-perfect threads on a coupling, and checking the proposed location of each pipe before they cut the holes in the floors or walls. The plasterer very nearly quit when Lavinia took his assistant's trowel to show him exactly how the ceilings should be done, but the builder persuaded him to stay on the job, so the man exhaled great clouds of cigar smoke whenever Lavinia stood too close to him. The painter, similarly beset, simply stopped working to stare at her whenever she decided to offer comments, and since the builder was paying the man and his crew by the day, he desperately began to find other things to occupy his client's attention. She spent four days crouched over while a crew of boys with sanding blocks went over the entire floor, leaving a smooth surface for the painter to varnish, but they quickly learned that Mrs. Hosken would reject any board that left even the smallest splinter in her glove. When the paperhanger arrived, Lavinia was ready with instructions regarding the sizing and the paste, and whenever he suggested that he had his own way of achieving the result she wanted, she tartly observed that her uncle in Galena knew the right way to hang wallpaper, and she would follow his example.

By April, the construction was nearly finished, and Lavinia returned home weary one evening after a long meeting with the draper, who appeared to have his own ideas regarding the fabric for the portieres in the dining room. She walked into the kitchen to find Will there. That was unusual by itself—he now spent most of his time with the other young fools from the Champion—but before she could formulate a comment, she noticed that he and his father had spread an inky newspaper across her clean kitchen table.

They looked up as she walked in, with Henry straggling behind her. "It's war, Lavinia," said William.

"What?" She stopped short, still thinking of portieres and printer's ink.

"Spain has declared war on the United States," Will explained. He looked at his father and took a breath. "I'm going to enlist."

Lavinia glared at them. She had barely taken notice of that business about the *Maine,* regarding the disaster as clear evidence either of the perfidy of those scoundrelly Spanish or of the manifest incompetence of the U.S. Navy, manned, no doubt, by drunkards and wastrels, but demoting the incident, in spite of the sensational headlines in the local newspapers, to insignificance. How could affairs so far away possibly be of any concern to her? She was inclined to treat the declaration of war with similar impatience, but the prospect of Will enlisting was a different matter entirely. Join the Army and run off to Cuba? Why if he wasn't shot, he'd probably catch some tropical fever or other, and she'd be nursing him for the rest of his life.

They argued over the question all evening—that is, Lavinia and Will argued while Mary sat in a corner sewing, her lips pressed white, and Nettie, finished with cleaning up after dinner, dusted every knick-knack in the parlor, wiping her eyes with the back of her sleeve. Finally, William rose to his feet to inform Lavinia that Will was a grown man and could do what he pleased, no matter how she or anyone else felt about it.

Lavinia's dudgeon rose when she found Eleanor in tears and learned that James, too, was giving serious thought to enlisting. What could he be thinking of? He was married and had three small children, not to mention a business to run. She told Eleanor to put on her hat, then took little Florence by the hand and walked them down the street and around the corner to Susan's house, with Henry following in the buggy.

Susan sighed. "Bertie and Ernest want to enlist, too."

"What about Martin?" asked Eleanor.

"No," smiled Susan. "'e says 'e'll join up when th' Spanish sail into San Francisco Bay, unless they cut off th' tobacco supply first."

Wafare, 1896-98

Lavinia had been muttering and sputtering under her breath ever since leaving Eleanor's house, and saw none of the humor in Martin's attitude. "Those fools! Those young fools! Mrs. Carne, we cannot—*we cannot*—permit them to do this."

Susan's sons were oddly deferential, but she felt that they were only being patient, giving her an obligatory hearing before they did what they wanted to do. Bertie jigged around the displays of ladies' boots while chuckling about American boys teaching the dirty Spanish a lesson, and she found James standing across the street from his store, staring at the façade with his arms folded. After he listened to her recitation of the obvious—that he had a wife, a family, a home, and a business—he scowled, shook his head and asked, "Do you think I *like* working here, Mother?"

Susan sat in her empty house and listened to the silence. People left; if they didn't die, they traveled halfway around the world chasing after a rumor, and failing that, they simply grew up and moved out. Perhaps there was no point in trying to keep the men from enlisting; if it wasn't the Army, it would be something else. She brooded until a small grey bird lit suddenly on a branch and let out a surprisingly loud whistle. Susan laughed in spite of herself, then walked downstairs to open the front door and let in the warm spring afternoon. She was starting to think like an old woman, she thought, an old, petulant woman who has nothing better to do than complain about things she can't change and perhaps aren't her business anyway. Yet while Ernest might do as he liked, whether or not her married sons would leave their families was very much her concern, and if they wouldn't be reasonable, she would have to take them in hand.

First she met with Bennett, who promised, after only a brief discussion, that if Bertie left the shoe department, he would dissolve their partnership and find another man. Then she took Bertie next door to see James, leading them back to the store room for a private talk. Susan laid out her plans calmly. If they enlisted, she would decline to renew her lease on the building. If they came back—*if* they came back—they would have to run the store, if there was a store to run, on their own. James began to argue, but she lifted a gloved finger, and he fell silent. However, if they stayed where they belonged, Dibble would draw up papers to make the store a partnership among the three of them. Bertie and James would run the business, as before, but Susan would invest enough extra capital to make the store something special. They would remodel the whole place, outside and in, and they would improve the breadth and the quality of their stock. They would attract a better class of customer, people willing to pay more for better goods, people who would find the place reminiscent of their favorite stores in San Francisco. Profits would rise; they would be able to hire more clerks and James would not have to work such long hours. Moreover, they would set up the partnership so that Susan had no vote at all—she would exercise no prerogatives to match her obligations, and would only expect to receive her share of the profits after, of course, the boys paid themselves appropriate salaries.

The men listened, James leaning back in his chair and Bertie dancing his feet nervously on the scraps of fabric and paper that littered the floor. When she finished, Bertie was smiling and chuckling, but James was biting his lip. He felt trapped. Going home was no solution; there were evenings—he hoped that Eleanor did not suspect this—that he dawdled at the store, closing the doors and shutters but remaining behind to sort shipments simply because he could not face the stuffy, crowded parlor on Race Street. He had hated working in the mines, but there had been something about the labor— the timbering, the drilling, the blasting, the shoveling—that was elemental, that had made him think back to his grandmother's stories about the Trevennas in the mines of Camborne. But now he was caught—he could not, on a miner's wages, afford the house he now owned, the furnishings and decorations, the clothing Eleanor liked to wear, the boots he bought from Bertie, his hats from San Francisco, the carriage that delighted the children, and on and on. He could not go back. He had considered enlistment as a reckless solution to an insoluble problem, acceptable only because the implicit heroism made it somehow honorable. Yet now that his mother had reduced the matter to more practical terms—now that she had, once again, stepped in to chart his course—he knew he could not go through with it.

"All right, Mother." He tried to smile. "Shall we shake hands on it?"

Susan searched his face for some gratitude or enthusiasm, but found only wariness. That, then, was her portion. Exhausted, she could devise no stratagem to keep Ernest and Will close to home, so they, like playful boys just let out of school, made their plans.

When Lavinia, again, stormed her porch, Susan thought wearily that while the Hosken woman never, ever asked for her advice or help, she rapped on her door whenever she stumbled on an outrage, as though it were somehow Susan's responsibility, or that its presentation would lead inevitably to redress. Susan was no less distressed, but she recognized the limits of what she could do. "They've no wives, no children. They don't much like workin' in th' mines, but they don't know what else t' do. Just three months ago, I 'ad all I could do t' talk Ernest out o' shippin' out t' Dawson."

Lavinia clucked her tongue impatiently. "You should have let him go, Mrs. Carne. Better the Klondike than Cuba."

Susan did not reply. She had thought that Alaska might be a fine place for her youngest son, even though, remembering the long years in Cornwall after the men had gone to America, she had hoped to hold the family together. She had been about to offer to pay for Ernest's passage and equipage, but he had mentioned that Joseph might be going with him, a casual remark that had thrown her wildly off balance. The idea was impossible: her brother had eight children, and even though he seldom worked more than two weeks in a row, he was a kindly husband and father, and his family was surely better off with him here. When she had called him to account, the image of a dog had come absurdly into her mind, a big retriever that has done something wrong, knows it, but wags his tail anyway, watching his mistress anxiously in hopes of forgiveness. Joseph had not been able to explain how he felt—he could scarcely put five words together to make a thought—but she had gathered that he found work, home and family all quite overwhelming. They had been standing in the stable, and when three of the children had run out into the yard, calling to each other at the tops of their voices, Joseph had winced and almost cowered back into the shadows next to the tack and bales of straw. Joseph was lost, but he had, somehow, found something solid in this dream of wandering off to the Klondike, and he was reluctant to let go of it, no matter how ashamed he might feel. She had reminded him of his responsibilities, over and over again, and finally he had mumbled that he would go only if Ernest went; indeed, that was his motivation in the first place, that his nephew might need a more experienced, older man to stand by him. Susan had thought to herself that her son was better equipped to look after her brother rather than the other way around, but she took that confession back to Ernest, insisting that if he went to Dawson, and Joseph with him, then he, and he alone, would bear the responsibility for the neglected wife and children. She had cornered him every way she knew, appealing to his better nature one moment and sneering at him the next, until she got what she wanted. Resentful and aggrieved, he had consented to stay in California.

Now, having irreparably damaged her relationship with her son, she had nothing left that would prevent him from joining the Army. She could not explain this to Lavinia, because she had kept the Klondike incident secret from most of the family, not wanting to make Joseph's humiliation and Ernest's disappointment matters for public discussion. So Ernest and Will took the stage to San Francisco, where they walked into the nearest recruiting office and joined a regiment of infantry. In the meantime, Congress unanimously passed McKinley's war resolution, the American fleet blockaded Havana, and Lavinia finished her house. She moved her family into it in May, and immediately invited the Carnes and Trevennas over to, as James put it, "show them how it was done."

Even Martin had to admit that it was an admirable home. Just off of the entry way, with its massive newel, an elegant dining room featured a bay window facing Pine Street, and beyond, in the enormous parlor, windows thrust out to catch the southern sunlight. In her well-appointed sitting room,

Lavinia declared, she would entertain certain special guests—she left it to their imaginations to decide just what criteria she had in mind. The pantry impressed even Susan, and the bathroom offered every modern convenience. Upstairs were three bedrooms, a small one for Henry, another for Mary and Nettie, and the last large enough, as James muttered to Bertie, for the whole family, but intended only for Lavinia and William, with a vast fireplace. Susan found the house uncomfortably raw, although Lavinia's furniture suited the fresh paint and up-to-date decorations, but William, in a burst of loquacity, assured her that they were planting trees all over the property, and that some day soon there would be shade and seclusion.

Susan wanted to rest, but she spent each day anxiously seeking news of the war. Ernest and Will had sailed through the canal to Florida, where their regiment was training for the liberation of Cuba. Everything she read, as well as everything she heard in the shops downtown, presented the war as a great adventure, a lark for young men in dashing uniforms who had left their loved ones behind to teach the Spanish cutthroats a lesson and return by Christmas, heroes all. She began to read about terrible atrocities, slaughter of women and children, but a woman at church assured her that these were flagrant fictions intended to sell newspapers and fan the outrage of the American public. In June, American troops began landing on Cuban beaches, but she did not know whether Ernest was among them. July passed without a single letter from Florida, and none of the newspapers even mentioned her son's regiment. At the end of the month, Spain sued for peace.

A week later, Lavinia received a letter from Will. He and Ernest were well, but they were eager to leave Florida to join the fighting. Could his mother send him some clean socks? Wool was too heavy; cotton would be better. The date on the letter was July 7, and Susan, sitting in Eleanor's parlor, realized that anything could have happened in the meantime. At that moment, there was a loud knock on the door, and Eleanor opened it to find a young miner standing there, his sweating horse tethered at the curb.

"Is Missus 'osken 'ere?" Eleanor looked back at Lavinia, who rose and came forward. "It's Mister 'osken . . . 'e's hurt."

Lavinia went white in an instant. "How badly?"

The boy shook his head. "I dunno. They 'ad t' carry 'im out. We took 'im to yer 'ouse, an' Miss 'osken told me where ye might be."

For five days, William lay in the big upstairs room. Mary shut the windows and drew the heavy curtains, capturing the sultry August heat and leaving no possibility for a breeze or any fresh air. Lavinia sat as straight as a post on a spindle-backed chair that she had set halfway across the room, not loosening so much as a button on the dress she had been wearing on the day they carried him there, her eyes fixed on her husband's bearded face while Mary, Nettie and Eleanor took turns tending to him. For five days, he lingered, never regaining consciousness, and for five days, Lavinia spoke to no one and scarcely acknowledged anyone else's presence. Early in the morning of the sixth day, Nettie gave a little gasp and reached up to touch her father's forehead. William was dead.

Susan was standing on her porch reading a telegram when Henry, alone this time, pulled up in Lavinia's buggy. She listened to his message and nodded. A light breeze set the leaves to trembling. "Tell Lavinia . . . " She showed him the paper in her hand. "Tell Lavinia that Will is comin' 'ome. Ernest, too. They're all right."

"Ah!" said Henry. He shuffled back to the buggy, waved his whip vaguely in the direction of his horse, and turned back down Auburn Street, heading for home. Susan wiped her sweaty eyelids with the back of her hand and then closed them, feeling the clean air.

23
The Arcade
1900

Bertie leaned over the counter, smiled and winked, and said, "Jimmy, you must leave your inkwell and come with me to see something fine." James rattled off hasty instructions to his clerk, took his hat, and followed Bertie out onto Mill Street, staying just far enough to one side to leave room for his brother's sporadic jig. Bertie waved to his friends inside the People's Cash Store, tipped his hat cordially to a man who walked out of a saloon, and leaned in the door of the barber shop to exchange greetings with a man in one of the chairs. The brothers crossed to the other side of Main Street, holding the brims of their hats against the March breeze that sliced down the hill, and walked up past the Hotel de Paris and the Holbrooke to stop at the corner of Church Street. Bertie winked again and pointed.

James looked diagonally across the intersection at the tall, broad building on the far corner. "It's the old Cabinet." The hotel had been closed for two years.

"Yes," said Bertie brightly. "Let's take a look."

The lobby had been stripped bare of furnishings; all that remained were the gas fixtures on either side of each window and doorway, a long oak counter, and on the wall behind it, a grid of pigeon-holes for mail and keys. They climbed the wide, curved staircase to the second floor, where Bertie opened a room here and a room there, revealing a few pieces of furniture and bedsteads, all covered with dust cloths. There were no curtains or draperies, and the windows were dingy. Bertie led James back downstairs, crossed the lobby, opened another door and revealed a spacious but completely empty sitting room with a high ceiling and tall windows that looked across towards the Holbrooke. He stood there for a moment, glancing at James out of the corner of his eye, then walked through to a long room decorated with tall mirrors and an assortment of heavy round tables. "Well? What do you think?"

"What do I think about what?"

"This," said Bertie, holding out his arms, wheeling in place and looking up to the corners of the room.

"What do you mean, Bertie?"

"I mean," replied his brother, "that I'm going to re-open the hotel. It's always been a hotel—first the City, then the International, then the Cabinet. The Temby brothers gave up on it, but I'm bringing it back." He smiled, winked, and demonstrated his jig, which seemed longer than usual and less involuntary.

James stared at him. "You're not."

Bertie kept smiling. "I am. I've taken the lease on the building, and I've hired Walter Body and his brother to fix it up." He jigged his way back to the lobby, clapping his hands. "It's not in bad shape, really. Needs some paint, of course, and all new carpeting. I want Body to refurbish all of the doors. People notice doors, you know. Some of the brass is all right; the rest we'll replace. And curtains—thick, heavy, velvet curtains. Red, I think. With tassels."

James ran the palm of his hand down the counter. "Where do you think you're going to get the money for all this?"

Bertie leaned in as though about to impart some great secret, and spoke in a low tone. "You'd be surprised—*very* surprised?—at the supposedly brilliant men in this town who are afraid to go in on a sure investment. I won't tell you all the names, but I'll just say this." He dropped into a portentous whisper. "If you want to expand your store, don't bother going to old Findley for the money. The man's a coward—has no imagination at all!" He sprang away from the bar and skipped towards the windows. "It's a sure thing! A sure thing!"

James took him by the arm and held him in place for a moment. "Bertie. Who is paying for this?"

Bertie actually giggled. "Who do you think? Mother."

"Mother!" James let go of Bertie's arm and watched his brother dance across the room. "You went to Mother for the money?"

"Of course," cried Bertie. "She has more than she needs. Even with Uncle Joe and his family, she has plenty. The Live Yankee just keeps paying those dividends, paying and paying."

"Bertie," said James, trying to sound friendly, "she's your mother. What if the business fails?"

"It won't! It can't!" Bertie gave an especially high hop and nearly clicked his heels together. "It's a sure thing! Besides," he said, moving closer and speaking so softly that James could scarcely hear him. "It's a new year." He stepped back and crowed towards the ceiling. "A new century! And the country's moving! What better time to commence a fresh enterprise?"

For two months, Bertie placed orders and signed contracts with hardly a glance at the bids and charges. Body brought in a crew of carpenters who worked their way through the hotel, room by room, sanding the woodwork, repairing the plaster, and replacing decorative moldings. A team of painters scraped, sanded, filled and scrubbed everything before applying two coats in a variety of colors: russet, auburn, moss and cerulean, with dashes of gold leaf on the most ostentatious decorations. They rubbed and polished the long counter in the lobby, then oiled it until the surface reflected the features of anyone standing behind it. Another crew buffed and sealed the oaken floors, another hung opulent curtains at every window, and another laid comfortably thick rugs in every room, impressive runners down each staircase and hallway, and exceptionally luxurious rugs, imported from the Far East, for the sitting room and dining hall. Four men polished the brass until it gleamed, and Bertie proudly installed three matching chandeliers, showpieces for the lobby, sitting room and dining hall, each offering over a hundred prisms of hanging crystal that dazzled anyone who paused to gaze. Finally, he brought in new furniture: soft mattresses with elegant brass headboards, carved oak night tables, tall armoires with engraved mirrors, an assortment of upholstered chairs and settees, and a complete set of new dining chairs ordered to match the tables where the guests would sit.

Before Bertie sent in Body's carpenters, James spent a difficult evening with his mother. Susan displayed no particular enthusiasm for the project but dismissed James' warnings as constituting a treacherous and unjustified attack on his elder brother. Bertie wanted to run a hotel, and she saw no reason why she should not help him do so. The building was a fine one, and the location was certainly irreproachable; the Holbrooke, right across the street, had been successful since the fifties. If her eldest son had decided to rise out of the shoe business and become one of the prominent men of Grass Valley, then she, Susan Carne, would support and applaud him. That the hotel presented enormous and indeterminate risks seemed clear to James— Grass Valley did not seem to need more rooms for rent, and the building had been sitting vacant because the previous proprietors had gone broke—but he felt completely unsuitable for his unexpected, unwanted new role as the family Jeremiah. Bertie had made his name in Grass Valley, publishing large, confident advertisements in the *Union,* building up his clientele in the boot and shoe business, and joining the local Republican party, while James whiled away the hours at the fire house. Susan would not listen, and the more he tried to explain his concerns to Eleanor, the more she treated him as though he had suddenly become an irrational child complaining of inexplicable and empty fears. Martin, as usual, had little to say. He regarded everything outside of his shop as beyond his interest or control, and he wanted only to be left alone to roll cigars and sort his leaf in peace. When James persisted, he simply fell silent, glancing occasionally towards the door in hopes of seeing a customer arrive, until his brother gave up. James managed to trap Bertie in a saloon—he was waiting to keep an appointment with one of his Republican cronies, and so could not leave—but when he pressed the issues, his brother smiled, winked, and somehow contrived to dance his jig while sitting in a leather armchair. James wanted to know how Bertie's wife, Hettie, felt about the hotel, but when he mentioned it, she gave a little series of gasps and began, in spite of her trembling hands, to comb little Earle's hair.

When the work was done, Bertie invited the entire family to inspect the results, arranging for them to gather at the dry goods store so they could walk down Mill together, cross over to the Holbrooke promenade, and stand on the corner to watch the new sign—the last, finishing touch—rise into place:

THE ARCADE HOTEL

Bertie escorted Susan and Lavinia, one on each arm, up the staircase, through the lobby, and to a pair of truly imposing chairs placed at the corner windows, all the while controlling his jubilance so that he made the entire walk without one hop or skip. As soon as they were seated, he sprang back and chuckled as a waiter appeared from nowhere to offer the overwhelmed ladies cool drinks in tall glasses. The rest of the family stood awkwardly, hesitant to sit in the perfect chairs, and gazed at the opulence surrounding them. The Hoskens huddled near Lavinia, raising their eyebrows at the extravagance but grudgingly impressed. James, defeated and resigned, lingered near the doorway with Martin, leaning on his good leg, no more impressed with Bertie's achievement than he had been with James' case against it.

Bertie announced the opening with a half-page advertisement in the *Union*:

> *Say Boys —*
> If you have got to pay for anything don't you think it a duty you owe
> yourself to get the best you can for your money?
> ### THE ARCADE HOTEL
> will furnish you with the neatest rooms in town, the best beds to be had,
> and spreads a table that is unsurpassed in the county at the same rates.

He posted placards at the livery stables in both towns and pasted them on every blank wall he could find. He printed off ten gross of handbills and saw to it that few prospective clients could avoid seeing one, sending Joseph's two boys over to the Narrow Gauge station to spend their afternoons thrusting circulars into passengers' hands and through any open Pullman windows they could reach, and hiring two young men to patrol Main and Mill to offer the inked sheets to anyone they saw, especially men walking out of saloons, stables and restaurants, and even—Bertie had instructed them to do this *very* discreetly—people leaving the Pacific, the Hotel de Paris, the Fillmore House and the Holbrooke. No one in town had ever seen such an advertising campaign, and when the *Union* sent a man to the other hotels to check on business, their managers had to admit that they were holding more empty rooms than usual. A steady parade of men and women climbed the sweeping staircase into Bertie's lobby; some to gawk at the new appointments, but some to arrange lodgings. By the end of the first week, over half of the rooms were occupied, and Bertie had to hire five more men to handle baggage, escort horses and carriages to the Fashion Stable, and serve drinks in the lounge.

To Susan's considerable surprise, Bertie persuaded Ernest to leave the Empire and take the job of hotel manager. In actuality, Bertie would manage the hotel himself, but he needed someone to be on hand for those times— and they were many—when he felt it necessary to buy a round of drinks in the saloon, walk down to Mill Street to meet someone, or step across to keep an eye on developments at the Holbrooke, which provided, he assured James, his principal competition as well as the standard by which the town would measure his service. He ordered Ernest a new tailored suit, in grey striped wool cassimere with a cutaway coat, and bought him a new black derby to go with it. Martin studied the new outfit and gravely proposed that Ernest apply for a post on McKinley's cabinet.

By Independence Day, the Arcade's rooms were nearly full most of the time, so Bertie mounted a new publicity campaign, announcing that his hotel was the very best facility in town for receptions and lodge dinners, and quite respectable enough for ladies' luncheons. Our chef can prepare any menu you desire! Our bar man can mix any punch known to the civilized world! We can accommodate any decor, any arrangement, any schedule! After the Odd Fellows held a "smoker" in the Arcade's lounge, the Free Masons bested them by arranging a complete dinner, but Bertie's reputation as a host was confirmed when the Women's Christian Temperance Union, with Mrs. Lavinia Hosken as Chairwoman of Social Arrangements, conferred on him the weighty responsibility of arranging their annual fête.

By 6:00 p.m., the coat-room rack displayed the most patrician walking-sticks in town, and the dining-room assistants were racing to get the last bowls of fresh flowers placed on the tables while the eager guests perused menus printed in a most ornate script on parchment with a forest green border. The feast began with fresh Pacific oysters, whisked up from San Francisco on beds of ice. The soup was a cream of zucchini, seasoned delicately with white pepper, and no sooner had the ladies and their husbands laid down their spoons than the waiters carried out a succession of entrées: sand dabs sautéed in a lemon-and-egg sauce, *filet de bœuf* with truffles and mushrooms, and quail stuffed with wild rice. By the time the waiters brought out the sweetbreads with fresh green corn, even the men were shifting happily in their chairs and gratefully mopping their foreheads with their handkerchiefs. They were relieved to turn to bowls of green salad, trimmed with julienned radishes and carrots, and when they had nibbled all they could manage, the bowls gave way to schooners of blackberry sorbet.

The Arcade, 1900

At the head table, Lavinia rose and stared at the assembly over the top of a grand epergne of silver and glass, its curves and points reflecting the light from the gas wall fixtures and the crystal chandeliers that floated over the tables. The ladies began to whisper for quiet, leaning towards their table companions with feathers nodding, and finally the room fell silent except for the irrepressible, covert tinking of silver spoons against crystal.

"Ladies," began Lavinia, and then, with a small, deferential smile, "and gentlemen. On behalf of the Women's Christian Temperance Union, I should like to extend our thanks to the gentleman who arranged this grand occasion and especially this magnificent feast—a *temperance* feast." Everyone in the room chuckled, nodded or applauded; in order to appease the ladies, Bertie had locked up the wine cellar for this particular event, but he had quietly taken the precaution of opening a small room off of the lobby where their husbands could discreetly retire for a quick eye-opener, compliments of the proprietor. "Surely no one can claim that Grass Valley need defer to San Francisco in such matters, and I give you our host—Mr. Albert Carne."

Splendid in his most formal evening dress, Bertie smiled and waved deprecatingly from the corner near the kitchen entrance, and those sitting near him saw one foot begin to scuttle back and forth on the carpet. He turned and gestured grandly towards his head waiter, whose entire entourage swept out of the kitchen, doors swinging, with trays of desserts: apricot charlotte, peach meringue, rice pudding and slices of devil's food cake. The dinner was an unqualified success even though a few of the ladies seemed perplexed that their husbands were so easily inclined to hilarity.

Bertie then began to promote the Arcade as the most suitable possible site for a wedding. His wife's sister, Annie Tregaskis, had declared her determination to be married there and set the date for the last Saturday in October. She demanded mauve and bone, with accents of melon, so Bertie himself went to San Francisco to buy bolts of fabric and lengths of ribbon. He consulted with his customary florist and accompanied him to the wholesale market to place their order. He interviewed three different musical ensembles, one all the way from Marysville, before making a selection, and he invited the Methodist minister, who cantankerously disapproved of holding the ceremony outside of the church, to visit the hotel, and by the time the man had finished three glasses of Bertie's best port, he was content and convinced.

The wedding was a glorious triumph. Bertie transformed his largest room into a chapel, complete with raised dais and altar, and he arranged the seating so that every guest had a clear view. The bride entered through a lofty floral arch—preceded by Bertie's six-year-old son, Earle, as the proud ring-bearer—and afterwards stood beneath the same blossoms with her new husband to receive congratulations. Bertie had insisted that his own chef bake the cake, and the apprehensive Annie wept with surprised delight when four waiters slowly carried it out to its place of honor. The evening finished when the bride and groom, having changed into their traveling clothes in the Arcade's most sumptuous suite, departed in a gleaming landau manned by a liveried coachman and groom—all, of course, due to Bertie's careful planning.

Jack happened to be visiting Grass Valley that weekend, so he sat in a corner, sharing a bottle of champagne with his son, Frederick, and watching the rest of the guests, most of them people he did not know, gather around the cake. James sat down at Jack's table and looked at him with an odd expression.

"Quite an occasion, isn't it?"

Jack nodded. "Bertie seems to have found his calling."

James looked over at his brother, who was giving instructions to a little knot of his staff. "Did you know that Mother is his partner?"

Jack's smile faded a little. "No." He thought for a moment. "Well, it looks like a good investment. I hear that there are nights when you can't get a room, and he has plenty of weddings and dinners."

The younger man shook his head. "I wish I knew more about it."

"What do you mean?"

"Bertie won't let Mother see the books."

"Has she asked him?"

"Well, no. But I asked if she could have a look. He said there was no need, but if she really wanted to—if *she* asked him—then he would have one of his clerks give her a report."

"Do you think he's trying to hide something?"

"I don't know, but I can't figure out how he's making a profit."

"Why not?"

"Do you know what he charged Trevaskis for the wedding?"

When James told him the figures, Jack looked around the room, appraising the decorations, the food, the wine, and the staff. He looked at Frederick, who shrugged, and the three men leaned in towards each other. What James wanted was simple: to find out whether the Arcade was actually making enough to pay its expenses. He had asked around a little, but no one was able or willing to tell him anything. Jack, on the other hand, still knew several of the more important men in town, and James thought it likely that he would be able to get the answers. Jack listened, carefully pushing the table cloth into little ridges with his fingers.

Jack and Frederick spent nearly a week in Grass Valley, moving from the Holbrooke over to the Arcade as soon as there was room. Each afternoon, Jack took Susan on a drive to enjoy the fall colors, but when she asked why Frederick never joined them, he would say only that his son was taking care of some business for him. On the day before he was scheduled to leave, he climbed the steps to her porch with Frederick right behind him. She offered them seats in the parlor, but Jack chose to stand near the fireplace warming his hands. "Winter's coming. I don't know what it is, but the cold up here is different than in San Francisco. Dries me out."

"Ye're gettin' older, Jack." Susan smiled up at him, and winked at Frederick, who flushed in surprise.

"Not a bit, not a bit." He sighed. "Susan . . . I don't know how to start." She took a breath as if to speak, but he held up a hand. "No, it's all right. Listen, it's about Bertie." He sighed again. "James tells me that you're his partner in the Arcade."

Susan waited for more, but both men simply kept looking at her, their faces concerned and apprehensive. "That's right."

Jack took a deep breath, held it, and let it out slowly. "Susan, I'm very impressed with what he's done with the hotel. But there's something you deserve to know. He's running the place at a loss."

Her mouth fell open slightly, and she laughed incredulously. "What d'ye mean? Th' place is full most o' th' time. Why, I 'eard just the other day that the 'olbrooke is lowerin' its rates just t' try t' bring people back."

Jack nodded. "That's so. The rooms are full, and the downstairs has two or three affairs each week. He's bringing in business from locals and travelers alike, and everything I hear is that people are pleased with the service he's giving them."

"Then what's wrong?"

"What he's providing costs more than he charges.'

"Even with th' place doin' so well?"

"That's right."

"It doesn't make sense."

"Maybe not, but it's true. Suppose I'm running a bakery. When I sell you a loaf of bread, I have to charge you at least what it costs me. And not just the flour and milk and butter and all. I have to pay my baker and his assistant, and someone to meet the customers. I have to keep the building up . . . "

"All right, Jack Trevenna, don't talk t' me like I was a child. I understand all that. But there's no sense in Bertie chargin' too little."

"You're right."

She looked at Frederick, and back at Jack. "I don't believe it. How d'ye know, anyway?"

Jack nodded to Frederick, who cleared his throat and began to speak. "I went to his suppliers—the florists, the grocers, the butchers—all of them. He's paying the best prices to get the best goods. Even if he has to have the best—better than most places in San Francisco—he doesn't have to pay so much. These men would take less, I'm sure."

Susan was frowning. "Ye've been spyin' on 'im."

Frederick started to reply, but Jack interceded. "I asked him to look around. Has Bertie ever shown you the books?"

She dropped her eyes for a moment. "No."

"Why not?"

"I've never asked 'im!" she flared up. "What d'ye want from me, Jack? T' be goin' down t' the 'otel every Wednesday to check up on 'im? Why don't I just run the place myself?"

Jack sat down next to her. He reached for her hands, but she withdrew them. "Susan, listen to me. I've nothing against Bertie. He's doing a fine job, better than I'd have thought, and better than I could have done." Jack was stretching his magnanimity a bit, but it seemed the right thing to say. "But I'm almost certain that he'll lose the place if he keeps going this way. You must talk to him."

"And tell 'im what?"

"Explain to him that he doesn't have to pay the first price that his suppliers ask. That he doesn't have to pay his waiters more than they'd earn in Sacramento. That he's got to make a profit on every dinner or wedding. That he's got to charge enough for the rooms so he can get through the times when half of them are empty."

She rose to her feet. "It's none o' yer business, Jack. The Arcade is goin' t' be th' best 'otel in town, and it'll be Bertie who'll take th' credit."

The men stood, and Jack sighed again. "And if he goes under . . . Who'll take the credit for that?"

Susan brooded over Jack's visit for a full week. He had no right. He had no right to be spying into Bertie's affairs. And he had no right to be making such accusations. How could he know? Had he seen the books? What did he mean by sending Frederick out to make inquiries of the men in town? Jack was a fool if he thought that no one would figure out who was asking the questions, and every man Frederick approached would now be wondering why Bertie's own cousin was so curious. It was so like Jack, living all the way off in San Francisco, to just drop in from time to time and hand out judgements and advice. And when you confront him with it, he tells you he's sorry that you can't see what a favor he's doing you.

Then again, he was right about one thing. She was a partner in the hotel, even if a silent one. There was no reason, no reason at all, why she shouldn't see the books. Bertie had impressed everyone, no doubt, but this was the same man that might still be working in the mines if his own grandmother hadn't arranged an opportunity and encouraged him to buckle to. Then Susan remembered that it was Jack who had set up the meeting with Bennett. Couldn't they do anything without Jack getting involved? Perhaps she should let Bertie alone. No, she would go down to the Arcade and take a look for herself.

The Arcade, 1900

The hotel lobby was nearly empty. Ernest was standing behind the counter sorting little slips of paper, and two of the bell boys were perched on a crate in the corner, smoking cigarettes and flicking the ashes onto the carpet at their feet. A man was sitting near the windows; all she could see was a pair of legs and a San Francisco newspaper. Ernest seemed startled to see her, but when she asked for Bertie, he opened the little door on the side and showed her into the office within.

Bertie was sitting at a desk littered with papers, and he was frowning at a scrap in his hand. He scurried around to bring her a chair and stood there, grinning, winking and chuckling spasmodically. When Susan explained that she had come to ask about the business, just out of curiosity, of course, to see how well they were doing, he lost control of his feet, and he began to flit about the room, jigging and hopping, even twirling as he reached a corner or a hatrack and realized that he had turned too far to see his visitor.

"Why, we're doing j-j-just fine," he stammered. "J-j-just fine!" He circumnavigated the room and landed in his chair, trying to sit with his hands folded on the desk in front of him, but compulsively re-arranging the papers that lay there. From beneath the desk came a muffled tapping and clicking, and Susan guessed that his feet were still dancing.

"Bertie," said Susan, trying to catch and hold his eye, "I'd like t' see the books."

Bertie's eyebrows shot up. "The b-b-books? The records, the ledgers? Why, of course! Perhaps if you come back tomorrow, or maybe next week."

"Can't I see 'em now?"

"Now? Why, certainly! No problem at all." He tried to pat one handful of papers into a neat pile, and Susan could now see that they were bills from various tradesmen; she recognized the letterhead of a merchant in Grass Valley and caught a glimpse of one Sacramento address and two others from San Francisco. "Of course, they're not quite up to date. We're so b-b-busy, you know, that our bookkeeper has more than he can handle! Maybe in a week or so—things are a bit quieter now—m-m-maybe then he'll catch up."

Bertie was always twitchy, but there was something about the way he was answering her questions that was more anxious than usual. "I'd like t' see whatever ye 'ave."

He opened his mouth as if to speak, but seemed to turn to stone for a moment, staring at his mother with raised eyebrows and the beginning of an hysterical smile on his lips. Susan was about to ask whether he were all right when he jumped to his feet, grabbed up wads of bills and receipts and scooped them into a drawer that was already so full that he had to jam the scraps into it. "No trouble at all! None whatsoever! Always glad to oblige!"

He shoved three large ledgers across the desk, and she opened the first, checking over the columns of debits from the renovation. As she ran her finger across the broad, lined pages, she realized that Bertie was leaning over her shoulder, so close that she could feel his breath on her ear. She sat back in her chair, startling him, and looked up. "Bertie, I'll be all right 'ere. Can't ye find somethin' else t' do?"

He waved his arms. "Of course! Of course! I'll just sit here and check over the dining hall menu for next week." He capered around to his side of the desk and reached for his chair.

"No, Bertie, wait." He stopped, frozen. "Just let me use yer office, just for a little while." At that, he nodded, up and down, over and over again, and, spluttering and galloping, managed to find the door and make his way out.

Susan took a deep breath, shut her eyes for a moment, and bent over the ledger. The records for the refurbishing were clear, complete and, as far as she could tell, accurate. Some of the bills seemed high, but Bertie had wanted to make the capital investments count so that the Arcade would deserve a reputation for high quality from the very start.

When she turned to the records of the actual operation, the handwriting became more hurried, and then actually so sloppy that she could scarcely read some of the figures. The explanatory notes dwindled to abbreviations and then vanished completely, so that while she knew that he had received a bill from a certain concern, she could not tell what was supplied. The records of payments became increasingly haphazard, and there were several notations that apparently indicated advances or loans made to bell boys, maids and waiters. One man had drawn, in addition to his weekly wages, the sum of $20 every other week, marked, ambiguously, "on account," and she could find no suggestion that he had ever paid anything back. As for the guests, not only had Bertie let some of them defer paying their charges, he had actually lent them money. She couldn't decide what was worse—that Bertie had made a mess of the business, or that Jack had been right and she had been a doting fool.

She sent Ernest to find Bertie, and when he arrived, she shut the door behind him and firmly told him to sit in his chair, and try to sit still. They were going to bring his books up to date, whether it took a week, or two weeks, or a month. They would check all of the entries, sort out the bills and receipts, and bring each account up to date. Bertie was overwhelmed; he found her calm authority far more intimidating than anger and tears, and he dreaded her reaction when she discovered that his difficulties were far worse than she knew.

The audit took two weeks. Susan could have finished it sooner by herself, but she needed Bertie there to translate illegible entries and answer questions, and just when she thought they had learned everything about a certain account, he opened another drawer—or, once, turned out his coat pockets—and found another scrap of paper. When they were finished, Susan had to conclude that Jack had described the situation even more accurately than she had suspected. Bertie was giving first-class service but levying second-class charges. No wonder the town was so impressed with the Arcade, and no wonder the other hotel keepers were so frustrated! She now remembered overhearing, at Annie's wedding, a comment that made no sense at the time, but which she now understood. A man smoking a thick black cigar had remarked to his companion that anyone could run a business like Bertie if he just had the right person behind him. He was chuckling when he caught sight of Susan standing quite near him, and he abruptly composed himself. She now realized that he, and perhaps others, thought that she was providing Bertie with a regular subsidy that permitted him to offer luxury while keeping his prices low enough to undercut his rivals. The truth was that Bertie apparently didn't understand how to make ends meet, and his aspirations far exceeded his means.

Jack had claimed that Bertie was paying wages that were higher than necessary, so Susan quietly went to visit the other hotels in town. Each manager had lost staff to Bertie, and each was glad to show his pay schedules to Mrs. Carne, hoping that she could bring her son's operation into line so that they might be able to compete on a more equal footing. When Bertie argued that higher wages brought in better workers, she took him through the hotel and pointed out the unpolished brass, the unswept floors, the linens that weren't quite clean, and the dishes that weren't quite washed.

Susan calculated that Bertie did not have enough cash on hand to pay even those accounts that were overdue. He stammered and spluttered for a good five minutes before finally confessing that he had gone to Findley for a short-term loan, just so he could continue to pay his staff during those times when he had laid out too much for preparations for dinners and weddings. The suspicious old banker had turned Bertie away when the Arcade was just an idea; now that it was bringing in so many customers, he judged the risk to be justified, but he charged a ruinous rate of interest. Susan wanted to scold her son for making himself so vulnerable, but she could not find the energy.

She did everything she could think of, but she had intervened too late. Findley's loan came due on the first of December, and the Arcade simply did not have enough cash to pay the note. Susan considered paying it herself. She could manage it, just barely, but the real consideration was Bertie. If she saved him this time, there would be another time, and another. She decided that it was better to let him fail. Findley instituted proceedings immediately, and when his lawyers and accountants had finished making their own inspection of Bertie's ledgers, they determined that his liabilities exceeded his assets by over five hundred dollars.

Cousin Jack

Susan found Bertie in his office, sitting behind a desk clean, for once, of papers, and staring at the wall. He was perfectly still: feet and hands lay quiet, and he did not greet her. "Bertie." He turned, his face absolutely blank behind his mustache. "Bertie, we 'ave t' pay 'em off. We've little choice."

He looked down at the desk as though puzzled by the uncluttered surface, then stared at the wall again. "Yes. Yes, we will."

Susan's eyes filled with tears and her throat felt swollen. Poor Bertie—he had enjoyed it so. If she had thought to hire a manager, someone who really knew the business, perhaps they could have avoided all of this. Now it was too late.

A few days later, the *Union* ran a discreet notice:

> Albert Carne, proprietor of the Arcade Hotel, yesterday afternoon made a voluntary assignment for the benefit of his creditors. A receiver has been placed in charge of the premises.
>
> The failure is attributed by Mr. Carne to be lack of sufficient accommodations to make the hotel profitable. While every room was occupied, the expenditures were in excess of the income, and rather than plunge himself further in debt, Mr. Carne considered the making of an assignment the proper course to take.

Susan knew that the article was not quite accurate. The Arcade hadn't been full every day, and even if there had been more rooms, Bertie would have kept reaching for the grandiose, the posh, and the elegant. Still, when the editor sent a boy to her house to ask if the notice was acceptable, she had let it go. Let Bertie put the best face on his humiliation.

The receiver, a man named Clinch, accepted bids on the fixtures for ten days, and by Christmas, everything was gone, and the building was empty again.

Susan invited her family to her house for Christmas dinner, but few accepted. Eleanor and James had taken their children to Lavinia's home, and Katie's older girls had insisted on fixing a special feast for their parents, enlisting the younger children to wash potatoes, fill pitchers and pass plates of cookies to their captivated father. Susan and Sarah fixed a small, quiet dinner for Martin, Ernest and Bertie; a forlorn gathering. Hettie had, on Christmas Eve, taken the stage to Sacramento, there boarding a ship for San Francisco, where she intended to stay with her married sister, and she had taken Earle with her.

24
Flight
1903

The cedar forest receded as the train approached the Chicago Park station, but Jack could see only a few farms that seemed inhabited, and at least two unfinished barns, lost in the middle of green fields deep in lupine, their posts and rafters left to shrivel and silver in the sun and snow. The station wall displayed several faded "For Sale" signs.

Susan was wearing a new suit of wool cheviot serge, all blue, with trimmings of black satin, the broad lapels slashing away from her simple white lawn waist. Her hands, comfortably hidden inside black silk gloves with polished pearl buttons, were lightly folded over the malacca handle of her parasol. She had piled her hair underneath a hat of straw, grey silk and blue feathers that curved low over one eye and swept up high on the opposite side. As she bent forward to look out at the station, Jack grinned, thinking that she had surprised him again. When he had invited her on this excursion, he had anticipated that she would wear something much simpler, more like the women he saw in the shops in Grass Valley, but she had descended her stairs wearing the costume and confidence of the most well-established lady in San Francisco. He did not mention his amusement, because he knew that she would either smile superciliously or complain that he never gave her credit for having good sense.

When they pulled into Colfax, Jack slouched down and peered over at the Central Pacific siding. "Ah!" he said. "It's there. Let's go." As he escorted Susan through the car, he noticed that several women glanced up, then looked again, their eyebrows raised slightly at the clearly cosmopolitan lady who was traveling on the Narrow Gauge. They walked across to the main platform, boarded the car and found their compartment, and Jack took the conductor aside for a quick, urgent conversation, passing him an envelope and a gold coin. Susan arranged her skirt on the leather seat and reached into her handbag to bring out a handkerchief, a small pearl-backed brush, and a tiny mirror. Jack, pacing restlessly back and forth between the corridor and the compartment, tried not to stare at her, but the impudence—or was it an affirmation of familiarity, a sophisticated gesture of intimacy?—amused him. Presently the conductor returned, smiling, and beckoned. Jack joined him in the passageway but had to wait while Susan, not hurrying at all, finished patting her forehead and eyelids with her handkerchief. They walked down the length of the train, past compartments and through the dining car, to the penultimate platform, where the conductor tipped his hat and left them confronting a man in a black suit and bristling auburn whiskers. Jack handed him a piece of paper, and after scanning it quickly, the man nodded and opened the door, ushering them into a private Pullman car decorated in oak, leather and red velvet.

There were several men in the car: one sitting next to a window, absorbed in a book, two carrying on a heated but quiet conversation, and two more making notes on a sheaf of papers. In the center of the car, just to one side, a man in a white jacket stood next to a small table where he had just set a bowl filled with sliced peaches drenched in thick cream. Behind the bowl, just setting his silver spoon on the white linen cloth, sat the President of the United States.

Teddy Roosevelt had broken out of the careful chambers and august halls of Washington, determined to visit the West, and with his celebrated drive and determination he had passed through nearly every state on the far side of the Mississippi, leading his little troupe of advisors and bodyguards across ranches and over mountains. They had whisked through cities like Milwaukee, Omaha and Denver—only large towns by Eastern standards—so the President could linger in Albuquerque and Wichita, small settlements where he could trade jokes with cowboys and take his entourage on horseback caravans after herds of startled cattle. Now he was heading for San Francisco and the Pacific.

He rose, laughed, and displayed the famous teeth beneath the bushy mustache and flashing lenses. Jack glanced at Susan. Her composure, so natural all morning, had become more studied; she was charmed. The President shook Jack's hand vigorously, declaring himself "dee-lighted" with the gift of the peaches, and graciously took Susan's hand, actually bowing over it as though meeting the wife of an ambassador. The white-coated servant pulled out a chair for Susan, then for Jack, and anticipated the President's insistent invitation by setting before each guest a bowl of peaches and cream.

Their host announced himself satisfied—no, astonished—by the peaches. Nowhere in the East could he find ripe peaches so early in the season, and certainly not of this size and quality. He punctuated his comments with spoonfuls of peaches and cream, reaching for his napkin after every mouthful to blot the white droplets that appeared in his whiskers and dribbled down his chin. Jack assured him that although they had enjoyed an unusually warm spring, the fruit farmers in California, even in the hills—here he nodded rather obscurely in Susan's direction—were accustomed to picking their first crop at this time of year. The President worked through his bowl, demanding boisterously that his guests address theirs as well, and he gestured to his servant to bring Susan more cream and to sprinkle fine sugar over the fruit, assuring her that his own dear Edith preferred her peaches served that way. Cocking an ear at her speech, he asked where she had been raised. "Why, I'm partly English, too!" he cried, and offered a recollection of damp Devon castles that he had visited years ago, while still a small boy.

Jack asked the President whether he were enjoying his trip through the West. Roosevelt laughed again, a sudden roar, his eyes nearly closing with the effort and a sudden flush suffusing his neck and face, making his earlobes glow. Susan, glancing discreetly down the car, noticed that none of the men paid any attention to their chief's clamorous behavior. He described the Grand Canyon in pious tones, and then, laughing again, called to a man near the door to "bring out Josh." His aide opened a wooden box and led out a small grey badger, whom the President solemnly introduced as "Joshua, one of my constituents from Kansas." Jack was making what he hoped was an appropriate remark over the ingratiating creature when Susan started violently. A strangely docile lizard was strolling across the thick rug, making his way to some destination under the table. The President laughed and looked under the table cloth, calling "Bill! Bill!" as though the reptile might come at command.

The three resumed their seats at the table while the badger climbed up to look out the window, and Jack asked about Panama. The President's smile dissolved and the lower lip pushed up stubbornly against the mustache as he leaned back from the table, displaying the gold chain that festooned across the belly of his vest. "We are offering them a square deal—a square deal." He repeated the phrase again and again, apparently pleased with the way it sounded. "Ten million now, and two hundred and fifty thousand—" He leaned in and fixed first Jack and then Susan with his eyes, gleaming under bristling eyebrows. "—a quarter of a million, each and every year for the next century." He sat back, thrusting a finger into his watch pocket. "And not for tyranny! Not to take what is not ours! Merely for the privilege of building the Canal and then managing it for the benefit of all!"

Jack asked, "Do you think our forces will be able to keep the peace?"

The President slammed his fist down on the table. "An excellent question, sir! An excellent question! Why, these are a people accustomed to insurrection! Nearly every year, sir! Each and every year! Many of them are utterly unfit for self-government—half-castes, Indians, wild pagans." He lowered his voice and nodded to both of them. "There are those who contend that we should leave well enough alone. But I say to them—my view is that we cannot be content to rot by inches in ignoble ease within our borders. America must face its duties around the world, or forfeit its right to shape the destiny of mankind. Our fleet must be able to pass, unencumbered, from one ocean to the other. We must keep order in Panama, or sacrifice our national honor. If we do not meet our obligations, then some other, stronger and more manful race, will do so for us."

Susan glanced at Jack, who was nodding almost as though hypnotized, his lips slightly parted. "Mr. President," she said, and both men looked at her, Roosevelt with a half smile, his eyebrows raised as though in question. "Mr. President—Mr. Trevenna and I both traveled across the Isthmus, many years ago. I could not imagine a longer passage, even by train, and I'm glad that th' Senate rejected th' Nicaraguan route."

Roosevelt's face expanded into a sunburst of teeth, whiskers, flaming cheeks and highlights reflected off of the lenses of his spectacles. "Dee-lighted! Dee-lighted to hear your views, Mrs. Carne! The honor is all mine, ma'am, I assure you!" The President nodded discreetly to someone behind her, and rose, thanking them profusely for their visit and assuring them that he would take no more of their time. Were they traveling to San Francisco! They were? And on the very same train? Then he would look forward with the greatest pleasure to their next encounter.

Susan had not visited San Francisco since before Zennora died. There had been afternoons, sitting on her porch in the green shade, or looking out of her parlor window at the drifting rain, when she had wondered when she had lost her restlessness. She had lived in Grass Valley for over forty years, and she could no longer quite remember precisely how the girl she had been felt about leaving home. She recalled the many ways she used to impress upon Hannibal that she disliked California; twelve years of discreet, relentless remonstrance. Yet since he died, her yearning for Cornwall had dwindled, and there must have been a day, a moment that passed unnoticed, when she stopped thinking about Camborne as a place to which she sought to return, a home that compelled her, but she could not locate the catalytic event that had, somehow, fixed her in America. Perhaps the agent of her alchemy had been something apparently insignificant—a moment when she had stumbled on the street, or filled a canister with flour, or brushed a wisp off of her cheek—or perhaps there had been no spur at all, and her passage through time had gently brought an unexpected, oblivious evolution.

Now she sat by the window and watched the green slopes turn brown, the forests give way to scrub, and the hills settle, their undulating grades sinking by degrees into endless flat fields. Only Jack's determination had brought her here. He had invited her over and over again, insisting that she would enjoy herself, assuring her that Annie and the children were eager to see her, and hinting that she should consider coming to live there herself, the widow of a prominent mining engineer and a major partner in one of the more important mines in Nevada County. She had consented partly just to get him to stop, to leave her alone, thinking that if she gave in, if she went to the City this one time, he might be satisfied.

He kept her so busy that she could scarcely pull off her clothes each night before gratefully drawing the sateen comforter up to her chin and falling instantly asleep. They dined on abalone at the Palace, the aroma of fine cigars floating past her nose from tables where whiskered men leaned back in their chairs to regard each other across straining buttons, and strolled leisurely along a gallery in the Great Court to look down at the smart carriages whose passengers promenaded augustly into the grand foyer with squadrons of bell boys swarming behind. They drove out to the beach, gaped at the notorious Cliff House, and spent the day at Golden Gate Park, ambling through glens and across lawns, and stopping to have a picnic lunch and watch a game of baseball before spending an hour in the steamy warmth of the conservatory, where, beneath a giant philodendron, Jack actually unbuttoned his collar. He declared that she must ride a cable car, so Frederick, by his father's orders definitely *not* on holiday, but assigned to keep their office running while cousin Susan was visiting, dropped them off at Market Street, where they climbed aboard a little car that doggedly dragged itself up to the top of Nob Hill, then west, then north again, and finally eased down the far side of Russian Hill, an incline so steep that Susan wondered, just for a moment, whether they would tip over. From the wharf they watched a regatta, dozens of yachts heeling over and slicing the water into white foam. They dined at a different restaurant every evening, always finishing the last course hastily to leave time for a play at the Alcazar, or the Orpheum, or the Bijou, all clustered where O'Farrell met Market, the sidewalks and placards shining in the arrays of incandescent lights, and candy butchers calling out monotonously until the last patron had run up the steps and through the lobby. One day they took Jack's two younger children to the Ringling Brothers' circus down in the Mission District, the girl and boy already in their teens, clearly reticent about the amusement but resigned to their father's program, yet they, along with Susan, sat fascinated with the acrobats and the equestrian display, and completely relinquished their affected boredom when a clown with a bright nose and impossible shoes tripped in the sawdust and sprawled at their feet.

They met Roosevelt once more. Jack had arranged for them to attend a reception for the President in City Hall. Frederick drove them down in the buggy, and they climbed the long stone staircase, surrounded by tall silk top hats and nodding feathers. The mayor, "Handsome Gene," had arranged for four orchestras to play in different parts of the building so that no one would be without music even for a moment, and His Honor stood in the center of a raised marble dais, shaking the hands of as many of his guests as his aides could propel in his direction, and taking the baton himself to conduct the largest orchestra in a special arrangement of "America" to honor the President's grand entrance. Roosevelt strode in, grinning and

387

waving, and scurried up to stand next to the mayor and magnanimously transfer the applause and cheers to him. The highlight of the evening was the moment when the President was to send the first telegraphic message around the world using the newly-completed Pacific Cable. Jack managed to find them a place along a gallery, pressed up against a broad pillar, where they could look down and see the dignitaries seated at a table where an operator had set up a key and a receiver. Throughout the hall, ushers demanded silence, and when everyone was ready, the President bent over the table and tapped out a message. They waited—one minute, two, five and on. Stern-faced attendants bustled the more tipsy guests, those unable to sustain the silence, to another part of the building. After twelve minutes, the message came through, and the gathering exhaled and then broke into cheers as the President grinned broadly.

Jack wedged them into the receiving line, and when they reached Roosevelt, he took the President's hand and said, "A pleasure to see you again, Your Excellency!"

Susan noticed that the man next to the President looked over sharply, but Jack kept on pumping his hand vigorously. "Ah!" said the President. Disengaging his hand from Jack's and turning to Susan, "Dee-lighted!" His face was all teeth and mustaches and cheeks and slitted eyes. Across his forehead was a sheen of perspiration that had matted his hair. He froze for a split second, then turned to the man who had been nudging her all through the line. One of the official aides drew them away, and a moment later they were standing in another part of the hall and Jack was looking away from her, smiling ruefully to himself.

On the way home, Jack announced that they would have to rise early the next morning to catch the ferry to Oakland. By mid-morning they were standing on a wharf that rose above a sandy beach where a crowd of people were gathered, all talking and calling at once. Susan held her hat against the wind that raced across from the Golden Gate, pressing patterns into the green water and kicking up the waves into whitecaps. Below her, the crowd swung back to reveal an automobile backing up slowly, down towards where the light surf rolled up across the sand. The boys clustered on the pilings began to cheer, and the men and women began to call out, "Old Pacific! Old Pacific!"

Jack bent down to Susan's ear. "That's the name of the car, but it's built by a fellow named Packard. He bought a car for himself, a Winton, but the machine kept breaking down on the road. Winton told Packard to go build his own car if he thought he could do a better job, so he did!" Susan looked down at the contraption. People around her referred to it as a "horseless carriage," but the only part that reminded her of a carriage was the upholstered seat, with its gently curved back and firm springs, looking as though someone had simply set it on top of the frame. The spoked wheels were strangely small, and fitted with pneumatic tires that seemed too soft to withstand the rocks and gravel of the roads. Where the horse should have stood was a sloping hood, decorated with a pair of bull's-eye lanterns, and instead of reins, the driver placed his hands on a wheel. Both he and his passenger wore caps pulled down over their ears, goggles that distorted their faces, and long dusters that covered their ankles.

"They expect that the trip to New York will take two months," said Jack. "They'll travel about fifty miles a day on the average, slower over the mountains, and faster back East, where the roads are better." She looked down at the machine, still rolling slowly down the sand. The body rode low on its springs, too low, she thought, to negotiate the deep wheel ruts in Grass Valley's roads.

The Packard had reached the edge of the surf, and several men ran down, their feet leaving deep prints in the wet muck, to ease the machine a few feet farther so that its wheels were actually resting in the wash. The driver kept looking back at the rear of the car and then out at the waves. The man sitting next to him rose to his feet and seemed to be making a speech to the crowd, but the wind carried the sound of his voice away from the wharf, leaving only the cries of the gulls that were balancing on the air twenty feet overhead. The cheering coalesced into one word: "Fetch! Fetch! Fetch!" Jack shouted over the noise that "Fetch" was the name of the driver, who, not even acknowledging the crowd, now made some adjustments with the controls in front of him—levers and triggers—until the engine began to make a loud popping. Bursts of blue smoke billowed out from somewhere underneath the vehicle, and the wheels began to spin, in fits and starts, in the wet sand. The men who had pushed the car ran over, but the driver waved them away, adjusting his controls and looking back at the edge of the water. Slowly, the rear wheels began to settle into the silt, and the passenger tapped the driver on the shoulder, shook his head, and waved the men in. They arranged themselves around the rear half of the auto, first pushing down, then lifting slightly, taking care to stay well clear of the spinning wheels. The Packard moved a few feet up the slope, away from the water, to sand that was firmer and drier. The driver shouted at the pushing men, waving them off, but they stayed with the car, laughing and cheering, as long as they could, two of them keeping their hands on the rear of the body until the contraption reached the hard roadway at the head of the wharf and left them behind, coughing in the dust and smoke.

All the way back to San Francisco on the ferry, Jack reviewed the current state of the development of the automobile. It was, he declared, the way of the new century, certain to relegate the horse to pastimes like hunting and pleasure riding. Oh, yes, some people complained about the noise and smell, but who had ever wanted to live next to a livery stable? What about the dust and manure that permeated the towns every summer? An automobile wouldn't attract flies, you could be sure of that. And it was reliably fast. Even back in 1895, when autos were still new, one of Duryea's machines raced from Chicago to Evanston—a distance of over fifty miles—in just over ten hours. No horse could do that, and certainly not a horse pulling even a two-seater buggy, much less a carriage. He laughed as he told Susan how Bailey had put an auto into his circus, advertising it as a "motor wagon" and presenting it as a curiosity. No more, he assured her, no more—the auto would become as common as a bale of hay, and a man seeking to buy one had many from which to choose: the Porter Stanhope, the Friedman Road Wagon, the Jaxon steamer, the Wanamaker Searchmont, the Clarkmobile Touring Car, and the Haynes Apperson. He had just heard of a new two-cylinder auto, with plush leather seats, manufactured in Detroit by a man named Ford. And for only $850!

When the ferry docked, Jack hired a cab to drive them to McAllister Street, and they disembarked next to a small sign that read, "California Automobile Company." A man in shirtsleeves returned Jack's greeting—they seemed to know each other—and offered them chairs next to a worn desk piled high with papers and bits of hardware.

The proprietor used a bit of rag to clean some black marks off of his fingers, then leaned across the desk with an ingratiating smile. "Think of it, Mrs. Carne. Convenient, inexpensive transportation wherever you want to go. You'll ride clean and comfortable. Our steel springs and pneumatic tires will make you wonder why you ever rode a coach to San Francisco. Noise? After two days, you won't even notice. Repairs? Hardly ever. Maintenance? Nothing to speak of. Certainly nothing like keeping a horse." He and Jack shared a knowing chuckle. "We can sell you a one-seater, just for you and a friend, or a two-seater, large enough for your family. Plenty of room for luggage. Even carry a cake to the neighbor's if you want, and it'll stay clean and safe. We can install any kind of top you like." He assumed a carefully serious expression. "Automobile manufacturing is a two hundred million dollar business. That's two hundred million this year. Next year—who knows?"

Jack was watching her, apparently anticipating some sort of reaction, and for a moment she felt like a girl who opens a present while her anxious parents wait for a delighted smile. Yet she found the whole business tedious—she had never taken a great deal of interest in carriages, and the horses she had owned had engaged her attention only when they gave her trouble. Why should she care about an auto? Jack suggested that they visit the shop. The proprietor opened a door to a place rather like a livery stable, with vehicles arranged in rows, four down each side, each with its own stall, surrounded by tools and pulleys and small carts. The proprietor pointed out cars in various stages of completion. "We can make you one with a gasoline engine, or a steamer if you want. More people seem to like steamers now." He stopped and turned to Jack. "Did you hear? The White racer did the mile at seventy-four miles per hour." Jack whistled. "Or, Mrs. Carne, we can make you an electric car. The ladies prefer them. They're quieter, of course, and cleaner. Just the thing for going visiting." Susan began to wonder how long they would have to stay here. "We can install any kind of top you like—leather quarter, waterproof black rubber, surrey canopy trimmed with fringe. Brass headlamps. Full fenders. And we guarantee the vehicle for one year. Anything wrong—just bring it right back, and the boys'll take care of it."

The man's brusque confidence began to annoy her. "I live in Grass Valley," she told him, hoping to deflate him somehow.

"Oh? Ah . . . Ain't that near Oakland? Well, I suppose we could send a man over. No extra charge." He nodded and folded his arms, satisfied.

Back in the cab, Jack smiled. "Some people just won't learn. I read just the other day that some farmers back East have threatened to arrest anyone driving a car and to shoot the ones that won't stop."

Susan could not think of an intelligent response. "Dabbety fay!"

He looked over at her, smiling warily. "Pearson wants me to buy one of his autos." She said nothing. "I'd like to become a partner in the company."

"Is 'e sellin' stock?"

"Well, not really. But I know he'd like to expand, and he must need some capital. He hasn't said 'no,' but we can't seem to agree on how much the business is worth." He tapped his fingers on his knee. "He's right about one thing, though—ten years from now, you'll see hardly any horses in San Francisco." Susan tried to imagine what the City would be like. Instead of dust, smell and flies, they'd have dust, smell and smoke, but apparently everyone would get there sooner. Farriers would give way to mechanics, and everyone would throw away tack to make stable room for the new contraptions. She realized that Jack was asking her a question. "Would you prefer an electric or a steamer?"

She had to smile. "Ye're already a partner, aren't ye, Jack? So what is this? Are ye offerin' t' buy me an auto?"

He laughed, a little nervously. "I wish I could."

"Jack, I bought th' carriage only because I got tired o' sendin' down t' the livery stable and because Katie and Eleanor like it when I take th' children out for picnics. The thing sits in th' stable most o' the time. What would I do with an auto?"

He looked at her. "Well, I thought you might find a use for it if you lived here in the City."

The remark wearied her. "I've told ye—I 'aven't made up my mind. I don't think I want t' leave Grass Valley."

Cousin Jack

She walked into Jack's house to find Annie regarding her, as usual, with what Susan interpreted as impatience at best, or vague suspicion at worst. She stayed there only because Jack insisted; she would have booked a hotel room except that he would have been openly hurt and disappointed. Once, when they arrived home late, finding everyone in the house asleep, she had asked him whether Annie suspected anything. The question had startled him; Susan rarely admitted, even by implication, that they had ever been anything more than cousins, thrown together by family connections that only the two of them really remembered and respected. Stammering, he had assured her that Annie had no reason to think anything improper. He had spent the entire next day treating Susan very carefully, almost formally, and after finding his behavior slightly irritating, she decided to enjoy the fact that she had, apparently, disconcerted him. He always seemed so sure of himself.

Joseph could feel no breeze, no breath on his face, but the leaves fell, a constant drifting, all through November. He remembered a snowstorm during his first winter in California, a day measured by the constant descent of large flakes that appeared out of the formless canescence and collected around his waiting feet. The leaves fell and fell, never hurrying, never ceasing as the elms and oaks gracefully relinquished their burdens but found no respite, no lightening. Then came a morning when he looked out at perfectly bare branches rising above lofted deposits of ochre, sienna and dun, and the quiet closed in around him.

Jack brought his entire family to Grass Valley for Christmas, installing them in two suites in the Holbrooke and hiring a new landau so that they could all ride about the town together. Annie had received a special invitation from Eleanor, one intended to make her feel welcome on her own, not just as Jack's wife, but she was dismayed to learn that there would be over thirty guests in the Race Street house—Trevennas, Hoskens and Carnes. Sarah, trying to reassure her, explained that the family preferred large gatherings, leaving Annie wondering whether she and her children had traveled all that way just to fill in the extra seats.

Since Zennora died, Susan had slowly opened the path to his final ruin, impelled not by cruelty or malice, but by her impatient practicality, and he, always respectful, deferred. He had not been able to find a way to keep Jesse's house; Zennora's deed trapped him on Quartz Street, and he could not afford to keep two homes. When he proposed himself as caretaker, Susan skipped a beat, letting the moment slip by. Two months after it sold, he crept onto the property and saw that the new owners had replaced the siding where Jesse had bored his final bolt-holes, and they had torn down the shed where he kept his tools. Homeless, he wandered home again.

While Eleanor, Sarah and Annie were baking cookies, Jack took Susan aside and asked her to come with him to see an inventor on the northwest edge of town.

"What does 'e invent?" she asked.

Jack checked over his shoulder and lowered his voice. "He says he's built a machine that actually flies under its own power."

Hannibal's mine seduced him into idleness. He imagined that he might help run the Live Yankee, as Jesse had helped run the North Star, but when the pounding in his ear ebbed enough for him to speak, Susan had already turned to Zebulon Day, pre-empting him, a conspiracy. Katie welcomed the money with tears and laughter, but he recognized the catastrophe, realizing that only the possibility of indigence had provided him the courage to face a work day at all. Now Katie stopped hectoring him and instead took charge of the four or five hundred dollars that arrived every month, and he had to pick his way through a house full of draperies, hats, scarves, clocks and china cats curled around cunning cannikins and crucibles. She treated his most casual remark as an inquiry and justified her plans in a biting, defensive tone. He retreated to the stable, where he contemplated his own banality and his memories of Jesse.

As Susan descended from the shelter of the buggy, a gust of wind peeled her hat off her head, and Jack ran across the damp uneven ground of the meadow to retrieve it, apologetically picking bits of grass off the brim before returning it to her. She tried to hold her hair down and settle the hat back in place, but the breeze pressed on her, flipping a curl back and forth on the side of her head and making her eyes water. Jack led her to a small clapboard house that looked as though it had not been painted in many years. He knocked on the door, waited, knocked again, called out, and finally, tentatively, turned the knob, leaned in, and called again. No one answered.

"Maybe he's in his shop." They picked their way around the house and across a bare dirt yard to a large barn. The door sagged on its hinges, stubbing heavily into the wet ground, but Jack managed to pull it open far enough to step into the darkness. He peered in, listened, and called out, "Hello!"

There was a sudden scuffling noise, the sharp sound of metal falling onto metal, and a voice. "Who is it? What do you want?" A man scuttled out of the gloom, crouching slightly and shielding his eyes against the light and the fresh air.

"Perkins? It's Jack Trevenna."

The inventor seemed puzzled. "Trevenna? Trevenna? Ah! Well! So it's you. Let's go back to the house." He gently shooed them out, dragged the barn door closed, and led the way to the house, to a room with an enormous black, cast-iron stove, a scarred pine table strewn with papers bearing bits of drawings and calculations, and an odd collection of wooden chairs. He stood before them, compulsively patting his lapels and pulling at the hem of his coat as though he hoped to stretch out the creases and wrinkles.

Carlyle Perkins wore a beard as long as Susan's hand, and his black, tangled hair draped over his collar. The brim of his otter-colored fedora drooped here and there, showing notches where he must have walked into a corner or an overhang. He wore neither collar nor tie with the stained shirt that he had buttoned all the way up to his neck, and his coat needed cleaning and brushing. His trousers bloused slightly as they disappeared into the tops of his calf-length, muddy leather boots, each with the laces carefully criss-crossed around the hooks, encircled around to bring the two sides of the vamp close together, and tied in a careful bow knot. Susan thought he looked like an unsuccessful prospector who had been camping in the mountains for years, one of those worn and weathered hill men who were younger than they appeared, but there was something in his face that fascinated her. The long mustache draped over his lips, but she thought she could see a smile in his crabapple cheeks and in the crinkles in his eyes, which were the palest brown she had ever seen, nearly transparent, and wide open. The eyes reminded her of Nick, just before he disappeared. They projected the same innocent wonder, the same undisguised, helpless vulnerability, suggesting that Perkins, like Nick, was keenly attuned to the ineffable currents that enfolded him. Yet there was a tendency to flinch, as though guarding a wound, so perhaps, like Nick, he had learned that others were ruthless, willing to use deceit and trickery at his expense, and she was sensing a scar. Both Hannibal and Jack had charmed and exasperated her with their own ingenuous eyes, but she had learned that her husband's apparent naïveté veiled a crafty man's tendency to reach too far and stumble, and that her cousin—her strange, casual lover—had learned, quite early, to control his candor, although not well enough to get what he really wanted.

"Well," exclaimed Perkins, rubbing his hands together and absently picking at a callous on one palm. "What brings you here, friend Trevenna?"

Jack introduced Susan as a local mine owner, and Perkins took her hand, very gently, and bowed repeatedly, jerking himself so forcefully that Susan thought of a toy that Eleanor had given the baby for Christmas, a wooden doll whose arms and legs sprang out when you pulled a string. "Mrs. Carne might be interested in joining our little venture." Susan looked sharply at Jack; she had said nothing to him about investing in anything.

The inventor seemed just as startled, but for a different reason. "Our little venture? Our little venture? I . . . ah . . . You will, I hope, forgive me, friend Trevenna. Our little venture?"

Flight, 1903

Jack looked slightly annoyed. "Yes. Your flying machine."

"Ah, yes, yes, of course," said Perkins, scraping at his callous so hard that he apparently broke the skin, for he jumped slightly and examined his hand as if he had been stung. "My airplane." He nodded and scanned the room, then strode over to the table to gather together his drawings and notes, scraping them into a rough pile and laying a large book over the mess. "So, you, ah, wish to invest?"

"Mr. Perkins," said Jack. "We talked about this only three months ago."

"Yes, yes, of course. Not at all. My pleasure. That is, well, of course we did. No question about it." He waited for Jack to say something, and, receiving no reply, continued. "Well, I hope you're satisfied with the prospects. No doubt about it, of course. The future. The future!" He waved his arms in the air, looking up at the ceiling as though it were the sky, and rapped a knuckle sharply on a low beam that traversed the room.

"Mr. Perkins," Jack sighed. "I'd like to see the airplane." Perkins simply stared. "We discussed this." The inventor abruptly sat in a chair and resumed scraping his callouses. "You said you had flown, under power, a distance of three hundred yards over level ground." Perkins gasped slightly and glanced apprehensively at Susan. Jack leaned forward and tried to fix the man with his eyes. "I'd like to see you do it. I'd like to see the machine."

Perkins looked puzzled. "See the machine? See the machine. Ah, the airplane. Well, ah, yes, the airplane. Hmm." He actually relaxed for a moment, his hands sitting still in his lap, folded calmly. "Well."

The Klondike was his last chance. One morning three months after Bert was born, Katie, holding the baby in her arms, with two little girls hanging onto her skirt and another squalling at the foot of the stairs, had announced that four was enough. Yet they kept coming, and after the sixth, Katie had impatiently rebuffed his questions. His children surrounded him. His wife and his sister had dismissed him, consigned him to insignificance. His family offered neither solace nor reward, but rather siege. He was not yet fifty; anything, surely, was possible. Perhaps he could remake himself. He could journey to Alaska, disembark into a community that harbored no assumptions, no preconceptions, no suspicions. Jesse had gone away, sailed to a place beyond the sunset, found something precious, and then sent for them. Yet Susan stopped the holes, cutting off his escape and binding him to the life on Quartz Street.

Perkins selected one sketch at a time, using a pencil to point out this feature or that. As he explained the principles and the engineering behind the craft he had depicted in careful lines and shadings, his voice, which had been high and tight, dropped into a more comfortable range, and his hands stopped flittering and instead soared on the pressure of imaginary zephyrs like the wings he sought to explain. "Lift. Da Vinci proposed wings, flapping like a finch, but consider the hawk, who soars and glides, carrying momentum into momentum. She lights on the tallest trees, stretches her wings and falls into the wind. She sails, riding the breeze that washes over her. You see the cross-section." He pulled out a sketch of several curved shapes, thin, bulbous at one end and tapering to a point at the other, placed in different attitudes all over the page. "An ærofoil. The air flows past, but you see—" He quickly sketched in straight lines on the bottom and curves on top, following the contour of the shape. "—below, here, the shorter distance, less resistance; the wind simply passes. But above, the breeze tarries on the leading edge, then hurries along and out. The speed picks up the wing, and so you have lift. The question is the angle, the curve. Too far this way, no lift. Too far this way, the wing dives." He was sketching as he spoke, quick, neat drawings with the precise, sharp point of his pencil. "Just so, and the wing will round to and stop in mid-air, just like the hawk confronting its prey. We ride the air, but if we lose our balance, the air will push us to earth. It's all pressure." As he drew and spoke, he looked up occasionally, checking, but Susan sensed that he knew they would not understand these invisible countervailing forces, not completely, even though it was all quite real to him.

"Forward thrust: propulsion. A propellor, a wing that spins. We lift, but forward, so we pull. But how much weight? How much power?" His discussion was becoming more and more elliptical, and he was looking up at Jack more often, as if assessing him to see how much he was absorbing, and Susan began to suspect that he was deliberately obscuring the crucial details. "Then—control. Not like a carriage, for we have not only yaw but pitch and roll. All very simple, all very delicate. A rudder, as on a ship, for yaw. Deflect the airstream, and the craft turns. This way—that way. All pressure; the surface and the wind." He was sketching even more quickly now, but no less exactly. "For pitch, a rudder laid on its side. Aft, where the tail catches the wind and swings as we wish. The hawk lifts her tail and rushes down to earth. But for roll—a difficult problem. More rudders, I think, set in the wing, but I haven't solved it yet, not yet." He paused, tapping his pencil and frowning at the paper in front of him. He looked up at Susan, the clear eyes no longer simple, and smiled, not nervous now, but as Jesse used to smile when she ran to him. "It's all right." He actually reached out and patted her hand. "We run wires through pulleys here, here, and here, and the pilot actually twists the wing. A Frenchman thought of it, actually. The wing lives in the air, just like the hawk."

He liked to slip out to the stable before breakfast and remain until dusk had so enveloped the walls that he could scarcely find his way out. He craved not so much the drink as the silence, and as his progress through the brown bottles slackened, he retraced the past, mulling over events like a man who finds a box of letters in the attic. The years seemed to fall into a paradigm, each little epoch marked by the woman who loomed over him: his grandmother, his mother, his wife, and, here at the end, his sister. There was no place for the men in the paradigm. They had come to California and left him behind, left him with the women, and when his mother had brought him, her arm around his shoulders, the men had regarded him with slight surprise, as though they could not quite imagine him. Susan's boys had deferred to him as their uncle, presuming an authority that he did not actually wield, and assuming an elder's disinterest in their affairs. Caught between generations, he huddled in the stable, falling deeper and deeper into the labyrinthine, insoluble past.

Jack broke in. "Mr. Perkins, this is all very well, but I want to see the airplane. I want to see you fly it."

Perkins sat back in his chair, considering his visitor carefully. After a long moment, he rose. "Very well. If you please." He ushered them out of the house and around behind the barn to a large shed. He opened the doors wide, and the daylight revealed a double-winged craft with a span of nearly twenty feet. The thin, delicate struts were built of strong, dry wood, and over the framework was stretched canvas so thin that they could see the members through it.

Jack folded his arms. "It looks like a kite."

Perkins nodded. "It does indeed. I took this craft out last year, towed it behind a horse, had to lash the creature to get him to run fast enough, but it sailed well enough in the end. The great problem was control; it's too small for a man to ride, and his weight would bring it down."

"Can you install an engine in it?" Jack wanted to know.

"Oh, yes. Of course." Perkins walked over to a corner and threw back a tarp. "But look at this. This is how I test my ærofoils. You see?" They looked down at an open, tapered box about twelve feet long. Perkins opened a crate to reveal a whole collection of tiny wing sections, each with a strong cord looped through from top to bottom, and others attached to the tips. "That is a sort of chute, a passage for wind. I take it out in the meadow on the windiest days. I point the chute into the wind, and the flared end picks up the breeze and funnels it back to the center, here. Then I can control the attitude of the ærofoil, and find out how well it works. If it's going to dive, much better to find out now than when you're up in the air."

"Mr. Perkins," said Jack, trying to keep his voice under control and speaking in a slow, measured rhythm. "I want to see you fly."

"Fly?" Perkins seemed to hear the request for the first time. He looked around, up at the clouds, and over at the tree tops. "Not today."

"Why not?" Jack growled. Susan had to concentrate to keep from smiling.

"No wind. Hardly a breeze." Susan realized that the wind had, indeed, died out completely. "You see, Mr. Trevenna, even a powered craft needs a good wind and a good start. I tried using sleigh runners after that blizzard we had last February, but when the snow is deep like that, you can't tell where the rocks might be. No, wheels work better, but you need a bit of a downward slope and, as I say, a fine, strong headwind. Especially here, you see. We're higher in elevation than San Francisco; the air is thinner. Conditions must be just right or the thing won't get off the ground at all."

"You can't fly today?"

"Not possible." The inventor chuckled and began picking at his calluses again. "I wait for weeks sometimes, for just the right day."

"You mean you can fly only in certain weather?"

Perkins smiled. "We've been trying to fly since Icarus. Someday, we'll be able to fly any time we wish. For now, God chooses the days, and then He gives us a glimpse of eternity."

More and more, his reveries followed him into the house, so that pretending the join the others was not enough to free him from his desperate contemplations. More and more, he looked up at Katie or one of the children to find an expression of petulant concern, and he caught his breath, lost, wondering how far and how disastrously he had fallen out of step. More and more, he felt that he was sinking, but the traces of the past had become so entangled with the conundrums of the present that he could not find his bearings well enough to extricate himself.

"My God!" Jack slapped his fist into his palm and stalked off a few paces. He returned to look the inventor in the eye. "Perkins! Did you actually fly?"

"Yes."

"Not a glider, but a machine under its own power?"

"Yes."

"But you can't do it today?"

"No."

"Can you at least show me the airplane?"

Perkins took out a large blue handkerchief and wiped his face all over before anwering. "You wish to see the airplane?"

"Yes."

"The one that I flew last year?"

"Yes."

Perkins considered, blew his nose into the handkerchief, folded it carefully and tucked it away into his coat pocket. "Why?"

"Why?" Jack was incredulous. "You and I are discussing the possibility

Flight, 1903

of my investing in your . . . your operation here." He looked around at the weathered barn, the open shack, and the scraps of ironmongery sitting in the underbrush. "I am proposing to give you enough money to move ahead, to develop this machine into something useful. You might become famous, or rich, or both. So might I. But you need my money and I need what you know. Now." He took a breath. "If I'm going to commit to this thing, then I want some sort of proof. I want to see it."

Perkins lowered his gaze, the lids drooping so that the impossible eyes nearly disappeared. "You say you wish to invest. You say you are interested in the future of powered flight. So you say." He looked at the wind chute. "How do I know you aren't building an airplane yourself? Or representing someone who is?"

"What?" Jack's jaw dropped.

"Oh, yes. Or perhaps you work for the government. The Army." He began drawing the tarp over the chute. "A man came to see me last summer. A man from the Army. No uniform, of course, but he told me what he was about. Imagine, he said, if soldiers could fly over enemy lines. They could locate the other troops, chart their movements. They might even carry weapons and fire on the enemy, or lob shells down onto them. No, I said. Not in my airplane. He smiled. You cannot stop what will happen, Mr. Perkins. No? Perhaps not. But nor will I comply. Good day, sir. And he left."

"You think I'm from the Army?"

"I think nothing. But I must be careful. Yes, I flew an airplane. Single wing, 42-foot span, aft rudders, twin propellors, eighteen horsepower engine. Flew six times off of that saddle over there, launching right into the face of the gale, so brisk it made my eyes water and I couldn't see, couldn't tell for sure when I left the ground except that I knew I was soaring. I could feel it. Even circled the hill once. The craft is sitting in that barn right there. You've seen the drawings, you have my word—what more do you want?"

"I want to see the plane, damn you!"

Perkins pulled the doors shut. "I must be careful. I hope you are an honest man, Mr. Trevenna, but there are those that are not. Good day, sir. Good day, Mrs. Carne." Scratching his calluses, the inventor walked back to his little house, leaving the visitors standing in the mud.

Without a word, they walked back to the buggy. Jack helped Susan up and then stood there, staring at the barn. They were halfway back to town before he spoke. "Well, automobiles would be safer."

She looked over at him. "D'ye think 'e was tellin' the truth?"

Jack stared out between the ears of the horse. "I don't know." He smiled at her. "I hope so. Just think of it. To fly!"

He turned back to the reins, and she looked at his profile, neatly outlined, like a weathervane. "Then why not go back? Offer t' go in with 'im. P'raps, in a little, 'e'll trust ye."

Jack looked at her and chuckled a little. "Let him make a fool of me? I don't think so."

"And if 'e *is* tellin' the truth? What if 'e *is* the first? Then who's the fool?"

"Let it go, Susan. This time, I know I'm right."

The Race Street house was crowded with children, full armchairs, and cups of hot punch. Susan deflected questions about their mysterious excursion while Jack exchanged a few discreet words with Frederick. The families sat down to Christmas dinner as the freshening breeze whistled past the windows.

On the day after Christmas, Joseph saddled his horse and rode slowly through a desultory drizzle to Auburn, where he rented a room in a boarding house. There was a bed, a table and a chair, and across the single, dingy window hung a torn scrap of canvas. To the center of the ceiling was attached a bracket for a chandelier from the days when the house had held prosperous miners' revels. He drew the chair over to a position directly beneath the bracket, climbed up to stand on the seat, reached up, grabbed on to the iron hooks for a moment, and lifted his feet, gasping. The bracket held. He lowered his feet to the seat of the chair, then stepped down, shrugged off his coat, laid it on the bed, and reached into one of the large pockets to bring out a short length of rope. He sat on the bed, rubbing his fingers along the splintery hemp, and then, quickly and expertly, tied a slip knot in one end. He stepped back up onto the chair, looped the free end of the rope through the bracket, and tied a bowline close up against the metal. He lifted the loop over his head and discovered that he was still wearing his hat, so he took it off, held it in his hand for a moment, and gently let it fall onto the bed below. Then he slid the loop over his head, past his face and down under his chin, and pulled to bring it tightly around his neck. He stood there, staring at the wall. In his ear sounded, again and again, his grandmother's name for the barley gruel she used to feed him, so thin that it was little more than water: "sky-blue and sinker, sky-blue and sinker, sky-blue and sinker." He stood, motionless, for a minute, then another, and another, until fifteen minutes had passed. Abruptly, he shifted his weight so that the chair fell out from under his feet. He fell, but not far enough, and the rope pressed on his windpipe, pressing until his eyes felt swollen. Slowly, so very slowly, the room began to shimmer, and then dissolved.

25
The Earthquake
1906

Susan and Sarah stood outside the house on Race Street watching the movers load the last of Eleanor's furniture. Lavinia, tugging at her shawl, hectored the man in charge, barking that they were packing the wagon wrong, all wrong. Her hair was white now, and deep, dry lines ran down from the corners of her mouth.

"Will you be coming to the station, Mother?" asked James. Susan shook her head. "Then we'll see you down there soon, won't we?" He looked at Sarah. "Both of you?" Clumsily, he stepped in, clasped Susan's shoulders with his hands, kissed her cheek, climbed up into the front seat of the carriage, where Eleanor and the children sat waiting, and flicked the whip over the horses' ears. As he turned the corner, Lavinia let out a sudden, exasperated hiss and called sharply to Henry, who was dozing in her buggy. They drove off, Lavinia looking back to stab an accusing forefinger at the movers and blare recriminations.

The town seemed deserted. Bertie had long since moved down to San Francisco to join Hettie, who would not even discuss the possibility of returning to Grass Valley, and now James was taking his family to live in Alameda, just across the bay, a flat town of ferry schedules and constant wind. Ernest had become restless again, and even Martin had declared his intention to consider the move to the City. Susan had tried to persuade them to stay, but they listened only politely, and she gave up when she discovered that Sarah, too, had grown tired of Grass Valley and wanted a change. They tried to convince her that the family would not scatter, that they would be together again in San Francisco, but she knew that living there would not be the same, that they would become estranged, pushed apart by time, space and the pressure of the city itself.

She was well acquainted with Jack's views. He believed that any man who wished to lead California through the twentieth century—any man with gumption, insight and energy—would leave the hills for San Francisco, but, wary of Susan's objections, he had carefully avoided getting involved in the boys' debates over the opportunities they imagined, the excitement and vitality of the City, and the dreariness they attributed to Grass Valley. He intervened only to serve, only after they had made up their minds, arranging for Bertie a job as a conductor on a street car line, and for James the opportunity to buy a home in a neighborhood where Jack himself owned property. Susan, strangely dizzy, felt as though the Sierra were tilting to a steeper grade, and that anything not irrevocably rooted would naturally and inexorably roll down towards the Pacific.

Restless, alone, Susan drove her carriage all over the district, each afternoon heading a different direction. She found French Lead completely unfamiliar: the owners had raised a new mill house of broad granite blocks, and where the cottages once stood were rail sidings lined with spare ore cars, bunches of dry grass growing up between the ties. At the Kentucky Ranch, she discovered such orderly, well-tended orchards and vineyards that she wondered whether she had taken a wrong turn; she could scarcely credit her recollection of the day when Hannibal had driven them all out there to spin his anxious dreams. She felt absolutely out of place in Nevada City and so left Broad Street to drive across Deer Creek and visit Lavinia, who kept her waiting on the porch, with Mary and Henry staring out from behind her, until she accepted that her visit had no specific purpose, and so, nonplussed, invited her in for tea. The house was perfectly clean and precisely arranged, as though no one lived there, and Mary poured into china cups that she took out of the buffet in the dining room after surreptitiously asking Lavinia where to find the key. When Susan tried to take a sip, she could barely swallow. She peeked past the delicately scalloped porcelain edge at the three Hoskens—Lavinia propped on the edge of her chair, Mary hovering before the kitchen door, and Henry standing like a broken tree near the window, his eye patch aimed squarely towards her—and felt as though she had invaded a sanctum, shattering some inexpressibly private and precarious equilibrium. She left as soon as she could.

The catalytic moment arrived in town. She wanted to visit the bank while Sarah went to the grocer's, but she had not taken three steps when she caught her breath suddenly, as though someone had yanked at her. When her pounding pulse slowed, she felt, strangely, that she had become able to watch the town unnoticed, and indeed, as men and women walked past her, no one nodded, no one glanced her way, and no one needed to dodge to avoid bumping into her. She looked down past Loutzenheiser's pharmacy towards Wolf Creek, up towards the Holbrooke and the white houses that gleamed on the crest of the hill, and across, along the curve of Mill Street with its brick storefronts, plate glass windows and covered walkways. The town had always annoyed her because it had been so pushy, so bumptious and intrusive, with its new buildings and bragging announcements and general self-importance. Now, invisible, she realized that the place had settled into the merely routine. Men simply walked from appointment to appointment, knowing in advance what would happen, and women strolled from shop to shop, confident that they would find what they needed and meet with no surprises. Even the few passing Chinese excited no notice. The town had become settled, predictable, mundane; even trite. There was no uncertainty, no risk, and no enterprise. As she stood there, she thought she felt the Sierra tilt just a bit more, and she had to shift her feet to keep her balance and prevent herself from staggering a little farther to the west. When Sarah returned, Susan told her that they would be going to visit Jack.

After the Trevennas' maid had unpacked Susan's bags in the upstairs front bedroom, Jack found that he needed brief moments, at unpredictable intervals, when he could be alone to compose himself. Susan had always been tricky to manage, and he knew now that if he betrayed too much enthusiasm, she would take the next train back to the hills, possibly never to return, if only to prove that she had a will of her own. If he handled her just right, there was a good chance that she would decide to stay. He felt sure that Jesse and Hannibal, if they had lived, would have followed his example, would have come to San Francisco, and Nick as well. Susan was a woman of talent, clear-headed and determined. She was wasted on the little town in the hills; she belonged in the more cosmopolitan, open-minded city. Besides, he wanted her near him.

She had visited him soon after Joseph's funeral, and on the night before she was to leave, he had stayed up too late, sitting by himself in the parlor. Finally, dizzy with fatigue and brandy and memories, he had crept in to stand by her bed, then kneel, and then lower his head onto the coverlet next to her shoulder. His next recollection was waking to her gentle, dry fingers stroking his hair. He lifted his head and looked into her eyes, shining in the moonlight that floated through the translucent curtains, and slowly, so slowly, he bent down and kissed her, finding her lips full and warm and welcoming. He slipped off his shoes and slid in next to her, still wearing his vest and trousers, and nestled, finding her waist through the soft flannel, feeling her turn and bend, laying her thigh across his and wrapping one arm around his head, now pillowed on her breast. Falling, falling, he slept again, drifting off, oblivious to her fitful breathing and the tears dripping slowly down to her pillow. He left her with the setting moon, well before dawn, pausing only for one more kiss and a smile. Yet at breakfast the next morning, she spoke to him just as ironically and briskly as had become customary, as though nothing at all had happened. He knew that Annie was jealous of his cousin, but he could not assess how much she guessed about their past, and so he had decided to ignore her suspicious glances and irritable replies. Her mistrust was rather amusing, actually; Susan was just past sixty, although she looked remarkably well for a woman of her age, while Annie was fifteen years younger, with her hair that much darker and her step that much lighter. At odd moments, Jack permitted himself a bit of preening at the idea of his wife and his cousin—his lover—covertly, discreetly competing over him, but he always caught himself, remembering that his sons would regard the entire affair as completely devoid of intrigue and interest, given that the principals were really too old to be thinking of such things. Shaking his head at all of them, Jack grinned to himself.

For three days, Jack drove Susan and Sarah through various neighborhoods, occasionally stopping to walk through houses that were available. Sarah quickly tired, and she decided to go stay with James and Eleanor until her mother was ready to make a decision, so Jack dispatched Frederick to escort her on the ferry to Alameda. Now he was left alone with Susan—Annie did not count, as her days were full of running the household and attending meetings of the Temperance Union and the Episcopal Women's League—so he arranged each day, house-hunting in the morning, resting in the afternoon, dining amidst arching feathers and rich cigars, and finishing in this theatre or that. There were moments when they could look across the table at each other and smile, each seeing in the other the shimmer of private encounters from long ago.

Susan donned her finest gown when Jack proposed that they dine at the Palace and attend *Carmen* at the Mission Street Opera House. He escorted her grandly to a box decorated with gilt flowers and dancing lions; she was surrounded with stiff collars, shining hair and jewelled fans. The opera began with soldiers and a young girl, but the audience seemed preoccupied, waiting, and when a certain officer walked onto the stage, the crowd applauded and cheered, "Caruso, Caruso, Caruso!" Wherever Caruso went, the glinting opera glasses followed him, even when a gypsy girl, a deep pink acacia blossom tucked in the corner of her lips, danced slowly across the stage, chanting a sensual melody to the eager soldiers. Caruso stood with his feet separated, as though holding his balance on the heaving deck of a ship, lifted his mustache, stuck out his chin, and sang until the railing under Susan's gloved fingers buzzed and hummed. Women in diamonds sniffled and sobbed while Caruso sang to the gypsy, his feet still planted, his chin jutting out above the orchestra, and his eyes staring fiercely. He climbed up and down the melody, lingering on a passage where his eyebrows stretched up and Susan felt that he was screaming at her. Caruso took nine curtain calls, his chin still thrusting defiantly up towards the upper balcony while he kissed his hand to the clamoring throng.

Jack took Susan through the lobby, picking a path through the departing men and women, and down a corridor that led to a door where an old man in brass buttons sat dozing. They passed men in soiled grey shirts and others wearing pieces of yellow dragoons' uniforms, and they stopped in front of a blue door. Jack knocked, and the door opened.

There were several other men and women there, all chattering in the dingy light glaring off of the mirrors, and in the center of the room stood Caruso in a red silk dressing gown. As Jack and Susan approached, the people with the singer drew back only a little, regarding the newcomers with what Susan interpreted as suspicion and resentment. Caruso took Susan's hand in both of his, bending over it to plant a kiss. He lifted his chin again, accepted a glass of red wine and slapped his belly with his free hand. As they turned to go, Susan realized that her glove, ivory silk, bore a smear of brown grease paint.

That night she dreamed that she was ten years old, walking on the beach near Mount's Bay and clapping her hands at the soaring gulls while the wind lashed her face with her hair. Then she was fully alert, with no transition into wakefulness, listening. She reached out and pulled the curtains away from the window, and the room filled with a cold grey light. It was nearly dawn; the air was perfectly still. She snuggled the comforter up under her chin and lay on her side, gazing at the roofs of the neighboring homes silhouetted against the pale eastern sky. She glanced at the clock on the night table; it was twelve minutes past five, so she closed her eyes to try to fall asleep again. In the yard behind the house next door, a dog began to yip and whimper.

At that moment, her bed began to sway.

A fisherman walking on Baker Beach stood staring as the undertow kept running, pulling the water away and leaving piles of kelp beached on the wet, exposed sand. He spun around to run up into the dunes, but the returning water caught him, engulfed him, picked him up off of his feet and carried him out to sea.

Cliff House shuddered as though a giant sledgehammer had struck its foundations. Every window shattered into slivers, the fragments coalescing into miniature twisters that picked up small objects and lacerated the walls, the upholstery, and the faces of the two people upstairs whom the noise had abruptly jolted from sleep.

At the Presidio, General Funston dreamed of gunfire. Awaking, still hearing the sound, he ran to his window to see fifty-foot eucalyptus trees snapping at the bases of their trunks and flying through the air. One especially large one lost its few branches and hit the ground rolling, advancing all the way across the parade ground and crushing three astonished sentries before crashing into a barracks.

At North Beach, houses swayed to and fro, the odd members of a row leaning forward while the even members leaned back, then changing direction like dancers in a chorus line.

On Market Street, a baker and his helpers were loading their first delivery while the next batch of loaves browned. Their horse began to fidget and suddenly reared. As the teamster grabbed for the reins, the wagon flew up about ten feet, snapping the traces like kite string, and came down to collapse into a pile of kindling and splinters mixed with cracked wheat and sourdough. In the kitchen, hurtling bread pans burned three of the baker's helpers, and one of the men flew helplessly against the searing hot oven door.

At the Palace Hotel, Caruso awoke, wet and shaking, from a dream that he was trapped in Naples, raising his hands against the blistering ash falling from Vesuvius. Above his head, the French chandelier was swinging so hard that it slammed against the ceiling. He tried to roll out of bed, but caught one foot in the Persian bedspread and lost his balance, reaching for the walls and tearing the satin as he fell on the thick Turkish carpet. He covered his face against the shower of plaster, staggered to the window, threw it open, and stood there gaping at a scene out of Dante. A man wearing only a night shirt and trousers, his suspenders flapping behind him, darted out of the hotel to meet a cluster of bricks that fell off of the façade and knocked him, senseless, to the cobblestones. A stark naked woman, fat and pale, ran down the middle of the street, screaming and jiggling. A milkman's cart rattled at full speed out of an alley and on, out of sight, its horse galloping headlong with no driver in the cab. The street buckled and a sudden fountain of flame roared up into the air. The tenor crossed himself and began to mutter the Ave Maria.

In Grass Valley, safely embedded in the foothills over a hundred miles to the northeast, the drowsing birds ruffled their feathers and warbled, and a few of the town's dogs sniffed the wind and whimpered. The bells in the taller steeples swung gently to and fro, but not far enough for the clappers to strike, so no one realized what had happened.

On Piety Hill, Lavinia Hosken had risen before dawn and was standing on her front porch estimating the number of stones she would need to build a path down to the street. She thought she heard a humming, and looked up. The trees were shivering, the leaves quaking like aspens in a breeze, but the air was perfectly still. The porch began to vibrate under her feet, and she reached for the broad turned post that stood on one side of the stairs. A jay, the largest she had ever seen, with impossibly bright blue feathers, landed on a drooping branch, looked straight at her, and jeered, a raucous call that echoed and repeated, pounding on her ears. She shrank against the post, her mouth hanging open, staring at the frenzy of the trees, her spellbound gaze finally drawn, compelled, to the glaring jay before her. Alone in the peaceful neighborhood, the house shook, rippling and dancing in the brightening morning, until the porch post cracked and the great beam fell like a carload of rab and tailings. Then the house settled, and all of Piety Hill was completely silent and motionless. The jay cocked his head to study Lavinia's body, stretched down across the stairs, the outraged face grimacing up at the sky and the arms wrapped tightly around the massive timber that lay across the chest. She did not move. The jay ruffled its feathers, jeered once more, and flew up, over the house, away from Piety Hill and southwest past Grass Valley.

On Sacramento Street, Susan lay in her bed, bewildered, as the dog next door began to scream, and a roar like titanic hail competed with the clamor of hysterical church bells. She threw back the covers, swung her feet to the floor and began to walk to the front window, but the boards heaved beneath her as though on a ship defying a violent storm, folding her up and throwing her against the wall, where her head hit the chair rail. She collapsed to her knees and kept moving toward the window, crawling on the tossing floor. She pulled herself up on the sill and pushed the curtains aside to peer out. The glass had already shattered, and the cool morning air bathed her face. The house across the street was shrugging like a man doing the Furry Dance back in Helston, now settling its weight on one side, now on the other. The entire front fell away, revealing the rooms like the back of a doll house. The whole structure staggered once more, the center of the ground floor sprang up as though a subterranean Goliath had kicked it with his heavy boot, and the walls crumpled and fell in on each other, sending showers of brick down into the street. She raised one hand to her open mouth. It felt wet, and she looked down at the sill to find red smears on the painted wood. The broken glass had scattered across the floor in spite of the curtains, and without realizing it, she had crawled through the mess and etched chaotic patterns into the palms of her hands. Her head began to throb.

Then the world stood still.

Susan looked down at her bleeding hands and wondered when the room would begin to shake again; the motion had lasted just long enough to seem inevitable, perhaps even normal, and this stasis felt unnatural, too fixed. Across the way, a cornice fell from above the windows of the upper story and crashed onto the pavement below. As if responding to a signal, horses in all of the nearby stables began to kick and whinny, and in the distance, Susan could hear the fire stations sounding their whistles and horns.

Jack kicked open the door and stood there, his mouth hanging open and his night shirt covered with dust. He walked towards her in a strange half-crouch, stopping and swearing softly when his bare feet found the shards of glass, and reaching out as if to help her up, even though he was still standing eight feet away. She rose, tip-toed over to him, and together, their arms around each other, they walked down the cracked staircase. Frederick was rubbing his shoulder; he had battered in the jammed bedroom doors in order to free his sisters. One of the maids was missing, but Jack found her huddled against an armoire, dazed and crying. They opened the front door and looked out into the street.

Cousin Jack

Fragments and sections of houses, with splintered boards and chunks of plaster, littered the broken street and sidewalk. Only a few chimneys remained standing; the rest had fallen, either plunging straight down into their houses or catapulting out into the street, there to smash into fragments. One house had collapsed completely, leaving only a pile of rubble, and they could see, discreetly revealed at the edge, a hand, the palm turned up and the fingers delicately extended. The house next door to the broken heap looked sound and pristine, and the family who lived in it had walked out onto the stoop to stare, bewildered, at the calamity beside them. Dust filled the air, suspended, hardly drifting at all. A man dressed in a black suit and a derby, his gold watch chain stretched across his vest, his mustache perfectly curled, walked briskly past them and nodded curtly to Jack. From the other direction, a gray mare trotted crisply up the street, her nose held close into her chest as though someone were pulling on imaginary reins. Jack chuckled, and Frederick let go with a long laugh. Across the street, the horrified family frowned at them, then began to smile.

Abruptly, Jack hurried back into the house, paused for only a moment to note the fallen bookcases and the crockery strewn across the floor, carefully picked his way through the chunks of fallen plaster that littered the staircase, and walked into his bedroom. The place was covered with a fine white dust, but when he opened his wardrobe, he found that although the pole had fallen down, sliding his suits into a jumble, the joinery had been tight enough to keep everything clean. He found a suit, a hat and a pair of shoes, and quickly dressed himself. At the bottom of the stairs, he found Susan wearing a silk Eton jacket and a small hat.

He smiled. "You seem to be on your way."

She smiled back at him. "I'm comin' with ye."

He raised his eyebrows. "You don't even know where I'm going."

She shook her head, still smiling. "Ye're goin' down t' your office, t' look after your papers and things. And I'm comin' with ye."

"What for?"

"Better see what's 'appened than stay 'ere and 'elp Annie and the girls clean up the mess. It's their 'ouse—let them set it to rights. I'm goin' with ye."

"We'll have to walk—the buggy won't get through the streets, the way they are."

"I agree."

He looked into the parlor to say good-bye to Annie, who was pulling the furniture away from the dusty curtains. Susan took his arm, and they walked out of the front door and down the steps. A few men were working at the collapsed house, throwing chunks of brick and plaster into a cart. One got down on his knees to try to pull a body clear of the mess. Jack and Susan walked down the street, around the corner, and turned onto California Street.

A furrow ran eccentrically through the worn bricks, veering back and forth across the roadway before taking a straight line directly through a house that now sagged towards its own middle, slowly tumbling into the sudden trench that had opened up in its foundation. Broken glass littered the sidewalk. At a livery stable, bales of hay lay haphazardly throughout the stalls, and a groom sat on a stool, twisting his cap in his hands and staring at the carcass of a horse: the shock had driven the animal, head first, clean through a wall. People on the street glanced from side to side apprehensively as they walked along, not casually, but not too fast either, rather carefully, as though testing each step for a tiny fraction of a second.

As they crossed Buchanan, a woman, her hair loose and her apron falling down around her ankles, ran out of a restaurant crying "Fire! Fire! Help!"

Plumes of black smoke pushed out of the side of the building, and a little gang of men ran around the corner and into the front door. Two carried axes. A man wearing a straw skimmer strode out onto the sidewalk, put his fingers to his lips and gave three piercing whistles. More men ran out from the nearby shops while the man with the skimmer looked up and down the street. He beckoned to Jack. "Come here, you!" Jack looked down at Susan, but she took her hand out from the crook of his elbow. He followed the man back inside, and a moment later came out again carrying a chair, which he set down in the street. Then back again, and out again, with four or five other men, clearing everything they could carry out of the burning building. Susan could hear bumping and crashing noises, and a man threw open a window and began to hurl out pieces of splintered timbers. She staggered as someone bumped into her from behind, and she turned to see a line of people handing buckets back and forth, extending from the burning building to a cistern sixty yards away. She stepped into the line, took a bucket from the man next to her, and handed it off to a boy on her other side. The buckets kept coming, back and forth, empty and full, and after fifteen minutes her skirt was heavy with water and sand. Then the buckets stopped, and she looked past the boy to the restaurant. The entire rear of the building was stained with smoke, and one corner of it was burned and black, with a section now open to the sky. The woman who had called for help now sat weeping in one of the chairs that someone had arranged in the street, and only Susan seemed to notice when a man picked up a marble-topped table sitting quite near her and walked around the corner with it. Jack found her—he had lost his collar and tie, and his hat brim had been crushed behind his right ear—and they went on.

There were fallen chimneys everywhere, and so much ornamental stone-work had fallen into the street that the houses looked curiously stripped. At Van Ness, Susan pulled Jack back from a fire wagon, drawn by four horses, the driver frantically trying to find a speedy path through the rubble, his mates hanging on to the railings as they pitched and swerved. At the shoulder of Nob Hill, they looked up to their left and saw the railroad mansions still standing, but when they looked down, towards the docks, they could see smoke piling up from a dozen different locations. Jack began to walk faster. At Stockton Street, they had to push their way through hundreds of people hurrying out of Chinatown. Susan had never realized how many Chinese there were in San Francisco; now it seemed that every one of them was moving south, each with at least one bundle, faces grim, queues swinging, eyes seeking a clear path through the throng. She missed her timing once, and a man wearing a blue silk smock nearly knocked her over. He hardly glanced at her and didn't offer to apologize, but kept going, his eyes fixed ahead. They struggled past Dupont and through the last streams of refugees walking down Kearney.

Jack had taken an office suite in a grey stone building just past Spring Street, only a few doors west of Montgomery. The door sagged on its hinges like a slack mouth, and he strode in, took the stairs two at a time, and drove his key into the lock on the door that said "Trevenna & Son." She followed him into the outer office and tried to dry her sweaty face while he found a cardboard carton and rifled his desk, stopping every moment or so to check a packet of papers, throwing the ones he wanted into the carton, and tossing the rest on a table. He took the box to Frederick's desk, pulled out a series of packets folded in brown paper and tied with twine, then stooped down next to the safe, twirled the knob from one side to the other, leaned on the heavy handle, and swung the door open. He crouched there as though considering, pausing long enough to take his hat off and run his fingers through his hair. The building shivered with an aftershock. Susan stepped in next to him, close enough to see the neat folders of papers stacked on the shelves in the little compartment.

"Jack?" He looked up at her. "If there's a fire, don't ye think th' papers'd be better off in th' safe?"

He shook his head. "Anything could happen. Anything at all. I'd rather keep 'em with me. Here, take these." He began handing up slim folders, stacking them in her arms. When the safe was empty, he rose, took the stack from her, and began to unfold each packet, laying the papers out flat. There were certificates for mining stocks, railroad bonds, water bonds, property deeds, trust deeds, and brokerage accounts. Susan later remembered only the ornate scrollwork in the corners of the heavy certificates and the parade of names of counties as she sorted through the deeds: San Francisco, Alameda, Fresno, Inyo, Placer and Nevada. Jack divided the papers in half, packed each stack into a folder and tied the laces tight. He took off his coat and began to unbutton his shirt. He happened to glance at Susan, noticed her surprise, and dropped his intent, determined expression to grin at her. "I'm all right. 'elp me out, won't ye?" He draped his shirt over a chair and held one of the folders against his belly, and she understood. She found a ball of twine in the clerk's desk drawer, slapped the second folder against his back and began to unroll the twine around and around, maintaining the tension until the folders were securely pressed against him. She tied a knot and he reached for his shirt, but she shook her head, giving him the free end of the twine and pressing his fingers into place while she wound around and around again, finishing with another knot. As she snipped the ends with a scissors, something in his face caught her eye, and she looked up to see him, his hands on his head, grinning down at her. She smiled back, but shook her head and finished the job. He put on his shirt and coat, and locked and double-locked the door behind them.

Outside, the breeze, usually so fresh and salty, brought only smoke. A blast shoved them, reeling, against the stone wall next to them, and when Susan recovered, settling her hat back on her head, she saw a battalion of troops marching down the middle of the street. In the rear, a squad of men surrounded an open touring car, all bright paint and polished brass, loaded down with boxes and bundles and great reels of wire. They stopped in front of the building on the far corner of Montgomery, and Jack approached the officer in charge. The man listened impatiently and jerked his head over his shoulder, back in the direction of the explosion. "Dynamite. We're taking down these buildings to stop the fire, keep it from spreading."

One cluster of buildings, quite close to the waterfront, had become a holocaust. The soldiers had left a trail of destruction, but a few of the blasted hulks still stood. Jack tapped the officer's shoulder. "Lieutenant—look! It's burning!"

The officer set his lips petulantly and looked back at the last place where his men had fired their charges. There were flames flickering out of the empty windows, and smoke was beginning to float out of the vents. "Would've burned anyway. Maybe this way, we'll slow it down. Step aside, sir!" Two of his men came running out, unreeling the wire behind them. The officer fastened the ends to a box that he brought out onto the hood of the car, called "All clear! Stand back!" and, after checking perfunctorily from side to side, abruptly shoved the plunger home. The concussion made Susan crouch involuntarily, and when the chattering hiss of falling fragments ceased, she discovered that her ears were ringing. All of the windows had shattered, and the pavement was covered with shards of glass. She had just time to wipe her eyes before Jack pulled at her elbow, drawing her away from the battalion and up the street.

They were walking fast now, and he was muttering to himself, "Damned fools." She glanced back and saw flames licking the window frames, the smoke already drifting out through the holes that the dynamite had blasted in the roof and upper walls. They turned the corner and walked up Kearney, trying to avoid the path of the fire. A crew of firemen were striving to save a small building. They had uncapped the hydrant, but they were not using it; their pump hose ran down through an open manhole into the sewer, and the spray fouled the air. After two more blocks, the fugitives found another crew of soldiers with dynamite, and the officer in charge ordered them to turn back. Jack led Susan back about twenty yards and ducked into the shelter of a doorway. They covered their ears and hid their faces in each other's coats, and after the shock of the blast, Jack took her hand and they ran up the street, skirted the group of watching soldiers, turned the corner, and didn't stop until they reached Dupont.

They were standing in the heart of Chinatown. The crowded shops, with their wooden scaffoldings and brightly-colored banners, sagged against each other as though frozen in mid-lurch during the tremors. They looked so helter-skelter that Susan could almost feel the earth still pitching and wheeling under her feet. She looked down and caught her breath. Loping past them were rats, some a foot long, fleeing just as resolutely as the crowds of people they had seen earlier. Ten or fifteen had stopped to nose in the rubble of a laundry, and she gasped when she realized that they were gnawing on a leg that stuck out from underneath the crushed boards and scattered bricks; the force that had killed its owner had ripped the clothing away and left the flesh open to the little scavengers. Jack pulled at her arm and she followed him up the street, stepping over bits of fallen trim and skirting piles of rubble, all that was left of the balconies that overhung the narrow right of way. On both sides, men and women were methodically picking through the wreckage of shops, taking bundles of cloth, racks of tools and baskets of shoes. Two old women were calmly loading up a cart with fish, vegetables and canvas sacks of rice. In the remains of a gambling house, three men lifted a small iron safe onto a wheelbarrow; when one noticed the white people, he called out a sharp warning. A few doors farther up, they passed a small boy, no more than seven years old, wearing black knickers and high-buttoned shoes, sitting on a stoop and weeping inconsolably, squalling like a small baby but strangely inert, as though fixed to his spot. Susan turned as if to stop, to comfort him, but Jack kept her walking at his side. They paused for a moment to let a small group of women pass; Jack politely tipped his hat, but then coughed under his breath and replaced it, his mouth twisted in a wry smile. Susan looked at the women again; all but one were quite young, and she could see that under their coats they were only half-dressed. One of them looked full into her face, a strangely invasive and confident gaze, and she realized that they must be the girls of a Barbary Coast brothel, following their proprietress to ostensible safety. One wept, sniveling in gulps as she clutched a tiny gilt clock to her chest. Something stung Susan's cheek, and when she reached up to brush it away, she saw sparks, glowing points of red and orange, floating through the air above her head. On a sagging balcony across the street, a man wearing a frogged collarless jacket was beating a wad of rags against the flames that were traveling up his railing; then he screamed and staggered back into the house, his long white beard on fire. When they reached Jackson, they turned to avoid a storm of sparks, falling like glittering snow, and headed up the slope with Nob Hill on one side and Russian Hill on the other.

They stopped at Powell to catch their breath, and they looked up the hill to see a small procession approaching them. In the lead was a man wearing a full dress suit, complete with top hat, silk vest, boutonniere, gold watch chain, creased trousers, and flawless spats neatly buttoned over his polished shoes. Something about the flourish of his black mustache and the jut of his chin seemed familiar: it was Caruso. There were two men with him, and as he stopped on the corner to bring out a white silk handkerchief and dab at the tip of his nose, they looked apprehensively down towards the bay, cringing away from the looting that continued two blocks below them. After tucking the handkerchief smartly into the pocket of his jacket, Caruso flourished his walnut walking stick and continued on. He seemed completely oblivious to the broken street and shattered buildings around him. As he passed, he tipped his hat, nodded, and said, "Buon giorno, Signora." Then the tenor was gone, continuing down towards Union Square, parading along as though he were out for a Sunday constitutional, his attendants scurrying in a half crouch, peering up fearfully at the ornamental stonework of the better houses, their arms ready to ward off falling gargoyles.

Jack and Susan kept walking through an eerie combination of peace and panic. Neither streetcars nor cable cars were running; the shocks had twisted the rails and wrenched the streets into corduroy. Many houses looked untouched; their doors remained firmly shut and apprehensive faces peered out from behind window curtains. Other homes leaned on each other or crouched down to touch the street; surely, they would collapse completely, but for the moment, they looked stable, as though their architects had anticipated just this situation. A sporadic stream of people left the neighborhood, some pushing baby carriages full of silver and framed photographs, some bandaged or limping, all heading the same direction as Caruso, down towards Market. Jack stopped one man and asked where he was going. The man stared at him, surprised and incredulous. Why, to the Ferry Building, of course. His next-door neighbor had heard, on good authority, that the suburbs west of Van Ness were completely destroyed, and the fire would surely engulf the city by nightfall. The only chance for safety was to board the ferry for Oakland, and leave San Francisco behind. Susan assured him that the damage in the Western Addition was no worse than on Nob Hill, but he shook his head and walked on, dragging his trunk behind him, the scraping sound joining with others to form the subliminal chorus of the exodus.

When they reached the crest of Russian Hill, they stopped to look down at the city beneath them. To their left was the bay, blue under the clear sky and more than usually crowded with yachts, clippers and merchant ships. Susan realized that their captains must have cut loose from the docks as soon as the fires began, eager to move out onto the water, but she could also see, near the docks just past Telegraph Hill, masts leaning at impossible angles, and she guessed that the water, driven mad by the upheavals in the bed of the bay, must have sent some of the ships crashing against their moorings, careening them against pilings and wharves, not sunk, but broken. Below them, Chinatown was burning fiercely; the streets where they had walked were now covered with smoke and flames. A looming cloud hung over the business district, denser every moment as more smoke rose to join the pall. South of the Slot were more fires, and Susan pointed to the Palace; flickers of orange and yellow were climbing up one corner, and a slow fountain of black smoke rolled up into the sky. Another explosion boomed, and Jack sighed. The fresh spring breeze was whipping about their faces, changing directions as capriciously as a sea gull, and they could see the eddies swirl in the smoky clouds. A gust swept in from the bay, and the flames in the Merchants' Exchange flared ever more brightly.

They walked down the hill to Van Ness, turning south towards Sacramento Street and home. They had gone no more than a few blocks when a company of militia marched up behind them, forcing them to retreat against a pile of rubble. As they balanced against the fallen timbers, waiting, one of the soldiers gave a sudden cry and pointed down the street. The officer in charge ran ahead and called out, "Stop!" then "Stop, or we'll fire!" A moment later, he gave a signal, and two of his men broke ranks to run out, crouch, take aim, and fire. A hundred yards down the street, a man fell, and the box he was carrying burst and scattered its contents. The officer swore loudly and snarled at the sergeant to re-form the lines. He noticed Jack and Susan cowering against the wreckage. "You!" He pointed at Jack. "Come with us!" Two haggard men, each carrying a rifle at the ready, strode up to Jack, took him by the arms, and marched him away. As the company set off down the street, Jack turned and called back to Susan, still transfixed, that he would meet her at home.

Jack slipped away from the militia after the sun went down. By the light of the fires, he found his way back to Sacramento Street, no longer walking erect through the city, but darting from shadow to shadow, crouched like a wild animal moving cross-country through a predator's territory. When he reached the house, Annie told him that no one had seen Susan since they left that morning, but Frederick had heard that the public parks had become the refuge of the lost, the homeless, and those who were simply too apprehensive to spend the night under a roof. Jack suddenly felt inexpressibly weary, as though the weight of the disaster had, just at that moment, leaned insistently on his back, pressing him to the ground. Annie's face was smudged and her hair, although pinned back, stuck out haphazardly. She made no attempt to stop him, so he turned and walked out, back into the fiery night in search of the missing woman.

He found her more easily than he had dared hope. Just five blocks from his house was Lafayette Square, and as Frederick had predicted, it had become a sanctuary for the displaced, the disoriented, and the terrified. He walked from campfire to campfire, even peering between the flaps of the few tents, and then, as he turned to walk down another makeshift alley, the light from the burning city caught her profile. She was no longer wearing the silk jacket, and her head was bare, the long greying hair in a thick braid thrown over her shoulder as she knelt on the damp grass to wrap a bandage around a child's arm. When Jack spoke her name, she looked up, smiled, turned to finish the bandage, gave the child a kiss on the cheek, and rose to face him.

"Jack, I want ye t' go back t' the 'ouse. Bring th' girls. Ask Freddie t' find all th' blankets ye can spare, an' water if there's any in th' cisterns. There're children 'ere who can't find their parents, and they 'ave no place t' sleep. If we don't 'ave enough blankets, they can share an' keep each other warm. They're 'ungry, an' some're thirsty—they're cryin' fer somethin' t' drink. There's a little girl over there—she can't find 'er mother, and she's 'urt 'er arm. I think it may be broken, but there's no doctor 'ere." A child ran to her, burying his face in her skirts, and she leaned over to hold him, leaning her cheek on his cap.

Jack did as he was told. Annie stayed at the house with Jack's older son, and the rest came to the square to help Susan. After nearly two hours, they had gathered together ten or eleven lost children, and Frederick had succeeded in finding parents for a few others, wandering through the square with a list of names and keeping an eye out for men and women who seemed more than usually anxious. By midnight, Susan had managed to get them all to curl up under the blankets and fall asleep; even though they were frantic and inconsolable, they were also exhausted. Two six-year-old girls could not stop crying, and Susan finally lay down next to them, letting them huddle against her, with her arms wrapped around them, and within five minutes their eyes were closed, two little faces winking in the flickering light. She rose, exhausted, and told Jack that she would stay the night, watching and waiting. He sent the others home with Frederick and found Susan standing on the high knoll at the corner of the square, oblivious to the night chill, gazing out at the city.

Cousin Jack

San Francisco was burning. The bay winds had driven the flames west through Chinatown to the foot of Nob Hill, up along the waterfront towards Telegraph Hill, and down through the shacks and warehouses south of the Slot. Market Street stretched like an infernal canal, passing the fire up and down its length. The Call Building, St. Mary's, City Hall and the Palace—all gone. The Ferry Building still stood, the wind at its back, the gate to the bay and safety. Like a curtain from a theatrical extravaganza, the smoke reflected the lurid light from below.

Jack and Susan gazed out over the city. "How long do you think it'll take to rebuild?" he asked.

She looked at him, puzzled. "What d'ye mean?"

"The fires'll burn out in a day or two. Most of the docks are all right, so there'll be no trouble bringing in fresh supplies. Clearing away the mess, that's the first problem. The mayor'll have to send crews around to decide what to leave standing and what to tear down. Take my house—there are a few cracks in the walls, but it seems all right. I don't know, though—I'd like to have someone look it over. But after they clear away the rubble, we can start over again."

"Start over again?"

"Iss fay." He grinned. "Think of it! To rebuild a city like this, but knowin' what it could be! What it was! I remember when I first saw it—everyone tearin' around, shacks 'ere, stone castle there, a great confloption lookin' like it 'ad simply burst out o' the earth."

Susan frowned incredulously. "P'raps the earth 'as taken it back again!"

He turned, startled. "What?"

"Look around ye, Jack. Look there, right before yer own eyes." The ground had slipped, opening up a trench that ran out of the square and through the street, and the fracture had sundered the stone perimeter wall, leaving a vertical jog of nearly three feet. "The earth 'as moved, right under yer feet, picked ye up and swatted ye down. The earth 'as taken this city o' yers, broken it t' pieces, and crumbled yer stone and brick right t' dust. And look out there" They both turned to gaze out over the smoke and flames below. "D'ye know why they can't put out th' fires? The mains're broken. The water that men like you took from th' mountains, it's all runnin' back into the earth. The earth takes its own."

He laughed. "Ye sound like a prophet out o' the Old Testament. Is that it? 'as God brought th' plagues of Egypt t' th' people o' California?"

"Don't mock me."

"Ye're mockin' yerself, Susan Trevenna. That's what ye're sayin', isn't it? That God is punishin' our pride? That 'e's takin' th' city that gold built? P'raps we should go back t' Grass Valley and take a look at th' deep mines. P'raps th' shafts an' th' tunnels 'ave all collapsed, takin' the town with 'em, down below."

She set her chin. "I'm tellin' ye what I see. The City is broken, and it's sinkin'."

He snapped at her. "Broken it may be, but we'll bring it back!"

She hissed back. "Were you ever really a miner, Jack? Did ye learn nothin'? Yer father an' mine knew that if ye work in the earth, ye work on its terms."

"When there's a cave-in, do th' men seal up th' mine?"

"Sometimes."

"Iss fay, sometimes, but more often they dig it out again. Ye're right. Jesse an' Joseph worked with the earth—*in* the earth—by its rules, but they gave nothin' up. They kept goin' back down, down into th' deep shafts. Even Hannibal died down there, sick as 'e was. 'e knew where 'e belonged."

Even as the tears welled up in her eyes, she shook her head scornfully. "Th' man was crazy with fever; 'e didn't know what 'e was doin'."

He pointed out towards the landscape of smoke and flames. "This is a cave-in, Susan. We'll dig it out an' prop it up, and as soon as may be, we'll be bringin' out the rock again, be it black tin or gold or dreams."

"Ye talk like one o' those madmen that used t' walk around th' streets 'ere. Always seein' things in th' future."

"That's where we're going to live, Susan, and our children and our grandchildren."

"No." She turned to face him, her arms at her sides. "Jesse an' Joseph knew when t' stop. 'ow deep t' drill. 'ow far t' drive out a drift. Nick knew it, too, and even Hannibal. You never learned that. Ye always thought ye could keep goin', farther down, farther out. Well, sometimes ye can't. Sometimes ye 'ave t' let th' ledge be, because it's been there before we came, and it'll be there long after we're gone."

"You're afraid." He said it quietly, evenly.

"You may think so. And I may think ye're a fool."

She paused, and he waited. Far below, they could hear the roar of the fire.

"Susan," he began. "Did you . . . Did you ever really love me?"

She stared at him, amazed. One side of his face was dark, and the other barely lit by the distant flames. She laughed. "Is that what it comes to, after all this time? Is that why ye've been wantin' me t' live 'ere?"

"That's part of it."

"Why d'ye ask me this? Why now?"

He looked away, out at the burning city. "Because I love you. Always 'ave."

She studied him, trying to remember: a boy climbing over the wall of the Gwennap Pit, a girl waiting for him. "No, ye don't." He turned towards her sharply. "Ye don't, Jack, an' don't think that ye do."

"'ow can ye say that?"

"I don't know what ye love—p'raps ye don't know yerself—but it isn't me."

"I wanted to marry you. Ye know that."

"It 'as nothin' t' do with that. We did what we 'ad t' do, every step. But you were always lookin' fer somethin', somethin' over my shoulder."

"What about you?" She said nothing. "Ye 'aven't answered my question. Did ye love me?"

She raised her sleeve to her face, trying to stop the tears. "I don't know. I thought I did. I ached fer ye, Jack. I can't tell ye 'ow much."

"Did ye love me, Susan?" He spoke softly, tenderly.

"I can't remember." She sobbed. "Idden that th' worst of it? To 'ave nothin'—not even th' memory." He reached out to take her by the shoulders, but she twisted away. "No, please." He waited while she slowly got her breathing under control. "I'm leavin'."

"Leavin'?"

"I'm goin' back t' Grass Valley."

"You can't leave now."

"There's nothin' left 'ere."

"You wait. Two years, three years. This is th' best opportunity anyone could ever 'ave."

"That's it, isn't it, Jack?" She smiled sadly at him. "Always lookin' for the opportunity. Th' best chance. T' be in at th' beginnin', all cock-a-hoop. No wonder ye buckle up t' this country so well."

"If that's 'ow ye feel, why don't ye go back t' Cornwall?"

Her eyes filled with tears. "I wish I could. But it's too late. Too late. It's been so long—I 'ardly remember it. I'm goin' back t' Grass Valley, and I'll likely die there."

"Susan!"

"Oh, not tomorrow, I pray, or next month, but one day. That's where I'll come to rest."

"Susan."

She looked up at him. The blue eyes hadn't changed; she remembered them, only them, just as candid and trustful as when they were children together, stretching out in the furze to name the shapes in the clouds overhead. "This 'as gone on long enough. Get back to Annie, and Frederick, an' th' rest. Put yer city back together again, stone upon stone. But mark this." She placed the palm of her hand against his chest, gently, as though offering a charm to keep him safe. "It'll 'appen again. The earth will move again. And nothin' ye can do—no wish, no dream, no prayer—will stop it."

She turned and walked back to where the children were sleeping.

The Earthquake, 1906

Five days later, Susan managed to book two places on a ferry to Oakland. Jack went with her as far as the Central Pacific terminus, and he stood on the platform and waved as her train pulled out, bound for Sacramento and Colfax. For the last time, through the smudged window, she gazed at him, the satin band of his new hat shining in the sunlight and his mustache carefully swept up at the corners. As the train picked up speed, she looked back at the smoldering ruins across the water. He was right, of course. They would rebuild. Men like Jack would push aside the ashes, tamp them down and raise a new city on the black foundation. The wheels clattered along the tracks, hitting their rhythm now, as she leaned back in her seat and shut her eyes, trying to block out that last image of Jack's optimistic smile. She would walk away, leaving the cataclysm behind her and retreating to her sanctuary in the hills. She was weary, so weary, but she was going home.

Virtual Hilarity is a compilation of the best humour gleaned from the Internet—with the advantage over Virtual Reality— you don't need an electronic helmet to have a really good laugh.

It is of course virtually indispensible to all practicing and potential 'After Dinner Speakers', 'Stand-up Comedians' and 'Lounge Bar Wags'. When you read this book, treat it as an experience and experience it as a treat!

And now for the good news . . . we're already working on volume 2.

Price £6.75   (US$9.95) ISBN 1 899526 70 6

Envision Publishing

4 South Street Fowey Cornwall PL23 1AR. UK. Tel: + 44 (0)1726 832 900
e-mail: alexander69@delphi.com www.cornwall-online.co.uk/envision

The Cornish Riviera

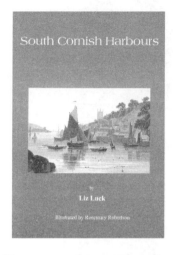

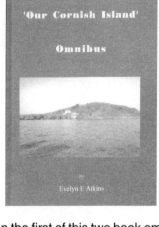

The rugged coastline that stretches west from Plymouth to Lands End is dramatic in its beauty but often a danger to seafarers. Before roads and railways connected this south west tip of England, the Cornish looked to the sea as their lifeline. The shipping of tin and china clay, fishing, smuggling and wrecking are bound into the granite of the many deserted quays that can be found in isolated coves and inlets. Illustrated. ISBN 1 899526 45 5

£7.99

In the first of this two book omnibus, **'We Bought an Island'**, Evelyn Atkins tells in a funny and sometimes moving way how, against formable odds, she and her sister Babs became owners of their own island. The second part of this two book volume is the follow-on title **'Tales from Our Cornish Island'** and brings readers up to date with their adventures.

ISBN 1 899526 40 4

£8.99

Alexander Associates

4 South Street Fowey Cornwall PL23 1AR. UK. Tel: + 44 (0)1726 832 900
e-mail: alexander69@delphi.com www.cornwall-online.co.uk/envision